THE THOUSAND DEATHS OF ARDOR BENN

"Hold on," said Quarrah. "That seems awfully complicated. This is a simple burglary we're talking about. Why don't I just slip into the palace in the middle of the night and take it?"

"Simple burglary?" Ard turned to Raek and let out an incredulous laugh. Apparently, Quarrah Khai thought very highly of herself. "We're talking about the Royal Regalia. Stealing the crown." He turned to Raek. "Can you remind me what the penalty is for treason? I can't seem to remember."

Raek made three simple gestures. The first implied getting shot; the second, hanged; and the third, slitting his throat.

"Obviously, the Reggies won't do all three," Ard said. "One is usually enough to ruin your day. This isn't an ordinary job, Quarrah. You think your spyglass is going to shine right into Pethredote's chambers? Figure out where he stores the regalia?" Ard shook his head. "Between us and our prize is every red-coat Reggie in the king's employ. Even if you did snake your way in and steal it, how long do you think it would take the king to notice that his crown and coat were missing?" He paused to see if Quarrah would retort, but Ard appeared to have made his point. "We have to do this right. Careful."

THE THOUSAND DEATHS OF ARDOR BENN

KINGDOM OF GRIT: BOOK ONE

TYLER WHITESIDES

www.orbitbooks.net

ORBIT

First published in Great Britain in 2018 by Orbit

1 3 5 7 9 10 8 6 4 2

Copyright © 2018 by Tyler Whitesides

Map by Serena Malyon

Excerpt from *The Dragon Lords: Fool's Gold* by Jon Hollins
Copyright © 2016 by Jonathan Wood

The moral right of the author has been asserted.

A CIP catalogue record for this book
is available from the British Library.

ISBN 978-0-356-51100-9

Printed and bound in Great Britain by
Clays Ltd, St Ives plc

Papers used by Orbit are from well-managed forests
and other responsible sources.

Orbit
An imprint of
Little, Brown Book Group
Carmelite House
50 Victoria Embankment
London EC4Y 0DZ

An Hachette UK Company
www.hachette.co.uk

www.orbitbooks.net

To Constance

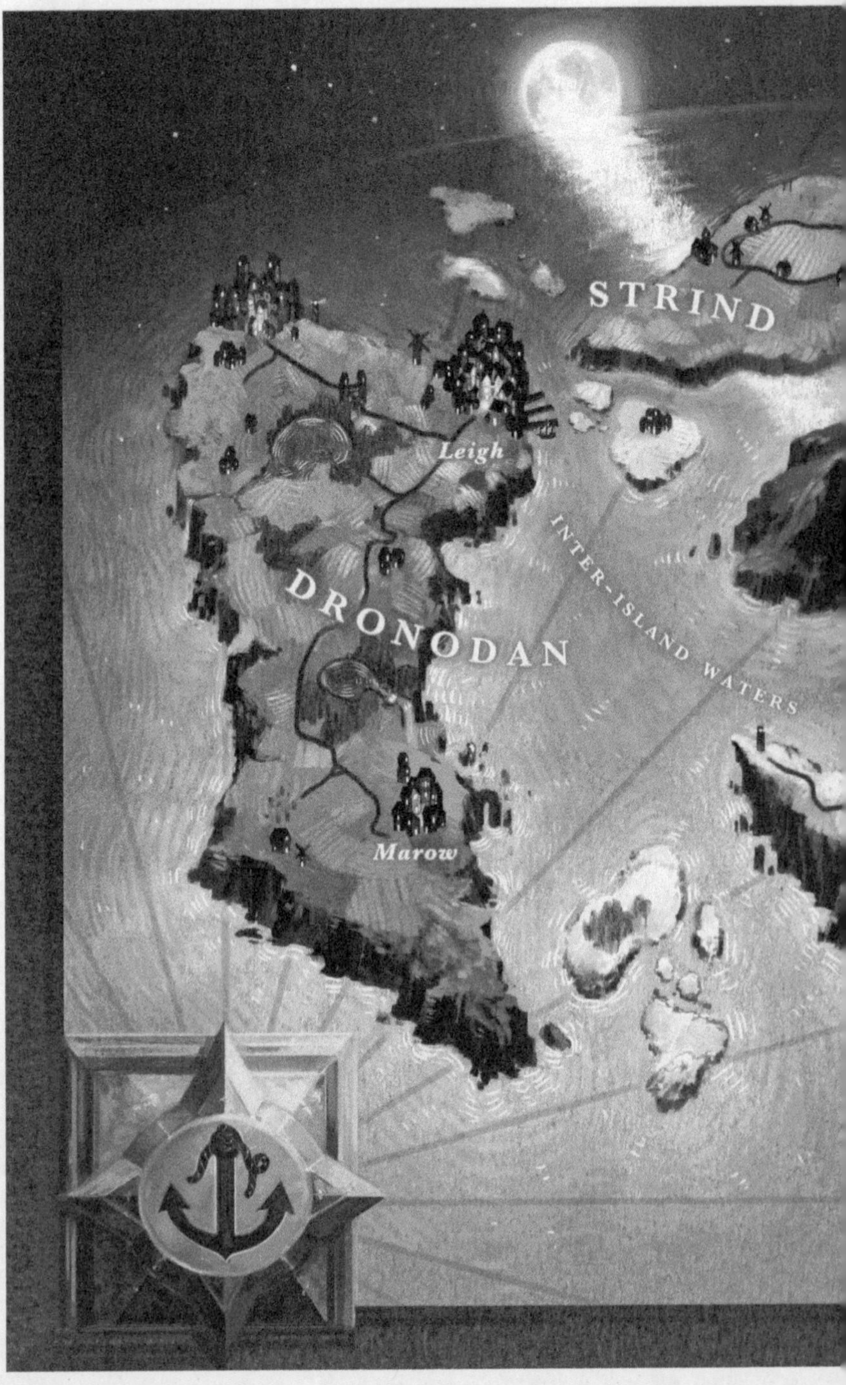
STRIND
Leigh
DRONODAN
INTER-ISLAND WATERS
Marow

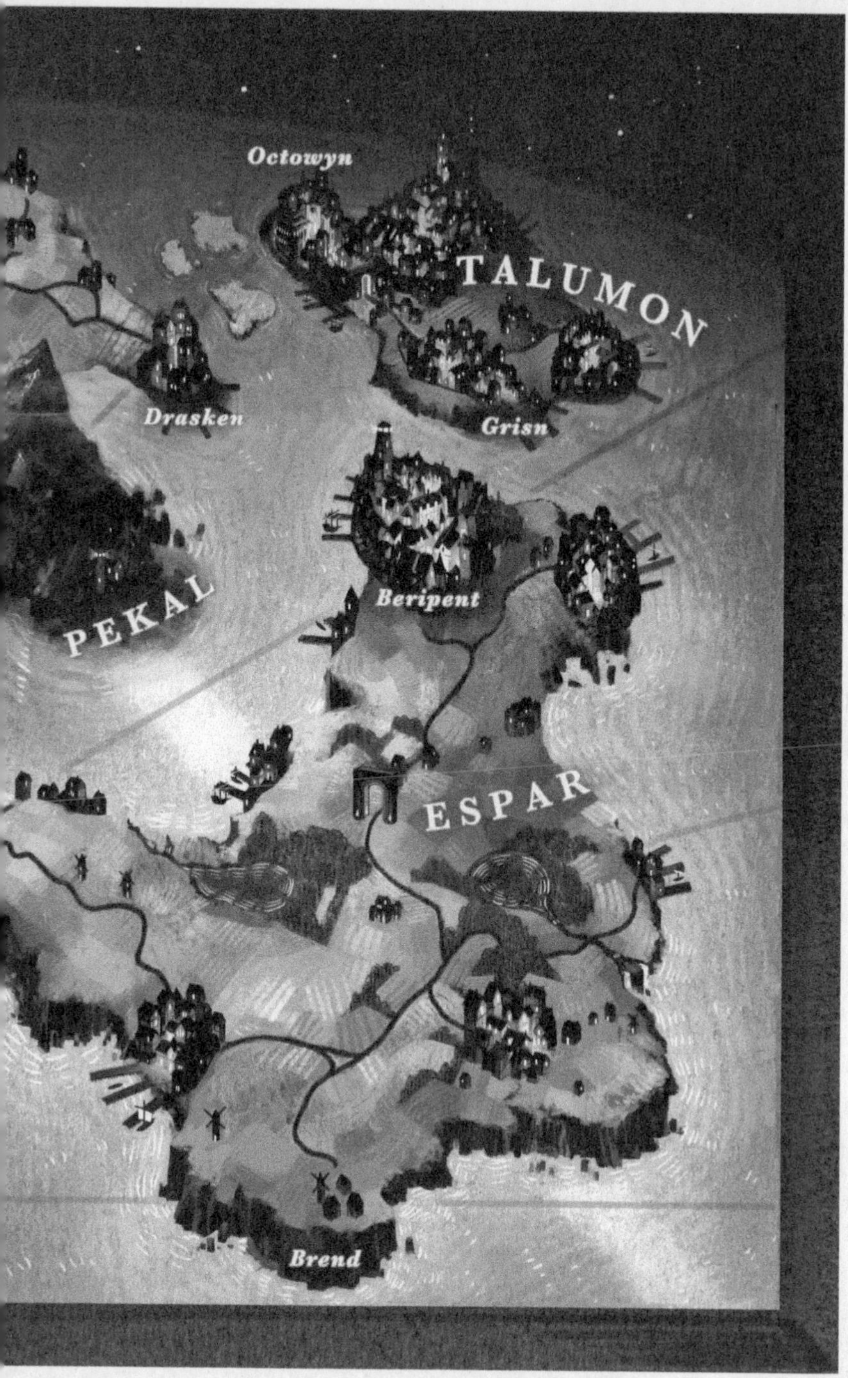
Octowyn
TALUMON
Drasken
Grisn
Beripent
PEKAL
ESPAR
Brend

*T*hey fed a corpse to the dragon.

They said the man had died a beggar in Talumon. Now his bones, if properly digested, will give us Grit. But what of his soul? If any part of him remains here through the Moon Passing, he will never reach the Homeland. His fate will be like mine.

The Harvesters don't concern themselves with such thoughts. I have been with them now for six days. I did not glimpse the dragon or her breath of flames as she fired the dung into Slagstone, but I marvel at her role in this natural process.

Back home, the streets of Beripent are aglow with Light Grit. Nobles warm their manors with clouds of Heat Grit. But I suspect now that they, like me, understand little of its origins.

Here, on Pekal, truth lurks behind every crag and tree. I am seeing things I have only known in writing. And at the end of my journey, I hope to put in writing things no one has ever seen.

The Harvesters have what they came here for. In the morning, they will collect the Slagstone from the dragon and their path will take them down the mountain. But I must slip away in the dark of night, for my path presses on. Upward. Higher.

To truth.

It begins here. Although, for me, I suppose this is something of an ending.

PART I

That Crimson Moon, each cycle filling the sky with its hues of blood, throws a light to sicken man, from which there is no cure. Alone in these floating lands, is there no one to shield the Wayfarer, far from that Homeland blessed? A Holy Torch is lit on each unholy night, to draw from the Moon its flames of red.

—Wayfarist Voyage, *Vol. 1*

The passing Eye spills flame above the frailty of human life. Blazing bodies upon the summit. The flicker of a lighting Torch.

—*Ancient Agrodite song*

PART I

CHAPTER

1

Ardor Benn was running late. Or was he? Ard preferred to think that everyone else in the Greater Chain was consistently early—with unreasonable expectations for him to be the same.

Regardless, this time it was all right to keep his appointment waiting. It was a stew tactic. And stew tasted better the longer it cooked.

Ard skipped up the final stairs and onto the third floor. Remaught Azel clearly wasn't the big fish he purported. Rickety wooden tri-story in the slums of Marow? Ard found the whole thing rather distasteful. Especially after Lord Yunis. Now, that was something! Proper stone mansion with a Heat Grit hearth in every room. Servants. Cooks. Light Grit lanterns that ignited with the pull of a chain. Ard half suspected that Lord Yunis wiped his backside with lace.

Different island. Different ruse. Today was about Remaught Azel, no matter how unaccommodating his hideout appeared.

Ard shifted the Grit keg from one arm to the other as he reached the closed door at the end of the hallway. The creaking floorboards would have already notified Remaught that someone was coming. *Interesting*, Ard thought. *Maybe there is something useful about holing up in a joint like this. Floorboard sentries.*

The door swung open, but before Ard could step through, a hairy, blue-skinned arm pressed into his chest, barring entrance.

"Take it easy," Ard said to the Trothian man. This would be

Remaught's bodyguard. His dark, vibrating eyes glared at Ard. Classic. This guy seemed like a tough son of a gun, although he was obviously past due for one of those Agrodite saltwater soaks. The skin on his arm looked like it might start flaking off.

"I'm a legitimate businessman," Ard continued, "here to do... legitimate businessy things."

He glanced past the large bodyguard to the table where Remaught sat, bathed in sunlight from the western window. The mobster wore a maroon velvet vest, a tricornered hat, and a shoulder cape, currently fashionable among the rich folk. Remaught seemed tense, watching his bodyguard detain Ard at the doorway.

"Search him."

"Really?" Ard protested, holding the Grit keg above his head so the bodyguard could pat his sides. "I left my belt and guns at home," he said. "And if I hadn't, I could easily shoot you from where I'm standing, so I find this whole pat down a little unnecessary, and frankly uncomfortable."

The bodyguard paused, one hand on Ard's hip pocket. "What's this?" he asked, his voice marked by a thick Trothian accent.

"Rocks," Ard answered.

"Rocks?" Like the bodyguard had never heard of such things. "Take them out—slow."

Ard reached casually into his pocket and scooped out a handful of small stones that he'd collected on the roadside before entering the building. "I'll need these for the transaction."

In response, the Trothian bodyguard swatted Ard's hand, sending the dusty pebbles scattering across the room.

"Now, that was quite uncalled-for," Ard said to the mobster at the table. "I find your man to be unnecessarily rough."

"Suno?" replied Remaught. "Three cycles ago, he would have fed you those rocks—through your nose. Going soft, I fear. Fatherhood has a tendency to do that."

Ard wondered what kind of father a mobster's bodyguard would be. Some fathers made a living at the market or the factories. This guy made a living by stringing people up by their toes at the whim of his boss.

The Trothian moved down, feeling around Ard's thighs with both hands.

"At the very least, you should consider hiring a good-looking woman for this step," Ard continued. "Wouldn't hurt business, you know."

The bodyguard stepped back and nodded to Remaught, who gestured for Ard to enter the room.

"Were you followed?" Remaught asked.

Ard laughed as he set the Grit keg gently on the table, stirring a bit of dust that danced in the sun rays. "I am never followed." He adjusted the gaudy ring on his index finger and sat down across from the mobster. "Except occasionally by a bevy of beautiful maidens."

Ard smiled, but Remaught Azel did not return the gesture. Instead, the mobster reached out for the Grit keg. Ard was faster, whisking the keg away before Remaught could touch it.

Ard clicked his tongue. "How about we see some payment before I go handing over the Grit in a room where I'm unarmed and outnumbered?"

Remaught pushed backward in his chair, the wooden legs buzzing against the floor. The mobster crossed the room and retrieved a locked safe box from the window seat. It was no longer than his forearm, with convenient metal handles fastened on both sides. The Regulation seal was clearly displayed on the front beside the keyhole.

"That looks mighty official," Ard said as Remaught placed it on the table. "Regulation issue, isn't it?"

"I recently came by the box," replied Remaught, dusting his hands. "I like to keep my transactions secure. There are crooked folk in these parts."

"So I hear," answered Ard. "And how do I know the safe box isn't full of sand?"

"How do I know that Grit keg isn't empty?"

Ard shrugged, a smirk on his face. They had reached the part of the exchange that Ard called the Final Distrust. One last chance to back out. For both of them.

Remaught broke the tension by reaching into his velvet vest and producing a key. He slipped it into the lock, turned it sharply, and lifted the lid.

Ard squinted at the coinlike items. They looked real enough in this lighting. Most were stamped with seven small indentations, identifying them as seven-mark Ashings, the highest denomination of currency.

"May I?" Ard plucked out a coin before Remaught granted permission. Ard lifted the Ashing to his mouth and bit down on the edge of it.

"Taste real enough for you?" Remaught asked. Ard's relaxed nature seemed to be driving the man continuously more tense.

Ard studied the spot where his teeth had pressed against the coin, angling it in the sunlight to check for any kind of indentation. He preferred to gouge suspicious coins with a knifepoint, but, well, Remaught had made it pretty clear that weapons were not allowed at this meeting.

The Ashing seemed genuine. And if Remaught wasn't planning to slight him, there would be 493 more in that safe box.

"You ever been to the Coinery on Talumon?" Ard flicked the coin back into the open box. "I was there a few years back. On legitimate business, of course."

Remaught closed the lid and turned the key.

"Coining," Ard went on. "Sparks, that's an elaborate process. Just the effort it takes to grind those raw scales into perfect circles... And you know they follow up with a series of chemical washes. They say it's for curing and hardening. I hardly think a dragon scale needs hardening…"

Across the table, Remaught was fidgeting. Ard suppressed a grin.

"Is something wrong, Rem? Can I call you Rem?" Ard pressed. "I thought this information would be of particular interest to a man in your line of work."

"Perhaps you can save the details for some other time," Remaught said. "You're not my only appointment today."

Ard leaned back in his chair, pretending that the mobster's words had really put him out.

"I'd prefer if we just get along with the transaction." Remaught gestured to the Grit keg. "What do you have for me there?"

"One full panweight of Void Grit," said Ard. "My source says the batch is top quality. Came from a good-sized block of indigestible granite. Passed through the dragon in less than five days. Properly fired, and processed to the finest of powder." He unlatched the cap on the Grit keg and tilted it toward Remaught. "The amount we agreed upon. And at an unbeatable price. I'm a man of my word."

"It would seem that you are," answered the mobster. "But of course you understand that I'll need a demonstration of the product."

Ard nodded slowly. Not all Grit could be demonstrated, especially indoors. But he had been expecting such a demand for this transaction.

Ard turned to the Trothian bodyguard, who leaned in the doorway like he was holding up the frame. "I'll be needing those rocks now."

Remaught grunted, then snapped at his bodyguard. "Suno! Pick up the blazing stones."

Wordlessly, the man hunted across the floor for the stones he had slapped away. As he searched, Ard quickly picked up the safe box, causing Remaught to jump.

"Relax," Ard said, crossing the room and carefully setting the valuable box on the wooden window seat. "I'll need the table cleared for the demonstration."

A moment later, Suno handed the rocks to Ard and lumbered back to the doorway, folding his dry, cracking arms.

There were nine little rocks, and Ard spread them into a loose ring on the tabletop. He unclasped the Grit keg and was about to reach inside, when Remaught grabbed his arm.

"I pick the Grit," the mobster demanded. "No tricks."

Ard shrugged, offering the container to Remaught. The man slipped his hand inside and withdrew a pinch of grayish powder. Ard pointed to the center of the stone ring and Remaught deposited the Grit in a tiny mound.

"That enough?" Remaught asked, as Ard brushed the pinch of powder into a tidier pile.

"More than enough," Ard said. "You trying to clear the whole room?" He clasped the lid on the Grit keg and set it on the floor behind him. "I assume you have a Slagstone ignitor?"

From his vest, Remaught produced the device Ard had asked for. It was a small steel rod, slightly flattened at one end. Affixed at the center point along the rod was a spring, and attached to the end of the spring was a small piece of Slagstone.

Remaught handed the ignitor to Ard, the tiny fragment of Slagstone wobbling on its spring. "With the amount of Void Grit you've laid down, I'd expect the blast radius to be about two feet." Ard said it as a warning. Remaught caught the hint and took a large step backward.

Ard also positioned himself as far from the table as he could, while still able to reach the tiny pile of gray Grit. He took aim and knocked the flat end of the steel rod against the table. The impact brought the spring down and the small piece of attached Slagstone struck the metal rod.

A respectable spark leapt off the Slagstone. It flashed across the wooden table and vanished instantly, with no effect.

"Ha!" Remaught shouted, as though he'd been waiting to make an accusation. "I should have known no one would sell a panweight of Void Grit at that price."

Ard looked up. "The Grit is legitimate, I assure you. This Slagstone ignitor, on the other hand…" He held up the device, gently shaking the spring as though it were a child's toy. "Honestly, I didn't even know they sold something this cheap. I couldn't ignite a *mountain* of Grit with this thing, let alone convince the spark to fall on that pinhead target. Allow me to throw a few more sparks before you let Suno rip my ears off."

The truth was, the tiny pile of powdered granite hadn't lit for two reasons. First, Remaught's Slagstone ignitor really was terribly inaccurate. And second, the Void Grit was definitely fake.

Ard leaned closer to the table, pretending to give the ignitor a close inspection. With his right hand hovering just above the pile of gray powder, he wriggled his fingers, spinning his heavy ring around so he could slip his thumbnail into a small groove and slide the face of the ring aside.

The gesture was subtle, and Ard was drawing Remaught's attention to the ignitor. He was sure the mobster hadn't noticed the fresh deposit of genuine Void Grit from the ring's secret cavity.

"Let's see if this does the trick." Ard repositioned himself, bringing the ignitor down, Slagstone sparking on impact.

The genuine Void Grit detonated instantly, the powder from Ard's ring creating a blast radius just over a foot. It wasn't at all like a deadly Blast Grit explosion of fire and sparks. This was Specialty Grit, and the particular demonstrated effect was far less dangerous.

A rush of energy emanated from the pinch of Void Grit, like a tremendous wind blasting outward in every direction from the center.

It happened much faster than Ard could withdraw his hand. Caught in the detonation, his arm was shoved backward, the Slagstone ignitor flying from his grasp. The stones on the table flew in every direction, the Grit pushing them to the perimeter of the blast, their momentum sending them bouncing across the floor.

The Void Grit was spent, but hovering around the table where the detonation occurred was a dome of discolored air. It would have been a spherical cloud if it had detonated midair, but the tabletop had been strong enough to contain the underside of the blast.

Remaught stumbled a step closer. "How did you do that?"

Ard wrinkled his forehead. "What do you mean? It's Void Grit. Digested granite. That's what it does." He bent down and retrieved a fallen pebble. "It voids a space within the blast radius. Clears everything out to the perimeter. The effect should last about ten minutes before the blast cloud burns out."

To prove his point, Ard tossed the pebble into the dome of discolored air. The little stone barely touched the perimeter before the effect of the Grit pushed it forcefully away.

Remaught nodded absently, his hand drifting to his vest pocket. For a brief moment, Ard thought the mobster might pull a Singler, but he relaxed when Remaught withdrew the key to the safe box. Remaught stepped forward and set the key on the edge of the table, just outside the hazy Void cloud.

"I'm ready to close the deal," he said, producing a few papers for Ard's inspection. Detonation licenses—or at least forgeries—which would allow him to purchase Grit.

But Ard wasn't interested in the legalities of the transaction. He dismissed the paperwork, picking up the keg of false Void Grit and holding it out to Remaught.

"Of course, I'll need a receipt," said the mobster, tucking his licenses back into his vest.

"A receipt?" That sounded frightfully legitimate to Ardor Benn.

"For my records," said Remaught. In a moment, the man had

produced a small square of paper, and a charcoal scribing stick. "Go ahead and notate the details of the transaction. And sign your name at the bottom."

Ard handed the Grit keg to Remaught and accepted the paper and charcoal. Remaught stepped away, and it took only moments for Ard to write what was needed, autographing the bottom as requested.

"I hope we can do business again in the future," Ard said, looking up from his scrawling. But Remaught Azel didn't seem to share his sentiment.

"I'm afraid that will not be the case." The mobster was standing near the open doorway, his Trothian bodyguard off to one side. Remaught had removed the cap from the Grit keg and was holding the cheap Slagstone ignitor.

"Whoa!" Ard shouted. "What are you—"

Remaught brought the ignitor down. A cluster of sparks danced from the impact, showering onto the gray powder housed in the open keg.

"Did you really think I wouldn't recognize an entire keg of counterfeit Grit?" Remaught asked.

Ard crumpled the receipt and dropped it to the floor, lunging for the key on the edge of the table. He scooped it up, but before Ard could reach the safe box, the Trothian bodyguard was upon him. In the blink of an eye, Ard found himself in a headlock, forced to his knees before a smug Remaught.

"I believe I mentioned that I had another appointment today?" Remaught said. "What I didn't tell you was that the appointment is happening now. With an officer of the Regulation."

A man appeared in the doorway behind Remaught. Not just a man—a veritable mountain. He had dark skin, and his nose was somewhat flat, the side of his face marked with a thin scar. The Regulator ducked his shiny, bald head under the door frame as he entered the room.

He wore the standard long wool coat of the Regulation, a crossbow slung over one shoulder and a sash of bolts across his broad chest. Beneath the coat, Ard thought he could see the bulge of a holstered gun.

"Delivered as promised," Remaught said, his tension at an all-new high. The Regulator seized Ard's upper arm with an iron grip, prompting Remaught's bodyguard to release the headlock.

"What is this, Remaught?" Ard asked between gasps for air. "You're selling me out? Don't you know who I am?"

"That's just it," said Remaught. "I know exactly who you are. Ardor Benn, ruse artist."

"Extraordinaire," said Ard.

"Excuse me?" Remaught asked.

"Ardor Benn, ruse artist extraordinaire," Ard corrected.

The giant Regulator yanked Ard to his feet. Prying Ard's fingers open, the man easily removed the key to the safe box before slapping a pair of shackles around Ard's wrists.

"Now wait a minute, big fella," Ard stalled. "You can arrest *me*, an amicable ruse artist trying to eke out a humble living. Or you can take in Remaught Azel. Think it through. Remaught Azel. *He's* the mobster."

The bald Regulator didn't even falter. He stepped forward and handed the key to Remaught with a curt nod.

"The Regulator and I have an understanding," answered Remaught. "He came to me three weeks ago. Said there was a ruse artist in town selling counterfeit Grit. Said that if I came across anyone trying to hock large quantities of Specialty Grit, that I should set up a meet and reach out to him."

"Flames, Remaught! You've gone clean?" Ard asked. "A mobster of your standing, working with a Reggie like him? You disgust me."

"Clean? No," Remaught replied. "And neither is my Regulator friend."

Ard craned his neck to shoot an incredulous stare at the Regulator holding him. "Unbelievable! A dirty Reggie and a petty mobster make a deal—and I'm the victim!"

Remaught addressed the big official. "We're good, then?"

The large man nodded. "We're good. I was never here."

The Regulator pushed Ard past Remaught, through the doorway, and into the creaky hallway, pausing to say one last thing to the mobster. "You got him to sign a receipt like I told you?"

Remaught scanned the room and gestured to the crumpled piece of paper on the floor. "You need it for evidence?"

"Nah," said the Regulator. "This lowlife's wanted on every island in the Greater Chain. The receipt was for your own protection. Proves you had every intention of making a legal transaction. Buying Grit isn't a crime, providing you have the proper licensure." He gave Ard a shove in the back, causing him to stumble across the rickety floorboards. "Give me plenty of time to distance myself before you leave this building," the Regulator instructed. "Understood?"

Ard glanced back in time to see Remaught nodding as the door swung shut. Ard and the Regulator descended the stairs in silence, the huge man never removing his iron grip from Ard's shoulder. It wasn't until they stepped outside into the warm afternoon that Ard spoke.

"Lowlife?" he said. "Really, Raek? That seemed a bit much. Like you were enjoying it."

"Don't lecture me on 'a bit much,'" answered the Regulator. "What was that whole 'ruse artist extraordinaire' slag?"

"You know I like that line. I saw an opportunity and I took it," Ard answered.

Raek grunted, tugging at the collar of his uniform. "This coat itches. No wonder we can always outrun the blazing Reggies. They're practically choking themselves on the job."

"You almost look convincing," Ard said. "But where's the Reggie helmet?"

"I couldn't find one that fit," answered Raek. "And besides, I figure I'm tall enough no one can see the top of my head. Maybe I'm wearing a tiny Reggie helmet. No one would know."

"Sound logic," Ard said as they turned the corner to the west side of Remaught's building. "You swapped the key?"

"Child's play," Raek answered. "You leave the note?"

"I even drew a little smiling face after my name."

Raek led them to a sturdy hay wagon hitched to a waiting horse.

"Straw this time?" Ard asked, finding it difficult to climb onto the bench with his hands still shackled.

"Should pad the landing," Raek replied.

"Look at you! Good idea."

"You're not the only person who can have one, you know." Raek pulled himself onto the bench beside Ard and stooped to grab the reins. "You're getting bored, Ard."

"Hmm?" He glanced at his friend.

"This little stunt." Raek gestured up to the third-story window directly above them. "It's showy, even for you."

Ard dismissed the comment. Was there a simpler way to steal the safe box? Probably. But surely there wasn't a more clever way.

Remaught had to be feeling pretty smug. In his mind, the exchange had gone off without a hitch. The mobster had been gifted a Regulation-issue safe box, partnered with a crooked Reggie, and taken some competition off the streets by having the ruse artist arrested.

By now, Remaught was probably reading Ard's note on the receipt—a simple message thanking the mobster for the Ashings and informing him that the Reggie was as fake as the Grit. This would undoubtedly send Remaught scurrying to the safe box to check its valuable contents. All he needed to do was thrust Raek's replacement key into the lock, and... *boom*.

Any moment now.

The idle horse stamped its hooves, awaiting Raek's directions.

"We're sparked if he moves the safe box," Raek muttered after a moment's silence.

"He won't," Ard reassured. "Remaught's lazy."

"He could have the bodyguard do it."

"Suno was going soft," Ard repeated what he'd heard from Remaught. "Something about fatherhood. I'm more worried that the window won't break…"

Three stories above, the glass window shattered. The safe box came hurtling out on a perfect trajectory, landing in the back of the hay-stuffed wagon with a thud.

Remaught Azel was blazing predictable. Classic mobster. Maybe Ard *was* getting bored.

"I'm actually surprised that worked," Ard admitted, as Raek snapped the reins and sent the horse galloping down the street.

"That doesn't give me much confidence. Tampering with the safe box was *your* idea."

"I knew *that* would work," Ard said. They'd tipped the replacement key with a tiny fragment of Slagstone and filled the inside of the lock with Void Grit. The detonation would have cleared everything within the blast radius, undoubtedly throwing Remaught backward. The box of Ashings, still latched shut, was hurtled outward by the force of the Grit, smashing through the glass panes and falling three stories to the hay wagon waiting on the street below.

"I had full trust in the Grit." Ard gestured behind him. "I'm just surprised the box actually landed where it was supposed to!"

"Physics," Raek said. "You trust the Grit, but you don't trust physics?"

"Not if I'm doing the math."

"Oh, come on," said the large man. "Two and a half granules of Void Grit detonated against a safe box weighing twenty-eight panweights falling from a third-story window…"

Ard held up his still-shackled hands. "It physically hurts me to hear you talk like that. Actual pain in my actual brain."

Behind them, from the shattered window of Remaught's hide-out, three gunshots pealed out, breaking the lazy silence of the afternoon.

"Remaught? He's shooting at us?" Raek asked.

"He can't hope to hit us at this distance," answered Ard. "Even with a Fielder, that shot is hopeless."

Another gunshot resounded, and this time a lead ball struck the side of the wagon with a violent crack. Ard flinched and Raek cursed. The shot had not come from Remaught's distant window. This gunman was closer, but Ard couldn't tell from what direction he was firing.

"Remaught's shots were a signal," Ard assumed. "He must have had his goons in position in case things went wrong with his new Reggie soulmate."

"We're not soulmates," Raek muttered.

A man on horseback emerged from an alleyway behind them, his dark cloak flapping, hood up. The mob goon stretched out one hand and Ard saw the glint of a gun. He barely had time to shout a warning to Raek, both men ducking before the goon fired.

The ball went high. Ard heard it whizzing overhead. It was a Singler. Ard recognized the timbre of the shot. As its name implied, the small gun could shoot only one ball before needing to be reloaded. The six-shot Rollers used by the Regulators were far more deadly. Not to mention ridiculously expensive and illegal for use by the common citizen.

The goon had wasted his single ball, too eager to fire on the escaping ruse artists. He could reload, of course, but the process was nearly impossible on the back of a galloping horse. Instead, the goon holstered his Singler and drew a thin-bladed rapier.

"Give me the key," Ard said as another horseman appeared behind the first.

"What key?" replied Raek. "The one I swapped from Remaught?"

"Not that one." Ard held up his chained wrists and jangled them next to Raek's ear. "The key to the shackles."

"Oh." Raek spit off the side of the wagon. "I don't have it."

"You lost the key?" Ard shouted.

"I didn't lose it," answered Raek. "Never had it. I stole the shackles from a Reggie outpost. I didn't really have time to hunt around for keys."

Ard threw his chained hands in the air. "You locked me up without a way to get me out?"

Raek shrugged. "Figured we'd deal with that problem later."

A cloaked figure on foot suddenly ducked out of a shanty, the butt of a long-barreled Fielder tucked against his shoulder.

Raek transferred the reins to his left hand, reached into his Regulator coat, and drew a Roller. He pointed the gun at the goon with the Fielder, used his thumb to pull back the Slagstone hammer, and pulled the trigger.

The Slagstone snapped down, throwing a spark into the first chamber to ignite a pinch of powdered Blast Grit in a paper cartridge. It detonated with a deafening crack, the metal gun chamber containing the explosion and throwing a lead ball out the barrel.

The ball splintered through the wall of the shanty behind the goon. Before he could take proper aim at the passing wagon, Raek pulled back the Slagstone hammer and fired again.

Another miss, but it was enough to put the goon behind them. Raek handed the smoking Roller to Ard. "Here," the big man said. "I stole this for you."

"Wow." Ard awkwardly accepted the gun with both wrists chained. "It looks just like the one I left holstered in *my* gun belt at the boat."

"Oh, this gun belt?" Raek brushed aside the wool Reggie coat to reveal a second holstered gun. "You shouldn't leave valuable things lying around."

"It was in a locked compartment," Ard said, sighting down his Roller. "I gave you the key."

"That was your mistake."

Behind them, the Fielder goon finally got his shot off. The resounding pop of the big gun was deep and powerful. Straw exploded in the back of the wagon, and one of the side boards snapped clean off as the Fielder ball clawed its way through.

"Why don't you try to make something of that Reggie crossbow?" Ard said. "I'll handle the respectable firearms."

"There's nothing disrespectful about a crossbow," Raek answered. "It's a gentleman's weapon."

Ard glanced over his shoulder to find the swordsman riding dangerously close. He used his thumb to set the Slagstone hammer, the action spinning the chambers and moving a fresh cartridge and ball into position. But with both hands shackled together, he found it incredibly awkward to aim over his shoulder.

"Flames," Ard muttered. He'd have to reposition himself if he had any hope of making a decent shot. Pushing off the footboard, Ard cleared the low backboard and tumbled headfirst into the hay.

"I hope you did that on purpose!" Raek shouted, giving the reins another flick.

Ard rolled onto his knees as the mounted goon brought his sword down in a deadly arc. Ard reacted instinctively, catching the thin blade against the chains of his shackles.

For a brief moment, Ard knelt, keeping the sword above his head. Then he twisted his right hand around, aimed the barrel of his Roller, and pulled the trigger. In a puff of Blast smoke, the lead ball tore through the goon, instantly throwing him from the saddle.

Ard shook his head, pieces of loosely clinging straw falling from his short dark hair. He turned his attention to the street behind, where more than half a dozen of Remaught's men were riding to catch up. The nearest one fired, a Singler whose ball might have taken him if Raek hadn't turned a corner so sharply.

The wagon wheels drifted across the compact dirt, and Ard heard a few of the wooden spokes snapping under the strain. They were almost out of the slums, but still a fair distance from the docks. Raek's stolen hay wagon was not going to see them to their journey's end. Unless the journey ended with a gut full of lead.

Ard gripped the Roller in both hands. Not his preferred way of aiming, but his best alternative since his wrists were hooked together. Squinting one eye, he tried to steady his aim, waiting for the first goon to round the corner.

The rider appeared, hunched low on his horse. Ard fired once. The man dropped from the saddle, but six more appeared right behind him. And Ard's Roller only packed two more shots.

"We need something heavier to stop these goons!" Ard shouted. "You got any Grit bolts on that sash?"

Raek glanced down at the ammunition sash across his chest. "Looks like an assortment. Anything specific you're after?"

"I don't know...I was hoping for some Visitant Grit," Ard joked as he reached over and pulled the crossbow off Raek's shoulder.

Raek chuckled. "Like you'd be worthy to summon a Paladin Visitant."

"Hey, I can be downright righteous if I need to be," he answered.

Ard didn't favor the crossbow. He preferred the jarring recoil of a Roller, the heat from the flames that licked out the end of the barrel. The lingering smell of smoke.

"Barrier Grit." Raek carefully reached back to hand Ard a bolt from his sash. The projectile was like a stout arrow, black fletchings fixed to the shaft. The Grit bolt had a clay ball serving as an arrowhead, the tip dyed bright blue.

The bolt was an expensive shot, even though Barrier Grit was one of the five common Grit types. Inside the clay arrowhead, a chip of Slagstone was nestled into a measurement of glittering dust: digested shards of metal that had been dragon-fired and processed to powder.

Ard slipped the bolt into the groove on the crossbow, fitting the nock against the string he had already pulled into place—a difficult task with chained wrists. The goons were gaining fast now. Definitely within range.

"What's the blast radius on this bolt?" Ard pulled the crossbow to his shoulder and sighted down the length.

"The bolts were already on the sash when I stole it," answered Raek. "I'm guessing it'll be standard issue. Fifteen feet or so. You'd know these things if you bothered to keep up your Grit licenses."

Ard sighted down the crossbow. "Seriously? We're riding in a stolen wagon, you're impersonating a Reggie, we're hauling five hundred Ashings we just swindled from a mobster...and you're lecturing me about licensure?"

"I'm a fan of the Grit licenses," Raek said. "If anyone could purchase Grit whenever and wherever they wanted, the islands would be a mess of anarchy."

"I'm not just anybody," Ard replied. "I'm Ardor Benn..."

"Yeah, yeah. I got it," Raek cut him off. "Ruse artist extraordinaire. Just shoot the blazing bolt already."

Ard barely had to aim, the goons were riding so close now. He leveled the crossbow and pulled the trigger. The bolt released with a twang, finding its mark at the foot of the leading horse. The clay ball shattered on impact, and the Slagstone chip sparked, igniting the powdered metallic Grit.

The blast was nearly large enough to span the road. The discolored cloud made an instant dome, a hardened shell trapping two of the horsemen inside it. Their momentum carried them forward, striking the inside perimeter of the Barrier cloud.

The two horses went down, throwing their riders and crumpling as though they had galloped directly into a brick wall. A third rider also collided with the outside of the barrier dome, unable to stop his horse in time to avoid the obstacle suddenly blocking the road.

The two men within the Barrier cloud wouldn't be going anywhere until the Grit's effect burned out. They were trapped, as though a giant overturned bowl had suddenly enclosed them. Although the Barrier cloud seemed like it had a tangible shell, it couldn't be moved. And this dirt road was compact, so they wouldn't have a prayer at burrowing under the edge of the dome.

Ard grinned at the successful shot. "Haha! That'll buy us some time to reach the docks. Teach those goons not to mess with Ardor Benn and the Short Fuse."

"Come on, Ard," Raek muttered. "You know how I feel about that name."

"It's a solid name for a criminal Mixer like you." Ard understood why Raek thought it was unfitting. Raekon Dorrel was neither short nor impatient. Several years ago, during a particularly sticky ruse, Ard had referred to his partner as the Short Fuse. It was meant as little more than a joke, but somehow, the Regulation ended up circulating it through the streets until it stuck.

"Still don't think that's a respectable weapon?" Raek changed the subject, pushing the exhausted horse as they moved out of the slums.

"I'll leave the Grit shots to you." Ard handed the crossbow back to the driver. "I'll stick with lead and smoke."

Here, the road opened to a few grassy knolls that led right up to the cliff-like shoreline. The steep path down to the harbor was just ahead, where the *Double Take* was moored and waiting. Ard could see flags waving atop several ship masts, but with the high shoreline, it was impossible to see the harbor clearly.

"Clear ride to the docks today," Raek said. Now that he mentioned it, Ard thought the thoroughfare, usually bustling with pedestrians and the occasional cart or carriage, seemed abnormally still for a summer's afternoon.

"Something doesn't feel right," Ard muttered.

"Now, that's what you get for eating oysters for breakfast."

"I think we should stop," Ard whispered.

"Definitely," Raek replied. "We wouldn't want to outdistance those goons…" Raek was cut off as the wagon wheels hit a shallow trench across the dirt road.

Ard saw the sparks as the wheels struck a buried piece of Slagstone. He didn't even have time to grip the side of the wagon as the mine detonated.

Drift Grit.

A lot of it.

The blast radius must have been at least twenty yards, the center of the detonation occurring directly beneath the wagon. The discolored air hung in a hazy dome as the Grit took effect.

Ard felt his stomach churn as a bizarre weightlessness overtook him. The jolt from hitting the mine sent the wagon floating lazily upward, straw drifting in every direction. The horse's hooves left the road, and the poor animal bucked and whinnied, legs continuing to gallop in the sudden weightless environment.

"What was that?" Raek shouted. He still held the horse's reins, though his body had drifted off the wagon bench, his long wool coattails floating around his huge form.

"We hit a mine!" Ard answered. And the fact that it was Drift Grit didn't give him much hope. Barrier Grit would have been an inescapable trap, but at least they would have been safe inside the detonation. Adrift as they were now, he and Raek would be easy targets to anyone with a firearm. "They were waiting for us."

"Remaught?" Raek asked. "Sparks, we didn't give that guy enough credit!"

They were probably ten feet off the ground, Ard's legs pumping as though trying to swim through the air. He'd forgotten how disorienting and frustrating it was to hang suspended without any hint of gravity.

Now upside down, facing west toward the harbor, Ard saw more than a dozen mounted figures cresting the steep trail and riding out to meet them. He didn't need to see them upright to recognize the wool uniforms and helmets.

"Remaught didn't plant the mine," Ard shouted to Raek. "The Regulators did it. They knew we were coming."

"Flames!" Raek twisted in the air to see the horsemen Ard had just announced.

A gunshot pealed, and Ard saw the ball enter the Drift cloud. The shot went wide, exiting the detonated area just above their heads.

"We're sitting ducks!" Raek called, sun beating down on his bald head, dark skin glistening. "We've got to get our feet back on the ground."

Even if they could, exiting the Drift cloud now would put them face-to-face with an armed Regulation patrol. Perhaps they could flee back into the slums. Nope. From his spot hovering above the road, Ard saw four of Remaught's goons riding toward them.

"I thought you said this ruse was going to be low risk," Raek said, also noticing the two groups closing on their position.

"Did I? You're putting words in my mouth," Ard said. "How long until this detonation burns out?" He knew there was no way to know exactly. A standard Drift Grit blast could last up to ten minutes, depending on the quality of the bones that the dragon had digested. Raek would make a more educated guess than him.

Raek sniffed the discolored air. "There was Prolonging Grit mixed in with that detonation," he said. "We could be adrift for a while."

There was another gunshot, this one passing below their feet. Ard didn't know which side had fired.

"What else have you got on that sash?" Ard asked.

"More Barrier Grit." Raek studied his chest to take stock. "And a couple of bolts of Drift Grit." He chuckled. Probably at the irony of being armed with the very type of detonation they were trying to escape.

More gunshots. One of the lead balls grazed the side of the bucking horse. Blood sprayed from the wound, the red liquid forming into spherical droplets as it drifted away from the panicking animal.

Raek drew a dagger from his belt. Using the reins to draw himself closer, he slashed through the leather straps that yoked the animal to the wagon. Placing one heavy boot against the horse's backside, he kicked. The action sent the horse drifting one direction, and Raek the other. The horse bucked hysterically, hooves contacting the wagon and sending it careening into Raek.

Ard caught Raek's foot as he spiraled past, but it barely slowed the big man, tugging Ard along instead.

Their trajectory was going to put them out of the cloud's perimeter about thirty feet aboveground. They would plummet to the road, a crippling landing even if they didn't manage to get shot.

"Any thoughts on how to get out of here?" Ard shouted.

"I think momentum is going to do that for us in a second or two!"

They were spinning quite rapidly and the view was making Ard sick. Road. Sky. Road. Sky. He looked at Raek's ammunition sash and made an impulsive decision. Reaching out, Ard seized one of the bolts whose clay head bore the blue marking of Barrier Grit. Ripping the bolt free, he gripped the shaft and brought the stout projectile against Raek's chest like a stabbing knife.

The clay arrowhead shattered, Slagstone sparking against Raek's broad torso. The Barrier Grit detonated, throwing a new cloud around them midflight.

The bolt contained far less Grit than the road mine, resulting in a cloud that was only a fraction of the size. Detonated midair, it formed a perfect sphere. It enveloped Ard, Raek, and the wagon, just as all three slammed against the hard Barrier perimeter. The impenetrable wall stopped their momentum, though they still floated weightlessly, pressed against the stationary Barrier.

"You detonated on my chest?" Raek cried.

"I needed a solid surface. You were available."

"What about the wagon? It was available!"

A lead ball pinged against the invisible Barrier. Without the protective Grit cloud, the shot would have taken Ard in the neck. But nothing could pass through the perimeter of a Barrier cloud.

"Would you look at that?" Raek muttered, glancing down.

The Regulators had momentarily turned their attention on Remaught's goons. Apparently, the Reggies had decided that an enemy of their enemy was not their friend.

"We've got about ten minutes before our Barrier cloud closes," Raek said.

Ard pushed off the invisible perimeter and drifted across the protected sphere. Since Prolonging Grit had been mixed into the mine detonation, their smaller Barrier cloud would fail before the Drift cloud.

"How do we survive this?" Raek pressed.

"Maybe the Reggies and goons will shoot each other and we'll have a free walk to the docks."

"We both know that's not happening," Raek said. "So we've got to be prepared to escape once these two clouds burn out on us."

"I plan to deliver you as a sacrifice," Ard announced. "Maybe I'll go clean. Become a Holy Isle."

"Right," Raek scoffed. "But they won't be able to call themselves 'holy' anymore."

"Just so we're clear, this isn't my fault," said Ard. "Nobody could have predicted that Suno would sell out his boss."

"Suno?" Raek asked. "Who the blazes is Suno?"

"Remaught's bodyguard," he answered. "The Trothian in need of a soak."

"How does he figure into this?"

Ard had worked the entire thing out as they drifted aimlessly in the cloud. That was his thing. Raek figured weights, trajectories, detonations. Ard figured people.

"Remaught wouldn't have double-crossed us like this," Ard began. "It would put too many of his goons in danger, sending them head-to-head with an armed Regulation patrol. Our ruse was solid. Remaught thought he got exactly what he wanted out of the transaction—a dirty Reggie in his pocket.

"Suno, on the other hand, wasn't getting what he wanted. The bodyguard recently had a kid. Must have decided to go clean—looking for a way to get off Dronodan and get his new child back to the Trothian islets. So Suno sold out Remaught for safe passage. He must have told the real Reggies that one of their own was meeting with his mob boss. Only, the Regulators checked their staffing, saw that everyone was accounted for, and determined..."

"That I was a fake." Raek finished the sentence.

Ard nodded. "And if you weren't an actual Reggie, then you wouldn't be heading back to the outpost. You'd be headed off the island as quickly as possible. Hence..." Ard motioned toward the patrol of Regulators just outside the Drift cloud.

"Flames, Ard," Raek muttered. "I wanted to wring somebody's neck for this setup. Now you tell me it's a brand-new dad? You know I've got a soft spot for babies. Can't be leaving fatherless children scattered throughout the Greater Chain. Guess I'll have to wring your neck instead."

"You already killed me once, Raek," Ard said. "Look how that turned out." He gestured at himself.

Ard knew Raek didn't really blame him for their current predicament. No more than Ard blamed Raek when one of his detonations misfired.

Every ruse presented a series of variables. It was Ard's job to control as many as possible, but sometimes things fell into the mix that Ard had no way of foreseeing. Ard couldn't have known that Suno would be the bodyguard present at the transaction. And even if he had known, he couldn't have predicted that Suno would turn against his boss.

Maybe it was time to close shop if they survived the day. Maybe seven years of successful rusing was more than he could ask for.

"There's no way we're walking out of this one, Ard," said Raek.

"Oh, come on," Ard answered. "We've been in worse situations before. Remember the Garin ruse, two years back? Nobody thought we could stay underwater that long."

"If I remember correctly, that wasn't really our choice. Someone was *holding* us underwater. Anyway, I said we aren't *walking* out of this one." Raek emphasized the word, gesturing down below. Their Drift cloud was surrounded. Goons on one side, Reggies on the other. But Raek had a conniving look on his face. "Take off your belt."

Ard tilted his head in question. "I don't think that's such a good idea, on account of us being in a Drift cloud and all. Unless your plan is to give the boys below a Moon Passing. You see, this belt happens to be the only thing currently holding up my trousers. Take it off, and my pants might just drift right off my hips. You know I've lost weight over this job, Raek."

"Oh really?" Raek scoffed. "And how much do you think you weigh?"

Ard scratched behind his ear. "Not a panweight over one sixty-five."

"Ha!" Raek replied. "Maybe back on Pekal. When you were with Tanalin."

"Do you have to bring her up right now?" Ard said. "These might be my final moments, Raek."

"Would you rather think about *me* in your final moments?" Raek asked.

"Ah! Homeland, no!" cried Ard. "I'd rather think about cream-filled pastries."

"Like the ones you used to eat whenever we came ashore from Pekal…with Tanalin."

"Raek!"

The big man chuckled. "Well, Ard, you're not usually the type to let go of things." He let out a fake cough, saying Tanalin's name at the same time. "But I have to say, you've really let yourself go. You're a hundred and seventy-eight panweights. Pushing closer to one eighty with every raspberry tart."

Raek had a gift for that. The man could size up a person, or heft an object and tell you exactly how much it weighed. Useful skill for a detonation Mixer.

"Still less than you," Ard muttered.

"Actually, given our current gravity-free surrounding, we both weigh exactly the same—*nothing.*"

Ard rolled his eyes. "And you wonder why you don't have any friends."

"Don't mock the science," said Raek. "It's about to save our skins. Now give me your blazing belt!"

Ard had no idea what the man was planning, but nearly two decades of friendship had taught him that this was one of those moments when he should shut up and do whatever Raekon Dorrel said.

In a few moments, Ard's belt was off, a surprisingly awkward task to perform while floating with both hands shackled. A gentle toss sent the belt floating to where Raek caught it. He held the thin strap of leather between his teeth while digging inside his Reggie coat for the gun belt.

"How many balls do you have?" Raek asked.

Ard made a face. "I'd think someone so good at mathematics wouldn't have to ask that question."

Raek sighed heavily, his developing plan obviously stifling his sense of humor. "Lead firing balls. In your Roller."

"Oh, right." Ard checked the chambers. "Coincidentally, I have two."

"Reload." Raek sent four cartridges drifting over to Ard, who caught them one at a time. The cartridges housed a premeasured amount of explosive Blast Grit in a thin papery material. At the top of the cartridge was the lead ball, held to the cylindrical cartridge with an adhesive.

Ard set the first cartridge, ball downward, into an open chamber. Twisting the Roller, he used a hinged ramrod on the underside of the barrel to tamp the ball and cartridge tightly into place.

It took him only a moment to reload, a practiced skill that couldn't even be hindered by his shackles. When he looked up, Raek was floating sideways next to the wagon, holding Ard's other Roller and making use of the belt he'd borrowed.

"What kind of arts and crafts are you up to?" Ard asked, seeing his friend's handiwork.

Raek had taken every spare cartridge from Ard's gun belt, a total of more than sixty rounds, and used the belt to lash them into a tight bundle. The barrel of the Roller was also tied down so the Slagstone hammer would make contact with the bundle of cartridges. The whole thing looked ridiculous. Not to mention incredibly dangerous.

"Our Barrier cloud is going to close any second," Raek said. "I'll get everything in position." He shut his eyes the way he often did when required to do complicated mathematics under stressful circumstances. "You should probably get the safe box."

Ard felt a sudden jolt of panic, remembering the whole purpose of the ruse. Glancing down, he was relieved to see that their stolen prize was still floating within the confines of their Barrier cloud, not adrift and unprotected like the poor horse.

Ard judged the distance, reaching out to feel the Barrier wall; solid and impenetrable. He shoved off, a little harder than intended, his body spinning and coming in at the wrong angle.

Ard's forehead struck the safe box. A painful way to be reunited, but it gave Ard the chance to reach out and grab it. For a moment he expected the box to feel heavy in his arms, but weight didn't exist in a Drift cloud.

Ard was just bracing himself to hit the bottom of the Barrier cloud when it burned out. He passed the spot where the invisible perimeter should have stopped him, momentum carrying him downward through the weightlessness of the lingering Drift cloud.

Ard slammed into the road, a clod of dirt floating up from his impact. A gunshot cracked and a lead ball zipped past. Normally, Ard enjoyed having his feet on solid ground. But with the goons and Reggies standing off on the road, he suddenly found himself directly in the line of fire.

"Ardor!" Raek shouted from above. "Get back up here!"

Lying on his back on the road at the bottom of the Drift cloud, Ard saw Raek and the wagon sinking almost imperceptibly toward him. The full strength of the Drift cloud had expired. Prolonging Grit kept it from collapsing entirely, but the effect of pure weightlessness would continue to diminish until both types of Grit fizzled out.

Gripping the safe box against his chest, Ard kicked off the road and sprang upward, the Drift cloud allowing him to float effortlessly upward.

"Gotcha!" Raek grabbed Ard's sleeve, pulling him against the flat bed of the empty wagon.

Raek carefully reached out, taking hold of a thin string. It looked strange, lying flat in the air like a stiff wire. "What we're about to do is among the more experimental methods of escaping."

"You mean, you don't know if it's going to work?" Ard said.

"I did the math in my head. Twice. It should..." He dwindled off. "I have no idea."

"Do I want to know what's tied to the other end of that string?" Ard asked.

"Remember how I lashed your other Roller onto that bundle of Blast Grit cartridges?"

Ard's eyes went wide. "Flames, Raek! That's going to blow us both to..."

Raek pulled the string. Ard heard the click of the gun's trigger on the other side of the wagon. The Slagstone hammer threw sparks, instantly accompanied by one of the loudest explosions Ard had ever heard.

The two men slammed against the wagon as it grew hot, fire belching around them on all sides. The energy from the explosion hurtled the broken wagon on an upward angle, a trajectory Ard hoped was in line with whatever blazing plan Raek had just committed them to.

They exited the top of the Drift cloud, and Ard felt gravity return around him. It didn't seem to matter much, however, since both men were sailing through the air at breakneck velocity. The burning wagon started to fall away behind them, like a comet soaring over the heads of the Reggies.

Raek reached out, grasping Ard's coat at the neck to keep the two of them from separating in the air. Ard had a lot of questions for his big friend. Namely, *How the blazing sparks are we going to get down?* But Ard couldn't breathe, let alone speak.

They were at the apex of their flight, any moment to begin the death-sentence descent, when Raek reached up with his free hand and ripped something off his ammunition sash. It was a Grit bolt, but the clay arrowhead was a different color from the Barrier bolts Ard had used earlier.

Raek gripped the shaft in one hand. Reaching back, he smashed the clay tip against Ard's left shoulder. The Grit detonated, throwing a fresh Drift cloud around them.

Ard felt the weightlessness return, along with a throb on his shoulder from where Raek had detonated the bolt. Guess he had that coming.

In this smaller, new Drift cloud, high over the road, the two men were no longer falling. They were shooting straight through the air, their velocity and trajectory maintained in the weightless environment.

In a flash, they had passed out the other side of the cloud. But before gravity could begin pulling them down, Raek detonated a second Drift bolt, this time shattering the clay tip on Ard's other shoulder.

They were flying. Sparks! Actually *flying*! High over the heads of their enemies, leaving both Regulators and goons behind. A few lead balls were fired in their direction, but there was little chance of getting hit, moving at the rate they were, spinning dizzying circles through the air.

One after another, Raek detonated the Drift bolts, the discolored clouds slightly overlapping as the two men shot horizontally through the air.

The concept of propelling an object over long distances through a series of detonated Drift clouds was not unheard-of. It was the basis for moving heavy materials used in the construction of tall buildings. But for a person to fly like this, unsheltered, the only calculations done impromptu and under gunfire. This was madness and genius, mixed and detonated on the spot.

The two flying men cleared the cliff shoreline, and Ard saw the harbor and docks just below. They exited the latest Drift cloud, the eighth, as Ard was made painfully aware from the welts on his back, and finally began to descend. Gravity ruled over them once more, and Ard judged that they'd slam down right against the first wooden dock.

"Two more!" Raek shouted. He crushed another Drift bolt on Ard's back, maintaining the angle of their fall and buying them a little more distance. As soon as they exited, Raek detonated the last bolt. They soared downward, past the docks and moored ships. Ard saw the *Double Take* below, docked in the farthest spot, a tactical location to speed their getaway.

They exited the final cloud and Ard watched the rapidly approaching water. He had hoped for a more elegant ending to their haphazard flight. Instead, he'd be hitting the bay at tremendous speeds, shackles locked around both wrists, holding a terribly heavy safe box.

Well, I'm certainly not bored, thought Ardor Benn. He took a deep breath.

~

It begins here. Although, for me, I suppose this is something of an ending.

CHAPTER

2

The night was red, bathed in a most unholy light. The Moon—that crimson orb gazing down like the giant blind eye of a Moonsick soul—filled half the sky as it rose above the eastern horizon.

Isle Halavend pulled his coat tighter about his neck, the hem of his pants damp from summer evening rain. Coarse things, trousers, swishing back and forth between one's legs with every step. But he couldn't very well walk the streets in his Islehood robes. People would wonder what he was doing away from the Mooring on the night of a Moon Passing. If he was out here, then who was minding the Holy Torch?

Ha! There were plenty of other Isles at the Mooring who could watch the Torch. Isles who still believed that the ancient ritual actual sheltered the people from Moonsickness. Leave it to them. Halavend had a more important task to complete tonight.

Isle Halavend wasn't alone on the road. Despite the late hour, citizens milled about as if the Moon were merely some second sun, granting them extra hours of rosy light. As if the bloodred sphere in the sky couldn't strike them all blind and mad with Moonsickness.

The citizens weren't wrong in their ignorantly assumed safety. Moonsickness wasn't a threat anywhere but Pekal. That was the way things had always been. But Halavend knew something that they didn't. Things were about to change, and he cringed under the glowing Moon.

Beripent was a complex city, with winding side streets, narrow alleys, and the tallest buildings in the Greater Chain. It was damp and smoky, with nearly a million citizens, and it had taken Isle Halavend hours to find the tavern where his source said the man would be waiting.

His muscles ached from the long walk, and his feet were nearly numb from the damp street. His head ached, too. Isle Halavend wasn't used to staying awake so late. And the physical strain of this night was coupled with a twist of anxiety in his chest. Halavend knew what would happen to him if his superiors learned of this covert outing. But he'd already carried on for so many cycles, despite the threats.

The old Isle stopped under a sign hanging in front of a two-story structure. The windows were lit from within, but dingy curtains had been drawn to block the unwanted gaze of outsiders. Several figures loitered on the steps of the Staggering Bull. A worrisome welcome, but Halavend hadn't come this far to let a few drunken vagabonds bar his entrance.

Reaching inside his coat, Halavend clutched the cold handle of the dagger on his belt. Who was he fooling? Halavend couldn't stab someone, even if his life was threatened. He had fallen far, but not far enough to murder another person.

The dagger was completely unnecessary, Halavend soon discovered. The loitering figures paid him no mind, and he pushed through the door, an unfamiliar stench welcoming him into the tavern.

The dim room was choked with bodies. It was warmer than Halavend could tolerate. The night outside was pleasant. He didn't understand why no one bothered to open a window.

It was noisy, too. A wash of slurred conversations that rattled in the old man's ears, making his head ache worse. It was as far removed from the Mooring's Coves as possible. And the smell...

A woman approached him, a fraction of his age, a tall wooden cup in one hand. Her skin was pale and her hair looked weeks unwashed, but her revealing dress seemed new and crisply ironed. She pressed herself close to him and spoke with breath that reeked of cheap ale.

"That's a nice hat."

Isle Halavend was frozen, his hand gripping the dagger hilt tighter than ever, though he had no intention of using the weapon. It had been so long since he'd been this close to a woman outside the Islehood. The Isles weren't barred from marriage, but tradition required their union to be with another Holy Isle. This woman wasn't even a Wayfarist. Or if she was, the Islehood's teachings were obviously lost on her.

"I'm looking for someone," the old Isle said. His voice seemed to get whisked away, mixing with the maddening hubbub in the Staggering Bull. How did anything useful ever get done in a place like this? He scanned the crowd, but all he had to go off was a charcoal sketch from his source. It was just too dim in here.

"Aren't we all?" said the woman.

Halavend took an awkward step back. "Go only to aid others in their Way." What was he doing? Quoting Wayfarist scripture at this Settled woman?

Her face turned to a sneer, and she moved away. Halavend hadn't meant it to be offensive, but she had clearly recognized the saying. Isle Halavend's hand finally slipped off the dagger, and he reached out to grab the woman's wrist.

"I'm looking for a specific person," he clarified as the woman turned back. "His name is Ardor Benn."

"Figures." The woman tugged her wrist out of the old Isle's grasp. "That's the man." She pointed across the tavern to a small table in a smoky corner, where a man sat alone. That couldn't be him. Everything Halavend had heard about Ardor Benn led him to believe that the man was gregarious, even finding ways to thrive in the spotlight despite being a wanted criminal.

"There's still time if you want in on the drinks," said the woman. "He's not shooting for another few minutes." She turned and strode off into the crowd, leaving Isle Halavend to puzzle over her words. He moved through the press of bodies, losing sight of Ardor several times in the bustling tavern.

There were all types of people here. From the varied complexions of the Landers, to the deep blue skin of the Trothians. Halavend was pleased to see the cultures mingling. Many of the Landers in the Staggering Bull were young enough that they probably never knew a time when Trothians weren't allowed in the Greater Chain.

To Halavend, it was another reminder of how many years he'd been cooped up in the Mooring. King Pethredote's rule had changed so much of society, but the Holy Isles remained largely isolated from such developments.

At last, Halavend reached Ardor's table and came face-to-face with the man, his old heart racing. Cycles of illegal study had led him to this meeting. A meeting that could turn the islands upside down. He was here at last.

And Ardor Benn was drunk.

The young man leaned back on his wooden chair, legs spread wide and one booted foot resting on either side of the table. His features were handsome: a square stubbled chin, deep brown eyes, and short dark hair. His fair skin was suntanned a rich brown, like a curing leather.

On the table between the man's raised feet, Halavend counted nine empty mugs. They were lined up neatly, as though on display. Behind them was a large wooden bowl filled with single-mark Ashings.

Of course. Isle Halavend sighed. The one night he dared venture out, risking everything, the man he needed was barely conscious. Halavend thought about leaving right then. There was no way he could offer this man a job in his current state.

"Three Ashings and an Ashlit, old man," Ardor said, his speech slightly slurred from the excessive drink.

"Three Ashings and an Ashlit for what?" asked Halavend, annoyed and rather disgusted.

"To buy me another drink," explained Ardor, a grin on his face.

"That much for a drink?" Halavend didn't have much experience outside the Mooring lately, but ten Ashlits made an Ashing, and there was no way the price of ale had soared so high.

Ardor chuckled. "The Ashlit is for the drink," he said. "The three Ashings are for the bowl." He gestured at the pile before him.

"Now why would I do that?"

"I'll be target shooting in about one minute," Ardor said. "I miss the shot, and you get all your Ashings back, plus I pay for three drinks a man."

Halavend pointed to the empty mugs on the table. "And nine fools have already bought into this?"

"I know!" Ardor laughed. "Isn't it great?" He tipped too far on his chair, causing both his boots to snap off the table so he could right himself before falling.

"You're drunk."

"And you're old." Ardor held out his hands. "Three Ashings and a drink."

"Drunkenness is idleness is drunkenness. One bringeth about the other to the making of a Settled soul." Halavend quoted another scripture without even thinking.

"You can't talk me down off this ledge like you're some kind of Holy Isle," Ardor replied. Halavend went rigid, wondering if the man somehow knew his station. But that would be impossible. They'd never met before, and Ardor would have no reason to suspect it.

"Spouting Wayfarism in a place like this will likely get you thrown out without your coat." Ardor stood up, drawing a Singler from his belt. Halavend stepped back, his hands raising in instinctive defense. "Relax." Ardor picked up the bowl of Ashings with his free hand. "It's time to collect."

Ardor Benn staggered past Isle Halavend, bumping into an empty chair. Miraculously, all the Ashings stayed in the bowl. Ardor cursed, then raised his voice over the clamor of the tavern.

"Shooting time!"

A few people began pushing aside tables and herding patrons against the wall. Halavend guessed the ones preparing the room were the ones who'd bought into Ardor's little bet. They were anxious to get their Ashings back and get the promised free liquor flowing.

In the press of people, Halavend found himself forced behind the table, into the corner where Ardor Benn had been sitting. The man had left a pipe burning, a thin plume of smoke mingling with the haze in the room.

The old Isle suddenly felt a rush of excitement. His head seemed to clear a bit, and his aching leg muscles soothed. Was this what it was always like for the common citizens? Had he been holed up in the Mooring for so long that he didn't remember what a thrill felt like? No. This was something more. A warmth from deep within.

"Twenty-seven Ashings!" Ardor shouted, swinging the bowl around for everyone to see. "And this morning—tonight...ah, whatever time it is. Right now, I will make a shot worth twenty-seven Ashings!"

A Trothian man with deep blue skin and a long ponytail stepped into the open space that would soon be a drunk man's shooting range. He pulled a high bar stool to the far side of the room and carefully placed a ceramic mug on the seat.

"One shot!" Ardor's voice was unnecessarily loud, now that everyone in the tavern had quieted to see how the gamble would play out. He waved the Singler above his head, and Halavend half expected him to pull the trigger on accident. A real surprise for the tenants on the second floor.

"Last call!" Ardor held out the wooden bowl of Ashings. "And a real bargain deal. Three Ashings say I can shoot that mug. Three drinks and your money back if I miss."

Seeing his inebriated state prompted several other people in the tavern to step forward, tossing three-mark Ashings into the bowl.

Halavend shook his head. Perhaps this was all a mistake. There had to be another ruse artist in the Greater Chain capable of carrying out Isle Halavend's important venture. The man Halavend saw now, deprived of his better judgment, waving a loaded gun through a tavern full of people, seemed a far cry from the best.

Ardor was aiming now, if that was what it could be called. The Singler in his outstretched hand wobbled so much, it looked like he was writing his name in the air. The distance was no more than twenty feet. But the target mug was small, even for a sober man to hit.

Halavend's muscles suddenly ached again. The air around him seemed clearer, despite the fact that Ardor's pipe continued smoldering next to the empty mugs. His headache returned. And he suddenly understood exactly what was going on.

The Slagstone hammer threw sparks as Ardor squeezed the trigger. The Singler spit flame, and in the same heartbeat, the mug on the other side of the room exploded, the lead ball chipping into the brick wall behind.

The tavern's occupants seemed to take a collective gasp. While the crowd was still parted, Ardor raised the gun's barrel and blew the smoke away from him. Tucking the bowl of Ashings under one arm, he sauntered—*staggered*—across the room. He fidgeted with the door, pushing for a moment before realizing that it needed to be pulled. Then he stepped out into the glowing red night and the door swung shut.

Isle Halavend moved around the table, maneuvering through the room as the crowd dispersed. If Ardor Benn got away now, Halavend would never forgive himself. He'd had the man across the table from him, but he'd doubted. And that was exactly what Ardor was counting on.

Halavend stepped into the street, the Red Moon so large it left only a little dark sky visible on the horizon. He adjusted his hat and sucked in the refreshing night air, scanning up and down the cobblestoned roadway.

Which way had Ardor gone? Halavend stepped over to one of the men slouched against the brick wall of the Staggering Bull.

"Did you see a man leave this place just before me?" Halavend didn't even think of reaching for his dagger now. Had he really been afraid of these loiterers before? The man didn't respond, so he bent and touched his shoulder. "He was slender, dark-haired. Did you see which direction he went?"

It was a woman who answered, seated on the bottom step of the tavern entrance. "He went that way."

Halavend turned to see her pointing down a narrow side street. "Homeland bless you!" he called, hurrying in that direction.

Down the street, several indistinguishable figures were bathed in reddish light, making their way to unknown destinations. Confound his old eyes! One of those figures had to be Ardor Benn.

The old Isle raced forward, wishing his joints didn't protest so. He was halfway down the side street when something emerged from a narrow alley in a blur of movement.

A cry left his lips, and Halavend's hand flew to the knife on his belt. His assailant was much quicker, swatting the knife to the cobblestones as soon as it appeared. Halavend's arm wrenched back painfully, and a strong hand closed around his neck as the attacker shoved him against the wooden siding of the nearest building.

Halavend heard the distinct click of a Slagstone gun hammer locking into place. He felt the barrel, hard and cold as it pressed into the soft flesh below his chin.

"Why are you following me?" asked a whispered voice. Halavend could just make out his attacker's face from the corner of his eye.

Homeland be praised! It was Ardor Benn. Though Halavend wasn't sure if he should feel relieved or terrified that the man had found him.

"Who are you?" Ardor asked. "You with the Beripent Regulation? I have broken no laws tonight. Unless, of course, you *are* with the Regulation. Then I suppose I just assaulted a Reggie."

"No, no." Halavend found it difficult to speak in a way that wouldn't jostle the gun under his chin. "My name is... Holy Isle Halavend. I'm here with no threat to you or your Settled soul."

Ardor suddenly stepped away, his face wrinkled in confusion as he lowered the Singler. "Holy Isle... That would explain the Wayfarist speak back at the tavern. But it doesn't explain a whole slew of other things."

Ardor holstered his gun and picked up a sack. Halavend heard the distinct sound of Ashings clicking together, likely the ruse artist's earnings from the tavern.

"First," Ardor said, "in case you hadn't noticed, it's a Moon Passing tonight. If you are who you say, then you're supposed to be watching the Holy Torch in the Mooring on a night like this."

"And you're supposed to be drunk," retorted Isle Halavend. "So I guess tonight we are both more than people take us for."

Ardor slung the sack over one shoulder, and Halavend spoke quickly before the younger man could walk away. He had to make Ardor believe that he was worth listening to.

"You detonated Health Grit behind your table." Halavend's words caused Ardor Benn to stop short. "An expensive detonation, probably mixed with Prolonging Grit, possibly even Compounding Grit. The pipe on the table was a smoke screen—quite literally. A way to envelop your corner in haze so no one would notice the detonation cloud hanging around you."

"And why would I do that?" Ardor took a threatening step toward the old man.

"Health Grit purges imperfections from the body," Halavend explained. "Within that cloud, you could drink all the ale in that tavern and not get drunk. But the others didn't know that you were merely acting. You had them bet against you, and in the end you probably earned double the Ashings that you spent on the Health Grit."

"Hmm," Ardor mused. "The longer you talk, the less I believe that you're actually a Holy Isle."

"My word is genuine, I assure you," said Halavend. He'd certainly earned the man's attention. "Though lately I haven't been as holy as my title might suggest."

"That might be the most honest things I've heard from the mouth of an Isle," Ardor said. "But none of it explains why you were following me."

"I need your help."

"Well, I'm not in the business of helping old religious folk," replied Ardor. But he didn't walk away.

"I know your business," Halavend said. "And I have a job fit for your unique set of skills."

"How do you know I'm the right man?" asked Ardor. "My last ruse didn't exactly go off without a hitch."

"Yes, I know. Two weeks ago on Dronodan. Outside of Marow," said Halavend. "As I understand it, there is a safe box with five hundred Ashings waiting for you at the bottom of the harbor."

Halavend had him now. Ardor stepped closer, his posture threatening once more. "How do you know that?"

"I did my research," answered the Isle. "That's how I know you're the right man for my job."

"I'm listening."

Isle Halavend retrieved his fallen dagger and glanced around the narrow street. A few late-night pedestrians had drawn uncomfortably near. Taking Ardor Benn by the arm, the old Isle directed him into the dark alley where the ruse artist had been hiding. This was one place the Red Moon's light didn't penetrate, but there was still enough ambient glow for the two men to see each other.

"Before I can continue, I must assure absolute secrecy of this information," said Halavend.

Ardor pinched his lips shut. "Secret's safe with me. A ruse artist understands the value of a good employer."

"I wish I could trust you, but this is much too important to test a man's word." Isle Halavend reached into his coat pocket and withdrew a bundle of cloth, securely tied. Pulling the ends of the string, the bundle unfolded to reveal two clay balls, both just a bit larger than an Ashing.

"These detonation pots contain two types of Specialty Grit," Halavend explained. "With your permission, I'm going to detonate them both at our feet before I explain anything more about this job."

Ardor scratched behind his ear thoughtfully. "I'd like to know just what kind of Grit we're dealing with before you blow us up."

"Of course." Halavend pointed to the detonation pot on the left. "This is Silence Grit. Are you familiar with its function?"

Ardor nodded. "No better way to keep a secret."

Silence Grit was derived from pieces of spruce wood, digested and fired by a dragon, and then processed to powder. Its effect contained all sound within the blast radius. People outside the Silence cloud wouldn't be able to hear anything within, just as people within wouldn't be able to hear anything outside. That would eliminate any possibility of an eavesdropper.

"The second pot is full of Memory Grit," Isle Halavend explained. "Have you used this before?"

"Now, that's a clever question," said Ardor. "I suppose I wouldn't remember if I had." He leaned forward as if to inspect the pot closer. "Digested human skull, isn't it? I worked a stint as a Harvester," explained Ardor. "Right unsettling to dig a human skeleton out of a fire-hardened mound of dragon dung. More so if you knew the guy going in."

Halavend felt a chill that caused him to fidget. He didn't like to think about where the Grit came from. Especially the types derived from human bones. He knew King Pethredote had instituted an initiative to ensure that the bodies used were not gainfully acquired, but the whole thing was still unsettling.

"When the Memory Grit detonates," Halavend went on, "we can stay within its blast radius and converse normally until the cloud closes. Once outside the effect, neither of us will have any memory of what transpired within the cloud."

"I don't see why that's necessary." Ardor seemed hesitant. And rightfully so.

"I can only trust you with information if you agree to take the job," explained Isle Halavend.

"But how will you know if I agree?" Ardor asked. "Once we step foot outside the Memory cloud, we won't remember anything either of us said."

"I will make a marking." Halavend produced a piece of chalk from his pocket. "A Y if you accept, or an N if you do not."

"How do I know you won't trick me?" Ardor asked. "You could explain the job in the heart of the detonation and mark a Y even if I say no. Once the cloud closes, I won't remember that you wrote down the opposite of what I said."

Halavend nodded. The man was as good as people claimed, thinking through every angle. "If you see me write anything contrary to what you agree with"—he took a deep breath and drew the dagger from his belt—"you can stab me. If there is any trickery, you'll find me dead when the Memory cloud closes."

Ardor Benn raised his eyebrows. "Wow." He took the proffered handle of the blade. "You've really thought this through."

"You have no idea the extent of research that has led me to this moment," Isle Halavend said. "Things are not right, Ardor Benn. I need your help to set them straight. What do you say? Can I detonate the pots?"

Halavend looked at the two clay spheres resting in his wrinkled palm. Using these types of Grit for personal reasons would get him barred from the Islehood. And the punishment would be far worse if anyone discovered what conversation they had been used to safeguard.

Ardor Benn nodded. "That's a lot of fanfare. Let's find out if your job offer lives up to the hype."

Isle Halavend hurled the detonation pots against the ground. They sparked and ignited on impact, enveloping the narrow alley in two overlapping clouds of Grit.

～

The night frightens me. There are wild things afoot in the cover of darkness.

CHAPTER

3

Ardor Benn rapped on the roof of the carriage and waited for it to stop. He was at the corner of the bustling Char, a place where no one paused to notice the comings and goings of others. It was several miles from the Mooring, but Ard preferred to make the final approach on foot.

Ard climbed out of the wagon, passed the driver six metal Ashlits, then flipped him an extra two. A tip. For avoiding Bort Street. That roadway was in such disrepair, a man could lose teeth from rattling along in a hired carriage.

Isle Halavend had given him the Ashlits for the ride, but Ard would have happily paid from his own purse. He was a ruse artist, not a thief. Being able to pay generously for goods and services was exactly why he ran ruses.

Rusing was a craft. An art form. Like the rich folks' orchestral music—some movements slow, some movements swift and thrilling, but Ard was always the conductor. Picking a wealthy Focus, planning the setup, executing the plan, getting the payout. That was rusing. Slighting your carriage driver, or slipping an extra apple into your bushel—that was baseless thievery. No creativity at all.

Ard set off into the busy Char, following a wide, paved pathway. Pruned hedges lined the sides, taller trees rising behind them. The vegetation was a symbol here. Life out of ash. Regrowth.

Ard passed the first preserved structure. It was little more than a crumbling square of blackened timbers. The ground around the burned ruins had been paved with flat stones to hold back vines that would try to climb the historic walls.

In front of the old building was a vendor's cart, colorful canopy stretched overtop. Ard couldn't see the wares due to the crowd of curious onlookers—visitors who had come from other cities across Espar, or sailed in from the surrounding islands of the Greater Chain. Beripent was a city worth visiting. And the Char, with its historical significance, was not a place to miss.

Ard passed another destroyed building, preserved and maintained with a perimeter of the same stone pavers. At this site, an artist sat on a short stool, painting oils over a stretched canvas. Sparks, why would anyone buy that painting? Who wanted to look at a two-hundred-and-fifty-year-old pile of rubble?

Ard knew the history, of course. Flames, every kid in the Greater Chain knew what happened in the Char. A dragon happened. A bull dragon.

This area had once been the center of Beripent's high society. The site of the old palace was just up ahead. King Kerith, inarguably the worst monarch in the history of the islands, decided he was the man to tame the dragons. Bring them out of the high mountains of Pekal and onto the rolling hills of Espar.

Now, moving a dragon—everyone knew that was suicide. But Kerith's Harvesters reported the location of a fertilized dragon egg and he had them kill the mother and extract it. Put it on display until it hatched. Blazing thing grew up three years, nearly to its full size, before it decided to raze the city and eat a bunch of citizens.

Grotenisk the Destroyer.

Grotenisk. As far as Ard knew, this was the only dragon to have ever been officially named. *Eat enough folks, and they're bound to name you,* Ard thought. *People can't curse you if you don't have a name.*

Grotenisk's attack made sense to Ard's mind. Only dragon to leave Pekal. Only dragon to attack an island. Ard wouldn't like it, either, getting plucked out of his natural habitat, raised away from his kind. No wonder the bull snapped.

Ard passed a man selling roasted nuts, his open flame contained in a barrel beside a historic wall of crumbling bricks. Here was a place where so many people had been burned or eaten. Now somebody was selling roasted nuts. Did no one else see the irony?

Supposedly, nearly ten thousand people had died in the damage caused by Grotenisk's attack. Fires raged for weeks. The dragon himself was said to have single-handedly killed a thousand people in the space of just a few hours. That was destruction like Ard couldn't imagine.

The vendor with the roasted nuts called out to him, but Ard was already late. Holy Isles had a reputation of being uptight to begin with. That poor Halavend was probably nearing a complete nervous breakdown.

Raek wasn't happy about Ard's choice to meet the old man. Could be a setup. Didn't have enough to go on. Raek could be right on all counts, and normally, Ard would have dismissed the Isle as a lunatic, and forgotten all about it. But Raek hadn't been in that alleyway during the Moon Passing two nights ago. He hadn't seen the fear and sincerity in the old man's eyes.

Now Ard was trusting his gut. And a single letter that had been chalked onto the brick wall when the Memory Grit cloud burned out.

Y.

He entered Oriar's Square, the heart of the Char. Activity was concentrated here, with enough vendors lined up to make the area look like a common marketplace. Musicians, performers, and artists were scattered among tourists, each competing for an Ashing.

Oriar, Ard thought. *The Folly of Beripent.* A public stain on the Islehood to this day. A failed attempt to save the city.

Ard glanced at the stone steps that had once led to the entrance of King Kerith's palace. This was the very site where Oriar had failed his detonation of Visitant Grit. Now the stairway led nowhere. Cordoned off with stout chains, the stone steps ascended more than fifteen feet before crumbling away to nothing.

Ard picked up his pace, navigating a few more pathways before emerging from the historic Char. Here, Ard could see the abrupt drop of the cliff-like shoreline, and smell the salty breeze coming off the sea. On a clear morning like this, he could even see the cloud-covered tips of Pekal's looming peaks across the InterIsland Waters.

The Mooring was nestled in a low spot at the base of a grassy knoll. It was a massive, oblong building, in the fashion of an overturned ship, though completely made of stone. The walls turned gently inward, domed. A construction feat made possible by the use of Drift Grit, just like the high-rise buildings of the rich folk. Pay enough, and the masons could float blocks of stone right into position.

Ard reached the entrance to the religious building and paused before the open double doors. He hadn't been here since he was a child. For a moment, Ard thought how his mother would be proud of him, returning to the Mooring, meeting with a Holy Isle. But the truth was, Isle Halavend seemed like something of a heretic, and Ard was here for a ruse. Although the thought was painful, it was probably best that his mother went on thinking he was dead.

The chamber inside was large, and the scuff of his boots echoed against the stone walls. Light Grit burned in a dozen mounted braziers, and a massive candlelit chandelier hung from the arched ceiling.

In the center of the room was a display, of sorts. It was a large glass box, an impressive piece of craftsmanship with bands of iron added for support. A detonation of Light Grit burned at the top, illuminating the contents of the transparent box.

It was an unfertilized dragon egg. It was mostly spherical, perhaps slightly oblong, standing almost as tall as Ard. Unlike a bird's egg, there was no shell. As Ard understood it, that came later, during fertilization. The dragon egg on display was gelatinous, its milky white color the only thing that really distinguished it from the preservative liquid suspending the egg in the display box.

This egg was old, likely infertile. Though if it had been fertilized, its white color indicated that the hatchling would have been a female. But hatchling dragons were a thing of the past now. They had ended with the Bull Dragon Patriarchy. Kind of impossible to have hatchlings when all the males were dead.

"Homeland bless you," a voice echoed through the waiting chamber. Ard stepped away from the gelatinous egg to find one of the Holy Isles—a woman Isless—ascending a wide staircase on the opposite side of the chamber. She looked to be only a few years older than Ard, dark-skinned, wearing the sea-green robes of the Islehood.

"Morning." Ard tugged at the bottom of his vest. He hadn't worn his gun belt and Rollers, of course. It would be quite inappropriate to wear such weapons into this holy edifice. Instead, he had a dagger in each boot and a short-barreled Singler snugged tightly inside his vest.

"What calls you to the Mooring, Wayfarist?" asked the Isless.

Ard didn't bother to correct her. He was no more a Wayfarist than she was a Trothian Agrodite. "I'm here to meet with Isle Halavend," he explained. "He's expecting me in Cove Twenty-Three."

The Isless gestured for him to follow her back down the stairs. Ard moved around the glass box with its illuminated egg.

"Isle Halavend is a wise Compass," she said as they descended the long flight of stone steps. "He's been with the Islehood a very long time. He will provide you with excellent guidance."

"I'm sure he will," Ard replied with a half grin.

It was much darker at the bottom of the stairs. A few Light Grit detonations provided a soft glow, but most of the illumination was from the colored skylights set high overhead.

Ard stepped off the bottom step and onto a floating wooden

dock, where another young Isle was waiting for him, long wooden pole in hand.

Every Mooring was like this, although the one in Beripent was easily the largest. The building was flooded after construction, diverting seawater to flow gently along the floor of the Mooring. At its deepest, the water was probably only three or four feet. Ard could even see the bottom in spots where direct light glinted through the skylights to touch the glassy water.

"The Homeland calls him to Isle Halavend," said the Isless to the young man. The other Isle nodded, leading Ard from the floating dock to a tethered raft. The Isle released the rope and dipped his pole into the water.

Pushing along the bottom, he directed the raft into the middle of the indoor canal. Built into the walls on both sides were small rooms—coves, as they were called. Each cove had a small floating dock to allow access to the wooden door.

"Have you been to the Mooring before?" asked the poling Isle.

Ard nodded. "It's been a while."

"The Homeland is grateful for your visit."

They passed another raft returning to the main dock, an aging Isless poling a man and woman in common citizen clothing.

"How did you meet Isle Halavend?" Ard's Isle asked. "Did the wind guide him to you?" It was common practice for the Isles to wander the city, approaching homes to invite Wayfarists to visit the Mooring for further spiritual guidance. In a way, wasn't that what Isle Halavend had done?

"Something like that," Ard answered, but his attention had turned to something in the middle of the waterway. It was a wrought iron fire pit, standing just above the water's surface. Although Ard couldn't see the pedestal holding it upright, he knew the large bowl must have been anchored into the Mooring floor.

"Have you seen it lit?" asked the Isle, when he noticed Ard's attention on the fire pit.

"The Holy Torch?" he answered. "No."

They were floating past it now, and Ard could see a few blackened logs resting in the bottom of the heavy bowl. It looked like it was designed for the ashes and embers to fall through the iron slats into the waterway.

"I would encourage you to join us next cycle during the Passing," said the Isle. "Any additional prayers help to strengthen the Torch's protective power."

Ard remembered his parents going to see the Holy Torch when he was young. They described the waterway full of rafts, with every Holy Isle in attendance along with hundreds of Wayfarist citizens that came and went to offer a prayer of thanks to the Homeland.

It was hard to accept that some little fire in that iron brazier kept all mankind safe from Moonsickness. Halavend probably believed it. The young Isle poling his raft certainly believed it. Sparks, even Ard's parents had always believed it unquestioningly.

There had to be something to it. There was a Holy Torch in every Mooring in the Greater Chain, and the Islehood had been lighting them for centuries—from the time the Landers first arrived on these islands. The Torch was a beacon to the Homeland. A lighthouse to attract its holy protection.

Espar, Strind, Dronodan, and Talumon had never been touched by Moonsickness. Even the little Trothian islets were protected, nestled safely between the larger islands of the Greater Chain.

Pekal was the only real danger. Poor souls who spent a Moon Passing on that mountainous island inevitably contracted the sickness. It made sense. There was no Mooring on Pekal. No Holy Torch. Centuries back, the Islehood had declared the island impure and unfit for such a sacred edifice.

The Holy Torch was the simplest explanation—that the Homeland's power protected them—but it required faith. There were other, more scientific theories behind the cause of Moonsickness.

Raek liked to talk about them, but Ard only ever listened with half an ear. Wayfarism denounced such theories, of course.

Ard wasn't sure what to believe, and he didn't waste a lot of time thinking about it. Ard had survived a Moon Passing every thirty days of his life and was yet to wake up blind, mute, and raging with violent madness.

Now past the empty brazier, the Isle dug his pole deep, crossing the canal until they bumped against a floating dock.

Ard stepped off the raft, thanking the Isle that had brought him. Should he tip the man for his service? Before Ard could dig an Ashlit from his pocket, the Isle had pushed his raft back into the open canal.

Ard stood on the dock for a moment. There was a bell mounted beside the cove door, but Ard decided to knock. After what seemed like a long pause, the wooden door cracked open. Isle Halavend's face appeared, and he anxiously beckoned Ard to enter.

A Light Grit torch illuminated the cove, the bright detonation set into a cleft in the wall above a desk. The silver-haired Isle was wearing his sea-green robes today. He shut the door quickly, and Ard was surprised to find that Halavend was not alone.

A Trothian woman leaned against the wall where the open door had shielded her. She looked only a few years younger than Halavend.

She didn't wear the common clothes of an island citizen like most of the Trothians who had taken up living in the Greater Chain. Instead, the woman's arms and legs were wrapped in red cloth from the elbows and the knees down. She wore a long leather tunic tied with a decorated belt of clay beads. The woman's hair was long and straight, cascading over her shoulders like an ink-black waterfall. Her skin was a royal shade of blue, well kept and glistening. But Ard had a hard time looking any Trothian in the eye for more than a moment. Hers were a pale steel gray, vibrating so rapidly that his own eyes began to water.

"Here's an unlikely pair if ever I've seen one," Ard said, glancing between the Trothian and the old man who had seated himself at the desk.

"You're late," snapped Isle Halavend, sliding a pair of spectacles onto his face.

"Do you ever get holy fish in that canal out there?" Ard asked, ignoring Halavend's comment. "Maybe a shark or two? That would sure liven things up around here."

Isle Halavend swiveled in his seat, his bespectacled face tense. "Ardor Benn! The Mooring is a sacred place. When you step onto that raft, you begin a symbolic journey to the Homeland. I asked you to meet me today for your employment, not for your mockery."

Sparks! Was this the same old man from two nights ago? The man who had seemed to tremble at the very smell of the Staggering Bull?

"This is your thief?" the woman asked Halavend. Her accent was noticeable, but not as pronounced as many of the Trothians Ard had associated with.

"Thief? Flames, no!" Ard cried. "I'm something a bit more specialized."

"Ardor is a ruse artist," Halavend said. "A person who gets what he wants through elaborate trickery."

"And he is the man for the job?" the Trothian asked.

"Perhaps regrettably," answered Halavend. "But he has the skills required."

"Perhaps regrettably?" Ard repeated. "That's a very different tune from the one you were singing when you found me outside that tavern."

"Don't confuse my position, Ardor Benn," said Halavend. "Just because I'm hiring you does not mean I'm comfortable going outside the law in this manner. If there were another way, Homeland knows I would take it."

Isle Halavend gestured to a bench against the cove wall, and the

Trothian woman seated herself. Ard preferred to stand near the door. Quicker escape, in case this was a setup.

"Who's your new convert?" Ard asked Halavend. It was a ludicrous question. All Trothians were Agrodites. As far as Ard knew, they couldn't denounce their religion, even if they wanted to. Certain things necessary for a Trothian's health were intrinsically tied to Agrodite ritual.

Take the saltwater soak, for example. To participate in the ritual was considered Agrodite. But if a Trothian missed too many soaks, their blue skin started to flake off, like Remaught's bodyguard. Supposedly very itchy, and somewhat painful. Hard to denounce a religion that kept your skin where it was supposed to be.

"This is Lyndel," Isle Halavend replied. "Her role in this is significant. I wanted her to meet you." She bowed slightly, crossing her wrists before her chest in the traditional Agrodite way.

Ard nodded. "Pleasure."

"Lyndel and I have been studying together for several cycles now," Halavend explained. "The wind had blown me far from Beripent when our paths crossed. She is an Agrodite priestess."

Priestess! Sparks. Every moment, this Halavend seemed more Settled than Wayfarist. King Pethredote's Inclusionary Act allowed Trothians to become citizens of the Greater Chain, but the Prime Isle still wouldn't let them near Wayfarism. The very fact that Halavend was harboring an Agrodite in his cove put them all in danger.

"So... are you lovers?" Ard asked.

"Homeland, no!" Halavend cried, his pale face flushing.

Ard held up his hands. "It's all right if you are. No judgment here. I'm sure old people feel things, too." They were both getting up there in years, but it wasn't like a Trothian and a Lander could bear offspring, anyway.

"Lyndel came to me for help," said Halavend, seeming anxious to change the subject.

"It is our language," explained Lyndel. "The Trothian tongue can only be spoken. There is no way to write it. Wayfarism is set in books. The books keep it steady. Never changing."

That wasn't completely accurate. Wayfarism had splintered into several religions throughout Lander history. They were all Homelandic. All stemmed from the same original beliefs. Still, there were far more Wayfarists throughout the Greater Chain than any other religion.

"The Agrodite religion is of the oral tradition," Halavend explained. "Songs, poems, and stories told from one generation to the next."

"I asked Holy Isle Halavend to write the Agrodite teachings," Lyndel said. "Let there be a record so my doctrine can be steady, too."

"I thought it was against your religion to read and write," Ard replied. "Now this old Isle's teaching you the alphabet?"

"It's not that simple," Halavend said. "What do you know of Trothian vision?"

Ard made a quick glance at Lyndel's blurry gray eyes. He knew Trothian eyesight was very different from his own. Suspicious Landers even claimed that Trothians could see through walls. Ard didn't believe that.

"I know Trothians can see in the dark," Ard answered. It was common knowledge not to sneak up on a Trothian bodyguard in the dead of night.

"The Trothian eye perceives only the energy of things," explained Lyndel. "I see your face; its shape and form make you identifiable. It is difficult to explain the differences, since I have never seen the way you see."

"Lyndel is incapable of seeing text on a page," Isle Halavend added. "The energy of the paper overpowers such fine lettering."

"Can't you write bigger letters?" Ard asked.

"We have tested several theories," said Isle Halavend. "They all work, but none are practical. Increasing the size of the text does make it visible to Lyndel's eye, but I can fit only a few words on each page. Using a lower-energy background can help, but the most effective materials were shale and slate—cumbersome. Even then, we had to find a high-energy medium to use in place of ink."

"That was most effective," said Lyndel. "But Halavend was made uncomfortable by the best ink substitute."

Ard raised an eyebrow. "What was it?"

"Blood," answered Lyndel. "Needed to be fresh and warm. As it dried, the text was once again washed out from my sight."

"So you'd have to kill a lot of animals to learn to read," said Ard.

"That was never my intent," answered Lyndel.

"Killing animals?"

"Learning to read," she corrected. "I came to Halavend so he could write the Agrodite doctrine to preserve it for future generations."

"Future generations that won't be able to read it any better than you," Ard pointed out.

"Our cultures are mixing. Now, more than ever," said Lyndel. "Our races may not be capable of procreating together, but I predict that the future will bring more and more *Muckmus* willing to read our doctrine."

Muckmus. It wasn't necessarily a derogatory term, just a Trothian word used to describe anyone who wasn't blue-skinned. Ard's people preferred the term Landers.

"As much as I like standing here talking about religion," Ard said, "I have a feeling it doesn't have anything to do with why you called me to the Mooring."

"On the contrary," said Halavend. "Religion has everything to do with it. Lyndel has a brilliant mind, and her beliefs are fascinating. By comparing our doctrines, we discovered something. A piece of evidence toward a theory never before considered. The further we researched, the more solid it became, until we were absolutely sure of its gravity. But it was a dangerous road to tread, disproving a significant piece of Wayfarist dogma, and realizing that the truth was actually in an all-new doctrine. Something that changes the very way we view our world."

"New doctrine," muttered Ard. "Sounds like something you should talk to the Prime Isle about."

"I attempted to tell Prime Isle Chauster last cycle," Halavend said. "He would not hear what I had to say. The facts that I presented go against common Wayfarist beliefs. I hid the fact that my findings had been reached through a collaboration with an Agrodite priestess. Still, the Prime Isle insisted I abandon my pursuit of these studies, lest I get barred from the Islehood, tried for heresy, and executed for my crime."

Ard knew the feeling. He had been strong-armed and threatened by authority before.

"What's so important about this new doctrine?" Ard asked.

"That is not something I'm willing to discuss with you today," replied the Isle. "But I assure you there is nothing more critical than following through with it."

"If it's so important, why not sidestep the Prime Isle altogether?" Ard asked. "Make your *new doctrine* known to the common citizen." *You could start with telling me*, Ard thought.

"It may come to that someday." Isle Halavend shot a worried glance at Lyndel. "But we cannot risk that kind of chaos at this point. This information would incite panic—the kind that could start a war. I'm prepared to die for this cause, but Lyndel and I still have critical work left to do. We do not have the support of the Prime Isle. Without his backing, we do not have the support of the king. Neither the law nor the Islehood will do anything for us. Which is precisely what led me to you, Ardor Benn."

Ard thought of the white letter chalked onto the alley wall. It was strange to think that he'd already accepted the job once, though he had no idea *what* he had agreed to do.

The old Isle looked up, his blue eyes trained on Ard. His voice was barely above a whisper. "I'm hiring you to steal the king's crown."

What? Ard studied Isle Halavend's wrinkled face. The old man hadn't proven himself to have much sense of humor. Was he serious?

"You want me to run a ruse on the king?" Ard said. "On King Pethredote—the crusader monarch." Halavend nodded once. "To steal his crown?"

"Not just his crown," continued the Isle. "We need you to take the entire regalia."

Ard scratched his head. Everyone in the Greater Chain knew about the king's Royal Regalia. Both crown and coat were golden amber, crafted from the eggshell of old Grotenisk himself.

"And I agreed to this?" Ard exclaimed. "Two nights ago when you cornered me in that alleyway? I thought this was a good idea?" Flames! A job like this was suicide! Mobsters and lords were his area of expertise. He'd never attempted something of this scale.

"Unfortunately, your job will not end with the theft of the regalia," said Halavend. "More will be required of you."

"More?" Ard cried. "Of course! Because stealing from the king is never enough."

"Are you familiar with Visitant Grit?" asked Isle Halavend.

"I wasn't raised under a rock," answered Ard. What child in the Greater Chain hadn't fantasized about detonating that Grit and summoning a Paladin Visitant? The Grit was created from the eggshell of a dragon. Once consumed and passed through the beast's digestive tract, it could be Harvested from the fired Slagstone and refined to powder. Visitant Grit, usable only by the worthy.

The king and his Regulation had exclusive control over all things relating to dragons. When a dragon skin was shed, the husk was removed by the Harvesters and delivered to the king so the scales could be refined into Ashings. When an entire dragon corpse was found, it, too, was extracted, the teeth and talons later removed for use in the coinery and Grit factories. But the fertilized shell of a dragon egg...that was controlled by the Islehood.

"You want me to steal the Royal Regalia just so we can process it into Visitant Grit?" Ard clarified. "That seems like the hardest way of doing it. Why don't we use a piece of shell from the Islehood storehouse?"

"There is no more shell." Isle Halavend's reply was sharp. "Whatever had been collected was swept out to sea when the storehouse flooded twenty years ago."

"I remember the flood," Ard said, though he'd been just a boy. A dam had broken and the resulting rush of water had devastated a good portion of western Beripent. "But I didn't know it wiped out the Islehood storehouse."

"That information was not made public for a good reason," said Halavend. "The bull dragons are thirty years gone. The entire dragon race is riding toward inevitable extinction. Everyone knows there won't be more fertilized shell. What we have is what we have. The general public cannot know that the Islehood's stored shell has been swept away. The Wayfarists need to believe that there is potential for a Paladin Visitant to appear. To say that the holy warriors are a thing of the past would shatter the kingdom. It is not the Paladin Visitants who keep the peace. Their appearances through history are but few. It is the *fear* of a Paladin Visitant who keeps anarchists from rising without a worthy cause."

"So the Royal Regalia is the only fertilized shell left," said Ard. Stealing it was a bold plan. And why the blazes did a Holy Isle want to summon a Paladin Visitant? "Let's suppose I succeed. I get you a detonation of Visitant Grit. The Paladin Visitants can level an entire army with a single word. You feared a war, but it sounds to me like you're planning one."

Halavend shook his head. "I would never intend to use the Paladin Visitant for violence. I may be a heretic, but I am not a killer."

Ard couldn't help but give an incredulous laugh. "Let me get this straight. You want to summon the most powerful warrior in history, but you're not going to use him to fight?" He put his hands up. "What use is a Paladin Visitant if there is no battle?"

"I have my reasons, Ardor Benn," said Halavend.

"I'd love to know them."

"Do you demand a full accounting from every employer?" Isle Halavend snapped. "Or do you merely expect one from me because I am a Holy Isle?"

Ard faltered. He didn't take jobs from strangers very often. Most of the ruses Ard ran were jobs that he or Raek drummed up. He'd catch wind of a rakish lord, or a devious mobster, and decide to show them that there was someone on the island more rakish, or more devious.

But from time to time, a fellow criminal would come to him, seeking vengeance. Wanting to see an enemy ruined without putting themselves at risk.

In those instances, Ard liked to know why. *Needed* to know why. His employers didn't always tell him, though he inevitably sleuthed it out during the course of the ruse. But a Holy Isle...this was new. If Halavend's motives stemmed from some new doctrine he'd uncovered with Lyndel, then Ard doubted he'd have much chance of uncovering it on his own.

"I'm not hiring you to know my reasons," said Halavend. "I'm hiring you to run a ruse. Steal the regalia, and process the shell into high-grade Visitant Grit."

"And what's the payout?" asked Ard.

"I will fund every expense of the ruse, so you and your partner will not take any financial risk," assured Halavend. "In addition, I will see to it that the Regulation clears your name of any crimes previously committed."

"What about my partner?"

"Yes, yes. Raekon Dorrel, too. The one the Regulators call the Short Fuse."

"Tempting offer," Ard remarked. It would be good to have their names cleared. But they'd survived this long without getting caught. Ard's usual payouts involved good sums of Ashings. "I don't see a lot of profit in it. The Ardor Benn I know wouldn't have agreed to those terms in the alleyway."

"The Ardor Benn I spoke with in the alleyway was convinced of the importance of this task," said Isle Halavend. "Under the cloud of Memory Grit, I was able to explain my new doctrine, and *all* my motives."

"But you're not going to do that now?"

"I cannot," replied Halavend. "There is too much at stake to let you leave this cove with such information."

"You're out of your mind, old man." Ard waved a dismissive hand. "You expect me to run the biggest ruse of my career under the assumption that I agreed with your motives in a cloud of Memory Grit?"

"No," answered the Isle. "Although that *was* the case with the Ardor Benn I spoke with in the alley. I knew I'd need something more material to entice you today." Halavend took a deep breath. "I am prepared to withdraw one million Ashings from the Islehood Treasury. To be paid upon delivery of the processed Visitant Grit. What do you say now, Ardor Benn?"

Ard's insides were churning. Sparks, he'd never heard of a job with this kind of payout! Not to mention full funding along the way. "A million Ashings... How do you intend to make such a withdrawal without raising serious suspicion?"

"I have the approval papers for a massive construction overhaul of the Mooring," said Halavend. "It's a forgery, but I'm a confirmed and trusted source. The Ashings will be long gone before anyone realizes what happened."

"And you'll be a criminal," Ard pointed out.

"Never mind that." He waved a wrinkled hand. "Do you accept the job?"

Ard had to admit, Isle Halavend was everything he looked for in an employer: thorough, committed, dependable, and shrouded in hidden motives. "I'll do it," he agreed. "But a ruse this size can't be performed alone. I'll need to contract a few other experts."

"The million Ashings will be yours to split how you choose. I'll fund whatever supplies or temporary services you need. Whatever the cost." Isle Halavend's forehead was creased. "Lyndel and I will continue our joint study. Visitant Grit has failed far more times than it has worked. Wayfarism teaches that only a select few are worthy of a visit. If we only have one detonation from the regalia, we want to make sure it's in the right hands."

In response, Ard held up his hands. "These?"

"Homeland, no!" cried Halavend. "Not you!"

"Good," replied Ard. "Find your own worthy hero to detonate that mess. You said a million Ashings payable in full upon delivery of the Grit."

Isle Halavend nodded.

"How long do I have?" Ard asked.

"As long as you need to do it right," answered the old Isle. "But you must know that time is against us. Homeland knows how many more cycles we can last before the devastation reaches us."

Ard raised an eyebrow and adjusted his vest. Halavend's cryptic words were unsettling. Sounded much more threatening than *new doctrine*. "This has been a most enlightening conversation. If there's nothing else, I'll be on my way. I have quite a royal ruse to plan."

"Actually, there is one more thing." Isle Halavend paused, as if debating whether or not to go on. "Your name," he finally said. "Why did you choose it?"

"A parent usually does that for you," he answered. "Not sure I understand the question."

"You're a known criminal throughout the Greater Chain. Surely you changed your name from what your mother picked. I'm just wondering why you selected *Ardor*?" asked Halavend. "A strong Wayfarist name. 'A deep burning. A passion.'"

Ard was surprised by the question. Why did it matter to Halavend if Ard abused a religious name? In a way, weren't they both betraying Wayfarism? Ardor with his name, and the Holy Isle in his association with a criminal?

"Seems to suit me," Ard answered. "After I eat a dozen or so pastries, I get quite a burning in my gut."

Without waiting for a reply, Ard opened the door and stepped out onto the floating dock. He rang the bell on the wall and waited for a raft to come for him.

Truth was, his name had always been Ardor. The last name was a change, but Ard had always kept his given first name. He didn't mind the Wayfarist association. He had nothing against the religion, despite his decision to abandon it.

He liked the name. He liked what it meant.

A deep burning. A passion.

A ruse artist had to care. He needed to immerse himself in the job to perform the trickery needed. Sometimes Ard feared he cared too much. It was a slippery slope, passion.

Ard didn't like the way Halavend had concealed his motives. According to that Υ chalked onto the alley wall, they were motives that Ard had agreed with just two nights prior. If that was true, then Ard felt himself itching to know what this was really about.

Ard took a deep breath and shook his head. He'd have to be careful not to get too wrapped up in uncovering the cause of this one. Wasn't it enough to simply get paid for a job well done?

A million Ashings and his criminal name cleared.

Ard rocked gently as he waited on the dock. He and Raek were good at what they did. But stealing the Royal Regalia?

Ard was going to need a thief.

～

The importance of my task is the only thing leading me on. Without such a dire cause, I surely would have shrunk in terror at the sacrifice the Homeland Urges me to make.

CHAPTER

4

Quarrah Khai was taller than she wished to be. Small people could fit into more places, squeeze into tighter spots. Quarrah wasn't large, by any means. But she wasn't the size of a child anymore. And that frustrated her. Especially on nights like tonight, when the easiest way to break in was through a gap too small.

Quarrah sized up the culvert once more. The grate was new, the metal rungs a bit tighter than the previous one. Sparks, it had only been two days since she'd surveyed the manor. What were the odds that Lord Wilt would change the grate?

She could use Blast Grit to blow it off, of course. But that would require every granule of her Silence Grit to cover the sound, leaving her nothing for the extraction.

Quarrah cursed and turned away from the culvert. Now she'd

have to go around the manor and enter through the window on the northeast side. The backup plan was never as smooth.

Quarrah moved through the landscaping of Lord Wilt's grounds without a sound. The next Moon Passing was still four days away, so the night was utterly black. She was dressed to match the darkness, her blondish-brown hair tucked beneath a tight-fitting cap that tied beneath the chin.

Her attire was uniquely suited for the job—knee-high black boots of a supple leather. Trousers that sported customized pockets along the thighs. Her long-sleeved shirt was snug against her upper body, with a series of belts that hugged her hips and crisscrossed her chest.

Quarrah preferred the belts to any sort of pack or satchel. From the leather straps, she could secure anything she might need. Access was quick, her movements unrestricted.

She paused below the window. Her backup plan was higher than she remembered. Why didn't they design these manors to be more accommodating to burglars? She found it downright rude, installing tight grates and high windows. There was no conveniently placed tree, either.

The exterior walls of Lord Wilt's manor were made of limestone. The mortar between the large blocks was smooth and flush, denying any kind of handhold. Quarrah wouldn't reach the windowsill unaided.

Reaching into a hardened leather pouch on one of her belts, she produced a tiny mesh teabag containing a pinch of powder. She had carefully preplaced everything on her belts, so she didn't even have to check the marking on the bag. Quarrah had a system, a consistent method, that enabled her to select the exact item she wanted even in absolute darkness.

The teabag in her hand would be Drift Grit. She'd been warned a dozen times about packing Grit like this, with a loose fragment of Slagstone in the bag to provide the needed spark. The fine mesh bag was not a secure way. Taking a hard fall could impact the

Slagstone and detonate every bit of Grit on her belts—a lethal error if she happened to be wearing explosive Blast Grit.

Detonation licenses required the powder to be stored in a Grit keg or a clay detonation pot. But clearly, that decision was not made with thieves in mind. Quarrah couldn't very well go smashing clay pots without drawing attention. So she'd devised a Grit teabag. Cheaper than buying blank detonation pots, though she did have to handle them with greater care.

Quarrah gauged the distance to the window, and dropped to one knee. She gripped a handful of the manicured grass with her left hand and slammed the Grit bag against an ornamental stone beside her. She saw a spark as the fragment of Slagstone hit the rock, detonating the Drift Grit.

The hazy cloud kicked up around her, bleeding instantly through the fine mesh of the teabag to form an eight-foot radius. Drift Grit always delivered a bit of a jolt upon detonation, and the action would have sent Quarrah floating off the ground if she hadn't anchored herself with a fistful of grass.

She glanced up at the window, crouching with both feet planted firmly against the ground. Letting go of the grass, she lunged straight upward, kicking off the ground with all her strength. Her body propelled through the weightless environment, exiting the top of the domed cloud on a path to the window. With that eight-foot head start, she was able to grasp the stone sill and hoist herself onto the ledge.

Drift Jumping was an expensive technique, and not many were as practiced at it as Quarrah Khai.

She peered through the window into a room full of bookshelves, a single desk tucked into the corner. The only illumination came through the open door from the hallway.

Quarrah examined the window. Two panels, each hinged to swing inward. There was a latching mechanism, but no lock. She had been counting on that for a second-story window.

She reached along her inner thigh and withdrew a long slender band of steel, hammered nearly as thin as parchment. Carefully, she slid the tool between the window panels, jostling it upward until she found the latch. Applying just the right amount of pressure, she felt the latch pop, one of the glass panels swinging inward.

Quarrah replaced the tool along her thigh and tucked up her legs. Releasing a clasp on her boot, she loosened a leather binding over her arch and slipped out of the sole. Those heavy things were useful in making a fast retreat down a cobblestone road, but they were far too noisy for creeping around a lord's manor in the middle of the night.

Once removed, the soles clipped onto one of her belts and she dropped from the windowsill to land on silent, leather-clad feet inside the study. She latched the window behind her, casting a quick glance to the Drift Grit cloud below. The detonation would burn out in a few minutes. Quarrah wished she could snuff out the cloud now, but once Grit ignited, there was nothing to do but let it burn.

She moved across the study, pausing where the hallway Light spilled into the room. The route she had *planned* to take was memorized. But that was useless since she couldn't get into the kitchen through the culvert.

Crouching, Quarrah withdrew a paper and studied her charcoal-sketched map. It was by no means comprehensive. She had pieced together only what could be seen while surveying the manor from a safe distance. Her spyglass had impeccable range, but there was a lot more to the manor than the outer rooms and hallways.

A door shut. Voices sounded in the hallway. Quarrah melted into the shadows. Sparks, it was hours past midnight. Why didn't people sleep when she needed them to?

"That's what I've been saying," spoke one voice. "But it doesn't seem to matter."

"He has unreasonable expectations," said another. "What's he going to do if nobody comes to see the hideous thing?"

They continued talking, but their voices faded as they moved into an unmarked area on Quarrah's map. It was true that many people found Lemnow's artistic style bold, even abrasive. But that "*hideous thing*" was worth eight hundred Ashings. The painting hadn't left Beripent since Lemnow created it some eighty years ago. Finally, a tour of the artwork had been announced, with a stop in every major city on Espar and Talumon.

Lord Wilt was the perfect Focus for her thievery. He hadn't been part of the original tour, but flooding in Tosbit had cut that location short. The painting had been transferred inland to Leez, and Lord Wilt found himself with an opportunity to host the famous artwork for a single day.

Quarrah had watched Lemnow's painting arrive at sunset. A covered wagon driven by two Reggies. It was a skeleton crew, since the others must have gone ahead to prepare the next stop. And Lord Wilt was far too cheap to hire additional security for the night. This was the opportunity of a lifetime. Quarrah was surprised that the grounds weren't crawling with would-be thieves.

She checked her map once more, then folded it and tucked it away. Drawing a dagger from her boot, she slipped into the bright hallway.

Quarrah moved with purpose, following the new route. Down the stairs at the end of the hallway. Tucking into a dim room as more servants passed. Around a corner. Down another flight of stairs. At last, passing the kitchen. See, all that risk could have been avoided if the grate hadn't been replaced.

Finally, she came to a halt before a heavy wooden door at the end of the hallway. A Light Grit torch had been detonated on a wall sconce nearby, a glowing cloud that hung where it had been ignited like a bright orb. Except this one was dimming.

It was common practice to mix Prolonging Grit into the detonation to keep the Light Grit working all night. Prolonging Grit could stretch the effect of any other type, but the result caused the potency of the primary Grit to wane.

Quarrah slipped the dagger into her boot and took a knee to examine the lock. It was a mortise lock, set into the door itself, allowing someone to use a key from either side. Her tools were out in a flash, a thin pin-like piece in her left hand, and a flat toothed device in her right. Her mouth held a third tool, hooked and pronged, but she doubted she'd even need it for a standard lock like this.

She inserted the tools into the keyhole and turned her head, pressing one ear against the cold lock. Her eyes were useless for a task like this, and would serve her much better by watching the hallway. This was a job for her fingers and ears.

The tools were like sensors to her, passing vibrations to her fingers. Her ears took in each sound as the picks rattled against the inner workings of the lock. Quarrah assembled the information in her brain, creating a mental model of the lock's insides.

A brief moment later—*snick!*—the lock was sprung and she pulled the door open, storing her tools as she slipped from the hallway.

It was drafty behind the door. She was at the top of a long, narrow stairwell that descended, presumably, to the dungeon where the painting was supposedly being stored.

Quarrah pulled the door shut and waited for her eyes to adjust to the darkness. Her eyesight wasn't as sharp as it used to be. Sparks, she was supposed to be in the prime of her life!

There was a dim glow at the bottom of the long stairwell. The two delivery Reggies would probably be spending the night near the Lemnow painting. She'd have to act fast.

Quarrah moved down the steep stairs, sliding her hands into a pair of thin gloves. The gloves were her own design, modified over the last four years to fit her needs.

They were fingerless, save for the middle finger, which housed a tiny fragment of Slagstone in the tip. At the base of her thumb, a slim pocket was filled with a pinch of Light Grit. She might not need to use the gloves, but it was better to have them ready so she wouldn't waste time fumbling in the dark.

Quarrah reached the bottom of the stairs and leaned cautiously around the corner. The dungeon was a simple stone room with no windows, the far side barred into two cells. Through the closed bars, Quarrah could see the large wooden crate the Reggies had unloaded from the covered wagon. The box had a red cloth draped over the top, likely to protect the contents from settling dust. The painting would be inside, wrapped in fabric, probably nestled into sawdust to keep it dry and padded.

The two Reggies Quarrah had expected were nowhere in sight. That would clean up her task considerably. She hated dealing with people. Especially the ones trying to stop her from taking what she wanted.

Quarrah moved quietly toward the locked cell. She was almost there when the sound of a boot scuffing on stone caused her to reel. One of the Reggies was on her in a moment, a huge man with arms that wrapped clear around her torso, yanking her feet off the floor.

An ambush cleft! She cursed herself for not anticipating it. These old dungeons often had a small cleft built into the wall. Invisible from the stairs, the space made an ideal hiding spot for a dungeon guard. Many a criminal jailbreak had been thwarted by a heavily armed guard concealed in an ambush cleft.

Well, Quarrah thought, *at least he didn't shoot me in the back of the head.*

The Reggie hefted her even higher. Sparks, the man was strong! There was little chance of her wriggling free or reaching her boot dagger.

Quarrah brought her hand up, reaching blindly for the man's face behind her. Craning her neck, she could see his sneer from the corner of her eye. He was wearing a knit hat to ward off the dungeon's chill. With any luck, that hat would catch fire.

Quarrah slammed her gloved middle finger against the Reggie's forehead. The piece of Slagstone in the fingertip reacted to the impact, throwing a shower of sparks across the bridge of his nose.

The man shouted, shaking his head. Swinging around, Quarrah threw her weight, bring both knees up and slamming her feet down against the man's thighs. At the same time, the back of her head butted into his face.

He dropped her, finally. Quarrah hit the stone floor, rolling to avoid igniting the delicate Grit bags on her belts. She was lucky the Reggie hadn't detonated any of them with his python grip.

Quarrah rose into a defensive crouch as the Reggie ducked back into the ambush cleft. Behind her, the stairs were wide open. Now was the chance to flee. And leave behind a poorly guarded Lemnow? It was only one Reggie. Quarrah pulled a teabag of Barrier Grit from her belt. She could take him.

The big man emerged suddenly, a clay pot in his hand. She flung the bag of Grit at the man's feet. It ignited just inches in front of him, instantly throwing a detonation cloud six feet tall.

The man was enveloped, but just barely. He dropped the detonation pot, but the clay exterior didn't strike with enough impact to break or ignite.

"You won't get the painting," he grunted. His nose was bleeding from their skirmish, and he was now helplessly trapped behind the invisible shield of the Barrier cloud.

"Watch me." Quarrah strode past the detonation and approached the locked cell. She'd have to work quickly now. The Barrier Grit would only hold the Reggie for about ten minutes. But Quarrah Khai was accustomed to working under pressure. She actually found the rush of a deadline quite thrilling.

Wait a minute. What kind of blazing lock was this? It looked like a piece of pipe, about the length of her forearm, but larger in diameter. It hung straight down from the gate latch, a loop of iron keeping the cell locked. The trapped Reggie chuckled when he saw her surprise.

Quarrah dropped to her knee and peered up into the pipe. Too dark to see. And she wasn't about to go reaching into something she didn't understand.

She positioned her left hand a few inches below the pipe lock and snapped her fingers. As her gloved middle finger slapped against the pouch at the base of her thumb, it detonated a pinch of Light Grit, instantly casting a glowing orb around her hand.

Quarrah slowly pulled her hand free, the movement not affecting the perfectly spherical shape of the light. The nature of all Grit was to detonate in a spherical cloud. Detonations often appeared domed, as igniting them against the ground or other hard surface prevented the bottom of the sphere from forming. And of course, some detonations could be contained in boxes or lanterns. But the Grit's natural shape was always a sphere.

The bright orb hovered just below the pipe lock, Quarrah stooping to peer inside. Now properly illuminated, she was glad she hadn't reached in. The interior of the pipe was lined with short needles, their sharp points all angling inward. At the top of the pipe was the locking mechanism itself, an ordinary thing that wouldn't normally pose a problem for someone with her skill.

"Increased security for the Lemnow tour," announced the Reggie from behind. "The pipe is welded around the lock, and the needles are coated with a tranquilizing agent. No better way to catch a thief."

Sparks, Quarrah thought. Was he actually boasting? Didn't he know that such language only prompted her onward, daring her to tackle the impossible?

The pipe lock wasn't impervious. It was just designed to make things difficult. That Reggie's big arm could probably slide past the needles if he was careful. Using one hand to open a lock with a key was easy. *Picking* a lock with one hand, however... This was going to be a challenge.

For a moment, she considered employing a less discreet tactic.

Quarrah could easily fill the pipe with Blast Grit and light a fuse from behind the safety of the Barrier cloud.

But what if the explosion was too strong? It might blow apart the cell gate and hurl hot pieces of metal at the crate. Lemnow's painting would be far less valuable with a hole through the canvas.

Quarrah removed one of her gloves and rolled her sleeve up to the elbow. Couldn't risk snagging the fabric. Her tools were out in a heartbeat, two in her right hand as she carefully reached up the pipe.

Unlike the mortise lock at the top of the stairs, this one would take all her senses. Her eyes focused on the needles, and in a moment, she had both slender tools driving into the locking mechanism.

It was maddening, keeping her arm perfectly still while one hand did the work of two. And all the while, the Reggie behind her seemed to be breathing heavily through his mouth in an obnoxious manner.

Quarrah felt a click. That was good. Then a series of clicks in quick succession. She held perfectly still. Sparks, her hand was cramping! The lock was nearly sprung. All she needed to do was twist one of the instruments...

There!

She slowly withdrew her hand, stowing the tools and donning her glove. More than half her time was up, and the Reggie inside the cloud knew it just as well as she did.

Quarrah slid the pipe lock free of the latch and set it aside, quickly pulling open the cell gate. As it swung on creaky hinges, she saw something in the illumination of her Light Grit. It was a string, unraveling quickly as the cell door opened.

Her foot shot out, bracing against one of the cold metal bars and stopping the gate from opening farther. She traced the string, one end tied to the bottom of the gate. From there, it trailed across the floor toward the covered crate. She drew her boot dagger, stooped, and cut the thin string.

Quarrah slipped into the cell and crossed to the covered box.

She'd heard the painting was large, but this packaging seemed excessive. The crate was square, the top just higher than her waist. She gripped the corner of the cloth covering and pulled it free.

Resting atop the crate was a crossbow, previously concealed by the red cloth, pointing at the entrance to the cell. The weapon was loaded and ready, a Grit bolt nocked. She saw now that the string was tied off to the crossbow's trigger. Had it drawn tight, the weapon would have shot.

Quarrah removed the crossbow bolt and stowed it on one of her belts. It would fetch a nice Ashing if she didn't decide to use it for herself. Lifting the crossbow, she set it on the floor beside the crate. She'd take it, too, if the painting didn't prove to be too cumbersome.

The crate itself was secured with a simple latching mechanism. Good thing, too. If she wanted to remove the painting without facing that Reggie, there probably wasn't time to pick another lock.

Quarrah flipped the latch, grabbed both sides of the crate's lid, and slid it open. Before she could move, a hand reached out of the crate and seized her firmly by the wrist. The Slagstone hammer of a Roller clicked back and the gun barrel pressed against her abdomen. A man slowly rose from where he'd been sitting cross-legged inside the crate.

"I appreciate your timeliness," the man said. "I don't know how much longer I could have sat in there. My leg was cramping something fierce." Quarrah began inching her free hand toward her belt. "I don't think so, Quarrah Khai."

The man shoved the barrel of the gun tighter against her stomach. This whole thing was a setup? Lemnow's painting was not in the crate. Was it even coming to Lord Wilt's manor?

Behind them, the Barrier cloud flickered briefly, and then snuffed out. The large Reggie strode into the cell.

"You knew I was coming," Quarrah said. Obviously. They knew her name; they knew her skill set. They had lured her to the dungeon. "A lot of effort to make an arrest."

"Oh, we're not here to arrest you," spoke the man in the box. He pushed her gently backward into the waiting arms of the big Reggie. The shorter man holstered his Roller and climbed out of the crate.

He wasn't dressed like a Regulator. Instead, he wore a stylish leather vest and billowing white shirtsleeves. He was undeniably handsome. Square jaw and a skiff of stubble across his chin. "My name is Ardor Benn."

Ardor Benn? Flames! The man standing before her was Ardor Benn? *Don't say anything,* Quarrah told herself. *Act like you've never heard of him.*

"So this is a setup?" she asked. Had Ardor Benn already stolen Lemnow's painting? Looking to remove competition?

"Don't think of it that way," said Ardor. "Think of it as . . . a job interview."

"Which you passed," added the big man holding her. "Like a dragon's slag."

Quarrah wrinkled her face at the rather crude analogy. "What is going on here?"

The man before her smiled warmly. "I'm Ardor Benn," he said again, arms wide, as if repeating his introduction should mean something. It did, of course. The ruse artist had been making waves in the criminal community for years. And if Ardor was the man speaking, then the big fellow holding her must have been the one people called the Short Fuse, though there was nothing short about him.

"Don't think she's heard of you, Ard," said her captor.

"Come on, Raek," he answered. "Don't be naïve. Quarrah Khai is a celebrated thief. She couldn't run those circles without my name cropping up. Everyone's heard of our famous exploits."

"Exploits?" Raek responded. "Are you referring to those harebrained escapades where we barely got away with our heads intact?"

"Exploits," Ard insisted. "The dagger of Alpana, the chalice of serenity, Felmann's viola…Do you think those items just walked off on their own?"

"So you're a ruse artist," she said. He was *the* ruse artist, but Quarrah was determined not to say anything that would play to his ego. She glanced around the small dungeon. "The painting isn't here, is it?"

Ardor shook his head. "Of course not."

"Was there even flooding in Tosbit?" she asked.

"That part is true," he affirmed.

"And we didn't even cause it," added Raek.

"A good ruse has a handful of true facts scattered throughout it," Ard continued. "When Tosbit flooded, we knew they'd have to relocate the painting. Raek and I reached out to Lord Wilt and asked if he would be willing to host a short exhibit here. He accepted, of course. But we knew he'd want to verify our generous offer."

"At that point, Lemnow's painting was on its way to Gilram to wait a week for the next exhibit," Raek added.

"It was a simple matter of closing the road outside Smona, which rerouted the painting and its entourage through Clind," continued Ard. "Meanwhile, Raek and I got a duplicate wagon and headed down the closed road to meet with Lord Wilt's messenger. We verified our own story—that Lord Wilt had been selected to host the painting for an exclusive evening—and then followed the messenger here."

Quarrah stared at the man. What he had just described was genius, or madness. "So Lord Wilt is just a victim of your little ruse?"

"He wasn't a victim. More like a beneficiary," Ard said. "We installed a new grate over the culvert below the kitchen." He smiled. "Free of charge."

"But you didn't get the Lemnow," she pointed out.

"Neither did you," Ard returned. "Still, I'm impressed with your skills. I need someone like you. Fast, adaptable, and as it turns out, rather fierce." He gestured at the dried blood on his companion's upper lip.

"You set all this up to test my skills?" It seemed a bit elaborate, even for Ardor's reputation.

"I set this up for two reasons," he explained. "First, to make sure that your skills are up to the level we need."

"And the second?" asked Quarrah.

He shrugged, a little smirk on his handsome face. "To prove that I'm good enough to pull a ruse on you."

"But not good enough to get the painting," Quarrah said again.

"That wasn't..." He sighed. "This ruse isn't about the painting."

"Then what's the payout?"

"You are," answered Ardor.

"Was it worth it?"

He shrugged. "Depends on if you say yes to my job offer."

"This must be some ruse you're planning," Quarrah remarked, "if it took a ruse of its own just to bring me on board."

"Oh, this is just the beginning," Ard said. "I've got a lot more tricks up these billowy sleeves."

"How long are you going to keep me guessing?" she asked.

"About the job?" Ard clarified. "This isn't the kind of job you talk about in the dungeon of some lesser lord's manor."

"If you expect me to join you without knowing the details, then you're even crazier than all the stories I've heard."

"Ha!" Ard pointed at Raek. "I told you she'd heard of me."

Quarrah opened her mouth to protest, but there was nothing to say. He had her. Words had a way of betraying Quarrah Khai, and this conversation had finally caught up to her. Ardor Benn certainly seemed as pompous as she'd heard in the stories. His laughter died, and the ruse artist suddenly became very serious.

"Two hundred thousand Ashings."

Quarrah didn't mask her surprise. Sparks! With that sum of money, she could buy anything she wanted. She could buy an estate in Beripent's wealthiest quarter. She could practically retire! Though who was she kidding? The money was compelling, but even a sum that large wouldn't stop Quarrah from thieving. It was her way of life, not simply her employment.

"And you both stand to make as much?" Quarrah asked.

"Double," answered Raek from behind her.

"If we're to be completely honest." Ard shot him a disapproving glance.

Quarrah quickly did the math in her head. That was a million Ashings among the three of them! Who could afford to pay such a sum? What had Ardor Benn gotten himself into? Sounded like trouble. Trouble that Quarrah would rather stay out of.

"I work alone," she finally said.

Ardor Benn looked flustered, turning to his big companion. "You said two hundred thousand Ashings would be enough to entice anyone."

"Don't put this on me," said Raek. "Some people have an insatiable greed."

"Well, I'm not willing to offer any more," he said. "I guess we'll have to find someone else to help us steal the king's crown."

"The...what?" Quarrah blurted.

Ard lifted a hand to cover his lips. "Oh. Did I say that out loud?"

"The crown?" Quarrah stammered. "As in, the Royal Regalia? You're going to steal it?" Her mind was suddenly swimming. Quarrah had stolen some pretty significant items in the last few years. That tapestry from Lady Burgot's palace. Lord Ermit's favorite breeding horse. She had even managed to swipe the Far Peak Diamond. But the king's dragon shell regalia...That would be the pinnacle of all thievery. Two hundred thousand Ashings aside, pulling off such a theft might finally leave Quarrah feeling satisfied.

"So much for secrecy," Raek grumbled. "I thought we weren't going to tell her any details."

"A slip of the tongue," Ard said. "I'm sure she won't mention it when the king's regalia goes missing."

Quarrah glanced back at Raek. The Reggie impersonator had

stopped trying to detain her, but his big hand still rested on her shoulder. Quarrah reached up and brushed it off, stepping sideways so she could see both men clearly.

Only twice in her thieving career had Quarrah teamed up with other criminals. One had tried to drown her, and the other had betrayed her to the Regulation. Those kind of experiences didn't make her too anxious to sign on with another team. But this was Ardor Benn and the Short Fuse. The duo was already a legend. And now they were inviting her to help them take the Royal Regalia. Plus, two hundred thousand Ashings certainly wouldn't hurt.

She was going to say yes. Quarrah could feel it pulling her insides, a job bigger than anything she'd previously tried, tempting her with its impossibilities.

"So we'd be partners, then?" Quarrah asked.

"If that's what you want to call us," replied Ard. "I would have liked to hire you as a single-service contractor, but I'm afraid your particular skills will be needed from start to finish. So I'm offering to bring you into this ruse with payment taken from my own earnings." He paused. "I guess that makes us partners." He stuck out his hand, an affable grin on his face. "What do you say, Quarrah Khai? It's gonna be fun. There'll be gunfights, dragons, swordplay, narrow escapes…"

"Explosions," Raek added.

Ard nodded. "Possibly even a Paladin Visitant."

Before she could think any more about it, Quarrah accepted Ardor's handshake to seal the deal. Well, she could always get herself out if it got too dicey. Quarrah would see the early signs of betrayal and vanish into the night—probably taking Ardor's coin purse with her.

"When do I see the money?" she asked.

"Upon completion of the ruse," Ard answered. "But…" He held up a finger as though anticipating that she might gripe about the payout schedule. "Our employer is fully invested and willing to fund all our operations."

"That means an upgrade on any gear you might need," Raek said. "You can finally afford to carry your Grit in proper pots."

"I like my gear," Quarrah defended. "Pots are too noisy."

"Suit yourself," Raek said. "But I'm not coming within twenty yards of you. Not while you insist on using those blazing dangerous teabags."

"She'll come around to your methods," Ard said to his partner. "Nobody mixes a Grit pot like the Short Fuse."

It would be a real time-saver to have someone else preparing her Grit. A world of possibilities was opening to Quarrah. And these men were intriguing. Partners who had successfully worked together for years. People who might actually care for each other.

"So, what's next?" she asked.

Ardor reached into the pocket of his leather vest and withdrew a scrap of paper. "Meet us in Beripent. Noon, three days from now." She took the slip, noticing an address scribed in charcoal.

"It's our new hideout," said Raek. "Recently purchased and renovated to fit our needs. All at the expense of our generous employer."

"The Bakery on Humont Street?" Quarrah read.

"A dangerous place, to be sure," added Ard. "Enough secret meetings there and none of us will be squeezing through a culvert grate."

Oh, he was a coy one. Quarrah narrowed her eyes in suspicion. "That reminds me. Do you have a way out of this dungeon?"

Ardor slipped the Roller from his holster and clicked back the hammer. "That's part two of your job interview." He pointed the gun toward the low dungeon ceiling. "It's called '*See how they run.*'"

He fired over her head, a deafening bang and a puff of white smoke. Quarrah stumbled backward. What was he doing? Ardor fired a second shot, and then holstered his gun.

"Better hurry," urged Ard. "Two shots in the middle of the night are bound to draw attention from Lord Wilt's security—they're already on edge, what with a rare Lemnow painting being stored in the dungeon."

Every muscle tensed as Quarrah waited to see how the two men would react to the unwanted noise they'd just made.

"Don't wait for us," said the Short Fuse. He tugged at his knit cap and straightened the collar of his wool coat. "All they'll find down here is a couple of Reggies and a thief."

"And no Lemnow painting," Ard pointed out. "I don't think Wilt's security will like your explanation."

Quarrah ground her teeth. There was no point in arguing. She never seemed to have the right words, anyhow. She turned and sprinted out of the cell, her soft-clad feet barely making a sound.

Oh, flames. Was this how it was going to be with these two? Quarrah had half a mind to disappear into the night and be done with them. But the other half of her mind agreed with Ardor Benn.

This was going to be fun.

~

The colors are so vibrant here. In comparison, the Greater Chain seems dull. It is as though this island is a thief, stealing the brightest hues and leaving what is left for mankind.

CHAPTER

5

Ard had himself a genuine chalkboard. The smooth, dark piece of slate was almost five feet wide, and nearly as tall, affixed to a wooden frame and propped against the wall in the hidden room above the bakery. The blazing thing weighed a load, but it made his meetings feel so much more official.

"Visitant Grit?" Quarrah repeated for the third time. "From the king's crown?"

Ard understood her hesitations. What right did a trio of criminals have in meddling with the holy responsibility of the Prime Isle? But that was the job. He crumbled off a bit of cinnamon scone and shoved it in his mouth.

"And this Halavend fellow." Quarrah pointed to the board where Ard had written the old man's name. "You trust him?"

"I do," he answered, barely intelligible while chewing.

"What about you?" she asked Raek. He was wearing a sleeveless shirt, his boots up on the chair beside him, sipping a dark tea.

"I haven't met the old Isle," answered Raek. "Ard filled me in on the job, same as you. But Ard wouldn't take a job if the source wasn't genuine."

"Thank you, Raek," Ard said, trying to catch a piece of scone that crumbled to the floor. "Isle Halavend *is* trustworthy. He has no reason not to be. He's an Isle, for Homeland's sake."

"Not a very holy one, by the sound of it," Quarrah mumbled. "Why would he come to you?"

"He said, and I quote, 'Ardor Benn is the best.'" He polished off the scone.

"I mean, why go to you instead of going to the Prime Isle himself? Or even the king?"

"That's a wonderful idea," Raek said. "'Hey, Pethredote. Just wondering if I could borrow your crown and coat this afternoon. I want to feed it to a dragon and then grind it up.'"

Quarrah glared at Raek, and Ard smiled. His team was gelling quite nicely.

"Halavend claims to have uncovered some big new doctrine in his studies with Lyndel," Ard explained. "Prime Isle Chauster didn't take kindly to that, so Halavend had to recruit us to get things done."

"So, where do we start?" Raek asked, swapping his teacup for an apple tart.

Ard grabbed the dusty rag draped over the chalkboard frame and wiped the slate clean. He flung the rag over his shoulder and plucked out a piece of white chalk.

"We start with a basic infiltration into high society," Ard said. "Quarrah and I will begin maneuvering ourselves into the royal circles."

"Hold on," said Quarrah. "That seems awfully complicated. This is a simple burglary we're talking about. Why don't I just slip into the palace in the middle of the night and take it?"

"Simple burglary?" Ard turned to Raek and let out an incredulous laugh. Apparently, Quarrah Khai thought very highly of herself. "We're talking about the *Royal Regalia*. Stealing the crown." He turned to Raek. "Can you remind me what the penalty is for treason? I can't seem to remember."

Raek made three simple gestures. The first implied getting shot; the second, hanged; and the third, slitting his throat.

"Obviously, the Reggies won't do all three," Ard said. "One is usually enough to ruin your day. This isn't an ordinary job, Quarrah. You think your spyglass is going to shine right into Pethredote's chambers? Figure out where he stores the regalia?" Ard shook his head. "Between us and our prize is every red-coat Reggie in the king's employ. Even if you did snake your way in and steal it, how long do you think it would take the king to notice that his crown and coat were missing?" He paused to see if Quarrah would retort, but Ard appeared to have made his point. "We have to do this right. Careful."

"Passing ourselves off as royal folk," Quarrah mused. "That's going to take a lot of time. And a lot of, you know...talking."

"You're right. It's going to take significant positioning," Ard said. "But I'd rather be slow than dead."

The four islands of the Greater Chain had been united under King Pethredote's rule for some forty years now, but a single kingdom had not always been the norm throughout history. Talumon and Dronodan, even Strind still had bloodlines that actively ruled under Pethredote's crown.

Ard shook his head. "And we won't be going as royalty. Even a lesser lord would likely be recognized by somebody's cousin's uncle. No. We need to mingle with them from a more believable angle."

"And what angle would that be?" Quarrah asked.

Ard shrugged. "Cook staff, tailors, and servants would all get us access. A musician or an inventor would get us access *and* notoriety..."

Quarrah leaned back in her chair. "Why don't you take Raek?"

Ard laughed. "You can't take that guy to the market in the Char, let alone infiltrate high society. For starters, his manners are atrocious."

Ard pointed to Raek, who promptly put whatever was left of his apple tart on top of his large bald head.

"Besides," Ard said, "the whole idea is to get *you* into the palace.

You need to be familiar enough with its layout so you can slip away and steal the goods undetected."

"I don't like it," Quarrah answered. "I'm not really suited for high society, either."

"Sparks, no! I certainly wouldn't take Quarrah Khai to a royal function," Ard assured. "But remember, you won't be going as yourself." He wiggled his fingers mystically.

Quarrah narrowed her eyes in suspicion. "I swear, Ard. If you make me a royal prostitute, I'm going to..."

Raek burst out laughing, and Ard shook his head emphatically. "Nothing like that, I hope. I've got someone working on options for us."

He twirled the chalk between his fingers once, and then turned to the slate and wrote two names: *Elbrig Taut* and *Cinza Ortemion*.

Raek moaned, pulling the tart off his head and finishing it in one bite. "Not the crazies."

"Who are they?" Quarrah asked.

"You haven't heard of them?" Ard asked. "Of course not. Those are the names I know them by, but I'll be sparked if that's what their mothers called them." He turned back to the chalkboard. "Disguise managers." He wrote the label beneath the two names.

"Crazies," Raek muttered again.

"And we'll need disguise managers to move into high society?" Quarrah asked.

"Naturally," answered Ard. "Certain jobs require a costume. You know what I mean?"

Quarrah raised an eyebrow.

"Take Raek a few nights back," Ard explained. "Dressed up like a Reggie when you met him in the dungeon. You've done that before, right?"

Quarrah answered with a blank stare and a shake of the head. Sparks, had he picked the wrong thief after all? He and Quarrah were both experts at taking things that didn't belong to them, but that seemed to be where the similarities ended.

"All right," Ard tried again. "Maybe you've dressed in something a bit more provocative than you might usually wear. A costume to seduce your Focus?"

"I wear black," she answered. "What you saw me wearing in Lord Wilt's manor. That's what I always wear on the job."

Ard sighed. Not much creativity in that corner. Cinza was going to have a blazing time working with her. "Anyway," Ard continued, "Elbrig and Cinza's services go far beyond a costume. They provide identities. Flesh-and-blood characters with documented records and backgrounds."

"But they cost a fortune," Raek protested.

"A cost we would normally avoid," Ard agreed. "But with Isle Halavend funding the ruse, Quarrah and I can buy identities from Elbrig and Cinza without cutting into our own Ashings."

"Let's say we get these new costumes," Quarrah said. "Then what?"

"Eventually, we position ourselves to be able to make the theft."

"But like you said, won't Pethredote know the moment his regalia goes missing?" she asked.

"Indeed," answered Ard. "And that's why we'll need a forger." He spun and wrote the word on the chalkboard. This thing really added nicely to the drama of his presentation. "Raek, how are we doing on that?"

"I'm still compiling a list of potential forgers," he answered. "Ones we've used in the past, as well as a few new kids who are gaining a reputation."

"The Forger will craft a replica of the Royal Regalia," explained Ard. "We'll swap it for the real one and trust that King Pethredote will be none the wiser."

"Then we get paid?" Quarrah asked.

Ard shook his head. "Then comes the interesting part." He turned and wrote the word *Pekal*. "Next we have to feed the regalia to a sow dragon."

"You ever been to Pekal?" Raek asked Quarrah.

She shook her head. "Nothing to steal there."

"On the contrary," replied Ard. "The mountains are littered with uncut dragon scales."

"Which are no good unless they're coined into Ashings." Quarrah picked up a pastry and took a bite.

Again, with the lack of imagination! If Ard only thought of things in terms of their current value, he never would have become a ruse artist. *Potential* value was often a hidden jackpot. Like a husk of uncut scales, needing only a little, albeit precise, work to transform them into a fortune.

"Ard and I used to be Harvesters," Raek said. "We have experience on Pekal, so that shouldn't pose too great an obstacle in the operation."

"We'll set some bait for the dragon, embedded with the pieces of shell from the Royal Regalia," Ard explained.

"The fragments of shell should be large enough to pass through the dragon's digestive acids without too much dissolving," added Raek. "We've got to have a sizable chunk to work with once it passes out the other end."

Quarrah wrinkled her nose at that. If she only knew how it really smelled! Especially if the job was botched and the dragon didn't return to fire the slag. Ard remembered watching Tanalin be sick from the reek of it.

Tanalin Phor was always so anxious to get in and get the work done. He preferred watching from a less toxic proximity. There were plenty of Harvesters to recover the indigestibles on a botched job. Ard always said that the work of a hundred men could easily be done by ninety-nine.

"Once the dung is passed, the dragon breathes fire to harden it," Raek said.

"That's disgusting." Quarrah set her half-eaten pastry back on the table.

Ard was always surprised by how little the common citizen knew about the process of obtaining Grit. The powder's impact on society was hugely taken for granted.

"It's not that unusual," Ard said. "Cats cover their litter. Dogs often scratch the ground or turn a circle to prepare the area. Dragons are fastidious animals. They clean up after themselves."

"Once the slag is fire-hardened, we'll need to bring the resulting Slagstone back to the Greater Chain for processing," said Raek.

"Where do you do something like that?" Quarrah asked.

"It'll have to be on Strind," Raek replied. "Nearly all the processing is done there. I'll head out in the morning to begin scouting for a factory that'll fit our needs."

Ard clapped his hands together. "That's it, then! We're well on our way to running the largest ruse in the history of the islands."

"That's it?" Quarrah asked. "What about *after* we process the shell? What's going to be done with the Visitant Grit?"

Ard leaned against the wall. Wasn't that the question of the year? "That's not up to us. We get paid once Halavend gets the Grit. How he chooses to detonate it is his own business."

Ard didn't really feel that way, of course. Halavend's motive for the Visitant Grit had been eating away at him for weeks now. He'd had a second meeting with the old Isle, briefer than the first, to receive the Ashings he needed to pay rent on the bakery. Despite Ard's pressuring, Halavend remained tight-lipped about his true reason for wanting the Visitant Grit.

The three of them sat in silence for a moment before Quarrah spoke. "The last time a Paladin Visitant was successfully summoned was over forty years ago. King Pethredote, himself."

Ard had been only a small child when Dietrik Pethredote had led the uprising and taken the throne. But everyone knew the story.

The Greater Chain was fresh off the rule of a respected queen who had died peacefully in her sleep. Her Majesty's son, King Barrid, assumed the throne, but he turned out to be a tyrannical imbecile. The moment he came into power, he disavowed any affiliation with Wayfarism and announced that he was a Settled man.

Less than a year into his reign, he banned all Wayfarist Voyages, claiming that such a religious exodus was economically devastating. In a way, Ard saw his logic. In the history of the Greater Chain, no one had ever returned who sailed away from the islands. Whether they all died or whether they reached the Homeland didn't change the fact that ships and resources were lost.

However, King Barrid's Settled policies didn't go over too well with the Prime Isless at the time. She encouraged the other islands to secede from the kingdom. Dronodan and Talumon did, and from that rebellion rose young Dietrik Pethredote, a Wayfarist zealot barely out of his teens. It had been a year of ugly inter-island war, but Pethredote put an end to the bloodshed.

With the blessing of the Prime Isless, Pethredote led an assault on King Barrid. He was severely undermanned and poorly prepared. But he had faith. And a clay pot full of Visitant Grit. In the most desperate throes of the attack, Pethredote detonated the Grit, summoning a Paladin Visitant within the blast cloud.

The very sight of the fiery Paladin incinerated King Barrid and a significant portion of his army. There were many casualties among the rebels, too, but at least they knew to shield their eyes and plug their ears. Mere moments after the Visitant cloud burned out, young Pethredote took the throne, his policies and rule unifying the islands once more under one crown—the very crown that Ard had been charged to steal.

"What if Isle Halavend is planning to do something similar?" Quarrah asked. "What if he's planning to choose a hero to detonate the Visitant Grit so he can remove Pethredote from the throne? Sparks, we could be helping him start an uprising."

It was a reasonable concern, since that was typically the use for a Paladin Visitant. But Halavend had assured Ard once again that his motives were nonthreatening.

"Halavend told me that he didn't intend to use the Visitant Grit to incite any sort of war," Ard assured them. "The man seems peaceful enough. I can't imagine him wreaking death and anarchy with a Paladin Visitant."

"Why else would he want the Grit?" Raek asked. "What other purpose does a Paladin Visitant serve?"

"Wayfarist doctrine claims that the Paladins are visitors from the Homeland," explained Quarrah.

"Look at you, spouting doctrine," said Ard. "I didn't take you as a Wayfarist. Doesn't stealing from wealthy Wayfarists go against the whole idea that we're supposed to 'lend aid to our fellow wanderers in these islands far from home'?"

"Just because I steal doesn't mean I stopped believing in the Homeland," said Quarrah. "Besides, I'm not the one with a religious name, quoting scripture."

Did Ard believe there was a Homeland? Sure. The Landers' ancestors had to have come from somewhere.

Wayfarist doctrine centered on a driving desire for progress. When the Homeland communicated, it inspired a person to change. An Urging for something more. The Islehood preached that the Urgings were fundamental, owing to the nature of the islands being a temporary dwelling place.

But the islands seemed far more permanent than the Islehood was ever willing to admit. Landers had been living in the Greater Chain for well over twelve centuries. Time had turned the Homeland into a mere belief. The vast majority lived and died on these islands. Only the Wayfarist Voyagers left.

That was the utmost sign of religious devotion. To enlist in a

Voyage and depart from the islands in search of the Homeland, never to return.

Let the Wayfarist zealots take their Voyages, but Ard certainly wouldn't be volunteering for the journey. Espar was home to him. And the islands spoke to him more than some imagined Homeland ever could.

"Just because Wayfarist doctrine claims to know where the Paladin Visitants come from, doesn't make it true," said Raek. "*Doctrine* is just a word that religious folk use to explain things they don't understand. Things they expect everyone to believe. Like the Holy Torch. The Islehood wants us to believe that lighting it protects us from Moonsickness."

"But you don't believe that?" Quarrah asked.

Ard wanted to interject, but Raek had already leaned forward, anxious to engage in the controversial topic.

"Moonsickness is a factor of elevation, according to the Shwazer Society," Raek began. "Pekal's summit is more than ten thousand feet higher than the highest point in the Greater Chain. The theory is that proximity to the Moon, on the night of a Passing, is what causes people on Pekal to get Moonsick. Of course, that theory is easily debunked. Pekal's harbors and surrounding waters are no higher than Beripent, so why does Moonsickness strike there, but not here? That leads me to Lubon's theory: that Pekal's soil is somehow contaminated from the Moon Passing. I don't buy into that, either. If the soil on Pekal were contaminated, why do folks only get Moonsick on the night of a Passing? Wouldn't they be affected on the other thirty days of the cycle?"

"You're not really proving a point," Quarrah noted. "You're just making me think that the doctrine of the Holy Torch is as good a theory as any."

"Raek does this," Ard explained. "Spends half his breath telling you what's not accurate so you'll believe him when he comes around with the hard facts."

"Personally, I lean toward the theory of Grumont, which combines elements of Lubon with the Shwazer Society," Raek continued. "It basically states that due to the geomorphic features of Pekal, the island itself becomes a conduit for Moonsickness, passing it from the summit all the way to the surrounding water, afflicting any human being unfortunate enough to be standing around."

Based on Quarrah's expression, Ard couldn't tell what she thought about Raek's ramblings. Sparks, Ard himself didn't know what to think, and he'd been hearing Raek's philosophies since he was a teenager—a far cry from his mother's faith-filled explanations of the world.

"See, I'm not convinced that the Wayfarists have anything right," Raek carried on. "I'm sure they think they do, but at the end of the day, a lot of the Islehood's preachings seem like scare tactics to me. Doctrines intended solely to keep people in line."

"Like the Paladin Visitants," Quarrah followed up.

"Like the Paladin Visitants," repeated Raek. "We don't even know what they really are, let alone where they come from."

"Isle Halavend seems to know something about the Paladin Visitants that we don't," said Ard, pleased by the way his interjection brought them back to the matter at hand. "He's determined to have one more detonation of Visitant Grit, but he assures me that it will be used to save lives, not take them. All his motives seem to hinge on whatever new doctrine he claims to have uncovered with that Agrodite priestess."

"New doctrine?" Quarrah whispered. "Like what?"

"Doctrine! Doctrine!" Raek cried, finishing another pastry and dusting off his large hands. "You'd think we were a bunch of Holy Isles sitting around in here."

"Raek's right," Ard said, though he was just as curious as Quarrah. "We need to stay focused on the job we've been hired to do. Never mind what Isle Halavend plans to do once we give him the Visitant Grit."

"Well." Raek stood up with a heavy sigh. "I'm off to Strind to scout for a proper factory. I'll be taking the *Double Take*."

Ard knew Raek wasn't going to take a ferry. The big man hated public transportation. City carriages were too cramped, and he'd only tried the Trans-Island Carriage System once before deeming it "unpredictable" and "unsafe." Ard grinned. This from the guy who had propelled them through the air, all the way to the docks of Marow, with nothing but a stolen sash of Reggie crossbow bolts and a mathematical equation in his bald head.

"What about us?" Quarrah asked.

"We have a meeting with Elbrig and Cinza tomorrow," Ard said.

Raek rolled his eyes, muttering, "The crazies."

"So soon?" Quarrah asked.

"We're not simply stepping into costume," Ard answered. "They're going to help us become someone we're not. That's going to take time."

He crossed the room, peering out the secret slot he had installed in the wall. Below, the shopfront was empty save for Mearet, the Trothian baker.

Ard opened the door and climbed down the small ladder, emerging from the faux brick oven they had installed, its chimney rising to disguise the upper door.

"Anything fresh this afternoon?" Ard asked Mearet as Quarrah navigated the secret entrance.

The stout woman shook her head, eyes a blur as they looked at Ard. "Big man take all the fresh on the way in." Ard thought she handled Landerian quite well, though her Trothian accent made some words difficult to understand.

"Yeah, well, Big Man has the appetite of a bull dragon," replied Ard. "But none of the charm."

"I heard that!" Raek called from within the false oven.

Mearet chuckled at the interaction, though Ard wondered how

much she really understood. Mearet's pastries were actually the reason Ard had been drawn to this building. He'd frequented the Bakery on Humont Street often enough. And when Isle Halavend agreed to pay for a base of operations, Ard thought it would be a simple matter to convert the upper room.

They were renting the space from Mearet for fifteen Ashings a cycle—probably more than it was worth in this part of Beripent. Ard told her that he and Raek were linguists. Hey, it wasn't far from the truth, since Ard had an affinity for words. And from what he'd recently learned about Trothian eyesight, he didn't have to worry about Mearet catching a glimpse of his chalkboard.

Mearet was a Trothian making an honest living in the Greater Chain. She represented everything the king hoped for when he opened the island borders thirty years ago. Besides, having Mearet as a landlady had its perks. Fine baked goods.

"I'll have doughnuts at morning," Mearet said.

"Ah, my favorite," Ard replied, though he was never awake in time to enjoy them fresh. The husky older woman nodded in respect and retreated into the back kitchen, leaving Ard alone with Quarrah as Raek secured the false front on the oven entrance.

"Elbrig and Cinza employ a significant security detail," Ard said.

"You want me to bring my belts in case of trouble?" Quarrah asked.

"Flames, no!" Ard cried. "You trying to get us killed?" They crossed the shopfront, Ard grabbing a croissant as they passed the counter. "Bring a cat."

"What?" Quarrah stopped fast and turned to stare at him.

"I said, bring a cat," Ard repeated, taking a bite. "I'll meet you at the southeast corner of the Char tomorrow morning. Eight o'clock sharp." He opened the door to the street, but Quarrah remained still.

"A cat?" she said again.

"You're still hung up on that?" Ard shook his head. "I'll see you tomorrow."

~

I stop to write whenever I grow weary. Seeing the words on these pages helps me. It gives me hope that my findings will reach you.

CHAPTER

6

Quarrah Khai did not bring a cat. She didn't think there was any possible way that Ardor Benn had meant what he'd said at the bakery. But the ruse artist seemed quite annoyed with her lack of preparation when he picked her up at the southeast corner of the Char.

Ard had arrived late in a double-horse public carriage, a large model that could accommodate up to four passengers. The driver was an older man, very overweight, his girth spilling over the bench. *Poor horses,* Quarrah thought, *hauling that man around all day.*

They'd been riding for at least fifteen minutes, the morning gray and drizzling. Ard had spent most of the time complaining about how they were going to be late. *He'd* been the tardy one! If being on time to their meeting meant so much, couldn't he have awakened earlier? Sparks, the man's hair was still poking up on the side of his head like he'd just rolled out of bed.

"Where does one even buy a cat?" Quarrah asked. It was the closest she was going to come to apologizing. Ard was sitting across from her on the hard bench, staring out the carriage window as Beripent flew by.

"No, no," he said, without looking up. "You don't *buy* a cat. They're everywhere. You simply snatch one up when you see it passing. A large bag works nicely."

"I had one, growing up," said Quarrah.

"A large bag?"

She rolled her eyes. "A pet cat. My mother got it for me when my father died."

"A fairly suitable replacement, I imagine." Ard didn't treat the topic tenderly, but that didn't surprise Quarrah. He seemed blunt whenever it came to things that couldn't benefit him.

"I never liked that cat," Quarrah said. "But I held on to her for years because she reminded me of my mother."

Ard finally looked at her. "Your mother died, too?"

Quarrah shook her head. "She left when I was ten. I never saw her again." Not that it was a bad thing. Quarrah had accepted her solitude from an early age, quickly overcoming any sense of abandonment, and instead finding strength in being alone. She didn't need anyone taking care of her. She made her own luck.

"Should've gotten a dog." Ard turned his attention away once more.

Seems like I just found one, Quarrah thought. Gratefully she didn't say it out loud. At least, she didn't think she had. Sometimes it was hard to keep track of which words happened in her brain and which ones came tumbling out of her mouth.

"What about you?" she asked. "Where are you from?"

"Here," Ard said. "Beripent. Born and raised."

"Do you still have family in the city?"

"Just Raek," answered Ard.

"Is he your uncle or something?" she blurted. Probably not. Was Ard being literal?

"You don't have to be related to be family."

Right, then. Not literal. "How long have you known him?"

"All the years worth remembering," answered Ard. "I was in school as a kid. Raek was a few years older. He lived a few streets down and started tutoring to make an extra Ashing."

"You were Raek's student?" Quarrah asked.

"Or he was mine," answered Ard. "We never could decide. But one thing was certain. Together, we were unstoppable."

"You were teenagers," Quarrah pointed out. "Who was trying to stop you? And from doing what?"

Ard shot her an annoyed glance. "That's not...You can't..." He sighed heavily. "I worry about your imagination sometimes."

The carriage began to slow. Ard muttered something and pressed his face against the window. Outside, the heavy driver raised his voice.

"Outta the way! That's a fine stunt to get yourself killed!"

Quarrah sat forward. "What's going on?"

Ard squinted. "Rough part of town."

The carriage came to a complete halt. Without her belts, Quarrah felt useless in a skirmish. She wore a boot knife, of course, but if this were a robbery, that would be sorely insufficient. Ard's hand brushed back his leather coat to reveal a holster. Good, the man had brought his Rollers.

"I'm not stopping here," continued the driver. "Get your blazing drunk face off the road and out of my way!"

Ard popped open the door of the carriage and slid one foot onto the step, Quarrah peering over his shoulder at the obstruction. There was a woman lying in the middle of the damp street. She was stretched lengthwise, arms raised above her head so that she nearly spanned the narrow road.

"What's she doing?" Quarrah whispered to Ard.

The woman sat up when she saw the occupants of the carriage. The vagrant was dressed in rags, hair grayed. Her nose had an unpleasant downward hook. She looked rather shapeless, with so much tattered cloth around her.

The hag crawled across the compact dirt, finally standing when she was beside the horses. She moved forward, one hand clutching the yoke as if to prevent the carriage from departing.

"Back inside," the driver said to Ard and Quarrah. He raised his short whip to strike the woman, but Ard reached up to stay the man's hand.

"What do you want, old woman?" Ard asked.

Quarrah had withdrawn into the carriage, but she could easily see the exchange from her position. The hag hobbled a few steps closer.

"Just an Ashlit." Her teeth were discolored or missing altogether. "Havin' a lovely ride wit' the wifey?"

Wife? Quarrah was glad he didn't turn around to see her blushing. She and Ardor Benn, a couple? It would take a drunk hag to assume something so absurd.

"My wife is as charitable as she is beautiful." Ard gestured to Quarrah. "We would like to give you something far more valuable than an Ashlit, madam."

Ard reached into his vest and withdrew a necklace of glittering pearls. Quarrah gawked at the piece of fine jewelry.

"This will fetch a fair price in certain parts of Beripent." Ard pressed the necklace into the old woman's dirty hand.

The woman let out a shriek, tears welling in her eyes. "Homeland bless you, pretty people!" The hag bowed, backing away.

"Drive on," Ard instructed the driver before closing the carriage door.

"What...was that about?" Quarrah hoped the shadows of the carriage would hide her flushed face. She was still thinking about the two of them as a couple.

"Giving an Ashlit to a woman in her state is the same as handing her a bottle of liquor," Ard said. "Turning those pearls into

Ashings will require work. I believe people should work for what they get."

Quarrah tried not to read into that statement. Thieves worked for their pay, too. "And you just happen to be carrying a strand of pearls in your pocket?"

"I intended for them to be a gift." Ard stared across the carriage at her. "To give at the right moment."

Quarrah felt her face flushing again. "Oh...well...I couldn't possibly..."

"For Cinza," Ard said, causing Quarrah's blush to increase until she thought her face might catch fire.

"I just thought...because of what you said about me being your wife..." Was her mouth still going? See, this was why she preferred to work alone. "I'm just wondering..." Quarrah took a deep breath. Words. Why were they so complicated? "Why did you tell that woman we were married? Because we're not married." Obviously. She probably could have done away with that last sentence.

Ard was simply smiling at her as though amused by her discomfort. "Safety precaution," he explained. "I make it a point never to reveal truth about myself to strangers. If I find myself engaged in criminal activity later today, and the Reggies question that poor woman, she will tell them that a married man generously gave her a piece of fine jewelry." He slouched on his hard bench. "Now, that doesn't exactly fit my typical description. Throws them off my trail, see?"

Quarrah nodded, finally recovering from her string of embarrassment. "Is everything a ruse to you?" she asked. "Life. Is it just one big ruse?"

"I don't think of it that way," Ard explained. "I prefer to see it as a never-ending series of small ruses that are linked together."

No doubt, Ardor Benn was a fascinating man. "Have you always been this way?" Ask questions. Get to know each other. Wasn't that what people did when they worked together? "When you and Raek were *unstoppable* kids. Were you swindling people?"

"Flames, no, Quarrah. Don't criminalize the innocence of my youth. Raek and I were honest fellows for a long time," Ard said. "Creative. Tenacious. Hardworking. But we were straight arrows."

"So what made you start rusing?"

Ard didn't say anything for a moment. Then asked, "What made you start thieving?"

Quarrah was aware of the way he had turned the conversation around, but decided to go along with it. After all, from what she understood, conversation was supposed to be a two-way street.

"After my mom left, I was taken in by a family that I barely knew. Reformed Expeditionists. Do you know anything about that religion?"

Ard shrugged. "Only a little."

"It's Homelandic, of course," said Quarrah. All religions were, aside from the Trothian Agrodotism. "It's similar to Wayfarism, except they're governed by stricter rules. I didn't understand the way their family functioned, and the parents were constantly pressuring me for information."

"You were just a kid," Ard said. "What kind of information did they want?"

"How was I feeling? Was I comfortable in their home? Were the other children kind to me?"

Ard let out an abrupt laugh. "That's not an interrogation, Quarrah. It's common courtesy! They were trying to be nice to you."

"It never felt that way." Quarrah leaned back. Was she really going to tell him this story? Ard hadn't even respected her father's death. Why did she think he'd treat this any differently?

"There was a boy in the family, just a year older than me," she continued. "He'd take Ashings from his father's safe box. I saw him do it over and over. After a while, the missing money went noticed.

The boy blamed me, and his parents never questioned it. They whipped me. And the boy watched without saying a word."

Quarrah drew in a deep breath. "Nothing was the same after that. I saw what they provided for their own children, and how they skimped when it came to me. After all, I wasn't of their blood, or their faith. I was untrustworthy. A thief. So I made a choice. If I was going to get punished for something I didn't steal, then I might as well steal it and take my chances. At least that way the punishment would be worth some Ashings in my pocket.

"They hid the key much better, but I started practicing with locks. Listening to them, feeling them. Learning them. Then one day, when everyone was out of the house, I broke into the safe box and took every last Ashing. I ran away. And I never even felt bad about what I'd done. I had enough Ashings to stay alive for a while, and it wasn't long before I found another safe box. And then another."

Sparks, saying it like that made her sound so greedy! It wasn't that at all. There was something to the thrill of springing a lock that made her feel useful. She didn't even care much what was inside, though Ashings helped take care of life's annoying necessities.

They rode in silence for several moments. Then Ard looked right at her. "Blazing misers got what they deserved. Wish I could've been a fly on the wall to see their reaction."

"Lots of yelling and crying," Quarrah said.

"You stuck around to watch?" He was grinning now.

"I was only close enough to hear," she answered.

"Still, you were ten years old."

"Eleven, by then."

"Oh, well, that changes everything," Ard said. "I'm not impressed anymore. I was impressed when you were ten..."

Quarrah found herself smiling without realizing that it had crept onto her face.

"This is it, I think." Ard's gaze was out the window once more. They appeared to be in a much nicer part of the city.

No sooner had Ard spoken than the carriage began to slow, the driver pulling his team to a halt at the side of the wide road.

Ard cracked open the door and leaned out to speak with the driver. "We have an appointment with the tenants of number seventeen. An extra three-mark Ashing if you call on them for me."

Three Ashings was a generous tip! That would be enough to get anyone moving. Quarrah heard the driver mumble something in reply. A moment later, the carriage shifted as the big man climbed down from the bench.

Ard produced a coin pouch from his coat, the leather dyed green, and passed it to the driver. The man nodded, always seeming short of breath, as he tucked the payment into his vest pocket.

Quarrah watched their driver waddle around the corner of the building, his movements heavy and belabored. "Times are hard," Ard said, seeming to notice the surprised expression on Quarrah's face. "An extra three Ashings can really help out."

"It helps that you're not funding any of this," answered Quarrah. "Would you have tipped the man so generously if it were coming out of your own pocket?"

"Absolutely," answered Ard. "Elbrig and Cinza are not to be approached casually. They're just as likely to shoot you in the kneecap as they are to invite you in."

"I thought you had an appointment with them," Quarrah said.

"I do," he answered. "But that doesn't mean they won't spook when they see the likes of *you* on the doorstep."

Quarrah grunted her disapproval and slouched on the hard bench. Ardor Benn was inconsistent, she was picking that up quickly. No, perhaps *inconsistent* wasn't the right label. He just operated by a different code than most.

His words were not spent lightly. She got the distinct impression that each one served a purpose. If it served him to admire her looks, he'd say so. If an insult better met his private agenda, then he'd say that, too.

"What can I expect from the people we're meeting?" Quarrah asked. When she had to interact with people, she normally liked to survey them first. Surprises, no matter what kind, were unpleasantries in her line of work.

"It's best to go into this meeting with no expectations whatsoever," answered Ard. "Cinza and Elbrig are a different kind of Grit, so to speak. I don't think they'll like you. At least, not at the start."

"What's that supposed to mean?" Quarrah retorted.

"It means you have to win them over."

"How am I supposed to do that if I don't know anything about them?"

"Well, it would have helped if you'd brought a cat."

Was he ever going to let that drop? "I still can't tell if you're serious…"

Ard held up a hand to silence her. "Do you hear that?"

Quarrah picked up the sound instantly. It was a woman's voice, pitched high and desperate.

Ard flung open the carriage door and leapt out in a single bound, tugging his long leather coat to conceal his Rollers.

"There." Quarrah pointed across the street. "Down that alley." Ard set off without a word, Quarrah jogging a few steps to catch up. "What are you doing?"

"Sounds like someone's in trouble," said Ard. "I'm going to help my fellow wanderer. Isn't that the Wayfarist thing to do?"

If Quarrah were alone, she never would have looked down the alley. Other people's problems didn't need to be hers.

Now that they were closer, Quarrah could hear the skirmish, punctuated by the grumbling voice of a man. In stride, she stooped and drew her boot dagger. She and Ard rounded the corner together, taking quick stock of the situation in the dead-end alley.

The woman seemed close to Quarrah's age, her ruffled red dress slipped off one shoulder. Her hair was in ringlets, but her feet were bare. Quarrah couldn't figure why the woman would be dressed for an evening out, when it wasn't yet noon. The distraught lady held a scrap of wood like a club, her knuckles bloody. A few raindrops mingled with her tears, further smearing her thick makeup.

Before her was a middle-aged man, thin as a rail. His clothes were also fancy, though disheveled in a similar manner. His hair was nearly to the shoulders, but not pulled back in the fashion of the rich folk. He brandished a dueling sword in his left hand.

The man turned to glare at Ard and Quarrah, lean face drawn in a sneer and his black goatee greased into a downward point. "Nothing to see here." The man's working-class accent betrayed the rich facade of his clothes. "Merely a lovers' quarrel. I'm sure you understand."

"Don't listen to him!" The woman tried to dart forward, but the man's sword came up to bar her path.

Quarrah heard the click of a gun hammer locking into place. She turned to find Ard pointing his Roller at the man with the sword.

"Let's hear both sides of the story before we decide to walk away," Ard demanded.

"I don't know this man," the woman whimpered. "I don't know him at all."

"Shut yer blazing mouth!" yelled the man, making an aggressive move toward her.

Ard clucked his tongue sharply. "Not another step."

"Did he hurt you?" Quarrah asked the woman.

"I was upstairs..." The lady could barely keep it together. "He came in. But I escaped down the back steps. Please, somebody call the Regulators. Take this horrible man away!"

"That's enough from your pretty mouth." The man took another step toward the woman.

A gunshot cracked through the dead-end alley, the abrupt sound nearly deafening Quarrah. From the corner of her eye, she saw Ard lower his Roller, a white puff of smoke lingering where the gun had been fired.

The man in the alley dropped his sword, staggering. His right hand flew to his chest, and Quarrah saw a deep red begin to soak his fine shirt. The stranger made a strangled, grunting sound as blood dripped from his lips. Then he collapsed in a heap.

Quarrah covered her mouth, feeling as though she, too, might collapse. Ard seemed incredibly nonchalant about the exchange, holstering his Roller and concealing it with his coat.

The woman raced past her dead assailant and grasped Ard's arm. The woman was shaking. Quarrah was shaking. Sparks! Ard had just killed a man!

"You're going to be all right." Ard reached into his vest and withdrew an embroidered handkerchief. "Something for your tears?"

"Yes, thank you." She clutched the kerchief to her face and muffled the sobs. Quarrah followed them around a corner, hesitant to leave the man bleeding out in the dingy dead end, rain pattering around his body. She saw faces peering out of nearby windows. The crack of a Roller in the morning was bound to draw attention.

"Are you the Regulation?" the shaken woman asked.

"Yes, madam," Ard said. "I'm not in coat at the moment, but I happened to be passing through the neighborhood when I heard what was happening."

The lies! He spoke the lies so smoothly. For a moment, Quarrah herself might have believed that Ard was an actual Reggie.

"Homeland bless you," the woman whimpered, dabbing her eyes with the handkerchief as they stopped before a multilevel apartment building. "I have to pull myself together." She moved up the stairs, pausing in the doorway long enough to look back at Quarrah. "You found yourself a respectable man, miss. Don't make the mistake of letting him go."

"What?" Quarrah stammered. "No. We're not together like that..." The traumatized woman closed the door, cutting off Quarrah's explanation midsentence.

"We should get off the streets." Ard led the way past their waiting carriage toward the building where he had sent the overweight driver.

"What do we do about the body?" Quarrah asked as Ard began noting the numbers on the apartment doors.

"What body?" Ard knocked on the door labeled with a seventeen.

"*What body*?'" Quarrah cried. "I don't know, how about the one in that alleyway back there?"

"I warned that blazing idiot," Ard answered. "I told him not to take another step."

"You can't behave like this!" When Quarrah had agreed to work with Ardor Benn, she hadn't known he'd be so reckless. "Shooting whomever you please. We should have called for the Regulation."

"The man was assaulting her," Ard exclaimed. "Besides, I make it a point never to call for the Reggies. That man was a criminal, and I dealt with him accordingly."

"*You're* a criminal, too!" cried Quarrah. "How would you feel if someone shot you in the chest?"

"I suppose I'd feel nothing, as I'd be dead." Ard pressed his ear against the door. "I don't think they're here. Flames! Something must have spooked them."

"Any chance it could have been some lunatic firing a Roller in the alley just outside?" Quarrah remarked.

"No sign of the driver, either." Ard stepped away from the door. "We'll wait for him at the carriage. Come on."

He set off once more, ducking against the drizzling rain as Quarrah moved to keep up. Ard reached the carriage first, flung open the door, and hoisted himself inside. Quarrah was right behind him, halfway in, when she noticed two people already sitting inside.

She hesitated, but Ard seized her arm, pulling her down onto the bench beside him.

The carriage door clicked shut and Quarrah stared at the strange duo seated across from them. It was a man and a woman who seemed to be slightly older than Ard. No, much older. Quarrah drew back. Perhaps they were younger?

There were several things about the two that made it nearly impossible to guess their age. To start with, both were missing hair, though clearly not from balding. Even the woman had shaved her head, leaving just a fuzz of new growth upon her scalp. In addition, neither had any teeth, their lips folding in like wrinkled pits above their chins.

"Quarrah Khai," said Ard. "Meet Elbrig Taut and Cinza Ortemion." He gestured across the carriage, and suddenly, Quarrah knew exactly why Raek had called them crazies.

They were clothed only in long underwear that buttoned up the front, the tan material ironed as though they might wear it to the symphony. Their builds were slight, and they both seemed shorter than Quarrah, though it was hard to tell while everyone sat.

"Oh, Ardy," said the woman. "Did you bring me a kitty?" Her toothless speech was difficult for Quarrah to understand.

Ard shot a sideways glance to Quarrah. "Not this time, Cinza. I'm afraid I left the task of finding a cat to someone else, and they didn't come through. Just goes to prove, if you want the job done right, do it yourself."

"It wasn't Raekon, was it?" Elbrig asked. "It would take that oaf weeks to catch a cat, loud and obtrusive as he is."

"It wasn't Raek," Ard said. Quarrah waited for him to call her out, but for once, he let the story lie. "Thanks for going through with the meeting."

"I wasn't sure about your new friend at first glance," Cinza said. "Knew she had potential, but I had to see her move. See her out and about."

"What do you mean?" Quarrah shifted under the stranger's piercing gaze. "You were watching us from the carriage?"

Elbrig chuckled. "How many people spoke to you on your ride from the Char?"

Quarrah thought back to the morning's trip. Besides Ard, there was the overweight driver, the panhandling hag, and the quarreling couple. Now the two strangers in the carriage.

"Six," answered Quarrah. "Including the two of you, but not Ard."

"Think again," said Cinza.

Had she forgotten something? Quarrah squinted her eyes, mentally running over the morning's ride from the moment Ard's carriage had picked her up. The driver, the hag, the swordsman, the distressed woman. That was all.

"The answer is two," said Elbrig. He reached down to a bag on the floor and withdrew a familiar green coin pouch full of Ashings.

"You stole that from the driver?" Quarrah muttered.

"I *was* the driver," answered Elbrig Taut.

No. How? He was so fat!

From the same bag, Cinza withdrew a strand of pearls and an embroidered handkerchief. Quarrah stared. Ard had given both of those items away. The hag had been old and hideous, the crying woman young and attractive. Quarrah studied Cinza's face across the carriage, but could see no resemblance to either woman.

"And the swordsman in the alleyway?" Quarrah dared ask.

Elbrig withdrew a white shirt, the front stained with crimson liquid, still wet. He stretched the shirt tight, and Quarrah saw that there was no hole from the lead ball.

Now she spun on Ard. "You knew?" How had she let him trick her again? "You staged all of this?" Did he keep doing this just to prove that he was always two steps ahead?

"Not my idea this time," Ard said defensively. "Elbrig and Cinza have an intense screening process for new clients. They want the chance to interact before making the decision to work with you. The pearls were the first test. If she refused when I offered, then it meant you had no potential."

"Like Raekon," muttered Elbrig.

"When Cinza accepted my handkerchief," Ard explained, "she was actually giving a final agreement. It meant you passed the inspection and warranted a meet."

Inspection! Like Quarrah was some kind of commodity to be sold at the Char marketplace. "You didn't kill anyone," she finally said to Ard. Quarrah didn't know if she should feel relieved to know that her new partner wasn't a killer, or upset to know that a man dying before her very eyes could be a stunt.

"I usually try not to. There was a blank Blast cartridge in my Roller," Ard explained. "And Elbrig has a thing for artificial blood."

"Faking your own death is surprisingly satisfying," said the toothless man.

"And liberating," Ard added. "I tried it once. Really gives you a chance to start fresh."

The entire exchange made Quarrah feel like a fool. Costumes! She should have seen through them!

"Still trying to wrap your head around it?" Elbrig asked. "The trick to a good disguise isn't in hiding your face. It's in drawing attention to something else. Something memorable." He leaned forward. "What's the first thing that pops into your mind when you think of the carriage driver?"

"He was obese," Quarrah answered without hesitation.

"What did his face look like?" asked Elbrig.

Quarrah opened her mouth to answer, but realized she had nothing to say. She felt shallow, but the driver's face hadn't made an impression when compared to his overwhelming girth.

"What about the man in the alleyway?" Elbrig said.

"He had a pointed black beard," answered Quarrah.

"When we see people," Elbrig stroked his bare chin, "our minds lock on to specific details. A good disguise enhances the details you want remembered, and drowns out the things we can't change."

"The old hag," said Quarrah. "I remember her voice. Her hair. Her nose."

"As planned," said Cinza, tapping her own nose, which now looked very different. Must have been some sort of putty. A sculpted nose, and Quarrah hadn't noticed?

"Her makeup," Quarrah said about the alley woman. "The red dress and blond hair in ringlets."

Quarrah suddenly understood the raw appearance of the couple before her. It was much easier to change teeth and hairstyles when you didn't have any to start with. This was a whole new level of dedication to craft.

"Now let's see what we can make of you," Cinza said, causing Quarrah to shift uncomfortably. "You have nice features, but they're underutilized."

So much attention. Half the reason Quarrah had become a thief was to skirt attention. Cinza leaned across the carriage, touching Quarrah's face. "Cheeks could use more color. Your hair is entirely too flat and shapeless. And your ears are a bit on the large side."

Quarrah scoffed, folding her arms defensively. "If I'm so imperfect, why did you agree to meet me at all?"

"I said you have *potential*," explained Cinza. "If a chef turned down all her ingredients, what would she use to cook a masterpiece? You have nice elbows."

"Elbows?" Quarrah straightened her arms self-consciously.

Cinza reached out and poked Quarrah softly in the breast. "Hmmm…"

Quarrah gasped, swatting away the strange woman's hands. "What do you mean, '*hmmm*'?"

"She could do with a bit more bosom," Cinza said. "Wouldn't you agree, Ardy?"

Ard looked down at the carriage floor, and for once Quarrah thought the blushing might have befallen him. "Whatever you say, Cinza."

"What about Ard?" Quarrah asked. She wasn't going to endure this scrutinizing alone. "What about his features?"

"Ardy?" Cinza cried. "He has a nearly perfect face!"

Quarrah rolled her eyes. She would have enjoyed seeing Ard brought down a little.

"It's true," replied Elbrig. "And while I hate to have him cover it up, I must insist that he start growing a beard at once."

"You have someone in mind for us?" Ard asked.

"A few good options," answered Elbrig. "You need to work your way into the social circles of the rich and royal folk to access the palace, yes?"

"That's right," Ard said. "But don't make us royalty."

"Blegh." Cinza pretended to throw up. "Royalty is a mess. We don't build those profiles anymore. Bloodlines are too blazing tight on these islands. Royalty's a bunch of Moonsick inbreds."

"We'll work you in from another angle," assured Elbrig. He turned to Quarrah. "Do you have any particular skills that might help us select your identity?"

"I can pick locks," she answered. "And pockets."

"You can bottle those skills for a while," said Cinza. "Any skills useful for a lady of high class?"

Quarrah considered it. She'd surveyed a lot of manors and estates, watched a lot of rich folk go about their frivolous daily activities. They always seemed so foreign. So proper. Did she have anything in common with the people she stole from?

"I can drink tea," answered Quarrah.

"She can drink tea!" Cinza cried merrily, slapping her knee. Elbrig nearly burst the buttons on his long underwear. It was meant to be a joke. They knew that, right?

"Well, that doesn't give us much to work with," said Elbrig. "We may have to charge extra for the amount of tutoring this one will require."

Ard nodded. "We'd like to get started right away."

"Of course," answered Cinza. "Tonight's the Moon Passing. Fifth Cycle starts tomorrow. We'll begin the day after that."

"Should give us time to get our documentation and wardrobe together," added Elbrig. "Half payment will be due upon signing. The other half will be paid out through the course of the tutoring sessions." Elbrig glanced at Quarrah. "Additional fees may apply."

"That's more than acceptable," answered Ard.

Cinza reached across the carriage and pinched his cheek affectionately. "Oh, Ardy. That's why we love doing business with you. You're just so blazing agreeable." She turned to Quarrah. "I meant what I said by the alley. This man's the catch of a lifetime. You better treat him right."

Quarrah rubbed her hands across her face, trying not to let herself get too flustered. They wanted a reaction out of her, but she'd remain composed. "We're not..." She sighed. "We are not a couple, spark it all!" So much for composed.

"No," Cinza said. "But you will be, starting day after tomorrow."

Elbrig threw open the carriage door and stepped out to the street, a startling sight with his toothless mouth, shaved head, and long underwear. Cinza slid out after him, blowing Ard a kiss. "See you at the bakery! Midday. Two days' time!"

The door shut, and Quarrah sat in stunned silence. Of all the strange folk she'd encountered in her life...the crazies. Raek was right.

"I suppose I should drive us back to the Char," Ard said.

"Don't do that again," Quarrah said as he moved for the door.

"Do what?"

"Play me like that." She fought to keep her voice steady. "I'm not here to be rused, Ardor Benn. I'm not here for your personal entertainment. You asked me to join you for a job, and I intend to do it."

She took a deep breath. "But if you trick me like that again, then I might be tempted to try out *my* particular skill set on *you*."

Ard stared at her for a moment before nodding. "I'm sorry about today. It wasn't my idea. Elbrig and Cinza needed to screen you. We're all on the same page now. It won't happen again." He popped open the door. "I promise, dear."

"Dear?" Quarrah repeated, as he stepped down to the street.

Ard smiled at her. "Just getting into character. You heard what Cinza said. And while I'm at it, how many kids do you think we should have? Is seven too many? I hope they have your eyes."

Quarrah blushed one more time as the carriage door shut.

~

The twilight plays tricks on my eyes. I mistook a rock for a bear. A vine for a snake. Perhaps my own insecurities cause me to see things the wrong way.

CHAPTER

7

Ard and Quarrah waited by the racks of baked goods near the bakery's shopfront entrance. Mearet bustled in and out, hauling sacks of flour from a wagon on the street to the storage room in the back. The driver of the delivery wagon was also a Trothian, and Ard heard the two of them conversing in their native tongue.

Ard wondered what the older generations thought about the

inclusion of Trothians into the Greater Chain. There had always been an undercurrent of mistrust and fear between the two races, dating clear back to speculative history—before any consistent documentation.

Supposedly, the Landers had sailed from the Homeland, arriving to find a chain of uninhabited islands. The Trothians came later, arriving in "ships that the eye could not behold." Ard remembered that phrase from school, though he didn't have a blazing idea what it meant.

Over the space of a few generations, Trothians slew hundreds of thousands of Landers before the tides turned. Some speculate that the Landers were able to summon the first Paladin Visitant. Others say that the Trothians willingly withdrew. Whatever the case, the Trothians took up residence on their small islets, and the races had been kept separate ever since.

Language, rituals, and the fact that Landers and Trothians could not interbreed all created natural divides. But King Pethredote had taken great steps to overcoming centuries of estrangement.

Brave pioneers like Mearet and the wagon driver were changing history, one cinnamon scone at a time.

"Breakfast?" He offered Quarrah a sticky glazed fritter.

"Lunch," she answered, pushing it away. "They're late."

Not by Ard's standards. It was only a few minutes past noon. Elbrig and Cinza operated on a similar clock. Besides, the waiting had given Ard plenty of time to watch Quarrah fidget while he ate his fill of pastries.

Quarrah was agitated today. Ard could tell by the way she shifted her weight, her hands clenched into fists. She was wearing all black, as though she might have to sneak into a dark place in broad daylight. Never mind that. Cinza would have her out of those drab clothes soon enough.

Ard rubbed a hand across his stubbly chin. It had been years since he'd grown a beard. Since Pekal. Tanalin used to say it increased his looks tenfold. Now he was afraid it would only make him look old.

Ard finished off his scone and started on something that looked like a strudel. The pastries were paid for as a necessary part of the ruse. Ard had been to the Mooring to see Isle Halavend just yesterday. Lyndel hadn't been present, and the meeting was as brief as ever. Ard gave the old Isle another list of his expenditures, as well as an estimate for the disguise managers' services.

Ard had pressed Halavend for his motives with the Visitant Grit, but the old man still refused to entertain the topic. He dismissed Ard, who received his reimbursement at a predetermined drop site in the Char, a safe box concealed behind vines that covered the crumbled wall of a historic edifice.

A bell chimed, causing Ard to look up from where he'd been tracing his finger through a flour-dusted tabletop.

"Elbrig!" Ard clapped his hands in warm welcome. The man didn't look at all like his natural self—the version they'd met inside the carriage two days ago.

In place of his bald head was a wavy blond hairpiece, looking extremely realistic. In place of his toothless gums was a mouthful of straight, white teeth. And in place of his long underwear, he wore dark trousers and a gray shirt with modest sleeves. Over one shoulder, Elbrig carried a sack so large it nearly dragged on the threshold.

Cinza appeared behind him with a similar bag. She wore a simple brown skirt and sensible leather shoes. Like Elbrig, Cinza looked a shade paler than she had in the carriage. She had a straight row of teeth, and a blond wig that reached past her shoulders, plain and uninspiring.

This couple standing in the bakery was the closest thing to Elbrig Taut and Cinza Ortemion that anyone got to see with regularity. Unaltered faces, simple hairstyles, and plain clothes. If they weren't playing a role, they didn't want to stand out. In their current apparel they were the kind of people who were looked at halfheart-edly and instantly forgotten.

"Thank the Homeland I've come," Cinza said, eyeing Quarrah. "Your wardrobe is in distress."

Quarrah glanced down and began to justify the usefulness of black for someone in her line of work. Elbrig cut her off.

"I like the new digs." He shifted his sack and snatched a dough-nut off the display rack.

"Even His Majesty had great things to say about this place." Ard pointed to a frame on the wall. It displayed King Pethredote's sig-nature, scribed in charcoal across a scrap of parchment.

Cinza peered at it. "Forgery," she muttered.

Ard shook his head. "Mearet swears to the Homeland that it's real. Said King Pethredote visited this establishment when she first opened some five years back."

"The Trothian can't even see what's on the paper." Cinza waved her hand, still unconvinced.

"Oh, I'm a believer!" Elbrig declared through a mouthful. "This is delectable."

"Mearet's the best," Ard said as the stout woman ducked into the back room with the final sack of flour over her shoulder. "Some-times I think she's just fattening me up for the slaughter."

Ard led them to the false brick oven. It took some assistance, but Elbrig was able to finagle his large bundled sack up the ladder and into the secret meeting room.

"Where's Raekon?" Cinza asked, scanning the room's chalk-board, table, and chairs.

"He's off to Strind. Investigating something," answered Ard. "Probably be gone for some time, so you don't have to worry about seeing him."

"I'd be more worried about *hearing* him," said Elbrig. "Big oaf, lumbering about like a dragon with a stubbed toe."

"What is it you don't like about Raek?" Quarrah asked.

"We like him fine," said Elbrig. "He's just so...undisguisable. Mountain of a man, with his head as round and shiny as the Moon. Can't trust someone like that, who always walks around looking exactly how they're supposed to look."

"You'll be proud to know that Raek has recently been successful in disguising himself as a Reggie," Ard pointed out. "On two separate occasions."

"Wonder what kind of Moonsick fool he was able to trick," Elbrig muttered.

Ard glanced at Quarrah, but decided not to say anything about it. Telling them that Raek's disguise had fooled her would not start them on the right foot. Quarrah needed all the good favor she could muster.

Cinza kicked a chair so that it slid to a stop in the center of the room. Then, grabbing Quarrah by the elbow, Cinza plopped her down rather forcefully.

"You could always ask me to sit, you know," Quarrah protested. Ard flinched as something appeared from the pocket of Cinza's simple outfit.

Scissors.

Cinza made two complete snips before Quarrah realized what was happening. She leapt from the chair, whirling on Cinza, who stood with scissors in one hand and two long locks of Quarrah's blondish hair in the other.

"What are you...?" Quarrah gasped, running her fingers along the back of her head. Her face was twisted in shock.

Cinza held up the scissors impatiently. "Well, I'm not done."

"You're not touching my hair," Quarrah whispered.

The disguise manager held up the locks she'd already claimed. "Might as well let me finish now." She shrugged. "Can't get any worse at this point."

Ard watched Quarrah take a few steadying breaths. "Cinza wouldn't cut it unless there was good reason," he tried to explain.

"Ardy's right," said Cinza. "Dirty blond hair of your length will hardly leave a lasting impression. We need to fix you up with something to make a mark. Something to draw attention away from that face."

Ard sighed. Cinza could be so tactless.

"What's wrong with my face?" Quarrah asked.

"Absolutely nothing," Ard said. And he meant it. There was an unrefined beauty to Quarrah's appearance. The juxtaposition of that light hair against her dark eyes. But Cinza was never satisfied with anyone's base appearance.

"The fact is," said Elbrig, "we'd rather not alter your face."

"At least we agree on that point," muttered Quarrah.

"Instead," continued Elbrig, "we want to draw attention away from it. Draw the eye to other, more distinguishing features."

"It's a compliment, really," Ard said. Coming from those two.

"Is that so, Mister Perfect Face?" Quarrah's hands were in fists at her sides, but she sat stiffly before Cinza.

"Nothing too radical," Cinza said. "A shorter cut makes it easier to get a wig on and off properly." This coming from a woman with a shaved scalp.

Elbrig moved across the room and plucked a little piece of chalk from the blackboard's frame. Ard knew the disguise managers would appreciate the chalkboard's dramatic flair. Elbrig turned with a grin to face his new pupils.

"Cinza and I have carefully selected two personas that should allow you to insert yourself into high society," he began. "Your point of access is the Royal Orchestra."

Elbrig flourished the piece of chalk and scrawled the word *orchestra*.

"You want us to join the king's orchestra?" Ard liked the plan already. Bold, public, with results that could get them access to many parts of the palace.

"I feel like I shouldn't have to point this out," said Quarrah, holding her head still as Cinza kept snipping, "but I don't actually play an instrument."

Ard wasn't surprised. He didn't know much about music, either. Learning an instrument was an indication of class. No one was forbidden from the study, but lessons and opportunities were made much more available to certain bloodlines, or families with enough Ashings to earn them clout among royalty.

"Pooey!" Elbrig scoffed. "I didn't say you needed to play an instrument. I said you were going to join the orchestra."

Quarrah tried to look at Ard, but Cinza tugged her head another direction. "Am I missing something?"

"Let me introduce you to the people you are about to become." Elbrig turned back to write some more. Now that Ard was sitting at the table, he wondered if the chalkboard came across so tedious when he used it.

"Ardor will take the role of Dale Hizror." Elbrig underlined the name, and scrawled a few more details as he explained them. "Raised in the rural leeward side of Strind, a township called Nint, Dale grew to young adulthood on a family-owned hog farm."

"Hog farm? Any chance I could convince you to change that to a horse ranch?"

Elbrig shook his head. "Must be hogs."

"Oink, oink," Cinza added, chuckling at herself.

"Young Dale's father was in possession of an old violin, which Dale began to learn by ear," Elbrig continued. "When Dale was nineteen years old, his parents were killed in a boating accident and he inherited the farm. The hog life had never suited him, so he sold the farm for ten thousand Ashings."

"Must have been a lot of hogs," Quarrah interrupted.

"With enough Ashings to live comfortably," Elbrig said, "Dale moved to Beripent to pursue his true passion—music. He lived in the city for nearly ten years, exhausting his funds as he auditioned for orchestra after orchestra. Discouraged, Dale left Beripent for a more familiar rural setting. Long story short—and we will get to the long story, just not today—Dale later discovered that his greatest talent was not in playing orchestral music, but in *composing* it."

Ard nodded. Composer. That was brilliant. Skilled composers were lauded as much as, or more than, the musicians who played their music. Taking the role of a composer would also prevent Ard from having to perform in front of anyone. It took massive amounts of knowledge and skill to compose, but the work was done in private. An ideal situation for an impersonator.

Elbrig crossed to his bag and withdrew a wooden portfolio. From it, he produced a folder, fat with papers. "Everything you need to know about Dale Hizror's public interactions is contained in this folder, beginning with a record of sale of the hog farm."

"Wait a minute," Quarrah cut in. "How do you have a record of that? I thought this Dale person was made-up."

"Not simply made-up," said Elbrig. "We like to use the term *created*."

Ard thumbed through the documents. "These are forgeries, then?"

"Absolutely not!" cried Elbrig. "Every document you hold is legitimate."

There were a number of sales receipts, signed tenant agreements, dozens of rejections signed by orchestras in the city. Sparks, this was an actual person!

"Was he real?" Ard finally asked. He didn't know much about the way Elbrig and Cinza did their work, but it wasn't a stretch to think that they'd been the cause of an unfortunate accident for the real Dale Hizror, stepping in to impersonate the dead man however they pleased.

"He's real to us," said Cinza. "And to any of the folks that meet him."

"I mean," pressed Ard, "will I be impersonating someone who actually used to be alive?"

"Shame on you, Ardy," Cinza said. "We don't take advantage of the dead."

"Too much uncertainty in that," added Elbrig. "If we tried to keep the dead alive through impersonation, there would be too many unknowns about their life. Conversations they had with people, key memories we wouldn't know about."

Ard gestured to the folder. "What about all these conversations?"

"I had them myself," said Elbrig, "while developing the character of Dale Hizror."

"So there is an actual hog farm?" Quarrah asked.

"Of course," said Elbrig. "In the township of Nint in rural Strind. I bought that hog farm fifteen years ago so I could resell it to establish roots for my character."

Fifteen years? Sparks, Ard knew these two were good at what they did, but Elbrig had been building this character for fifteen years? And now he was going to sell it off to Ard. Suddenly, the high price they had agreed upon seemed reasonable.

"You're selling us a product that you've been developing for more than half my life." Quarrah seemed even more shocked than Ard.

"It's not so crazy, is it?" Cinza rounded out the back of Quarrah's short cropped hair. "You can't sell a tree for lumber if you only planted it last year."

Ard was astonished by the amount of detail presented in the folder, let alone the backstory Elbrig had only begun to explain. Ard felt capable of juggling a lot, mentally. He'd once run four ruses simultaneously. But what Elbrig did was a different thing altogether.

"How many of these long-term identities are you currently developing?"

"We have dozens of burners," answered Cinza. "That's what we call the ones with minimal history. Not much more than a good costume, those."

"The more established personas run at a higher price," said Elbrig.

"And we save those for premiere clients worthy of cashing out on the work we put in."

Ard noticed how Elbrig had skirted his question. They were secretive people, and Ard didn't press it.

"Clients like Ardy," Cinza said with a smile. "We're dusting off the best for you, my boy."

"Thanks," replied Ard. "But I am curious to know how we take an unknown composer with no formal training and present him at the royal circles. Emerging composers are an Ashlit a dozen. But I'll need to gain enough notoriety to get close to the king."

"Of course," said Elbrig. "That's part of the deal. Every spring, the king selects a composer to debut a new composition at the Grotenisk Festival."

Ard nodded. The Grotenisk Festival was a long-standing tradition. People came from all over the Greater Chain for the festivities. Spring—a time to celebrate regrowth. A time to celebrate killing the dragon that destroyed half the city.

"This year"—Elbrig smirked—"King Pethredote is going to choose Dale Hizror."

"That's quite an impression I'll need to make."

"It'll be easier than you think," answered Elbrig. "You see, we're going to convince those Moonsick royals that Dale Hizror composed the Unclaimed Symphony."

Ard felt an uncontrollable smile spreading across his face. This was why he'd hired Elbrig Taut. He was the only other person that seemed to think on the same scale Ard did. The Unclaimed Symphony. Flames, this really was going to be the ruse of a lifetime.

"What's the Unclaimed Symphony?" Quarrah asked.

Cinza snipped the scissors aggressively beside Quarrah's ear. "Don't you know anything about high society?"

"I know lots of things," Quarrah said. "Things I can steal. Tangible things. I can't steal music. I've looked into it. Too many copies floating around. A stolen stack of parchments is rather useless on the thief's market."

"The Unclaimed Symphony is indisputably King Pethredote's favorite piece of music," answered Elbrig. "Personally, I don't find the composition too riveting. In my opinion, its popularity is largely owing to the mystery that shrouds it. You see, no one knows who wrote the Unclaimed Symphony."

"Hence the name," Cinza cut in.

"It was deposited at the palace four years ago," explained Elbrig. "And it's driven the royals mad ever since."

"And we're going to convince everyone that Dale Hizror wrote the symphony?" Ard said. "I imagine this type of claim has been made before."

Elbrig nodded. "Half a dozen times. But each claim was ultimately disproven."

"What makes you think our attempt to prove it will be any different?" asked Quarrah.

"Because Ardor Benn will be selling the bit," answered Elbrig. "The claims made before came from actual aspiring composers, not ruse artists."

"So . . ." Quarrah said. "You're saying that Ard will successfully convince people that he's a famous composer because he's actually not one?" She rolled her eyes. "Besides . . ." Quarrah's tone furthered her skepticism. "If we do succeed in convincing everyone that Ard wrote the symphony, won't that prompt the real composer to come forward and dispel the claim?"

"I will ensure that does not happen," said Elbrig. "I'm developing a character who disposes of threats like that."

"Flames, Elbrig!" Ard cried. "You can't kill the real composer!"

"I doubt it will come to that," he answered. "But it's best to have someone waiting in the wings."

Cinza produced a hand mirror from the large sack and held it in front of Quarrah. "What do you think?"

Ard liked the haircut. It framed Quarrah's face in a new way, bringing out features he hadn't noticed before. Quarrah didn't say a thing. The look on her face implied that she didn't hate it, but Ard knew she wouldn't come right out and say that to Cinza.

Ard had to admit, he enjoyed the way Quarrah handled herself. She was confident but vulnerable. There seemed to be no pretenses with Quarrah Khai, and that kind of honesty was attractive to him.

"What's my role in all of this?" Quarrah turned away from the mirror to face the chalkboard.

Elbrig tossed the piece of chalk across the room and Cinza caught it. "You'll be taking on the role of Azania Fyse, Dale Hizror's lovely and soft-spoken fiancée."

"Fiancée?" Quarrah repeated. Ard thought he saw her cheeks growing slightly more pink.

"It's the easiest way to connect the two of you in social circles," explained Cinza, reaching the chalkboard and writing Quarrah's new name.

"Do we have to be connected?" Quarrah asked.

"I suppose not," said Elbrig. "It's certainly more convenient. Finding an alternative would incur an additional fee..."

"Just shut up and marry me," Ard said to Quarrah. It was amusing to watch her fluster under comments like those. Endearing, really, which was why Ard found himself wanting to pester her. Besides, it was good practice. Ard's jibes would be nothing compared to what happened in daily conversation with the rich and royal.

"So that's it?" Quarrah said. "I'm just supposed to hang on Ard's arm? He gets the hog farm and a whole rags-to-riches backstory, and I get 'lovely and soft-spoken'?"

Ard was trying not to laugh. He was known for getting passionate, but Quarrah had a way of getting fired up in a single snap. Like an explosion from the spark of a Slagstone ignitor.

"Patience!" Cinza cried. "That's supposed to be one of Azania's best qualities." She lifted an eyebrow. "I've got my work cut out...

Now, the two of you met through music. Dale is a composer, and Azania is a budding vocalist."

"A singer?" Quarrah cried. "You're making me into a singer?"

"The other option was a violinist," said Cinza, "but in order to pull that off, you'd need to play the violin, which we know you don't do."

"I don't sing, either!" Quarrah insisted.

"No, I imagine you don't," answered Cinza. "But we can work around that. Teaching you to open and close your mouth properly is going to be a lot easier than teaching you fingerings and bowing. We're already into the Fifth Cycle. Only five more until the First Cycle and the spring festival. That may seem like a lot of time to you, but this is going to be complicated. Trust me. Azania the soprano is the way to go."

Quarrah sat back in her chair. "I really don't sing."

Ard felt like she was missing the point. Quarrah was no more a singer than he was a composer. But Elbrig and Cinza were going to transform them. Of course, they couldn't turn Ard into an actual composer, but they were going to make him passable in public. The same would be done with Quarrah if she trusted Cinza's methods.

"I was under the impression that King Pethredote favors instrumental music," Ard said.

"It's true," replied Elbrig. "But even the king's personal tastes cannot compete with what is trending among the nobility. Vocal soloists are gaining popularity, and while the king approves all the music played by his orchestra, the repertoire is mainly chosen by the conductor. Besides, we trust the king will change his opinion when he discovers the identity of his favorite composer and learns that Dale Hizror is writing a new cantata."

Quarrah threw her hands in the air. "Ard's going to write a cantata?"

"Of course not," Elbrig said. "We have people for that. But his beautiful face will be what sells the new composition."

"Let's establish your look," Cinza said to Quarrah. She crossed to her sack and withdrew a wig of vibrant red hair.

"Ginger?" Quarrah asked. "That seems a bit flashy."

"Well, that's the point," said Cinza. "I didn't cut off your bland hair just to replace it with a wig of a similar color. Red is uncommon and, as you said, flashy. It will draw some attention away from your face."

Cinza began situating the bright wig on Quarrah's head. Elbrig moved around the table with another wig in his hands. The hair was black, shoulder-length, and already tied back in the noble fashion. Ard noticed a built-in prosthetic forehead ending in bushy eyebrows that would conceal his real ones.

He slipped the piece onto his head and examined himself in Elbrig's mirror. He was surprised how much it changed his appearance. The artificial forehead, though not yet tacked down, subtly changed the shape of his face. There was a single streak of white hair rolling off the front of the wig, a distinctive touch that Ard knew wasn't there by coincidence. He thought it aged him a bit. Made him look distinguished.

"We'll also shape your beard once it gets to length," said Elbrig. "Dale Hizror wears the sideburns long with a gentleman's mustache on the lip. Best to have a real mustache on first introduction. Everything must stand up to scrutiny. After you've established yourself in court, I would recommend moving to a fake mustache and adhesive."

Ard stroked his upper lip. Fake mustaches and wigs. This was all rather exciting.

"Spectacles." Cinza held them out for Quarrah.

"Let me guess," Quarrah said. "To cover my face."

"That's one benefit," Cinza answered. "Wide-rimmed spectacles like these are actually coming into vogue with the royal women. I've heard that some even wear them with a plain glass lens. No magnification. Purely for fashion. Something of a ruse in itself, fake spectacles. Anyway, these should also help with the squinting."

"Squinting?" said Quarrah.

"Haven't you noticed how she does that?" Cinza asked the two men. Ard chose to say nothing, but Elbrig agreed. "From simple observation, I'd say your eyesight's failing. Sad thing, young as you are. So the spectacles should help."

Quarrah slipped them onto her face, the red painted rims wide and ovular. Ard did admit, between the wig and the spectacles, Quarrah's face seemed rather drowned out. A shame, really. But then, that was the point to a disguise.

"The wardrobe will also help with the transformation," said Elbrig. "We have a few outfits for you both to try on. They'll fit loosely today, but we'll have them tailored to your figure."

"Now go ahead and kiss each other," said Cinza.

"What?" Ard and Quarrah replied in unison.

"You're supposed to be in love, for Homeland's sake," Cinza cried. "That means you'll have to dispel any awkwardness between the two of you. Best to get started on that now. What better way than a passionate kiss?"

This time, Ard felt *his* face growing red. And Quarrah's cheeks nearly matched her new wig.

"Here?" Quarrah stammered. "Now?"

"Maybe we should work up to that," Ard said. It wasn't that he found the idea unpleasant. In fact, in many ways he would have found it easier to kiss Quarrah if she *weren't* so endearing.

Ard stood up awkwardly. Quarrah was already on her feet, and Ard thought it might be so she could make a quick getaway.

"Sure," Elbrig said. "No sense rushing into things. All we have to do is teach you both to read music, basic understanding of music theory and form, instrument ranges, lyrics, knowledge of composers past and present…not to mention mannerisms specific to your characters, nuances, idiosyncrasies, backstories. Oh, yeah. And we also need to create infallible proof that Dale Hizror is in fact the composer of the Unclaimed Symphony."

Ard rubbed his forehead. This *was* going to be a lot of work. With only six cycles until the Grotenisk Festival, he and Quarrah would have to learn quickly. They weren't just putting on costumes. They were becoming new people altogether. And Elbrig was right. With that long list of things to learn, they wouldn't have time to fall in love.

Quarrah was standing beside him now. In one swift motion, Ard turned on her, his arms slipping around her thin waist. He kissed her lips before she could react to his advance.

It was easy. Ard just did what he'd done for the last seven years. Pretended she was Tanalin Phor.

~

I saw a dragon today. Never before have I beheld such a magnificent creature. She was wearing a gown of scales, the deepest green, and her leather wings were like the shoulder capes of the noblemen.

PART II

No Settled hand can ignite that Holy Torch. Like a sentinel from the Homeland. A watchman on the highest peak. An impenetrable shield, else fire cloak these forgotten lands.

—Wayfarist Voyage, Vol. 1

Hail the Fire. The day is long. And thirty more shall pass before the torch is lit anew.

—Ancient Agrodite poem

CHAPTER

8

Isle Halavend waited in Cove 23. It was dangerous to keep inviting Lyndel to the Mooring, but he needed the books and manuscripts for their research. Taking those outside would be far more risky. Besides, the Agrodite priestess had been sneaking in for nearly a year now. No one had discovered her yet.

King Pethredote's inclusionary policies toward the Trothians had no jurisdiction over the Mooring. The Prime Isle was the king's counselor, but Chauster could not allow Trothians to convert to Wayfarism. Isle Halavend understood the reasoning, though the whole situation seemed to him like a cruel conundrum.

All Trothians were considered Agrodites. All the ones who valued their health, at least. The thick blue Trothian skin needed *Fajumar*, a daily soak in the salty water of the sea, though most could manage several days before the flaking became painful.

The saltwater soak was considered by Landers and Trothians alike to be an Agrodite ritual. And Prime Isle Chauster simply couldn't allow anyone to join Wayfarism unless they willingly denounced all association with other religions.

Hence, the cruel conundrum.

Another way to resolve the situation would be for the Agrodite spiritual leaders to change their view of the *Fajumar*. Considering the saltwater soak to be a practice of health, and not a religious ritual, would remove the stumbling block between Trothians and Wayfarism.

It was a suggestion Halavend had once made to Lyndel. To his surprise, she was adamantly opposed. The inseparability between Agrodite ritual and Trothian well-being was what gave her people their culture. Take that away, and Lyndel feared that the Trothians would soon be little more than blue-skinned Landers.

Halavend lifted one corner of the desk and heaved it a few inches to the side. The smooth wood dug into his fingers, and the weight of the desk made them tingle. When had he gotten so fragile? Moving the desk was as taxing an activity as he ever tackled anymore.

Halavend knelt slowly, using the chair to brace himself as his knees cracked in protest. He seized the edge of the rug, usually pinned to the floor by the legs of the desk, and whisked it aside.

Beneath the rug was a wooden trapdoor. Lyndel had helped him install it, once they decided that her visits to the Mooring would be a regular thing. A small, contained detonation of Blast Grit had blown a hole in the stone floor, Silence Grit to cover the sound.

Isle Halavend withdrew. He didn't have the strength to pull open the trapdoor today. Besides, Lyndel would have an easy time pushing it open from below.

He rocked back on his knees for a moment, summoning the strength to rise. Trapdoors and secret meetings. Was he really the heretic Ardor Benn had accused him of being?

In the three and a half cycles that had passed since hiring the criminal, Halavend had met with Ardor a handful of times. The ruse was already costing more than anticipated, and Halavend worried that his secret withdrawals from the Islehood Treasury would soon be noticed.

Perhaps Ardor would hasten his work if he knew what consequences awaited failure. But Halavend couldn't tell him of his plans with the Visitant Grit, despite the young man's pressing questions. Ardor needed to hurry, but a few more cycles shouldn't matter. The latest census still counted thirteen sow dragons on Pekal.

Halavend was still on his knees when a soft tapping sounded at the trapdoor. "It is safe, Lyndel." His voice was raspy. It was past noon. Was that his first utterance of the day?

The wooden door lifted, and Lyndel's face appeared, that dark blue skin blending into the shadows. She boosted her thin form through the opening, gently closing the trapdoor as she slid out from under the desk.

She really wasn't much younger than he was. Amazing what an extra decade could do to a man. Yet, Halavend had a hard time imagining Lyndel so fragile, even ten years from now. Perhaps fifty years at a desk in the Mooring had not treated his body kindly.

"How is the tunnel holding up?" Halavend asked.

The hidden passageway was one of the outdated, original aqueducts built to deliver water into the Mooring. Most had collapsed over the years, but the one running under Cove 23 had been navigable.

"Last cycle's rain was not good for the tunnel." Lyndel rose, taking Halavend by the arm and helping him up. "We hope it does not rain like that again."

It was now the Seventh Cycle, and it had been an unusually wet autumn. The fast-approaching winter weather could present problems. Heavier rains, winds, and erosion. So long as the tunnel didn't collapse while Lyndel was down there. Halavend couldn't bear losing another soul in this venture.

"You should sit," Halavend offered. "Have a drink. We have much to discuss." He had been in the cove for hours already, and the Light Grit torch on the wall was growing dim, sustained only by Prolonging Grit.

"You have found the answer?" Lyndel seated herself on the bench, taking a sip from the mug of salt water he had prepared for her. So strange, the Trothians' ability to drink water directly from the sea. Halavend liked providing the refreshment for her, just as she liked to occasionally bring him a new quill or scribing charcoal. These little offerings celebrated their differences, and the desperation of their study reminded them that they weren't so different after all.

"No real answers yet." Halavend shook his head. At times it felt as though any search into the matter was an utter waste of time. For centuries, scholars and Isles had hypothesized about why Visitant Grit worked for one, and not for another. What hope did Halavend have to prove what no one else had been able to?

Lyndel.

She had changed everything, from that first time she approached him in the Char with a plea to document her religion. Comparing Wayfarism and Agroditism had already led them to one terrifying discovery. Perhaps it could also provide the answer they sought regarding the Paladin Visitants.

"In the history of the Greater Chain, there are only sixty-eight recorded instances in which Visitant Grit was successfully detonated," said Halavend, pointing to the paper he'd been writing on.

"How many failures?" Lyndel asked. She was always full of questions that inspired Halavend to dive deeper and search harder. It was one of the things he enjoyed about her company. Especially now that Isless Malla was gone.

"Possibly hundreds more," said Halavend. "Of course, the failed attempts are not nearly as well documented. Merely the location and basic events surrounding the failure. The Prime Isle selects only the most worthy to receive Visitant Grit. A failed detonation does not reflect well on the Islehood."

"Do you believe that it is worthiness?" Lyndel asked.

Halavend sighed. He wasn't sure what to believe anymore. What was worthiness? According to Wayfarism, it was determined by both action and belief. A worthy Wayfarist was one who believed that the Homeland existed. That the Homeland could inspire and Urge the island dwellers to one day return to their true land.

A worthy Wayfarist was constantly changing and improving, understanding that they were lost and far from home. They limited their association with nonbelievers—Settled folk—and did what they could to help other Wayfarists. Was such worthiness truly what qualified someone to successfully detonate Visitant Grit?

"I've compiled information about the people who created the successful detonations." Halavend changed the subject. He didn't want to answer Lyndel's question about his beliefs on the matter of worthiness. Certainly, other factors were at play. More quantifiable factors.

"Here, I've notated the name, age, gender, religion, and location of each detonation. The only column that correlates perfectly is 'Religion.' All sixty-eight successful detonations were done by Wayfarists."

"Of course," said Lyndel. "Your Islehood has always controlled fertilized dragon shell."

"Not always." Again, Halavend was amazed at the loss of history among the Trothians. Without a written language, their version of history was full of inaccuracies. Songs and oral poems were impactful, but the meaning could easily be altered from generation to generation.

"The first recorded summoning of a Paladin Visitant occurred in 745. That's discounting several that supposedly happened before written history," Halavend explained. "But it wasn't until 748 that the kings of Dronodan, Talumon, Espar, and Strind all agreed to allow Prime Isle Kleyton to sanctify the shell as an official Wayfarist proprietary. That was long before the Regulation, so the armies of the kings swept the islands and claimed any sizable pieces of shell."

"The Trothian islets as well?" Lyndel asked.

Halavend nodded. "History refers to it as the Sanctification of 748. A holy war that lasted nearly two years. But with the full muscle of the Greater Chain behind the movement, the Trothians had little hope in resisting. All known fragments of shell were claimed, and the Islehood has had exclusive rights to it since."

Isle Halavend tapped his scribing charcoal lightly on the desk. "But that leaves a window of three years from the time the Visitant Grit's power was discovered until it came under Islehood control. Documentation was so poor that we cannot possibly know the results of them all. It's possible that Settled folk—even Trothians— could have succeeded during that time."

Halavend wasn't considering the two years of Trothian resistance that followed the Sanctification. Even if the armies had failed to possess all significant fragments of shell, it was unreasonable to think that a Trothian could have processed it into Visitant Grit. Lyndel's people had never had factories of their own, and it wasn't until the tenth century that Trothians were able to obtain limited permits to access Pekal and use Strind's factories.

"So, possibly it is *not* the worthiness of the man that brings the Fire Walkers," said Lyndel. That was a literal translation from the Trothian *Kram Udal*. Halavend actually found it a fitting description for the Paladin Visitants.

Lyndel was polite to even consider his religion's beliefs. Wayfarism claimed that the Paladin Visitants were holy beings sent to protect mankind from destroying itself. Agroditism preached that the *Kram Udal* were actually dragons, condescending to take human form, and inflicting punishment against any who saw them.

"It's possible," said Halavend. "But looking at the documented facts, all we know is that every successful detonation has been performed by a Wayfarist. In every instance, the one who detonated the Visitant Grit was hand selected by the Prime Isle to use it in dire need."

"What were these needs?" asked Lyndel.

"Do you recall that verse from the first volume of *Wayfarist Voyage*?" asked Halavend. He quoted the short passage. "*'Behold, the Homeland sendeth those fiery figures. Those Paladin Visitants, who alone can save mankind from its own annihilation. In the day of their coming, mankind is transported as one. As a flock of birds upon the wind, drawing ever closer to that Homeland blessed*.'" He glanced up at Lyndel over the rim of his spectacles.

"I remember it," Lyndel said.

Of course she did. They had certainly discussed it many times. The idea that a Paladin Visitant had the power to save mankind from annihilation had been the primary motive behind hiring Ardor Benn to procure the Visitant Grit. Halavend had to believe that there was much more to the Paladin Visitants than their ability to decimate entire armies with their presence.

"So the Prime Isle authorizes a hero to detonate the Grit in an effort to preserve mankind?" Lyndel clarified, proving that she not only remembered the verse, but understood its meaning. "Then, if not the worthiness of the person, possibly it is the worthiness of their task?"

Halavend scratched his silver head. He had been wondering the same thing.

"How does your Prime Isle select a person to handle the Grit?" asked Lyndel.

"It depends on the situation," said Halavend. "Visitant Grit is only authorized on rare occasions, when there is a task requiring special help. Take a Wayfarist Voyage, for example.

"Every few years, the most devout Wayfarists receive an Urge from the Homeland," Halavend explained. "This ultimate sign of devotion is a journey. Back to the Homeland. Away from the islands."

"That is a death trip," said Lyndel. "There is no life beyond the sea."

"That is a matter of faith," Halavend answered. "Regardless, a ship full of faithful Wayfarists sails away. Although none have returned, we assume the journey to the Homeland is perilous. For each Voyage, the Prime Isle traditionally selects one person to carry a pot of Visitant Grit. The Grit is to be detonated if unmanageable hardships befall the ship."

"And these detonations have worked?"

Halavend shrugged. "No one has returned to let us know. But we believe they have worked. We believe their feet have once again touched the Homeland. That is ultimately the purpose of a Paladin Visitant. To see that mankind can survive to be brought closer to the Homeland."

"These are stories of faith and belief," said Lyndel. "Impossible to study."

"True," said Halavend. "Which is why we should focus on the documented occurrences."

He had the books on the desk before him. Several passages were fresh in his mind. Isle Halavend reached out and opened *Wayfarist Voyage*, Vol. 7. His fingers flipped across the pages until he found the section.

"In this passage, year 958," Halavend explained, "there was an uprising on Talumon. The insurgents were a violent band of Settled souls, making significant advances toward capturing the city Helizon. The Prime Isle authorized an army captain, a worthy Wayfarist woman named Phenro, to take a hundred warriors and a pot of Visitant Grit to put down the rebellion."

Isle Halavend squinted at the page through his spectacles and began to read. " '*And fifty of her hundred men had fallen at the city gate, when Phenro dashed the clay upon the earth. Summoned from a bygone place, he came cloaked in fire and glory. A Paladin Visitant as a bonfire within the cloud. And the enemy was brought down as dry wood burns to ash.*' "

The account of Phenro was like many other successful Visitant Grit detonations. The Paladin had come in battle. Throughout history, before the islands had been united, successful summonings had caused entire kingdoms to rise or fall. In times when the Greater Chain had been united, the Paladins had given aid in quelling rebellions and decimating gangs of anarchists.

Their assistance was always significant, of a sort that changed the course of the future. But for every successful detonation, there were a hundred failed attempts.

Captain Oriar was perhaps the most notable failure. Had he managed to summon a Paladin Visitant, Oriar could have stopped Grotenisk from razing all of Old Beripent. Was that not as worthy a cause as quashing a group of violent insurgents on Talumon?

"Phenro was considered worthy," Halavend said. "And her cause of keeping the kingdom's peace goes without question. But there are other passages that cause me to doubt. Instances where a Paladin Visitant has appeared for less worthy a cause."

He opened to a bookmarked page in the third volume of *Wayfarist Voyage*. "An excerpt from the Conquests of Jendair," Halavend prefaced. "He successfully summoned a Paladin Visitant in the year 892, while forcing a colony of Trothians from a small islet north of Dronodan." He adjusted his spectacles and read aloud.

"*'The Paladin came as a flame from a dragon's throat, resplendent, his figure bathed in fire. The fury of a bull was his voice, and all who heard him speak perished at the words. Swept from the islet were the unknowing Trothians, burned asunder at his glorious coming.'*"

Halavend closed the book. "Jendair did not perish," he continued. "He and his soldiers had prepared for the Paladin Visitant with plugs for their ears, and masks for their eyes. The regent queen of Dronodan later returned the islet to the Trothians, but hundreds had already lost their lives."

"Why did this Jendair attack?" Lyndel asked. "Was that before the treaty?"

"There has always been one treaty or another among our people," Halavend said. "It would seem treaties are made to be breached. In this case, Jendair was attempting a conquest at the Urgings of the Homeland. His success with the Visitant Grit would imply that his cause was a worthy one."

Halavend paused. He had felt the Urgings many times. But he didn't believe that the Homeland would inspire progress through conquering and bloodshed, even if the decimated people were Settled Trothians. Perhaps history had scribed something wrong about the purpose of Jendair's conquest. Or perhaps the Homeland Urged differently now than it did in times gone by.

"What do *you* think?" Lyndel asked.

Halavend pushed the book away from him. "I think history is what we have interpreted it to be. The Islehood has been the only consistent organization to keep records. It is impossible to see what truly happened without viewing it through the lens of Wayfarism."

"Is that not the lens we need?" asked Lyndel. "Wayfarists are the only ones who have successfully summoned Fire Walkers. You must consider that when selecting the right person to ignite the Grit from the Royal Regalia."

Halavend was impressed by Lyndel's ability to set aside her own beliefs if the evidence led her in a different direction. It was one of the primary reasons he trusted her so much. What had begun as a religious dictation project had turned into something so much bigger. Lyndel kept crawling through that dark tunnel because she believed that the preservation of her people was more important than her own life. Lyndel kept staring over Halavend's shoulder at text she couldn't see, because she was committed to the research and understood the true scope of what the two of them were doing.

What *were* they doing? At times it felt like nothing more than chasing their own tails. Halavend felt suddenly discouraged by the stacks of books and parchments on the desk. What did they contain that would actually help? It was a fact that Wayfarists were alone in their summoning success. But that had to be due to the fact that only Wayfarists were given the opportunity to detonate Visitant Grit. Was it a matter of worthiness or probability?

"Possibly it would serve us to study the most recent detonations," suggested Lyndel.

"It has been forty-three years since even an attempt has been made."

"What does that mean?" Lyndel asked. The facts were rarely

enough for her. She pushed him to find a reason. "Has there been less need for Fire Walkers?"

"Pethredote's reign *has* brought tremendous peace and prosperity. Not to mention a renewed religious vigor toward Wayfarism. In many ways, there hasn't been a need for Visitant Grit. But even if there had been, Prime Isle Chauster couldn't authorize it. There is no more dragon shell. And without that, there can be no Visitant Grit."

"Who was the last to successfully detonate the Grit?"

"King Pethredote," answered Halavend. "In 1204."

"Then possibly we should study him. What kind of man is Pethredote?" asked Lyndel. "Or rather, what kind of man was he forty-two years ago when he detonated the Visitant Grit and took the throne?"

"I remember the events well," said Halavend, "though I didn't meet the king until many years later. In my twentieth year, I had followed the Urge to join the Islehood and dedicate myself fully to the Homeland. It was a tumultuous time, with King Barrid opposing the Voyages, and ultimately, Dronodan and Talumon breaking away from the kingdom and waging war.

"Prime Isless Hin, the one before Chauster, was a significant motivator in the secession. After all, it was in the best interest of Wayfarism to remove Barrid from rule. She selected young Dietrik Pethredote, a religious zealot with a bloodline that was considered marginally noble in Espar. Pethredote made an agreement with the Prime Isless and the independent islands to become a crusader monarch."

"Crusader monarch?" Lyndel asked.

Halavend scratched his head. How could he explain this? "It was a political move instigated by the Prime Isless. Pethredote was required to devise a comprehensive plan for the way he would rule the Greater Chain. When his terms were accepted by Dronodan and Talumon, he was given the Visitant Grit and sent to Beripent.

If he succeeded in dethroning King Barrid, Pethredote would rule without marriage or an heir."

Halavend opened the book and read the passage he had marked for Lyndel. "*As to the worthiness of His Highness King Pethredote, there can be no question. Certainly, the Homeland Urged him into such a bold confrontation. With his passion for Wayfarism and his noble heritage, King Pethredote was uniquely suited to deliver the Greater Chain from a ruler whose personal ambition and greed had led to suffering and oppression.*

"*Evidence of his worthiness is manifest in the circumstances surrounding the Visitation. So confident was young Pethredote that he challenged King Barrid, calling him out of the throne room and shattering the pot of Visitant Grit upon the palace grounds.*

"*King Barrid was burned away as chaff, his eyes beholding the mystical Paladin in his hazy cloud of Visitant Grit. The tyrant's army, too, was seized in shock at the fiery arrival. Three hundred men and a hundred horses perished in the blink of an eye. But young Pethredote had prepared his followers and they fell to the ground with eyes sealed against the holy being, hands clasping their ears, should he speak.*

"*And all the while, Pethredote felt the warmth of the Paladin's flame as the magnificent figure stood over him, shielding the worthy young man on the brink of ascending to the throne of a divided kingdom.*""

"Pethredote felt his warmth," said Lyndel. "But the Paladin did not touch him?"

"Of course not." Halavend closed the book. There was much mystery surrounding the nature of the Paladin Visitants, but one thing was an indisputable fact. Any interaction with the fiery figures would result in sudden incineration. One could not touch a Paladin Visitant, hear its voice, or even look upon it.

The only reason historians even knew the general form of the beings was thanks to Vethdrow. Her successful detonation in 1038 had been mixed with Illusion Grit. At great personal risk, Vethdrow and several scholars returned to the site of the detonation several days after the Visitant cloud had burned out. A second blast of

Illusion Grit had shown them the image of what had transpired. And miraculously, all who observed the afterimage of the Paladin Visitant survived to record their findings.

"Pethredote's detonation seems no different from other examples you have read to me," said Lyndel. "Immortal warriors who caused death."

"I agree," said Halavend. "Still, we have to assume that the Paladin Visitants can do more than slay enemies with their presence. The scripture says they can protect mankind from its own annihilation. That is critical for our overall plan."

Lyndel nodded. They rarely spoke of the true reason they met together. What was left to be said on the matter? They had been down that road dozens of times. Isless Malla had died for it, Homeland keep her. The pieces were all in motion now. Talking about it would only cause Halavend to second-guess himself and end up paralyzed with fear and regret.

It was better to spend his efforts discovering the right person to detonate the Visitant Grit once Ardor acquired it.

"We will find the answers," said Lyndel. She must have seen his furrowed brow. "As the Trothians say, a man finding seashells looks down."

Halavend smiled. He enjoyed learning nuggets of Trothian wisdom, even if he didn't always understand them.

"If you stop searching," said Lyndel, "we will certainly never find anything."

Lately, Lyndel's words seemed to be the only glimmer of light in a world of discouraging darkness. "Thank you, Lyndel. I wondered what your thoughts are regarding..."

Isle Halavend stood suddenly, his ears picking up sounds of commotion outside the cove. Lyndel must have heard it also, and she moved in two long-legged strides to her concealed position behind the wooden door.

Halavend's heart was racing. He'd have to stall whoever was

coming. Hold them at the dock to give Lyndel time to slip through the trapdoor into the old aqueduct.

He took a deep breath to steady himself, wrinkled hand shaking as he cracked open the door and peered out.

The Mooring was indeed filled with commotion, but the voices were not approaching Cove 23.

There was a raft in the waterway, but an Isle had fallen overboard. He was still floundering as he got his feet under him, his seagreen robes soaked, and the water lapping at his chest. It was a very rare occurrence for someone in the Mooring to fall into the water, let alone a Holy Isle!

There was an Isless on the raft, driving her long pole to the bottom of the canal in an effort to anchor them. There were also two officers of the Regulation, Rollers holstered beneath long wool coats.

Halavend opened the door farther, to spy yet another figure onboard the raft. A young man in ragged clothing, lying on his side. His wrists and ankles were bound, and he lay very still, the two Regulators watching him cautiously.

"Are you all right?" the Isless called to the man in the water.

"Continue along," replied the Isle, wading across the waterway to the cove on the other side. "I will wait on the dock."

The bound figure bucked violently, wobbling the raft as the Isless withdrew her pole.

"Steady!" shouted one of the Regulators.

"Hold him!"

But the ragged man rose to his knees, slamming his forehead into the chest of the nearest Regulator. The man toppled overboard, striking the water with a significant splash, his helmeted head vanishing beneath the surface as he struggled to right himself.

The ruffian was on his knees now, straining against his bonds. He turned his face toward Cove 23, mouth agape and silent. Isle

Halavend gripped the open door, staring across the waterway at those eyes.

Red. Crimson eyes like pools of blood. Blind. Mute. Violent. Moonsick. This lost soul had already reached the third stage.

Halavend should have ducked back into his cove and shut the door. It had been years since he'd seen Moonsickness. And what he knew about it now painted the picture before him in a completely different hue.

The Moonsick man tried to rise, but the second Regulator brought a wooden club down with a crack across the back of his head. The blow barely seemed to affect him, and the Regulator struck again. And again. Halavend saw a spatter of blood pepper the raft. By the Homeland! That beating would have killed an ordinary man.

The Regulator struck twice more with the club, the final swing connecting with the young man's face. The bound figure finally slumped onto the raft, still writhing. The Regulator on board dropped onto him, holding both ends of the club and pinning the shaft across the lad's throat.

"Hoy!" called the Isless poling the raft. Halavend stood numbly in the doorway, unaware that the woman was calling to him until she shouted a second time. "Lend us your dock!"

The Regulator that had fallen overboard was wading toward Cove 23! Halavend stepped onto the small dock, swinging the door shut behind him. Lyndel was probably into the tunnel by now. The Regulator wasn't likely to enter Halavend's cove, but commotion of this sort necessitated an abrupt end to their study session.

Halavend was still staring at the raft, the Moonsick man wriggling, pinned down on the wet wood as the Isless poled them across the waterway toward Halavend. He felt sick himself. That face was burned in his mind. Bloodred eyes, slack jaw, trembling with a violent rage.

Isless Malla.

Was that how she had looked? Oh, Homeland keep her, poor girl. Halavend felt the guilt pouring around him, filling his insides. Was her sacrifice on Pekal worth such a horrid, unholy fate?

"Mind if I pull myself up?" asked the Regulator who had waded over to his dock. "Afraid I'll topple the raft if I try to climb on board."

There was a short ladder built onto the opposite end of the dock, lowering into the water for such unlikely instances. The man ignored it, hoisting himself, dripping, onto the damp planks beside Isle Halavend.

"What…" Halavend started, his lips dry. "What happened?" His eyes were still fixed on the raft as it drew nearer.

"Sad set of circumstances," answered the Regulator. He was shivering from the chill of the late autumn water, soaked to the bone in his wool coat. "Part of a Harvesting crew. He was separated in a storm and his mates had to leave Pekal before the Moon Passing."

"This lost soul endured the night with no Holy Torch to ward off the sickness," explained the Isless, drawing the raft alongside the dock. "He arrived on the beach five days into the new cycle, and Pekal's harbor Regulation rushed him to Beripent."

Halavend could see the man clearly now, though he was grateful that the Regulator's coat draped over that horrid face. There was more blood on the raft than Halavend could stomach. And was that a shred of gory scalp clinging to the Regulator's sleeve? Surely such a beating would have damaged the young lad's brain.

Never mind that. The sick man was as good as dead already. And many healers over the years had validated the theory that those infected with Moonsickness felt no physical pain.

The healers had performed tests, sticking a Moonsick patient in the leg with a needle. The poor soul wouldn't even react. In some cases, a needle had not been strong enough to penetrate.

Supposedly, Moonsickness created a toughening of the skin, a durability of the bones, and a hardening of the internal organs. Somehow, all this happened without killing the poor sap. In fact, the symptoms largely helped prevent their deaths, with bones like iron and skin that was nearly tough enough to stop a Roller ball.

Unsettling.

At least Isless Malla hadn't felt the suffering. Homeland be praised for that small relief.

"Why the Mooring?" Halavend didn't realize he had his back pressed to the door, as though Moonsickness were some sort of contagious malady that could be contracted in close proximity. "Why did you bring him here?"

Very few infected with Moonsickness ever made it out of Pekal's mountainous slopes. Those who did were usually taken to a remote Regulation Stockade on Strind, where the sick patients could live out their miserable days in isolation.

"We were instructed to bring this man to the Prime Isle," said the Regulator, stepping from the dock to the raft.

"In this state?" Halavend cried, pointing at the squirming man. He had done a considerable amount of study on Moonsickness. Those afflicted became very dangerous, especially in the third stage.

"This man is a danger!" Halavend insisted. "He mustn't..."

The Isless pushed off the dock, slipping out into the Mooring waterway once again. "Prime Isle Chauster asked to see him," she said. "This man is his nephew."

Halavend slumped against the cove door. That poor wretched creature was someone's nephew. Someone's son. Moonsickness was ignorant of love. It could strike the Settled criminal and Holy Isless alike. And, though no one would believe him, Halavend knew it had nothing to do with Pekal, or the absence of a Holy Torch. He knew the truth. The new doctrine.

Moonsickness was coming.

Halavend stared at the raft as it drifted down the waterway, its deranged passenger still thrashing under the weight of the blood-stained Regulator.

This was the future of every soul on the islands.

～

My greatest fear is what will happen to my eyes.

CHAPTER

9

Cats catch killer kittens cussing quickly. Cats catch killer kittens cussing quickly. Catch cats kitten killers quickly kissing..." Quarrah trailed off as the words stopped making sense.

"Oh, poo!" Cinza leapt from her chair. "Diction, Quarrah! Diction! How can the king become obsessed with your lovely voice if he can't understand what you're singing?"

Quarrah drew a deep, calming breath through her nose. "First of all, I won't be singing about cats and killer kittens," she said. "And second, I won't actually be singing at all!"

She might have tried to control the volume of her voice if Ard had been studying at his usual table in the corner, but he and Elbrig were out on some assignment, leaving Quarrah and Cinza alone in the upper room of the bakery.

Cinza took two big steps toward her, pressing her nose inches from Quarrah's face. "That is precisely why diction is so important! The only thing the audience will be seeing is your mouth wagging onstage. What will they think if your words don't line up with what they're hearing? This isn't the freak fair. It's the king's blazing orchestra!"

"Just give me a minute." Quarrah pulled her face away from Cinza's, adjusting her large-rimmed spectacles. She'd been at this for three cycles now. Some ninety days of work and most of the time she felt as if it were her first lesson, as though the day—no, the week—before had taught her nothing.

On her evenings off, Quarrah wandered the streets of Beripent, remembering how it felt to blend into the shadows, to go unnoticed. And the next morning she was back at the Bakery on Humont Street, Cinza Ortemion right in her face, teaching her how to stand out in a crowd. Drilling her on diction, lyrics, pitch, pose, blah, blah, blah...

Quarrah sat down on a chair beside Ard's blackboard. Why did she stick around to endure such musical torture? Quarrah had no doubt she could vanish into the heart of the city, and neither Ard nor Cinza would ever find her. But if she ran, Quarrah would never feel the thrill of swiping the king's regalia.

It wasn't that Quarrah had anything against King Pethredote. On the contrary, the man had done amazing things for the Greater Chain. But he represented a new level of untouchability that tempted Quarrah's inner thief. She knew the job was too big to tackle alone, but with a team of experts they just might succeed.

And then there was the matter of two hundred thousand Ashings. Even if Ard's elaborate ruse took a year, that was more money than she was likely to make in ten working thefts alone.

The challenge of the theft and the promise of Ashings had enticed her to the ruse in the first place. But those weren't the only things that kept her from leaving.

Whenever she felt like progress would never be made, Ard would come into the room and make some comment about her improvement.

*   *   *

Quarrah didn't believe half the things Ardor Benn said. He was a ruse artist, paid to manipulate people's emotions. But sometimes, on the hardest of days, Quarrah didn't care if he was manipulating her. The compliments felt good.

Ard made Quarrah feel like she belonged. And that was a feeling she hadn't experienced since before her mother left. This sense of inclusion was fulfilling, satisfying an emotional deficit that had grown deeper than Quarrah realized.

So she didn't run. Quarrah stayed. And she sang and sang. And sang.

"From the top!" Cinza motioned for her to rise. Quarrah did so reluctantly, brushing a strand of bright red hair from her eyes. Blazing wig. The huge thing was like an octopus consuming her skull.

"Approach your space," coached Cinza.

Quarrah eyed a particular spot on the floor and strode purposefully toward it. When she reached the spot, she stopped abruptly so her wide-hemmed dress would ripple and swirl.

"Meh," Cinza said. "Next time, approach the space without looking at it, remember?"

"How can I see where I'm going if I don't look?" Quarrah asked. Years of sneaking around manors in the dark had made her hyperaware of her footing. Walk without looking? No wonder the royal folk got robbed!

Cinza ignored the question, snapping her fingers instead. "Cue the music. Pose, pose!"

Quarrah struck the singing pose Cinza had taught her. Feet together, shoulders back, hands clasped at the navel, chin slightly lifted to elongate her neck. For what it was worth, Cinza claimed the royal men would really take a liking to her neck. Despite the comment being rather unsettling, Quarrah took it as a compliment—the closest she'd get from Cinza.

Cinza was humming the opening instrumental measures. She raised one hand to cue Quarrah, speaking in rhythm. "And...go."

"Wait." Quarrah momentarily broke the pose. "Which one am I singing?"

Cinza rolled her eyes. "The cantata."

"Can't I do the aria?" Quarrah countered. "I know it so much better."

"That's precisely why you needn't sing it," snapped Cinza. "The purpose of practice is not to sound good. You're ready with the aria—a thing I thought I'd never say. It's the cantata that concerns me."

"It's just..." Quarrah sighed. If all went according to plan, she would be performing the aria in just a week. Shouldn't she focus on that? Quarrah wouldn't perform the cantata for cycles. And that was only if Ard impressed the king enough for the piece to be selected for the Grotenisk Festival.

"Cue the music!" Cinza shouted again, humming. Quarrah snapped into her pose. She drew a deep breath, supporting from the diaphragm, and began singing from memory at the top of the cantata.

"'Grotenisk! Grotenisk! Devourer of life. Terror of kingdoms. Bringer of strife. In peace we brought thee from that dangerous peak. In compensation for our gesture thou didst prey upon the weak. Grotenisk! Grotenisk!'"

Quarrah knew her pitch was awful, but that wouldn't really matter. It was tempo and rhythm that Cinza harped about.

The strange woman stood before Quarrah, humming the accompaniment and waving her hands as though conducting an invisible orchestra in the bakery's upper room. When the performance finally arrived, there would be an actual orchestra, of course, and it was imperative that Quarrah learn to follow the conductor so she could stay on track.

Quarrah knew the first movement rather well. The libretto was originally a poem written in 1086, and read aloud to mark one hundred years from the dragon's attack on Beripent. The author was one Isless Vesta, who Quarrah decided was much too verbose.

The movement focused on the attack, the heavy lyrics set to a dark and brooding melody. The second movement was a slow and mournful funeral march. Quarrah was supposed to sing a long list of names—prominent people in Beripent whom Grotenisk had chewed up. In Quarrah's opinion, the whole movement was obsolete in today's age. But Cinza assured her that the names would mean something to the royal descendants in attendance at the Grotenisk Festival.

The third movement began a more hopeful tone, the lyrics talking about the survivors banding together to rebuild a new Beripent. And the cantata finished with a triumphant fanfare, acknowledging a new city, alive with commerce and culture. The whole thing took about an hour to sing. Lots of pointless repetition.

As for the origin of the music . . . well, that was a bit of a mystery. Elbrig had arrived one day with the complete musical score, as well as a separate solo soprano part that Quarrah would be "singing."

Over the weeks, Elbrig's lessons had instructed Ard to transcribe the orchestra parts from the score onto separate sheets. It looked like terribly tedious work, drawing all those small dots and perfectly straight lines. But Ard was good at it, and he never seemed to complain.

Ard would need to be incredibly familiar with the piece, since he was claiming to have composed it. Quarrah didn't want to know who the actual composer was, or how Elbrig obtained the music. He made the same assurances with this cantata as he did with the Unclaimed Symphony. The actual composer was taken care of. Out of the picture. Not a threat.

Quarrah hit a high note moving toward a key change. It sounded horrible, and Cinza's uninhibited laughter didn't buoy her confidence. Quarrah paused, counting the measures of rest before coming in again, imagining an orchestral accompaniment that she'd only ever heard hummed by Cinza.

"No!" Cinza clapped her hands in Quarrah's face. "You came in early on the recitative!"

"I was within a count," said Quarrah, dropping her pose. Sparks. Standing like that made her chest feel as though it was going to split right down the middle.

Cinza stepped forward, bringing her hand up like she might jab Quarrah in the stomach. Quarrah tensed until she saw that it was just a threat. She exhaled, relaxing. *Then* Cinza jabbed her just below the ribs.

"Ow!" Quarrah stepped back, swatting Cinza's hand away. "Why?"

"There are certain reactions people expect," said Cinza. "I bring up my hand, and you flex. When you open your mouth to speak or sing, people expect the words to match the movement of your lips. If that doesn't happen, it's like a jab to the gut when you're not expecting it."

"Why can't *you* follow *me*?" Quarrah asked. "I'm the one hanging out in the public eye with a blast of Silence Grit in my mouth."

"And how will I be able to see you, dear"—Cinza's tone was falsely sweet—"when I'm under the stage making you sound like a decent soprano?" She stepped back, pointing for Quarrah to take her place again. "Pick it up at the recitative."

Quarrah took a deep breath and began again. For the recitative, Isless Vesta had borrowed a passage from the seventh volume of *Wayfarist Voyage*. It was about Oriar's failure to successfully detonate the Visitant Grit against Grotenisk.

"'Oh, that chosen of the Islehood, even Captain Oriar. Who, through his unknown Settled sins, brought ruin to the masses. Who stood upon the palace step of Beripent, and cast the Grit upon the stones. When feigning righteous deeds, the midnight blast enveloped Oriar. But he was left alone. No Paladin Visitant was his rearguard. No flaming form to bring the dragon low. Just a cloud of darkest night where the bright warrior should have been.'"

"No! Did you forget to breathe?" Cinza cut her off. "You can't afford to go red in the face like that. You look like a constipated street dog."

"So many words," Quarrah gasped.

The door opened, and Quarrah straightened at the sight of Ardor Benn, Elbrig entering through the false oven chimney just behind.

"About time you got back," Cinza chided. "Saved me from the mournful mewling of a dying cat."

Quarrah flushed, putting a hand to her eyebrow. What was it with Cinza and cats?

"I doubt that." Ard crossed the room and set a plate of pastries on the table. "I find Quarrah's voice to have a rather captivating natural tone. Sure, she's untrained, but I think there's a surprising amount of raw musical talent in that throat of hers."

See? There he went with the compliments again. Was there any truth behind his words?

"Say goodbye to the beautiful beard, Quarrah," Ard said, rubbing a hand over his chin. It had grown quite full over the past three cycles, and she'd become accustomed to it.

"Elbrig's playing barber in the morning," Ard continued. "Only the mustache and sideburns get to stay. Got to look convincing for tomorrow night's big debut."

Sparks! Was the reception really tomorrow? The thought made Quarrah's knees weak.

"Although, I must confess," said Ard, "the winter cycles would be much more comfortable with a full beard. It's like wearing a permanent scarf."

Autumn had been wholly gobbled up in tedious preparations. The Eighth Cycle began with the Moon Passing tonight, and that meant the official onset of winter.

"Not a chance," said Cinza. "Dale Hizror would never wear a full beard. I should know; I've actually met him."

"It was a funny story," Elbrig said. "I'll fill you in later. For now, we need to go over a few final details regarding tomorrow night's reception." Elbrig gestured for Ard and Quarrah to seat themselves on the padded couch.

It had been a feat to get the thing into the upper room, requiring the removal of the faux oven and chimney. But, as Quarrah had discovered from lounging during her brief breaks, the comfort of the couch was worth the effort.

Ard plopped down, looking comfortable in his new attire, shoulder cape spilling stylishly down his left arm. Quarrah dropped beside him, earning an instant reprimand from Cinza.

"Sit like a noble lady, Quarrah Khai," she said. "Put your blazing knees together. Your dress isn't a Trothian tent."

Flustered, Quarrah snapped her knees together. Like Cinza was one to speak about elegant behavior. Her first impression had been bald, and toothless, wearing a dirty pair of long underwear.

Without looking over, Ard reached out and placed a comforting hand on Quarrah's knee. They had grown physically close over the last three cycles, and it wasn't uncommon for Ard to place a hand around her waist when they stood side by side. Or occasionally peck her on the cheek when he went out. And for no good reason!

Well, there was a reason, Quarrah knew. Azania Fyse and Dale Hizror were supposed to be engaged. Their courtship would be proper, restrained, in the fashion of the royal folk. But sometimes it was difficult to differentiate Ard's considerations from Dale's affections.

Quarrah definitely felt something stir inside when Ard touched her. So unlike most of the advances from other men she'd experienced over the years. Companionship wasn't something Quarrah Khai had ever actively sought, but that didn't mean it hadn't come close to finding her.

Like that next-door tenant who had always happened to take his dog out when Quarrah came up the steps. Or that man who lived across the street from the *Starboard Keel*, who consistently entered the tavern moments after her. Or that muscly fellow who'd been hired to repair her roof at that run-down tenement in the Eastern Quarter.

Quarrah hadn't sought those men, but circumstances had brought them into her life. Like Ard, they had done most of the talking. Quarrah patiently learned their names, their interests, where they kept their safe boxes. She tried to feel *something* for them—the way they obviously felt things for her. But there'd never been any real connection. In the end, when the men had grown too close for Quarrah's comfort, she'd pack her bags and vanish into the smoky haze of Beripent's anonymity.

Ard was so different from any other man she'd met. He wasn't pushy or needy. He was arrogant, but not the intolerable type that Quarrah found so obnoxious. Maybe she was a fool. Maybe it was all an act with Ardor Benn, but this was supposed to be an act for her, too. And somehow, oddly, that made his hand on her knee actually feel... *right*.

"I have your invitations to the reception." Elbrig handed them both a folded piece of parchment, sealed with a pressed drop of hardened wax. "I also have confirmation that you are on the guest list, so you shouldn't have any trouble getting into the palace." He clasped his hands in a teacherly fashion. "Now, let's go over your objectives for tomorrow evening's debut."

"We introduce ourselves to Beripent's upper crust as eager newcomers to the big city," said Ard, "but don't give away the fact that I am the composer of the Unclaimed Symphony."

"Exactly," agreed Elbrig. "Over the years, there have been too many imposters coming forward to claim the composition. In order for this to work, the realization must be made internally. That is to say, we leave a trail of bread crumbs that will allow Beripent's rich and famous to come to the conclusion about your identity on their own."

Elbrig kicked out a chair and sat down across from the couple on the couch. "So let's review the bread crumbs. You need to naturally steer the conversation toward a handful of key points. What are they?"

Naturally, Ard answered first. All the bread crumbs were about him. Quarrah was simply the soft-spoken fiancée. If they managed to successfully build Dale's character, then Azania would be pulled into the fame by mere association.

That was fine with Quarrah. Let the ruse artist have the spotlight. Her time to shine would come: wearing black and creeping through the shadows to steal the regalia. For now, Quarrah just had to be sure she didn't make a fool out of Azania Fyse. Sparks, this was going to be an awkward reception.

"I was in the city of Octowyn during the summers of 1229 and 1230," Ard said, Elbrig nodding his approval. "I dislike quill and ink, preferring charcoal scribing tools when writing. Though deprived of formal schooling, I am proud of my mother's Dronodanian heritage and her insistence on education. And I proposed to Azania with a bouquet of blue irises," Ard finished. "The flower of my family crest."

Quarrah knew the reasoning behind each conversational bread crumb, no matter how disconnected they initially seemed. Cinza and Elbrig had gone over them a dozen times.

Octowyn had a conservatory that taught a style of musical calligraphy that uniquely formed the flags of semiquavers. Ard had been dutifully practicing the style under Elbrig's tutelage for weeks now. The score of the Unclaimed Symphony was written in that way, so it would make sense that Dale Hizror had spent some time in Octowyn.

Supposedly, the original score was written in two mediums. The staves and notes were in common ink and quill, but all additional markings were done in charcoal—an unusual choice for composers, since charcoal was more likely to smudge than ink.

Elbrig said the pages of the score were numbered in old Dronodanian numerals. It was an obsolete numbering system, but one Dale would have learned if his mother was proud of that island's heritage.

Lastly, upon the final page of the Unclaimed Symphony was said to be drawn, in charcoal, a small flower. Elbrig had been making Ard practice the sketch over and over again until it so closely resembled the one in the score that no one would question it.

How Elbrig knew so much about the original score of the Unclaimed Symphony, Quarrah didn't know. Unless being performed, the score was locked away somewhere in the palace. And aside from King Pethredote and the conductor of the Royal Orchestra, few were said to have ever even seen it. That, at least, made the whole thing interesting to Quarrah. Maybe she would steal the original score when all this was over.

"A few notable figures to watch out for at the reception," Elbrig went on, drawing a small paper from his pocket and glancing at the names listed. "Cantibel Tren, the orchestra's first violinist. She's frighteningly knowledgeable on music theory, so it's best to avoid such discussions with her." He referred back to the list. "Lorstan Grale. You'll want to talk to him, but not for very long. He's been the conductor of the Royal Orchestra going on ten years. He's met a lot of composers. But he's never met Dale, lucky for you."

"Hopefully no one has," Ard pointed out.

"We're not that lucky, I'm afraid," said Elbrig. "Noet Farasse. He's the guest composer at tomorrow's function. The orchestra will be playing several of his compositions at next week's concert. The reception is in his honor, so I'm afraid avoiding him would actually draw suspicion."

"And Ard's met him before?" Quarrah asked.

"Not Ard," answered Elbrig. "But Dale Hizror has. Eight years ago, when living in Beripent, Dale auditioned for the Southern Quarter Orchestra. Violin. Of course, he didn't receive a spot, which eventually led him to pursue composing instead of performing. Noet Farasse was the conductor of the Southern Quarter at the time. There is a chance he'll remember your audition."

"That was eight years ago," Ard said. "Farasse must have seen hundreds of prospectives since then. You really think he'll remember Dale, who didn't even manage to get in?"

Elbrig raised his eyebrows. "When developing a character, Cinza and I tend to do things to stand out. That way, each public interaction carries weight and is worth the time we spent developing that persona." Elbrig glanced at Cinza. "Dale's audition was... memorable."

"Oh, great," Ard said. "What did I do?"

"There was something of a tantrum thrown when your name was not called at the end of auditions," answered Elbrig. "It resulted in hundreds of pieces of violin on the stage."

"Ah." Ard nodded, and Quarrah thought he even looked a little embarrassed on behalf of his character.

"I'll fill you in on all the details shortly," Elbrig said. "Noet Farasse might recall it in shocking clarity." He looked once more at the list of names on his paper. "Another person you'll need to meet is a woman named Kercha Gant. She's the soprano that will be featured in Farasse's aria next week."

"Why do we need to meet her?" Quarrah asked.

"Because you're going to replace her," answered Cinza.

"The aria?" Quarrah asked. "The aria I've been working on is Farasse's composition?"

"Now you're catching on," Cinza said. "It's just as important to solidify *your* position as it is Ard's. That's why Kercha is going to be feeling a little under the weather this week. Lorstan Grale will be desperate to find a new soloist for the concert. You need to make a good enough impression on the conductor tomorrow night that your name will come to mind as a replacement."

"What's going to happen to Kercha?" Quarrah hadn't signed up to see prominent musicians murdered.

"Furybeth extract." Cinza produced a small vial from her pocket. "It's a slow-releasing toxin that won't kick in for several days. But, boy, when it does…"

Elbrig plugged his nose and spoke with an altered voice. "I'b not feelig bery good."

"Congestion," explained Cinza. "A singer's worst nightmare. Kercha's sinuses will swell like she snorted a bunch of grapes."

"Surely someone of her standing has the funds to acquire plenty of Health Grit," Ard said. "How do we make sure Kercha Gant stays down long enough for Quarrah to replace her?"

"That's the magic of Furybeth," said Cinza. "It so closely resembles the symptoms of a terrible head cold, she won't risk wasting her Health Grit on it."

It was common knowledge that Health Grit had little to no effect on common illnesses. In fact, some claimed it made the illness last longer, the symptoms more intense. Health Grit strengthened any living creature, which led some healers to think that flus and colds were somehow alive inside a human host. The very notion made Quarrah shudder.

But Health Grit was wonderfully effective for aches and pains, allergic reactions, injury, and, of course, toxins and poisons like this Furybeth extract. Cinza was counting on Kercha Gant not to suspect her condition to be the result of foul play. The vocalist's ignorance would keep her down while the poison ran its course.

Cinza tossed the little vial of extract to Quarrah. "You can just drop it in her drink at any time during the reception."

Quarrah's eyes grew as she realized what Cinza was implying. "Me? You want *me* to drug the soprano?"

"If I recall correctly," said Cinza, "being sneaky was one of your only useful skill sets."

Quarrah looked at the tiny glass container in her hand. Drugging a stranger's drink at a social event was very different from lifting a safe box in the dead of night. Where was Quarrah going to draw the line with these people?

"Let's see what else." Elbrig checked his list once more. "Yes. You should steer clear of Waelis Mordo, Rispit Born, Ardor Sicero, and Chal Ovent," he said. "They're all backbiting gossipers who grow quickly jealous of popular newcomers."

Quarrah silently reviewed the names Elbrig had just listed. This was ridiculous. How was she supposed to remember all this, plus the pose, the lyrics, and her own fake name?

"Oh, and of course, King Pethredote," said Elbrig. "Though it's unlikely that he'll actually be there. Over the last few years, he's grown more selective about which events to attend. Age is finally catching up to him, I suppose."

There was a knock at the door. Everyone froze, and Ard's hand slipped off Quarrah's knee. Nobody knocked at the bakery's hidden door. Mearet, the baker, knew better than to bother them, and as far as Quarrah knew, no one else was aware that the upper room even existed.

The door flew open. Ard leapt to his feet, a Roller appearing in his hand. A tall, broad figure squeezed through the small doorway, winter coat unbuttoned and bald head exposed.

"On a scale of one to ten, how much did everybody miss me?"

"Raek, you old scoundrel!" Ard holstered his Roller. "I nearly put a ball in you. Give us a little warning next time."

"I gave the secret knock." Raek shut the door behind him.

"I didn't know we had a secret knock," said Ard. Quarrah was relieved to know that she wasn't the only one.

"Well, it wouldn't be very secret if everyone knew it." Raek dropped his coat on the floor as he crossed eagerly to the plate of pastries.

"Hello, Raekon." Elbrig's greeting was rather flat. "How unpleasant to see you here."

Raek paused to stare at Cinza and Elbrig, as if attempting to see past their faces. "Trying to decide if you look as ugly as the last time I saw you two." He picked up an apple tart and fit the entire thing into his mouth.

"How was your trip?" Ard asked. "Useful, I imagine. You were gone long enough."

"These things take time," Raek answered through the mouthful.

The big man had been gone for three full cycles. Quarrah felt like she'd become an entirely different person in that amount of time. In a way, wasn't that exactly what the disguise managers had been hired to do?

"I've got our Grit factory," announced Raek. "Mordell and Sons. It's on the southern coast of Strind, about an hour outside Hothrow. Small, but not too small. Quick access to and from the water. Private security. I stashed the things we'll need to move the Slagstone in and get it processed."

"Good work." Ard helped himself to a pastry as though he'd accomplished something, too.

That was it? Good work? Quarrah doubted that Raek was as thorough as she would have been. Surveilling a building was her specialty. She manipulated locks and doors like Ard manipulated people.

How many access points? Doors, grates, vents? What kind of locks, and how many hinges on the doors? How many security guards, and at what times did the shifts change?

Quarrah was surprised at how comfortable it felt to drop back into her favorite thoughts. She'd spent so much time being Azania lately: posing, curtsying, memorizing lyrics. She had almost forgotten what it was to be a thief.

"Looks like you're all in the middle of something," said Raek. "Just wanted to pop in before I chase down another lead."

Ard nodded. "Quarrah and I have an event tomorrow. Our first foray into royal society. I'll fill you in on everything later tonight. Where are you off to now?"

Raek retrieved his fallen coat. "I think I've selected a forger to make the replica of the Royal Regalia," he said. "Thought I'd set up a meeting so you can decide if he's the one we should use."

"Sounds great," answered Ard. "Glad to have you back." The bald man nodded and slipped out the door.

"What an unpleasant interruption," Cinza remarked. "Let's get back to business. What do you say if someone asks your thoughts on Crementi's Symphony in F Major?"

"I enjoyed the exposition," Quarrah said, "but I found the development a bit drawn out."

Sparks, what was she even saying? It was easy to recite the phrases Cinza had taught her, but Quarrah didn't really know what they meant. It was one thing to say them here, in the comfort of the bakery, where everyone knew she was an imposter. But to declare such statements in public, and attempt to pass them off as her own?

What had she gotten herself into? *Oh, flames.* Quarrah Khai was in over her head.

~

I am learning so much. The island is a ruthless tutor, but I find its lessons fascinating.

CHAPTER

10

Remember," Ard whispered, popping open the carriage door, "you look dazzling."

He meant what he said. Cinza had really put the final touches on Quarrah. If Ard didn't know better, he certainly wouldn't suspect that beneath those thick-rimmed spectacles and that cascade of red hair was Quarrah Khai.

It wasn't just her looks, Ard realized. Quarrah carried herself differently when she was Azania. She stood to her full height without a hint of apology, though her heels and hair actually made her look slightly taller than Ard. She seemed confident but approachable. If Ard weren't Dale Hizror, he would have been jealous of the man.

But beneath it all, Ard knew Quarrah was shaking. He could feel the slight tremble in her fingers as she placed her palm against his in the traditional style of escorting one's betrothed.

"Just breathe," Ard whispered. "You look perfectly natural. Like you've done this a hundred times."

This compliment was slightly exaggerated, but that was Ard's specialty. Like a carpenter's tools, his words served important functions, and he treated them carefully. A public ruse like this did not come naturally to Quarrah, which was all the more reason to tell her she was doing great.

Cinza's methods were too hard on Quarrah. She learned the skills, but Ard knew the lessons left her discouraged. Ard's crafted words needed to repair any damage the disguise manager inflicted and make Quarrah *feel* like she could do this.

Ard always said that forty percent of any successful ruse was planning. The remaining sixty percent was confidence. If Quarrah believed she could be a talented soprano, others would buy into it, regardless of her actual skill.

Detonations of Light Grit hung in the night air like giant, stagnant fireflies, illuminating the steps as Ard and Quarrah approached the palace. That kind of illumination was an expensive effect, since the Light Grit blasts above didn't appear to be diluted with cheaper Prolonging Grit. Their blaze was bright, but each blast would last only ten minutes or so.

Overhead, Ard saw the young servant responsible. The boy was igniting fuses and gently tossing Light Grit teabags from a balcony. They fell only a few feet before detonating midair, resulting in more hanging clouds of bright light.

Quarrah's dress, the color of ripe strawberries, shimmered in the glow, her fox-fur coat pulled close about her slender neck. Last night's Moon Passing had marked the official onset of winter, and the chill air nipped at Ard's freshly shaven chin. He missed the beard already.

They reached the top of the stairs and paused on a wide landing before the palace doors. There was a wooden podium with a finely dressed man checking invitations against the guest list.

Several palace Regulators were standing at attention, Rollers holstered, sashes of Grit bolts across their chests, with crossbows in hand. Their uniforms were cut in the same style and pattern as the blue Reggies of the streets. But red was the color of the palace guards.

Quarrah was growing visibly more nervous as they waited in line. Ard needed to get some wine in her quickly.

"This building is incredible, isn't it?" Ard drew Quarrah's attention to the fine stonework around the entrance. "More than two hundred years old, and still in perfect condition."

"The mortar on the right of the keystone has been weakened from settling," said Quarrah. "A well-placed detonation of Void Grit…"

Ard wrapped his fingers around her hand and squeezed uncomfortably hard. Sparks! That was definitely Quarrah speaking. She needed to get into character before they went inside.

Quarrah cleared her throat, straightened her back a little, and said, "Lovely. It's absolutely lovely," in a tone that was quite unlike her.

Ard and Quarrah finally stepped up to the podium. "Good evening," said the attendant. Quarrah curtsied like Cinza had taught her.

"Dale Hizror," Ard said, slightly changing the timbre of his voice to match the coaching Elbrig had given him. "This is my fiancée, Azania Fyse." He handed two invitations to the man, who briefly checked them against a list of names on his podium.

The attendant looked up and nodded. "Enjoy the evening, sir and madam."

Ard heard Quarrah exhale sharply, an unintentional sigh of relief as he whisked her along, passing through the grand palace entrance.

Once inside, a cordon of velvety ropes created a pathway, funneling all the guests through the open foyer.

Ard watched Quarrah's head turning like an owl hunting prey. *She's mapping the place*, he realized with a slight smile. There was a reason he had picked Quarrah Khai to join his ruse. Her unique perspective and attention to detail made her a valuable part of the team. Especially when it came to directions. Ard usually had a hard time even remembering which door he'd entered through. He was always more concerned about what happened *in* the room.

They rounded a corner and ascended some stairs, never out of sight from a red-uniformed Regulator. At last, they passed through open double doors to the room where the reception was being held.

Ardor Benn had finagled his way into plenty of fancy, important places, but the reception at the king's palace was unlike anything he'd seen before.

There was a hearth on every wall, each burning with a large cloud of Heat Grit. Ard had never seen so much of the stuff in one place. Heat Grit was clean, smokeless, and convenient to ignite, but it was usually only used by the wealthy as a supplement to regular fire. This was unrivaled extravagance.

Several serving tables were arrayed with such fine food that Raek would have lost all dignity right there. Taller tables with high stools were positioned around the room. Ard immediately identified those as the focal points of conversation.

On each table was a vase of flowers. Flowers? It was winter! They must have been transported from the very southern tip of Espar. That alone would have cost more than most citizens earned in a year.

In the center of the room was an ornamental tree, its roots housed in a giant pot, framed by a low bench. High overhead, Ard noticed a handful of hanging Light Grit chandeliers, of a fashion he had seen only a few times, in the richest manors of the Greater Chain.

A servant stood beside the wall-mounted Slagstone ignitor switch, ready to operate it with a sharp tug of a cord. Housed within the stone wall would be a small chamber full of Prolonged Light Grit. When detonated from the switch, the blast would be forced upward through a network of thin pipes embedded in the walls. The glowing Light cloud would ultimately emerge through openings in the chandelier, forming luminescent orbs that hung where candles would normally be.

When the illumination began to fade, the servant would signal a worker in the room below, who would give a few pumps on a bellows, forcing fresh Light Grit into the chamber, ready for detonation.

It was a brilliant piece of engineering, although an inefficient use of Light Grit, essentially hiding half of the glowing detonation in the pipes concealed within the walls. But it was convenient. And impressive. Ard had learned that those qualities always trumped frugality when it came to the rich and royal.

There were more people in the room than Ard expected. That would make it easier to avoid the ones Elbrig had warned them about, but harder to find the ones they were supposed to connect with.

The patrons stood around, sipping wine, nibbling cheese. There was a buzz of conversation that was almost stifling.

At least there wasn't any dancing at these preconcert receptions. Dancing required music. Music required musicians. And all the best musicians would be in attendance to enjoy a night off.

Ard had learned from past experience that dancing led to trouble. How could it not, when two dancers found themselves locked together for the duration of an entire musical selection? Dancing was just an excuse to bleed each other for valuable information.

"Shall we get something to drink, my love?" Ard didn't wait for Quarrah to answer, leading her across the expansive room.

They had just passed the centerpiece tree, when a woman, boisterous laughter on her lips, stepped back from her tall table.

"Excuse me," Ard apologized, unavoidably bumping into her.

"Not at all." She smiled broadly. "Care to join us?"

"Actually," Quarrah cut in, her voice somewhat annoyed, "we were getting a drink."

"Come now, Azania." Ard glanced sharply at her. "There will be plenty of time for drinks. Let's meet these good people."

Ard didn't mean to antagonize his fiancée, but the woman who had bumped into him had made an invitation, and Ard wasn't going to pass that up. Besides, their whole purpose in coming to the reception was to spread their names around this social circle.

Quarrah maintained an unamused face as they stepped over to the tall table. There was little Ard could do to ease Quarrah's discomfort. She was supposed to be going for lovely and soft-spoken, but more and more, Azania seemed to be shaping up into a blunt and tense personality. If she didn't turn it around soon, people would start to scatter when they saw her coming.

They made their introductions around the table. Fortunately, none of the folks Elbrig had cautioned them about were among the group. But this was a talkative bunch, and a nice mix. Four of them were of noble standing. One was a wealthy property owner, and the other two were musicians.

"And what is it you do, Mr. Hizror?" asked a nobleman.

"Oh, a little of everything," Ard answered humbly. "I've spent much of my life traveling."

"Really?" chimed the property owner. "Where's the most interesting place you've been?"

Ard stroked his mustache. "I once took a tour of lower Pekal. It's one thing to see the mountains from the InterIsland Waters, but to stand at the base of them…" He whistled softly. "As far as the Greater Chain, I love the old cities along the coast of Talumon. In fact, I spent the summers of '29 and '30 in Octowyn. Beautiful place."

"There's a music conservatory there," said one of the musicians, a woman with a low-cut dress.

"That's right," Ard answered. "Marvelous campus."

"Ever been to Strind?" asked the property baron. "I own a lot of land there."

"Of course," Ard replied. "I was actually raised on Strind, believe it or not."

"What part?" asked the man.

"Little township." Ard waved his hand. "I'd be surprised if you've heard of it."

"What's the name?"

"Nint," answered Ard.

The landowner nodded his head. "I know Nint. Just outside of Billis."

Ard laughed, slapping his hand gently against the table. "You're kidding! That's fantastic! I miss that rural air sometimes."

There was a slight lull in the conversation. But Ard wanted the hints he'd just dropped to percolate in the minds of his current company. He was doing rather well already. The conversation seemed quite natural.

"These flowers are not irises!" Quarrah abruptly reached across the table and seized the centerpiece. "Dale proposed to me with a bouquet of blue irises. That's the flower of his family's crest."

Sparks, Quarrah! What was she doing? Ard knew that thieving required great subtlety. Could she not employ that same skill to conversation? He blamed it on nerves. Nerves made people do strange things.

Ard covered the awkward moment with a laugh, taking the vase from Quarrah's hand and placing it back on the table. "My Azania," he said. "She loves all things bright, blue, and beautiful. Something of a delicate flower herself, really." He put his arm around her waist, the fine fabric of her dress smooth against his palm.

"So, a country man of Strind with a flair for romance," asked the flirtatious noblewoman who had bumped into Ard. "What brought you to Beripent?"

"The music," he answered. "I wish I could say I was an instrumentalist, but it's been years since I've dusted off the violin. Now I'm something of an aspiring composer."

Impressed nods went around the table. "Then you must meet Noet Farasse," said the woman musician. "He's here tonight, of course. We're performing his Unified Aria at the concert next week."

"That would be wonderful!" Ard exclaimed. "Would you mind pointing him out to us, so we can remain on the lookout for an opportunity to approach?"

The other musician, a tall, slender man, took a brief step away from the table before returning to point through the crowd. "He's at that far table with Lorstan Grale." Ard squinted in that direction, feeling Quarrah do the same. There were two men seated on stools, an air of unapproachability isolating them from everyone else in the room.

"Farasse's the broad one with the green shoulder cape," said the musician.

"Thank you," said Ard. How convenient that the conductor was at the same table as the composer. "And I know my fiancée was quite looking forward to meeting next week's soloist."

"Ah, Kercha Gant," said one of the noblemen. "She's over there." He pointed to the opposite side of the room. "She's looking tempting in that blue gown tonight, wouldn't you say?"

Ard cleared his throat. "I'm sure I wouldn't notice such things," he said coyly, offering his hand to Quarrah. "Come, my dear. Now would be a great time for that drink you spoke of earlier." He bowed to the people at the table and gently guided Quarrah away.

"That was good, working in Octowyn," Quarrah whispered when they were out of earshot. "And did you notice what I did with the flowers?"

"Yeah," Ard muttered. "I noticed."

They reached the serving tables, and Ard filled a small plate to share with Quarrah. A few half slices of artisan bread, cheese, and some sort of bite-sized vegetable with bacon wrapped around it. Raek would like those. Of course, he'd like them even better without the vegetable.

"What would you like to drink?" asked an aproned bartender. An assortment of bottles and glassware were spread across the draped bar. A far cry from taverns like the Staggering Bull. Ard would have liked a simple ale, but Dale wouldn't be likely to drink such a common beverage. Especially at an event like this.

"I'll have a scotch," Ard said. "A red for the lady."

The bartender nodded, pouring a dark wine into a stemmed

glass for Quarrah and selecting a tumbler for Ard. From a jar on the table, the bartender pinched a tiny amount of powder and dropped it into the glass.

"What's this?" Ard said. "I asked for a scotch." He wasn't fond of people dropping unidentified substances into his beverages. Kercha was supposed to be the only one drugged tonight.

"It's a new technique the king is rather fond of," replied the bartender, adding a pinch of a second substance to the empty glass. "A powerful mix of Cold Grit and Compounding Grit."

Ard was familiar with Compounding Grit, derived from digested and processed quartzite. Like Prolonging, it only worked in tandem with other Grit types. When detonated at the same time, it increased the effect of the primary Grit.

But its use was fairly limited. Not all Grit types could be compounded. Drift Grit, for instance, created a cloud of weightless space. Compounding couldn't make it *more* weightless. But combined with Light Grit, for example, it could create a nearly blinding cloud.

Compounding Grit was dreadfully expensive. And now the nobles were putting it in their drinks?

The bartender picked up a Slagstone ignitor, the kind with a trigger which grated the explosive stone against a steel rod. Holding the glass in one gloved hand, he sparked the ignitor and detonated the mixed Grit.

A tiny blast cloud formed inside the glass, the temperature dropping so quickly and drastically that the glass began to frost. Holding the glass steady, the bartender poured an ounce of water into the contained Cold cloud. Upon contact with the extremely frigid detonation, the water instantly froze into a perfect sphere of ice.

The bartender carefully lowered the frosty glass, the ice sphere resting in the bottom while the small detonation cloud hung suspended in the space where he had detonated it. At last, he poured the scotch, the amber liquid causing the freshly frozen ice to crackle in the bottom of the glass.

Now, *that* was something! Citizens of Beripent were up late tending fires to stay warm on a winter night like tonight, and the nobles were making iced drinks.

Ard and Quarrah took their beverages, the plate of food, and headed toward the far table where Kercha Gant had been spotted.

"I'll engage her in conversation," Ard whispered to Quarrah. "Once she's distracted, you can slip the Furybeth extract into her drink."

He saw Quarrah stiffen at the mention of the task ahead. This was undoubtedly the riskiest thing they would attempt tonight.

"You'll be fine," Ard reassured. "Just like picking a pocket. Except you're putting something in instead of taking something out." He had full confidence in Quarrah as long as she remained collected.

"What if I don't see an opening?" Quarrah asked.

"Play it safe," answered Ard. "If the conditions aren't right, we can always strike up another conversation with Kercha Gant later in the evening. Give ourselves a second chance."

"I'd rather do it right the first time," said Quarrah.

Ard nodded in agreement. "Just don't say anything to draw attention to yourself."

"Sometimes words come out," Quarrah whispered.

"I hadn't noticed," replied Ard.

They had reached the tall table where Kercha Gant stood with four other women. It would appear that Ard was the only man brave enough to draw near.

"Mind if we join you?" Ard asked.

Kercha turned, examining him from head to toe before shrugging dismissively. Ard took that as a yes. He stepped forward, letting Quarrah occupy the spot closest to Kercha in case an opportunity presented itself to reach the woman's drink.

"Dale Hizror," Ard introduced. "It's an honor to meet you. My fiancée and I are so looking forward to hearing your performance of Farasse's Unified Aria next week."

"Fiancée, huh?" Kercha glowered at Quarrah. "That's a blazing shame." She lifted her glass and took a big gulp of wine. At least it wasn't going to be difficult to convince her to drink something.

"What are you drinking?" Quarrah asked.

Ard tensed. Come on, Quarrah! Hadn't they just agreed that it would be better for Ard to do the talking? And drawing attention to the woman's beverage was among the most foolish things she could do!

"If you're going to tell me that I've had too much," snapped Kercha, "then I'm going to tell you to find me again after you've had his baby." She gestured to Ard with her glass and took another draught. "Nights like this...nights away. The only relief I get anymore."

"You have a child?" Ard asked.

"Four cycles old, the little brat," Kercha answered. "I haven't slept a wink since he was born."

Ard couldn't help but glance down at her. *That* body had a baby four cycles ago?

"You really should try Silence Grit," said a woman across the table. "I used it with all three of my babies."

"Silence Grit?" Ard asked. "I don't understand."

"You wouldn't," muttered Kercha. "Men..." She took another swig. If Quarrah didn't act soon, there would be no drink left.

"The nights *do* get long," continued the woman, "and Homeland knows a lady needs her sleep. A blast of Silence Grit under the baby's crib can make for a much more restful night. I know a Mixer who adds just the right amount of Prolonging Grit so it will burn all night. Of course, it starts to wear through after a few hours, but it's muffled. After a while you'll learn to sleep through that, too." The woman took a sip of her own beverage, a fruity light-colored drink. "It does wonders. The baby can cry all night without bothering you."

"I'll try anything at this point." Kercha lifted her glass and drank the final swallow. Ard glanced at Quarrah. Well, there was an opportunity missed. Quarrah barely seemed to notice what was going on. She was crumbling a piece of bread nervously over her plate.

"Well, for what it's worth," Ard said, "I think you look absolutely radiant."

"I think you look like you need something to eat," Quarrah muttered.

"What was that?" Kercha turned. The women on the other side of the table fell perfectly silent, watching like sharks behind a fishing boat.

"I mean, you don't get to be that thin—especially so soon after having a baby—without skipping a few meals," Quarrah insisted.

Ard placed a hand of caution on Quarrah's back. What was she doing? Now that the drink was gone, they needed a second conversation with Kercha if they hoped to administer that extract.

"Perhaps if you ate something," said Quarrah, "you'd have more energy to take care of your screaming child."

"I eat!" Kercha insisted. "I eat plenty, all right?" As if to prove the point, the soprano reached out and snatched the remaining bacon-wrapped morsel from Quarrah's plate. Without turning away, she shoved the bite into her mouth and chewed obnoxiously. "There!" she swallowed forcefully. "Are you happy now?"

"Quite." Quarrah backed up, tucking a strand of red hair behind her ear.

"It really was a pleasure meeting you," Ard said, following his companion as she peeled away from the table. "What was that?" he hissed in Quarrah's ear. "What kind of second chance are we going to have now?"

Quarrah glanced at him, her face smug under those wide-rimmed spectacles. "We don't need a second chance."

Ard paused, milling over her words until the cleverness of Quarrah's deed dawned on him. "The food?" he whispered.

Quarrah nodded. "Bacon-wrapped Furybeth."

Ard leaned forward and kissed her cheek. That was a brilliant development, when he thought Quarrah had been completely out of the loop. Prying that drink out of Kercha's hand would have been nearly impossible. So Quarrah had baited her. Like a sow dragon.

That wasn't a thief's strategy, using words to lure Kercha to eat something. Quarrah was thinking like a ruse artist, and that gave Ard an unexpected feeling of pride.

"Let's talk to the others so we can get the sparks out of here," Quarrah said.

Ard was pleased to see that Lorstan Grale was still sitting with the composer at their isolated table. As they approached, Ard decided he would play out the scenario as if Dale had never met Farasse. Besides, their previous encounter would be wildly embarrassing to a more mature Dale. He wasn't likely to lead a conversation with it.

"Gentlemen," Ard said. "May we borrow a few moments of your time?"

"'Borrowing' would imply that you intend to give them back," said Farasse, turning his broad shoulders to see Ard and Quarrah. His face was bearded and his hair long enough to pull back.

Ard gave a good-natured chuckle. "I'm afraid we'll have to steal them, then." He pulled out a stool for Quarrah, but remained standing behind her.

"Noet Farasse," said the composer, putting out his hand.

"Oh, I know." Ard accepted the handshake. "You're the man of the hour. So much anticipation for next week's compositions. Especially the Unified Aria. Great piece of music. I heard it performed by the Northeastern Orchestra last year." It was a bit of useful information he'd picked up from Elbrig.

"Yes," said Farasse. "Tunea was the soprano for that one. She choked a bit on the words of the second stanza."

"'*Founders in peace, their wistful eyes closing. A new generation sprouts in fertile soil,*'" spouted Quarrah.

Ard had no idea what the words meant, but the sentence clearly impressed Farasse, who grinned broadly.

"You know the piece?" he remarked.

"Very well," Quarrah answered.

"Yes," Ard jumped in again. "Azania, here, is an extremely talented soprano. And I'm not just saying that because we're soon to be married."

"Lorstan Grale," said the other man, beckoning for Quarrah's hand. She allowed him to take it, and he kissed her softly on the knuckles. The conductor was slight of build, with salt-and-pepper hair, and large ears that poked through. He had a pointy beard that made his chin seem long, and a gap between his teeth. The man wore square-rimmed spectacles upon his wide nose. Probably useful for reading a musical score on a podium, but he didn't seem to need them otherwise, peering over the rims at Ard.

"You introduced your lovely fiancée, but I didn't catch *your* name," said Lorstan.

Ard grinned. Someone had called Azania "lovely." Cinza would probably count the whole evening a success just for that. "Dale Hizror," he answered.

Noet Farasse scratched his thick beard. "Dale Hizror," he repeated. Ard could tell he was trying to make the connection. But it had been eight years. Surely he had forgotten the incident.

"Hold the wagon!" Farasse looked excitedly at Ard. "Did you audition for the Southern Quarter Orchestra? Would have been several years back now, when I was conductor there. Violin?"

Ard nodded reluctantly. "It was a challenging time in my life."

Farasse clapped his hands. "Hot sparks! I've told that story countless times over the years. Never gets old."

"What's the story?" Lorstan Grale asked.

Ard looked down, scratching his nose. Nothing like being embarrassed for something he hadn't actually done.

"So, we finish a round of auditions," Farasse launched in, "and we're announcing the list to the people waiting. Well, we get to the end of the list, and this whippersnapper comes marching up on the stage and insists that there's been some mistake. I extend my apologies but explain that decisions are final. And that's when he loses it."

Farasse began to laugh at what he knew was coming. "So he smashes his violin. I kid you not. *Smashes* his violin into a thousand chips right there on the stage. He's yelling something." Here, Farasse shook his fist in impersonation. "'You wouldn't know talent if it sat up and bit your nose!' until eventually, the Regulators come in and pull the kid off the stage."

Ard was standing rigid. Several people at nearby tables had keyed into the animated conversation, and Ard actually felt a little sheepish. But that was ridiculous. That tantrum had been thrown years ago, by Elbrig's portrayal of Dale Hizror. Ard's version of the man was much more composed. Refined, even.

"Quite the blazing temper," finished Farasse, glancing up at Ard.

"I'm afraid I get that from my mother," Ard replied. "She was a typical Dronodanian. You know how fiery they can be."

Farasse nodded. "I used to be married to one."

"Then you can imagine what it was like to have my mother as a teacher," Ard said with a bemused chuckle. "I couldn't have received a stricter education had I gone to the University in Helizon. So you understand why I might have expected more out of that audition. But you'll be pleased to know that, unlike a good cheese, I have grown more mild with age. I'm not even likely to smash your dinner plate on the floor if you send me away."

"I often wondered what became of that youngster," mused Farasse. "You're here." He gestured around the royal reception room. "And that's an impressive sign. What have you done with yourself?"

"Attempting to follow in your footsteps, actually," answered Ard. "I've begun composing. Hopeful to have something performed in a few cycles."

"That's wonderful," answered the composer.

"It's challenging work," continued Ard. "The harmonies and progressions tax my brain in a wonderful way, but scribing the score can be painstaking."

"Here's a professional tip." Farasse leaned forward, cupping one hand against his mouth in a mock whisper. "Hire someone to scribe the staves for you. Give your hand a rest. Trying to hold on to a quill for so long will cripple your knuckles."

"Oh, I only use quill and ink when absolutely necessary," Ard said. "I find those charcoal scribing tools much easier on the hand." He paused to let that bit of information sink in. "But I appreciate the tip. When I sell my first composition, I'll set aside a few Ashings to hire out the tedious work."

Farasse chuckled, clapping Ard on the shoulder. "Looks like you turned out all right, kid," he said. "Tell you what. Why don't I save a seat for you and your beautiful Azania at the concert next week."

"Really?" Quarrah chimed. "Oh, we'd be honored." Then, seeming unsure about whether she should have agreed to that, Quarrah swiveled around to look at Ard. "Wouldn't we?"

"Of course, dear," said Ard. Though, if everything went as planned, Farasse would only need to save one seat, since Quarrah would be onstage mouthing the aria while Cinza's voice was projected out to the concert hall.

"You can have the tickets sent to 448B Avedon Street in the Central Quarter," Ard informed him. The apartment was one of Elbrig's, and Ard was expected to pay rent for its use. Dale had to live *somewhere*, and they couldn't risk running a connection back to the bakery. Leaving the Avedon address was essential, since Farasse and Lorstan Grale would need to contact Quarrah to replace Kercha Gant.

Lorstan Grale sat quietly, studying Ard in a different way than he had when they'd first stepped up to the table. The conductor stood slowly, reaching for Ard's hand this time.

Ard nodded courteously, taking the handshake in parting.

Lorstan turned his wrist, pulling Ard's hand closer as he peered at it through his square spectacles.

"Pleasure meeting you, Dale Hizror," said the conductor, the gap in his teeth causing a soft whistle to escape when he said the name.

"Until next week." Ard took Quarrah's hand as they stepped away from the two men.

Well, that couldn't have gone much better, Ard thought. They'd hit every talking point that Elbrig had assigned, and Kercha Gant would soon be feeling ill. Ard paused as they passed the bar. Just one more frozen scotch and they'd be on their way.

~

It is no wonder the dragons are solitary.
What reason would such a commanding creature
have to socialize with others?

CHAPTER

11

Isle Halavend barely waited until Lyndel had crawled out from beneath the desk before launching into his findings. Since their last meeting, he'd studied some accounts of *unsuccessful* Visitant Grit detonations, and he wanted Lyndel's perspective.

"Captain Oriar's failure to summon a Paladin Visitant against Grotenisk's attack is well documented in Rishna's *The Folly of Beripent.*" Halavend adjusted his spectacles and began to read the excerpt he was so excited to share.

"'*Why the Prime Isle selected Oriar as the city's champion against such a furious dragon is certainly a matter to be questioned. There is no doubt about Oriar's Wayfarist devotion at the time he faced Grotenisk, though later investigation revealed that his youthful years were somewhat more Settled than he let on. Could this duplicitousness be the cause of his astronomical failure?*'"

Isle Halavend paused, thinking about the events surrounding Oriar's fruitless detonation. "It was confirmed that the Visitant Grit *did* ignite on the Old Palace Steps in the Char. Survivors even reported that the detonation cloud was large enough to envelop most of the staircase..."

Halavend finally looked to Lyndel. She stood stiffly beside the desk, arms wrapped in the red cloth of her religion, with a leather satchel slung over one shoulder.

"What's wrong?" Halavend asked. It was uncharacteristic for Lyndel to seem disinterested in his findings. She had not even taken her seat on the bench.

"There is something," said Lyndel. "A matter unrelated to the topic of our current research. It is the shell."

Halavend closed *The Folly of Beripent*. That didn't seem unrelated at all. Wasn't that what they'd been studying since the moment he hired Ardor Benn? Searching for answers about dragon shell. Visitant Grit. What made one person more likely than another to succeed in summoning a Paladin Visitant?

Lyndel reached inside her leather satchel and withdrew something as large as a dinner plate, draped in tan cloth. Leaning forward, she set it on the desk and cast aside the covering.

"Homeland be blessed." Halavend's breath caught in his throat as he slipped the spectacles from his face.

It was a piece of fertilized dragon shell. Stark white. The shell of a female hatchling.

"Where did you come by this, Lyndel?"

The Sanctification in 748 was said to have put every significant piece of shell in the Islehood's control. But it was possible a fragment had been overlooked. Had the Trothians been keeping it all these centuries?

From what Halavend had researched, this piece looked large enough to be processed into Grit. It might not yield a large detonation cloud, but it could be sufficient for their purposes!

"Do you know what this means?" Halavend stood up, his old body seeming to ache less with this rush of adrenaline. "The king's Royal Regalia might be unnecessary. Ardor Benn can take *this* fragment to Pekal. It will advance our plan and eliminate unnecessary risk."

"The shell is not real," Lyndel stated.

Halavend looked up sharply. "What do you mean?"

Lyndel pointed to the white fragment, thick as a book. "Trothian divers discovered this piece in an underwater cleft between our islands. It is not real."

Halavend knew that Trothian divers had an uncanny ability to hold their breath. Some reports claimed that they could remain underwater for over an hour.

Halavend carefully lifted the fragment of white eggshell in both hands, although there was no need to be gentle. Eggshell was as durable as any other part of a dragon. "Not real?"

Lyndel pointed to a worn spot near the edge. Halavend squinted. Confounded old eyes. He set down the shell and slipped back into his spectacles.

"This material," said Lyndel, "has worn away. My sight easily detects the variation in energies. This piece is of Lander craftsmanship."

Studying the piece, Halavend saw the worn spot where the shell seemed a slightly different color, as though a coating had rubbed away to reveal a different material beneath. Shell wasn't supposed to wear like that, no matter how long it had been underwater.

"Washed into the ocean from Pekal?" Halavend mused. "No. If it's man-made, it surely would have come from the Greater Chain."

"My people say this fragment has been in the sea for maybe twenty years," Lyndel said.

"Twenty years?" A terrible thought occurred to Isle Halavend. One that made his head throb. He deposited the shell on the desk. "Please wait here, Lyndel. I will return shortly."

He moved for the door, Lyndel positioning herself so she couldn't be seen when it opened. Halavend had Cove 23 scheduled for the entire day. No one would bother Lyndel.

In a moment, he was on the cove dock, the Mooring's interior bitingly cold during the winter cycles. Isle Halavend moved onto his raft, lifting the pole from its bracket and pushing off.

Books.

Halavend needed books. He needed the verification of records before he even dared make such an accusation.

In a moment, he had crossed the wide Mooring canal to a dock on the far side. Here, a stone staircase had been cut into the wall. The floating dock that served as a landing was large enough to accommodate many rafts, and Halavend tethered his to a post, dropping his pole into the bracket on the side.

Hiking up the hem of his sea-green Islehood robes, Halavend began ascending the cold steps. There was a short railing, but he stayed close to the wall to avoid seeing the drop to the water below.

The entire upper story of the Mooring served as the Islehood library. The Holy Isles and Islesses on duty could take books to the Coves for personal study, but removing any materials from the Mooring was strictly forbidden.

Halavend reached the top of the stairs and passed through a stone archway. An Isless welcomed him, but he barely acknowledged her, moving toward the bookshelves that ran from wall to wall, partitioning the long room into mazelike corridors.

The vast Mooring Library contained much more than Wayfarist doctrine. Its volumes were ordered into sections, storing information about almost everything in the known world.

Nearly twelve centuries of history were stored here, though the first five hundred years were mostly speculation, since no significant written documents had been kept. Isle Halavend had once been very fond of the Mooring Library. But his most recent discoveries had somewhat soured a lifetime of research. It didn't matter how much information, how many books were at his disposal. It all meant very little in light of the new doctrine he and Lyndel had uncovered.

Halavend knew his way among the shelves better than most of the Holy Isles. He even knew the exact location of the record he was searching for—an uncommon thing in a room with thousands of books.

He moved past the volumes documenting inter-island commerce, and turned into an aisle marked *Islehood Assets and Resources.* One side was full of records, with a complete accounting of the Ashings in the Islehood Treasury.

The Islehood Treasury wasn't in the Mooring, of course. It was a secure location closer to the palace, and heavily guarded by the king's Regulation. There was a steady ebb and flow of money through the Treasury—Ashings withdrawn to help a Wayfarist whose Supplication was accepted, Ashings deposited by way of donation or tithing.

The Holy Isles were the only ones allowed access to the funds themselves. There was supposed to be a level of trust and honesty from someone in his position, but for cycles now, Halavend had been skimming from the Treasury to fund the ruse for Ardor Benn.

For every small deposit that he had made, Halavend would secretly smuggle out as many Ashings as could fit in the pouches sewn on the inside of his robe. He took them from various accounts and departments, hoping that the incremental losses wouldn't be noticed until the year-end audit. It would be the Second Cycle by the time the numbers were checked and double-checked. An investigation to the missing Ashings would surely be launched, but Isle Halavend hoped his work would be done by then.

But Halavend wasn't interested in the accounting books today. The other side of the aisle contained books documenting other assets owned by the Holy Islehood: land, livestock, ore mines, shipyards, and a variety of other resources scattered throughout the Greater Chain.

Today, there was one particular resource that interested Isle Halavend. A resource that the Islehood had controlled for centuries.

Halavend slipped his spectacles onto the bridge of his nose and peered through the lenses at the array of titles before him. His eyes settled quickly on the volume he needed. Good, it was on a lower shelf. He was getting too old for the ladders, and he'd rather not ask a younger Isle to help him reach it.

Halavend's wrinkled fingers slipped around the spine of the book. *Index of Dragon Shell, Vol. I, 748–950.* There were three more volumes resting beside the first, the latest covering the years 1151 until the flood of 1218, which had completely decimated the Islehood's stores.

With all four volumes tucked in his arms, Isle Halavend made his way back to the library's exit. It was amazing that the volumes weren't more expansive. But then, the rarity of fertilized dragon shell might have something to do with its value. Halavend had heard that hatchling dragons had a tendency to smash their shells into useless fragments as a way to discover and test their own strength. Most of the shards found on Pekal were too small to survive the digestive tract of a baited dragon.

The few sizable fragments were brought to the Islehood for documentation and storage. Under rare circumstances, the Prime Isle would approve a piece of shell to be sent to Pekal and fed to a dragon. Once fired and extracted from the Slagstone, it would be processed into Visitant Grit and bestowed upon a worthy Wayfarist to use in some dire circumstance.

Isle Halavend rounded a corner sharply, head down, and collided with a person coming the other direction. His spectacles slipped from his face, and the topmost volume in his stack tumbled to the floor.

"Isle Halavend," said the man. "You seem to be in a tremendous rush. '*Hearken speedily to the Homeland's Urges*' does not mean running through the Mooring Library."

It was Prime Isle Chauster.

Halavend hadn't seen Chauster since the Second Cycle, when he had approached the Holy leader with his findings regarding Moonsickness. The exchange had been unpleasant, and Halavend didn't take it as a good sign that Prime Isle Chauster remembered his name.

Halavend made to retrieve his fallen belongings, but Prime Isle Chauster was quicker. More than ten years younger than Halavend, Frid Chauster was a tall, slender man with angular features and long hair pulled back in the popular style, though Halavend thought it was really too thin to maintain that fashion. Instead of the sea-green robes of the common Isle, the Prime wore garb of a dark violet, with white trim and an embroidered anchor across his chest.

Halavend tensed as the Prime Isle lifted the book from the library floor. The man was too astute to miss the connection. Halavend began preparing a cover story as Chauster straightened, handing him the spectacles. He held on to the book, turning it over in his hands so he could see the title.

"The dragon shell index," he read. "A curious text for an Isle to study, considering the absence of shell in today's society. This wouldn't have anything to do with that particular subject you approached me about some cycles back? I thought I was clear when I instructed you to abandon that topic."

"I have," answered Halavend. Technically, it was true. Halavend had resolved his first topic of study when he hired Ardor

Benn. He no longer needed to investigate that new doctrine. Halavend considered his findings to be fact, now that the pieces were moving.

"The Homeland appreciates your obedience to my counsel," answered Chauster. Halavend kept his mouth shut. His previous exchange with Chauster could hardly be considered counsel. The Prime Isle had refused to hear more than Halavend's introductory statements before the direct threats began.

"So, what is your interest in the shell index?" Chauster followed up, glancing at the book.

"I'm writing a few thoughts on Teriget's detonation of Visitant Grit in 1157," answered Halavend. "I thought it would be useful to see a drawing of the shell fragment used to create the Grit."

"Teriget was indeed a blessing from the Homeland," Chauster said, proving his knowledge of history. "Her successful detonation protected Kipsing at a desperate time. 1157." He looked at the three remaining books in Halavend's hands. "And yet you have all four volumes of the index."

Halavend shuffled awkwardly, but he had a response prepared. "I wanted to cross-reference Teriget's fragment against several others used in successful detonations."

"Ah," said the Prime Isle, "I see."

"Perhaps," Halavend began. It was a bold statement he was about to make, but Homeland knew he had to do something to make himself appear less guilty. "Perhaps you would grace me with your presence in Cove Twenty-Three. I would be honored to have you check your knowledge against my notes."

"Well," answered Chauster. "Some other time, perhaps."

Halavend hoped the Prime Isle didn't see the tension release from his old body. Prime Isle Chauster was far too busy a man to pay a visit to Halavend's cove and spend time looking over notes regarding a bygone event.

"Homeland bless your research." Chauster finally handed back the book. Isle Halavend bowed slightly as the tall man stepped past. He found himself rooted in place. Chauster was almost out of earshot when Halavend called after him.

"I heard about your nephew." He regretted saying it the moment the words left his mouth. It was not his place to bring up such a tender subject.

"What did you say?"

Halavend finally turned to find the Prime Isle standing two shelves away, staring back at him.

"I was in the Mooring when your nephew was brought in." Halavend didn't ask how the young man was faring. He would still be in the third stage, if his violent tendencies hadn't already led to his death. There was no cure for Moonsickness. The boy was as good as dead from the moment the Crimson Moon had passed.

"Yes." Chauster took a step closer. "My brother's son. He has already perished."

Halavend hung his head. "Homeland keep him."

"The boy should have known better," answered Chauster. "Harvesting is a dangerous business. It could happen to any of those souls on Pekal."

"Moonsickness is a terrible thing." Halavend's mind once again conjured an image of the young man on the raft. His eyes like pools of blood. "Homeland save us all if the sickness ever leaves Pekal." Was that also too bold? Too much an allusion to the topic that Chauster had refused to hear?

"That is why we light the Holy Torch," answered the Prime Isle. "But the draw of Pekal will always tempt the young and the reckless. The boy followed in his father's Settled footsteps. Can we expect any less than an early demise for such as them?"

Halavend didn't respond. It was common knowledge that the Prime Isle's own brother had been something of a Settled soul. He, too, was dead some fifteen years, though not from Moonsickness.

Prime Isle Chauster sniffed and tugged at his violet robe. "You have spoken out of turn, Isle Halavend. You will not do so again."

Halavend nodded his silver head. "My apologies." He shuffled away from the Prime Isle, face flushed and heartbeat pounding in his ears.

Halavend should not have drawn any more attention to himself. Part of him had hoped the Prime Isle would hear him out, now that Moonsickness had touched his family. A foolish hope. Chauster's threats were more veiled this time, but they were present enough to let Halavend know that his position hadn't changed. He didn't want to hear anything of the new doctrine.

Isle Halavend passed through the archway and descended the stone steps to the dock. He felt pressure to return quickly to Cove 23. Leaving Lyndel alone was always concerning. If someone were to discover a Trothian—an Agrodite priestess—hiding there...

Halavend poled through the still, flat water, his books resting in a specialized glass case in the center of the raft. Books and water did not mix. Ardor Benn would have some cutting remark about the irony of a library built on a waterway. But the ruse artist didn't understand the symbolism of the Mooring. He was a Settled criminal, to whom the Homeland had probably never called.

He tethered his raft anew outside the door of Cove 23. Lifting the four thick books from the glass case, Halavend's sandaled feet slapped against the wooden dock as he pushed open the cove door and stepped inside. Seemingly of its own accord, the heavy door shut, revealing the spot where Lyndel had waited behind it.

"You were gone long," she said, clearly made uncomfortable by waiting alone in the cove.

"The Prime Isle was in the library," he answered.

"You spoke to him?"

"I didn't have much choice." Halavend deposited the four volumes on his desk. "I told him I had dropped my studies."

"Do you think he knows?" she asked. "About the coming Moon-sickness?"

Halavend shrugged. "It would seem he knows *something*. Why else would he refuse to hear my theories?"

He looked at the fragment of counterfeit shell that Lyndel's divers had recovered, then began thumbing through the pages of the first volume. He felt the stiff pages whirring past his fingertips as he opened to the back of the book.

"You have an idea about this fake shell?" Lyndel asked.

It wasn't an idea so much as a suspicion. If these volumes verified that suspicion, Halavend didn't know what he would think.

There was a method to the documentation of shell fragments, beginning with color. White meant the hatchling dragon was a sow. But much rarer was the golden amber shell, indicating the hatchling was a bull.

Lyndel's fragment was white, disregarding the worn spot that revealed its falsity.

The index then listed shell fragments by shape, starting with the number of sharp points along the edge. The false one on the desk had six.

Next came the tedious part. Listed below the white shell fragments with six points was a series of page numbers. Marking his spot with a scrap of parchment, Halavend turned to the first indicated page, number thirteen.

The page contained a drawing of a white shell fragment. Although not to scale, meticulous measurements were given from point to point, as well as overall width, length, and thickness.

Page thirteen was clearly not a match for the fragment on the desk. Halavend flipped back to the index to check which page he should turn to next.

"What are these books?" Lyndel asked, peering over his shoulder as she often did when he plunged into the text. She was a patient woman, Halavend had learned. Much more patient than he would be, watching someone read and write text he couldn't even see.

"The Islehood has kept a record of all the dragon shell fragments collected over the years." The next page wasn't a match, either, so Halavend moved on.

"And you think this piece will be in the record?" asked Lyndel.

"I surely hope not."

Lyndel withdrew. She was understanding his moods more and more as their studies wore on. There were times when conversation was the needed catalyst, leading them to possible theories quicker than any manuscript. Then there were times like this, when the only useful thing was to put his nose in a book and study in silence.

The first volume yielded no match to the shell fragment. Halavend was halfway through the second when Lyndel ignited a fresh pinch of Light Grit in the wall brazier. She must have seen him squinting, his face drawing closer to the page as the illumination faded from its mixture with Prolonging Grit.

Lyndel didn't benefit from the light, with her unique ability to see in the dark, but it was so like her to be mindful of his needs. Her selflessness was an attribute that Halavend looked up to, not just in her treatment of others, but in her overall concern for the human race.

If Halavend wasn't careful, he found himself trying to ignore what his studies really meant for mankind. He was obsessed with finding answers, and it was less emotional to get totally lost in the puzzle of the research. But not Lyndel. Every question she asked and every theory she suggested was motivated by a desire to see her people survive the coming Moonsickness.

Halavend set aside the second volume. Perhaps it wasn't what he had feared. Perhaps the scrap of fake shell had merely belonged to a criminal sculptor. What did Ardor call them? Forgers. Perhaps a forger had tested his skills by making a sample of falsified dragon shell, only to cast it into the sea once satisfied with his own competence.

Isle Halavend had just begun his search of the third volume, when he found the match. Page nine. An artist's rendering of the same shell fragment lying on the desk. Halavend's suspicions were confirmed as he tested the fragment against a measuring stick.

He called to Lyndel, who was at his side in a heartbeat. The book was open, the matching fragment beside it. She didn't need to see what was on the page to know what he had discovered. Halavend pulled off his spectacles and pressed the palms of his hands over his tired eyes.

"What does all this mean?" Lyndel finally asked.

"It could mean any number of things," said Halavend, finally willing to verbalize some of the theories he had been concocting as he studied. "We know this piece of shell is not real. Yet we found a diagram of this very piece recorded in the Islehood index."

"So someone stole the real shell," Lyndel said. "Replaced it with a false piece that looked identical."

"The very ruse that Ardor Benn is currently running," said Halavend.

"But who?" wondered Lyndel. "This could mean the real shell is out there. If we find the person who made this replica, we find the true fragment."

"There is another possibility," said Halavend. "And I fear this one more than the first."

"What is it?"

"Your divers said this piece had been underwater for some twenty years." That was the comment that had sent him scurrying to the library in the first place. "Twenty years ago, the Egrebel Dam broke. The resulting flood obliterated two of the Islehood's storehouses, destroying the contents and washing them out to sea. One of those storehouses contained the Islehood's fragments of dragon shell."

"What are you suggesting?"

Halavend took a deep breath. "That this is one of those fragments from the storehouse. That the Islehood indexed a fake fragment *before* the stores were washed away in the dam break."

"What caused the Egrebel Dam to break?" asked Lyndel.

Halavend thought back to the disaster. "Structural failure. The dam was very old, and the winter's rains had swelled its levels."

"Your people do not check the dams?" Lyndel asked. "Strengthen old wood?"

"The dams are stone," said Halavend, but that wasn't the point. Of course they did. Maintenance crews were always making improvements to existing structures.

"Then how did it fail?" pressed Lyndel.

"What are you suggesting?"

"What if the breach was not an accident?" said Lyndel. "What if someone wanted to wash away the Islehood's shell fragments?"

"I can't imagine…" Halavend began. But nothing was making sense anymore. From the fake fragment to Prime Isle Chauster's defensive behavior. It was at least worth investigating the Egrebel Dam break.

"What year is this piece?" asked Lyndel.

Halavend slipped his spectacles on once more and glanced at the page. "It says this fragment was brought from Pekal and indexed in 919."

"Was Visitant Grit successfully detonated after that year?" Lyndel asked.

"Of course," he said. Pethredote himself had done it within Halavend's lifetime. "Why?"

"The thought occurred to me that perhaps there were more false pieces in the Islehood storehouse," said Lyndel.

Halavend couldn't ignore the probability. What were the odds that the only piece of fake shell happened to be the one that Lyndel's divers discovered? It was more likely that this was one of many falsified shell fragments that the Islehood had stored.

"Still, *some* of the shell must have been real," said Lyndel. "For the successful detonations."

Halavend nodded. "Maybe that's the answer we've been searching for. Perhaps every detonation of Visitant Grit is successful. Perhaps the Prime Isle delivers fake Grit to some people in order to perpetuate the idea that not everyone is 'worthy.'"

"That is a harsh claim against your Prime Isle."

Lyndel's words caused Halavend to feel a twinge of guilt. He had made the accusation so quickly. Did it take an Agrodite priestess to remind him of his own faith?

Now that he paused to give it more thought, the idea seemed ludicrous. The Islehood wasn't manipulating the people's faith in that way. He wouldn't allow himself to believe that the organization he'd dedicated his life to would do something like that. He was a Holy Isle, for Homeland's sake!

Halavend sighed. Lyndel's discovery had opened so many new questions. How was he supposed to keep up when questions on his other topics still remained unanswered?

"Ardor Benn is preparing to hire a forger to create a replica of the Royal Regalia," said Halavend. "If you lend me this scrap of shell, perhaps that forger might be able to provide us more information about it."

"You trust this forger?" asked Lyndel.

"I barely trust Ardor," answered Isle Halavend. "They're all Settled criminals, and I pray the Homeland will forgive me for my association with them."

"You are a good man, Isle Halavend," Lyndel replied. "Perhaps even a worthy one."

He looked up at her sharply. Was Lyndel really implying that *he* could be the one to detonate the Visitant Grit? He, a Holy Isle dabbling into criminal deeds? No, Halavend certainly did not consider himself worthy enough to summon a Paladin Visitant.

But he was running out of time. Not only did he need to find a worthy hero, but he needed to convince said person to carry out an illegal plan that had been created by the joint efforts of a Holy Isle, an Agrodite priestess, and a ruse artist.

Halavend closed the dragon shell index, shaking his head. And Lyndel considered him? *Homeland save us all,* Halavend thought, *if we grow desperate enough to see worthiness in me.*

~

I will pursue the truth at any cost.

CHAPTER

12

Ard shifted in the saddle, glancing back down the long dirt road. A few leafless trees stood in clusters along the way, but the flat expanse of the countryside seemed to sprawl endlessly. Far behind, Beripent hunkered like a smudge of grease on the horizon. The distant city was hazy with smoke from the wood-burning hearths. The citizens weren't so frivolous as to warm their homes with Heat Grit.

Ard glanced at Raek, who rode alongside him on a chestnut horse. He hadn't asked where his partner had scored the two mounts. Raek would give him the receipt for Halavend's reimbursement later . . . *if* the horses had been rented legitimately.

They had an appointment with Tarnath Aimes, the man Raek had selected from their list of potential forgers. Where Tarnath lived was too far outside Beripent for a rented carriage. It would be hours of traveling in both directions, and the distance would be covered much more quickly on horseback.

"Quarrah would hate it out here," Ard said. "So flat. Wide."

"Doesn't that sum up every island?" Raek replied. "Aside from Pekal."

Central Espar was considered the most mountainous, but even those peaks looked like low hills compared to Pekal's height. The wild island loomed at the center of it all, the summit so high that most days it was shrouded in clouds.

"I mean, no buildings," Ard explained. "No nooks or corners to hide around. Just the open road."

Ard found the country rejuvenating. Not that he'd want to live out here in this Homeland-forsaken wilderness. Not enough people for his liking. Not enough coming and going. Not enough opportunity.

"You two seem to be getting along rather well," Raek pointed out.

"Quarrah and me?" Ard replied. "Our characters are supposed to be engaged. It's all a bit of an act."

"Right."

"What's that supposed to mean?"

"It's just that I haven't seen you show this kind of interest in someone." Then he added, "Since Tanalin."

"That's blazing nonsense," said Ard. "I've shown plenty of interest. What about the haberdasher girl? Remember her?"

"Vaguely," Raek answered. "What was her name, again?"

"Collia. No, Colenia... Anyway, it started with a *C*."

Raek grinned. "My point exactly."

Ard twisted the leather strap of the horse's reins through his fingers distractedly. "She's not Tanalin," he said. "Quarrah's nothing like her."

"Does she have to be?" Raek asked. "It's been seven years, Ard. You're a whole new person. You can't keep holding out for someone who thinks you're dead. Who's to say Tanalin would even look twice at Ardor Benn?"

"I'm still myself," he answered. "Dashing, brilliant, charming..."

"Humble," Raek added. "Don't forget humble."

"I didn't want to list them all," said Ard. "You've known me longer than anyone, Raek. Have I really changed that much?"

"Ardor Benn is a far cry from that lanky teenage kid who got his trousers stuck on the Pelfid family's fence while trying to throw that pigeon trap onto the roof. You were hanging there like a limp flag when I found you."

"Those pants were made by a delirious tailor," Ard rebutted. "Who sews pockets that hang open like that? And besides, I was going to train those pigeons to bring me Grit pots. Would've worked, too, if you'd designed a better trap."

Raek chuckled. "Ardor Castenac was a dreamer. Ardor Benn is a dreamer *and* a taker. Not sure Tanalin would appreciate the latter."

Ard noticed the way Raek had brought the conversation back to her, despite his efforts to derail it.

"Tanalin won't understand why you didn't come back," continued Raek. "Even if she understands why you did it, she's going to wonder why you stayed dead so long."

"It's this lifestyle, Raek," said Ard. "Come on, you know Tanalin. She's a straight arrow. Probably even more so now, because of what happened. As long as I'm rusing, I can't risk getting her involved. But this is it. This is the big score! With half a million Ashings, I won't have to live this lifestyle anymore."

"So, what? You're just going to hang up your rusing hat, find Tanalin, and sweep her off her feet?" He chuckled. "Please let me know how that goes."

"That's not what I'm doing." Ard's hopes for him and Tanalin were never too clear, even in his own mind. Had it really been seven years? He'd gotten far too deep into something that was supposed to be only temporary. With every passing cycle—passing year—he felt the reality of being with Tanalin slip further away.

He hoped she had moved on. No, he *wanted* to hope that, but he couldn't really bring himself to feel it. In his mind, Tanalin was holding out for him the same way he was holding out for her. But that was ridiculous. Tanalin Phor thought he was dead.

Ard kept track of her secretly, as best he could. From what he gathered, Tanalin was still working on Pekal, but she'd risen in the ranks. He'd heard she was a Tracer in the king's own Harvesting crew! Flames, Tanalin was probably making enough money now that he didn't need the half million Ashings.

But Raek was right. How was he supposed to mend things after all this time? Tanalin was headstrong, independent, trusting. But she could be stubborn, too. Not quick to forgive a massive stunt like the one Ard pulled.

"You and Quarrah makes sense together, Ard," Raek went on. "I mean, you're both on the Regulation's wanted list, so your dangerous lifestyle wouldn't be a problem." He grinned. "You could be like the next Elbrig and Cinza."

"Gross." Ard shuddered. "You know, Quarrah asked me the other day if those two were brother and sister?"

"Now, *that's* gross," Raek said. "I swear I saw them kiss once."

"They did!" Ard agreed. "They demonstrated once for Quarrah and me. Said we had no chemistry."

"Was that before or after she wondered about them being siblings?"

"That's what sparked the question." Homeland only knew how Elbrig and Cinza were related, but Ard remembered Quarrah's disgusted reaction.

Quarrah made him laugh. Not always on purpose, but that was part of her charm. She was talented, clever. And at times downright awkward. Sparks, *was* he falling for her? Ard didn't know what to think. After so many hours of practicing with Elbrig and Cinza, the line between Dale's affection for Azania and Ard's feelings toward Quarrah was blurring.

"They were wrong, by the way," Raek added. "You and Quarrah have plenty of chemistry."

"Glad it's convincing," said Ard. Maybe he was even convincing himself. "It's a lot of work to maintain a fake relationship."

And the ruse was only growing more demanding. Five days had passed since Quarrah had served Kercha Gant the Fury-beth extract. With the concert fast approaching, it had become clear to Farasse and Lorstan Grale that the soprano soloist would need to be replaced. Quarrah's impressive regurgitation of the aria's lyrics must have stuck in their minds, because just last night an invitation had arrived at Dale's residence, requesting Azania's vocal talent.

Elbrig and Cinza would be seeing to her success at the rehearsal. They had some servant disguises established at the concert hall. It would get them inside, allow them to make the necessary modifications to the stage, and position Cinza in a situation that would enable her to sing for Quarrah.

Rehearsals would be trickier than the actual performance, due to their stop-and-go nature. The orchestra had been practicing for several weeks, but luckily, the soloist was only expected to attend two rehearsals preceding the concert. Cinza had it all worked out, but Quarrah still seemed a nervous wreck when Ard and Raek had left the bakery that morning.

Ard wished he could have donned Dale Hizror's disguise and gone with her to the rehearsal. But Raek's meeting with Tarnath Aimes wasn't something easy to reschedule. In fact, Raek had coordinated everything through a servant boy, with instructions to meet them at Panes junction, an hour past noon.

Ard happened to be on time for once. Squinting across the flat stretch of countryside, he thought he could see a horseman waiting at the crossroads ahead.

Ard shifted the satchel Isle Halavend had given him at their last meeting. The old man had seemed even more uptight than usual, and Ard realized that he should probably exercise some measure of frugality in the ruse. However Halavend was withdrawing Ashings was bound to be risky. There would be no million-Ashing payout if their employer was caught and executed.

Isle Halavend had again urged Ard to work as quickly as possible, reminding him that time was of the essence. Whatever that meant. In the same breath, Halavend had apologized for distracting Ard with the contents of this satchel, but it was a matter that needed looking into. It was no trouble for Ard. He needed to meet with a forger anyway, and if Raek's research held up, Tarnath Aimes was the best source to check it.

The boy waiting at the junction couldn't have been over fourteen years old. He had a mess of curly black hair on his head, and his skin was pale, like he rarely went outside.

"It's this way," said the lad, turning his horse down the road toward Panes.

They rode for another hour before they reached the town, the boy tight-lipped despite Ard's best efforts to engage him in conversation. A youthful messenger who spilled trade secrets was more liability than help. This one seemed to earn his keep.

Panes was just big enough not to be considered a township—located halfway between Beripent and Ergomun. For a visit, Ard enjoyed the city's casual approach toward life. But it was lacking several things that Beripent had—the pollution, the stench, the poverty, and the crime. It would be too hard to live like Ardor Benn and blend into the general population.

The boy led them past a tavern attached to the side of a hotel, and came to a stop before a multistory brick building with a cobbler's shop on the ground level. All three dismounted, hitching their horses to a post by the shopfront before entering.

It was quiet inside, the smell of fresh leather and adhesive filling Ard's nose. Shelves lined the walls, full of every type of shoe. From the sturdy boots of a field laborer, to the tall riding boot. From the square-toed ankle shoe of the nobleman—the uncomfortable type Ard wore when playing his role as Dale—to the laced heel of the noblewoman.

There were two small mobile benches, and a low mounted mirror on one wall. A workbench occupied the far side, scraps of leather and bits of braided shoelace littered across its scuffed surface. There were a variety of foot molds, some of which had been placed inside damp leather forms to give them the proper shape.

The only thing missing was the cobbler.

The quiet boy stepped behind the workbench, instructing Ard and Raek to remain where they were while he disappeared up a stairwell. A moment later, the youngster returned, waving for them to follow.

The wooden stairs creaked as Ard and Raek made their way up. The boy opened a door at the top of the stairs and gestured for them to pass. "Tarnath will see you."

Ard stepped into the room to find a heavyset man sitting on a bar stool. Tarnath's face was round, and his eyes deep set in his pale face. Both ears were pierced, with golden studs poking out through black hair that fell in tight curls to his shoulders. His beard was bushy and thick, like the hair on his arms. Golden chains were draped around his thick neck, and his shirt fell open to reveal a chest that looked as furry as a dog's backside.

Before him on the table was a thin woman, lying on her side in a rather provocative position with her eyes closed. A thin sheet draped over her shapely body, toes poking out the bottom, and bare shoulders visible at the top. The woman had blond hair, full lips, and a seductive expression. She remained absolutely still as Ard and Raek entered the room, her face toward Tarnath.

"Isn't she something?" Tarnath asked. His thick fingers were gripping a small, pointy tool. The heavy man leaned forward and poked the woman's eye with the metal utensil.

She remained perfectly motionless. Unflinching.

Ard took a startled step closer as Tarnath dragged the pointy metal tool under the woman's eyelid. Sparks! What kind of sorcery was this? Torture? Twisted pleasure? Ard couldn't decide. But the woman on the table seemed completely unresponsive. He might have thought she were dead if it weren't for the rosiness of her cheeks.

"Who is she?" Raek asked.

"Name's Gella," Tarnath said, switching the metal tool for a delicate paintbrush. "Making her for a client of mine."

"Making her?" Ard repeated as the man brushed soft strokes across the woman's face.

"Wax, my boy!" Tarnath threw back the sheet to expose her body. But what Ard saw was clearly not human. The shape had been roughed out, but the body was made of an opaque white material, like an unburned candle.

"A wax figure," muttered Ard, feeling duped. "That's clever."

"Hopefully clever enough for my client," said Tarnath. "She thinks her husband is unfaithful." The forger reached out a thick hand and patted the wax woman. "Gella, here, is going to be a test. Position her just so upon the bed. Then hide in the room when the husband comes in." He chuckled. "I don't really care what the outcome is. Suspicion has already paid me a handsome Ashing."

Tarnath set down the small paintbrush and turned on his stool to face the two men in the doorway. He waved at the boy with the back of his hand. "Leave us to business, Kippo." Now that Ard saw them in the same room, the family resemblance was obvious. The lad stepped onto the stairs, pulling the door closed as he returned to the shoe shop below.

"My boy says you have an offer for me," Tarnath said. "Ardor Benn, and the Short Fuse. I'm flattered."

"You should be." Ard was somewhat pleased that his reputation had preceded their meeting. "I have a question for someone with your expertise."

He reached into his satchel and withdrew the fragment of white dragon shell that Isle Halavend had given him. Lyndel, the Agrodite priestess, had insisted that the shell was not real. And now Ard was trying to sniff out its origins.

"What can you tell me about this?" Ard set the fragment on the table beside the wax woman.

"Well, well," muttered Tarnath, picking it up. "Fertilized sow dragon shell."

"My friend says it's a..." Ard began.

"Forgery," Tarnath finished. "Yes, yes. Look how it's worn along the edge to expose the resin. Would have been hard to spot in its day, but this piece is decades old. Weathered."

He found a pair of spectacles and slipped them onto his nose. Unlike Quarrah's, these had multiple lenses, which could be lowered into place for magnification. "Where did you come by this piece?"

"That's not something I can talk about," answered Ard. "Ever seen anything like it?"

"Only a Moonsick fool would forge dragon shell." Tarnath reached up and dropped an extra lens over his spectacles. "The Islehood controls this product. There's no market for it whatsoever."

"Yet someone clearly took the time to make this piece," Raek pointed out.

"His name was Reejin," answered the forger. He tapped his finger on the side of the shell fragment. "That's his mark etched into the edge."

"You found that awfully quick," Raek said.

Tarnath glanced up and smiled. His eyes looked huge and watery under the magnification of his lenses. "Knew exactly what I was looking for."

"You know this Reejin?" Ard asked. This was good news for Isle Halavend.

"I did," answered Tarnath. "He's dead now. Shot to death in a Beripent alley some years back."

"I hate it when that happens," Raek said.

"I had the chance to study with him." Tarnath slid away the extra lenses on his spectacles. "Many years ago. Had a bit of a reputation, Reejin did. A bold cat, as they say. Lots of rumors. Some said Reejin worked for the Islehood. Others said he was cheating the Islehood. Whichever was the case, Reejin gained notoriety among forgers for making counterfeit dragon shell."

"Did he get paid for it?" Ard asked.

"Reejin never seemed to be hurting for Ashings," said Tarnath. "I was working around the clock trying to make ends meet with counterfeit Grit, paintings, instruments, anything that would fetch a price. Whatever arrangement Reejin had was a deluxe one. While I was apprenticed to him, someone used to bring him genuine shell fragments to forge."

"Who?" Ard asked.

"Don't know," answered Tarnath. "I don't even think Reejin knew. Fragment would show up, and he'd forge it and return both pieces to the drop site. By the time he got home there was a bag of Ashings on his doorstep." Tarnath shook his head. "Yep. Reejin had it good. He was one of the lucky ones."

"Except for the whole shot-to-death-in-an-alley part," Raek reminded.

Tarnath shrugged. "Hey. Beripent's a dangerous city. Highest crime in the Greater Chain. Why do you think I'm out in Panes? How do I compete with a city full of forgers?"

"You specialize," said Raek. "The forgers in Beripent are still gun shy when it comes to fake shell. Every lead I sniffed down sent me in your direction."

Tarnath set down the piece of shell and removed his intricate spectacles. "Now, hold on a minute, gentlemen. You want me to forge you some fertilized dragon shell?"

"I wish it were that simple," Ard said. "Our offer will likely be the most complex of forgeries."

"More complex than a woman?" Tarnath chuckled, gesturing over his shoulder to the wax figure. "I somehow doubt that."

"You clearly have a lot of confidence in yourself," said Ard. "Good. You'll need it to pull this off."

"Who says I'm taking the job?" Tarnath asked.

"This isn't the kind of offer you turn down," said Ard. "Understand?"

"Is that a threat?" The forger laced his pale fingers across his leather artist apron and rested them on the bulge of his stomach.

"It's more of a mercy," Raek added. "A chance to decline now, before we really explain anything."

Tarnath squinted thoughtfully at the two men. "What kind of payout are we talking?"

"Five thousand Ashings," answered Ard without hesitation. Like Elbrig's disguise, the forged regalia was a commodity. Halavend would reimburse Tarnath's fee without dipping into the million Ashings owed to Ard.

The forger raised his bushy eyebrows. "It's right to be suspicious of a sum that large, don't you think? How do I know you'll make good on your end?"

"We'll give you the money at the same time you give us the product," Ard answered.

"Eight thousand," Tarnath haggled. "I'm the best forger on Espar when it comes to dragon shell."

"Done." Ard shook hands with the burly man.

"Now, what exactly do you need me to make?" Tarnath asked.

"We want you to create an identical replica of the Royal Regalia," answered Ard, his voice soft as a caution against eavesdroppers.

Tarnath's eyes grew wide. He looked from Ard to Raek, seeming to carry on an internal debate about whether or not they were serious. Then he let out a nervous laugh, swiveling on his bar stool to face the wax woman. "Did you hear that, Gella? King Pethredote's Royal Regalia! These fellows are out of their blazing minds!"

"Says the man talking to a wax figure," Raek replied.

"Unfortunately, we're very serious about all this," Ard said.

"And that alone is rare," said Raek. "Ard has a hard time being serious about anything."

Tarnath ran a hand through his shaggy beard. "Absolute oysters! That's a suicide job."

"This isn't the kind of offer you turn down," Ard repeated.

"Now, *that* was a threat," added Raek.

"You don't understand my methods." Tarnath stood up for the first time since Ard and Raek had entered the room. "I saw the Royal Regalia *once*. More than ten years ago. From the back of a crowd. I can't conjure up that image with enough detail to make a convincing replica."

Ard reached into his satchel and withdrew a small stack of papers that he had requested from Isle Halavend. "All the information in the Mooring Library about the Royal Regalia." Ard handed the pages to Tarnath. There were detailed descriptions, and drawings from every angle.

Tarnath rifled through the pages before looking up. "This is helpful for a start, but this isn't how I work." He set the papers on the table next to the wax woman. "I'm a tangible artist. In order to re-create something, I have to see the colors up close. Feel the textures with my own fingers..."

"That's simply not going to happen," Raek said.

"But what if it did?" interjected Ard, stroking his mustache. Elbrig had suggested an artificial one, now that Dale had made his crucial first impression. But Ard found the mustache helped him think.

"What do you mean?" Tarnath's voice was hesitant.

"What if I could get you close enough to the regalia so you could gather your information?" answered Ard.

"That would be . . . impossible," whispered the forger.

"How long would you need with it?" pressed Ard.

Tarnath shook his head. "Only a moment. I can draft a clay model with the information from these pages. I'd just need a minute with the regalia to solidify the fine details before I finish crafting the replica. But the regalia is in the palace. How would you . . ."

"I expect the king to invite me to the palace soon," said Ard.

Tarnath scoffed. "Now, that seems a bit arrogant. Even for Ardor Benn's reputation."

"Clearly, you don't know him," Raek said.

"I'm working an angle," Ard continued. "I'll be attending a concert with the king's orchestra in a few days. Pethredote should be there, but he won't likely be wearing the regalia."

"Even if he was," said Raek, "how could you get Tarnath inside? The crazies?"

Ard shook his head. Another disguise would be too expensive, and Elbrig wouldn't have time to train Tarnath on a character suitable for a royal event.

"If we can't get Tarnath inside the palace," said Ard, "we'll have to find an opportunity to get the regalia out."

Raek scratched his bald head. "That doesn't make much sense. If we could successfully steal the regalia, why would we need a replica?"

Ard grinned. "I'm not talking about stealing it yet. I'm talking about having Tarnath make his inspection during a public address from the king."

"You want me to inspect the regalia," Tarnath muttered, "*while* Pethredote is wearing it?" He looked again at the wax woman. "Sparks, Gella! They really are nutty!"

"Be ready to move at a moment's notice," Ard instructed the

forger. "We'll need you in Beripent quickly should an opportunity present itself." He turned to leave.

"Oh," Raek said to Tarnath, pausing in the doorway. "While you're at it with the wax figures, you might want to sculpt one of Ard. I know a lady who wouldn't mind keeping him propped up in the corner of her bedroom."

Ard reached up and smacked Raek across the back of his bald head. "Quarrah's not a pervert."

Raek chuckled. "Oh! I was talking about the Trothian baker."

~

I'm certainly not the only person qualified for this task. Sometimes I wonder if I am insane for having agreed to do it. But the choice was mine alone.

CHAPTER

13

Quarrah Khai adjusted her dress, took a deep breath, and turned back for a drink of water. Her fingers found another éclair instead, and she shoved the entire thing into her mouth.

"Relax." Ard's voice was barely above a whisper. "Everything's in place. You're going to be amazing."

"You should get back to your seat." Quarrah swallowed the dessert and chased it down with a gulp of water. "The intermission Light Grit will burn out any second."

"My tardiness won't bother anyone," Ard said. "They'd expect me here. Backstage with you." He, too, helped himself to an éclair, shrugging only moderate approval of the pastry. "Besides, I'd rather wait until the Lights go out so I don't have to see Farasse's smug face. He talked through the entire first half of the concert."

Quarrah fanned her face with her hand. She wasn't really listening to Ardor Benn. He had slipped backstage to the performers' lounge to help calm her nerves, but at this point, her nerves were too far gone. She was a ship, lost at sea, tackling unmanageable waves that were much too big for her.

The first half of the concert had been a steady flow of increasing anxiety. She'd thrown up twice before intermission, and was now nervously stuffing down anything edible, hoping she wouldn't regret it onstage.

Her part was coming fast. The Unified Aria started the second half of the concert, with one of Farasse's short instrumental pieces as the final number. Whether she would be conscious to hear it was yet to be determined. Quarrah had the distinct shortage of breath that oft preceded passing out.

Ard reached out suddenly, seizing her gloved hand. He lifted it to his lips and kissed it softly, his eyes locking with hers. Sparks, that didn't help the nerves.

Ard was definitely looking the part of Dale Hizror at the moment, long-haired wig pulled back and tied with a bright ribbon, thick mustache, and full sideburns extending almost to his chin. The wig's prosthetic forehead had been tacked firmly into place, the shape of his head different from what she was accustomed to. But the eyes were the same. Ard's eyes.

"Azania Fyse." Ard bowed as he released her hand. "I am supremely confident that you will leave this audience in speechless wonder." Why did he have to say things like that? Didn't Ard know that her insides were already a puddle of mush?

He stepped over to the door and pulled it open. "If you'll excuse me." He slipped out of sight.

Ard was good. Talented in so many ways. He had gone from downing pastries and bad-mouthing Farasse to a proper gentleman in the blink of an eye. Quarrah's transition into character wasn't half as fluid. She needed to start acting like Azania now if she had any hope of looking like her onstage.

Quarrah crossed the room a few times, trying to practice the nuances of her character's movement. The heels on these shoes were downright absurd. Every step was like an audible announcement of her approach.

A young man's face appeared in the open doorway. "If you are ready, madam, I'll see you to the stage."

She nodded, downing one final sip of water to soothe her dry throat, before taking the arm of the young stagehand. They moved down a narrow backstage hallway, painted black and barely illuminated by a Light Grit detonation the size of a candle flame. When they rounded the corner, Quarrah saw the thick curtains hanging along the side of the stage. She almost lost the éclair she'd just eaten.

The young stagehand deposited her in the darkness beside Lorstan Grale who smiled warmly and took her hand in both of his. "Are you ready, my dear?" he whispered.

Ready? Flames, no! Quarrah had never felt less prepared for anything in her entire life.

Onstage, the orchestra musicians had taken their seats. Cantibel Tren, the first violinist, was providing the tuning pitch. It was a cacophony of independent sounds, and Quarrah felt like she could have let out a few much-needed shrieks of fear and no one would have noticed.

"Does one ever feel truly ready for such things?" Quarrah replied to the conductor.

Lorstan Grale chuckled. "The nerves can steel with experience. I've been doing this for a long time." He let go of her hand as the orchestra's whining faded to silence. "I'll gesture for you to follow me out," he whispered, stepping past the side curtain to uproarious applause from the audience.

Don't pass out. Breathing is important. Why did Cinza tie my dress so tight?

Quarrah practiced breathing the way Cinza had taught her. In through the nose. Out through the mouth. In through the nose…

Lorstan Grale gestured to the side of the stage for her entrance. This was it. Quarrah slipped something from a secret pocket in her glove and popped it into her mouth. Then her legs were propelling her onstage, the applause a wash of indecipherable sounds.

Find the mark. Find the mark.

Quarrah kept her focus on the finely crafted wooden flooring. Several feet from the conductor's podium was a very important mark chalked onto the flat black stage. She stepped across it, letting the long hem of her dress swirl around her feet.

Safely in place, Quarrah struck the pose Cinza had drilled into her over the past three cycles. Only then did she look up.

Quarrah hadn't been expecting the light. Light Grit detonations hung above the stage, mirrors positioned to reflect the light directly upon her face. She felt instantly hot, like the amplified lights might melt the inordinate amount of makeup that Cinza had applied on her.

The rest of the Royal Concert Hall was enveloped in darkness. So dark that Quarrah couldn't see anyone sitting out there at first. Instead of finding comfort in that, she found it oddly unsettling. Like she was being watched by unknown eyes. The expert thief in her wanted to turn and run.

Lorstan Grale took the podium. He looked once to Quarrah, who nodded. She didn't think about the action, but muscle memory from her practice sessions took over. Lorstan rustled a few pages on his podium and lifted his baton. He prepped, his baton came down, and the orchestra launched into the opening of Farasse's Unified Aria.

Quarrah took a deep breath, careful not to choke on the item in her mouth. She was on an unalterable course now. From the downbeat, Quarrah had sixty-four measures before her first notes. Sixty-four measures to get everything into position for Cinza to effectively take over as the soloist.

Quarrah felt a slight thump at her feet and she knew the disguise manager was making the first move. Concealed in the crawl space below the stage, Cinza was removing a precut portion of the flooring between Quarrah's feet. The process took some force, but the orchestra's vigorous opening provided ideal sound cover for any bumps that may occur. And Quarrah's long dress hung like a curtain to hide the trickery, so long as she didn't move from the chalk mark she was straddling.

Quarrah stared out, her eyes adjusting to the reflected light enough that she could see the audience rows. She scanned the faces for Ard, but individuals were difficult to make out. There was a balcony, too, but Ard had said Farasse saved their seats on the ground floor.

The hall was full, but that was to be expected. Attending a concert was a thing of status. Even more, when it was the king's own orchestra at the Royal Concert Hall adjacent to the palace. To the patrons here tonight, it mattered less about whether they enjoyed the music, and more about being seen at such a prestigious event. Supposedly, King Pethredote himself was out there. Ard hadn't seen him, as the king had a private box on the Grand Tier.

Quarrah tried not to fidget as she felt something between her legs. It was Cinza's head, unencumbered by a wig of any kind. The disguise manager would have a set of teeth in, but other than that, Cinza would be in her raw and natural state, sliding her narrow shoulders through the trapdoor she had just removed from the stage.

Cinza's head rose uncomfortably high, coming to rest between Quarrah's thighs. For stability, Cinza wrapped her arms around

Quarrah's legs until she was positioned just right, her lower half under the stage, and her upper half hidden beneath the thick folds of Quarrah's dress.

The dress itself was of singular design. The thick burgundy fabric made intricate folds and scallops, trimmed with black lace. From the outside, nothing appeared unusual about the front seam, pulling away from the hips in two rich draperies. But Quarrah had felt the chill of winter on her thighs as they entered the building, the lace front deceivingly thin and breathable.

As uncomfortable as the arrangement was for Quarrah, she figured it was far worse for Cinza, who was stuck between her legs with a stifling dome of fabric hanging around her as she sang through a lace window.

Cinza tapped Quarrah's knee three times to indicate that she was ready. Good. There were still eight measures before their entrance.

Quarrah rolled the small item out from beneath her tongue. It was a hazelnut, shelled and roasted. Raek had painstakingly hollowed it out to create an open cavity inside. Next, the Mixer had poured high-grade Silence Grit, mixed with just a touch of Prolonging Grit to make absolutely sure that the effect would last the length of the fifteen-minute aria, but not too long after. If things went as planned, she'd need to be able to accept congratulations shortly after the piece's conclusion. Last, Raek had inserted two minuscule shards of Slagstone before sealing the opening with a tiny beeswax plug.

Quarrah maneuvered the nut across her mouth until it rest between her molars. The edge of the hazelnut was growing soft from being under her tongue, despite the dryness of her mouth.

Bracing herself against the unpleasantness, Quarrah bit down swiftly on the nut. She felt the spark between her teeth as the tiny fragments of Slagstone grated together. The Silence Grit detonated, like a sudden puff of air originating within her mouth.

There was a bitter taste, and Quarrah fought to keep her lips sealed, containing the blast. The cloud filled her mouth, with any residual spilling down her throat to sufficiently mask her vocal cords.

Every trial they'd run in the bakery's upper room had worked, but Quarrah couldn't help but feel uncertain as the orchestra swelled toward her entrance.

From the corner of her eye, Quarrah saw Lorstan Grale lean out slightly, his free hand cueing her to come in. She didn't need the cue. Cinza had drilled the counting into her head and Quarrah felt like she knew the aria as well as Noet Farasse himself.

She opened her mouth and boldly sang the first note. Not a sound escaped her lips. But from beneath her wide dress, Cinza's pure soprano notes pealed out to fill the Royal Concert Hall.

In his soft chair on the seventh row, Ard felt his entire body relax, muscles loosening that he hadn't realized were tensed. Praise the Homeland, that was *not* Quarrah's voice coming from the stage.

Quarrah Khai was many things, but a singer was not one of them. Had Cinza's trickery beneath the stage not worked, Farasse would likely have chased Quarrah off the stage with a loaded Singler.

"She was absolutely effortless on that opening line." Farasse leaned over to whisper in Ard's ear. "The impact there really sets the tone for the entire piece."

Ard gave a knowing nod without replying. It was his first concert as a legitimate attendee, but even Ard knew that common etiquette demanded silence during a performance. Farasse obviously felt like the exception, perhaps due to the fact that they were performing his compositions.

Ard squinted to see if he could see the discolored detonation cloud in Quarrah's mouth. There was no trace of it from where he was sitting, but other patrons carried special magnifying glasses crafted specifically for watching performers onstage. Ard hoped they wouldn't spot anything amiss.

Quarrah was already to the third stanza. "*'A shattered glass repaired. A scattered dust of Grit cannot ignite. Bring us henceforth inward. Let our dwellings be as ceramic pots, our actions as Slagstone striking. Hail the victor; worthy one. Our glorious crusader monarch, whose peace is ever Compounding.'*"

Farasse swiveled in his chair, peering upward over his broad shoulder, then whispering again to Ard, "It's one thing to have this performed with the Northeastern Orchestra. But it's another to have His Majesty listening. What do you suppose he's thinking?"

Ard shrugged silently. The Unified Aria probably wasn't the first song to be written about King Pethredote. The lyrics spoke of how the great crusader monarch reestablished peace across the islands of the Greater Chain. Ard had heard Quarrah practicing it a hundred times. It talked about King Pethredote's worthiness in summoning a Paladin Visitant. It talked about his magnanimous reign.

Personally, Ard found the whole thing distasteful. Sure, he agreed with the lyrics, but he didn't agree with Farasse's reason for writing them. The Unified Aria was the work of a self-righteous sycophant. And that was one personality Ard couldn't abide.

Still, sitting next to Farasse was useful in establishing himself. Before the concert began, Ard had managed to plant a few more clues implying that Dale Hizror was the composer of the Unclaimed Symphony. There was another reception in two weeks, followed by a concert the week after. If he could keep up the game, the royal folk might come to their own conclusion in another cycle or two.

"Wow...Flawless approach to that high C," Farasse muttered. He wasn't necessarily speaking to Ard anymore, but the man seemed compelled to narrate the aria.

To her credit, Quarrah *was* doing an incredible job. If Ard didn't know better, he would have been easily convinced that the voice he was hearing belonged to the young woman onstage. Her mouth

formed the words perfectly in sync with Cinza's hidden performance below. Her diaphragm contracted naturally under the tight
corset as she drew breaths between phrases. Everything looked perfect and natural.

"*'A stronger steel of justice. A gentler touch of grace.'*" Quarrah began
what Ard recognized as the final line of the aria. "*'Homeland see him
well to guide us. Hail the crusader monarch.*'"

Quarrah finished strong and confident, the orchestra cutting off
their final sustain under Lorstan Grale's baton. Ard finally relaxed
to the point where he wasn't even gripping his armrests anymore.

The audience broke into rich applause. Farasse leapt to his feet,
hands thundering together as Quarrah took the first bow in a series
of many. Ard imagined the frantic work of Cinza beneath the dress,
ducking her shaved head below the stage, fixing the floor panel
back into place. Quarrah exited, then returned a moment later with
a bouquet of flowers to continue bowing at the gracious audience.

Well, they liked her, Ard thought. That would certainly strengthen
the position of the ruse going forward. He glanced up toward the
glass box on the Grand Tier, hopeful to catch a glimpse of the king's
reaction.

Suddenly, Lorstan Grale was quieting the audience with a gesture. Patrons seated themselves to hear the conductor's remarks as
Quarrah stood nearby, cradling the flowers, her back rigid in that
practiced pose.

"Before we play tonight's final number," Lorstan Grale's voice
was soft enough to prompt everyone in the hall to hold very still,
"I wanted to acknowledge the beautiful voice you just heard. Our
soloist, Azania Fyse, is something of a newcomer to Beripent's
musical scene, but she was able to fill in for Kercha Gant in a flaw-
less manner."

There was some applause, and Quarrah had the presence of
mind to bow again. This kind of attention was good, and Ard was
impressed with the way Quarrah was handling it.

"And if this young vocalist was not impressive enough," continued Lorstan, "I'd like to introduce her fiancé, Dale Hizror, who also happens to be in attendance with us tonight."

Ard's heart rate quickened as the conductor peered out across the audience. "Mr. Hizror, would you please come forward?"

Ard stood up stiffly. Sparks, what was going on? Had they seen through his disguise? He glanced at Farasse, but the composer seemed genuinely puzzled, if not a little perturbed that Dale was receiving attention at a concert featuring Farasse's compositions.

Slowly, Ard moved into the aisle, resisting the urge to adjust his wig. He needed to trust Elbrig's costume and coaching. Besides, acknowledgment was what he needed, right? What was more notable than getting called to the stage in front of the king and a hall full of wealthy nobles?

Ard ascended the side steps to the stage, his march feeling as though it had taken hours instead of mere seconds. He approached the conductor, locking eyes with Quarrah as he stepped past her. She looked genuinely panicked, and that, strangely, put him at ease.

This was his thing: acting smooth under pressure. He was a ruse artist, able to talk his way out of any scenario. Whatever the reason behind getting singled out, Ard was going to deal with it to prove to Quarrah that he was a master of his craft.

"I believe this man warrants a special introduction." Lorstan Grale slapped a hand around Ard's shoulder. "Some of you had the opportunity of speaking with him at last week's reception. I, for one, learned something very interesting the moment I shook his hand." Lorstan Grale seized Ard's right hand and raised it before the audience. "Dale Hizror is none other than the composer of the Unclaimed Symphony."

A collective gasp came over the audience, followed by a wave-like murmur. Ard glanced at Quarrah, a broad smile passing over his face. As it turned out, there would be no need for talking them out of trouble after all! And the ruse had just accelerated. Ard felt the giddiness of victory spreading though his body. For once, something had turned out *better* than planned!

"Give us proof!" cried a faceless voice from the audience.

"Of course." Lorstan Grale held up his hands for order. "I would never make such a statement without backing it up. When the Unclaimed Symphony was deposited on the palace steps, the score was packaged in parchment, sealed with a drop of wax. Pressed into that wax was an emblem of a blooming iris. For years, the king's men searched for the identity behind this emblem. It wasn't until last week that I found it—in the signet ring of Dale Hizror."

Ard glanced at the ring on his right hand. It was part of the costume he had purchased from Elbrig. If the ring had such important ties to the Unclaimed Symphony, why hadn't Elbrig mentioned it? Here, Ard had been dropping subtle clues, when all he really needed to do was flash the ring to the right people.

"Upon further investigation," continued the conductor, "I discovered that Dale Hizror is trained in the musical calligraphy style of the Octowyn conservatory, which matches the penmanship of the symphony's original score. He was also schooled in classic Dronodanian, matching the numeration of parts and movements found through the score. I have little doubt as to the true identity of this man, and lack only a confession from him to confirm my suspicions." Lorstan Grale let Ard's arm fall as he turned to face him. "Well, sir. What do you have to say regarding this matter?"

Ard looked over the stunned audience. He'd have to play this right so he didn't enrage the people. He wanted them to celebrate his role as composer of the Unclaimed Symphony, not spite him for it.

"A sparrow and a dragon are not that different," Ard began. "Both hatch from eggs; both can fly freely upon the breeze. We esteem one greater because of what it can accomplish. It gives us Grit. It breathes fire. It demands fear and respect." He paused, glancing at Farasse, who was poised at the edge of his seat to hear Dale's statement.

"I had no intention of going about my life as a dragon," continued Ard, "when I could fly just as well as a sparrow." The answer was much too poetic for Ard's liking, but it worked for Dale Hizror. "I *am* the composer of the Unclaimed Symphony."

This time, the audience erupted into full chaos, and it took several moments for Lorstan Grale to calm them. Ard briefly caught the red face of Noet Farasse, who seemed to be on the verge of throwing a tantrum to rival the one he recounted about young Dale Hizror.

Ard finally risked a glance at the king's private box, but the glass was dark. The purpose of the ruse was to get close enough to steal the regalia. Setting himself up as the king's favorite composer was the perfect opportunity. But it would only work if His Majesty believed.

When the conductor finally managed to settle the crowd, Ard saw a handful of figures he hadn't noticed before. Regulators—their wool coats and helmets barely visible as they lurked in the back of the concert hall. Had they been there all evening?

Lorstan Grale turned to Ard. "I must ask the question all of us have wondered. Why did you choose to remain anonymous when your symphony was so warmly received?"

"When I wrote that symphony, I knew it was special," Ard answered. He and Elbrig hadn't rehearsed these answers, so he'd have to be careful to speak only in broad, vague terms. "There was something about the piece that made me want to see it fly unhindered. I wanted each note to be esteemed for its own merit, with no association to a face."

Sparks, there were more Regulators pouring through the back door. What was going on? They whispered to one another, fanning out behind the back row to cover the hall's exits.

"So," continued the conductor with his impromptu interview, "after all these years away, what made you return to Beripent?"

Ard glanced at Quarrah. Her posture suddenly seemed a little more Quarrah, and a little less Azania. He could tell by her expression that she had spotted the Regulators, too.

"It was my dear Azania who brought me back to Beripent," answered Ard. "She is simply teeming with talent, and I knew I had to do all I could to integrate her into Beripent society. Give her the chance to work with the most professional and gifted individuals in the Greater Chain."

Oh, no. One of the Reggies was coming down the aisle toward the stage. He had a lot of stripes on his shoulders, and his helmet was a darker shade of blue.

"Suppose I hadn't seen the ring. Did you ever have the intention of coming forward to claim your work?" Lorstan Grale seemed oblivious to the sudden influx of Reggies.

Ard, on the other hand, had put so much focus on the officers, he could barely construct a reply. "It's hard to say. I think…"

The Regulator reached the edge of the stage, leaning forward to get Lorstan Grale's attention. "I hate to cut in like this," he said quietly, "but I'm afraid we have a possible security threat in the building. I'm going to need to address the audience for a moment."

Lorstan Grale swallowed visibly. "Of course." He gestured for the man to take the stage. Ignoring the steps, the Regulator hoisted himself up until he was standing between Ard and Quarrah.

"Ladies and gentlemen." The Reggie's voice was booming, projecting through the hall as well as Cinza's. "I apologize for the interruption. You understand that safety and security is our top priority, especially at an event where His Majesty is present." He cleared his throat. "We have received information that a known criminal is in our midst tonight."

Well, there it went, slipping sideways. Had someone spotted Cinza as she crawled out from beneath the stage?

The Regulator chief reached into his coat and withdrew a paper. "The man is a ruse artist by the name of Ardor Benn."

Blazing sparks!

The Regulator unfolded the paper to reveal a charcoal sketch of Ard's face. It wasn't a very good one—what was the deal with those eyebrows? But it got the point across.

It took all of Ard's self-control not to bolt. Quarrah edged closer to him, the bouquet of flowers hanging limply in one hand. This was really happening? This, on the heels of successfully establishing himself as the composer of the symphony?

"Here's how we're going to proceed," continued the Reggie chief. "My Regulators will make their way through the concert hall, checking faces and confirming identities. The word we received said that Ardor Benn would likely be mingling among us in disguise." He held up his gloved hands. "Now, no one panic. Everyone remain seated. If he's here, I assure you my Regulators will smoke him out. Although I'm afraid this could take some time."

Wall ignitors sparked, and the entire concert hall brightened with multiple detonations of Light Grit piped in the same manner as the palace reception room. The Regulator chief leapt down from the stage to direct his officers. In seconds, the Reggies had fanned out along the aisles, making their crossbows and Rollers highly visible.

Ard turned to Quarrah, her face flushed nearly as red as her wig. Ard didn't know why *she* was so nervous. It wasn't Quarrah's likeness that the Reggies were passing around.

Perhaps Raek would make a move and attempt some daring extraction. He was supposed to be watching the concert hall from outside. Surely his partner had noticed the sudden assembly of Reggies.

"This is terrible," Lorstan Grale muttered to Ard. "Just terrible. Do you think it's possible? A villain in our midst?" The conductor moved away as a pair of Regulators ascended the steps to the stage.

Quarrah's nervous hand slipped into his. Ard would have liked to lay out some brilliant plan of escape. But the fact was, he didn't have one. Even if he did, it would have been impossible to share the details with Quarrah. Cantibel Tren and half a dozen other musicians were seated easily within earshot.

Another Regulator had taken the stage, and despite Lorstan Grale's protests, the Reggies were positioning themselves to verify the identities of the musicians. No one was beyond suspicion, a fact that should have made Ard feel proud of his reputation. For once, he wished people might not think him capable of so much.

One Reggie moved down the line of violinists, pausing only feet away from Ard and Quarrah to have a short conversation with Cantibel. She seemed to answer his questions adequately, speaking to the identities of several male musicians.

Then the Regulator turned toward Ard.

Trust the disguise. Trust Elbrig's coaching. Ard wondered if his sweat had caused the adhesive to slip on his false forehead.

"I just have a few questions for you, sir." The Reggie was holding a scribing charcoal in one hand, and a list of names in the other. "Can you state your—"

A gunshot sounded.

Ard's hand instinctively swung for his gun belt, but Dale Hizror didn't carry a weapon. Screams lit up the concert hall, and the patrons swarmed for the exits like a school of fish, Reggies taking up defensive positions at every doorway in an effort to contain the situation.

The Regulator questioning Ard promptly dropped his charcoal and paper in exchange for a Roller, turning away to find the source of the gunfire.

On the stage, the musicians were also in turmoil. Some abandoned their expensive instruments, while others tried to tow them along.

Quarrah had cast aside her bouquet of flowers and dropped into a defensive crouch. To Ard, her dress had never looked more like a disguise than it did in that moment. The body and stance were so clearly Quarrah Khai. The gown looked ridiculously out of place, spilling about her tensed figure.

Ard dropped to a knee beside her, his shoulder cape drooping across his arm as he touched her shoulder. "We have to get out of here," he whispered, casting his eyes over the chaos.

"Who fired that shot?" Quarrah asked.

"I don't know," Ard answered. The well-timed gunfire had to be Cinza or Raek. There would be time to ask later. For now, they needed to take advantage of the chaos and escape.

Ard saw the fallen list of names and the scribing charcoal. Snatching them up, he quickly scanned the paper until he found Dale Hizror. He crossed out the name, copying what had been done to the names of the male musicians the Reggie had already investigated. Ard dropped the list as Quarrah sprang up, grabbing his sleeve and pulling him across the stage.

They ducked behind the curtains and Quarrah gestured down a narrow backstage hallway. Other musicians were navigating toward the back exit, too, but the way was sealed off with a blast of Barrier Grit at the door, a pair of Reggies standing guard with loaded crossbows.

"Please return to the stage!" one of them shouted at the panicked musicians. "The situation is being handled, but it's necessary for us to get a proper accounting of every man and woman!"

"Oh, flames," Quarrah muttered, pulling Ard back around the corner. She dashed partway down the narrow hallway and opened a door, pushing Ard into the performers' lounge, where Quarrah had been so nervously awaiting her performance. Funny, in many ways she seemed calmer now that the Regulators were searching for them and their lives were in danger.

Maybe Raek was right about Quarrah. Maybe she and Ard *did* go well together.

Quarrah shut the door and leaned against it. Gratefully, no one else had sought refuge in the lounge, so they would be able to speak openly.

"We have to assume that the Reggies are covering all the exits," Ard said.

"They have to make sure the king gets safely away," added Quarrah, "but they're also hopeful to use this opportunity to trap you."

"I don't understand!" Ard slammed a fist against the table of desserts. "How did they know I was going to be here? And in disguise, nonetheless."

The implications sickened him. Only a handful of people knew about Ard's attempt to infiltrate the king's orchestra. Were they dealing with a spy?

"Not all the exits are blocked," Quarrah said. "There's a glass skylight above the mezzanine."

"You consider that an exit?" Ard cried. "It's probably fifty feet up."

"Thirty, if we jumped from the mezzanine," said Quarrah.

"You can't jump thirty feet," said Ard. "Why are we even discussing this?"

"We need to do *something*," cried Quarrah. "If we stay here, our false identities are shot. The Reggies aren't going to stop until they find Ardor Benn."

Ard put a hand to his fake forehead, running through a number of possible scenarios. He couldn't jeopardize Dale Hizror's character. Especially not now, after Lorstan Grale had acknowledged him in front of the king. If the Reggies were determined to find Ardor Benn, then perhaps he should give them what they want.

Ard reached down and scooped a large dollop of sweetened cream from the top of a plum pudding.

"Oh, seriously?" Quarrah protested. "Why don't we just fill ourselves with pastries? That might stop a ball from passing through your gut."

But Ard wasn't planning to eat it. Stepping over to a standing mirror, Ard slapped the cream against his face, massaging it over his thick sideburns and mustache. Reaching into his vest, he drew a short knife from a leather sheath. It was a poor excuse for a weapon, but it was the only thing Elbrig would approve for Dale to carry.

Ard placed the sharp edge of the blade against his cheek and dragged carefully downward, shaving off the sideburns along with the makeshift shaving cream. He understood now why Elbrig had suggested adhesive facial hair. It would have made the task of transitioning between himself and Dale much quicker.

Well, he'd certainly be needing adhesives now.

As soon as the deed was done, Ard stepped over and blotted his face on the tablecloth.

"You can't turn yourself in," Quarrah said, as Ard worked his fingertips under his artificial eyebrows and peeled back the false forehead. With it came the long wig, and Ard scratched his fingers through his real hair to alleviate the itchiness of the hairpiece.

"Turn myself in?" Ard crossed to the wardrobe beside the mirror. "Now, that wouldn't be very clever at all." He stripped off his shoulder cape and his vest, donning a long black coat from the wardrobe.

He now held an incriminating bundle of clothes, as well as the wig and forehead, which simply couldn't be left behind as evidence for the Regulators. "Stuff these down your bloomers." He tossed the items to Quarrah.

"Excuse me?" Was she seriously blushing now?

"The bustle on your dress is wide enough to hide the bulge," Ard explained. "Now stuff those down your bloomers, or I'll come over there and do it myself."

That gave Quarrah the motivation she needed. Turning away from Ard, she hiked up the front of her lacy burgundy dress and began packing the cape, vest, and wig into her bloomers. Ard scoured the room for anything else that might be useful in their escape, but it was a performers' lounge, not a mobsters' hideout.

Quarrah turned back to him, letting her dress fall to her ankles. She shifted uncomfortably, scratching at her crotch in a very unladylike fashion.

Ard nodded knowingly. "The wig itches." He stepped over to Quarrah, positioning himself directly behind her. "Azania Fyse," he whispered. "I'm afraid Ardor Benn is going to need a hostage."

Ard put one hand around her middle and brought his short knife up to her throat. They moved as one toward the door. Quarrah sighed heavily at the way things were developing.

"This is your plan?" she hissed. "You're going to get us both shot."

"Nonsense." Ard threw open the door to the backstage hallway. "The people loved you tonight. They won't let the Regulators take unnecessary risks."

They ducked out of the performers' lounge to find the hallway vacant. Ard relaxed his grip so they could move swiftly while not being seen.

"I have an idea," Quarrah whispered as they paused by the curtains. The Regulators seemed to have successfully herded all the musicians back onto the stage and the patrons into the seating area. A frantic feeling still emanated from the concert hall, but the Reggies were getting things under control to resume their search for Ardor Benn.

"We're going to need Drift Grit," continued Quarrah.

"How much?"

With so many Regulators in the venue, there was bound to be Grit. Crossbow Drift Bolts were standard issue on the Regulation sash, but each bolt created a blast radius of only about fifteen feet.

"We need enough to Drift Jump from the stage to the skylight," said Quarrah.

"You're back to the skylight?" Ard hissed. "Drift Jumping is a great way to get yourself killed."

His last Drift Jump had been unusual, propelled haphazardly

over the docks of Marow with Raek. Usually, the jumper simply sprang from the ground. Ard knew plenty of people who had done it wrong. If the person didn't stick the landing, they would come crashing down through the Drift cloud from a dangerous height.

"I do it all the time," replied Quarrah.

"At fifty feet?" Ard noticed Quarrah's lack of reply. If one Reggie Drift bolt created a radius of fifteen feet, then two should make thirty, right? That would be a sixty-foot diameter, if he could somehow detonate them in the center of the room.

But no, Ard remembered Raek saying something about how the effect didn't truly double with twice as much Grit. Raek had probably gone on to spout some equation about energy loss and consumption, equal to the weight of a horse's behind...

Sparks! Where was Raek when he needed him? Simultaneous Grit detonations were a complicated thing. Raek had once described it to Ard by saying that a single detonation was like tossing one stone into still water. It created a unique set of ripples, originating from a specific point. Once those ripples were rolling across the water, a second pebble could be tossed beside the first, creating a new set of ripples that would outlast the first.

However, if someone were to throw a fistful of stones at the same time, the ripples would be indistinguishable from one another, making what appeared to be a larger splash than any single stone.

Ard's takeaway from that was: more Grit bolts equalled bigger boom. And without Raek to run a complex mathematical equation, Ard was going to have to calculate it his way.

Overkill.

"You ready for our scene?" Ard took his stance with the knife to Quarrah's throat. "Remember. Whatever happens, I'm your enemy out there."

Ard shoved Quarrah past the curtains, stepping into the Light of the reflected detonations above the stage.

"Ladies and gentlemen!" Ard's voice was loud enough to demand attention over the hubbub of the concert hall. "I believe someone was looking for me?"

Two dozen Rollers and a dozen Reggie crossbows trained on him instantly. That got the blood pumping. But garnering some attention as Ardor Benn was exactly what he needed to do in order to steer any possible suspicions away from Dale Hizror.

"Let's not be pointing those things in the direction of this beautiful young lady." Ard kept his body close behind Quarrah's to prevent any clear shot. "Let me explain how things are going to go here. The two Regulators nearest me are going to deposit their weapons and bolt sashes in front of Lady Azania. This simple act will prevent me from slicing open her elegant neck. And between you and me, I don't think her vocal cords will sound nearly as impressive *outside* her throat."

Ard waited until the nearest Reggies realized that they were the ones to relinquish their weapons. They unclipped their belts and sashes, stepping toward Quarrah.

"Slowly," Ard cautioned, visibly tightening his grip on Quarrah. The last thing he would need was for some hotheaded Reggie to slam the sash down, detonating all the various Grit bolts in an effort to entrap him.

Fortunately, the two Reggies were compliant and a decent arsenal was now at his disposal. He pushed Quarrah forward as the Regulators retreated. Glancing down, Ard took stock of what was available.

Two crossbows, four Rollers, two dueling swords, and the Grit bolts on the sashes. Ard tried to remember what Raek had taught him about the coding system for the clay-tipped Grit bolts.

Blue for Barrier. Green for Drift. Yellow for Blast Grit.

"All right, sweetheart," Ard said to Quarrah. "Slowly reach down and pick up eight bolts with green tips." *Eight ought to do the trick, right?*

Ard and Quarrah bent as one. He kept his knife to her throat but managed to reach around and grab the nearest Roller. Judging by the weight of it, the thing was still loaded. Once Quarrah succeeded in picking the bolts off the sashes, they stood together.

By now, the Regulator chief had reached the stage, stepping past a frightened looking Cantibel Tren and Lorstan Grale, and stopping beside his two disarmed Regulators. The chief had his empty hands in the air and a composed look on his face.

Only minutes ago, Ard and the chief had been standing side by side before a large audience. Had no one truly recognized him? Did it only take some fake hair and a shoulder cape to make people think he was someone else entirely? It was funny how blind people could be.

"Ardor Benn." The chief's tone was calm and unthreatening. "Please put down the weapons and step away from the lady."

"Who told you I would be here tonight?" Ard demanded.

"Put down the knife and gun, and I'd be happy to share that information with you."

Clearly, the chief had been trained in hostage negotiation. No sense in wasting time talking. Ard had a lot to do tonight. He had exposed himself as a ruse artist and been positively identified. In order to exonerate Dale from suspicion, he'd have to race back to the bakery, don the fake sideburns and mustache that Elbrig had encouraged him to wear, and return to the concert hall before everyone departed.

"Everybody back up!" Ard waved the loaded Roller toward the Regulators on the stage. Dragging Quarrah as he strode forward.

He couldn't imagine doing this with a real hostage. It simply wasn't his style. There was no *class* in threatening an innocent person. Ard feared what this might do for his reputation.

They had reached the front of the stage, standing near Lorstan Grale's podium. Raising his Roller, Ard pulled back the Slagstone hammer and felt the cylinders lock into place. Aiming at the dark glass of the skylight overhead, he pulled the trigger. It shattered, eliciting screams from the patrons as glass rained down on the seats.

"It's been a pleasure." Ard tucked the Roller into his pants and took all eight bolts from Quarrah. He gripped them like the bouquet of flowers that Quarrah had dropped, the round clay tips bunched at one end. "You can tell Noet Farasse that he picked the right soprano, even if the lyrics of his aria were atrociously fawning. I may not be of noble blood, but I surely enjoy a night at the symphony. Good evening, everyone!"

Ard reached out and smashed the heads of all eight Grit bolts against the podium stand. The effect, as Raek had described it, was like many stones splashing through the still surface of a quiet pond.

There was a slight outward rush of energy. Just enough to kick everything up off the floor and send it adrift in the sudden weightless environment. Chairs and music stands were suddenly afloat alongside a stage full of startled musicians and expensive instruments. The Reggies nearby, including the chief, were pulled off their feet and sent, arms pinwheeling, into the air.

The only reason Ard didn't drift away was because he was holding on to Quarrah. And Quarrah, obviously experienced in detonating Drift Grit at her feet, had the wherewithal to seize the edge of the anchored podium.

Ard glanced up, squinting against the mirrored lights above the stage. The air seemed hazy and discolored all around them, but he had no idea if the detonation cloud had reached as high as the shattered skylight.

He noticed people in the mezzanine, holding on to the backs of their seats as their feet came off the ground. That was a good sign, at least.

Ard leaned forward, pressing his mouth close to Quarrah's ear. "All right," he whispered, though no one was likely to hear him over the screams in the weightless room. "How do we make this jump?"

Quarrah gently released the edge of the podium, drawing into a crouch, her burgundy dress hanging weightlessly around her like a sail. In the utter chaos of the hall, Ard hoped that no one would see him let go of the knife. It floated out of his grasp so he could hold on to Quarrah with both hands.

Quarrah looked up, and Ard assumed she was checking the angle to the skylight. "On three," she said, whispering the numbers back to Ard. They sprang upward, both of them kicking off the stage with as much force as they could muster.

In the weightless environment, the two figures hurtled upward, angling out from the stage and over the heads of the terrified patrons. The skylight was growing rapidly closer. Now past the blinding stage lights, Ard could see stars in the square of dark night above.

The cloud of Drift Grit ended just two or three feet shy of the broken skylight. Ard and Quarrah exited the top of the cloud, the distinct feeling of gravity returning below them. The momentum from their jump propelled them the needed distance, and Ard's shins clipped the rim of the skylight as they toppled onto the gently angled roof.

"You have to tell Raek what we just did!" Ard said, lying still for just a moment while he tried to orient himself. "He's never going to believe that we pulled off a Drift Jump that large without his calculations."

A handful of gunshots sounded from the hall below. If Ard and Quarrah had successfully made the jump, then it was possible that a skilled Regulator might be able to follow them up. Ard rolled onto his knees, shins throbbing from the landing. Quarrah was already on her feet, looking as lithe as a cat on the rooftop. She must have lost her high-heeled shoes in the jump because her bare toes curled around the shingles.

She stepped over and hoisted Ard to his feet. "We have to get moving," Quarrah said. "The Reggies will reposition themselves outside to catch us as we come down."

"*I* have to get moving," Ard corrected. "Now that I've made it out of the concert hall, taking a hostage would only slow me down. Besides, I need you to stay behind and corroborate our story. Give me time to return as Dale Hizror." He gestured for her to hike up her dress. "I'll need my costume back."

"What's our story?" Quarrah asked, digging ungracefully in her bloomers, the chill night air causing her to shiver once.

"Ardor Benn caught you and Dale fleeing backstage," said Ard. "He knocked Dale unconscious and stashed the body in the lounge before using you as a hostage. That'll give me a reason to seem confused and disoriented upon my return. Then tell them that Ardor abandoned you up here once we came through the skylight."

He accepted the vest, cape, and wig from Quarrah, tucking them under one arm as he drew the stolen Roller from his pants.

"You should be able to get down on the southeast corner of the building," Quarrah suggested. "There's a tiered outdoor balcony with a canopy covering. The support ropes should hold your weight."

Had she noticed that when they'd come in? Ard was once again impressed with Quarrah's ever-observant eye.

"Thanks." Ard thought it was unusual for a captor to thank his hostage for her help. "Raek will have seen the commotion. He'll have the escape carriage waiting." Ard turned in the direction Quarrah had indicated, but paused. "Oh, and Quarrah. At least *try* to look scared when they come up to retrieve you. I doubt Azania Fyse has spent much time on rooftops."

Quarrah nodded, but the message didn't seem to sink in. She stood, balancing on the ridge of a gable, her bare feet as comfortable on the tiles as most people were on the dirt.

"Maybe sit down," Ard suggested. "Scream a little. I'll be back in a half hour or so. And by the way, you really did an exceptional job with the aria tonight." He bowed to her in the fashion of royal courtship, her gorgeous figure silhouetted against the night sky. "Beripent's rising star."

Then Ard turned and dashed across the rooftop.

~

There is a beautiful elegance to the sounds of this place. The chatter of birds at dawn, and the rustling of wind through the canyons are almost like a symphony to my ears.

CHAPTER

14

"Ardy!"

He awoke with a start, sitting bolt upright on the couch. The smell of fresh baked goods filled his senses, and morning light cast dusty rays through the window of the bakery's upper room. Had someone shouted his name?

The door from the hidden entrance banged open and Elbrig Taut came tumbling into the room. "Sparks, Ardor Benn! Would you care to explain what you're doing?"

"I think I was sleeping," Ard replied. "And I think I was enjoying it."

"Obviously, you were sleeping!" Elbrig cried. "But why were you sleeping *here*?"

Ard rubbed his tired eyes. That was a good question. Everything was a bit of blur after last night's escapade in the Royal Concert Hall. Ard had successfully made it off the roof and into Raek's waiting getaway carriage. They rode like there was a dragon chasing them—all the way to the Avedon apartment. There, it was a quick matter of applying some adhesive to his upper lip and cheeks and slapping on the artificial facial hair. He donned his wig and disguise, freshly tacking down the forehead, before racing back to the concert hall.

The whole thing went off rather smoothly. Dale Hizror was found puttering around the back patio, dazed and confused from a supposed blow to his head. Azania Fyse confirmed his story, and the two of them departed without an ounce of suspicion befalling them.

At the first opportunity, Quarrah had slipped away into the night. It was kind of unsettling for Ard to realize that, after all these cycles of working together, he still didn't know where Quarrah slept at night. She assured him that she had a safe place where no one would bother her. The woman surely valued her alone time.

"I set you up in a spacious apartment with six windows, a double-wide hearth, and an enormous poster bed," grumbled Elbrig. "And you choose to sleep *here*?" He was picking up Ard's vest and shoulder cape, which had been heaped carelessly on the floor.

For years, Ard and Raek had shared lodging. Currently, it was a musty little place not far from the bakery. With Ard spending more time at the Avedon apartment, Raek was probably enjoying the place to himself.

"Put these on. You must leave at once." Elbrig threw the vest and cape at Ard. Then he moaned in despair. "Look at the state of your shirt! You can't sleep in those clothes, Ardy. They need a good pressing, and there's simply no time for that."

"Whoa, Elbrig," Ard said, tugging on his vest. "What's the hurry? Where am I supposed to be?"

"You're supposed to be where you should have been!" cried Elbrig. "448B Avedon Street."

"Why are you so worked up? It's too early for this." Ard had seen vigor and intensity from Elbrig on many occasions. But this was edging more toward panic.

"A visitor, Ardy!" he cried. "Dale Hizror has a visitor at his door!"

"Well, the visitor will have to wait," Ard said, pulling on his long leather coat and tying on his shoulder cape. "Dale had a rough night."

Elbrig reached out, grabbing Ard's clean-shaven face with both hands and looking him straight in the eyes. "King Dietrik Pethredote!" he hissed. "The king of the Greater Chain is calling at your door, and you're not there to answer it!"

Ard felt his stomach tighten with anxiety. Sparks, the king had left the palace to make a personal call? Last night must have really made the right impression.

"Did I lock the door?" Ard muttered. "What if the king's Reggies force their way in?"

"We can hope he's calling to congratulate you, not arrest you," Elbrig said. "And if he were to let himself in, King Pethredote would find a perfect gentleman's apartment."

"Umm…" Ard scratched his chin. "Have you been inside lately?"

Elbrig's expression instantly darkened. "What have you done to 448B, Ardy?"

"Nothing," Ard said. "*I* didn't do anything. But Raek may have moved a few crates of stolen Rollers into the apartment a few days ago."

"What?" Elbrig's hands balled into fists.

"We're just storing them for a friend." Ard crossed the room and dropped into a chair to pull on his boots. "Have you met Darbu? Solid Trothian. Barely speaks a lick of Landerian, but he moves product at an impressive rate. Said he'd swing by this morning and get the guns out of our hair."

"Before or after the king?"

"Yeah, I can see how this might complicate things," Ard said. "I'll just keep the king on the front step."

"It's winter!" Elbrig moaned. "Oh, Raekon has ruined us!"

Ard reached down and snatched his wig and false forehead from the floor. He didn't even remember peeling it off last night.

"What is this carelessness?" Elbrig cried, snatching the wig from Ard's hand and placing it loosely on his head. "This hairpiece is a significant part of Dale Hizror's identity. Would you leave your *real* scalp lying about like this?"

"I imagine if I did, I'd have other things to worry about," answered Ard.

"Hold still." Elbrig took something from his pocket. It was a little bottle of adhesive and a fresh mustache and sideburns. Where had the ones from last night ended up? Did he leave them at the Avedon apartment?

Ard pinched his lips together as Elbrig used a tiny brush to paint below his nose. The stuff smelled awful, and Ard didn't want to know what it was made from. Elbrig made a few stripes from his ear to his jawbone, and then dabbed a bit across his forehead, between his eyebrows, and across his temples. Elbrig capped the bottle and tucked it away. To speed the tackiness of the adhesive, he blew in Ard's face, his breath smelling strongly of rosemary.

"Maybe the king won't wait around for me," Ard said, trying not to move his lips as Elbrig pressed the mustache into place. Missing this opportunity to build confidence with the king would be unfortunate. But getting caught with five crates of illegal guns would be more so. "It's a twenty-minute carriage ride to Avedon Street."

"You'll need to do it in half that time and hope the king is a patient man," said Elbrig, securing the sideburns and artificial forehead. "This meeting could be very beneficial for your ruse. I've got a horse waiting for you outside. Make up a good story about where you've been. And Homeland help us all if the king gets cold."

Ard stood up and cast a glance over the room to make sure he hadn't forgotten anything. His eye caught the chalkboard, and he suddenly remembered why he'd come to the bakery last night. He'd needed to be in his thinking space. He'd needed to scratch out some thoughts on his chalkboard. Only one word was written there now, but it reminded Ard why he hadn't been able to fall asleep at the apartment.

GUNSHOT?

"Elbrig," Ard said. There wasn't time, but he had to ask. "We nearly got made last night. The Reggies knew I was going to be at the concert in disguise."

"Yes, yes." He shooed Ard toward the door. "Cinza filled me in on the whole thing."

"Did she fire the gunshot?" Ard asked.

"Gunshot?" Elbrig cried. "What are you talking about?"

"When the Regulators moved to question me, someone shot a Singler and set the hall into chaos. Saved my skin."

"It certainly wasn't Cinza," said Elbrig. "She only lingered long enough to hear that windbag conductor present you as the composer of the Unclaimed Symphony. Once the Reggies started pouring into the hall, she slipped out the back. She said the charcoal sketch of you was downright ghastly."

"Raek didn't fire the shot, either," Ard mused. He'd asked his partner the moment he climbed into the getaway carriage.

"Well, perhaps it was King Pethredote," Elbrig said sarcastically. "You should ask him. I hear he's waiting to talk with you." He shoved Ard toward the door.

Ard checked through the slot to make sure no one was in the bakery below. He scrambled through the false chimney, and crossed the shopfront, pausing just long enough to snatch a fresh cinnamon doughnut. He was rarely awake early enough to eat them warm. This was indeed a special day.

Ard found Elbrig's horse waiting just outside. Stuffing the doughnut into his mouth, Ard leapt into the saddle and dug in his heels.

Ard rode so fast that he worried the hair might fly right off his face. He had a solid story in place by the time he reached Fariv Lane.

Ardor Benn was about to talk to the king! It was one of those days that he wished he could tell his parents about. They had always spoken of King Pethredote with the utmost respect and appreciation. He had improved life tenfold for the working-class citizen.

Ard's father used to tell him of times before the crusader monarch—when taxes were double, and education for the common citizen was unheard-of. When the Regulation was a cesspool of crooked officers who enforced their own law. When Heat and Light Grit were so expensive that only the rich and noble could afford any.

King Pethredote was known for his Paladin Visitant. He was known for ending the war that King Barrid had started. But anyone with a glimpse at history could see that his influence went far beyond that. King Pethredote's policies had done exactly what a crusader monarch was intended to do. Inter-island relations hadn't been this stable in centuries.

Sparks, Ard's train of thought was starting to sound an awful lot like the adulatory lyrics of the Unified Aria.

Ard turned onto Avedon Street and slowed his horse to a trot. He'd never seen the roadway so crowded! Outside his closed apartment door were at least twelve red-uniformed Regulators on horseback. And maybe a dozen more of the blue-coat street Reggies. A crowd of citizens had gathered, filling in the empty spaces like sand poured over a pile of rocks.

At the center of it all was a royal carriage, parked in the very middle of the street, creating an effective blockade. It was a gaudy thing, raised absurdly high, with painted wheels and decorated horses. The carriage door was open, and the step stool in place, but Ard saw no one inside.

Sparks. Had the king gone into the apartment and found the

weapons? Had this whole thing turned into a setup? Nothing to do but move ahead and hope for the best.

Ard urged his horse forward, pressing into the crowd and forcing the citizens to make way. He was halfway to the carriage when he spotted the king. Good. He was still outside.

King Pethredote almost blended with the crowd. He wasn't very tall, with a stocky build that had grown soft around the edges with age. His trimmed beard was mostly gray, matching the hair on his head. His skin was brown and somewhat wrinkled, but his blue eyes seemed to twinkle with a youthfulness. The man was dressed like a noble, with a heavy wool coat under a long red shoulder cape that nearly touched the ground. He did nothing in particular to stand out, but Ard knew immediately who he was by the way the crowd interacted with him.

The king stood among the citizens, shaking hands and exchanging brief words. The people around him were awed by his very presence. Pethredote commanded a certain reverence in the street.

This was the most powerful man in the Greater Chain. And he was calling at Ard's door. Of course, this man was also the Focus of Ard's ruse. But years of trickery had helped Ardor Benn to separate the person from the job. He had cheated plenty of honest nobles. Ard had full confidence that King Pethredote would rule just as effectively without a coat and crown of dragon shell.

One of the horseback Regulators saw Ard approaching and repositioned her mount to cut off access to the king. In response, Ard swung down from the saddle and proffered the reins to the Reggie.

"I believe His Majesty is waiting for me," Ard said.

Her eyebrows raised with the acknowledgment of who he was. "Of course, Mr. Hizror." She took his horse's reins. "Go ahead."

Ard ducked through the ring of Regulators until he reached the empty carriage. As soon as he stepped into sight, the king turned away from his adoring crowd to address the person he had come to see.

"Dale Hizror!" King Pethredote exclaimed, his arms wide in a warm gesture.

Ard did the only sensible thing and took a knee, head bowed low in respect. King Pethredote swept forward and took him by the shoulders, pulling him back to his feet. Ard stood face-to-face with the king!

For once, Ardor Benn had no words. He tried, but they came out jumbled. He took a deep breath to compose himself, remembering to subtly change the timbre of his voice to match Dale Hizror's. "Apologies for my tardiness."

The king grinned. "You cannot be late to an appointment you didn't know you had."

Wise words, and a forgiving schedule. Ard liked this guy already.

"You must be an early riser," he continued. "I had been hopeful to catch you before you went out this morning."

Early riser? Ard didn't want to commit his character to such a terrible practice. "Actually, I didn't even make it home last night." This was the story he'd crafted on the ride over. "My dear fiancée was a bit shaken up after last night's debacle. Understandably, she did not want to be alone."

"How lucky for you," said the king with a roguish wink. "May we go inside?"

"In . . . inside?" Ard felt his heart skip a beat.

"This is your residence, is it not?" King Pethredote gestured to the door labeled 448B. Ard wondered for a moment how the king had found him. Probably Noet Farasse. The composer would have been quick to tell His Majesty that he knew the residence of the man who wrote the Unclaimed Symphony.

"It is indeed," Ard said, with what he hoped was a confident tone. "But perhaps we would be better suited to converse in Your Highness's carriage."

"Oh?" the king remarked. "And why is that?"

Think, Ardor. Think of something clever. "Lately, the flue has been acting up. Drafting smoke back into the room something terrible. At times the place looks more like a tavern than a proper gentleman's apartment." Especially with five crates of guns lying around.

"Shouldn't be a problem this morning, if you were out all night," replied the king. Well, flames. One good story had to shoot the other one. That was the problem with making things up on the fly.

"Besides." King Pethredote stepped over to the carriage's open door and reached inside. "I've brought something to share." He produced a bottle of scotch. "Too early for drinks?"

"Never," Ard replied. But he and the king couldn't very well stand around trading swigs from the bottle in front of the whole neighborhood. Well, at least he might get a good swallow in before being hauled off in shackles.

"Please." Ard gestured toward the apartment door. "Let's take this inside."

Immediately, two palace Regulators were at the king's side as they moved toward 448B. Ard absently withdrew the key, his mind running full speed while trying to think of any way out of this. The Reggies would probably perform a brief inspection of the room before the king was allowed inside. Perhaps Ard could use the element of surprise to knock them out, slam the door, and escape through the back window. That would be the end of Dale Hizror, and the ruse to steal the Royal Regalia would be back to square one.

Ard pushed open the apartment door, bracing himself for the inevitable as the Regulators casually swept in. Pethredote didn't even wait for the all-clear sign, stepping over the threshold just behind Ard.

Holding his breath, Ard scanned the spacious room. Somehow, *miraculously*, the five conspicuous Roller crates were gone. Homeland be praised! Darbu, their Trothian contact, must have picked them up from Raek earlier this morning. The space in front of the double-wide hearth was now vacant.

Ard felt his muscles relax in silent relief, glancing over the room to make sure there weren't any other incriminating things on display. He didn't spot anything illegal, but the place could have done with a good cleaning.

Ard's dirty socks littered the floor, and the table was crowded with paper wrappings from that sandwich place down the street. Ard was sure the large bed wasn't done up, but at least he'd left the four-poster curtains closed so the king couldn't see his wrinkled blankets.

"By the Homeland," King Pethredote remarked. "I'd say you need to hire a new housekeeper."

"I'm afraid I haven't got one at all," Ard admitted, closing the door behind him while the two Regulators stood stoically beside the windows.

The apartment really was quite nice. Everything from the artwork on the walls to the color of the rug had been hand-selected by the disguise managers as a fit for Dale Hizror's tastes. There was a composing desk in one corner, where Ard continually practiced his notation. That at least added a bit of veracity to the place. Then again, Ard sometimes doodled little mustaches and hats on the semibreves, so perhaps it was best if no one inspected his work too closely.

"Aspiring composers don't have a lot of Ashings—or time—to spare on keeping house," Ard continued.

"Aspiring?" King Pethredote cried. "You, good sir, have already achieved! You can only imagine my surprise when I learned your identity at last night's concert."

Ard faltered for a half a second before realizing that the king wasn't talking about his identity as Ardor Benn, the ruse artist whose presence at the concert had incited mayhem.

"Yes," Ard replied. "Well, it wasn't necessarily my plan to come forward about the symphony. But Lorstan Grale is an astute man, and I figured it was only a matter of time before I was found out."

Ard hoped that statement didn't hold true for his real identity. "Can I take your coat and cape?"

"Thank you." He unclasped them and Ard helped him slip out of the heavy winter fabrics. There was a chill inside, but Ard couldn't very well light a fire after all that nonsense about the flue backing up. With the king's wool coat and cape draped across one arm, Ard crossed the room to the large wardrobe and pulled open the door.

Blazing sparks! Raekon Dorrel was in there!

Ard slammed it shut, casting a quick glance over his shoulder to see if any of the other three people in the room had noticed the large bald man crammed into the otherwise empty wardrobe. The king was studying his bottle of scotch, and the Reggies were staring out the window.

Ard wanted to risk a second peek, just to make sure that his eyes hadn't tricked him. What was Raek doing in the wardrobe? He must have just finished business with Darbu and didn't have time to get out of the apartment before the king and a host of Reggies arrived outside.

"Just remembered," Ard said, crossing the room. "Terrible moths in that wardrobe. Big ones that have a knack for chewing things up. I'll just put your things on my bed if that's all right." He reached the large four-poster and drew back one of the curtains.

And there was Darbu. Sitting on top of five crates of illegal guns.

Ard dropped the king's coat and cape and let the curtain fall back. "Definitely time for a drink." He retrieved two glass tumblers from a rack and used his forearm to sweep the table clear of its paper wrappings. It was a rather undignified thing for Dale Hizror to do, but Ard needed some liquor in him quickly to steady his nerves.

The king took a seat at the table, removing the cork from the bottle. "Will you indulge me for a moment?"

"Anything you ask, Your Majesty," Ard said, recovering some

composure as he settled into his chair. "It is you who have indulged me with your personal visit."

"The Unclaimed Symphony," the king began. "What you did with the episodes of the Rondo in the fourth movement was absolutely incredible. And bold, not to return to the tonic key for the final iteration of the theme. Very unexpected."

"That's something of my specialty," Ard replied. The king poured a shot of liquor into each glass.

"Tell me, Dale," said the king. "Are you a Wayfaring man?"

Ard picked up the glass and downed the scotch in a single gulp. "Absolutely," answered Ard. "In fact, I attribute much of the inspiration for the Unclaimed Symphony to the Urgings of the Homeland. I had always intended the development of that piece to represent the Homeland's commandment for us to drive forward and progress." It was a rehearsed answer. A poetic one that he and Elbrig had devised.

"Isn't that the very reason we love music?" Ard went on. "Every composer starts with the same available notes, but stretching before him is a seemingly infinite number of creative possibilities. Just as I can make something of those simple notes, I believe the Homeland can make something of me."

The king nodded, pouring Ard another shot. "As spiritual as you are talented." He downed his own drink and deposited the glass on the table. "Surely the Unclaimed Symphony is not your only composition."

"No," answered Ard. "But it is the only one that has been performed outside my head."

"I intend to rectify that tragedy," stated Pethredote. "Are you familiar with the Grotenisk Festival held in Beripent during the First Cycle?" Ard could feel it coming. This was what they'd hoped for!

"Yes, of course," said Ard. "Wonderful event. I've personally attended twice." It was an unapproved detail that Ard threw in, and he hoped it didn't contradict anything from Dale Hizror's file.

"Then you know it has become tradition each year to debut a new musical work," King Pethredote said. "It is my hope that you will accept my invitation to be the featured composer at this spring's festival."

Ard did his very best to look shocked. Then he let that emotion give way to excitement. The latter was totally natural. King Pethredote was playing perfectly with their plans for the ruse.

"I would be honored." Ard took a small sip from his glass. "That's only two cycles away. A rather pressing deadline."

"I understand," he replied. "I'll have my people bring by a thousand Ashings. Think of it as a commission for the project."

Ard nearly choked. One thousand Ashings? Someone would just stop that by like a neighbor dropping off a loaf of bread?

"Unless that sum is insufficient to cover your needs over the next two cycles."

"Oh, no," Ard said. "It's quite sufficient." He could live years on that. "I already have the score prepared, though scribing out the parts can be quite laborious."

King Pethredote waved his hand. "I have people for that! You are Dale Hizror. I can assure you that you'll never find yourself copying parts out of a score again." He poured himself another. "What's the piece?"

"A cantata," answered Ard. "Borrowing Wayfarist text from Isless Vesta's poem on the rebirth of Beripent after Grotenisk's destruction. A suitable topic, considering the festival."

"Indeed." Pethredote had an excitable look on his face. "Cantata. I imagine your beautiful companion will be the featured soloist?"

"Azania is already studying the part," answered Ard. "Unless another soprano would please His Highness more." It was a risky offer, but Ard was confident that Pethredote would choose Quarrah.

"Azania Fyse is a darling," answered the king. "Hearing her

debut your cantata would greatly please these old ears. How is she faring after last night's fiasco? I had already been whisked away when I heard that she was taken hostage by that savage man. Homeland be praised she was not killed."

"Azania is resilient," answered Ard, remembering Quarrah walking comfortably along the edge of the roof. "She will be fine."

"My people tell me they have been unable to find the man responsible," said the king. "They called him a ruse artist, but he seemed more of a violent thug to me. Opening fire during a Regulation inspection like that…"

Ard didn't point out that the criminal in question had not fired the first gunshot. The identity of *that* shooter was the second mystery of the night, following the question of how the Reggies had known Ard would be at the concert.

"I'm sure the Regulators will catch the criminal," Ard said. Another statement he hoped would never come true. "Word on the street has it that the man had no intention of harming anyone. They think he had come to the concert merely to prove a point. To listen to music only suitable for the ears of the rich and noble."

"Anyone who saves their Ashings for a ticket is welcome to the Southern Quarter, or half a dozen other concert halls on Espar," replied the king. "I can't fund free concerts year-round. That's what the spring festival is for. A concert for the common citizen. I'm not so exclusive as to deny them such a simple delight."

"No, indeed," answered Ard. "Your generosity is spoken of through all the Greater Chain. And now I can boast that I have experienced it firsthand."

"My scotch?"

Ard smiled. "Your commission of my cantata for the Grotenisk Festival."

King Pethredote nodded. "If the conditions are acceptable to you, here's how I'd like to proceed." He scratched a hand through his beard. "So much of the festival is about hype. I'd like to present you to the public, announce you as the composer of the Unclaimed Symphony, and get them excited for your upcoming cantata."

"A public announcement?"

"At the palace," said the king. "In two weeks' time."

Ard felt the tingling sensation of giddy success. This could be the opportunity they needed for Tarnath Aimes to get close to the regalia so he could complete his forgery.

There was just one thing he needed to check.

"What do I wear to such a public presentation?" Ard asked. "Should I try to match your attire?"

King Pethredote laughed. "I'm afraid that would be impossible, since I'll be wearing the Royal Regalia."

Now it was Ard's turn to laugh. "How foolishly presumptuous of me." Good. He'd confirmed that the king would be wearing the dragon shell. "I'll just wear something green."

King Pethredote slapped his hand gently on the table and stood up. "Keep the scotch. I must get back to the palace, and you must get composing."

To Ard's horror, he moved toward the four-poster bed to retrieve his coat and cape. Ard leapt up, passing King Pethredote in two big steps. But the king was close now. Too close for Ard to pull back the curtain. Instead, Ard simply stuck his hand through and began waving desperately. Darbu must have correctly interpreted Ard's gesture, because within a moment, he felt the Trothian press the king's coat and cape into his grasping hand.

Ard pulled it out from behind the curtain and helped slip it onto Pethredote's broad shoulders. The king clasped his shoulder cape and moved to the door, one of his Regulator escorts pulling it open for him.

"It was a pleasure, Your Majesty." Ard bowed once more.

"The pleasure was mine, Dale Hizror," replied the king. "I shall see you at the palace in two weeks. Midmorning."

King Pethredote and his Regulators strode out of the apartment, shutting the door behind them. It had barely latched when Ard leapt up from his bow, staggering forward to ram his key into the lock. Ard quickly moved to the window in time to see the king climb into the royal carriage. The Reggie horsemen led the way, and the entire processional moved down Avedon Street.

"Not a bad guy, old Pethredote."

Ard whirled around to find Raek sitting at the table, pouring himself a scotch. Ard motioned for his friend to pour him another.

"Sparks, Raek. Couldn't you have warned me that you were still in the apartment? I used a Trothian gun dealer as the king's coat hook!"

"Hey, Pethredote's policies have always been inclusionary toward Trothians," said Raek. "I'm sure he wouldn't mind."

"Should we tell Darbu it's safe to come out?" Ard asked. The Trothian could surely hear them, but he understood so little Landerian, he would likely wait until the others called for him.

"No rush," replied Raek. "Congratulations, by the way."

"On keeping your big shiny head hidden in that wardrobe?"

"That thing was not made for a man my size."

"That was an obvious oversight on Elbrig's part," Ard said. "Next time I'll make sure he furnishes the apartment with Raek-sized wardrobes."

Raek drained his glass in a swallow. "You want me to tell Tarnath about the public appearance in two weeks?"

"Might be just what we need to get him in contact with the regalia," Ard answered.

"You got something in mind?"

~

I do not feel like a guest here. Most days I feel more like an intruder, trying to catch a glimpse of the island's well-kept secrets.

CHAPTER

15

How is your ruse artist?" Lyndel asked Isle Halavend, as she took her usual place on the bench in Cove 23.

"He is proving to be as good as I had heard," answered Halavend. "Ardor has taken an elaborate disguise to infiltrate the king's own orchestra."

"A bold position," said Lyndel. "One he will need if he is to gain access to the Royal Regalia."

Halavend nodded. "Ardor told me the king came to visit him. His Majesty has commissioned him to debut a new composition at a festival in the spring, two cycles from now. The festival is to honor the defeat of Grotenisk and the rebuilding of new Beripent."

"I am familiar with it," said Lyndel. "I know many Trothians who have attended in years past."

"Yes," Halavend continued. "That is what makes the festival so wonderful. It is a coming together of all classes and races. Anyone is free to attend the concerts in the Char."

"Will Ardor have a chance to get close to the king as he prepares this new music?"

"He has already won the king over by claiming to be the composer of a famous symphony," Halavend explained. "Tomorrow morning, King Pethredote intends to present Ardor publicly from the palace."

"This all seems positive," said Lyndel. "Why do you look troubled by Ardor's success?"

"Ardor Benn told me that his location was betrayed at the concert two weeks ago," explained Halavend. "Homeland be praised that he made it out unscathed."

"A traitor?" Lyndel asked. "Someone involved in the ruse?"

Halavend shrugged. "Ardor does not know what to think. Since that incident, the ruse has gone on smoothly. Better than planned, in fact."

"He must be more careful," said Lyndel. "He does not know the consequences, should he fail." She paused. "Perhaps we should tell him."

"I have considered it," answered Halavend. "I don't think it would be wise. Ardor is a man easily carried away by his passions. His very name implies it."

"But perhaps that passion would drive him," suggested Lyndel. "If Ardor learned the truth, he would be more motivated than ever."

"Ardor Benn can be motivated by a million Ashings," Halavend said. "If he knew the reasons behind his job, I fear there would be no payment sufficient to stop him from telling others."

"But a day must come when everyone will be told the truth," said Lyndel.

"Yes, but not until our part is finished," Halavend replied. "If the truth gets out now, Prime Isle Chauster would easily link it back to me. You know I am willing to die for this cause, but not until the Visitant Grit is prepared. Not until you and I have discovered the true factors that make a person worthy to detonate it. Otherwise, what hope will mankind have in surviving the coming Moonsickness?"

"I suppose you are right," said Lyndel. "We will keep the truth between us. As we always have."

Halavend nodded. Their secrecy was more important than ever, especially considering all the things he'd learned since their last meeting. He knew the implications of his new discoveries were damning, but Halavend needed Lyndel's help to piece it all together.

"Ardor Benn's forger recognized the counterfeit dragon shell found by your divers," Halavend began. "Years ago, there was a man named Reejin who made a living creating replica shell fragments. The operation was very much illegal and funded by an anonymous source."

"That's it, then," said Lyndel, a hint of excitement in her voice. "We find this Reejin, and we can trace the shell back to the person who hired him."

"Reejin is dead," declared Halavend. "Twenty-eight years ago. Shot by bandits in the slums of Beripent in 1210. Two years after the plague that claimed the lives of the Bull Dragon Patriarchy."

"Are you saying these events are somehow connected?"

"I'm beginning to think that everything is connected," Halavend answered. "I'm just not sure exactly how. Reejin was commissioned by an unknown source to make replicas of hundreds of shell fragments. Plague strikes the bull dragons, eliminating any possibility of new shell, and two years later Reejin ends up dead. No more shell to forge. Reejin was obsolete."

"You believe someone had him killed?" asked Lyndel.

"Likely the same person who hired him to make the shell," answered Halavend.

"You don't think it is a coincidence."

"If it is," said Halavend, "then all my findings since our last meeting are riddled with such coincidences. There's a Wayfarist saying. *'A coincidence that strikes but once in a while is a blessing from the Homeland. A coincidence that strikes with frequency is a warning.'*"

"You have a suspicion?"

"More than a suspicion, I fear," whispered Halavend. "I believe Prime Isle Chauster is at the center of all this."

Lyndel drew back in surprise, but Halavend remained stone-faced. Since discovering the shell, he had learned too much to be surprised. He had steeled himself for the horrible accusations he was going to make against the head of the Islehood.

"Did you know that Frid Chauster had a brother?" Halavend asked.

Lyndel shook her head. "Another of your Holy Isles?"

"Quite the contrary," said Halavend. "The brother, Domic Chauster, was considered Settled by the Islehood, especially toward the end of his life."

"That must have been a burden for a man of Chauster's position," said Lyndel. She was an Agrodite priestess. Perhaps she had faced similar familial strain. Did Lyndel have siblings? Sometimes Halavend realized how little they really knew about each other's personal lives. The research bonded them, and there was little time for much else.

"It was widely known among the Islehood that the Prime Isle and his brother did not have a loving relationship," said Halavend. "But I have since discovered evidence to the contrary. I paid a visit to the brother's widow this week. A woman named Shristen. She lives here in Beripent."

"Visiting the widow of Chauster's brother does not seem a safe action," said Lyndel.

Halavend waved her worries aside. "It is common for the Isles to venture into the city to visit citizens, extending invitations to seek Guidance from the Homeland at the Mooring. I didn't tell her my name, but we engaged in an interesting conversation. Shristen said she hadn't been visited by an Isle since her brother-in-law had become Prime Isle. She thought such visits were forbidden due to her Settled late husband."

"Are they forbidden?" Lyndel asked.

"There is no official statement from Prime Isle Chauster against visiting his brother's family," said Halavend. He didn't tell Lyndel that it seemed to be an unspoken rule among the Isles and Islesses. Frid Chauster was a stern man. His brother was Settled. Who would be bold enough to cross that line—a line that Prime Isle Chauster himself wouldn't even approach?

THE THOUSAND DEATHS OF ARDOR BENN 257

"She was grateful for my visit, poor woman," continued Halavend. "Her husband is nearly twenty years gone, and last cycle she lost her only son to the Moonsickness."

"He was the one you saw in the Mooring?"

Halavend nodded, trying to blink away the memory of the sick young man. Glipp Chauster. There would be more on him later.

"Shristen was quite open about her husband's relationship with his brother," said Halavend. "Apparently, it was not the strained brotherhood that the Prime Isle led us all to believe. According to Shristen, Frid Chauster and Domic were actually quite close, from childhood until the cycle he died. In fact, they met together often, in private."

"Why would Chauster lie about such a thing?" asked Lyndel.

"He wanted there to be a social disconnect between him and his brother," explained Halavend. "If his brother's actions were ever made known, there would be no connection back to the Prime Isle."

"What actions do you speak of?"

"I looked into the breach of the Egrebel Dam in 1218," said Halavend. "A maintenance crew had recently performed improvements to the structure."

"Then it shouldn't have ruptured," Lyndel pointed out.

"The last person to work on the dam was Domic Chauster," said Halavend. "Reports say he stayed behind to make a final check on the dam's systems. It broke the next day."

"So Domic planted something in the dam to cause a failure," Lyndel said.

"A pot of Blast Grit would be sufficient," said Halavend. "And I believe he did it under the orders of his brother."

"The Prime Isle wanted to wash out the storehouses and destroy the shell."

Halavend nodded. "Because the shell was fake. It was fine to send false pots of Visitant Grit with the Wayfarist Voyages. No one ever knew if they worked anyway. But the Prime Isle knew that none of the detonations would succeed, because he had already hired Reejin to falsify the shell. He couldn't keep up the lie forever, so the breach of the Egrebel Dam took away the pressure. The other Isles understood why Chauster couldn't authorize more Visitant Grit: because, tragically, the flood had demolished all of the Islehood's shell reserves. But the general public was kept from the truth so they wouldn't despair."

"What, then, do we suppose happened to the *real* shell?" Lyndel asked. "If the dam breach served the purpose of washing away the counterfeit, then that leaves the original fragments unaccounted for."

"My thoughts exactly." Halavend's heart raced at the way she understood him, even anticipating his train of thought. "I examined many shipping records from the years when Reejin was counterfeiting. During that period, I found fourteen similar discrepancies.

"In each instance, a processing factory on Strind documented the weight of an outgoing Grit shipment. But when the shipment was received in Beripent's harbor, it was recorded to weigh many panweights less." He help up a finger to stop Lyndel from thinking it was a scribing error. "All of these discrepancies occurred on the same ship, under the same captain. One Mardin Wolsyn. And in every instance, the ship deviated from the most direct course, sailing into the deeper areas of the InterIsland Waters."

Lyndel nodded. "They were dumping genuine Visitant Grit overboard."

"Yes," Halavend whispered. Aside from detonating it, dumping Grit into the ocean was one of the few effective methods of destroying it.

"And what of this captain, Mardin?" Lyndel asked, though Halavend assumed she had already guessed the answer.

"Dead," he answered. "Drowned when his single-man skiff went down off the coast of Dronodan."

"And the Prime Isle's brother, Domic Chauster?" asked Lyndel.

"Poisoned himself a few cycles after the Egrebel Dam broke," said Halavend.

"I am beginning to see the repetitive nature of this coincidence."

"Sadly, this is just the beginning." Halavend took a deep breath. "Shristen told me that her son, Glipp Chauster, had been trying to contact his uncle for several cycles. The Mooring records indicate that the young man made more than a dozen visits here in the five cycles before his death. Each time he asked to meet with Prime Isle Chauster, but the Isle or Isless on duty had strict instructions not to let the boy in."

"Was the boy considered Settled, like his father?" Lyndel asked.

"Yes. And that was the Prime Isle's reasoning for shunning him," said Halavend. "However, according to the boy's mother, Glipp was finally invited to see the Prime Isle on very short notice. But not at the Mooring. Prime Isle Chauster wanted to meet his nephew on Pekal."

"Pekal?" Lyndel mused. "And now the boy is dead. Taken by the Moonsickness. I assume his uncle was not waiting for him on Pekal?"

"No, indeed," said Halavend. "But Chauster *had* been on the island the week before, preaching Wayfarism to the harbor Regulation. That way, he had a documented visit to Pekal. If anyone found out about the planned meeting with his nephew, it would appear as though Glipp had made an error and come a week too late."

"How did Glipp get approval to enter Pekal on such short notice?" Lyndel understood that there was significant paperwork involved to access the island.

"The Prime Isle provided him with the proper documents," replied Halavend. "Along with payment for the trip. Such tourist visits to Pekal are not cheap. When Glipp arrived to find his uncle gone, the lad decided to do one of the lower loop hikes through Pekal. The guide said a storm blew in and young Glipp was lost.

Forced to endure a Moon Passing on the island. There are few enough instances of Moonsickness these days, it seemed a terrible coincidence to have the Prime Isle's nephew contract it under such strange circumstances."

Lyndel nodded. "More likely the boy was abandoned on the hike. What of the guide?"

"She never reported back to work in the new cycle," Halavend answered. "No one has seen or heard from her since."

"It would seem that the Prime Isle wanted his nephew to contract Moonsickness," said Lyndel.

"The first stage causes the inflicted to go mute," said Halavend. "There is no more natural way to silence someone who knows something they shouldn't."

"So, what did Glipp Chauster know?" asked Lyndel.

"We may never find out for sure," said Halavend. "Shristen said that lately Glipp had taken an interest in his father's old ship manifests to Pekal."

"Was Domic Chauster a Harvester?" Lyndel asked.

Halavend nodded. "He signed on only cycles after his brother was made Prime Isle. Domic quickly rose to the rank of Tracer, working for the king's own Harvesting crew. Quite a prestigious position."

"Glipp had apparently spent significant time studying his father's manifests, and conversing about them with a Trothian neighbor."

"What kind of information do these manifests contain?" Lyndel asked.

"I wondered the same thing, so I procured a copy of every manifest from Domic Chauster's time." Halavend ruffled through some documents until he found the one he was looking for. "This is from his last Harvesting expedition, before Domic resigned. It lists everyone and everything that went to Pekal on his ship. As I compared this list to other manifests, I realized that the crew was much smaller than usual. Seventeen Harvesters were employed on that run." Halavend paused. "All dead now."

"Did the crew die on Pekal?" Lyndel asked.

"None of them, actually," said Halavend. "But that was the last expedition any of those Harvesters made. And aside from Domic's demise after the dam breach, all of the Harvesters on that expedition died within a year. Some fell sick with fever. Some were killed in accidents or muggings. Some simply vanished."

Lyndel sat forward slowly. He could tell she was beginning to suspect the things he did. *A coincidence that strikes with frequency is a warning.*

"But the size of the crew wasn't the only thing different about this final manifest," said Halavend. "All previous manifests for the king's Harvesting crew had been signed by a Gennet Brel. She was an advisor to King Pethredote at the time, and responsible for overseeing his Harvesting crew."

"She did not sign Domic Chauster's last manifest?" Lyndel asked.

"She did," said Halavend. "But the king made an addendum in his own hand."

"What did he add?"

Halavend turned to the second page of the manifest and tapped his finger on the spot next to the king's own signature. "Dried Turroc root and Stigsam resin."

"I know Stigsam resin," said Lyndel. "We call it Bemdep. Trothians use it with charcoal to make a waterproofing pitch."

"As do we," said Halavend. "But twelve barrels? I thought it strange to take unprocessed resin in such large quantities. The same goes for the Turroc root. It's a staple food, but a thousand panweights of dried root is enough to feed an army, let alone seventeen Harvesters on a single expedition."

"What is it like?" Lyndel asked.

"Turroc root?" said Halavend. "It's like a potato: bland and starchy. You've probably seen it in the Char. The vendors like to fry them and dust them with salt and pepper."

"Stoshk?" Lyndel stiffened. "What year did Domic's Harvesting crew make this expedition?"

Halavend looked down at the page's heading. "1208."

"And what cycle?"

He squinted. "The Eighth." Historically, it was an unremarkable time. It wasn't until the Ninth Cycle... It suddenly occurred to him. "This ship was the final Harvesting crew to visit Pekal before the plague befell the Bull Dragon Patriarchy."

"Turroc and Stigsam," said Lyndel. "Trothians call them by different names. Stoshk and Bemdep. Don't you remember? They are spoken of in '*Izmit's Drowning.*'"

"*Izmit's Drowning*" was an ancient Trothian poem, lengthy, if Halavend remembered correctly, about an Agrodite priestess who died around the year 550. Izmit wandered fifteen years on Pekal before attempting to swim the distance to the Trothian islets. She didn't survive the feat, but her religious insights on dragons were put to verse so they might be remembered and passed through generations.

Halavend had transcribed the poem under Lyndel's dictation several cycles ago. The tale couldn't have been true, for obvious reasons. Spending one Moon Passing on Pekal was enough to sicken a person, let alone fifteen years. Likely, bits of the story had changed over the centuries of retelling. As an Agrodite legend, Halavend was likely the only Holy Isle familiar with Izmit's tale. But he hardly knew it well enough to recall the reference Lyndel was making.

Lyndel was doubled over now, head nearly between her knees, long dark hair falling almost to the floor as she recited something in a low voice. The recitation was in Trothian, and Halavend waited patiently as she raced through her memory.

After only a moment, Lyndel sat up, her eyes still closed in concentration as she translated the excerpt into Landerian.

"'And I settle, wilting. I am as a dragon with a belly of Stoshk and Bemdep. I shall not see another day.'"

Lyndel opened her pale gray eyes, vibrating fiercely as she looked to Halavend. But he was thoroughly puzzled. "Explain."

"At the start of each new year, it is an Agrodite ritual for the priestesses to soak this dried Turroc root in Stigsam resin."

"Why?" Halavend asked. Stigsam wasn't edible, so what would be the purpose of combining it with Turroc?

Lyndel shook her head. "Tradition," she said. "You have your Holy Torch, we have Stoshk and Bemdep. When the root absorbs the resin, it undergoes a change. The odor is pungent, and the fumes can induce visions for the priestesses."

"But you don't eat it," Halavend clarified.

"That is the very point!" Lyndel cried, rising to her feet. "Stigsam-soaked Turroc root is a powerful poison. 'As a dragon with a belly of Turroc and Stigsam. I shall not see tomorrow.'"

Halavend felt the realization settle upon his old shoulders. After all he'd uncovered the last year, this was nearly too much to take in. "Homeland save us," he whispered. "There was no plague in 1208. The bull dragons were poisoned!"

He lifted a hand to cover his mouth. King Pethredote had sent the poison to Pekal. He had signed for it himself in a special addendum. He had eliminated the seventeen Harvesters so their dark deed would never be known. Oh, Homeland! The Prime Isle was not alone in his corruption. The crusader monarch was sitting on a throne of lies.

Lyndel reached out in comfort, her dark hand contrasting on his sea-green robes. "Let us make sense of all this," she whispered, sitting on the bench once more. "What do we know, in order of events?"

Halavend lowered his hand and took a deep breath. He needed to be a scholar now, to piece everything together. He thought back to the very start. To the moment when all of this started piling up.

"Pethredote took the throne in 1204," Halavend began. "He was the last successful person to detonate Visitant Grit. Two years after becoming king, he selected Chauster to be the next Prime Isle. Then, in 1208, the Bull Dragon Patriarchy perished, beginning the species' course to extinction. The Islehood's remaining shell fragments were falsified, and the forger killed by 1210. Lastly, the Egrebel Dam broke in 1218, cleaning up any evidence of the falsified shell."

Those were the facts. But the implications surrounding them were far worse.

"Does the king always select who will become the Prime Isle?" Lyndel asked.

Halavend shook his head. "Prime Isless Hin was already old when Pethredote took the throne. She suggested that he choose her successor—someone Pethredote could work well with. Someone young enough that they could serve many years together. He selected Frid Chauster, and Prime Isless Hin departed on the next Wayfarist Voyage."

"How did the two know each other?" asked Lyndel.

Halavend rubbed his head. It was difficult to remember back that far. "I believe Chauster was Pethredote's Compass—his private spiritual guide. Chauster was brand-new to the Islehood. It was quite a shock to learn that he would be the Prime Isle." Now he'd been in that position so long, it was hard for Halavend to think of anyone else. "We must assume that both men have been plotting together from the start."

"But we have no real proof against either of them," Lyndel pointed out.

That was by careful design, of course. Any evidence they might have been able to cobble together would only lead them back to Domic Chauster, the Settled brother. That was why the Prime Isle had publicly denounced him.

"Why?" Halavend muttered. "Why would they do such things?"

"To me it seems plain," said Lyndel. "Your king wanted to eliminate any possibility of a future Paladin Visitant. He wanted to be the last to successfully summon one."

Halavend nodded. It certainly seemed that way. "So Prime Isle Chauster eliminated any existing dragon shell, and King Pethredote made sure that there would never be more."

"What are we going to do about this?" Lyndel finally asked. "There is truly no one to trust, if your king is guilty of this crime."

"*Our* king," Halavend corrected. "You agreed to be his subject the moment you stepped foot on Espar."

"Pethredote may have opened the way for my people to dwell on your islands, but he will never be my king," said Lyndel. "You know I only stay in Beripent for our studies. Once this is over, I will return to the Trothian islets."

Halavend sighed. He would miss her company. If he even lived long enough to see this finished.

"I must warn Ardor Benn of our suspicions immediately," the old man answered. "He is to meet with the king and be presented to the public tomorrow. We always knew Pethredote was powerful, but he may be far more dangerous than we initially suspected."

"Indeed," agreed Lyndel. "A man of his position would likely do anything to keep a secret so large. This is growing risky."

"It was always risky, Lyndel," said Halavend. "We've been walking a dangerous road from the moment you first approached me in the Char."

"But I fear you have taken additional risks," she said. "The Prime Isle was already suspicious of you since you went to him with our findings about Moonsickness. Then you visited his brother's widow..."

"It was necessary," answered Halavend. "To find out what we just learned."

"I know." Lyndel nodded. "But you must be prepared to defend yourself."

Halavend laughed bitterly. "I'm not going to carry a Singler in the Mooring, if that's what you're implying!"

Lyndel reached down and drew a dagger from a sheath in her tall boot. She stood up slowly, holding the weapon out to Halavend.

"You must be joking!" he cried. The last time he had carried a knife, he had been searching for Ardor Benn. It had hardly made him threatening. He was an old man. He'd survived this long without needing to use a weapon.

"This is a Trothian Assassin Blade," Lyndel said. "I insist you take it."

Assassin Blade? What was Lyndel, a priestess, doing with *that*? Then again, he understood so little of her religion. Something unholy for a Wayfarist Isle wasn't necessarily unholy for an Agrodite priestess. But still, an Assassin Blade?

"The pommel can be removed." Lyndel unscrewed the little ball to demonstrate. "Grit is funneled inside and tamped into a groove at the center of the blade. The blade itself is composed of two separate pieces." She replaced the pommel and turned the dagger over. Where one side of the blade appeared to be tempered steel, the other looked like dark stone.

"Slagstone," she explained. "When thrust into an object, the two halves of the blade grate together, throwing a spark into the loaded groove. The Grit will detonate, making the attack very powerful."

Halavend held up his hands. "A barbarous piece of weaponry, to be sure. And one I cannot willingly accept."

Lyndel took a step closer, lowering the dagger. "I fear for you, Halavend. Each time I crawl through that tunnel, I wonder if I will find you murdered. You live under the Prime Isle's gaze. I have always worried he would uncover our meetings. Then I worried he would find out about your association with the ruse artist. Now this. Your Prime Isle is a dangerous man. He has killed before—maybe not with his own hand, but you yourself have uncovered a trail of bodies that lead back to him."

Clutching the two-toned blade gently, she extended the hilt to Halavend once more. "Take it. Or I shall leave it here anyway, and you can explain to the next Isle how a Trothian Assassin Blade came to be in this cove."

Relentless. Both in her pursuit of the truth, and in her insistence that Halavend arm himself. Lyndel was a rare ally in an age when the king and the very head of the Islehood were tainted with corruption. And Lyndel was all he had now that Isless Malla was dead.

Halavend reached out, his pale old fingers curling around the handle of the dagger. "It won't come to violence," he whispered.

"But if it does," replied Lyndel, "at least you will be ready."

The weapon felt heavy in his hand. Unnecessary. Who would come for him, Prime Isle Chauster? King Pethredote, himself? Ha!

No, he thought. *They will send someone.* A bandit in the street. A collapsing archway as he passed under. Poison in his cup.

Halavend tightened his grip on the blade.

~

Truly, nothing is grander than the dragons on these slopes. It is hard to believe that anything could threaten the existence of such powerful creatures.

CHAPTER

16

King Pethredote was dirty. Just when Ard felt like he'd met someone worth respecting, Isle Halavend had to go and spoil it. See, this was why Ard had given up believing in heroes. Any time he'd met one, the rug got swept out from under Ard's feet and he realized that the person he'd looked up to was a massive disappointment.

Ardor Benn followed his Reggie escorts through the palace, silently trying to remember the route to the throne room so he could report it to Quarrah.

Isle Halavend had quickly informed Ard of his findings that same morning. Ard had stopped by the Mooring on his way to the palace for the public presentation. Halavend had spelled out some pretty serious accusations against Prime Isle Chauster, too. The whole conversation left Ard's head spinning. He figured it would be for a while. Until he could fully wrap his mind around all the terrible things Isle Halavend had stated.

Since that revelation, Ardor had felt the meaning of his given name ignite like a detonation of Grit in his chest. Today's conversation with King Pethredote would be very different from the one on Avedon Street two weeks ago. Today, Ardor Benn was going after the king with all the zeal he had. He needed verification of Halavend's accusations. Ard needed to know for himself what kind of man Dietrik Pethredote was.

Ard made sure his personal quest for answers wouldn't jeopardize what the team had planned. Today's public announcement was about to make Dale Hizror's popularity explode. And if everything went smoothly, by noon, Tarnath Aimes would head back to Panes with all the information he needed to create a foolproof replica of the Royal Regalia.

The palace Reggies guided Ard to a tall set of double doors, seizing the iron handles and pulling them open. A servant stood inside the throne room, welcoming Ard with a subtle bow. "His Majesty is on his way up now. He will join you shortly."

Ard thanked the servant, careful to use Dale's slightly altered voice.

The throne room was a triangular shape, angling away from where Ard had entered. Along the far wall was a wide archway leading outside, heavy doors propped open. Curtains were drawn across the threshold, but daylight filtered through. Beyond, Ard knew, was the high balcony above the palace steps from which the king often made his public addresses. Ard could hear voices from the throng of citizens below, already gathering to hear the speech.

The actual throne was impossible to overlook, positioned in the center of the room. Ard had heard about it since childhood, but seeing it in person was more magnificent than any description.

It stood more than eight feet off the floor, a stone chair with a high back. But the height was not due to a raised pedestal or dais. The throne itself had been mounted directly atop a gigantic skull.

The skull of Grotenisk the Destroyer.

The creature's teeth were nearly as tall as Ard, and the skull was the length of three men. To further the magnificence of the king's throne, a blazing fire had been lit in Grotenisk's empty skull. The vacant eyeholes were aglow with a golden fury, and flames lapped through the teeth, curling up toward the arms of the throne. Two large chimney pipes vented smoke out the back, rising like twin pillars behind the stone chair.

It was more than a throne. It was a display. The skull was impressive. But Ard had seen the real thing on Pekal. And it was far more terrifying when the skull was attached to an enormous body, covered in scales, and breathing fire.

The living dragons Ard had seen weren't bulls, of course. Those had died out long before his time as a Harvester.

The Bull Dragon Patriarchy had always seemed like a rather fragile arrangement. It was probably great for the dragons in charge, but not the most considerate social structure for assuring the longevity of a species.

Three bull dragons.

Throughout history, there had never been more than three bull dragons living on Pekal at any given time. It was a statistic that could easily be maintained, since the gender of the hatchling could be determined by the color of the gelatinous egg. The bulls could fertilize as many white female eggs as they wanted. But the fertilization of an amber egg, which would lead to a male hatchling, would only occur when there was a vacancy in the Bull Dragon Patriarchy.

Ard stepped forward, feeling the warmth of Grotenisk's fire. According to the history books, this dragon had been a bull, not yet grown to maturity. With his death, one of the two remaining bulls on Pekal would have fertilized a male egg to keep the Patriarchy in balance.

But that was hundreds of years ago. Today, the Bull Dragon Patriarchy was gone, the trio of male dragons dead within a week. Wiped from the island so quickly that none of them had a chance to fertilize a new golden egg. And if Halavend's new findings were correct, then King Pethredote had been the cause of it.

Ard turned his attention away from the centerpiece. The throne was intimidating. Some might even find it terrifying. Not a very practical place to sit, though. Unless the aim was to cook a royal backside.

The walls of the room were pocked with half-circle alcoves set into the stone. They housed a variety of treasures, each gated with an iron grid and heavy lock. The throne room was an exhibit hall, Ard realized, stepping closer to examine the valuables.

The nearest was a spear with a rusted steel head. The craftsmanship was nothing extraordinary, and Ard would have dismissed it quickly if it weren't for the ceramic plaque mounted beside the alcove.

— YEAR 986 —

THE SPEAR OF KING KERITH

WITH WHICH HE SMOTE GROTENISK

A FINAL BLOW

Ard took a few steps forward, aware of the watchful eyes of the Regulators by the door.

The next exhibit seemed to be little more than a scrap of petrified wood, about shoulder height, a few corroded metal bands wrapping around its length. The plaque labeled it as a piece of the mast from the First Voyagers, who were supposedly the ancestors of all Landers. It was a nice sentiment, but Ard didn't believe for a moment that the wood was genuine.

Ard hoped the Reggies didn't see him scoff. If the alcove's claim was true, this piece of wood was over 1,200 years old. More likely it was a common piece of driftwood masquerading as a valuable relic. Ard grinned. It would seem that he and the driftwood had quite a lot in common.

Rumor had it that the Royal Regalia was usually stored somewhere in the throne room. It wouldn't be here today, of course. Ard was counting on the king to be wearing it.

He briefly scanned the other alcoves. A jeweled sword, a dragon tusk, an empty Grit pot. Each display held some significance to the monarchies of the Greater Chain. Predominantly the monarchy of Espar, dating back to a time before the islands were unified under one kingship.

"We keep the fire burning at all times." A voice caused Ard to whirl around.

King Pethredote was standing in the doorway. He looked much more regal with the extravagant Royal Regalia draping his frame.

A large fragment of dragon shell spanned the king's forehead like a crown, rising at least ten inches to a jagged point. A few other shell pieces wrapped around the back of his head, fastened together with metal rings that passed through drilled holes. How their ancestors had managed to drill through the shell was truly an impressive feat of craftsmanship.

The coat was constructed in similar manner, though the shell fragments were even larger. A good thing, too, since Ard was counting on them to survive the intense digestive acids of a dragon.

The coat itself hung past Pethredote's knees, hugging firmly around his stout middle. His shoulders were capped with more fragments, and pieces hung down his arms to the elbow. Unlike the white counterfeit shard from Halavend, the shell of the Royal Regalia was an amber gold. There was a polished shimmer to it, the way sunlight sparkled on tinted glass.

Ard knew he should drop to one knee in a humble bow. It was the proper thing to do when one found himself in the same room as the king. But today, he couldn't muster it. Today, the man before him was not worthy of Ard's respect.

The king gestured to the burning throne. "My servants always keep the fire going as a symbol. The dragon burned our city. Now we burn the dragon."

"I'm familiar with the throne's significance," Ard replied. "And I presume it keeps you plenty warm during the winter cycles."

"Ah, my boy. A sense of humor!" King Pethredote smiled. "A well-placed detonation of Cold Grit makes it a pleasant seat, even in the heat of summer."

A strange sound drew Ard's attention across the throne room. It was a snapping *croak*, like the noise of a giant toad.

"Ah, Millguin!" Pethredote shouted, moving toward the source of the sound. "Shush!"

Ard followed King Pethredote around the fiery throne as he approached one of the gated alcoves that Ard had overlooked. It was a small habitat, set behind tight metal bars. A stout tree limb was canted across the alcove, and perched upon it was a lizard.

The creature was nearly the length of Ard's arm, tail draped casually off the side of its perch. Its leathery skin was a muddy green, wrinkled like a discarded parchment. A fleshy beard dangled from its jaws, and large dark eyes flicked back and forth without the slightest movement of the head.

Pethredote unlatched the gate and reached into the habitat as Ard read the ceramic plaque beside the alcove.

MILLGUIN

KARVAN LIZARD—PEKAL

Pethredote stepped back, the lizard clinging on to the king's arm. Its sharp claws raked against the shell of the regalia as it settled upon Pethredote's shoulder.

"A baby dragon?" Ard tried to tint his voice with just the right amount of shock and awe. It was a ridiculous statement. Ard had encountered plenty of Karvan lizards on Pekal during his time as a Harvester. But Dale Hizror wouldn't know much of the creatures.

"Homeland, no!" Pethredote chuckled, reaching up to stroke the lizard's beard. "Millguin is a Karvan lizard. Fully grown. Docile. She feeds on leaves and crickets. Nothing so ferocious as a dragon. The only thing they have in common is habitat. Both dragons and Karvan lizards are indigenous to Pekal. But these little fellows do a bit better in captivity."

Ard stepped closer, pretending to be curious. "It's a pet, then?"

"A gift," Pethredote replied. "I've grown very fond of Millguin. She sits upon my shoulder when I'm found pacing the corridors on sleepless nights."

Sleepless nights. Ard didn't have to think hard about what might cause Pethredote an uneasy conscience. Time to find out for sure about Halavend's accusations.

"A gift, you said?" Ard pressed.

Pethredote nodded. "They say the lizards can live a century. Prime Isle Chauster gave me this one, some thirty years ago."

"Of course," said Ard. "He must have meant it as a symbol of your dominance over the Bull Dragon Patriarchy."

Oh, flames! Was he really going down this road so openly? Why couldn't he just keep his mouth shut and do the job? He liked to pretend that he didn't care, but when it came to looking someone in the eye who he thought was lying, Ardor felt a burning zeal to flush him out.

The king went absolutely rigid, his blue eyes piercing Ard. Those eyes were changing. Ard saw them transition from sociable and generous, to downright malevolent. Ard was in deep water now. Nothing to do but swim with the current.

"It's all right," Ard assured. "I know about what happened. The Turroc root and Stigsam resin."

"I don't know what you're saying." The king's voice was barely audible.

"I knew Glipp Chauster," Ard lied, using information he'd picked up from Halavend that morning. "He told me about the dragon poison."

The king suddenly clapped his hands for the Regulators at the doorway. Ard felt his stomach sink. He had overstepped the line, and now Pethredote would have him dragged away in chains. Instead of a celebrity, he would become a spectacle.

"Give us the room," Pethredote ordered, causing the Regulators to step out of the doorway without hesitation. The moment the double doors closed, the king whirled around to face Ard. "What exactly are you accusing me of?"

"I'm accusing you of protecting the Greater Chain against an inevitable attack," Ard said. "We rely too heavily upon those creatures. Over the last century, we have pressed harder, invading their territory. Testing more indigestibles for new, undiscovered Grit. We even cart away their dead so we can use bits of the carcasses."

Ard pointed at the king's burning throne. "If Grotenisk did as much damage as the historians say, imagine what a *swarm* of dragons could do if they grow tired of mankind's poking and prodding. Your Highness, there are many people who feel as I do on this matter."

King Pethredote was studying Ard. On his shoulder, Millguin mimicked his unblinking gaze.

Ard's reasoning was weak. Never in the history of the Greater Chain had a dragon flown out of Pekal. Isle Halavend believed that Pethredote poisoned the dragons to eliminate fertilized shell and solidify his place as the final summoner of a Paladin Visitant. But that angle was too blatant to use in conversation. And Ard needed to keep the king's suspicions away from the shell of the Royal Regalia.

Millguin croaked, breaking the long and awkward silence.

"The citizens grow restless." King Pethredote gestured through the curtained archway. His voice had turned cold and businesslike, a far cry from the tone he'd used as they shared a few drinks in Dale's apartment.

Pethredote returned Millguin to her alcove habitat, the lizard obediently moving down his arm onto the wooden perch. "We should begin the address," muttered the king, closing and latching the gate.

"Your secret is safe with me, of course," Ard said. Why was he still pushing this? Wasn't the look in the king's eye enough to confirm Halavend's suspicions? "With the extinction of the dragons, the safety of the Greater Chain will be assured for our future children and grandchildren. You have accomplished a brave deed, Your Highness, despite the need to perform it in secret."

King Pethredote suddenly spun around, catching a fistful of Ard's vest as he pulled him close. Ard felt the shards of dragon shell rubbing against him, their smooth, cool texture at odds with the king's outburst.

"This is not something you speak of," Pethredote hissed. "Not even here in the privacy of this throne room. Do you understand me, Dale Hizror?" Ard nodded, but the king wasn't finished with his threat. "I don't care if you are an esteemed composer. I don't care if you're a nobleman, a Trothian, or the Prime Isle himself. Some things are never spoken of under any circumstance, whether you are in favor or against. I don't know what Glipp Chauster thought he knew, but I assure you, the Turroc and Stigsam were used for the good of every man, woman, and child alive today. To ensure that nothing could erase the peace and prosperity that I have brought upon the Greater Chain."

The king released his grip and pushed Ard away. The older man seemed short of breath, his blue eyes full of a rage that could barely be contained.

"You tread on thin ice, speaking to me like that, Dale Hizror." The king adjusted the shell headpiece. "And your words have put me in a rather disagreeable state. I've half a mind to send you away. But alas, a crowd awaits, and rumor of my announcement on your behalf has already spread." He strode toward the archway where the curtain billowed slightly in the winter breeze.

"You will follow me out," ordered the king, "but you will not speak to the crowd."

Ard felt his trembling insides begin to still. That had been risky, even for someone with as silver a tongue as Ardor Benn. But the provocation had been successful. He could confidently report to Isle Halavend that his suspicions about the poison were confirmed. Perhaps that would earn him the right to know the Isle's motives for the Visitant Grit.

The king had all but confessed, which painted a rather large target on Ard's back, as Halavend would no doubt point out. Everyone else who had dug into the king's conspiracy against the Bull Dragon Patriarchy was dead. But Ard wasn't some retired Harvester whose murder could be attributed to a violent mugging. He was Dale Hizror, the composer of the Unclaimed Symphony. Ard was counting on his growing popularity to serve as some form of protection.

Besides, Ard had only risked confronting the king because of what he was about to do on the balcony. Any doubts that Pethredote had toward Dale Hizror would soon be relieved. If the plan worked, Dale would no doubt be counted among the king's most loyal subjects.

Pethredote parted the curtains to a ray of sunlight as he stepped onto the balcony. Ard followed closely, the winter chill refreshing on his flushed face. The crowd below was even larger than he had anticipated. Did so many people actually care about which composer would be featured at the spring festival? Or was it just an excuse to see their beloved king? They might make a different noise if they knew what Pethredote had done.

Everyone has a skeleton in the closet, Ard thought. Pethredote's closet must have been large, to accommodate the corpses of all three Patriarchal dragons.

"What a beautiful winter day!" King Pethredote's voice quieted the crowd. "Spring seems a distant thing, but it will be upon us before we know it. And with it, the Grotenisk Festival!"

He let the people cheer for a moment. Ard watched the king's pleasant demeanor rebuild at the adulation of the supportive crowd. Their encouraging shouts floated up like bricks in a cloud of Drift Grit to reconstruct a crumbling wall. A wall that Ard's words had broken.

"Each year, the festival brings an influx of tourism to Beripent. With that comes a chance for merchants and peddlers to earn some extra Ashings," the king continued. "Entertainment, too, is at its prime during the week, with a series of public concerts to be enjoyed at no cost. The pinnacle performance of the last three years has been my personal favorite—the Unclaimed Symphony. But that marvelous work no longer goes unclaimed. It is with great pleasure that I present to you the composer, Dale Hizror!"

Ard stepped up to the balcony's edge to applause from the crowd. He looked down at the faces of the citizens gathered below. Why would they care? Merchants, miners, fishermen, carpenters. What did it matter to them who composed some orchestral symphony that caused a stir among the nobility? And yet they clapped and cheered all the same. Maybe it was because music at the Grotenisk Festival was like a window into royal life.

The applause died as the king began to speak again. "In light of discovering Dale Hizror's true talents, I have commissioned him to compose a cantata to be performed at this year's festival. I'm sure it will be a spectacular work, and I, for one, look forward to its performance with great anticipation."

Any moment now. The king had finished his public acknowledgment of Dale Hizror. It was time for Quarrah to make her move.

The king licked his lips. "The performance will take place on an outdoor stage in the Char..."

Gunshots.

Two cracks from a Roller split the winter afternoon. The crowd below peeled away from the palace steps like ants whose hill had been disturbed. Screams and shouts filled the air as people made desperately to get away. It was a very similar scene to the concert hall two weeks ago. Except this time, Ard knew who'd fired the gun.

King Pethredote stumbled backward in surprise, his guards moving from the wings of the balcony to escort him to safety. But Ard reacted faster. He stepped in front of the king, his arms spread wide as if to protect Pethredote with his own body.

A third shot rang out from Quarrah's Roller. Ard slapped his shoulder, falling back against the king.

Concealed beneath Ard's shirt was a miniature teabag, less than a quarter pinch of Void Grit resting beneath a fragment of Slagstone. Wrapped around that was a sausage casing that Raek had filled with fresh pig's blood.

The Slagstone sparked under the force of Ard's slap, detonating the carefully measured Void Grit. Ard felt a stab of pain as the Grit formed a walnut-sized detonation cloud, pressing against his chest. At the same time, the force of the Void Grit ripped a hole right through his shirt, rupturing the sausage casing and spattering the blood in an impressive spray.

Pethredote grabbed Ard, lowering him to the balcony floor.

Ard's dripping hand reached out, smearing blood across one of the regalia shell fragments on Pethredote's chest.

One of the Reggie guards had his Roller trained on the scattering crowd below, while the other hurled a Grit pot at Pethredote's feet, a cloud of Barrier Grit springing up around Ard and the king. The Reggie guards positioned themselves defensively around the impenetrable Barrier dome, but at least for the next few minutes, the king and the composer were isolated and untouchable.

Ard sputtered and grunted, continuing to paw his bloody hands across the king's regalia. Pethredote looked panicked, kneeling beside the bleeding man.

"Get us out of here!" the king shouted to his guards through the Barrier dome. "This man needs a healer, for Homeland's sake! He's going to die in here!"

Ard knew as well as Pethredote that nothing could break through or move the Barrier cloud. Burrowing under the perimeter of a Barrier dome was one of the only known ways to escape. But that would be impossible here, with the balcony's stone floor.

It had been part of the plan, of course. It was standard procedure for the guards to contain the king in the safety of a Barrier cloud should there be a public attack. Ard's stunt with the fake blood had caused the king to hesitate on the balcony instead of retreating through the curtained archway, ensuring that the guards would resort to Barrier Grit.

The king reached for Ard's shoulder, but he swatted the hand away. The last thing Ard needed was for Pethredote to discover that there was actually no wound.

Come on, Raek.

There was an explosion beneath them. Ard felt the stones under his back shift and crumble. It was relieving to know that Raek hadn't misjudged the amount of Blast Grit to mount on the underside of the balcony. Too much would have blown him and the king to bits within the Barrier dome. But Raek was a genius on this matter.

The explosion was perfectly calculated to crumble a controlled portion of the balcony. Beneath Ard, the stones sloughed inward. The king cried out in terror, gripping Ard's shirt as they plummeted out the bottom of the Barrier dome.

The fall to the palace steps would have likely killed them both, especially with the rubble of the collapsing balcony coming down on top of them. But the same spark that had ignited the Blast explosion also detonated a large cloud of Drift Grit. Shards of broken stone hurtled through the weightless cloud like Roller balls, pushed by the explosion. But Ard and the king fell comfortably downward.

They had entered the Drift cloud with very little momentum, and that same force carried them down. It was a strange sensation, as though they were falling while time slowed around them.

Whether by Raek's design, or a slight miscalculation, the Drift cloud did not reach completely to the palace steps. Ard and the king exited the bottom of the cloud and plummeted the remaining four feet under gravity's usual care.

The king's regalia clattered noisily against the stone steps, the impenetrable shell protecting Pethredote from the impact. Ard sputtered and choked some more, although this time it wasn't acting. The force of the landing had jarred his back, stealing his breath.

Pethredote scrambled over to Ard, chunks of crumbling balcony falling around them like deadly hailstones. The king lifted Ard's head from the steps, cradling it in both hands.

"Help!" he screamed. A few street Regulators sprinted to the king's aid, ducking under the discolored haze of the hanging Drift cloud.

"We need to get you out of here, Your Highness." Ard heard Raek's voice before he saw him, wool Regulator coat hanging across his broad shoulders. At least he was wearing a Reggie helmet this time, despite Raek's complaints about how none would fit his bald head.

"No!" shouted the king. "He's been shot."

A medical coach pulled up at the bottom of the steps, marked with a pair of white flags. A wiry driver leapt down from the bench, gesturing frantically for Ard and the king to be brought over.

"I'm a healer!" the man shouted. Ard didn't recognize his voice or his face, but he knew that Elbrig Taut was beneath that clever disguise. Raek bent and scooped Ard into his muscular arms, descending the steps two at a time while the king scrambled to keep up.

The healer threw open the door of the medical coach and Raek passed Ard into the waiting arms of a curly-haired man with jewels in his ears. Elbrig ushered the king inside, following closely as he commanded the imposter Reggie Raek to drive the horses.

Tarnath propped Ard into the corner of the bench as Elbrig shut the coach door. Two small Light Grit lanterns illuminated the windowless vehicle.

"By the Homeland, sire! You've been injured!" Elbrig gestured to the blood that Ard had smeared across the regalia.

"I'm fine," answered Pethredote. "But this man's been shot."

Elbrig snapped his fingers at Tarnath. "Help the king out of his regalia so I can examine the wound."

Ard watched through squinted eyes as Tarnath grasped the fragments of shell on the king's coat. "Get your hands off me!" demanded Pethredote. "I'm fine. But this good man is dying!"

Elbrig reached out and took the king's wrists. "I'm sorry, Your Majesty, but you've been through a terrible ordeal. You may not feel pain due to the shock of recent events. You are the king. Regardless of other patients, it is my first priority to see to your well-being."

Tarnath had managed to run his hands across several pieces of shell, checking the metal loops that connected the fragments, and partially untying the leather back straps that held the coat on the king's body.

"This is outrageous!" Pethredote pushed away from Tarnath, and the forger sat back. Apparently he was done making the necessary observations about the regalia.

Pethredote's insistence to see Ard healed was a positive sign. Although Dale's words about the poisoned dragons had riled the king, Pethredote clearly had no intention of seeing the composer dead.

Elbrig finally turned to give Ard the medical attention he was feigning to need. Pressing both hands firmly against Ard's blood-soaked shoulder, Elbrig glanced back at the king.

"It's bad, sire. I'm afraid there is little we can do without the proper tools," he explained. "We need to detonate a Compounded blast of Health Grit directly into the wound."

The windowless medical coach came to an abrupt halt. Tarnath pushed open the door as Raek jumped down from the driver's bench. A second carriage, surrounded by Regulators on horseback, had intercepted the coach at an intersection.

Raek's broad face appeared in the doorway. "King Pethredote, your Majesty. An armed carriage has arrived to escort you back to the palace."

Pethredote didn't move. "I'd prefer to stay with Dale Hizror. See that he receives proper attention."

"I'm sorry, sire," insisted Raek. "That's just not a possibility. The shooter is still out there. It is our foremost duty to see you safely back to the palace."

Pethredote finally nodded, taking Raek's arm as he exited the coach. His crown was a bit crooked, and his coat dangled awkwardly from the leather straps Tarnath had loosened. Ard watched through half-closed eyes as the king crossed the street and entered the other carriage.

Raek jumped back onto the driving bench and Tarnath closed

the door. Ard sat up sharply, taking a deep breath and stretching his sore shoulder. That little Void Grit detonation was going to leave a bruise.

"Well, I'd say that went off rather swimmingly," said Ard. "You see what you needed to see?" he asked the forger.

Tarnath nodded. "It'll take some time to put the replica together, but I should have it done before the Grotenisk Festival."

Two more cycles, Ard thought. Dale Hizror would spend most of that time recovering from today's wound. It was perfect. Ard would remain fresh in the king's mind without having to make too many appearances as Dale Hizror. Azania, too, would be excused, as it would be expected for her to tend her recovering fiancé.

Two more cycles. Then they would steal the Royal Regalia and he could go back to being Ardor Benn full-time.

Elbrig reached out and adjusted Ard's adhesive mustache. "Sparks," Ard muttered. "Was it crooked?"

"Just a little," answered Elbrig.

"Do you think the king noticed?"

"Absolutely not," answered Tarnath. "He was pretty shaken up."

"Don't skimp on the adhesive next time," coached Elbrig.

Ard leaned back, feeling the pains of his daring stunt as the coach bounced along the cobblestones. What did Elbrig expect, falling from a balcony like that? That would be enough to put a crook in anybody's mustache.

~

There is no substitute for experience. Papers and books could only take us so far. In a case like this, I needed to be on the island. See it. Touch it. Breathe it in.

PART III

Who is watchful in the night, O ye Settled souls? The Holy Torch will tend itself. The Islehood is but a humble observer of such unspoken power.

—Wayfarist Voyage, *Vol. 2*

Red is the night, when that ember, whose brazier is the mountainside, watches over all.

—*Ancient Agrodite poem*

CHAPTER

17

Quarrah Khai was looking her best. Or rather, Azania Fyse was. The red wig had been reshaped for the occasion, trimmed a little in the front to let the ringlets fall at different lengths. Cinza had her in a pale blue gown for this reception. Not that it mattered much; Quarrah would be out of the cumbersome attire just as soon as Ard finished his chumming.

He did a lot of that, Ardor Benn. Ard's version of Dale Hizror was undoubtedly more charming than whatever character Elbrig had originally created. It surely wasn't a problem. The disguise managers provided a canvas with the outline sketched in place. But the details, the life of the painting, was left to the person who purchased the character.

Quarrah rocked back on the raised heels of her shoes. What life had she breathed into Azania Fyse? Quarrah had been playing the role for cycles now. But Azania was flat. Boring. Lifeless.

Quarrah felt like a wild animal, caged and on display. Like the captive Grotenisk from the lyrics of Dale Hizror's cantata. The costume did that to her, blazing wig and dress. The spectacles, however, she'd grown secretly fond of. With a slight magnification in the lenses, there was no disputing that her vision improved behind those obnoxiously colorful frames. When this was all over, Quarrah would purchase some sensible spectacles. A pair that held snug to her face with a lightweight wire frame.

Quarrah didn't know how much longer she could continue like this. The chill of winter had mostly run its course, and the promise of spring was in the air. It had been nearly two cycles since Ard had fallen from the king's balcony with a fake wound. Most of that time had been spent cooped up with Ard in that smelly apartment on Avedon Street, reading letters of well wishes from bootlicking nobles. Gratefully, it was improper for Azania Fyse to spend the night, so she still had her evenings to wander the city, eventually finding sleep at one of the two tiny tenements she rented.

King Pethredote had seen to it that Dale receive home deliveries of high-grade Health Grit. Ard was overly pleased with this unexpected bonus, as they now had quite a bit of the expensive stuff stored up.

Quarrah and Ard had only begun venturing out two weeks ago, when rehearsals for the Grotenisk Cantata were scheduled to begin. They rehearsed in the Royal Concert Hall, which was quite convenient for Cinza, who already had her routes beneath the stage well established. Lorstan Grale was always in attendance, but he had handed the baton to Dale Hizror. Now Ardor Benn was conducting the cantata.

Sparks. He *was* good. Conducting the king's Royal Orchestra? Six cycles ago, Ard didn't know a thing about music. But he must have been convincing, as the orchestra didn't complain. Not even the sour Cantibel Tren, who had been more than willing to correct Azania's key change in the second movement. Quarrah took the criticism with a nod, her mouth full of detonated Silence Grit. It was Cinza who grunted in frustration, her head lodged between Quarrah's thighs, and her grip tightening around her knees.

It was good to have Ard on the podium, however. He knew that Quarrah couldn't answer any direct questions, and structured the rehearsal to accommodate the ruse. Had Lorstan Grale remained in control, their secret surely would have been discovered by now.

Ard clinked a fork against his empty glass. A bit of ice rattled in the bottom, a favorite fad of the nobles. This time, there was a grape frozen in the little ice sphere.

Good. Ard was finally going to get this night moving along. She'd waited half a year for this moment. Literally.

"My esteemed colleagues and friends," Ard began, as the crowd in the reception hall quieted. "And Noet Farasse," he added, to laughter from the group. Farasse and Ard had developed a strange relationship since the announcement that Dale Hizror was the composer of the Unclaimed Symphony. They were openly hostile toward one another, but in a way that implied only good humor.

"Two nights ago," Ard continued, "I behaved irrationally and unacceptably." He reached up and brushed his fingers over his artificial mustache. It was a little mannerism that Ard was fond of whenever he portrayed Dale Hizror. Quarrah suspected that it was mostly to reassure himself that the thing wouldn't fall off while he was speaking.

"Those of you who were at the rehearsal know exactly what I'm talking about," said Ard. "And likely, news of my temper has already spread to those that weren't there." Ard dropped his chin slightly, a look of regret and embarrassment passing over his features. If Quarrah didn't know that this was part of the ruse, she would have thought he felt genuinely sorrowful.

Ard was referring to the exchange with Sem Braison, the timpanist in the king's Royal Orchestra. Sem was an affable fellow, quick to laugh, and quicker still to apologize for laughing.

The orchestration for the cantata presented a revolutionary challenge for the timpanist, requiring him to retune the pair of kettledrums midmovement. Sem had become quite skilled at turning the lugs and tightening the large drumheads. But the final movement didn't seem to provide him enough time to make the necessary changes, and Sem often struck the final drumroll only to find that the pitch was a half step too low.

At the last rehearsal, Dale had grown infuriated by Sem's

inability to make the change. And despite Sem's profuse apologizing, Dale Hizror had stepped down from the podium, crossed to the back of the stage, and used his knife to slash the drumheads to shreds.

"Sem Braison." Ard pointed to the timpanist, who stood among the crowd. "It is with profound sincerity that I publicly beg your forgiveness. What do you say, good man?"

Sem, comfortable in the back of the orchestra but unaccustomed to much attention at a reception, stepped forward hesitantly.

"I say, good evening, sir," answered Sem, to mild laughter from the group. "And it was quite a distinction to be at the receiving end of your perfectionism. How many musicians can say that the composer of the Unclaimed Symphony quite literally cut them down?" More laughter, Sem's included. "Indeed, it should be me apologizing, as I was unable to properly perform the notes you so carefully crafted. I do intend to play it right at the festival concert, however."

"How hard can it be?" droned Cantibel Tren, taking a drink from her frosty glass. "You only have two notes to choose from at any given time."

Sem laughed off the insult as Ard continued. "I, too, expect you to play it right. But in order to do that, I believe you'll need new drumheads." Ard clapped his hands, and two servants promptly appeared in the doorway. Between them, they bore Sem Braison's pair of timpani on a low wheeling cart, brand-new calfskin heads stretched across the frame.

About blazing time.

The nobles applauded their approval at Dale's gesture, as Sem made his way toward the repaired drums. The big speech, the delivery from the servants...It was all about the drama with Ardor Benn. If it had been up to Quarrah, she would have slipped the replica regalia through a window and crept inside to pick it up. But, no...

Ard had to hide the forged regalia inside a drum and parade it publicly in front of everyone at the reception.

"The heads are tanned calfskin Striker," said Ard, drawing all kinds of unnecessary attention to it. "I believe that is your favorite maker. I've also taken the liberty to install a new lug system. With improved threads on the bolts, and a reduction cog in the handle, this should allow you to make the tuning changes in the short measures I have written."

It was Raek's design and clever engineering. Quarrah respected the work he did and fully understood why Ard needed him. The big man could turn a hazelnut into a miniature Grit pot, or a drum into a smuggler's case.

Sem was circling the large drums, his hand rubbing along the upgraded frames. Quarrah found she wasn't breathing easily. All right, Ard. That was enough talk. The new drumheads were certainly opaque enough to conceal the regalia bundled inside, but Sem was the expert on this instrument. It wasn't wise to let him examine the drums so closely with such a crucial package stowed inside.

"Now, now," Ard said, as he pulled Sem's hands away from one of the drums. "You're still in public. You can get to know her later. Three days until the festival concert. I trust that is enough time for you to master the new tuning mechanism?"

"Thank you" was all that the excited Sem could manage.

Ard gestured to the servants, who stepped up to wheel the timpani cart away. "The reception hall is no place for a musical instrument. There could be spilled drinks, crumbled cake." Ard shrugged. "Who knows, maybe even a madman with a cheese knife."

Quarrah forced herself to laugh alongside the others. The drums were on the move at last, and with them, the item they had spent cycles to position. It was finally time for Quarrah Khai to do what Ard had hired her to do.

She moved toward Ard as the timpani exited the reception. Acting wasn't Quarrah's strong suit. She'd play this next part subtly, and let Ard sell it for her.

"I'm not feeling very well," Quarrah whispered, as Ard welcomed her with a hand about her waist. It was a rehearsed line. A trigger. But Ard responded so convincingly that Quarrah was momentarily afraid that he thought she was being sincere.

"Oh, my dearest." Ard's tone and volume picked up the attention of the nearest nobles. "Another episode?"

She lifted a lace-gloved hand to her forehead and nodded. "I'm afraid I need a moment."

"Of course." Ard led her through the crowd toward the door where the timpani had just exited. Several guests stared without reservation, so Ard decided to address them. "Regrettably, my sweet Azania and I must make an early exit tonight."

Another planned line to which Quarrah countered. "No, no, Dale. You're the guest of honor. I couldn't ask you to leave your own reception..."

A young palace Regulator stepped forward. "I could see to her safe return home, sir," he said to Ard. "I could summon a carriage."

That certainly wasn't a planned line, but thankfully, Ard responded to it well, getting them back on script. "Thank you, but that won't be necessary. I'll see her home myself. Poor thing hasn't quite been herself since that attack on the concert hall. Understandable, really. That lunatic criminal had her by the throat. She has since experienced occasional episodes of anxiety. Headache, nausea, shortage of breath. It will generally pass, but not in such a public atmosphere."

The crowd was watching sympathetically, several of the women nodding in understanding. Ha! If they only knew that the Drift Jump out the skylight had been *her* idea!

"Perhaps there is a quiet, dim place where I could take a moment,"

Quarrah suggested. "You could remain here and I could join you when I recover."

"There is a small service room down the corridor," answered the Regulator. "It isn't much, but it should be quiet."

"That would be wonderful," Ard answered. "If you'll show us the way, I'll see her comfortably inside and return to the festivities."

The Reggie nodded and stepped into the hallway, Quarrah leaning heavily on Ard's arm as they followed. They didn't need the Regulator's guidance. Quarrah had spotted the service room cycles ago, on their second venture into the palace. She had mapped it in her mind, and later determined it would be the perfect staging area. The entrance to the throne room was just around the corner.

Ard had described the throne room to her, including details on where he suspected the Royal Regalia might usually be housed. But Quarrah hadn't found those details nearly sufficient coming from Ardor Benn. The man could describe a filled doughnut with frightening clarity, but when it came to a secure room, Quarrah needed to see it herself.

She'd received that opportunity two weeks ago. Dale's pretend shoulder wound was healed enough to warrant another visit to the palace. This time, Ard took Quarrah with him. After Ard raved long enough about the magnificence of Grotenisk's skull, the king allowed them both into the throne room for a look.

The regalia had been there, displayed on a wooden mannequin, third alcove from the end. To reach it, Quarrah would have to bypass a mortise lock on the hallway door leading into the throne room. It was supplemented by a bar on the inside, but that would only be in use if someone wanted to shut themselves inside the room.

The second lock was even simpler than the first. A standard pin lock on an iron gate that closed off the display alcove. Quarrah could pick that in her sleep.

After all these cycles, it was surprising to discover such simple locks surrounding the regalia. But then, its location in the throne room was a formidable enough obstacle. With Regulators crawling the hallways, and consistent lighting, Quarrah never could have broken into the second-story room using her traditional stealthy methods.

The Regulator they were following reached the service closet and pulled open the door. A bit of illumination from the hallway Light Grit spilled into the dark room. Stacked inside were things typically useful for servants; trays, barrels, brooms, linens.

The only thing out of place was a low cart with the set of timpani. Only moments ago, Sem Braison's repaired drums had been stashed in the closet according to Dale Hizror's previous instructions.

"I'll get her settled," Ard replied to the Regulator as he pulled the closet door shut behind him and Quarrah.

The room was instantly plunged into complete blackness, only the outline of the door glowing where hallway light leaked through. Quarrah heard Ard rustling, followed by a crack of shattering clay as a pot detonated against the wall. A small cloud of Light Grit hung against the stones, smaller than her fist but providing sufficient light for a few minutes.

"You took your time in there." Quarrah stepped over to the pair of timpani.

"What are a few minutes in the grand scheme of things?" Ard dismissed.

But minutes were important to Quarrah. At times, a minute was all that separated a thief from a prisoner.

Picking the larger of the two drums, Quarrah felt beneath the rim and unclasped a series of latches. Raek's improvements to the drums actually had nothing to do with facilitating Sem Braison's tuning changes. Grabbing the *T*-shaped handles mounted to the top of the lug bolts, Quarrah lifted, the entire drumhead swinging upward on a concealed hinge. Quarrah reached inside the drum and withdrew a cloth bag.

The replica regalia was actually housed in the *other* drum. This bag contained her belts and tools, items Quarrah had been itching to wear for weeks now.

"Face the wall," she whispered to Ard. He turned obediently as she began to disrobe. The pale blue dress was not easy to slide in and out of, but at least Cinza had designed it with the laces on the side so she didn't need a second pair of hands to undress.

Quarrah dropped the dress behind an empty barrel, standing in her bloomers as she carefully reached into her wig and removed the pins that held it in place. Her natural hair was matted beneath, but in a moment she'd pull a cap over it anyway.

Having deposited the wig and spectacles with the dress, Quarrah reached into her bag and pulled on a tight black shirt. She quickly replaced her bloomers with fitted pants, keeping herself directly behind Ard in case he decided to steal a glance.

In another moment, she was ready. Various belts adorned her legs and torso, each carefully stocked with items she might need. Her lock-picking tools were in place, and Raek had outfitted her with Grit pots of nearly every type: Blast Grit, of course, though she hoped they wouldn't need to blow their way out of the palace. Then there was Light, Drift, and Barrier, mixed with various levels of Prolonging Grit. Those four basics she could understand, but Raek hadn't stopped there.

On a job like this, she didn't see much purpose for Cold and Heat Grit. Health and Memory Grit would only be needed if things went seriously wrong. Void Grit, Silence Grit, Illusion Grit, Shadow Grit. This was the final stretch of the ruse. Raekon Dorrel did not want Quarrah to be caught unprepared.

Quarrah pulled on her mostly fingerless gloves, feeling the tiny fragment of Slagstone against the tip of her middle finger. The sewn pockets on the backs of her hands, as well as her palms, had been loaded with her usual choice of Grit.

"All right," Quarrah said.

"Oh, I can turn around now?" he replied smugly.

"I thought you'd figure that out by now," answered Quarrah. "I've heard you say that you have eyes in the back of your head."

"I closed them while you were changing, of course." Ard grinned. "You ready to do this?"

"This may be the only thing I've felt ready to do since you hired me."

"Good luck, Quarrah Khai."

She stepped up to the open kettledrum. The wooden legs on the instrument looked a little spindly, but they had practiced at the apartment. The drum would hold her weight just fine.

Ard provided his shoulder as a brace while Quarrah swung her leg into the oversized drum. A second later, she was settling into its depths, curled tightly like a cat on a rug. She saw Ard smile before the calfskin drumhead swung into place, sealing her inside.

Quarrah heard the storage room door open, and felt movement as the instrument cart rolled forward, carrying her and the drums into the hallway. The cart paused, and Quarrah heard Ard's voice, presumably speaking to the Regulator waiting outside the service room.

"She's in quite a state tonight. I had my servants stow these drums in there, but Azania can't stand the sight of them right now."

"We could find her another room," came the muffled reply of the Regulator.

"Absolutely not," whispered Ard. "I just got her settled. Moving her would be a grave mistake. Better for me to push these kettle-drums a healthy distance away and come back for them later."

They rolled down the hallway, wheels of the instrument cart groaning against the added weight of a person onboard. What if the cart's axle snapped? Had they tested that possibility? Quarrah grimaced. If it were up to her, she'd be doing something far more trusted and safe. Like leaping along the palace rooftops. Or scaling the exterior stone walls.

It certainly wasn't comfortable inside the kettledrum. Quarrah once again cursed her taller-than-average stature. A more petite thief might have been able to sit up instead of experiencing the pain that Quarrah currently felt in her neck and knees. She didn't feel claustrophobic, though. Wedging herself into tight places was part of Quarrah's job description.

Ard would leave the kettledrums near the throne room entrance and return to the reception so as not to raise any suspicions. Quarrah would climb out of the timpani, pick the locks, replace the real regalia with Tarnath's replica, and slip back into the drums. A short time later, Ard would retrieve the drums, and return her to the service room so she could transition back into Azania Fyse. They'd spend the rest of the evening at the reception, with a promise to deliver Sem's new drums to the concert hall by tomorrow's rehearsal. That would give them time to get the drums out of the palace, rendezvous with Raek, and remove the stolen regalia from the timpani.

Tomorrow's rehearsal would come with no sign of Dale Hizror or Azania Fyse. Sure, their abandonment would leave Lorstan Grale scrambling to conduct the cantata, with only three days to find a replacement soprano. But that was hardly Quarrah's concern. By the time the cantata was scheduled to be performed, she would be on Pekal with Ard and Raek.

The cart came to a halt and Quarrah tensed, preparing to spring into action.

"I can't tell you how grateful I am to see the likes of you." Ard's voice came filtering through the calfskin drumhead. Who was he talking to? How was Quarrah supposed to pop out of a drum if the hallway wasn't vacant?

"Two strapping palace Regulators are just what I need." Ard tipped her off.

Two guards. According to their surveillance, there shouldn't have been guards in this hallway at this hour. It was customary to have them standing at attention during the day, when the throne room was unlocked. And throughout the night, servants were admitted every four hours to stoke the fire in Grotenisk's skull. But Ard had taken all of that into consideration. The fire had been tended just a half hour ago.

"I was wondering how you would feel if I left these drums under your watchful care for just a few moments," Ard said. Quarrah grimaced. Was he really going to leave her with a problem like this?

"Say," continued Ard. "What's that on your vest? Did you spill some soup?"

There was a bang, a crash, a grunt, a groan. Quarrah reached up and pushed gently on the calfskin drumhead, shifting herself uncomfortably to peer out. A hand seized the rim and flipped the drumhead covering fully open.

Ardor Benn was standing there, his lip bloody and his knuckles bloodier. Quarrah took his hand and leapt out of the kettledrum in a single bound, examining the results of the commotion she'd heard.

One guard was slumped against the large door to the throne room, unconscious. The other lay facedown on the stone floor.

"Sparks, Ard," she whispered. "What was that?"

"Smooth talking," he answered, stepping up to the second drum. "What?" He shrugged. "It's common knowledge that Dale Hizror has a bit of a temper."

"That's not a temper," Quarrah pointed out. "That's downright assault."

"Dale only has to last the night," Ard answered, unclasping the latches on the second drum and lifting the rim. "Come tomorrow, he'll be an enigma once more."

Ard reached into the drum and hoisted out a large bag with leather straps for handles. It was the replica regalia, supposedly an indistinguishable match to the original in weight, size, color, and texture.

Ard deposited the large bundle on the floor beside Quarrah. "I need some Barrier Grit," he answered, closing the lids on both drums.

"For what?"

He gestured to the two unconscious guards. "They're going to have a lot to say when they wake up. I want to make sure they're contained. At least until you have a chance to get out with the real regalia."

Quarrah undid one of her Grit belts and offered it to Ard, who studied it with a surprised expression.

"Raek labeled the Grit pots for you?" There was a hint of dramatic hurt in his voice.

Quarrah rolled her eyes and dropped onto one knee to examine the lock on the throne room door. It was as simple as she'd anticipated, and her tools were out in a flash.

"Why doesn't Raek label *my* Grit pots?" Ard carried on, unbuttoning his vest and lifting his shirt to fasten the belt around his bare middle. "He's always telling me I have to memorize the color code. That Moonsick cheater, playing favorites like that…"

Quarrah paid no attention to Ard as he dragged the first man down the hallway to the nearest unlocked door. She had her eyes closed, and her ear pressed against the door just above the mortise lock.

It wasn't challenging, but it required significant focus. Like jumping from stone to stone across a pond. With the slender instruments pinched between her fingers, Quarrah felt a bit of her lost vigor returning. She felt in control again. Confident. The opposite of how she felt when she played the role of Azania Fyse.

A final *snick* sounded in her ear, and Quarrah felt the throne room door unlock. She rose to her feet, glancing down the hallway. There was no sign of Ard or the unconscious guards. It must have taken her longer than she'd thought to pick the lock. All the time she'd spent memorizing lyrics, and practicing poses, Quarrah had never suspected that her true talents might grow rusty.

She pulled open the heavy door just enough to slip through. Stooping, she grasped the leather straps of the bag that held the replica regalia and moved into the throne room, closing the door behind her.

In the palace, Quarrah had grown accustomed to the steady, consistent glow of Light Grit detonations. But here, the only light came from the bonfire that raged within the frightening skull of Grotenisk the Destroyer. The throne seat was cloaked in shadow, and the flicker of the fire made the whole room seem shifty and mysterious.

Quarrah needed to act quickly. Ard's disposal of the Reggie guards was like a burning fuse. They no longer had the luxury of lingering casually at the reception. She needed to swap the regalia and get out of the palace before news of Dale's assault reached the Regulators. Or worse, the king.

On silent thief's feet, Quarrah Khai passed the skull of Grotenisk. The fire popped loudly, causing her to jump. Fire was a wild creature, moving and cracking of its own accord. She felt its heat and smelled its smoke, two more characteristics which distinguished it from the tameness of Light Grit detonations. She liked the flicker of firelight better. It almost made her feel as though she were out in the common neighborhoods of Beripent.

Quarrah passed the small gated habitat where Millguin was housed. The Karvan lizard was so still, Quarrah would have thought her sleeping if it weren't for the wide, dark eyes glinting in the firelight. "Creepy pet," she muttered. "Don't watch me."

At last, Quarrah drew quietly up to the alcove where she had seen the regalia on display. But what was this? The iron gate and standard pin lock had been replaced! Now there was a heavy wooden door, cut to the specifications of the alcove's opening, blocking her view of the regalia within.

The lock was unlike anything Quarrah had seen before. She stooped to inspect the mechanism. At its center was a pin lock, which should have led to a sigh of relief. But the device around it looked like a deadly game trap. Two jagged metal plates were held open like jaws, and the trap's trigger seemed fused to the lock.

Quarrah snapped her fingers, the fragment of Slagstone on her middle finger striking the pocket of Light Grit in the palm of her glove. It ignited, a small cloud of steady light hovering just inches in front of the trap.

She could see it clearly now. The device was a clever piece of engineering designed to slam shut the moment the lock opened. Whatever key had been forged for this particular lock must have had a long shank, allowing the jaws of the trap to spring around the shaft without closing on the person's hand. Quarrah, obviously, had no such key. And her tools required her hands to be close against the lock. Flames. The trap would snap around her wrists!

Well, wasn't this why Ardor Benn had hired her? Quarrah thought back to her "*audition*" more than six cycles back when Ard had tested her adaptive skills against that supposed Lemnow painting. Quarrah would do now what she'd done then.

Improvise.

What were her options? A detonation of Blast Grit would tear the mechanism to shreds, and Raek's generosity with the Silence Grit could cover up such a detonation. But this wasn't the kind of job to go leaving evidence.

There wasn't much point in replacing the Royal Regalia with a replica if she left the lock blasted off and the door dangling. Quarrah didn't know if Tarnath's counterfeit pieces would hold up under that kind of scrutiny.

No, the trap lock had to be removed intact. Not only that, but

Quarrah would have to find a way to reset it after she exchanged the regalia.

She needed something to jam the metal jaws, stop them from clamping shut. A tiny bit of Barrier Grit would do the trick. But then she wouldn't be able to reach past the detonation cloud to access the lock.

Perhaps Void Grit? Its repelling properties might be strong enough to push back the toothed jaws of the trap. Of course, that same power would repel her hands, pushing everything outward. That wouldn't work. Unless...

Reaching down to her belt, Quarrah removed a clay pot of Void Grit. Raek had labeled this one, mixed with Compounding Grit to magnify the potency of the Void Grit's outward push.

Using the tip of her boot knife, Quarrah picked away at the wax plug that Raek had applied over the filling hole. Upending the pot, she poured the tiniest bit of the white Grit into the palm of her hand. She wasn't too worried about the Slagstone sparking inside. Detonation pots were made with an anti-ignition agent mixed into the clay.

Quarrah brushed the loose Grit to the side of her palm and into the mesh pocket at the base of her thumb. The Light Grit that had been in there before would have burned away with her latest detonation.

Her lock-picking tools in hand, Quarrah reached past the dangerous jaws of the trap. She worked quickly and easily to bypass the first internal pin, knowing that the trap wouldn't spring until she touched the second.

In a moment, she was in position, holding perfectly still. Though she couldn't see the inner workings of the lock, Quarrah knew her pointed tool was hovering a hairbreadth below the pin. Carefully, she transitioned both tools into her left hand.

Turning her right palm upward, Quarrah snapped. Her middle finger came down, Slagstone fragment sparking against the mesh pocket at the base of her thumb. The Compounded Void Grit ignited instantly, throwing its effect faster than she could blink.

Three things happened nearly simultaneously. The Void Grit pushed the pointed tool upward, thrusting it into the final pin and forcing the lock open. As a result, the trap's metal jaws snapped shut. But they had only closed halfway when they encountered the expanding cloud of Void Grit. The jaws wobbled, half-closed, the mechanism's powerful springs fighting against the repelling strength of the Compounded Void Grit.

At the same time, Quarrah's hands were thrown downward. The force jammed her fingers, and her wrist barely caught the teeth of the trap as it exited the Void Grit cloud. Quarrah cupped the stinging injury with one hand as a line of blood appeared through the torn cuff of her black shirt.

At least it had worked! The Compounded Void Grit had pushed the open lock upward, rattling against the latch but unable to fall back into the detonation cloud. Quarrah grasped the edge of the lock and maneuvered it loose. As soon as it was free, the powerful Void Grit expelled the lock with full force, tearing it from Quarrah's grasp and sending it clattering across the floor.

The orb of Light Grit suddenly winked out. Quarrah hadn't added any Prolonging Grit, so it didn't fade or give her any warning. The throne room was once more a flicker of shifting shadows from the fire in Grotenisk's skull.

Quarrah seized the edge of the wooden door and tugged it back, grateful that her potent detonation of Void Grit hung just out of the door's path.

There was a sound. A soft *pop*. Different from the crackling of the bonfire throne behind her. Quarrah didn't even have time to glance up. Something struck her in the chest with such force that her breath was knocked away.

She hit the stone floor, sliding backward and striking something solid. Grunting, she tried to focus as she pushed herself up. The air around her was discolored. Hazy.

Sparks! She was inside a cloud of Barrier Grit!

The dome had sealed all around, a radius of maybe fifteen feet. Standard Regulation Grit bolt. She found the shattered fragments of the clay bolt littering the floor around her. Peering through the haze, Quarrah saw the open alcove where the Royal Regalia was supposed to have been.

A naked wooden mannequin stood in the display space. Rigged over the right shoulder was a Regulation crossbow, the trigger wired to a peg on the wooden door.

Quarrah slumped down again, her chest aching and her wrist bleeding. The actual regalia was nowhere in sight, and the replica rested in its bag, just out of reach beyond the border of her temporary Barrier prison.

This whole night had been a setup.

~

*It's worrisome to think that after all this effort,
I could still fail.*

CHAPTER

18

Ardor Benn dabbed his bleeding lip with a handkerchief, took a deep breath, and stepped through the doorway to rejoin the throng of guests still enjoying the reception. He had to put in at least a few minutes of face time before excusing himself to check on Azania.

Quarrah was fast, as he'd seen the night they'd met in the dungeon of Lord Wilt's manor. She was probably nearly finished by the time he had properly secured the two guards.

As long as no one found them, the guards wouldn't pose a threat. They were in a small room, bound, gagged, and secure inside a detonation cloud of Prolonged Barrier Grit.

Prolonging Grit had a strange effect on Barrier clouds. Over time, the impenetrable wall would soften. Eventually, the Barrier would decay enough that the guards would be able to press through and escape. Of course, that would take more than a half hour. By that time, he and Quarrah would be making their public exit from the palace.

"Ah, there you are!" called Jat Eygar. He was a trombonist in the orchestra. Ard knew all of the musicians by name now. It was a personal touch that might offset any doubts they had about his musical abilities.

"Yes," Ard answered. "I had to get my beautiful fiancée situated comfortably, you know."

"By the Homeland!" Jat exclaimed. "What happened to your lip?"

"Never argue with a soprano whose nerves are on edge." Ard dabbed self-consciously at the split. "It's really nothing."

"His Majesty will be glad to see you've returned." Jat dropped the issue before it became more awkward. "He was asking after you."

"King Pethredote?" Ard asked. "He's here at the reception?"

"Arrived only seconds after you left with Azania," answered the trombonist. "He's over by the drinks. Was talking to Lorstan Grale." Jat pointed across the busy reception hall, but Ard couldn't see through the crowd. He nodded to the musician and excused himself.

Pethredote didn't normally make an appearance at these receptions, but Ard took it as a sign of good fortune. It was risky to run a ruse like this when the most powerful man in the building was unaccounted for. Pethredote's presence here actually put Ard's mind at ease. He could engage the king, which would keep him from wandering down to the throne room. It would also solidify Dale's alibi should anything go wrong.

Ard pushed through the crowd, stepping around a group of chatting women, and finally caught a glimpse of King Pethredote. That was when everything started to spiral out of control.

Oh, flames. The king was *wearing* the regalia!

Pethredote was adorned the same way he'd been when Ard had met him for the public presentation. The fragments of amber shell shimmered in the glow of the Light Grit chandeliers, his fractal coat hanging just past his knees. The crown was on his head, tufts of his graying hair visible beneath the elaborate headpiece.

Ard clenched his teeth to steady himself. If the regalia was draped around the King, then what was Quarrah going to steal from the throne room? This was the unpredictable variable that presented itself in every ruse. The musicians had said he rarely came to the receptions, and when he did, Pethredote certainly never wore the Royal Regalia!

Ard crossed to the king, pasting a smile on his split lips. "Your Highness! You're looking rather spectacular this evening! I suddenly feel rather underdressed."

Pethredote turned away from Lorstan Grale, taking Ard in a comfortable embrace and chuckling at his comment. "You look fine yourself, Dale Hizror. I decided the regalia would become me at this evening's reception. The Grotenisk Festival comes but once a year. What better way to honor the festivities than to wear the shell of the beast whose death we celebrate?"

"Absolutely," Ard said, though his mind was spinning madly at this terrible setback. Quarrah would find the alcove empty. She'd return to the drums with the replica, and they'd have to try again at a later date. The prospect of maintaining Dale Hizror's character was discouraging, especially since he had just openly assaulted two guards. Ard would have to think up a good story for that one. And, sparks, maybe he would end up conducting that cantata after all!

"Where is the beautiful Azania Fyse?" asked Pethredote.

"I'm afraid she isn't feeling herself," Ard answered. "Though I hope she will rejoin us shortly."

The statement was true. Azania was ill—resting in that dim service room. Quarrah, on the other hand, was probably feeling more herself than she had in cycles.

Ard's attention shifted to the reception hall's entrance. A pair of red-uniformed Regulators was cutting through the crowd. The palace was always crawling with Reggies on reception evenings, but Ard could immediately tell that these two had a purpose of some urgency.

Ard took a respectful step backward as the two Regulators reached the decorated king. The first positioned himself before Pethredote, his stature and mannerisms creating an instant buffer, while the second Reggie leaned close to the old king's ear.

Whispered words were exchanged, and in the din of the reception hall, Ard had no hope of hearing them. He watched the king's mouth, but reading his lips through that trim gray beard was not a skill Ard had developed. Still, the expression spoke volumes.

The king went rigid, crystal blue eyes burning with a sudden intensity. Ard's breath caught in his throat. His wig suddenly felt very warm, and sweat began beading beneath his artificial forehead.

The Regulators stepped away and the king made to follow them, his brow creased beneath the amber shards of dragon shell that adorned his head.

"Your Majesty," Ard said, stepping forward. "I have a concern that demands your attention."

Pethredote turned back, raising his hand in an apologetic gesture. "An urgent matter beckons. We'll have to discuss your concern later."

Neither Pethredote nor the Regulators hesitated, and Ard quickly fell into pace behind the old king, benefiting from the path that the Reggies cleared through the curious reception guests.

"It's rather urgent," Ard persisted, following the king into the hallway. "Cantibel Tren has expressed some concerns about the upcoming performance."

"From what I understand, she can be difficult," the king responded. The reply was automatic, and Ard could tell his attention was elsewhere.

"Yes, but she has taken the liberty to rewrite several notes in her part. The result has put her out of line with the chordal harmony of the composition." It wasn't true, of course. Ard was bad-mouthing one of the most talented musicians in the Greater Chain. If this gossip led back to Cantibel, there would be fallout. But dealing with an angry violinist seemed little bother compared to what might happen if Pethredote caught Quarrah in the act of thievery.

"Talk to Lorstan Grale about it. Or deal with Cantibel as you see fit," answered the king. "I insist that you return to the reception at once."

"Of course," answered Ard, desperate to draw out the conversation and stay by the king's side. "But it isn't that simple. You see, several members of the Royal Orchestra are faithful to Cantibel Tren. Replacing her could unravel the entire group. We would be left scrambling to find a dozen new musicians with only three days until performance. I was wondering if perhaps you could speak with her…"

They rounded the corner, finally reaching the entrance to the throne room. Ard couldn't tell if the kettledrums he had left by the doors were still there. The entire hallway was choked with Regulators!

There must have been fifty of them, lined up before the closed doors of the throne room. They stood in silence, Rollers ready in their holsters, and crossbows strung and loaded.

"Homeland afar!" Ard muttered. "What is going on?"

King Pethredote finally turned to face him, eyes cold even though the tension was not directed at Ard. "Return to the reception hall at once. This is no matter for you."

"With all due respect, sire," said Ard. "Any matter involving your safety is a concern of mine."

"I have ample protection, Dale Hizror." King Pethredote motioned at the ranks of Reggies lined before the doors. "And this is less a matter of safety as it is security. There is a thief in the palace tonight. I received word that a strike would befall the throne room. I took precautions."

Sparks! Pethredote received word? How? It was a fact Ard had been pushing to the back of his mind since his position was made known at Farasse's concert. Someone was giving Ard's whereabouts to the Reggies.

But who even knew about tonight's theft? Elbrig and Cinza had intentionally been excluded from the plan. Tarnath Aimes hadn't been given any more information since he'd delivered the replica regalia. They were all contractors, and Ard had paid them flat fees for their services.

Isle Halavend knew, but the old man could hardly be considered a suspect since he was the instigator of his whole ruse. Besides, Ard hadn't told the Isle specifics about which night they were going to attempt the theft.

Tonight's extraction of the regalia had been left to the three people who would share the final million-Ashing payout.

Ard. Raek. Quarrah.

That didn't leave any reasonable suspects. Quarrah was on the receiving end of this betrayal, and Raek was...well, he was Raek. Sparks, Ard trusted his partner as much as he trusted himself.

King Pethredote turned away from Ard, probably expecting that Dale would obey orders and return to the reception hall. Instead, Ard caught the king by the arm. He didn't know exactly what he was going to say, but he needed to stall longer. Give Quarrah a chance to escape out the balcony.

This time, as King Pethredote faced Ard, his steely gaze was intended for the disobedient Dale Hizror. Under the pressure of the king's stare, a strategy suddenly presented itself to Ardor Benn.

"You didn't wear that regalia in honor of Grotenisk's death." Ard's voice was low and his head tilted toward the king's ear. "If there was a threat of theft in the throne room, you can be certain that the subject of such a heist would be the Royal Regalia."

Pethredote paused. Ard was afraid he might not reply at all. Or if he did, that Ard wouldn't hear the whispered response over the hammering heartbeat in his ears.

"And why would you assume such a thing?" the king finally answered.

"Everything in that throne room has value," Ard answered. "Everything is one of a kind. A thief would be a fool to attempt selling any of it. It's too loud. Too expensive. But the Royal Regalia represents the monarchy. Perhaps this theft isn't about swiping an item to make a pretty Ashing. Perhaps it's about undermining your kingship."

Pethredote nodded. "My source told me as much. The regalia was intended to be the subject of tonight's theft. I ordered a trap left in its place. The thief should be contained within."

"A trap?" *Oh, flames.* This was worse than Ard had supposed. "What kind of trap?"

"A Barrier Grit detonation," whispered the king. "By the time the cloud collapses, the thief will be surrounded by Regulators. A fused Light Grit alarm was tripped only moments ago, signaling my men that the trap was sprung. They await my command to enter."

Once more, Pethredote tried to step away, but Ard held fast to the king's arm, an action to which Pethredote seemed unaccustomed. He looked again at Ard, the king's limited patience seeming to evaporate. Ard had to think of something good, or Pethredote was likely to turn a few Reggies on him.

"Perhaps storming into the throne room isn't the best course of action," Ard hastily threw out.

"And why not?"

"Whoever is inside was hired to steal the regalia as a strike against you," said Ard. "But why? You are the beloved crusader monarch. Your rule has been long and prosperous. You've stabilized inter-island relations, lowered taxes, improved Regulation, increased support of Wayfarist Voyages. You've made working conditions safer for the common citizen and provided basic education for their children. What reason would anyone have to go against you?"

"What are you saying?" The king's quiet tone implied that Pethredote was already considering what Ard was about to point out.

"I'm saying, that there has only been one notable blemish on your otherwise impeccable record." He didn't need to spell it out. Turroc root and Stigsam resin. Poisoning the Bull Dragon Patriarchy.

"We mustn't take chances." Ard's lips were mere inches from the king's ear. "If the thief finds himself with no retreat, is it worth the risk that he could spill such *sensitive* information to a room full of Regulators?"

King Pethredote finally pulled away in such an abrupt manner that Ard recoiled. The king glanced toward the throne room doors, then scanned over the lines of armed Regulators at his command. Ard's words had clearly upset the old king. His cheeks were rosy and his breathing heavy as he seemed to ponder what the best course of action would be.

"I will enter the throne room alone," King Pethredote announced, causing an awkward shuffle among the waiting Regulators. "I need to assess the situation before making the arrest."

One of the Regulators stepped out of the front line, as the king approached the doors, his uniform a deeper red than most palace Reggies, with stripes sewed onto the shoulder.

"Chief Aufald, Your Highness," he said, by way of introduction. "I must counsel against this action. It's very possible that the thief will be armed and dangerous. The Barrier Grit detonation will only contain the enemy for another few minutes. I cannot allow you to be alone in there when the cloud comes down."

"Chief's right." Ard stepped toward the king. "You can't go alone. Let me come with you." He exchanged a knowing look with Pethredote, which Ard hoped would help solidify the decision to trust him. Pethredote had nothing to lose by taking Dale Hizror. From that meeting in the throne room cycles ago, Ard had made it clear that he knew the true demise of the bull dragons.

"I can handle myself with a gun," Ard continued. "And I needn't remind you that I've already taken a ball for you once."

The king nodded. "Give this man a Roller."

The nearest Regulator slipped a gun from his holster and handed it to Ard. *Well, this is new,* Ard thought. *Reggies handing me their weapons?*

Chief Aufald slipped a crossbow from his shoulder and ratcheted back the string. "At the very least, I must accompany you also."

The king grunted, squinting his eyes in hesitation. "Very well," he muttered, a cold, disconnected haze settling over his face. Ard suddenly felt concerned for the future well-being of Chief Aufald. According to Isle Halavend, the king was not afraid to arrange *accidents* to eliminate people who discovered his big secret.

Ard followed Pethredote and Chief Aufald until they stood before the closed doors. There was no sign of the timpani drums, and Ard assumed the Reggies had moved them when they formed ranks. The missing drums were actually something of a relief to Ard. One less thing to explain at the moment.

"The lock was sprung when we arrived," spoke the nearest Regulator, his voice barely above a whisper. "No sign of the two Regulators who had been standing guard here. We believe the thief entered through these doors."

"Of course," said Pethredote. "This was the intended access point."

"What if the thief has already escaped?" Ard tried not to sound too hopeful. "The balcony would make an easy exit."

The king shook his head. "We planned for that possibility. My men installed a locking bar on both sides of those doors."

"If the thief is prepared, he might have Blast Grit," said Ard. "He could blow his way through the doors if desperate to escape." He was probing the king now, testing the new security systems so he'd know exactly how to get out once he rescued Quarrah.

"The balcony doors are laced with Barrier Grit," answered the king. "Detonating Blast Grit would ignite the security fuses and throw a Barrier blockade into the doorway to prevent anyone from passing in or out."

Ard let the matter drop. This setup was well planned, with expensive traps designed by clever Mixers.

Pethredote nodded, and the Reggie pulled open the throne room door. The king strode forward, Aufald at his side, and Ard quickening his step to keep up. As soon as the three men had crossed the threshold, Pethredote barked an order, and the Reggie outside closed the door behind them.

It was dim inside the throne room, and Ard's eyes had a hard time adjusting to the flickering illumination of the bonfire skull.

On the far side of the room, the familiar discoloration of a dome-shaped detonation cloud shimmered slightly in the firelight. The Barrier Grit trap. Ard immediately saw the victim within—a hunched form in dark garb, indecipherable in poor lighting at such a distance.

"Show your face!" Ard called, careful to be the first one to engage her. Quarrah ducked her head lower, remaining crouched in an indistinguishable heap on the floor.

Good, Ard thought, *at least she's well practiced in doing the opposite of what I suggest.*

Chief Aufald nocked a Barrier Grit bolt onto the crossbow's string and lifted the weapon, ready to recapture the thief in case the first cloud burned out.

King Pethredote strode across the dim chamber, his gait cautious. The rattle of the regalia's shell fragments accompanied the pop and crack of the bonfire.

"The game is up, thief," Pethredote called. "It was a fool's hope to think you could succeed."

Don't reply, Ard thought frantically. *For Homeland's sake, don't say anything, Quarrah.* What was the likelihood that King Pethredote would recognize Azania's speaking voice? Quarrah didn't attempt to change her timbre as Ard did when portraying Dale Hizror. She had tried it in practice sessions, but Cinza said she sounded like a choking horse and demanded she stop.

Even if Quarrah didn't speak, the king would reach the Barrier cloud in seconds. He'd see that the trapped thief was a woman. Aufald would apprehend Quarrah the moment the cloud burned out. And something told Ard that it wouldn't take long for the king to see through her disguise. A red wig and a loud pair of spectacles would only go so far. Under scrutiny, Azania's identity was sure to dissolve quickly.

Ard put his thumb on the Slagstone hammer of the Roller, but stopped himself from pulling it back. What was he going to do, shoot Chief Aufald? Shoot the king? There were fifty Regulators waiting in the hallway outside.

Ard supposed a right hook to the king's jaw might give them an opportunity to pry the regalia away from him. But that was a brute option. Where was the Ardor Benn finesse in that? The result would leave a disgruntled king who knew he'd been robbed. Pethredote would alert every Regulator in the Greater Chain. They'd never make it to Pekal with the shell fragments.

The point of this entire ruse had been to quietly swap the regalia with a replica. That was the reason they'd waited cycles for

Tarnath to forge his piece. And it was the only way his team would have the breathing room to carry out the second half of the ruse and create the Visitant Grit for Isle Halavend.

Pethredote was nearly to the edge of the Barrier cloud, Quarrah still huddled to hide her face and figure. Aufald stood a few paces back, sighting cautiously down the crossbow with Ard at his elbow.

Ard had to act now. He couldn't stand by and watch Quarrah get taken. Not even to preserve the character of Dale Hizror. Ard had gotten Quarrah into this mess. He'd insisted that she go along with the costumes, the singing, the receptions. And now his mistakes were going to ruin her.

He thought of his hand on Quarrah's knee as they sat through tedious rehearsals in the bakery's upper room. He thought of how confident she'd been, standing on the palace roof after breaking them out of Farasse's concert. He imagined the soft brush of her face against his, giving her a habitual peck on the cheek whenever they parted.

Ard suddenly found himself standing in a very different place, in a time just before the debut of the ruse artist, Ardor Benn. He was on Pekal with Tanalin Phor. He'd roped her into his plan, and now Tanalin stood beside a stolen Drift crate, a look of terror on her face as the Harvesting crew closed in on them. The decision he'd made that night was really no different from the one he faced now.

Well, sparks. Maybe Raek was right. Maybe he was falling in love with Quarrah Khai.

Ard made his move, seizing Chief Aufald's crossbow at the butt. He spun the man around, ducking as he squeezed the trigger.

The crossbow string snapped, and the clay bolt struck the throne room doors about four feet off the ground. Clay shattered, Slagstone sparked, and the Grit ignited, throwing an impenetrable cloud against the twin doors and sealing them shut.

Aufald reeled, but Ard was still carrying through with his surprise attack. An upward fist caught the Reggie chief just below the jaw. His head snapped back, helmet tumbling to the stone floor as Aufald collapsed, unconscious.

Ard shook out his fist, the pain of the blow numbing against his already tender knuckles. It was remarkable what a single well-placed strike could accomplish.

At the commotion, King Pethredote whirled around, a small Singler appearing from his boot. Ard sensed the movement and dove for the cover of the burning throne. He saw the flash of the muzzle as the Blast Grit cartridge exploded, sending a lead ball screaming in his direction.

The king's aim was wide, and Ard dropped to his knees beside the fiery skull. Heat from Grotenisk's bonfire was intense at such proximity, but at least the firelight was bright enough for him to see what he was doing.

Ard scrambled to lift his silk shirt and vest, exposing the Grit belt that Quarrah had given him outside the throne room. He glanced at the clay detonation pots, each securely housed in its own hardened leather pouch. Each clearly labeled in Raek's scrawl. This was blazing convenient!

Ard quickly found what he was looking for. There were only three of this type, and honestly, that was more than Ard had hoped for.

On the far side of the skull throne, Ard heard Pethredote repositioning. He didn't know what kind of weaponry the king was toting. Pethredote could easily be carrying a second Singler. And if the king was adept at reloading, he might already have another shot prepared.

Ard held the three clay pots awkwardly in one hand. Detonating them at the same time would increase the blast radius, but Ard didn't really know what the exact dimensions would be. Best to do it now, while Pethredote was fairly close.

Ard smashed the three pots against the floor, seeing little sparks dance across the clay shards as the Grit ignited. The detonation cloud flew up around him. Ard couldn't see the perimeter, so that certainly gave him enough space to operate in.

"Quarrah!" Ard called. "The moment that Barrier cloud burns out, I want you to engage the king. We have to take him down and get the regalia!"

Ard pulled back the Slagstone hammer of his Roller and fired a threatening shot toward the ceiling, using the intimidation to emerge from behind the skull.

King Pethredote bolted from the shadows, moving hastily toward the hallway doors. Ard fired a second shot, intentionally wide of the king, but close enough to get him to veer aside. At the same moment, the shimmering cloud of Barrier Grit extinguished around Quarrah. She sprang from her place on the floor, tackling King Pethredote from behind and dropping him to the floor.

Ard was there in a moment, swatting the Singler from the king's hand and putting the barrel of his Roller against Pethredote's forehead. The dragon shell crown had tumbled from his head in the struggle. It lay on its side, casting jagged shadows in the firelight.

"Dale Hizror," muttered the old king as Quarrah knelt on his back. "You are a traitor to the Greater Chain."

"Yeah, yeah." Ard turned to Quarrah. "Where's the fake regalia?"

"It's in the bag on the floor over there."

Ard crossed to retrieve it. "We need to put it on him."

"What are you talking about?" Quarrah cried. "I think our opportunity for subtlety has passed. Let's just take the real regalia and get out of here."

"It's never that simple." Ard opened the bag and produced the fake shell crown and coat.

"It could be," answered Quarrah.

Ard shook his head. "If the king knows we stole the regalia, we'll never make it to Pekal."

The king lifted his head defiantly. "Whatever you're planning will fail!"

Quarrah shot Ard an incredulous look. "Whatever happened to not spilling our entire plan in front of the Focus?"

"It's all right," answered Ard. He waved his hand through the air around them. "Memory Grit. Processed from the digested skull of a human being. The stuff usually gives me the creeps, but this is one use I fully endorse."

Quarrah's eyes went wide at the realization. "How long do we have?"

"Oh, less than ten minutes," replied Ard.

"And then we won't remember any of this?"

Memory Grit was rather uncommon. Ard doubted Quarrah had ever found herself victim to it. Strange sensation, losing a portion of one's memory.

"And neither will he." Ard pointed a boot at the downed king. "If we can swap the regalia and get out of here, it will keep the ruse intact. Pethredote will come to his senses wearing the coat, and he'll naturally think that the theft was a failure."

"You will not get away with this!" the king hissed. "I will find you out. You can't escape!"

It was true that Dale Hizror was finished. Ard had attacked Chief Aufald *before* he'd thought to detonate the Memory Grit. Pethredote was right. Ard wasn't going to get away with this one. But he'd make blazing sure that Quarrah did.

Ard placed the barrel of his Roller once more against the king's forehead. "Get up." Quarrah released him and the king slowly knelt before standing. "Now, remove the regalia. *Slowly.*"

Quarrah came alongside Ard, her voice soft in his ear. "Are you sure this is going to work?"

Ard reached up with his left hand and peeled away his adhesive mustache, leaving his upper lip tingling from the abrupt removal.

"There's a Reggie chief on the floor there," Ard said, peeling off his artificial sideburns. "Drag him over here and take his helmet and coat."

Quarrah slipped silently away as Pethredote finished unclasping the buckles. As he slowly maneuvered his arms, the royal coat fell from his shoulders, crashing against the cool stone floor.

"Now put this one on." Ard used his foot to slide the fake regalia toward Pethredote.

Quarrah returned, the Reggie helmet on her head, his crimson wool coat over one shoulder, and Aufald's unconscious body dragged across the floor. As Pethredote buckled the counterfeit regalia into place, Ard removed his dark wig and prosthetic forehead. Quarrah gathered the real coat and crown and began loading them into the black bag.

Ard looked at the pieces of the puzzle around him. A Reggie helmet and coat, an unconscious Aufald. A large black bag loaded with the actual Royal Regalia, and a stunned Pethredote wearing a fake. The balcony doors rigged with impenetrable Barrier Grit. The hallway doors desperate to burst with fifty waiting Reggies. An adhesive mustache and sideburns. A wig. The dim flickering throne room cloaked in a cloud of Memory Grit, which would burn out in minutes.

Ard looked at Quarrah. He had to get her out. Above all else, he couldn't see Quarrah arrested and executed. He'd given up his entire life to keep Tanalin Phor innocent. And now he was willing to do it for Quarrah.

Ard turned to her, his heart hammering in his chest. "I think I love you, Quarrah Khai."

Her eyes grew big in the flickering light. "What?"

"I said, I think I love you." It seemed a strange place to profess it. Certainly less than romantic, with a loaded Roller to the king's head. "Deep down inside. But I won't let myself. Because of Tanalin. I can't let her go, Quarrah. And no matter how much I *want* to love you, you're not Tanalin Phor."

Quarrah stammered. "Why are you saying this?"

"So you'll understand why I'd give myself up to make sure you escape," said Ard. "And because neither of us will remember this conversation in a matter of moments." He grinned at her. "Now help me get everything in place."

Quarrah suddenly became aware of herself. It was like awakening from a dream, unsure of when she had fallen asleep.

The last thing she remembered was hunching low under a dome of Barrier Grit, trying to conceal her face as King Pethredote approached. There had been a scuffle and Pethredote shot at Ard. And now she was here, standing on the opposite side of the throne room, wearing some ridiculously oversized wool coat.

Quarrah glanced down at her attire. It was a Reggie coat. No, not just any Reggie coat. Quarrah was wearing the crimson uniform of a Regulator chief! She felt the weight of the helmet atop her head as well. And there was something on her face!

Quarrah reached up, touching her upper lip. An adhesive mustache had been pasted on, along with a pair of long sideburns. Under the helmet, Quarrah now realized she wore a dark wig, tied back in the fashionable men's style.

She was wearing Ard's disguise! What the blazing sparks?

No sooner had she realized it, than the throne room doors burst open from the hallway. Lines of Regulators poured in, weapons loaded and ready.

Quarrah staggered backward, but the Reggies flooded past her to the situation in the center of the throne room.

Two figures stood beside the burning dragon skull. One was King Pethredote, the shell crown atop his head, and his stocky frame draped in the regalia coat. The other was Ard. Not Dale Hizror, but unmistakably Ardor Benn.

His disguise removed, Ard stood with shaven face, his arm

outstretched as he pointed a Roller directly at the king. He was surrounded in a moment, the ranks of Reggies brutally forcing Ard to
his knees, the Roller swatted out of his hand.

Quarrah lifted a hand to her temple. *Ahhh!* What was going on?
The scene unfolding before her was dreadfully confusing. It was as
though she had begun reading in the middle of a book.

Clearly, she had failed to steal the regalia. King Pethredote was
wearing it, for Homeland's sake, and there was no sign of the black
bag that held the counterfeit. Across the chamber, the alcove she
had broken into was sealed up tightly. She absolutely remembered
breaking in, but now the trap lock was back in place as though she
had never managed to spring it.

It was all so puzzling. And although she couldn't understand it,
she knew that Ard was somehow behind this baffling turn of events.
It was obvious that Quarrah's ridiculous attire was in place to allow
her to escape unnoticed. Ard would be furious if she squandered
the opportunity.

Casting one final glance at the mess of Regulators around the
throne, Quarrah turned away, walking calmly for the hallway.
She kept her face downcast, shoulders squared, and Reggie helmet
pulled low.

Everyone had their attention fixed on the struggle at the heart of
the throne room. All they saw was another Reggie coat.

In a moment, Quarrah was away. She rounded a corner and
let her anxious breaths catch up with her. She was alone, and her
thief's instinct to run was stronger than ever.

Fleeing was what Quarrah Khai would do. But this was Ard's
ruse. She had to predict what he would want from her. Dale Hizror's character was ruined. The first thing people would do was
search for Azania Fyse.

Quarrah needed to return to the service room and change back
into her wig and dress. She needed to return to the reception hall

looking for Dale Hizror. She needed to act dismayed when word came of Dale's arrest. She needed to deny any knowledge of Dale's true identity as Ardor Benn.

Maintaining Azania Fyse would be dangerous, but it could buy them a little more time. It could provide her another opportunity to return to the throne room and finish what had gone so terribly wrong tonight.

But, oh, flames, it also meant she'd have to perform at the Grotenisk Festival. She'd have to stand on that blazing stage and silently mouth the words in front of thousands of citizens.

Maybe getting arrested was the better end of the deal.

~

I'm willing to do it. I wouldn't have come this far if I wasn't resigned to give myself up.

CHAPTER

19

Isle Halavend paused halfway up the stone steps to catch his breath. Below, the Mooring waterway rippled from a passing raft. The architects really should have considered a better handrail. But then, perhaps Holy Isles were not meant to stay in active service at such an age.

He began upward again, feeling the Trothian Assassin Blade rub against his upper leg. The terrible weapon was housed in a hardened leather sheath, well concealed beneath his Islehood robes. At her last visit, Lyndel had checked the Grit to make sure it was still packed tightly into the groove between the two halves of the blade.

Void Grit. A thrust from the weapon would detonate it, clearing a space with tremendous force. Halavend didn't know how much Grit was packed into the dagger, or how large the blast radius would be. It was a horrifying thought anyway. Homeland see that he never had to use it.

Halavend felt ashamed for secretly carrying the Assassin Blade. He was a Holy Isle, not some hired killer. But Lyndel had been right about a sense of increasing danger. The sharks were circling. Halavend could sense it.

He reached the top of the stairs and entered the vast Mooring Library. He wasn't after books on the shelves today. Lyndel was coming in a few hours, and he needed to give her another allotment of his manuscripts and journals.

It was prohibited to remove unapproved materials from the Mooring. Halavend would be condemned just for having written these manuscripts, let alone smuggling them out.

The process of removing them was slow. Halavend and Lyndel had been at it for cycles now. Quickest to go were the Agrodite documents, the first written scripture of the Trothian religion. What Lyndel would do with those writings, he didn't know, since none of her people had the ability to read them. He supposed they would be reliant on Lander allies in future generations—not an unrealistic hope, seeing how well the races had meshed in just the last thirty years.

There were no more Agrodite documents to smuggle away, but what remained was, in many ways, even more condemning.

Halavend steadily made his way past the bookshelves to the far end of the library. There were several tables here, a few younger Isles seated before stacks of books. Behind them, rows of locked cubbies were built into the stone wall.

Isle Halavend checked the numbers, pausing before locker 32.

He fished into the pocket of his robe and withdrew a key, which he used to open the small iron gate.

The private lockers were available for use by any of the Holy Isles. The Islehood could be competitive at times, despite the Wayfarist doctrine of aiding one another without payment. It was wise to guard one's research, locking it away at the end of a long day.

Halavend reached into the cubby, but paused before touching any of his documents. The trip wire was broken. Someone had entered his cubby before him.

Halavend picked up the broken piece of uncooked string noodle. It was a crude system, but it appeared to work. With careful placement, he made it impossible for the books to be removed without breaking the brittle dried noodle. He could remove the uncooked string, of course, but someone unaware of its presence wasn't likely to see it in the dim cubby. And if they did see it...well, it was just a string noodle.

Isle Halavend snapped the already-broken piece between his fingers. Third time this week. Someone was snooping in his locked cubby. Halavend had little doubt as to who it could be. The only individual with a key to each locker was the Prime Isle.

This was why the dagger strapped to Halavend's leg felt necessary. Chauster was no longer casually suspicious. The Prime Isle was actively digging for any legitimate reason to see Halavend tried and removed.

As long as Chauster waited for a reason, Halavend felt he could cover his tracks. It was impatience that Halavend feared. The bodies surrounding Prime Isle Chauster's treachery hadn't been fortunate enough to receive a trial. They had gone quietly. One by one, until anyone who might have known anything about the elimination of dragon shell was gone.

Halavend had moved beyond suspicion. It had been two cycles since Ardor Benn had reported a confession from King Pethredote about poisoning the Bull Dragon Patriarchy. With that confirmation, Halavend and Lyndel had been able to link everything together with full confidence.

Now Halavend couldn't decide who he feared and distrusted more. The king, or the Prime Isle? Evidence tied the two together at every point along the path of hidden corruption. The two most powerful figures in the Greater Chain were masquerading as upright Wayfarists, when Halavend knew them to be the basest of Settled souls. Homeland be closed to them. It made Halavend sick.

Isle Halavend withdrew the books from his cubby. These were not his incriminating documents. These contained bland research, an exposé on Teriget's detonation of Visitant Grit in 1157. The topic he had told Chauster he was studying last time they had spoken.

He closed the locker, and turned to walk away. He hadn't gone five steps when he turned back to the bank of cubbies, his rehearsed expression making it seem as though he had forgotten something.

Stepping up to the lockers once more, Halavend inserted a key and pulled open the iron gate. His heart raced as it did each time he accessed the hidden documents. An astute observer would notice that Halavend had not returned to the same locker, but to the one directly beside it, using a different key.

The adjacent locker that Halavend now accessed contained a few loose pages and a dusty book. Groping toward the back, Halavend slid his finger into a notch and pulled aside the false panel. It wasn't clever engineering, just a plank of wood, painted black and cut to fit the back of the cubby. The lockers were deep enough that many an Isle had rejoiced at finding a lost page or quill, if they went to the effort of detonating Light Grit. Halavend was counting on no such thing happening in locker 33.

He slid two thin journals from hiding before tipping the false panel back into position. Nestling the forbidden books among his other research materials, Halavend locked the iron gate and strode away from the wall of cubbies, his step livened by the rush of his illegal activity.

Even in death, she was helping him. Selfless, devoted, Isless Malla. It was her locker that hid his findings. No one knew he had the key. She had been gone more than nine cycles now, Homeland keep her. Had it really been that long? It seemed like yesterday that his young pupil had been at his side.

Had the Islehood been pressed for cubby space, a locksmith would have been hired to forge a new key or replace the gate altogether. But there were lockers still available, and hiring an outsider to work in the Mooring Library was a process.

But Halavend had the key. Another secret in a list that seemed to grow endlessly. Isless Malla had given it to him before she departed on her fatal mission. He gritted his teeth. There wasn't a day that went by that he didn't curse his poor health and crippling age. It should have been him on Pekal. It wasn't right that the young should die and the old live on. Though, if Ardor Benn failed, living would mean very little for anyone.

"Isle Halavend," called a soft voice to his left.

He startled, gripping the edges of his research books to conceal the journals in tow. The speaker was a woman. A young Isless with whom he had conversed a handful of times. He turned to face her, finding her eyes bright and eager. The same vigor for life that he had admired in Isless Malla.

"It's a blessing from the Homeland that I should see you passing," said the young woman. "Isless Wyren," she introduced. "Do you remember speaking with me before?"

He nodded. Did she think he was going senile? "Of course. What can I offer you?" He tried not to fidget, lest his anxiety make him seem suspicious.

"I'm writing a document on the Dronodan-Talumon protest against taxation of coffee," Isless Wyren said. "It took place in 1182. I was wondering if you have any personal insights that I might be able to include. You know, from someone who lived during that time." She gestured back to a stack of papers and an inkwell she had left on a nearby table.

"Am I that old?" Halavend remembered the protest from his boyhood years, but what insights could he possibly provide this bright young Isless? Age hadn't made him wise. It had made him skeptical, cynical, and distrusting.

The young woman twirled a quill nervously between her fingers, hopeful for advice. Wasn't this just how his tutelage to Isless Malla had begun? And look how that had ended, Homeland keep her soul.

"I'm afraid I can't help you." Halavend glanced away from the look of disappointment that shadowed Isless Wyren's face. "Perhaps the information you seek could be found in something previously written. Isle Jadrod wrote a paper that addressed several tax protests through the years, if I remember correctly."

"Yes," she said. "I have read Jadrod's paper. But I have found that history is best depicted by those who lived through it."

"I was merely a boy in 1182. The coffee tax hardly affected me," replied Halavend. "We're all living through history. The things happening today become papers and books of future Isles and Islesses. Simply living through them doesn't give us special insight. Does your presence in the Mooring today qualify you to speak knowledgeably on current topics happening abroad?"

Halavend's words were straightforward, and Isless Wyren seemed to ponder them for a moment. "I suppose not," she answered. "There is so much happening in the Greater Chain. I would only be qualified to speak on topics that have affected me directly. Anything else would be secondhand information. And that is no different from reading it in a book." The young Isless paused. "Like the village in southern Espar. Did you hear what supposedly occurred there last cycle?"

Oh, Halavend had heard, all right. It was the kind of news he had been dreading for a year now. Ever since his joint-doctrine studies with Lyndel had uncovered the startling truth.

The village was called Brend, a small farming community on the southernmost coast of Espar. Halavend had never heard of the place until the reports began trickling into Beripent toward the end of last cycle.

It was Moonsickness. The first ever reported case of the fatal sickness being contracted outside of Pekal. And if the messengers were to be trusted, it wasn't just a single victim. The entire town had been decimated. A few of the Moonsick victims found their way to the next township several hours' ride north. Well into the third stage of the sickness, they were killed by a rancher when they fell upon a herd of sheep and began tearing the animals apart by hand.

Messengers were sent down to Brend, and the reports were horrific. Blind and mute, families murdered each other in a demented rage. Peaceful villagers turned on one another in episodes of psychotic barbarity. Each report listed a different number of Moonsick victims, but the reports were unified on the fact that the entire village was wiped out, leaving the quiet, remote farming community a gory mess.

"It couldn't be true, could it?" asked Isless Wyren. "We lit the Holy Torch. Its protection covers even the farthest reaches of Espar."

The Holy Torch. What could Halavend say on the matter? The ancient practice was false. Meaningless. Halavend and Lyndel had disproven that doctrine while uncovering a new truth. There was no Holy Torch. Well, in a sense there was, but not as the Wayfarists believed it.

The sickening of Brend only solidified what Halavend knew to be true. And it meant that they were already too late. Brend was the first to fall. Even if Ardor Benn's ruse was successful, there was no way to be sure that the Paladin Visitant could fulfill the Wayfarist scripture and protect them from the coming annihilation. How would the fiery figure even do such a thing?

"The reports must be made of rumors," Halavend finally replied. Isless Wyren looked frightened. Telling her the truth would only cause her panic and despair. He would continue doing what he'd done for a year now.

Lie.

"There is no way Moonsickness could touch Espar," Halavend reassured. "Believe in the Holy Torch, dear Isless. Believe that the Homeland's protection will cover the Greater Chain as long as we are faithful."

He couldn't tell her to believe in Ardor Benn, a ruse artist, whose current job gave them the only glimmer of hope in eventually stopping the coming Moonsickness.

"Thank you, Isle Halavend," said the young woman. "You are indeed a wise Compass."

Halavend turned away from Isless Wyren and moved quickly toward the stairwell, not daring to look back. He had lied to her because the truth was too frightening to face. It was a burden he had to bear alone, now that Isless Malla was gone.

He had Lyndel, of course. But her visits had to be few and secretive. For the majority of his time in the Mooring, Halavend was alone. It was terrible to feel so isolated in a place where he had spent most of his life.

The Mooring was a foreign landscape to him now, and the Isles and Islesses who occupied it seemed like vultures, waiting to feast upon his carcass should Chauster grow impatient in his suspicions. If it weren't for Lyndel's company, Halavend felt he might have gone mad, as though the Moonsickness had taken him after all.

Just a while longer. Ardor Benn was making significant progress. The last update said they were close to stealing the Royal Regalia.

From there, they would need to take the shell to Pekal and pass it through the digestive tract of a sow dragon. Ardor assured him that preparations were in order to process the Grit, and Halavend didn't want to know what criminal deeds would make that possible.

Then it would be up to him. Halavend would have the pot of Visitant Grit and the final stage of his plan would be executed. But by whom, he still didn't know. One chance to summon a Paladin Visitant. One chance at picking a worthy candidate to ignite the Grit. Perhaps it could be young Isless Wyren.

He paused by the archway at the top of the stairs, finally looking back across the vast library. Wyren was gone, tucked back into her study table to write about inter-island taxation of coffee from over fifty years ago. What was the Mooring but an institute of useless knowledge?

There was no worthiness. At least not in the sense that Wayfarist doctrine preached. Lyndel was as likely a candidate as some studious young Isless. For that matter, more and more Halavend believed that a Paladin Visitant might come to anyone, regardless of the way they lived their life. Sparks, it might even be Ardor Benn.

Halavend sighed. Homeland help him. He had lost his faith.

—

I hope my findings will be known to future generations. There is power in the written truth, and it must be protected.

CHAPTER

20

In Ardor Benn's long list of experiences, he had never broken out of a Regulation Criminal Stockade. Strangely enough, he had broken *into* one. It had been an odd job between jobs that he and Raek had picked up about three years ago. Shent Tasken, a Talumonian mobster with a reputation to uphold, hired Ard to infiltrate the Stockade east of Lalot.

Ard's mission was to deliver a parcel to a prisoner who was locked up for life. Ard wasn't supposed to know the contents of the package, but as always, the zeal of his name kicked in and he was fueled by a burning passion to find out.

The parcel held the hairpin of the prisoner's wife, whose cousin turned out to be an old affiliate of Shent Tasken. It was a complicated matter, but Ard was able to sort it out by the time he made the delivery.

The job was purely for Tasken to gloat. As it turned out, the prisoner had double-crossed the mobster and landed himself in the Stockade. Ard had delivered the wife's hairpin as a way for Shent Tasken to cause emotional suffering to his imprisoned enemy. As a way for the mobster to prove that he had found the wife.

It was nasty business. Not at all the type Ard usually went in for. And the payout hadn't been extraordinary. But Ard was grateful to have done it now, as the knowledge he had gained let him know all the typical Stockade defenses and procedures.

Regulation Criminal Stockades were different from the common citizen's jail. The latter was really more of a scare tactic, used for short-term discipline of penitent citizens who failed to pay their taxes, purchased Grit without a license, disputed property lines, or committed other petty legal violations.

The Stockades were another thing altogether, and the inhabitants were the worst breed that the Greater Chain had to offer. Murderers, anarchists, arsons, contrabandists, goons, and mobsters. And now, one ruse artist extraordinaire.

Ardor Benn sat in the dark, his eyes trained on the sliver of light at the bottom of the door. He had been introduced to his Stockade cell around midnight, after being dragged from the throne room by fifty armed Regulators.

Ard's solitary cell was like a cold cellar, with a slanted door opening aboveground and steps descending into the isolated room. It was cool, damp, and maddeningly dark. He'd watched the sun rise through the crack beneath the door, unable to sleep a wink. It was still bright outside now. Probably late afternoon.

He took a drink from a keg of musty water and finally brought himself to eat the stale bread that had been set out for him. The hard, tasteless loaf was a far cry from Mearet's fresh pastries at the Bakery on Humont Street.

So far, Ard had spent most of his time thinking. It was one of his specialties. Before a complicated ruse, Ard would often dive deep into his mind, running potential scenarios, testing every variable imaginable. Time passed at a different rate when he was thinking, and nothing could break him from his reverie—not food, not company, not sleep.

Ard had easily been able to achieve this level of focus in his dark cell. Homeland knew he had a lot to think about.

King Pethredote had an informant. That was the reason everything had gone sideways in the throne room. The reason why Ard was locked away here. Someone was obviously feeding information to the king. But who?

Quarrah was beyond suspicion, since it had been her neck on the line. And it clearly wasn't Raek. He'd known the man for more than half his life. They'd been pals together in their Eastern Quarter Beripent neighborhood. Ard had been there when Raek's parents had been caught in a storm and perished at sea. They'd failed together at the University in Helizon. Ard for being too distracted, and Raek for being smarter than the professors. They'd Harvested together on Pekal. Raek had helped take care of Ard's parents—folks that became like his own after he'd been orphaned.

No. Ard wouldn't even entertain the thought that Raekon Dorrel might betray him. They'd been through too much together.

So who else knew of their plans?

Isle Halavend obviously knew what they were planning, but Ard had been careful not to give the old man too many incriminating details. Besides, the Holy Isle could hardly be considered a suspect. Halavend wanted this ruse to succeed more than anyone else. He was risking his life by working with Ard, making illegal withdrawals from the Islehood Treasury. As far as employers went, Halavend was the most trustworthy Ard had ever had.

But Halavend didn't work alone. Ard knew that he shared everything with the Agrodite priestess, Lyndel. Ard knew very little about her. He had only spoken to Lyndel once, on their first meeting in the Mooring. But Halavend spoke frequently of her. And they seemed to be meeting multiple times a cycle.

Ard had questioned Halavend about Lyndel before. The old Isle had vouched for her, saying that her motives were as pure as his own. Sounded pretty altruistic, and it meant very little to Ard, who wasn't privy to such motives. In Ard's mind, Lyndel was the most likely suspect.

But Isle Halavend could be speaking with others as well. He had mentioned a young Isless on more than one occasion. Malla, was it? But Ard didn't know how she played into it all.

Whoever it was, the king's informant had struck twice now. The

Regulator takeover of the Royal Concert Hall had been salvaged by quick thinking and Quarrah's experience in Drift Jumping. But the failed theft in the throne room last night hadn't turned out nearly as well. The truth was, with a stretch of memories missing, Ard was having a hard time figuring out exactly what had happened in there.

He remembered *part* of his plan—the part he had devised before igniting the Memory Grit. But it was a mystery how the events in the throne room actually played out.

Ard's half-baked plan had been to strip Pethredote of the real regalia and dress him with the counterfeit. Had they succeeded? If so, how would any of them know?

They would have needed to smuggle the regalia out of the throne room before the Reggies swarmed the place. A tricky feat, since the only exit led into the hallway where the enemy had been waiting.

Still, if anyone could sneak past fifty armed Reggies, it would be Quarrah Khai. He had to assume she made it safely away, though he could only imagine how perplexed she must have been when the Memory cloud burned out.

If swapping the king's attire had been successful, and Quarrah had managed to get the shell out of the palace, then she and Raek might already be on their way to Pekal. That would probably mean no rescue attempt for Ard.

But maybe the theft had failed. If that was the case, Ard would have asked Quarrah to maintain the role of Azania Fyse. Doing so would preserve the ruse. Quarrah might get a second shot at stealing the regalia, or rescuing Ard from the Stockade.

Of course, there was no way Quarrah could remember if Ard had asked her to continue as Azania. Therein was the great conundrum of Memory Grit. It affected everyone within the blast cloud, and that often involved the person who detonated it.

It was a double-edged sword. All one could really do was consider the facts from before the detonation occurred and compare them to the facts after the Grit's effect burned out.

So, the facts were these.

When the Memory cloud in the throne room burned out, Ard had shed his disguise as Dale Hizror and was holding King Pethredote hostage. Aufald, the Regulator chief whom Ard had attacked, was nowhere to be seen. And in the chaos of being surrounded by Regulators, Ard hadn't managed to spot Quarrah or the black regalia bag anywhere.

It wasn't much to go on.

There was only one thing that seemed out of character for Ard. He had to have known that the Memory Grit was about to burn out. So why would he have struck such an aggressive stance against the king? It was almost as if Ardor Benn *wanted* to get arrested.

And that was what troubled him. Ard had a keen sense for knowing when it was time to abandon the ruse and save his skin. What were a million Ashings if he wasn't alive to spend them? Putting a Roller to Pethredote's head mere moments before the room filled with Regulators seemed inconsistent with his survival sense. What could mean so much that Ard would risk imprisonment—execution?

It was Quarrah. It had to be.

She'd gotten into his head over the last few cycles. Raek had called him on it, but Ard hadn't been willing to entertain the thought of another woman taking a piece of his heart, which remained devoted to Tanalin Phor. Even here, in the darkness of the Stockade's solitary cell, Ard had a hard time admitting that he would have sacrificed himself for Quarrah Khai. But he had once given up everything from his former life to exonerate Tanalin on Pekal. How strong were his feelings for Quarrah?

It was this kind of thinking that caused the hours to pass remarkably fast. Perhaps too fast. The Grotenisk Festival was only two days away. Should Ard have attempted some sort of escape by now? He wasn't sure how much time he would have in here. The king would certainly dispose of Ard. But he'd have to do it publicly. Too many notable people at the reception would have heard of Dale Hizror's treason. They would demand public justice.

The Grotenisk Festival was likely the only thing that had preserved Ard's life this long. As much as he might like to, Pethredote couldn't very well start off the festivities with a public execution. Nothing said growth and progress like shooting the most current musical celebrity.

King Pethredote was playing a careful game. To satisfy the citizens, he had to hold off on the execution. To satisfy the nobles, he had to bring justice on Dale Hizror. Keeping Ard in solitary imprisonment, where he couldn't divulge the king's secrets, seemed like the only course of action... at least for the time being.

Ard was resilient, but he didn't know how long he'd have to endure this. He had to believe that the others would mount a rescue. Raek would Mix some daring explosive to get him the blazes out of here.

At the top of the stairs, Ard saw a sudden break in the line of sunlight beneath the door. He stood up cautiously, stooping slightly as the ceiling was rather low.

Ard shuffled across the hard dirt floor until he stood against the bars. Outside his cell was a small landing before the short flight of stairs ascended to the exterior door.

Ard heard a rattling against the lock and the door swung open. The cell was instantly flooded with blinding sunlight. Ard felt the rays strike his face, and he instinctively shut his eyes against the brilliance.

Footsteps descended the stairs, Ard heard them shuffle to a stop just outside his cell. The door at the top of the stairs slammed shut, and familiar darkness dominated once more.

Ard blinked hard, his ability to see anything completely obliterated by the drastic change in lighting. There was a sound of shattering clay, and Ard saw a Slagstone spark in the darkness. Instantly, an orb of Light Grit sprang up from the detonation, hovering over the shoulder of the unexpected visitor.

At last, Ard's eyes adjusted properly to take in the scene. The man waiting outside the jail cell was not a Regulator, as Ard had expected.

It was Lorstan Grale.

"I must say," began the conductor, "your actions have left me in quite a precarious situation."

"What are you doing here?"

The man reached up and scratched the side of his balding head. "Considering the unfortunate circumstances, I found it necessary to speak with you regarding the upcoming performance."

"The cantata?" Ard asked. Lorstan Grale had traveled from the heart of Beripent to discuss music?

"The debut performance will go on as planned," answered Lorstan. "And in your absence, the king has asked that I conduct the work. I have a question regarding the tempo of the exposition. Cantibel Tren is telling me one thing, and our soloist is saying another. I thought I could resolve the matter with a quick condescension to your current state."

"Ha," Ard scoffed. "Welcome to my humble abode. Not as lavish as 448B Avedon Street, but it's feeling homier the longer I stay." He squinted at the conductor. "Is Azania all right?"

"Dear Azania has been forced to endure scrutiny beyond compare," said Lorstan Grale. "I hope she has managed to preserve the delicacy of her voice under such stress."

Well, it helped that the voice belonged to Cinza Ortemion.

Ard smiled. So Quarrah *had* made it out. She had managed to preserve her character, despite the tremendous amount of suspicion that was undoubtedly cast on her due to Azania's connection with Dale Hizror.

"I wanted to tell her so many times." Ard hoped that his

comment would solidify Azania's cluelessness about Dale's deception. "I never meant to string her so far along. I didn't want to hurt her."

"What's expected from a selfish, criminal lifestyle?" Lorstan Grale withdrew a handkerchief from his pocket and wiped the tip of his ruddy nose. "The king has made it clear that no one is allowed to speak with you. It took all my persuasion to be allowed down here. Now, I'm sure I have already said too much. I insist you explain the tempo of the exposition, or my great persuasion will have been for nothing."

Ard held on to the bars of the cell and leaned back. "Afraid I can't help you. As I'm sure you know by now, I didn't actually write the blazing cantata."

"They said you were an imposter," answered Lorstan. "I was not sure how deep your deception ran."

"Deep deep," replied Ard. "I'm talking bottom-of-the-ocean deep." He leaned forward until his forehead touched one of the bars. "Remember the Unclaimed Symphony?" Ard grinned. "Didn't write that, either."

"Now, *that* I knew," answered Lorstan Grale.

"What?" Ard took a step back. Lorstan Grale had been the primary voice to confirm Dale's ownership of the mysterious symphony.

"You couldn't possibly have written the Unclaimed Symphony," said the conductor.

"And why is that?" Ard asked.

Lorstan Grale smiled. "Because *I* did."

Ard's breath caught in his throat. If Lorstan Grale was the true composer of the Unclaimed Symphony, then he must have known that Dale was a fraud all along. Sparks, Lorstan had been playing him! But why?

"I can see how this might confuse you," Lorstan Grale said. "Technically, it *was* Dale Hizror who composed the work. It's difficult to keep them all straight." Lorstan stepped forward and pressed his face between two of the cell bars. "Ah, flames. Maybe I'm getting too old for this, Ardy."

And with that, Lorstan Grale spat out a set of artificial teeth.

Great blazes! It was Elbrig Taut!

"Now let's talk about the tempo of the exposition," Lorstan continued. "Do you conduct it in one, or in three?"

"Three," answered Ard, his whole body tingling from the revelation. And suddenly, Ard felt as if he were in the upper room of the Bakery on Humont Street, Elbrig quizzing him on musical terms and beat patterns.

"Good." Elbrig winked one eye as he replaced the set of teeth that had fallen into his hand.

"So you've been..." Ard stammered. "The whole time...you were..."

Lorstan Grale nodded. "My disguises come with a customer satisfaction guarantee. I wouldn't have promised that I could get you into the high social circles of Beripent's musical scene unless I knew I could deliver."

"You were already in place as Lorstan Grale to make sure everything played out the way we planned." Ard suddenly felt like the *second-best* ruse artist in the Greater Chain. "You knew I could sell Dale Hizror as the composer of the Unclaimed Symphony..."

"Because Dale Hizror *is* the composer of the Unclaimed Symphony," answered Lorstan Grale. "And it helped that I was there to speed along the convincing. The ring was legitimate, as were all the other clues I coached you to plant. People were catching on by the time I announced you at Farasse's concert."

"I was afraid they were going to catch on to more than that," Ard admitted, remembering their risky escape out the skylight. "I was just waiting for that Reggie chief to peel off my forehead."

"And he likely would have," agreed Elbrig, "if I hadn't distracted him by firing that Singler."

"That was *you*?" Ard threw his hands up in astonishment. "But

I talked to you about that at the bakery. You said you knew nothing about it!"

"And I answered truthfully," he replied. "Elbrig Taut knew nothing about that gunshot. The Singler was fired by Lorstan Grale."

"Sparks, Elbrig," Ard muttered. "You're incredibly gifted."

Lorstan Grale grinned an Elbrig grin. "I have help from a lot of imaginary friends."

"So, what's the plan?" Ard asked, hope welling inside him. "Where do we stand with the ruse? Did Quarrah get the regalia out of the throne room?"

"She doesn't have it," said Elbrig. "At least, she didn't leave the palace with it. I was there to see her off. Quarrah was empty-handed."

"She hides things in her bloomers," Ard remarked.

"The regalia is *far* too large and heavy," answered Elbrig. "She would have been clunking around like a cow with its hind legs in a trap."

"Maybe she got it out of the throne room and hid it somewhere good in the palace," Ard mused.

"Whatever is the case, dear Quarrah won't be getting back to it in her current state," said Elbrig. "I'm afraid she is quite locked down at the moment. Azania is basically a prisoner in the Avedon apartment, and we haven't been able to reach her. I've persuaded the king to let me speak with her about the cantata, but not until tomorrow."

"You'll let her know your secret?" Ard didn't see any other way for Elbrig to get to her without revealing himself as Lorstan Grale.

"I'm loath to do it," he replied. "But, needs a must."

"Thanks, Elbrig."

"Don't thank me yet," he said. "What happened in the throne room, Ardy?"

"Memory Grit," Ard answered. "Don't remember much of it."

Ard considered a few possibilities. The king had been wearing the regalia when the Memory cloud burned out. Whether it was the real one or Tarnath's replica was impossible to know. Regardless, one version of that coat and crown was missing.

"You didn't happen to find a large black bag lying around the palace, did you?" Ard asked. "It would have the regalia inside. Could be real. Could be fake."

Elbrig shook his disguised head. "There has been no sign of it. And Sem Braison's kettledrums were both empty after the debacle."

"Who told you about the kettledrums?" asked Ard. Details of the actual theft were supposed to have stayed among the original three.

"Raekon," answered Elbrig. "Honestly, there's very little he hasn't told us at this point."

"We must have hidden the extra regalia in the throne room," Ard muttered. "Unless Quarrah got it to another part of the palace. Either way, she has to go back and steal it."

"It won't be possible," Elbrig said. "She'd be away for too long. They're barging into the apartment at random to check on her, Ardy."

"Then she's got to do it when no one will have eyes on her," Ard mused. "When they're all distracted by something else." He snapped his fingers. "The Grotenisk Festival!"

"That's when *everyone* will have their eyes on her," Elbrig said. "Have you forgotten that Quarrah is singing the cantata?"

"But she's not," Ard replied. "Cinza is. Quarrah's just standing there mouthing the words."

"And that's why *everyone* will have their eyes on her."

"Maybe we could disguise someone else," Ard theorized. "We hire someone to go out on the stage so everyone thinks they're looking at Azania. Meanwhile, Quarrah sneaks away to make a sweep of the throne room."

"Excellent idea," huffed Elbrig. "I nominate Raekon. I'd love to see him in that silver gown with red ringlets." He shook his head.

"Even if we could find someone with a similar look, they wouldn't have the training. It would be a disaster. Plus, at such close proximity, the orchestra would know it wasn't her."

"Okay, then what if we hid her somehow?"

"Oh, yes," said Elbrig. "Let's put the soloist behind a wall, so no one can see her."

Ard rolled his eyes. "I'm just brainstorming, here. I don't hear you adding any ideas."

"Because nothing will work," Elbrig said. "We've been coaching Quarrah Khai for six cycles. It has to be her up there, which means she won't be available to loot the throne room. Unless you know how to make someone be in two places at the same time."

A grin spread across Ard's face. "Illusion Grit."

"Ahem," sputtered Elbrig. "Have you used that before?"

"Well... not successfully."

Illusion Grit was unique in many regards. It was the only known Grit that was geographically specific. The use was quite simple, though it had taken centuries for the island's inhabitants to understand how it worked.

Whenever Illusion Grit was detonated, it recorded anything seen within the blast cloud. If a second pot was detonated in the same location as the first, it would conjure a very lifelike image of whatever had occurred in the first blast.

Illusion Grit, by its nature, operated in a pair of detonations. The first recorded the image, and the second reproduced it, if ignited on the same spot of land. The blast clouds were linked across time to the specific location where the detonations took place.

That second detonation would effectively reset the area. If a third blast of Illusion Grit were detonated on the same site, it would no longer produce the first recorded image. Rather, that third blast would be considered like the first, recording whatever occurred within the cloud.

Ard had used the stuff only once, purchasing two extremely

expensive pots to use in a ruse against an unhappy mobster. He and Raek needed a distraction, so Ard had danced on a table at the Smokey Husk Pub on Talumon. The dancing was tasteless and had been done earlier in the day, inside a cloud of Illusion Grit without an audience.

Later that night, when the mobsters filed in, Raek had ignited a second detonation of Illusion Grit on the same table. While Ard's recorded image performed the dance once again, the real Ard attempted to sneak behind the bar and smuggle out a barrel of hidden Ashings. The illusion worked great until somebody threw a glass bottle at Ard's head. It passed right through, and his image just kept on dancing.

"I don't know…" Elbrig said. "The cantata is roughly an hour long. We'd need at least a quarter panweight. You have any idea how much that stuff costs? It's only a human jawbone. I don't see why those are so scarce. I thought the Nameless Remains Initiative was supposed to change that."

The price was high for all human-derived Grit, even after Pethredote's initiative. Basically, any dead body that remained unclaimed for three days was shipped off to Pekal to become dragon fodder. This turned out to be mostly beggars and vagabonds, as well as many criminal corpses from the Stockades.

Before the initiative, human Grit was even rarer, since Harvesting crews only received bodies willingly donated by family. And no good Wayfarist would donate a body to Pekal. That was an unholy island, and a corpse that spent time there might never find its way back to the Homeland.

"We should go back to the good times with the kings of old. Back when you could make decent money turning in dead bodies for the Harvesting crews," said Elbrig.

Ard shuddered. "That's just a recipe for serial killers. Regardless," he continued, "price is not an issue for us. I think we can get enough Illusion Grit to make it work. Talk to Raek about the detonation. He can rig a series of fuse pots that go off one after another. If they're timed right, there shouldn't be any visual glitches. The secondary image doesn't re-create any of the original sound, but that's all right. Quarrah doesn't produce any sound, either."

"It's a bold plan, Ardy," said Elbrig. "But you're winning me over. We'll have to detonate the first chain of fuse pots tomorrow night. It's an outdoor stage, so it'll need to be done at the precise time that the actual concert will be happening. If the natural evening light doesn't match, it might be noticeable."

"Do you think Quarrah can slip away for that?"

"She doesn't need to," said Elbrig. "I'll just explain that I need to take her to the Char so she can practice singing on the new stage. Even if her Reggie escorts stand nearby and watch, they won't realize that we're recording the image with Illusion Grit."

"Won't they see the haziness of the detonation cloud?" Ard asked.

"I'll make up something to tell the Reggies," answered Elbrig. "But that could create a problem for the performance."

"What about a smoke screen?" Ard asked. "Light some real fires at the edge of the stage and mask the discoloration of the detonation with some torches on the stage." He'd done that very thing to disguise his cloud of Health Grit on the night Halavend came looking for him.

"Ooh, I like it!" exclaimed Elbrig. "And it sets the mood nicely for the Grotenisk Cantata. We can rig up the stage something fancy. Cinza will be in her usual place, singing from below. We'll have to record the image without the orchestra, of course, but as long as Quarrah counts her rests properly, I should be able to keep the orchestra on track with her image, while Cinza provides the voice that everyone is expecting."

"How will Quarrah's image get onstage?" Ard asked. "The

Illusion cloud can't move. And we shouldn't make the detonation big enough to cover the whole stage."

"True," said Elbrig. "The larger the Illusion cloud, the more likely we'll end up recording the image of something we don't want repeated. Blazing flock of birds are already trying to roost on the acoustic shell, and they just erected the stage two days ago."

"Birds would be bad," Ard agreed. He could imagine them suddenly appearing, flying through the detonation cloud and magically vanishing as they passed out the other side.

"We can only risk making the Illusion cloud big enough to barely cover Quarrah once she's in position on the stage," said Elbrig.

"But she's still got to walk from the wing of the stage to her mark," Ard pointed out. "How?"

"On her real two feet," answered Elbrig. "I can't see another way. Quarrah will actually have to walk onstage. Once she hits her position, she'll drop through the hatch where Cinza is waiting. At the same time, we will ignite the second chain of fuse pots, and Quarrah's image will appear so it looks like she never left. The cantata gives her an hour, but she'll need to be back to take her bows in person by the time the Illusion Grit burns out."

"No pressure," Ard muttered. If she didn't make the deadline, the Illusion cloud would burn out and Azania Fyse would simply vanish into thin air. "That won't leave her much time to actually search the palace."

"It would be better if you were with her, Ardy," said Elbrig. "You might actually have a chance of finding the regalia if you put your heads together and see if you can't figure out what happened under that Memory cloud in the throne room."

"Wouldn't that be nice?" Ard gestured around the dim cell. "Any helpful advice regarding my current situation?"

Elbrig removed a brooch from his shoulder cape. He beckoned for Ard and dropped it into his hand. "The gemstone is merely painted clay. Your friend, Raekon, has taken the liberty of filling it with Shadow Grit and a fragment ignitor. It should work like a regular Grit pot. There isn't much inside, however. Just enough to conceal you while crouching low."

"Shadow Grit?" Ard said. "You could bring me anything, and you chose Shadow Grit?"

"What would you have preferred?" Elbrig asked.

Ard shrugged. "At the very least, a good blast of Compounded Void Grit could have bent these bars enough to allow me through."

"And then what?" asked Elbrig. "You punch your way past every Reggie in the Stockade Yard? That doesn't sound like my Ardy."

"Thanks." Ard closed his fingers around the false brooch, still unsure what he'd do with it.

"All you have to do is cross the Stockade Yard without being seen," explained Elbrig. "Your friends will take care of the rest."

"So there is a rescue plan?" Ard couldn't suppress a smile.

"Your friends are working on something," replied Elbrig.

"How will I know when it's time to move?"

"Tonight's the Moon Passing, so just sit tight."

"Tomorrow night, then?"

"Patience, Ardy," said Elbrig. "They're not going to spring you out until the last possible moment. We need the king distracted so it takes him longer to catch wind of your escape."

"The Grotenisk Cantata?" Ard sighed, resigning himself to two more nights in this pit.

"The music is riveting," answered Elbrig. "Watch for some sort of signal from Raekon around dusk. That should still give you time to reach the palace and meet with Quarrah while everyone is focused on the concert happening in the Char."

Elbrig squared his shoulders, squinted his eyes, and subtly transformed back into Lorstan Grale. "You said the exposition should be conducted in three, correct?"

Ard nodded.

"Well, I'm glad my little visit wasn't *completely* useless."

Lorstan Grale turned and strode up the stairs as the faded Light Grit orb burned out.

~

I have discovered a clever little bird that can disguise itself as a flowering branch. Things here are sometimes more than what they seem.

CHAPTER

21

Quarrah stared across the table at the Regulator Inspector. The Avedon apartment felt like it was getting smaller with every passing hour. Quarrah was tired. Not just desperate for sleep, but *tired*. The ruse had gone completely off the rails, and Quarrah Khai felt like she was single-handedly holding it together.

"Can you tell me where you were at the exact time that Dale Hizror was found assaulting the king in the throne room?" asked the Inspector.

"No, I cannot," answered Quarrah. "It would be impossible for me to answer, since I do not know the exact moment that Dale Hizror was discovered."

"Many people have confirmed that you were absent from the reception hall for a lengthy period. The period in question, in fact," said the Inspector. "Can you tell me where you were?"

"Yes," answered Quarrah. "I can tell you the exact same thing

I told the last four Inspectors. I was in a darkened service closet near the reception hall, recuperating from a moment of crippling anxiety."

"What brought on the anxiety attack?"

"Any number of triggers can set me off," she answered. "Perhaps it was the noise of the busy reception. So many faces, I felt like I was constantly on display. Perhaps my dress was too tight. Or maybe it was just the smell of a strong cheese."

She hoped her reasons would be considered legitimate for Azania Fyse. Quarrah had simply named a few things that triggered a genuine sense of anxiety in her. Except for the bit about the cheese. Quarrah wasn't sure why she said that.

"And you were in that service closet the entire time?"

"Yes." It was getting so much easier to lie convincingly. She'd been trembling in front of the first Inspector, but she'd answered these same questions over and over. Quarrah thought Ard would be very proud of her. To her knowledge, she hadn't contradicted herself yet. And she hadn't even blurted aloud any incriminating thoughts. Quarrah had come a long way from that first reception when she'd poisoned the soprano, Kercha Gant.

"Can you describe the contents of that service closet for me?" asked the Inspector.

"It was dark. I was huddled in a corner with my eyes closed."

"Try," said the Inspector. This guy was a bit less sympathetic than the last four.

"There were linens, barrels, buckets," listed Quarrah. "Maybe some serving ware."

"Did you notice any musical instruments in the closet?"

"There were two kettledrums," answered Quarrah. "But the sight of them put me off. I asked Dale to wheel them away."

"Are you aware that those kettledrums were found just outside the door to the throne room?"

"I don't see what that has to do with me," said Quarrah. The drums were empty when she left them. No evidence against her there.

"At what point did you return to the reception?" asked the Inspector.

"Once my head stopped reeling and my heart rate slowed," she answered.

"Did you speak with Regulator Dunbury?"

"Who?"

"The Regulator who volunteered to keep watch over the service closet while you recovered."

"No," answered Quarrah. "He was no longer there when I came out." Good thing, too. The action at the throne room must have drawn that young Reggie away, allowing Quarrah to slip into the closet and transform back into Azania.

"Did you see anything unusual when you emerged?"

"A few Regulators rushed past me," she answered honestly.

"Were any of them wearing the crimson coat of a palace Regulator chief?"

"Not that I noticed," said Quarrah. "You suspect a chief was involved in this?"

"Chief Aufald entered the throne room with Dale Hizror and His Majesty," the Inspector explained. "He was later found locked in the alcove where the regalia is normally kept, deprived of his helmet and coat. Both items were then discovered in the room across from your service closet."

Quarrah would have liked to have dumped them farther away, but it was risky enough crossing the hall with the chief's coat and helmet while dressed as Azania once again. As for Ard's hairpiece and adhesive facial hair, Quarrah had repeated a good trick and tucked them in her bloomers to smuggle them out of the palace. But this time, she burned them the moment she was alone in the Avedon apartment.

"Do you know what item Dale Hizror was attempting to take from the throne room?"

"How can you be sure he was trying to steal anything?" Quarrah retorted. Was Ard really going to get all the credit here? Seriously. At least the Inspector could give some credit to the anonymous thief. The king had clearly glimpsed her before the Memory Grit detonation.

Quarrah had decided that was what had happened. She'd never experienced Memory Grit before, but she'd read a lot about it. It was the only way she could account for the confusion she'd felt in suddenly finding herself wearing a disguise on the other side of the throne room. She'd had a lapse in memory, and there was no telling what might have occurred during those few minutes. Quarrah had seen the king wearing his regalia, so clearly, they had failed to steal it. She only hoped that Ard had somehow managed to get Tarnath's forgery out of the throne room.

The Reggie Inspector shuffled his papers and cleared his throat. "Have you left this apartment since returning here after the arrest of Dale Hizror two days ago?"

"No." She'd wanted to, desperately. But slipping away from the apartment wasn't really an option. The king had sent her home with a handful of Regulators who had stood constant guard outside 448B. Pethredote insisted that it was for Azania's safety. Quarrah couldn't help but think that it was also his way of keeping an eye on someone he suspected to be Dale Hizror's accomplice.

"Has anyone come to visit you in the last two days?"

"No." Also an honest answer, and one that made Quarrah increasingly nervous. She understood why no one from the team could stop in and say hello, with Reggies posted all around. But couldn't they have sent her a note? A message? Something?

Quarrah typically enjoyed her time alone, but this was something torturous. With the Regulators at the windows, she hadn't even dared to take off her wig. The blazing thing looked like a rat's nest now, and it itched so badly, Quarrah wanted to scream.

"Did you ever suspect that Dale Hizror was not the man he said he was?" the Inspector asked.

"Of course not," Quarrah replied.

"Did his appearance ever seem altered? Perhaps due to a disguise?"

"Surely, I would have noticed something like that," she answered.

The Inspector narrowed his eyes, leaning across the table. "See, that's what I think, too. How could you be engaged to marry a man, and not know that his mustache was fake? What about when the two of you were being intimate?"

Well, there was a new question! Quarrah raised her eyebrows in genuine surprise, her cheeks flushing.

"It is suspected that the man had an artificial forehead," continued the Inspector. "For Homeland's sake, how could you miss something like that?"

"I find your question wildly inappropriate," Quarrah said, fanning her face with her hand. "Dale and I enjoyed a refined courtship of the classic Dronodanian style. Physical intimacy was to be reserved until after the wedding."

The Inspector sighed, leaning back on his chair. "Did you love him?"

"No," answered Quarrah. She enjoyed the shocked look on the Inspector's face as he sat forward again.

It was an answer she had come around to during the first interrogation. That Inspector had commented on her apparent lack of emotion surrounding Dale's arrest. Quarrah couldn't fake it. She couldn't turn on the tears, the way she'd seen Cinza do. So she had to justify her lack of heartbreak. Her story had made the rest of the interrogations so much smoother.

"You did not love the man you were going to marry?" asked the Inspector.

"It's not so uncommon among the rich and royal," replied

Quarrah. "I was a nobody when I met Dale Hizror. He had money—not a lot, just enough to get me interested. But he also had connections to high society."

"So you were simply using him to advance?"

Quarrah studied her manicured fingernails. "Is that a crime?"

"Interesting." The Inspector made a note with his scribing charcoal. "Does the name Ardor Benn mean anything to you?"

"He was that madman who held me hostage after my performance of the Unified Aria," said Quarrah.

"It is suspected that Ardor Benn and your Dale Hizror are, in fact, the same man."

"Impossible," whispered Quarrah, hoping she got the tone right. All this acting was exhausting.

"Ardor Benn," the Inspector said again. "He is a ruse artist of some renown throughout the Greater Chain." Oh, Ard would be thrilled to hear that. "With his reputation, it seems highly unlikely that he was engaged to you for love. We suspect he saw your vocal talent and wanted to exploit it in an effort to move himself into the social circles of high society."

"Are you saying that Dale was *using* me?" Quarrah tried to sound hurt, aware of the hypocrisy in her statement.

"Seems you were quite the pair," said the Inspector. "What did he promise you?"

Two hundred thousand Ashings, and an opportunity to steal the king's regalia, Quarrah thought, biting her tongue. "A future together," she answered. "Full of wealth and opportunity." There, that was a better way to say it.

"Did Dale speak to you about any plans for your future? What sort of things did he have in mind?"

A future with Ardor Benn. What if their engagement had been real? What if they were committed to each other beyond the partnership of this joint ruse? For years, Quarrah had only pictured a future where she was alone. But maybe this was something worth considering...

With Halavend's final payment, they'd have enough Ashings to leave the life of crime forever. They could buy a country home. Quarrah had always liked the dry, leeward side of Dronodan. Maybe they'd have a kid or two. Someone for Ard to keep talking to when she wanted a little time on her own to walk the shoreline cliffs.

Quarrah almost burst out laughing at the thought. Ard could no sooner stop rusing than she could stop thieving. More likely, their future together would be one of close calls and big victories. They'd hone their skills as a partnership until no one in the Greater Chain felt safe.

Either of those options would be better than parading around receptions in fine clothing and masquerading as lovers—although that seemed like an accurate picture of high society. Maybe she was fooling herself, but it seemed like she and Ard had something more real than that.

Sitting side by side on the couch in the bakery's hidden room, conversing in the carriage on the way to a reception, or frantically devising a plan in the performers' lounge at the Royal Concert Hall. Those were the moments Quarrah felt something. A future where she could be herself and Ardor Benn would find her perfectly interesting.

The apartment door suddenly opened, a red coat Reggie stepping over the threshold. So much for privacy! What happened to knocking? See, this was why Quarrah couldn't even take off her wig.

"If you'll excuse us!" cried the Inspector. "I have a few more questions to ask."

"His Majesty, King Pethredote, is here to see Lady Azania," replied the Reggie at the door.

Quarrah stiffened in her seat. The king was here? Now? She hadn't spoken with Pethredote since Ard's arrest. Sparks, she'd certainly never spoken to him alone. Quarrah knew the king's big secret, and that made her feel awkwardly leery around him. Ard had been a much-relied-on element in previous conversations with the king. Ard was the spark that kept everything going. Without him, Quarrah was afraid she'd come across like a dud detonation.

The Inspector stood, collecting his papers. "We shall resume this later." He was halfway across the spacious room when King Pethredote stepped through the doorway. He was dressed in the finest of clothes, but unadorned with the regalia. The Inspector bowed, reminding Quarrah that she should do the same from her chair. When she finally lifted her eyes, the door had closed, leaving Quarrah completely alone with the king.

"Did you know this is my second personal call to 448B Avedon Street?" the king asked, standing behind the chair where the Inspector had been. "Last time, I shared a bottle of scotch with Dale Hizror at this very table."

Yeah. That scotch was long gone. Along with every other drop of liquor in the apartment that might calm her nerves and help the time pass.

"But I hear you're more of the red wine persuasion." He set a bottle on the table. Had he been holding that the whole time? The king stepped over to the rack and selected one stemmed glass.

"I will admit," he said, returning to the table and taking a seat across from her, "the place is much tidier than it was on my first visit."

Ard could be something of a slob, but Quarrah couldn't stand clutter. She liked to be able to take in a room at a glance. Clutter could hide important things. Besides, what else was there to do but straighten up, while she'd been stuck in Ard's wretched apartment?

King Pethredote uncorked the bottle and poured some of the burgundy liquid into the glass. Then, reaching across the table, he presented the drink to her.

"Lady Azania. Please." He gestured.

Quarrah hadn't made a sound since the king had come in. Now she was downright frozen. The man who had poisoned the bull dragons was inviting her to drink from a bottle he had brought.

She cleared her throat, but couldn't bring herself to touch the glass. "Won't you join me?" Quarrah asked. "It seems mighty impolite to drink in front of His Majesty."

"This particular vintage doesn't agree with me." King Pethredote waved his hand. "But you go ahead. Feel no reservations."

Oh, sparks! Quarrah could almost feel her throat closing off from the poison already. How was she supposed to get out of this?

"What's the year?" She finally managed to lift the glass, and passed it under her nose cautiously. Smelled fine.

"1208," said the king. "The final year of the Bull Dragon Patriarchy."

Quarrah's breath caught. He knew. King Pethredote must have realized that Quarrah knew his secret. Taking a drink of this wine would be the end. Quarrah would be another body on that long list of poor souls who once knew the king's dark deed.

Spill it? That would buy her a few more heartbeats, but the king would probably just pour another from the bottle on the table. She'd have to spill them both. But tactfully. How could she make it look like an accident?

She set down the glass.

"Is something wrong?" asked the king.

"I just..." Quarrah stammered. "The glass is not... Dale wipes them out so poorly. I'll just get a different glass, if you don't mind."

She stood, intentionally slamming her knee into the underside of the table as hard as she could. It did the trick, toppling both glass and bottle. The dark red liquid ran across the wooden tabletop, filling the grain and pouring off the edge like a river that had swelled its banks in a flood. The king pushed his chair back, leaping up instinctively, and Quarrah made some attempt at an apology.

Reaching out, King Pethredote caught the bottle just before it rolled off the edge of the table. He righted it, and Quarrah felt sick to see that there was still a considerable amount that hadn't spilled.

The king set the bottle on the table and Quarrah saw his hand stained red. Dripping, as it were, with the blood of all those he had silenced.

"When I was a young boy, my mother took me to the amacea festival on Helizon's University Hill," said the king. He just stood there, hand outstretched over the mess on the table. Quarrah moved swiftly to grab a cloth from beside the washbasin. "Have you seen those flowers?"

"No," answered Quarrah, offering him the cloth. She hoped her answer aligned with Azania Fyse's profile. She couldn't remember all the details.

"Extraordinary colors," continued the king, wiping his hand. "Petals as large as my hand. But the amacea flowers last only a week. We arrived on the sixth day, and had to shoulder our way through the crowds to get a glimpse. While we were gazing in awe at their beauty, the gardener came through and began cutting down the flowers so he could harvest next year's seeds. The crowds were outraged, and rightfully so. We'd come from afar and had an expectation that the flowerbeds would be there in full color."

Was he trying to make a point? If so, Quarrah wasn't getting it. Oh, she got the point with the wine, all right. But what was the king saying now?

"Are you quite ready for tomorrow night's festival concert, Azania, dear?" asked the king. He had finished cleaning his hand, and he draped the stained cloth over the back of the chair.

"I . . ." She stammered. "I will do my best."

"I don't think there has ever been more excitement for the Grotenisk Festival," King Pethredote said. "Are you aware that thousands of citizens have learned your name in anticipation of the concert?"

"I am flattered." *Terrified* would have been a more accurate description of her feelings.

"The gardener made a mistake that disappointed the people," King Pethredote said. "If I were the gardener, I would have waited until the amacea festival was over. Then I could cut down all the flowers and no one would even care."

Quarrah felt a chill pass through her. She understood now. The only reason Quarrah wasn't dead or imprisoned was because of tomorrow night's concert. So what would happen when she sang her final note?

"It's hard to be king," said Pethredote, his voice soft. "Harder still to be the crusader monarch. Dale Hizror crossed me, Azania. He thinks he knows things about me, but he knows nothing. I am a good man. A worthy man." His voice was escalating, becoming unhinged in an unnerving manner. "Everything I did, I did…for… my…people!" With every one of those final words, he slammed his open palm against the wine-soaked tabletop.

The spastic action caused Quarrah to let out a little cry of alarm, recoiling as droplets splattered under his hand. When the king was finished, his face was speckled, his shirt and shoulder cape stained.

Now he was calm again. Frighteningly calm.

King Pethredote slowly lifted the cloth from the back of the chair and wiped his face. The wine shimmered darkly in his gray beard. He sighed heavily, and lifted the bottle of wine from the table. Tipping it back, he swallowed a long draft.

The king set the bottle back on the table and crossed the room to the door. "I am very much looking forward to tomorrow night's cantata," he said, tossing the cloth to the floor. "Which reminds me…Lorstan Grale is waiting in the street outside. He'll be conducting the piece now that Dale Hizror is out of the picture. Grale has a few questions for you. I'll send him in."

Quarrah stood beside the table, petrified, staring at the red droplet stains on her dress. The king pulled open the door and stepped out into the street. A moment later, Lorstan Grale entered alone, shutting the door softly behind him.

"I'm resting my voice," Quarrah said, holding up a hand as though he had already requested it. If Lorstan Grale asked her to sing anything, it would quickly become apparent that Quarrah's voice was not the one he was used to hearing.

"Not for long," the man spoke, crossing to the table. "We'll be heading to the Char this evening so you can try out the newly built stage before tomorrow night's concert."

"I'm not feeling up to it," Quarrah replied.

"You will be, once I tell you what I'm going to tell you." He ran his finger through the spilled wine, and then sucked it clean. "You might want to sit down for this."

~

The mountain's threats are constantly present. Although sometimes they are veiled in scenic grandiloquence or hidden in inky shadows.

CHAPTER

22

Ard sat in his solitary cell, absently twirling the Grit-filled brooch between his fingers. From the line of light beneath the door, he could tell it must be nearing sunset now.

Shadow Grit. That was all Elbrig had given him for the escape. How could Ard make the most of Shadow Grit?

Ard knew its function, of course. The detonation created a cloud of darkness so dense that nothing inside could be seen from without. People in the Shadow cloud, however, could see outward. It made sense. A person sitting in a dark room with an open door could easily see outside, although it would be difficult for people outside to see in.

Shadow Grit was processed from digested oak wood. Other types of wood were processed into Light Grit, and Ard found it ironic that oak reacted differently, yielding darkness rather than light.

Ard imagined that Quarrah would be a fan of Shadow Grit, what with her interest in sneaking around. Using it required some subtlety. Detonating a blast in broad daylight would be rather obvious. It would appear as a spherical cloud of blackness, effectively concealing everything within, but drawing a fair amount of attention to the black cloud itself.

For stealthy purposes, Shadow Grit worked best in dimly lit areas. Places where the impenetrable blackness would seamlessly blend into the natural shadows. Places like Ard's underground solitary cell.

But even if he managed to sneak outside, Ard was far from free.

Regulation Stockades were always located a respectable distance from the city, with a single gate in the ten-foot-high stone wall. Four octagonal towers, partitioned into jail cells, formed the corners of the perimeter. Atop each of these, a pair of Reggies would be positioned behind battlements. That meant at least eight people in optimal tactical position, armed with crossbows, long-range Fielders, and plenty of spare ammunition.

Ard knew his solitary cell was in the middle of the Yard, a walled-in stretch of compact dirt at least a hundred yards long. He'd have to survive a run across the open ground before even reaching the wall.

From the research Ard had done for the Tasken job, he'd learned that all of the mortar in the walls was laced with Barrier Grit. Any attempt to blast through would result in an impenetrable cloud, sealing the breach and allowing the Regulators to take control of the situation.

Aside from jumping the wall, the main gate was the only way out. But even if he managed to get that far, the field outside was riddled with Grit mines, leaving the single access road as the only safe route to or from the Stockade. If Ard's research was still current, the mines were small measurements of Blast Grit, meant to kill or disable anyone fleeing on foot. The Blast Grit mines were a brutal defense. And quite hard on the local wildlife, Ard imagined.

The Grotenisk Festival would be starting in the Char soon. Elbrig, Cinza, and Quarrah would be busy preparing for the cantata, readying things for Quarrah's Illusion Grit departure.

That left Raek alone to make the rescue. With the same knowledge about the Stockades as Ard, Raek had to know that the task was near impossible. Still, if anyone could figure out how to get Ard out, it would be Raekon Dorrel.

The line of daylight beneath the door was barely perceptible when the signal finally came. An alarm horn pealed out, an unmistakable announcement that a prisoner was on the loose. The first horn was answered by a second, and then two more. All the corner towers had responded, locking down their cells to prevent other escapees. Ard imagined the Reggies frantically running through the Yard above, making necessary checks and setting safeguards.

Well, Ard thought, *I'm guessing that's the signal to move out.*

The lock at the top of the stairs rattled. That would be the Reggie on guard, checking the solitary cell to make sure that Ard wasn't the prisoner whose escape had been announced.

Ard crouched low, hurling the Grit pot brooch at the stone floor between his feet. The artificial gemstone shattered, and Ard saw sparks from the Slagstone fragment, instantly igniting the processed powder and throwing a cloud of darkness around him.

The Reggie reached the bottom of the stairs. Above, the door had been left ajar, a rectangle of faint dusky light. Ard held his breath, staring directly at the uniformed man, the cell bars separating them by no more than arm's length.

The Regulator fidgeted, squinting. His hand clenched and relaxed. Then he quickly drew his Roller. "You in there, crook?"

Ard watched the man's gaze pass directly over the spot where he crouched in the darkness. He felt completely invisible, though the effect of Shadow Grit was hardly *that* powerful.

"Ah, flames," the Reggie mumbled, holstering his Roller and shouting up the stairwell. "It's him! He's blazing gone!"

In a final inspection, the Regulator pressed his face up to the bars, scanning the impenetrable darkness.

Ard stood abruptly, his head and shoulders exiting the Shadow cloud. To the Reggie, he would have appeared suddenly, a disembodied head and arms. The Regulator fumbled for his gun, but Ard had the element of surprise. Reaching through the bars, he seized the man by the lapels of his wool coat and jerked him forward.

The Reggie's face slammed into the metal bars. His helmet rolled off, and he groaned, a cut across the bridge of his nose. Ard pulled him in for a second strike, this one proving too much. The man slumped down, unconscious.

"Maybe I *will* punch my way out of here, Elbrig," Ard muttered, reaching for the ring of keys on the Reggie's belt. Without the cloak of Shadow Grit, Ard knew the Regulator never would have dared draw so close to the cell.

He tested three keys before finding the one that fit the lock. Once freed, he stripped the blue coat from the Reggie and pulled it on. He dragged the unconscious man behind the bars and claimed his Roller and fallen helmet.

Ard relocked the cell and moved quickly up the steps toward the ajar door. He cocked the Slagstone hammer of the Roller and held the gun ready. With only six balls loaded, he'd rather not shoot his way out.

Cautiously, Ard peered outside. It was almost fully dark already, and Ard hoped the rescue plan wasn't too far behind schedule. He had a date with Quarrah in the palace. And she was under a tight time limit.

The Yard was in a fair amount of chaos. Since the alarm triggered the lockdown of the towers, the final group of prisoners who had earned time in the Yard were suddenly left in the open as darkness settled in. It was a rare opportunity to be out of the towers in the dark, and one of the prisoners must have grown bold.

Ard spotted one prisoner on his hands and knees a short distance from the others. A few Reggies surrounded him while more struggled to maintain control of the remaining prisoners.

Ard ducked his head low and took a militant Reggie stance at the door as a searchlight panned across the Yard. He had forgotten about those. Atop each tower was a parabolic mirror mounted on a swivel. The Regulators could detonate a powerful blast of Light Grit, intensified by Compounding Grit, which would be further magnified by the mirrored bowl. The Reggies could then direct the brilliant beam in any direction across the Yard or the field outside.

The searchlight passed, and Ard decided to make his move. He walked purposefully from the cellar-like door, around the mound of dirt that comprised the top of his underground cell.

One of the four searchlights was trained on the gate—the only practical exit. Ard squinted. There was activity over there, and not just from the Regulators standing guard.

There was an open-top carriage parked inside the Yard. Two nervous horses were hitched, stamping their hooves in the compact dirt as they fidgeted at the repetitive blares of the alarm horns. And there, crossing slowly behind the carriage, was a man in sea-green robes, his silvery hair looking brilliant in the searchlight.

By the Homeland! That was Isle Halavend! It would seem Raek was not making the jailbreak totally alone.

It was customary for members of the Islehood to visit Criminal

Stockades to provide spiritual guidance for the inmates, since they could not visit the Mooring. But it was no coincidence that Isle Halavend now stood fifty yards away, casting an anxious glance toward the mound of Ard's cell. The old man had risked a great deal with this rescue. He really was much braver than Ard gave him credit for being.

A Regulator appeared behind the carriage, conversing in an urgent manner with Isle Halavend. A middle-aged Isless joined them a moment later, and the three seemed to agree on something. Halavend cast one more furtive glance over the darkening Yard. Then he accepted the arm of a young Reggie, who helped him and the Isless climb into the carriage.

The Regulators snapped into a practiced formation, weapons facing inward at the Yard as they cleared a perimeter for the large gate.

Sparks! Ard tensed. They were going to open the gate!

But of course! With a prisoner on the loose inside the Yard, it wasn't safe for two visiting members of the Islehood. It would be Stockade protocol to escort the Isles safely away. It must have been Halavend's plan for Ard to climb aboard the carriage. But his opportunity was quickly slipping away, and Ard doubted that Isle Halavend would be bold enough to stall for him.

Ard would have to sprint. It was fifty yards at the most, and the path was clear. As long as one of the searchlights didn't pass over him, he might make it to the carriage unnoticed.

One of the Regulators was on the driving bench, taking the reins. The metal gate began to roll open, its heavy wheel carving along a well-worn groove in the hard earth. Ard quietly clicked the gun's hammer closed so he wouldn't accidentally pull the trigger.

Speed and stealth. It was time to think like Quarrah.

Ard sprang from his spot against the dirt mound and set off toward the Islehood carriage. His boots pounded the packed earth, each step throwing puffs of dirt like mini detonations beneath his feet. Spurring him forward. Faster.

He saw a searchlight coming in on his left. Ard hesitated for just a moment, wondering if he should stop and let it pass, or try to outrun the light. In his second of deliberation, the magnified beam passed directly over him.

He froze, grinding to a halt, watching the light continue on its course across the Yard. Maybe the watchers from the tower hadn't seen him. From that distance, he surely looked like a legitimate Reggie. Then the searchlight suddenly swiveled back around, the oppressive beam shining right on him.

Was there some sort of procedure he was supposed to follow to let them know that everything was okay? After a moment of squinting against the light, Ard tried a simple wave.

He took a few steps toward the gate, and the searchlight tracked him. Well, this simply wasn't going to work.

Get off me. Get off!

Ard needed to draw the searchlight away. Give them something else to point at. How about this risky idea? Ard cast his glance back toward the center of the Yard, making it look like something had drawn his eye. Then, to really sell it, he drew his Roller and fired twice into the dirt mound of his solitary cell.

Instantly, the searchlight moved off, snapping over to the mound to see who Ard had supposedly been shooting at. It was a simple tactic that would buy him only a few seconds. He knew when the searchlight came back, it wouldn't leave him.

"Over there!" Ard shouted to a pair of Reggies running toward the sound of the gunshots. It was easier to fool the ones in the Yard who didn't have a bird's-eye view.

Ard sprinted toward Isle Halavend's carriage, not even slowing as he reached the edge of the searchlight that hovered on the activity at the gate. Ard used his momentum, throwing himself down, landing on his side, and sliding directly under the back axle of the wagon. He lost his Reggie helmet in the stunt, and his teeth felt gritty from dust as he came to a halt beneath the shadowy undercarriage.

The harness bells jingled, and Ard heard the horses pick up their feet. He swiveled onto his back, discovering two long metal rods installed on the bottom of the carriage.

Well, that was blazing convenient!

Ard didn't even have time to tuck the Roller into his pants. He grabbed one end of each rod, while tucking his feet into the other ends, and hoisted himself off the ground as the carriage rolled forward.

The Reggies at the gate might have taken more interest in the unclaimed helmet, or the loaded Roller left behind in the dirt, if there hadn't been a sudden explosion in the field outside the Stockade.

Ard saw the Blast Grit detonate, maybe fifteen yards on his right as the wagon rolled onto the illuminated road. It was clearly an activated mine, spraying chunks of earth and rock in every direction. The blast of fire and smoke was certainly enough to blow the legs off whatever unfortunate individual had misstepped. No sooner had the explosion occurred than two of the large searchlights honed on the mark.

The Islehood carriage didn't slow, the escorting Regulators jogging alongside for protection. Ard saw a handful of other Reggies pass through the gate with Fielders raised to their shoulders.

Ard craned his neck toward the spot where the explosion had occurred, bracing himself to see whatever bloody mess might be left of the person that had tripped the mine. But on the other side of the smoking aftermath, Ard saw something that nearly caused him to drop off the carriage.

Ard saw himself.

He was standing upright, defiant, with feet spread wide in a haughty stance. His face was turned upward, gazing directly toward the powerful searchlight that illuminated him.

One of the Reggies on the road called a command, and half a dozen Fielders cracked, their hammers sparking and long barrels flashing. But the version of Ard that stood in the minefield didn't so much as flinch. At the same moment that the guns fired, a dome of Barrier Grit detonated around the stationary Ard.

The carriage was moving at a good pace now, and Ard—the *real* Ard, hanging under the carriage—could barely see as the Regulators reloaded and fired again. But firing on a cloud of Barrier Grit was futile. The other Ard was safe for the moment. Trapped, and pinned down, but protected from gunfire for another ten minutes or so.

After a moment, the Regulator escorts who ran alongside the Islehood carriage shouted something to Halavend before peeling off to return to their posts at the Stockade.

Ard hung in silence as the carriage rumbled down the road. He wasn't sure if Isle Halavend knew he'd climbed aboard, but Ard didn't dare reveal himself now. The Reggie driving the carriage wouldn't be happy to see him, and the middle-aged Isless was unfamiliar to Ard. It was likely that Halavend was using her as an alibi. By taking an Isless who knew nothing of the ruse, Halavend would increase his chance of making the whole thing look coincidental.

Isle Halavend had risked a lot, coming to the very Stockade where Ard was detained. If anyone was suspicious of their connection, it wouldn't be hard to connect the dots from Halavend's Islehood visit to Ard's timely escape.

The Light Grit detonations that illuminated the road were fewer as they moved farther from the Stockade. Ard knew there would be a stretch of dark road before they reached the outskirts of Beripent.

The carriage slowed, then suddenly lurched to a halt, causing Ard's feet to slip off the ends of the rods. Why were they stopping here?

Ard lowered his back to the dirt, giving his cramped and trembling muscles a needed rest. From this position, Ard glimpsed the feet of three horses in the road ahead, though he couldn't see who was saddled on them.

"Here, now," spoke the soft voice of an old man. Isle Halavend. "We don't want any trouble."

"No trouble, indeed." This second voice was even more familiar to Ard. It undoubtedly belonged to Raekon Dorrel. "We're good Wayfaring chaps, humbled to come across a pair of traveling Isles on a lovely night like this."

"Let us pass." This was an unknown speaker, but Ard placed it as the Reggie who drove the carriage.

"Just wondering if you have any extra cargo you'd like to drop off," said Raek. "We'd be happy to take any valuables off your hands."

Ard smiled, finally letting go of the handhold rods and lying flat on the dirt beneath the carriage. He felt a little bad for the Isless and driver, who wouldn't know that Raek's threat had a harmless double meaning.

"Drive on!" Halavend cried to the driver in a bold voice. "Have faith that the Homeland will deliver us!"

The reins snapped, and the carriage rolled forward, forcing Raek's horses to the side of the road. Ard was left exposed, lying on his back in the dirt, but Isle Halavend didn't even look back.

Ard sat up to look at his rescuers. One horse was riderless. On the back of another was Raek. And the final rider was the forger, Tarnath Aimes.

As Isle Halavend's carriage faded into the darkness, Raek dismounted and crossed to where Ard sat. "Fancy, finding you lying around in the middle of the road out here." Raek offered his gloved hand. "You look just like a wanted fellow they're keeping in the Stockade."

"Must be a handsome chap." Ard clasped his old friend's hand and leapt to his feet. "That was bold of Isle Halavend." Ard shed his Regulator coat and tossed it to the roadside.

"Protecting his investment," replied Raek. "The old man got a message to me, offering any way he could help. Of course the handles under the wagon were my installment. I figured you'd know what to do. It was just like the Unther ruse, when you hitched up under that carriage and got into his manor. That's why I painted Lord Unther's symbol on the back of the Islehood carriage."

"Hmm. I didn't even see the symbol," Ard admitted. "I was just doing what came naturally. Mostly, that involved not getting shot at."

Tarnath leaned forward in his saddle and studied Ard's face. "I think my version was better looking."

"Absolutely," answered Raek.

"Your version?" Ard followed Raek to the horses.

"Who did you think was standing in that minefield back there?" Tarnath asked. "Unless you have a twin that the Short Fuse didn't tell me about."

So it was a wax figure. One of Tarnath's incredibly lifelike statues. "There's only room for one face like this in the Greater Chain," Ard said, stroking his chin. "I insist you melt that imposter at once."

"I'll take that as a thank-you," replied the burly forger.

Ard swung into the saddle of the horse beside Tarnath. "My wax double detonated Barrier Grit. How did you do that?"

"The whole body is embedded with fragments of Slagstone, and the clothing is full of Barrier Grit," Tarnath said. "The moment a ball strikes, the Slagstone sparks and detonates a pocket."

Clever. The wax figure hadn't detonated the Grit to prevent the balls. It only appeared that way because the Barrier cloud formed at the same moment that the first Fielder ball made impact.

"We used a series of Drift clouds to float over the minefield and position the wax double," Raek explained. "That explosion of Blast Grit was my own, rigged up with a really long fuse. Got their attention. And once the searchlights lit up the place, they thought they'd found who they were looking for."

"It ought to keep those Reggie fools busy for a while," Tarnath said. "They won't dare venture into the minefield, so they'll keep taking cracks at him from the road. Any time they hit the target, a fresh Barrier cloud will surround the wax figure."

"Hopefully, that'll buy us enough time to get back to Beripent," said Raek. "None of those Reggies will be too anxious to report to the king about your escape. As long as they think they have you pinned down, I don't expect they'll send word to Pethredote."

"Meanwhile, I'll be in two places at once," said Ard.

"And with the Illusion Grit, so will Quarrah," added Raek.

It really was brilliant, playing this same trick two different ways.

"How is she?" Ard asked.

"Very nervous, I imagine," answered Raek. "Haven't had a chance to speak with her."

"Last night's Illusion Grit worked all right?"

"Perfectly," he replied. "Let's get moving. The cantata starts in less than an hour. Once Lorstan Grale starts the piece, we'll have just shy of an hour until Quarrah has to be back onstage for the applause."

"I know exactly how much time we'll have," Ard answered, turning his horse down the darkened road. "Nobody knows that piece better than me. I wrote it, remember?"

"You didn't *actually* write it," Raek said. "I feel like I need to point that out."

Ard looked over at Tarnath Aimes. "Thanks for the likeness."

The forger nodded, jewelry twinkling in the distant Light Grit detonation. "I've worked on uglier folks."

"You coming back with us?" Ard asked.

"I'll ride with you to the Panes junction," he replied. "Don't know exactly what you nuts are up to tonight, and quite frankly, I don't want any part in it." He held up a bag, and Ard heard Ashings clink. "The Short Fuse paid me right, and my work here is done."

"Fun's just getting started," said Raek.

"Right," replied Ard. "Breaking me out of the Stockade was just our warm-up."

Ard led them off, galloping down the road toward the smoky glow of Beripent's outskirts.

~

Sometimes I feel like I'm doing this alone. But then I remember that others solemnly cheer me on. They are counting on me to succeed.

CHAPTER

23

Quarrah could hear the crowd from inside the tent. The common citizens made a different sound than the noble audience at the Royal Concert Hall. She had been nervous then, to perform Farasse's Unified Aria, but the memory was nothing compared to the nerves she felt now.

Setting aside her anxieties about going onstage, Quarrah was actually quite excited. Soon, she'd be a thief again, sliding through the night like a shadow. And if Raek's rescue had been successful, she and Ard would be meeting up within the hour.

Quarrah looked at herself in the tent's tall mirror, a cloud of Light Grit burning above her head. She looked good, there was no disputing that. Part of her preferred Azania's appearance, with the thick hair, ornate gowns, expensive jewelry.

Strip away the pearl necklace, the stylish thick-rimmed spectacles, and the ringlets, and by comparison, Quarrah Khai looked rather plain. Her black thief's garb, which wouldn't fit beneath her shimmery silver gown, was already in place beneath the temporary stage, and she couldn't wait to slip into it. Quarrah Khai was indisputably the more interesting character, but she thought perhaps Azania was more pleasing to look upon.

Quarrah spun around as the tent flap rustled. Lorstan Grale entered, his green shoulder cape a splash of color against the rest of his dark attire.

"You look radiant," he said, as the canvas flap settled behind him. "A picture of fire and ash." He gestured from her vibrant red hair to her fitted silver gown.

Quarrah didn't expect Lorstan Grale to break character. The fact that he was actually Elbrig Taut made Quarrah's head spin. Even after learning his true identity, Quarrah found it impossible to see him as anything but the conductor.

No one else knew his secret identity. Not even Raek. But Lorstan Grale had been the only person permitted to visit Azania at the Avedon apartment. He'd revealed himself as Elbrig and laid out the most insane plan for the cantata. So insane that Quarrah knew it had Ard's fingers all over it. She'd been whisked away to the outdoor stage to sing through the piece last night, getting everything set up just right.

"I came to inform you that we will begin in moments," Lorstan Grale said. "As I'm sure you know, King Pethredote is in attendance tonight."

That was actually good news. For one thing, it meant Pethredote had not yet received word of Ard's escape from the Stockade. It also meant he wasn't suspicious of a second raid on the throne room, as long as he had Azania Fyse in his sights. That was the whole purpose of this elaborate trickery.

"His Majesty will be viewing from a private box with increased security, but he wouldn't miss the Grotenisk Festival's opening concert," said Lorstan. "Homeland knows he's dressed for the occasion."

"The regalia?"

Lorstan Grale nodded.

The question nagged. Was the king wearing the *actual* Royal Regalia? Or had she and Ard had been successful on their first attempt, leaving Pethredote wearing Tarnath's forgery tonight?

What had really occurred within Ard's clever detonation of Memory Grit? One version of the regalia was definitely hidden somewhere in that throne room. She and Ard would have a limited amount of time to find it, and Quarrah hoped to the Homeland that it would be the real one.

"I wish you the best of luck," said Lorstan Grale. "I know there is a lot riding on the next hour."

Quarrah caught the double meaning. It was Lorstan Grale's way of speaking to her as Elbrig, without breaking character.

"My reputation is on the line, too, you know," he continued. "I need to make myself very clear about something. Should you make a mistake tonight, I won't be able to trust you in the future."

"I don't think you have to worry," Quarrah said. "I'm considering retirement if this all pays off."

"That's not exactly what I mean." His expression seemed rather merciless for the topic at hand. "If you are caught making a mistake tonight, you will not sing again. That is the price you pay for playing under my baton."

Lorstan Grale turned abruptly, pushing through the tent flaps. The waiting crowd began to cheer as he appeared on the raised stage.

Quarrah stood stiffly, breathing in the calming manner that Cinza had taught her. It had taken a stern look from Lorstan Grale, but Quarrah now understood exactly what he was implying.

If you are caught making a mistake tonight, you will not sing again. That is the price you pay for playing under my baton.

Sparks! Elbrig was threatening to kill her if she was caught! It seemed brutal after working side by side for so many cycles. But then, Quarrah was sure that Elbrig Taut hadn't become the king's favorite conductor by worrying about what his friends knew.

Quarrah and Ard had learned of the conductor's true identity through dire necessity. But Elbrig actually liked Ardor. He trusted Ard not to divulge his secret, even while detained in a Reggie Stockade with potential for torture. Such trust clearly did not extend to Quarrah. Elbrig would put a lead ball in her without thinking twice.

Well, what did she expect? No honor among thieves. Or disguise managers, as it were.

Elbrig wouldn't be her only problem if she were caught tonight. But even if she succeeded, Quarrah had a feeling of dread whenever she thought about the final applause. She was still rattled from the king's veiled threats during his personal visit. Quarrah perfectly understood that her performance of the cantata was a shield. What would happen when that shield came down?

No choice but to go ahead with the plan now. She'd have to deal with that problem if she got that far.

Sparks, how had she gotten herself here? This ruse had pushed her in every conceivable way. Would she have joined Ardor Benn if she'd known all the uncomfortable things that would be required of her?

But there were undeniable benefits, too. For the first time, Quarrah felt like she had partners who cared about her. She had Raek's concern for her physical safety, mixing only the finest Grit with the best equipment, so there wouldn't be any accidents. She had Ard's concern for her emotional well-being. His thoughtfulness, care, and, dare she say *love*? Whatever it was, she trusted it. And that was new for Quarrah Khai.

Quarrah parted the tent flaps just enough to peer onto the stage. The temporary structure had been erected in Oriar's Square, the very heart of the Char, putting Quarrah less than a ten-minute run from the palace. The stage itself was raised a good five feet, with steps ascending on the side. The orchestra musicians were all seated, and Cantibel Tren was setting the tuning pitch for the other instrumentalists.

An acoustic shell had been built across the back of the stage near where Sem Braison tuned his newly acquired timpani. The wooden shell clearly indicated a front to the stage, which would be very beneficial to Quarrah's planned departure. The Old Palace Steps helped, too. The tall ruins, where Oriar was said to have detonated his failed blast of Visitant Grit, rose beside the stage, further boxing in the musicians.

As a result of the wooden shell and Old Palace Steps, the massive crowd of citizens had gathered where they could easily view the stage. The majority certainly wouldn't be able to make out the lyrics of the cantata, and many near the back wouldn't be able to hear anything but the highest notes from the brass.

There would be a few stragglers behind the stage, those less interested in gossip and more interested in feeling the power of the orchestra. There would also be a few Reggies—at least a handful operating the aerial Grit effects. But Quarrah was confident that she could slip out from under the stage without drawing too much attention.

Lorstan Grale had demanded smoke as a theatrical nod to the subject matter of the cantata. And there was certainly smoke. Instead of a railing at the front of the stage, a long trough had been installed, designed to hold a slow burning oil which vented significant dark smoke. And if that wasn't enough, torches sat in braziers against the acoustic shell, and flickering fires burned in metal barrels on both sides of the stage.

Cantibel Tren had been very upset by all the smoke and fire, but Lorstan Grale had insisted. To provide a steadier light for the musicians to read their music in the dark spring night, small Light Grit detonations glowed above every other music stand.

In truth, the smoky atmosphere was necessary to convince the audience that the image of Azania was indeed live. The cloud of Illusion Grit would have a hazy quality just like any other type of detonation. And the radius needed to be large enough to encompass Quarrah's entire body, but small enough not to capture anyone else.

Mixing the Grit to the proper ratios wasn't her concern. Raek had proven his skill many times over, and Quarrah was confident that the fused chain of Grit pots would work flawlessly tonight.

"The Grotenisk Cantata," Lorstan Grale announced to an anxious audience. "Music by Dale Hizror, classic text by Isless Vesta. Tonight's soloist—Azania Fyse." He gestured toward the tent, and Quarrah took a deep breath.

Strangely, *now* she wasn't as terrified as she had been the night she performed Farasse's aria. Perhaps it was the demographic of the audience, common citizens who would be far less critical than the average nobleman. Or perhaps it was because all she really had to do was walk out to a mark on the stage and then make a secret departure.

Quarrah quickly ascended the stage steps in her outrageous heeled shoes. Thousands of hands thundered together enthusiastically, like the roar of a hundred waves crashing at once.

Sparks, they haven't even heard the music yet! What kind of applause would there be when she finished? Quarrah needed to make sure she was back in time to find out.

Quarrah's footsteps resonated over the hollow stage as she searched for the mark. She needed to stand in a very precise location for two reasons.

First, the spot they had marked doubled as the trapdoor through which she would drop to make her escape. And second, the mark was where Quarrah had stood last night when singing the cantata unaccompanied under the initial cloud of Illusion Grit. If she wasn't in the exact same spot tonight, the real Quarrah wouldn't line up with the illusion image.

Quarrah found the mark and struck the performance pose that Cinza had taught her. At this point in their past experiences, Quarrah would expect to feel Cinza's head coming up between her legs, concealed in the heavy folds of her dress. This time, however, the trick needed to play out a little differently.

Once the Illusion Grit was detonated a second time, Quarrah's image would be completely incorporeal. Cinza would pass right through it if she attempted to take her usual singing position. Instead, Cinza would sing from beneath the stage. They had installed a grate at the front, with a conical tube designed to project Cinza's voice out to the massive audience.

Lorstan Grale took the podium, baton in hand. The audience was so silent that Quarrah might have thought everyone had vanished if she weren't staring at them. This next bit needed to happen in perfect synchronization. Starting high overhead.

Aerial Light Grit displays had made their debut at the Grotenisk Festival some fifteen years ago. Tonight, they would kick off the cantata, at Lorstan Grale's request. The distraction would hopefully allow real Quarrah to transition to illusion Quarrah without anyone noticing an unavoidable glitch.

A cue was relayed to the Regulators behind the stage. Quarrah imagined them steadying their huge specialized crossbows, lighting the fuses on the Grit pots. She heard the slap of the bowstrings, and in the night sky, Quarrah saw the sparking tail of the fuses as the pots hurtled to tremendous heights.

She tried not to look up. She tried to steady herself for the drop. Lorstan Grale was watching, however, his baton ready to give the downbeat the moment the aerial detonations ignited.

Flames, Quarrah was suddenly very nervous. *More* nervous than her first performance.

There it was. A series of Compounded Light Grit detonations, punctuated with the bang and fire of a little Blast Grit. They lit up the dark sky over the Char like half a dozen miniature suns.

The audience gasped in collective amazement. Every head turned skyward. Lorstan Grale's baton came down in a resounding instrumental chord. A Grit pot shattered at her feet. Quarrah wasn't even sure where it had come from, but a hazy cloud instantly enveloped her.

For the briefest of moments, she was standing in the same place she had been the night before. This second blast of Illusion Grit linked the location through time, and a previous image of Quarrah appeared in the same spot. She was wearing the same dress, red wig done in an identical manner.

Then the trapdoor in the stage opened, and Quarrah, the real, tangible Quarrah, dropped out of sight.

"About blazing time," Quarrah muttered, landing in a crouch on the ground next to Cinza. The strange bald woman was pushing the trapdoor closed, hopefully quick enough that no one above noticed Quarrah's illusion image seeming to stand in midair.

Cinza paid absolutely no attention to Quarrah, her expression extremely focused. *Counting rests,* Quarrah realized, *to come in at the right time.*

Good thing Cinza's attention hadn't flagged. In the next few seconds, Quarrah's silent Illusion Grit image would open her mouth to sing and it would be up to Cinza to provide the expected voice.

Quarrah decided that she, too, ought to be keeping track of the music in her head. It was the only way she'd know how much time she had before she needed to be back on that stage.

It was fairly dark beneath the stage, but Cinza had a Light Grit detonation the size of a candle flame, burning just behind them. Staying low, Quarrah turned to find her thieving attire carefully laid out beneath the dim light.

Well, that was awfully nice of Cinza to lay her clothes out. It almost made Quarrah feel like royalty. Except, instead of a silken gown displayed upon a featherbed, it was thief's garb lying in the dirt. The silken gown was what Quarrah needed to shed. And quickly. Every moment wasted meant less time to search the throne room for any clues they might have left for themselves.

In a moment, Quarrah had made the transformation, her costume change accompanied by Cinza's crystal voice echoing through the grate under the stage. The best part was trading those wretched heels for Quarrah's black leather boots. High heels were ridiculously impractical. Whose idea was it to make her taller, anyway? A tall thief was far more likely to bump her head while crawling out from beneath a stage.

No one noticed the lithe thief emerge from the rear of the stage like an extra shadow in the darkness. The acoustic shell rose like a Stockade wall as Quarrah slipped past the aerial-shooting Regulators and a cluster of citizens who wanted to be close to the music.

In a moment, Quarrah Khai was on an open trail leading directly out of the Char. She moved at a run. Not a sprint, as she didn't want to arrive completely winded. Creeping past guards required careful regulation of breath. Exhaustion could get a thief caught, and Quarrah wasn't going to make that mistake.

With every footstep she sang through the music in her head, humming the instrumental bits to keep herself on track.

The palace came into view, its pinnacle turret always illuminated by a blast of Prolonged Light Grit like a lighthouse. Quarrah cut around the outer wall that fenced the manicured grounds until she reached the southeast corner.

She saw the horses first, tired heads drooped, standing beside a dim pathway that skirted the Char. Without her spectacles, Quarrah's vision wasn't sharp enough to see the two men until she was a stone's throw away.

"Quarrah." Ard stepped out of the shadows as she drew to a stop. Sweat dampened her hairline, and her face was flushed. All helpful things to mask the reaction she had to seeing Ardor Benn again. Quarrah hadn't anticipated the way her chest would tighten at hearing him say her name. Had Ard missed her the same way?

And it wasn't just her emotions. Instantly, Quarrah felt the ruse settle once more. They had been a snake without a head for a while. Knowing that Ard was at the helm again gave her unspeakable peace.

"*Fire and death*," she muttered. "*The bodies torn in a rain of blood.*"

"Okay." Ard smiled. "So good to see you, too." He raised an eyebrow. "Aren't you supposed to be singing some dreadful cantata right now?"

She waved her hand, drawing in steady breaths to regulate her exertion. "That was so last night." She hummed a little bit.

"It's just a catchy tune?" Ard asked.

She held up a finger. "I'm trying to keep track of where they are in the music, so I know how much time we have."

"Ah," said Ard. "Hence, the whole '*fire and death*' thing."

She nodded, humming again. "Don't mind my muttering."

Raek appeared between the horses. "I've loaded Ard with enough Grit to take on an army," he explained. "You get him up to the roof. He'll get you both inside."

"You're not coming in with us?" Quarrah asked.

"Three's company for an operation like this," he answered. "I'll keep my eye on these two." He patted the animals. "Lots of folks wandering the Char tonight. Opportunistic thieves would leave us without a getaway."

Ard and Raek would need a quick escape if the theft was successful. Quarrah would make a separate retreat on foot. Back to the stage to fill Azania's high-heeled shoes and take her bows.

"Besides." Ard strapped a Reggie crossbow through a harness on his back. "Raek isn't the sneaky type. Just look at him."

"Hey," replied Raek. "You've been spending too much time with Elbrig and Cinza. I'm plenty sneaky. Why, just this morning I was able to sneak half a dozen of Mearet's doughnuts right down my throat."

"That's the end of the cantata's first movement," Quarrah cut in. "We should get moving."

Luckily, the second movement was a long one. She'd need most of the fourth movement to get back to the stage, so that left only about thirty minutes for her and Ard to get in, find the missing regalia, and get out.

"Have fun! Don't break your legs!" Raek called, waving them off.

Ard moved down the path, Quarrah jogging a few steps to catch up. *Don't break your legs?* What kind of good-luck wish was that?

Quarrah hummed a line. "We'll hop the wall and make our way across the grounds," she explained. "We need to get to the roof?"

Ard nodded. "We'll access the throne room from the balcony this time."

The outer wall was more of a formality, a necessary boundary to ensure the preservation of the palace's surrounding grounds and gardens. Any lowlife criminal could jump it. They wouldn't encounter the real security until they were inside the grounds.

Ard beat Quarrah over the wall, hoisting himself and landing behind a bush. Quarrah dropped beside him, crouching side by side in the shadows, studying the illuminated palace.

The balcony was positioned directly above the grand entrance, but making a direct attempt at the front of the palace would be madness. Too brightly lit. Even from a distance, Quarrah saw six red-coat Regulators standing on the balcony, with another six on the steps below.

"We'll climb up over there." Quarrah pointed to a shadowed nook where two turrets met.

"Climb?" Ard whispered. "Why don't we Drift Jump to the roof?"

"That's too much Grit," Quarrah answered. "The detonation would have to be massive."

"We did a big one at the Royal Concert Hall," said Ard. "That didn't seem like a problem, and we shot through a skylight."

"I'm not saying the jump's impossible. I'm saying it's not smart. A Drift cloud that large is bound to get noticed. There are at least four Reggies on a rotating sentry at any given hour of the night. We'll have to slip between them as they circle the palace. If they walk into a giant Drift cloud, I think that'll raise some concerns."

"I might raise some concerns about climbing," he said. "What if I get a blister on my trigger finger?"

Quarrah ignored him. Where was she? The middle of the boring second movement. *Long shall their fates be remembered. Valiant, brave, and strong.* Was that the right line? *Sparks.* It was hard enough to remember all the lyrics when she was standing still and focused.

Quarrah led the way, keeping her figure low as she dashed from one ornamental bush to the next. What was it with wealthy people and their highly decorated grounds? Didn't they realize that they were providing ideal coverage for stealthy intruders?

The rotating guard had just passed when Quarrah and Ard reached the dark nook. They pressed against the wall, blending into the shadows.

Quarrah paused her humming to give some instruction. "There should be enough handholds." She ran her fingers over the cool palace wall. "This is limestone. Judging by the size of the blocks, these were positioned with Drift Grit. The best place to grip will be between the blocks, where the mortar has started to erode."

"I'll follow you." Ard's voice was uncharacteristically shallow. Quarrah was surprised to see an expression that she'd never seen on Ardor Benn before. Sparks, was he *scared*?

Quarrah glanced back up the wall. She had to admit, it was a frightening height. Or it would be to someone unaccustomed to scaling walls.

For a brief moment, Quarrah wanted to draw attention to it. What a rare opportunity to feel comfortable about something that seemed to terrify Ardor Benn. But then she remembered that night in the performers' lounge before Farasse's concert. Ard had only said and done things to calm her nerves.

There was a time to poke fun, and a time to bolster. Part of Ard's success was knowing that balance. Nothing would be served by ruffling Ardor Benn's feathers now. She might tease him later, but at the moment, Quarrah needed to instill in Ard the same confidence he so frequently gave her.

"Tie a small pot of Drift Grit to the back of your hand," Quarrah suggested. "An old climbing trick. More often than not, you'll feel yourself slipping. If you know you're going to fall, smash the pot against the wall. Could save you from a broken neck."

Quarrah hadn't employed that trick in years, but it had helped her deal with heights when she was beginning. By detonating a cloud of Drift Grit, the climber would hang suspended just as she began to fall, giving her time to find new holds and continue climbing.

Ard didn't say anything, but Quarrah could tell that he liked the idea. However, tying something onto the back of one's hand was tricky. That was largely what had prompted Quarrah to design her special Grit-filled gloves.

In a moment, Quarrah had done it for him, using two wide strips of leather, some string, and the smallest pots of Drift Grit from her belt. All the while, she hummed the music or mumbled lyrics about those who had died under Grotenisk's fury.

"What about you?" Ard asked.

"You'll be climbing below me. I expect you to catch me if I slip."

Without waiting to hear his reaction, Quarrah gripped a lip of stone where the mortar was chipping, and hoisted herself up.

She climbed quickly, though probably not as fast as she would have, had she been alone. Quarrah was aware of Ard beneath her, and set a pace that wouldn't outdistance him.

It was about time the tables had turned. Quarrah had been playing by Ardor's rules for cycles now. But tonight, he was doing things her way. Ardor Benn would never have agreed to such a thing when they first met. But maybe Quarrah wasn't the only one who had changed.

And their faith. Their faith will carry them in death. Will carry them to the Homeland.

With lyrics running through her head, Quarrah reached the gable and boosted herself onto the pitched rooftop, offering a hand to Ard. He hadn't used the Drift Grit pots she'd lashed on. That was a good sign.

They were both breathing heavily, seated side by side at the edge of the gable, nearly fifty feet above the dark palace grounds. Most of the tactical climbing was behind them now, but their ascent wasn't close to finished yet.

Some fifteen feet across from their perch was a ledge. That was the best route, but it was too far to jump without the assistance of Drift Grit.

Quarrah withdrew a Grit pot from her belt and threw it at a stone block halfway across the gap. The clay shattered, sparks igniting the loose Grit.

A detonation cloud appeared, hovering between their gable and the ledge. They would need to spring from their perch with enough momentum to enter the Drift cloud at the proper trajectory. Once within the blast area, their bodies would speed weightlessly along that same route until they exited the cloud. On the other side, gravity would return, and they would land on the ledge with natural weight.

Quarrah had performed countless jumps like this one, both in practice, and in thefts. Inexperienced Drift Jumpers tended to flail or spin during the weightless extension of the jump, creating a very obvious problem when exiting the other side of the cloud.

Ard suddenly pitched something into the darkness. On the far side, just above the intended ledge, Quarrah saw a second cloud form, overlapping the one she had detonated.

"What was that?" Quarrah asked, interrupting the music in her mind.

"Drift Grit," answered Ard. "Looked like your blast wasn't big enough."

"That was intentional," Quarrah said. "The landing point needs to be outside the detonation cloud. It's much easier to get your feet down under natural gravity."

"Oh, Quarrah." Ard readied himself for the jump. "Haven't you learned my philosophy by now? Anything worth doing is worth *over*doing."

He leapt. Pushing off the gable, his momentum easily bore him into the overlapping Drift clouds. Ard did exactly as Quarrah had feared, his arms and legs kicking as though he were swimming. He drifted headfirst, then upside down, finally striking the wall above the ledge with his back.

Quarrah rolled her eyes. For as precise as that man was with words, he was rather haphazard with physical stunts. She leapt from the steep gable, entering the clouds with her body at a perfect angle. She sped upward and across the gap, striking the far wall with all the momentum she had started with. Her shoulder took the brunt of the impact, and her palms would have been terribly scuffed if not for her fingerless gloves. See, that was why she preferred a natural landing.

Ard had managed to right himself, using the stone wall to move weightlessly along the ledge. When he cleared the blast radius of the second Drift cloud, his weight returned, planting him securely on the ledge. Quarrah was right behind him, and they moved in silence until they reached an arching windowsill providing access to the actual roof.

Humming softly to herself, Quarrah cupped her hands and gestured for Ard to step up. He slipped his boot into her hands and she boosted him. Getting a second foothold on the top of the window frame, Ard was able to grip the edge of the roof and hoist himself up. By the time he had steadied himself and turned to offer a hand, Quarrah was beside him.

They moved across the roof, making for the front of the palace. The rooftop wasn't steep like the small gabled end they had perched on. In fact, several flat landings had been built onto the roof, to allow royalty to come up and enjoy the sprawling view of the island landscape. Honestly, up here, Quarrah was much more afraid of coming across a Regulator guard with a Fielder than she was of falling.

At last, they were in position, crouching just above the balcony that led into the throne room. Some twenty feet below, Quarrah could see that the balcony was still in disrepair from the staged assassination attempt against Pethredote two cycles ago. Stone masons had begun bricking in the damage, but there were still wooden planks secured over the hole that Raek had blown out beneath the Barrier dome that had surrounded Ard and the king.

Quarrah wasn't sure what Ard's plan was. She'd been so isolated in the Avedon apartment that there hadn't been a chance to talk to Raek. But Elbrig had filled her in on the throne room's new security features. It was probably a good idea to pass on the knowledge to Ard before he tried anything brazen.

"Let me catch you up," she said. "Both sides of the doors are barred. That means they can only be opened with mutual approbation from within and without."

"Yeah," he replied. "Raek's original plan was to detonate Silence Grit and then blow the doors off their hinges with Blast Grit, but that's not going to work."

"Why not?"

"Pethredote said there were veins of Barrier Grit embedded into the doors," whispered Ard. "A single spark will detonate the Grit and seal off the entrance." He reached into one of the hardened leather pouches of his belt and produced a sizable Grit pot.

"What's that?"

"A little cocktail Raek mixed up," answered Ard. "We stopped at the bakery and he slapped it together in remarkable time. The primary Grit is Void, and the blast radius ought to be the width of the balcony."

"We're going to blow open the doors with Void Grit?" Quarrah hissed. "There's no way it's strong enough."

"Raek added Compounding Grit. Should give it the extra push we need to snap the bars and knock in the doors. And the whole thing should happen without excessive sparks, so we won't risk igniting the Barrier Grit."

"What about the Reggies on the balcony?" Quarrah counted four of them in palace red.

"I'll drop the pot between them," Ard said. "With the detonation originating there, it'll deliver the biggest punch to the doors. If I time it right, the Reggies will be on both sides of the blast center, so the Void Grit will throw them to the sides of the balcony and keep them pinned where they can't get a clear shot into the throne room."

"Won't that crack their heads against the railing?" Quarrah asked.

"That's why they're wearing helmets," answered Ard. "And for the record, this was all Raek's idea."

"What do we do once the Void Grit has blown open the doors?" Quarrah asked. "That's sure to get some attention."

"Then we jump."

"Jump?" Quarrah's voice was a bit more forceful than she intended.

"Raek did the math," Ard assured her. "He knows how much we both weigh. He mixed the Grit to our specifications."

"What's that supposed to mean?" Raek knew how much she weighed? She didn't recall telling him her size. Was nothing sacred to these people?

"If we step off the roof and fall into the Void Grit detonation, we should be aerodynamic enough to penetrate a good distance into the cloud before it throws us out."

"It's the 'throwing us out' part that has me worried," said Quarrah.

"As long as we penetrate deep enough, Raek said the Void cloud will spit us out through the open doors and into the throne room. We have to make sure we come down on the door side of the detonation's center, otherwise we'll get pitched off the front of the balcony. And he wanted me to tell you that we'd be exiting fast. So...tuck and roll."

Quarrah lifted a hand to her face. Only a moment ago, hadn't she been the one full of confidence? Maybe this was how a good duo worked—both partners strengthening each other through the swells of crazy ideas.

"If the Grit has enough strength to snap the wooden door bars, don't you worry that it'll snap our bones the second we enter the cloud?" Quarrah asked. She'd experimented a little with Void Jumping. It was extremely dangerous.

"That's why Raek said 'don't break your legs,'" Ard replied. "If we do it right, he said we'll be fine. Think of Void Grit as an intensely powerful wind, pushing everything outward from the center, where the ignition spark occurs. If a strong wind hits you broadside, it can throw you back a step. But if you lie down in the windstorm, it blows over you with less resistance."

Quarrah raised an eyebrow, still not sold on the haphazard plan. "You trust Raek's calculations?"

"Absolutely," answered Ard. "He's the best Mixer I've ever known. If the plan doesn't work it'll be because we jumped the wrong way." He looked at Quarrah. "Ready?"

"I don't think so," she said. But there was no sense in waiting until she would be. Quarrah nodded.

"Here we go." Ard hefted the Grit pot. Below, the four Regulators were momentarily positioned two on either side of the door.

Ard judged the distance and tossed the Grit pot in a gentle underhand arc. Quarrah tensed, drawing a deep breath as the clay pot struck the floor of the balcony. Sparks danced as the Slagstone reacted to the impact, and Quarrah heard the sound of rushing wind as the Grit detonated.

The four Reggies, who had stood with bored posture only seconds ago, were suddenly hurtled to both sides. They skidded across the wide balcony, slamming into the stone railings like leaves in a hurricane.

At the same moment, there was a crack of splintering wood. From her angle, Quarrah could barely see that the Compounding Void Grit had done its damage, the doors pinned open on their hinges.

Ard sidled forward, dropping his legs over the edge of the roof. "You saw where the pot broke?" He didn't bother to whisper anymore.

There was no sign of the broken pot now. Those shards had been promptly expelled by the Void Grit, exiting the cloud like balls from a Roller. But Quarrah had paid close attention to where it struck.

This was a precision jump. If she and Ard didn't leap into exactly the right spot, or if Raek's calculations were slightly off, the Void Grit would repel them forcefully into the night sky. Or into the palace wall. Or smashing into the door frame.

"You'll probably want to point your toes." Ard gave her a rakish smile. "See you inside." He slipped off the edge of the palace roof.

Oh, sparks. Now she'd completely lost her spot in the cantata. She'd just assume that the second movement had ended. That gave them about fourteen minutes to search the throne room during the third movement. Quarrah started humming the opening measures as she eased herself carefully over the edge of the roof.

Ard dropped into the cloud of Void Grit, careful to keep his legs together. His descent slowed immediately, like falling into water.

No, like falling into a windstorm. It was a painful torrent, reminiscent of that time Ard got dragged behind Lord Fewler's horse. Not fun. And quite disorienting.

His ability to breathe was completely stolen away, but the entire unpleasant experience lasted less than a second. Ard was ejected from the Void cloud with the force of two dozen men punching him in the abdomen. He hurtled through darkness, wondering if he was being launched skyward off the front of the balcony.

Then he was tumbling, skidding across a hard stone floor. Ard rolled upright, scrambling for the crossbow on his back. His eyes adjusted to the flickering firelight from the burning dragon skull, casting long shadows across the throne room.

There was no time to check for Quarrah. No time to soothe the aches and scrapes from his wild entrance. There was another way into the throne room, and it had to be blocked. The thunderous opening of the balcony doors would have alerted the Regulators in the hallway. Even now, as the ringing from Ard's tumble faded from his ears, he could hear someone jostling the hallway lock.

Ard had successfully blocked that door on his first venture into the throne room. His plan was to employ the same technique now. A bolt of Barrier Grit from his crossbow would seal the entrance, giving him and Quarrah a little bit of time to search the room.

Ah, flames. The crossbow! His breakneck entrance had snapped one of the crossbow's arms clean off. Well, that explained the throbbing pain below his left shoulder blade. It was a miracle none of his Grit pots had accidentally detonated.

Ard cast the crossbow aside and drew the Grit bolt he had intended to shoot. He sprinted toward the opening hallway doors, vaguely aware of Quarrah flying into the throne room behind him.

The big doors had only swung inward about a foot, when Ard heard a Roller crack. He saw flames as the Blast Grit cartridge ignited, hurling a lead ball in his direction. Ard flinched, hearing the projectile whiz overhead. Then he threw the Grit bolt as hard as he could.

It struck the left door, shattering the clay tip and throwing a hazy cloud of Barrier Grit. The detonation spilled through the opening between doors, encompassing two of the Regulators who were pressing through the gap.

It wasn't an ideal closure, but it would certainly do the trick. Unfortunately, the trapped hallway Regulators would now be able to observe Ard's actions in the throne room. But the Grit would prevent the doors from opening for about ten minutes, which was all the time Quarrah could afford anyway.

Quarrah appeared at Ard's side, her nose bleeding and her cheek scraped from the painful tumble into the room. The Void Grit must have ejected her face-first.

"Trapped," Quarrah muttered.

"I know." Ard gestured at the Reggies. "I'd say I'm a decent shot even without a crossbow."

"I was talking about *us*." Quarrah pointed back toward the balcony exit. "There's no way we're getting back through that Void cloud."

She had a good point, but Ard had already thought it through. "Raek mixed Prolonging Grit into that crossbow bolt. It'll hold a lot longer than the Void Grit. We can escape back out the balcony and Drift fall down to the stairs like I did with Pethredote."

"What about the Reggies on the balcony?"

"They took a pretty nasty tumble against the railings," Ard said. "We can hope they won't get up for a while."

"'*Seeds of a nation rising through ash,*'" Quarrah muttered rhythmically.

"Third movement?" Ard asked. She nodded, continuing with the next line.

They were finally in the throne room, and the clock was ticking. It was time to find what they had come for. Ard strode past

Quarrah to examine the alcove that she had intended to rob two nights ago. It was empty now, save for a naked wooden mannequin behind an unlocked gate.

"It wasn't like that when I came before." Quarrah wiped her bleeding nose. "They'd replaced that gate with a wooden door. And they'd made an improvement to the lock."

"According to Elbrig, this is where they found Chief Aufald in the aftermath," said Ard. "We must have hidden him in here while he was unconscious."

"So I could walk out wearing his coat and helmet," finished Quarrah.

Ard cocked his head, staring at the display alcove. It was maddening not to know what they had done under the influence of Memory Grit. In a way, Ard felt like he was running a ruse on himself.

"Let's re-create the scene," Ard suggested. "Before I detonated the Memory Grit, you were there"—he pointed—"confined in a Barrier dome." Quarrah moved to the indicated spot and dropped into a crouch, humming. "I was back here when I turned on Aufald." He jogged across the long room.

"King Pethredote fired on me," narrated Ard, "so I took cover behind the skull." He moved into position, dropping to one knee behind the elevated throne. "Where was the bag with the replica regalia at this point?"

"I had set it there while I worked on the lock," answered Quarrah. "I think it was just outside the Barrier dome."

"How long had you been trapped before I arrived?" asked Ard.

"It seemed like forever," replied Quarrah. "But I'd say about eight minutes."

"That means your Barrier cloud prison was about to burn out," said Ard. "We know Pethredote was standing between us. Your sudden freedom from the dome would have given us the surprise we needed to subdue the king."

Ard stepped out from behind the fiery dragon skull throne as Quarrah rose and moved from her position. They met each other halfway, Ard holding out his hands to indicate an imaginary Pethredote.

"I think we made the switch," Quarrah said, beating Ard to the same statement. Sparks, this woman was fascinating. A climber, a thief, a thinker. She had played a convincing lady of the courts, yet as she stood before him clad in tight-fitting black garb, he knew he was seeing Quarrah in her greatest role.

A gunshot caused them both to drop instinctively. There was a crack overhead, and a puff of dust and splinters as the lead ball struck the ceiling rafters. What the blazes? Ard didn't understand math like Raek, but he knew the trajectory of that shot was impossible.

Retreating to the far wall, a second gunshot rang out. This time the ball pinged off the Barrier cloud that Ard had detonated around the hallway doors. Who was firing at them? And from where?

"I thought they weren't going to be getting up for a while." Quarrah made a frantic gesture toward the balcony.

Ard squinted through the haze of the Void Grit cloud. There were Regulators out there, but not the four guards that had been pushed aside in the detonation. Tall ladders had been propped against the balcony railing. It was hard to see in the dark, but Ard counted three Reggies bracing the long barrels of their Fielders and firing into the throne room.

The incongruent trajectories of the lead balls could be explained by the fact that the shots were being made through the cloud of Compounded Void Grit. While the balls were small and moving incredibly fast, the pushing force of the Void Grit was still enough to skew the shots.

A muzzle flashed, and another ball tore into the throne room, going wide and chipping into one of the alcove displays on the opposing wall. So much for history. King Pethredote must have authorized any conceivable action against a second intrusion, even at the cost of damaging the one-of-a-kind items on display.

The displays!

"The regalia has to be concealed in one of these alcoves," Ard said, his back to the wall next to Quarrah. "We can rule out the displays that would be too small to hide the coat and crown."

Quarrah nodded in agreement. "I'll check the ones in this direction. You move that way and I'll meet you on the other side." She slipped away without another word, staying close to the wall as another Fielder spit a ball into the room.

They'd have to search fast. Ard approached the first alcove on his route. It was a bejeweled dagger, mounted directly to the stone wall. Nothing behind which he could have hidden a coat and crown of dragon shell. He moved on without pausing to read the plaque explaining the dagger's historical significance.

The second alcove was equally fruitless, displaying a husk of uncut dragon scales. Not an entire husk, of course. That never would have fit. This was a portion about the size of Ard's torso, hanging by decorative chains.

The scales were deep green—almost black. Each was roughly the size of his palm, with a stone-like ridge running the length. Ard knew from his previous visit that the plaque said these scales belonged to none other than the great Grotenisk himself. Ard found it odd that so many relics of the Destroying Dragon were proudly displayed in the king's throne room. Proof of death, he supposed. A reminder that they had slain the powerful beast against all odds.

Ard dropped to his knees and peered behind the hanging husk. In the flickering firelight he saw nothing but vacant space.

The next alcove presented the same frustration. It was a leather duffel bag supposedly used to transport Teriget's pot of Visitant Grit. The bag was certainly large enough to contain the regalia, but Ard could see that it was empty by the way it hung limply from a peg on the wall.

Two more Fielder balls were announced with a crack from the balcony sharpshooters. One struck the back of the throne, but the other actually came unsettlingly close to where Ard was standing.

He made a break across the room to examine the alcoves on the far side. As he passed the ajar hallway doors, he turned, sticking out his tongue and making a rude face at the two Reggies trapped inside the Barrier cloud. Just because he and Quarrah were under pressure didn't mean he couldn't have a little fun.

On this side of the room, Ard remembered a few of the displays. He had examined them on his first invitation into the throne room—how many cycles ago? The nearest was the spear of King Kerith. As useless a hiding place as a dagger. The next was a piece of wood, claiming to be part of the mast from the First Voyagers.

Ard only paused at Millguin's alcove long enough to see if the big lizard was there. She was spread lazily across a rock on the floor, big glassy eyes watching him.

"Where did we hide it?" Ard whispered to the Karvan lizard. "Come on. You must have been watching us that night." But even if Millguin could speak, the king's pet would have been caught in the same Memory Grit detonation as the rest of the throne room. "Useless lizard."

Ard didn't find anything hopeful until he reached the eighth alcove. It was a wooden barrel, the top missing, and a few of the planks broken. The plaque on the wall said it was the barrel in which Prince Raliph survived seven days aboard a pirate ship outside the InterIsland Waters.

Ard rose onto his toes, peering through the bars of the locked gate. But the darkness inside the barrel was impenetrable in the dim lighting. Producing a pot of Light Grit from his belt, Ard reached through the gate and tossed it into the open barrel. Light sprang up, and Ard had to turn away, momentarily blinded by the brilliance. In a moment, his eyes adjusted and he rose onto his toes once more.

The barrel was empty. He could see the bottom, perfectly illuminated by the blast of Light Grit. Cursing, Ard moved to the next
alcove.

Quarrah was waiting for him there, her expression matching
the despondent way Ard felt. This final alcove held a white gown.
The wedding dress of Queen Melsioba from 1060. It was set upon a
mannequin frame, much like the one that was supposed to display
the regalia. Ard studied at the dress, taking sudden note of the way
it bustled outward below the waist.

"Under the dress..." he began. But Quarrah shook her head,
showing him the open lock in her hand.

"I already checked."

"Now, now." Ard couldn't resist. "In the future, you leave the
checking under ladies' dresses to me."

Quarrah sang a line from the third movement, and Ard turned
his attention back across the room. Time was running short, but
they would have to examine each other's work. Maybe one of them
would see something that the other had missed.

But what was there to see? Just a bunch of useless displays.

Perhaps Ard had detonated a blast of Shadow Grit around the
regalia and left it in one of the alcoves. But a Shadow cloud would
look strange during the daylight hours. And there was no way it
would still be burning after two days. Prolonging Grit only went
so far.

Were they on a fool's search? Had the hidden regalia already
been discovered by the king's men and moved to a safer location?
Aside from the alcoves, what else was in this large room? Just an
empty throne and the ever-burning skull of a dragon.

Sparks, that's it!

It was suddenly so obvious! Ard raced forward, heedless of the
periodic Fielder balls piercing the room.

"It's here," Ard whispered.

"The throne is solid stone."

"Not the throne." He smiled, his face lit by the bonfire flames. "The skull."

"But the fire..." Quarrah started.

"If we succeeded in taking the real regalia from Pethredote, then we're talking about fertilized dragon shell," said Ard. "It's unbreakable, impenetrable, and impervious to decay."

"And fire," Quarrah muttered. "We put the regalia in the fire." She chuckled in disbelief. "That's so..."

"Me," Ard said.

"I was going to say *insane*," replied Quarrah. "But I'm beginning to think the two are synonymous."

Stashing the regalia in Grotenisk's fiery mouth was absolutely something Ardor Benn would do. The bonfire was an ideal place for hiding such a treasure. Ard was proud of his past self for thinking of it so quickly.

"So, if it *is* in there," Quarrah said, "how do we get it out?"

It was a good question. One that Ard doubted his past self had asked when hastily making the deposit in the flames. Even if they managed to fish it out, the fragments of shell would be red hot. By they time they cooled enough to handle, the Reggies would be swarming the room, repeating the arrest from two nights ago.

"Cold Grit," Ard suddenly realized. "The king told me that detonations of Cold Grit are used to cool down his throne. We can use the same principle to cool down the skull."

"'*Saplings of hope stretch skyward, skyward. Saplings of hope stretch high,*'" sang Quarrah tunelessly.

"I get the point. We're running out of time." Ard turned to his Grit belts. Labels. Well, that was an improvement. Maybe Raek *was* listening to his requests.

He found two pots labeled COLD GRIT. Quarrah probably had some, too, but his would be enough to envelop the inside of the skull. Using more Cold Grit wouldn't make the detonation any colder. A higher quantity of the Grit would only expand the blast radius. Compounding Grit was the only way to intensify the effect.

Drawing a small knife, Ard turned over the clay pots and gouged out the wax plugs on the bottom. "You have any unmixed Compounding Grit?" Ard asked. "We'll need it to drop the temperature low enough."

Quarrah reached into a pouch on her thigh and produced a small cloth bag. There was no sense in keeping unmixed Compounding Grit in a clay pot. As a secondary Grit, it would only create an effect if detonated with a primary Grit. Ignited on its own, it would merely burn out in a single burst with no effect.

Ard slipped the knife away and accepted the little cloth sack, pulling open the drawstrings.

"How much are you going to use?" Quarrah asked.

"Raek would have some mathematical equation for this. And those blazing little scales. Have you noticed how much mixing equipment that guy has?" Ard upended the clay pot and dumped the Cold Grit into the bag.

"You're going to use it all?" Quarrah observed.

Ard shrugged. "The colder the better. I don't want to get burned."

He emptied the second pot of Cold Grit. Both powders were of a shimmery substance. If he remembered correctly, Cold Grit was processed from digested chunks of nickel, and Compounding Grit was derived from quartzite. The sack was brimming now, fine powder spilling out the top as Ard attempted to cinch the drawstrings.

"What about the Slagstone ignitor?" Quarrah asked.

"Won't need one." Ard gestured to the bonfire in Grotenisk's gaping maw. "The second this pouch hits fire it's gonna blow."

Another Fielder sounded from the balcony, but Ard didn't pause to see where the ball struck. Getting out of this throne room was going to be a real problem. That seemed to be a trend.

Ard shook his head. He couldn't distract himself with thoughts of escape right now. One issue at a time. That was a motto to live by, and a big reason why Ard was so successful.

Turning to face the dragon skull, Ard pitched the little satchel of Compounded Cold Grit directly between the jagged front tusks. A cloud billowed from the dragon's mouth like ethereal fog. The temperature dropped instantly, the fire's warmth disappearing from Ard's face as though someone had suddenly extinguished the blaze. But the fire burned on, its dancing patterns of light and shadows unfazed by the sudden plunge in temperature.

Ard stepped forward, his hand reaching out as a vagabond might do to warm himself on a winter's street fire. But there simply was no warmth.

His confidence growing, Ard stooped to look into the fire, his head passing between the two front tusks, a row of smaller teeth just overhead. The fire was bright, the skull full of burning logs, cinders, and ash.

There! Homeland be praised! There was the regalia, in a heap toward the back of the skull, a scattering of black charcoal dusted across its glittery amber surface.

Ard withdrew his head, a daring look on his face. "It's in there, Quarrah. The regalia's in the fire, but it's out of reach. I'm going to climb in and get it."

"You're going to climb into the dragon's mouth?" Quarrah asked. "That's just fodder for bragging."

"No one has to know that the dragon was over two hundred years dead."

Ard was going to need a few historical relics to pull off his hare-brained plan. He raced back to the alcove with the leather duffel bag, reaching through the bars and pulling it from its peg. From there, he made his way to the first alcove. With a sharp tug, King Kerith's old spear came free of its display fastenings and Ard extracted it through the bars.

"All right, Grotenisk," Ard muttered, moving back to the throne. "Remember this old spear?" The plaque said that Kerith had used the weapon to smite the final blow against the raging dragon. Now, some two hundred and fifty years later, Ard reintroduced the two relics by shoving the spear into the coals.

He swept side to side, doing his best to knock the burning wood to the edges of the skull, creating a makeshift pathway down the center. Flames were still flames, even if they didn't feel hot, and the spear was now smoldering.

Ard swung his leg up to clear the row of bottom teeth. Ducking his head, he hoisted himself into Grotenisk's mouth.

The dragon skull was big, but it certainly wasn't spacious. Ard crouched in the small aisle he had cleared, maneuvering himself forward while using Kerith's spear to sweep a path through the coals.

It was incredibly hot, even with the Compounded Cold Grit lowering the ambient temperature. Without the Grit he would have incinerated. Without the fire, the intensity of the Cold Grit would have frozen him. He was maneuvering through a dangerous balance of elements.

Ard reached the heaped regalia in a series of quick shuffles. He reached down to grab a piece of dragon shell, but drew back his hand. Much too hot to handle.

Using his boot and the smoking tip of the spear, Ard began scooting the fragments into the leather bag he had stolen. Surprisingly, several of the metal fastenings had survived the fire, though the padding and straps had obviously been burned away.

The crown was in pieces, but Ard was able to bag all the significant fragments. He might have missed a few little ones, but the tiny scraps weren't likely to survive the dragon's digestive tract, anyway.

"Ardor!" Quarrah's voice called from outside the skull. She'd have to be patient. It would take a moment to get all these hot pieces of shell into the bag.

"Ard!" Quarrah shouted again. "The Void cloud is out! The Reggies are moving in from the balcony!"

Well, so much for dealing with that problem later. How rude of those Regulators to barge in before Ard had a chance to finish his current problem.

Ard shut his eyes, trying to think his way out of this as he sucked in a deep breath. The smoke caught in his chest, making him cough. With a large fire burning around the clock, how was the throne room not always a smoky mess?

Ard's eyes snapped open. If the smoke could get out, then maybe they could as well. The chimney pipes! Ard remembered seeing them in the center of the room. They rose from the back of Grotenisk's skull like dual columns behind the king's throne.

"Quarrah! Get in here!" Ard shouted. "And try not to catch on fire!" It was sound advice for any occasion, really.

Gunshots sounded in the throne room. Squinting through the bright fire, he saw Quarrah climbing over the teeth and dropping to a crouch inside the dragon's maw.

Quarrah shuffled on her black leather boots, moving with much more grace than he had. "For the record," Quarrah said as she crawled along the path Ard had cleared, "I think this is a terrible hiding place."

"For us, or for the regalia?" Ard shoveled the last few pieces of shell into the bag.

"You decide."

"We need Drift Grit." Ard pointed up the nearest chimney pipe. They were almost directly beneath it, the pipe barely wide enough to accommodate Ard's shoulders. Raek wouldn't have fit, for sure.

"We're going up the chimney?" Quarrah passed him a pot of Drift Grit from her belt.

"I thought the thief in you would appreciate this." Ard reached his arm as far as he could up the pipe. "We vanish like smoke."

He smashed the pot against the metal chimney with a resounding clang.

Though he didn't see it, Ard knew the Slagstone ignitor had sparked, detonating the blast of Drift Grit. Contained in the pipe, the detonation was forced in both directions, filling the chimney with the characteristic weightless effect. A portion of the Drift cloud spilled out the bottom of the pipe, enveloping the spot where Ard crouched, and causing the leather bag to float lazily.

More gunshots. At this point, every available Reggie would be climbing up the balcony ladders and spilling into the throne room. Had the Regulators seen them duck into Grotenisk's mouth? Maybe they'd assume the two thieves were burning up and leave them in peace.

Ard grabbed the duffel bag and maneuvered it into the bottom of the chimney. Giving it a sharp upward toss, he sent the Royal Regalia floating up the metal pipe on a one-way journey to the palace rooftop.

"All right." He seized Quarrah by the arm and pulled her into the bottom of the Drift cloud. "Up you go."

Whether Quarrah liked this plan or not, she didn't argue. Lining up her shoulders, she threaded herself headfirst into the pipe. Ard helped align her in the weightless environment, and she gave a solid kick, propelling upward through the narrow chimney.

Outside the skull, Ard saw the flash of a gun barrel. Lead balls laced through the dragon's teeth as the Regulators began shooting blindly at the two criminals who had climbed into the skull. But the balls didn't find their mark, as Ard was streaming upward through the pipe at Quarrah's heels.

It was a claustrophobic feeling, the metal chimney pipe tearing Ard's shirt and singeing flesh as he shot upward. Once in transit, there was no changing positions, and Ard was grateful that he'd entered the narrow pipe with both arms above his head.

He crashed into Quarrah on the exit, his hands frantically

grabbing at her feet as she hoisted herself out the top of the chimney. A moment later, the two of them collapsed on the roof under natural gravity, covered in soot, burns, and scrapes.

Ard began to laugh. "We did it," he muttered, staring up at the stars. "We blazing did it!"

Quarrah sat up abruptly. "Not much time left. I have an audience that will soon be expecting my bows."

Ard grimaced against the raw scrapes on his arms as he rose to his feet. "Azania's finished," he said. "Just come with me to the bakery."

"I wish I could," she answered. "But that would leave Lorstan Grale with a few too many questions to answer."

It would be inconceivable that a conductor could lead an hour-long piece of music and not know that his soloist was a fraud. Quarrah had to get back for Elbrig, and that was an agreement Ard would help her honor.

"I'm worried, Quarrah," Ard said.

"I'll be fine," she replied. "The third movement is probably just ending. I'll have time."

"It's not that..." Ard took a deep breath. If they were going to split up again, Quarrah needed to know what really happened leading up to Dale Hizror's arrest. She needed to know about the king's informant. "Last time you broke into the throne room...the whole thing was a trap."

"I gathered that," she replied. "The moment the crossbow shot me in the chest."

"But it's more than that," Ard continued. "Someone told Pethredote we were coming to the throne room that night. He knew we were trying to steal the regalia."

Ard studied the shocked look on Quarrah's face. The expression was genuine, furthering his feelings toward her innocence in this.

"And it wasn't the first time someone sold us out," continued Ard. "The same informant tipped off the Regulation that I'd be at Farasse's concert."

Quarrah shook her head. "Who?"

"I don't know," Ard answered honestly. He'd nearly split his brain over the matter, sitting in that dark cell thinking. "Elbrig and Cinza both knew we'd be at that reception." The disguise managers had certainly put together that the end goal of the ruse was to steal the regalia. But if they were selling secrets to the king, then why would Elbrig visit Ard in the Stockade and risk revealing himself as Lorstan Grale?

Quarrah suddenly drew a deep breath, as though startled by an idea of her own. Her hand flew to her lips. She looked at him, and Ard could tell what she was thinking. Homeland knew he'd thought it, too, but only ever for a brief second.

"Ard," she whispered. "What if it's Raek?"

He looked at her, his stomach knotting. Then the fear of her question quickly gave way to vexation. How dare she even suggest such an idea? She didn't know Raek like he did!

"He was the only other person who really knew what we were doing that night," she pressed. "And on the night of Farasse's concert, he was out of harm's way. Like tonight."

Ard shook his head. "But tonight wasn't a setup," he said, fighting to keep his voice low. "If Raek wanted to betray us, he wouldn't have sprung me from the Stockade." Quarrah had gone too far, suggesting that Raek might be a double-crosser.

Ard breathed slowly, feeling the cool spring night air fill his lungs. "You don't know him like I do," he whispered. "Raek would never..."

But it was hard to ignore the facts. Ard, Raek, and Quarrah were the only three who ever knew all the plans. Raek had never put himself in danger, while Ard and Quarrah had both experienced serious setbacks that nearly did them in.

"No," Ard insisted. "I can't explain it. But it's not Raek. Just be careful tonight. The king might know that Azania Fyse is not who she's supposed to be."

"The king won't try anything tonight," she replied. "Not while the public's eye is on me."

Ard picked up the leather duffel bag, noting the satisfying clink of shell fragments. Grotenisk's fire had not only been a clever hiding place, but it had also been proof that the regalia Ard now held was the real one. Tarnath's replica would have melted to a puddle of resin in that heat.

"We have to be more cautious than ever," Ard said. "We shouldn't mention our suspicions about the king's informant to anyone…not even Raek." It pained him even to say it—and he certainly didn't believe it. But until he had a better idea of who the king's informant was, Ard needed to start keeping things closer to the vest.

"I should go. The cantata is probably starting into the fourth movement by now," Quarrah said.

Ard nodded. The night was still a huge victory. Quarrah was skilled and smart. She'd survive the bows. "Something about the cruel flames of Grotenisk's skull…" Ard tried to recall the lyrics.

"'…*the unforgiving flames a symbol of his hatred*,'" Quarrah quoted.

"Nah. Poor Grotenisk was really just misunderstood. I mean, I thought he was pretty helpful down there."

"You just have to get to know him," Quarrah added. "Spend some quality time in his mouth."

Ard grinned. It would seem Quarrah Khai had a sense of humor, after all. "So." He glanced across the dark rooftop. "Any ideas on how to get down?"

~

I am always aware of the time frame. Aware that all will be lost if I am not where I need to be when my time runs out.

CHAPTER

24

Quarrah sprinted.

She knew she'd arrive at the stage completely winded, panting so hard she'd look like a dying horse. But at least she'd be there to take her bows.

Raek had taken her as close as he dared on horseback, but the last quarter mile had to be done on foot. One thing was certain: the music in Quarrah's head did *not* match up with the music she heard as she hastily approached the back side of the stage.

She was behind schedule. In her mind, Quarrah was singing "*a city, a beacon to the Greater Chain.*" But Cinza's voice, as it came into range, was already at "*Fateful Grotenisk no more to gloat.*"

Sparks! That was the final verse!

She scrambled through the flap and under the stage, her eye instantly training on the faint glimmer of light where Cinza was stationed. With the low stage overhead, Quarrah half crawled to reach her, finding her gown, wig, and spectacles carefully laid out and ready. Cinza must have set them for her during rests, or in the pause between movements. This would speed things considerably.

Quarrah unbuckled her Grit belts and shed her black garb as quickly as she could. Standing in her underwear, Quarrah had a terrible thought that Cinza might force her up through the trapdoor like this if she didn't get into the dress quickly.

She hiked the shimmery silver fabric up and began lacing the sides. No corset on this one. The dress itself seemed designed to squeeze her breathless. An extra pair of hands suddenly snatched the laces on her other side, and Quarrah repositioned herself to allow Cinza to continue singing while helping tie.

The dress was smudged with dirt, but Quarrah hoped the smoky atmosphere of the stage above would conceal that. Hopefully it would conceal a lot of little discrepancies. Quarrah's hands were soot-smeared from the chimney escape, and without a mirror, she wondered if her face was, too.

The wretched wig came next. Quarrah found some comfort in thinking that this was likely the last time she'd have to wear it. Cinza held out the two hairpins, and Quarrah carefully slipped them into place, securing the hairpiece. She had to be careful not to prick herself. Those things were unnecessarily sharp.

"'Life! Life! From death springs life.'"

Cinza belted the final lines, maneuvering Quarrah into position beneath the trapdoor. In the dim light, the two women finally took a moment to look at each other. Cinza's eyes grew wide, and her expression told Quarrah that her face was definitely not presentable.

Cinza held out a mug of water as she hit the final sustain, the orchestra playing out as she held the note. Quarrah plunged her gloved hand into the drink and wiped frantically at her face. Was that dried blood under her nose? Better her glove was filthy than her face. Hopefully that was better. Hopefully she hadn't smeared her makeup to look like something horrifying. Quarrah jammed the red spectacles onto her face.

As Cinza added vibrato to her tone, she pitched a small pot of Drift Grit at Quarrah's feet. It filled the space under the stage and Quarrah anchored herself against the weightlessness by pushing on the low floor above her.

Cinza Ortemion cut off her note with a dramatic flair as the cantata ended. Outside, Quarrah heard more aerial Light Grit detonations designed to make the audience look up. At the same moment,

Cinza yanked open the trapdoor. Quarrah knew exactly what to do. She sprang upward through the Drift cloud, popping up in the middle of the stage. The trapdoor slammed under her, and when she touched down, she was standing at her usual mark.

For a strange moment, the Illusion Grit kept burning. If someone looked closely, they might have seen two versions of Azania Fyse sharing the same space. But the Illusion burned out so quickly, it would likely seem a mere trick of the eye.

The audience was applauding now, their attention back on her. It was a roar louder than anything Quarrah had ever heard, and it made her smile. No, this was more than a smile. This was a giddy grin.

It had worked!

Praise the Homeland! The cantata heist had been successful in every way. Ard was free. They had the regalia. Everything was finally going right!

Quarrah took a bow. Then another. And another. Lorstan Grale had stepped off his podium. He was bowing, too, and gesturing proudly at Quarrah. Someone stuffed a bouquet of flowers in her hand. She bowed again. Was the crowd ever going to quiet down?

The crowd quieted. Instantly. Unnaturally.

Quarrah looked up, but the crowd was looking down, every head bowing in reverence. The smile melted from Quarrah's face. Only one person commanded this kind of respect.

King Pethredote strode onto the stage, the amber regalia shimmering in the firelight. It was a stunning forgery. Quarrah never would have suspected it was fake, if she hadn't just stolen the real one.

The king paused beside Lorstan Grale, the two men clapping hands together and exchanging brief words. Then Pethredote was moving toward Quarrah.

What was he going to do? The king had made it clear that he would deal with her once the cantata was over. But she hadn't expected him to act so soon. And in front of thousands?

No. Pethredote wouldn't hurt her here. There would still be time to get away.

"Azania Fyse." Pethredote reached for her hand, and she gave it to him instinctively. Her wet hand, the silver glove stained with soot and dried blood. He lifted it slowly to his lips and kissed her knuckles.

Quarrah was trembling. Oh, she hated this man. So spotless on the outside. So rotten on the inside. He lowered her hand, but didn't let go. Turning, he addressed the crowd.

"Tonight, you have heard the voice of a flower in full bloom."

Great, there he went with the flower analogy again. Was this the part where she got cut down?

"No doubt, you all would like to shower our dear Azania with adoring praise," continued the king. "But the night grows late, and I must ensure that such a lustrous talent as hers be safeguarded in a crowd so large."

The king gestured to the side of the stage. Next to the ruins of the Old Palace Steps was a private carriage, hitched to a chestnut horse.

"I had my servants prepare my carriage in advance so I could make an easy departure," said the king. "But I must insist that you take the carriage instead, Azania Fyse."

This couldn't be good. Something told her that carriage wouldn't be going to Avedon Street.

"What about Your Majesty?" asked Quarrah, fighting to keep her voice steady.

"My servants are already preparing another carriage," replied the king. "Though it will be some time before it will arrive, with the crowds such as they are. I am more than delighted to remain on the stage and congratulate this fine orchestra."

"So am I," said Quarrah. She turned awkwardly to the orchestra behind her. "Um...Congratulations!" *Ah, flames.* She was making a fool of herself. She needed to get ahold of this situation.

King Pethredote gestured to the carriage once more. "I insist, Lady Azania. Surely, you would not turn down your king."

Well, when he put it that way, what choice did she have? "I would be honored," she lied.

The king finally released her damp glove, and Quarrah stepped past him, moving slowly for the stairs at the end of the stage.

On display for thousands of eyes, Quarrah Khai was marching to her certain doom. She passed Lorstan Grale. For one hopeful moment, she hoped he'd do something to save her. Like when he'd fired that shot at the Royal Concert Hall.

But Elbrig didn't even look up from where he stared at the stage. Her life wasn't worth his reputation or his disguise. And with Ard and Raek securing the regalia, Quarrah would be totally alone against whatever fate awaited her in that carriage.

She descended the steps, a line of Reggie's holding back the crowd that had now risen to its feet. They were reaching for her, calling her name, applauding again.

The king's private carriage was incredibly nice. Easily spacious enough to carry four passengers, it had a door on either side with a small glass viewing window and embroidered curtains that could pull shut for privacy. The door on her side was already open, a red-uniformed Reggie holding it for her.

Quarrah paused in front of the carriage's fold-out steps. She glanced over the crowd one last time in a silent plea for help. Then she moved up the little steps and ducked into the carriage.

The seats were made of leather, padded like no other carriage Quarrah had sat in. A tiny Light Grit detonation was burning in a miniature lantern that had been mounted into the wall of the carriage above her backrest.

She settled in as best she could while one of the servants folded away the steps and shut the door. Then Quarrah heard the driver give a shout, and the carriage lurched forward.

Well, Quarrah thought, *here I go. Off to my certain doom.*

Peeling back the curtain, Quarrah peered out the window at the faces in the crowd. The carriage was trudging through the densely populated square, and some admirers were pushing through the throng in an attempt to keep pace with the carriage.

She let the curtain fall shut, leaning back and closing her eyes. For the first time, she felt some comfort knowing that she was the center of the crowd's attention. Pethredote wouldn't try anything so public. Surely, Azania's fame was some insurance against his plans.

More likely, this carriage was headed to the shoreline where she'd be thrown off the cliff with a block of stone tied around her ankles. Or maybe there would there be goons waiting to dispatch her in the Avedon apartment.

The trick, then, would be to get out of this carriage before it reached its intended destination. But for her escape to go unnoticed, she'd have to wait until they moved onto an open road outside the Char. Jumping out of a moving carriage wasn't going to be pleasant, but Quarrah figured it was a much better alternative than whatever the king was planning for her.

Assuming she survived such a stunt, Quarrah would need to dispose of her wig and dress and slip quietly back to the Bakery on Humont Street. Ard and Raek would be anxious to make plans for the next phase of the job.

An excursion to Pekal was going to require a crew, but after what Ard had told her on the palace roof, who could they trust? A traitor had sold them out—on more than one occasion. Going forward would demand a hard, honest look at everyone who had been involved. Even Raek.

Quarrah's eye snapped open. Was that smoke? She sniffed sharply. The smell was not the pure wood smoke of a campfire, but she recognized the distinct, somewhat chemical odor.

A fuse was burning.

Her body went rigid, eyes scanning. She'd been a fool to close them. Now she could see a smoky haze filling the carriage, thickest at her feet. This certainly meant explosives. Probably a keg of Blast Grit strapped to the underside of the carriage.

Grabbing the curtain, she whipped it back to check out the small window. Still in the Char, but outside Oriar's Square. Here, it was so dark that she couldn't see how many onlookers still surrounded.

No matter. It was time to get the blazes out of here, regardless of how many people witnessed her escape. Quarrah grabbed the carriage door and gave it a push.

Locked!

So that was what those servants were doing when they checked the doors. Pressing her forehead against the thick glass and peering through the little window, she could see a simple pin lock rattling against the exterior of the carriage. But she couldn't pick a lock that she couldn't reach.

None of this would pose a real problem if she only had her Grit belts. A mere pinch of Blast Grit would have blown the small lock to smithereens. But Azania Fyse had a terrible habit of walking around completely defenseless.

She reached across the carriage and gave the other door a shake, but it was obviously locked, too. Quarrah coughed as the smoke continued gathering, her heart pounding. It was impossible to know how long the fuse would burn. Pethredote probably wanted it lengthy enough to see the carriage out of Oriar's Square. She may only have minutes left. Possibly seconds.

Quarrah slammed her shoulder into the locked door. The whole carriage jostled, but the lock wouldn't give. She wondered what the driver of this doomed vehicle was thinking. Maybe if she made enough ruckus, the driver would realize something was wrong.

She shouted, slapping her gloved hand against the driver-side wall. Twice more, she heaved against the carriage doors, but it didn't even slow.

Desperately, Quarrah turned all of her attention on the small window. Over and over, she punched the glass until her knuckles were throbbing and bleeding. She needed something stronger to break through, but a quick scan of the carriage revealed nothing useful.

Sliding off the edge of the padded seat, Quarrah dropped onto her knees to check the carriage floor. She knelt back on her heels, feeling the point of her uncomfortable shoe dig into her backside. How about that?

Quarrah reached behind, tugging one of her impractical shoes free from her foot. Wielding the thing like a hammer, she slammed the point of the heel into the glass. The first blow resulted in a spiderweb crack, and the second completely shattered the window. She tossed aside the shoe and kicked off the other as she rose to her bare feet. Hunched in the carriage, she considered her next step.

She could probably reach the lock, but she didn't have any tools to pick it. Not to mention the risk of slicing her arm to shreds on the jagged edge of the window. Quarrah considered her resources. Maybe there were additional useful aspects of Azania's frivolous attire.

In less than a minute, Quarrah had slipped out of the silver gown and gloves. After all, Cinza had designed this outfit for a hasty costume change. Bunching the excessive fabric, Quarrah shoved it partway through the shattered window frame.

Now for the lock-picking tools.

She reached up and plucked the two slender wig pins from her red curls. It felt good to shake that hairpiece loose, like bidding farewell to the most obnoxious part of Azania Fyse.

With the hairpins in one hand, Quarrah reached through the padding of fabric, her hand groping down the side of the door until she felt the lock. One-handed, out of sight, on a bumpy road...not to mention a sinister length of fuse burning unseen beneath her feet.

This one would have to be opened completely by feel, since the subtle clicks of the lock's inner workings would obviously be drowned out by the moving carriage. Quarrah knew the lock wasn't complicated. It had no reason to be. While King Pethredote obviously didn't trust Azania, he had no reason to believe that she was an expert lock pick.

The hairpins were frustrating tools, a bit too long to hold comfortably in one hand. The pointy tips kept slipping inside the lock, but Quarrah remained steady and determined.

After a moment, the lock popped open. At the same time, the door swung open, Quarrah barely catching herself on the jamb so she didn't spill face-first onto the road. She clung there like a reluctant hatchling bird trying to work up the courage to leap from the nest.

The hard ground whirred past, the carriage gaining speed as it made its way along the final road leading from the Char. The trees were still dense here, with people making their way home along footpaths. But ahead, Quarrah could see a line of buildings at the Char's edge.

"Lady Azania!" shouted the carriage driver.

Quarrah jumped, treating the landing the same way she had when exiting that Compounded Void cloud. She struck the road, rolling. Rolling until she launched headlong into a pruned hedge.

Sparks! She'd done more than enough tumbling for one night! Quarrah pushed herself up, barely reorienting herself in time to see the carriage explode.

It lit up the night like one of Lorstan Grale's aerial detonations. Fire belched outward, and burning scraps of carriage were hurtled in every direction. From her spot at the base of the hedge, Quarrah saw pedestrians running, screaming.

An exploding carriage was enough to draw everyone's attention, and that was surely the king's plan. It was really the perfect way to dispose of Azania Fyse. Pethredote had publicly given up his own carriage to take her home. If the thing exploded en route, it would look like someone had been attempting to assassinate the king. Azania would be an unfortunate casualty, but the people would silently be relieved that it hadn't been their good king.

Quarrah rose on shaky bare feet and ducked into the wooded grounds of the Char, bidding a silent farewell to Azania Fyse. If the Regulator Inspectors took the time to pick through the remains of the smoldering wreck, they'd hopefully find a bit of red hair, or a scrap of silver gown. Everyone would think her dead, and, in a way, Azania truly was.

No more costumes and invented pasts. No more singing and posing. She was just Quarrah Khai now. And nothing felt better.

~

I often feel as if this island is out to get me.

PART IV

Keep the fury at bay. Let not your eyes darken and your tongue become stiff. It is not requisite for the Holy Torch to cure, but to make safe these islands with its own brilliance.

—Wayfarist Voyage, *Vol. 2*

Slintah was made sick in the red of night. A trespasser on land aflame.

—*Ancient Agrodite song*

CHAPTER

25

I think things are going rather well," Ard said, walking alongside Quarrah. It was dawn, the morning's purplish hues more vibrant after the red night of the Moon Passing.

Rather well? Was Ard talking about the ruse? "I have a different way of describing this job," Quarrah mentioned.

"Sure, we have a traitor in our midst," Ard continued, "I got imprisoned in a Reggie Stockade, and you nearly got blown up in a carriage. But isn't that what makes it all interesting? Keeps us on our toes. Despite all those setbacks, we still managed to steal the Royal Regalia."

Ard shifted his large backpack. Like the one Quarrah carried, Ard's pack was laden with enough personal supplies to last a week. But unlike Quarrah's load, Ard also carried the shards of dragon shell tucked in the bottom of his pack, wrapped in leather and brushed clean of the soot from Grotenisk's bonfire.

That was the most either of them had said about the king's informant since that night on top of the palace. But Quarrah felt the threat of a traitor like a constant undercurrent pushing against them. She had decided, like Ard, that it couldn't be Raek. The man was just too invested in Ardor Benn to turn on him. But if not Raek, then who?

"I mean, I'm just going to say it," Ard went on. "We are pretty blazing good at what we do."

Quarrah couldn't fully agree. She wanted to celebrate every small victory along the way, but there was still so much of the ruse to unfold. They were headed to Pekal now. The island of the dragons. Quarrah was afraid that all her expertise and accomplishments would mean very little when she found herself staring at a fire-breathing sow.

Ard dug in the pocket of his long coat, the cold springtime wind whipping his lapels as he withdrew identification papers for him and Quarrah. The man in the booth yawned as Ard approached, the breaking daylight and a mug of coffee clearly not enough to fully rouse him from the long night of the Moon Passing.

"Androt Pen," Ard introduced, passing the papers to the man in the booth. "And this is Floria Migg. We have spots reserved on the first carriage to Talumon."

The tired worker glanced at the papers, checking for whatever signatures he seemed to need. He nodded his approval and slid the papers back with a mumbled "Forty Ashings."

Ard apparently knew the steep cost and already had the coins counted. He dumped the payment on the counter, and the man handed Ard the tickets.

"Funny things, official papers," Ard told Quarrah, tucking them back into his coat as they strode toward the launching area. "The more people need them to get around, the better people get at forging them. The better people get at forging them, the less value they have."

Quarrah knew that Tarnath Aimes had done this particular batch of papers. After creating the counterfeit regalia and lifelike wax figure of Ard, Quarrah assumed that Tarnath had no trouble calligraphing the needed signatures.

Quarrah had been back to her old self for almost a full cycle, sitting around waiting for Ard and Raek to finish their preparations for the expedition to Pekal. It wasn't long after her escape from the king's carriage that Quarrah caught word around town—Azania

Fyse was dead. The people mourned for a few days. Quarrah heard the king even released an official statement expressing some remorse that it "should have been him in that carriage." What a blazing load of nonsense.

A tiny part of Quarrah was sorry to be done with Azania Fyse. She'd always found the character flat and uninteresting, but she knew what her purpose was. She didn't get to decide where to go, what to wear, what to say. That was all predetermined by Cinza Ortemion. But as long as Quarrah stuck to the instructions and coaching from the disguise managers, she would properly fulfill her role in the ruse.

What was her role now? As a thief, she'd accomplished what Ardor Benn had hired her to do. They had the Royal Regalia, so what was Quarrah's purpose on the team now? Honestly, she was starting to feel a little like extra baggage. Like she was just along for the ride until they finished the ruse so she could collect her two hundred thousand Ashings.

The sun was just beginning to crest the eastern horizon. It would take some time to get situated, but theirs would be the first carriage to depart in the Second Cycle. And as innocent as their travel plans seemed at the booth, Quarrah knew that the timing was essential.

Ard and Quarrah followed the paved path toward the edge of the bluff overlooking the InterIsland Waters. Aside from the palace hill, this was one of the higher points along the coast. Several miles outside of Beripent, it made for the perfect launching station for the Trans-Island Carriage waiting there.

Quarrah spotted the carriage immediately. She had seen drawings of them, seen them in flight. But this was the closest Quarrah had actually been to one.

It was an oblong balloon of sorts—thick flax sailcloth draped around a lightweight wooden framework. She thought it looked sort of like an airborne loaf of bread, with a more aerodynamic nose. The actual carriage sat below the balloon, lashed to it with some intricate webbing. The whole contraption was tethered to the bluff by a series of stout chains.

Large sails hung limp on both sides of the wooden carriage. In the faint morning light, Quarrah could just make out the propellers. They extended on sturdy arms behind the side sails, each propeller blade longer than she was tall.

Quarrah saw only a handful of Reggies, though the station was bustling with employees, checking balloons and overseeing other operations. There were several carriages getting prepped for later departures, but only one was straining against its tethers, ready for liftoff.

Traveling this way was expensive, and the paperwork alone had always prompted Quarrah to finagle her way onto a safer, albeit slower, ship when moving between islands.

Thanks to Pethredote's funding for developing inventions, Trans-Island Carriages had been in operation for nearly fifteen years now, each cycle bringing some new addition for safety or efficiency. Not even the swiftest sailboat could match the speed of the carriages. But Quarrah knew there were still many people like her that would rather keep their feet on the ground with a traditional ferry.

Raek claimed he didn't like the system, though Quarrah had a sneaking suspicion that he was actually fascinated by the carriages. His professed dislike probably stemmed from the fact that someone else had done the math. Someone else had planned the detonations and measured the Grit. But not this morning. Raek could finally have it his way, strapped into the pilot's station.

Quarrah knew that it was partly the danger of the carriages that had enticed Ard to use one for their passage to Pekal. This wasn't a boat that could be boarded or sabotaged, allowing a traitor to slip away while the rest of the crew perished. Once this thing launched with everyone on board, it meant they would all make it to Pekal. Or, as Quarrah pointed out, they would all crash and burn.

Quarrah and Ard approached the wooden carriage, massive

balloon lurching against its chains. Now that Quarrah saw the thing up close, she was pretty sure she didn't want to get inside. The carriage looked frightfully flimsy, hardly suitable to bear anything into the sky. Sparks, it looked like the bottom might fall right out!

"It's built to be lightweight," Ard said, probably noticing her uneasiness. "It's just like a giant Drift crate. Once the pilot detonates the Drift Grit, everything inside the carriage will become weightless." He gestured upward. "That way, the balloon only has to lift the weight of the carriage, not its contents."

Quarrah knew the *theory* behind the Trans-Island Carriage System. They'd talked it over and studied plenty of diagrams in the bakery. From here, Quarrah could see the intake at the bottom of the large balloon where the pilot would detonate the Compounded Heat Grit. Hot air was supposed to make this thing fly?

Quarrah shook her head. Raek got overly excited about the science, but it was all rather puzzling to her. It was indeed a bold bit of technology and engineering. And it was a perfect example of the type of progress and forward thinking seen under Pethredote's rule.

"All aboard," Raek's voice sounded at the carriage entrance. Quarrah and Ard stepped around the workers who were adjusting the side sails and found Raek looming in a small doorway. He was wearing a pilot's jacket and hat, though both looked a little small for his large frame.

"You're late," Raek muttered.

"I had a feeling you wouldn't leave without us," Ard said.

"We thought about it," answered Raek. "But you're packing some rather important cargo."

"It's always about the pastries, isn't it?" Ard pulled a wrapped scone from his coat and handed it to Raek.

The imposter pilot chuckled. "If I eat this, we'll never get off the ground." He rubbed his ample stomach.

"Nothing a little Drift Grit can't fix." Ard grinned, jabbing Raek in the gut.

Quarrah and Ard stepped through the carriage doorway and Raek pulled the door shut. A single Light Grit lantern illuminated the interior of the carriage.

Quarrah saw what had to be the pilot station at the front, with racks nailed to the walls, full of Grit pots. A small glass window was set into the nose of the carriage to allow the pilot to see out. The array of controls was nothing like the helm of a proper ship, with levers and switches and knobs. Quarrah knew how to sail, but she was glad she wasn't controlling this curious vessel.

Glancing to the rear of the carriage, Quarrah saw the passenger seats. They were cushioned and designed to seem luxurious. Loose chains secured the feet of the chair to the floor of the carriage, and another ran from the backrest to the ceiling. Quarrah thought they looked like something from a torture chamber, with a jumble of straps hanging from the headrests.

The expected passengers stood in the aisles, studying Ard and Quarrah with a mixture of expressions, as Ard counted under his breath.

"...seven," he finished. "Good. Looks like everyone's here."

These weren't ordinary passengers. Tarnath Aimes had forged their paperwork after Raek confirmed each person's position in their makeshift Harvesting team.

"Let me introduce you to the gang," Raek said, having to stoop for the low ceiling of the carriage. "They're a colorful bunch."

He pointed to two men standing on opposite sides of the carriage. They weren't as tall as Raek, but they were certainly as broad. Both had long dark hair pulled into multiple braids. One had a series of tattoos across his arm and neck, while the other had a jagged scar beneath one eye. They were exactly the type of men Quarrah would avoid on the streets. Not that she couldn't outrun them and leave them chasing their tails.

"The Kranfel brothers," Raek began. "Lan and Jip." Both stood before a massive crank handle that jutted out of the carriage's sides. Those would be attached to the propellers behind the sails outside.

"Harvesters," Raek continued. "They'll be pulling a lot of weight. Along with myself, Quarrah, and Ulusal."

The muscular woman leaned against the back of a chair, her arms nearly the thickness of Quarrah's legs. Her deep blue Trothian skin had a sheen to it, as though she'd come fresh from an Agrodite soak. Ulusal was built thick, like Mearet, but much taller.

Quarrah knew her position on the crew was to be little more than muscle, toting Drift crates and other equipment. A typical Harvesting crew had at least twenty people working the position of Harvesters, but they were going to get by with five. But Raek, Ulusal, and these Kranfel brothers were clearly better suited for the labor than Quarrah.

"We've got Sojin Wint, and Moroy Peng as Tracers." Raek indicated first to a lean woman with light hair, and then to a wiry man already seated, as if impatient for the launch.

Their slender physiques were in line with what Quarrah understood about Tracers. They spent a lot of time running the steep slopes of Pekal, following the dragon once it consumed the bait, and plotting the safest course for the rest of the crew to follow.

"This young lady is our Caller." Raek gestured at a dark-skinned girl standing against the far wall. "Nemery Baggish."

She couldn't have been fifteen years old. The girl seemed shocked to have her name called, like a heavy slap on the back that caused her eyes to stick wide open. What was someone so young doing with a criminal crew like this? Nemery should have been in school, worrying about making friends.

It was a hypocritical thought, especially coming from Quarrah. At Nemery's age, Quarrah Khai had been fully engaged in her thieveries. It hadn't been much of a choice for her. Really, stealing was the only way young Quarrah could have stayed alive.

But Quarrah had always worked alone. In doing so, she had been governed by her own moral code. Nemery's impressionable mind would surely be tainted by these rough characters.

"Lence Raismus." Raek pointed to the final person in the carriage. He was by far the oldest of the crew, his hair thin and white. A few small tattoos adorned his arms, but his pale skin was so wrinkly that Quarrah couldn't tell what they depicted.

"This piece of slag can only hear half the things you say," said Raek. "Like he's got Silence Grit detonated in his ears. But they say there's no better Feeder in the Greater Chain."

Despite his age, there was a spryness to Lence's figure that made Quarrah believe that the old man could keep up with the crew. At least, she hoped so. Falling behind on Pekal led to only one fate.

"That leaves one position." Raek addressed the rest of the crew. "This is *Captain* Ardor Benn. I know his reputation precedes him, and some of you are here for that very reason." Raek turned back to Ard. "Every one of these Moonsick rats has experience on Pekal. Some used to work for legitimate Harvesting crews. Others ran smuggling jobs on the island. Point is, they'll know what to do once we get there, and we won't have to coddle a single one of them."

Ard nodded. "And the Harvesting equipment?"

"It's all stowed in the compartments at the back of the carriage," answered Raek.

Quarrah had noticed that this part of the carriage was only a fraction of what she'd observed outside. Small doors were barred shut against the back wall, and it stood to reason that those led to storage compartments accounting for the rest of the carriage's floor space.

The exterior door to the carriage cracked open, startling everyone inside. A worker peered into the closed space, his face smudged with some kind of lubricating grease.

"I need everyone to strap in," he said. "We're preparing for launch." He looked up at Raek. "Pilot at the helm, sir."

Raek nodded. "Let's get this bird in the air!"

The worker ducked out, as Raek strapped himself in at the front of the carriage.

Ard dropped his large pack into a vacant chair and threw a strap around it. By no coincidence, there were plenty of open seats on this ride. Usually, the station would cancel a flight with so few passengers. Operating these machines took a lot of Grit, and the station wouldn't recoup the cost unless at least fifteen people paid. So Raek had purchased the vacant seats under the false names of passengers who would never show up.

Ard seated himself in the front-most chair, Quarrah quickly slipping into the one beside him. She mimicked Ard's actions, pulling straps over her shoulders and across her lap, cinching the buckles tightly.

"You heard the man. Strap in," Ard said to the other crew members, who stood motionless. "Unless you want to be knocked about like teeth in a fistfight."

Quarrah knew that Ard's words were mostly intended as a scare tactic. The flight was actually supposed to be rather comfortable. They'd remain floating in the contained Drift cloud, unaffected by the actual speed of the carriage. It was the same principle as a lump of Slagstone in a Drift crate. Raek had explained it to her quite thoroughly in the bakery.

A *fully contained* Grit cloud, one that was prevented from reaching its desired spherical shape, was moveable, as long as it remained boxed in. Items inside reacted as if the cloud were stationary, despite the fact that it was being carried up a mountain, or flown across the InterIsland Waters.

The seats and straps in the carriage were likely due to the fact that few people knew how to handle themselves in a cloud of Drift Grit. Most flailed around like injured fowl, pushing off nearby items and picking up momentum until they became a danger to themselves and those around them.

Raek pulled a knob, and Quarrah saw a spark at the top of the carriage. There was a haziness in the air, and Quarrah felt the sudden and distinctive weightlessness of Drift Grit filling the entire vessel. The tag ends of her safety straps drifted upward and the pit in her stomach was an indicator that gravity no longer held them. Beneath her, she felt her chair float a few inches off the floor, the chains keeping it anchored but basically weightless.

There was a general muttering of expletives as the crew members found their seats in remarkable time, restraints cinching snugly across shoulders and laps.

Raek leaned forward and blew a shrill note on a mounted whistle. Outside, there was a series of loud snaps as the chains released. A tug at her insides, and Quarrah knew that they were airborne.

Somehow, the intense heat inside the big balloon was pulling them upward, like a massive sailing ship high in the sky. Raek maneuvered a pair of levers. According to the diagrams Quarrah had seen, those would correspond to the side sails, angling them in a fashion to best catch the wind and direct their course.

"Starboard, crank!" Raek hollered back. Quarrah glanced over her shoulder to see the tattooed Kranfel, Lan, seize the large crank handle in front of him. He could operate it seated, his specialized harness allowing him to lean farther forward in his seat.

As Lan Kranfel cranked, Quarrah heard the purr of the starboard propeller engage, the sail popping as the vessel turned.

"Port, crank!" Raek shouted. On the left side of the carriage, Jip Kranfel engaged his turn crank. "Steady on!"

It bothered Quarrah most that she couldn't see. She strained to catch a glimpse out the pilot's window, but that was just a square of sky-blue glass. Were they over the InterIsland Waters already? How high were they now? Quarrah could curl up inside a sealed kettle-drum and not feel a bit claustrophobic. But this…

Ard reached down and unclipped the buckle at his waist. Slipping out of the shoulder straps, he pushed himself forward, floating easily through the Drift cloud interior of the carriage, but keeping one hand on his chair's headrest to anchor himself.

In this new position, floating nearly horizontally, Ard spun to look over his new crew. "Ladies and gentlemen," he said. "I welcome you to the first Trans-Island Carriage ride to Pekal."

"What's this?" called Moroy Peng, the wiry Tracer. "Short Fuse told us we were flying to Grisn so we could catch a boat out to Pekal."

"There's no station on Pekal," seconded Sojin Wint. "How are we supposed to land this thing?"

"The Short Fuse didn't tell you the plan?" Ard asked.

"Waiting for you to get here, Ard." Raek unwrapped the scone and stuffed half of it into his mouth. "Not my fault you were late." He adjusted a lever on his pilot console. "Besides, I thought *you* would like the honor of sharing our brilliant landing plan with the crew."

"Definitely," Ard said. "We take off, redirect the carriage to Pekal. And then we let out a little hot air, and we land."

"Or a lot of hot air, in Ard's case," Raek added, crumbs floating away from his mouth.

Quarrah rolled her eyes. The fact that they didn't really have a landing plan wasn't going to go over big with the crew. The stations were equipped with heavy nets, cables, and poles to slow the carriage and guide it earthward. She knew Ard's plan was far more... experimental.

"That's it?" Moroy cried. "You're just going to ram this thing into the mountainside?"

"Now, that's a rather tactless description..." Ard said.

"Even if we survive, you're going to get us all caught," muttered Sojin. "You don't think the harbor Reggies will see this chunk of wood flying over the shoreline cliffs?"

"It's barely morning," Ard replied. "And last night was a Moon Passing. That means the island was evacuated to avoid catching

Moonsickness. The Reggies won't be back to the harbors until this afternoon. I assure you that we'll arrive long before they do."

"How can you be so sure?" called one of the Kranfel brothers.

"Does anyone know how fast these carriages move?" Ard asked. *Oh, boy.* Quarrah knew that look on his face. Ard had something to prove. He glanced over his shoulder. "Hey, Raek. How fast are we going?"

"Wind is good this morning," answered the big man. "And the cool air helped us rise quickly. I'd say we're moving at about forty-five knots."

"Thank you." Ard turned back to the crew. "Do a little math, which isn't my strong suit. But even I can figure that puts us on Pekal in just over an hour."

"Sparks," Nemery cursed. "It takes a ship ten hours to reach the harbor. Nine, if it's a small craft and the conditions are right."

"What about the Redeye Scouts?" asked Jip Kranfel.

Quarrah had heard of Redeye Scouts, daredevil sailors hired by the king to watch the Pekal harbors on the night of a Moon Passing. Their name came from the shocking number that contracted Moonsickness, their eyes turning blind and blood red. There was said to be a safe distance one could sail from Pekal during a Passing, but if it wasn't perfectly observed, the influence of the Holy Torch would not protect the risky sailors. It used to be ten miles, but Quarrah heard the distance had recently been increased due to consistent Moonsickness among the scouts.

Foolhardy smugglers and poachers sometimes tried to wait out the Moon Passing beside the Redeye Scouts, and then access Pekal through the harbor. But no smuggler was quick enough to make harbor at dawn, bypass the checkpoint wall and gate, scavenge for valuables in the mountains, and depart before early afternoon, when the Regulation arrived with a full report from the Redeye Scouts.

"The Redeyes are hired to watch Pekal's *harbors*," Ard said.

"We'll be coming in from the sky, so we won't even need to go near them."

"The Reggies will figure it out," said Moroy. "It has to be pretty obvious that this carriage isn't headed to Talumon. Once word spreads, they'll send every Reggie in the Greater Chain after us."

"Pilot error." Ard gestured toward Raek. "The Reggies can't see our entire flight to Pekal. The authorities will assume that something went wrong with the carriage and we crashed in the Inter-Island Waters. They might send a search party for us there, but not on Pekal."

Quarrah could see that Ard's logic upset the Tracer. Moroy clearly hadn't learned how futile it was to go up against Ardor Benn in a verbal argument. Words were Ard's gift, and he had the ability to make something completely irrational sound like a great idea.

"How do we get back?" asked Sojin Wint. "If we crash this thing on Pekal, how are we supposed to get off the island with a full load of fired Slagstone?"

Quarrah knew that Raek had made arrangements for their transportation off Pekal on a ship. But Ard had never mentioned a strategy to remove the mound of Slagstone that would contain the regalia shell fragments. Quarrah was sure he had a plan. He was Ardor Benn! But with a traitor in their midst, the ruse artist was safeguarding that vital bit of information, even from her.

An annoyed expression crossed Ard's face. "I shouldn't have to explain everything to you misfits. I'm doing my job, and I expect you to do yours. You can all shut your lips in the meantime."

Quarrah was seeing a different side of Ard. Typically, he tried to flatter the people around him, building them up so they had the self-confidence to perform at the level he expected from them. But these motley crew members weren't the delicate Focus of some ruse. They were hired help. *Criminal* hired help. It was fitting for Ard to handle them roughly.

"Excellent!" Ard clapped his hands merrily while floating. Just like that, his familiar countenance was back. "I hope everyone enjoys the flight." He swiveled around and reseated himself, pulling the straps tight across his lap and shoulders.

"Port, crank," Raek called.

Quarrah glanced at Ardor Benn, but he had his eyes closed, like he might catch a nap on the way to Pekal. As though they wouldn't be crash-landing in less than an hour.

~

I saw a dragon fly overhead. It was only a short distance, but the grace of her flight was awe inspiring.

CHAPTER

26

Shouldn't we be slowing down?" Ard shouted, gripping the straps on his seat.

"Blazing tailwind," Raek called from the pilot's station.

"We didn't account for that?"

"How was I supposed to account for a tailwind?" Raek shouted. "It's not like I could lick my finger and hold it up three days in advance." He swiveled in his specially designed harness, two Grit pots in his hands. "We're going to have to shear the wings."

Raek swung forward, carefully tossing a Grit pot to each of the Kranfel brothers, who sat at the cranks. Ard flinched as the pots sailed through the weightless environment, but the brothers caught them gently.

"I need you to load those into the crankshaft," Raek explained. "Tamp them down to the end and give it a turn. They should detonate and blow off the wings."

"Blow off the wings?" Moroy shrieked.

From the seat behind, Ard heard the young girl Nemery muttering a prayer to the Homeland. He glanced over at Quarrah. She was pale, mouth slightly agape as she clutched the edge of her seat like it might protect her.

"On my mark," Raek called.

"Ready!" shouted Lan Kranfel.

"Ready!" said his younger brother.

"Now!"

The two men heaved against their cranks, and Ard heard the grating of clay as the pots were crushed. At the same moment, the whole carriage shook with a deafening boom.

"Yeehaw!" hollered Jip Kranfel.

"Moonsick idiots!" shouted Moroy.

Raek pulled himself forward and peered out through the glass viewing window. "Not going to do it..." Ard heard him mutter.

By this point, Ard was really starting to rethink the landing plan. Not that they could have prepared any better. Weather was a variable no one could predict.

"What do you see out there?" Ard called, desperate to float to the front of the carriage, but not willing to abandon the safety of his seat harness.

"Rocks," answered the pilot. "Lots of jagged rocks."

"That sounds like a delightful place to land," Ard answered. "Do you see anything softer?" Was it too much to ask for a well-positioned mountain pond?

"I'm thinking about throwing you out for a landing pad," Raek replied. He was wiggling levers, but Ard couldn't tell if they were actually doing anything. "There's a clearing below us. We'd have to drop fast," Raek explained.

"How fast?" Ard asked.

"Almost straight down," said Raek. "Too much residual heat in the balloon for that. The Grit's burned out, but we'll never get the air discharged in time."

Ard drew his Roller and put two balls through the thin wooden ceiling of the carriage. The resounding shots caused everyone to shout something in alarm, and Ard grinned at the insults and threats.

"Will that do the trick?" Ard asked, holstering his gun and brushing little chips of wood out of his hair. The holes wouldn't be enough to lose containment of their Drift cloud, but those Roller balls would really tear through the sailcloth in the overhead balloon.

Raek checked the gauges on his console and glanced through the front window again. "We're going down at a rate of... *Holy slag!* Everybody hold on to something!"

Ard alway found it strange to be inside a contained Drift cloud because it was impossible to tell how fast he was really moving. Glancing through the front window now, he saw the green mountainside coming up fast! *Sparks!* Maybe one shot through the balloon would have been enough...

"Ard. Ard. Ardor!"

He looked over at Quarrah, every muscle in her body tight. Did she realize she had just said his name three times? She didn't seem like she really wanted to start a conversation.

"Anticipation is the worst part," Ard lied. "Maybe just shut your eyes..."

"Maybe you should shut your mouth!" Quarrah shrieked.

Behind him, one of the Kranfel brothers laughed. There was the unmistakable sound of one of the Tracers retching. Then the carriage made impact.

It was a disorienting jumble of cracking wood and jolting force. The housed Drift cloud was suddenly released from its containment as the hull of the carriage smashed. The cloud rushed out, assuming its natural spherical shape, which it had been denied while in the box. The cloud still enveloped them, but it served them no protection. The crew was strapped into seats that were anchored into the carriage, and the carriage was splitting like a boiled potato against the mountainside.

The crash was over faster than Ard expected. With a jolt, everything came to a halt.

Ard lifted his head, but everything was blurry. He blinked hard, calling out to Quarrah and Raek. There was something wet on his forehead. *That would be blood*, he realized as it dripped from his forehead and splattered on his knee.

Ard knew he had been thrown out the front of the Drift cloud. He thought he was still in the carriage, but there was blue sky above him. Gripping his restraining straps, Ard worked them loose, falling from his seat the moment they came undone. He wiped his bloody brow and turned to take stock of the wreck.

The carriage was in pieces, the bulk of it rising at an angle from where Ard knelt in the dirt. There was dark smoke venting out the back.

"Blazes, Ard." Quarrah crawled through the torn earth toward him. "That plan sounded a lot better when we were sitting around a chalkboard eating pastries." She was favoring one arm, her chair toppled sideways on the ground behind her.

"Have you seen Raek?" Ard asked. Or the Kranfel brothers? Or Nemery Baggish? *Sparks!* Half the crew was missing. And the ones he could see didn't appear to be in great shape.

Lence Raismus looked unconscious, his seat dangling at a precarious angle. Ulusal was tearing at her safety restraints, and Moroy Peng was half-buried under a pile of rubble.

The spherical Drift cloud hung to one side of the carriage, full of debris. Ard saw Sojin Wint floating in the center of it, the Tracer struggling against the straps of her chair. The top chain was still anchored into the carriage ceiling, pulled tightly, holding her chair horizontally in the weightless cloud.

A wooden panel next to Moroy was suddenly heaved aside, and Raek appeared, dirt smeared across his bald head. "Smoke!" he shouted, peering at the back half of the carriage, where their cargo was stored. "Smoke means fire. We've got to get everybody out of here!"

Ard felt the urgency strike him. There was a lot of Grit back there. Blast Grit. If the fire found it...

Ulusal dropped from her chair, crashing across the sloped floor of the carriage to land beside Raek. The Trothian woman helped him pull back a piece of debris, and Ard saw Moroy scamper out of the wreckage and disappear outside.

"We'll get the old man." Raek gestured to Lence Raismus. "You two find Sojin."

Quarrah was already on her feet as Ard rose, head throbbing. In order to reach the floating Tracer, Ard and Quarrah would have to climb up the exterior of the carriage. Ard was still thinking about it when Quarrah took off, hoisting herself atop the carriage framework and scrambling upward to the Drift cloud.

Ard turned, scouring the wreckage for his pack. He found it, still strapped into the seat, headrest burrowed into the moist soil. Pulling the pack free, he untied a coil of rope and shouted to Quarrah.

She was crouched at the edge of the Drift cloud, smoke curling up around her. From her position, Quarrah wouldn't be able to reach Sojin's seat without leaping into the weightless cloud. Ard would have to serve as an anchor for the jump.

Holding on to one end of the rope, Ard threw the coil up to where Quarrah was waiting. She knew what to do without any explanation, quickly lashing the other end of the rope around her middle.

Shouldering his pack, Ard dug his boots into the ground as Quarrah sprang upward. He gave her slack as she soared up through the large Drift cloud, ramming into Sojin Wint. The force of the collision pushed both women upward, the anchored chair swinging on its chain like a pendulum.

The rope went tight in Ard's hands, their momentum yanking him forward. He leaned back, holding them in place. Quarrah and Sojin now floated upside down. They were exchanging a few words, but Ard couldn't hear the conversation. Then Quarrah slipped a knife from her belt and began slicing at the straps that held Sojin to the chair.

Ard saw Ulusal and Raek moving outside, carrying Lence Raismus between them. The old man was conscious now, muttering something about finding his Feeder equipment.

"Ard!" Quarrah shouted. "Reel us in!" Sojin Wint was clinging to her rescuer in the weightless environment.

With the rope in both hands, Ard sprinted out of the carriage wreckage and across the grassy clearing, tugging Quarrah and Sojin through the Drift cloud and away from the smoking debris. They were being towed earthward, but it would still be a bit of a drop from the bottom of the cloud to the meadow.

The ruined carriage suddenly exploded, blowing the top out of the back and sending smoldering scraps of wood into the ground like deadly spears. Ard fell to the ground, losing his grip on the rope. Rolling over, he popped his head up through the grasses to see Quarrah and Sojin stumbling toward him.

The two women reached Ard the same time Raek did. "Come on," his friend said, hoisting Ard up. "Rest of the crew's over here."

The four of them moved around the decimated carriage and up the grassy hillside. Ard was squinting one eye against the blood dripping down his face. He did a quick count of the beleaguered faces he saw waiting.

"Hey! Look at that! Nobody died!" Ard exclaimed. Miraculously, everyone was conscious and accounted for, though everybody appeared to have their share of bumps and bruises.

"You're a blazing maniac, Ardor Benn!" shouted Moroy Peng.

He started to say more, but then decided to storm off toward the trees.

"Moroy!" called Sojin. "Moroy!" She jogged up the hill after him, both Tracers disappearing into the woods.

"They'll be back," Ard reassured the others. "Tracers always tend to be the prigs of the bunch." Ard used to get a good laugh out of Tanalin by impersonating the ones from his old Harvesting crew. He didn't have the energy to do so now. Sparks, his head hurt!

Ard studied his new crew, realizing that they were waiting for instructions. He sort of felt bad for them. This was nothing but a bunch of petty criminals, some too young, and others too old. Little did they know that Ard had just brought them into a bigger game. Like a runner competing in a horse race. It almost wasn't fair. By casting their lots with Ardor Benn and the Short Fuse, the king would consider them personal enemies.

"First things first . . ." Ard couldn't finish the sentence. The dizziness from his head wound and the exertion of getting everyone away from the carriage caught up to him, and he almost fainted. Raek caught him, lowering Ard to a seated position on the grass.

"First things first," Raek took over. "Our captain needs a few minutes to recover. The rest of you get down to that wreckage and see what we can salvage."

Raek led the way, Ard watching through dim eyes as the others followed him. Quarrah suddenly appeared at his side, wincing as she examined the wound on his forehead.

"Guess that's what I get for sitting in the front," muttered Ard as he slipped out of his pack. He was glad to know the regalia shell was safe at his side, rather than scattered across the meadow.

Quarrah gently touched his brow. "That's going to leave a blazing scar. You've got to get that stitched up."

"Nah," Ard said, reaching blindly for his pack. "I'll just use my pot of Health Grit. That should at least stop the bleeding. Maybe even close the cut."

Raek had brought half their stash of Health Grit, divvying it equally among the crew members. Each person's detonation would be enough to mend a small injury, but Ard knew that Pekal had a way of dealing out big ones.

Quarrah dug in the pack for the item. "Is it a good idea to use it so soon?" She handed him the clay pot.

Ard shrugged, putting on a smile for her. "Well, I don't plan to get injured again. That would be purely reckless."

Quarrah squeezed his hand, and Ard realized that his smile was now genuine.

"I'll get down there and help," she said, standing up. "Don't want anyone calling me a prig."

Ard waited until Quarrah was about halfway down the hill before lying down in the tall grasses. Reaching up, he struck the Grit pot against the ground next to his head. The first attempt wasn't hard enough to shatter the clay, but the second one sparked the detonation.

The Health cloud was probably only two or three feet in diameter, but it was plenty to envelop Ard's entire head. He closed his eyes and felt the Grit working on him. It seemed to stabilize his mind, washing out the dizziness and pain and letting him think straight. The cut on his forehead tingled, and Ard knew the flesh was trying to seal itself.

The Health Grit burned out long before Ard was ready. A headache returned, but it was nothing like before. Slowly sitting, Ard reached up and ran his fingers across the wound. It was heavily scabbed, feeling more like a week-old injury than a fresh one.

Ard watched his misfit crew at work. Quarrah was helping young Nemery Baggish with her Caller's equipment. Lence Raismus was also standing beside the girl, his large Feeder's pack on the ground beside him as he pointed at one of Nemery's amplification horns resting in its hardened leather case.

Farther down the hill, the Kranfel brothers were loading their slag picks into a Drift crate that Ulusal was repairing with some pitch. The picks stood about Raek's height, with heavy wooden shafts wrapped in rawhide to improve grip. The tips of the slag picks were fashioned from fragments of dragon teeth, one of the only materials durable enough to make a dent in a pile of fired Slagstone.

Raek must have seen that Ard was alert, because the big man promptly moved up the hill toward him. There was sweat on his bald head from the effort of extracting the equipment from the rear compartment of the ruined carriage.

"One of the Drift crates took a serious beating," Raek reported. "Smashed to firewood when the Blast Grit blew."

"That doesn't give us much carrying capacity," Ard said. The single Drift crate they had left might not even be enough to house the entire Slagstone.

"The rest of the equipment should pull through," Raek answered. "Everything needs a little love and repair, but we can have it all in full working order within an hour or two."

That was plenty of time. Even if the Redeye Scouts had seen the carriage go down, the harbor Regulation wouldn't arrive until that afternoon. Based on their location, Ard estimated it was at least a fifteen-minute hike from the harbor to the crash site. By the time the Reggies arrived, Ard and his crew would be long gone.

"You figured out a plan for the Slagstone yet?" Raek asked.

Ard shot him a sideways glance. Of course he had. Moving the fired Slagstone off Pekal was an essential step. Ard wouldn't have come without a plan in mind. Still, he had been careful not to tell a soul. Problem was, he needed Raek's vast knowledge as a Mixer. The plan was really just a good theory at this point. Raek's expertise would make it happen.

"You're not thinking about the harbors, are you?" Raek asked.

"Flames, no," Ard said. "That's far too expected."

"And impossible."

Like the other islands of the Greater Chain, Pekal was lacking in any regular sense of a beach. Dark cliffs completely surrounded the island, making Pekal look like some sort of tower that had risen from the sea.

The island only had three natural harbors where the rock cliffs were tempered enough to gain access into the mountains. All traffic to and from Pekal had to pass through one of those points, so the Regulation had established significant security—lighthouses, which doubled as lookout ports, built on the high rocks at the edge of the harbors. A wall spanned the accessible areas, with a heavy gate, and firing niches for Fielders and crossbows.

"I imagine you've got something more clever in mind?" Raek asked.

Oh, what was the point in keeping this a secret? Raek clearly wasn't the king's informant, no matter what logic Quarrah might have tried to spell out. It would be safe to tell Raek.

"I've got an idea," Ard said. "It's complicated, but I think—"

A gunshot interrupted him. It was the distinctive crack of a Roller somewhere in the trees behind them. In the direction where Moroy had stormed off.

Then another.

The sharp man-made sounds caused a collective freeze among the crew, each looking up from his or her current project.

"What the blazes?" Ard's hand flashed to his own Roller as Moroy Peng burst through the trees beside the wrecked carriage.

"Get up! Get up!" he screamed. "They shot Sojin! We've got to move!" Moroy's lean form, trained for sturdy running on these mountains, staggered with frantic fear. The crew erupted, quickly stowing equipment and scrambling for weapons. Raek leapt down the grassy hillside, calling commands to get everything loaded into the Drift crate.

Ard sprinted forward, the dragon shell fragments clinking in the big pack across his shoulder. He caught Moroy as the Tracer reached Quarrah and the others. "What's going on? Who's out there?"

"Sojin's dead!" His eyes were filling with tears of panic. "You said they wouldn't be here for hours! You said they wouldn't see us land." Moroy turned. "They're here! Sparks, the Reggies are here!"

Another gunshot rang out, and this one was followed by a torn tuft of grass not ten feet away as the ball struck. The need for survival quickly outweighed any need for answers. Ard picked up one of Nemery's leather cases, his eyes locking with Quarrah's as another lead ball cracked into the hull of the ruined carriage.

Lence Raismus had already retreated, making his way toward the Drift crate that Ulusal had propped open. Quarrah hefted another of Nemery's cases and Ard pushed the young girl forward in a mad dash for cover.

New gunshots rang out, but these were returning fire from the Kranfel brothers, shooting their long-barreled Fielders blindly into the forest. The tactic was less about hitting a target and more about warning the approaching enemy that they, too, had weapons.

Ard and Quarrah reached the others, huddling between the Drift crate and the smoldering ruins of the carriage. Raek held Moroy by the shoulders, attempting to get any useful information out of the terrified Tracer.

The Drift crate was mostly full, all the salvageable food and gear loaded inside. They tossed Nemery's cases into the wooden box, but Ard hesitated for a moment with the pack on his shoulder. He didn't want to let the shell fragments out of his grasp, but he might need the mobility of running without a load on his back.

Ard tossed the pack into the crate and Ulusal closed the door. She began loading Drift Grit into the hopper chamber, where the spark would fall, funneling the detonation into the wooden box.

As the gun balls increased and the sound of the shots drew nearer, Ard determined the direction of the assault. Gratefully, the bulk of the carriage sat between them like a bunker, taking a fair amount of fire and buying them time to make a getaway.

"All right." Ard addressed the crew. "We need to get into the trees before they have a chance to flank us. Raek, Ulusal—you carry the Drift crate. Kranfel brothers keep laying down fire while the rest of us make a run. Once we reach the trees, we'll return the favor and you can join us."

"What about Sojin?" Nemery asked. Sparks, this girl was so young. What was she doing here?

"They shot her in the blazing neck!" Moroy cried, weeping. "She wasn't twenty feet from me."

Nemery's eyes welled and Ard felt a pit in his stomach. How was this happening? They hadn't been on Pekal for half an hour and one of the crew was already dead! It didn't make sense. According to their calculations, the Regulators shouldn't have been able to reach the harbor until midafternoon.

Something was amiss. The situation stank of trickery, a stench Ard was becoming all too familiar with. Such a speedy response to their arrival, followed by a flurry of lead.

Someone knew they were coming. They knew how. They knew when.

Oh, flames.

"Poachers!" cried a voice from the far side of the glen. The gunfire ceased as the speaker continued. "Let's take a moment and talk like civil folk. No need to fill each other with metal!"

Lan Kranfel pulled back the Slagstone hammer on his Fielder, but Ard's hand stretched out, stopping the tattooed man.

"We should hear him out," Ard whispered. Talking could determine who had sent them and how they had arrived on Pekal so promptly. That might lead to answers about the traitor in Ard's crew.

"Blazing Reggies!" Moroy screamed. "You killed her!"

Ard waved a hand at the distressed man, but the comment didn't seem to upset the speaker.

"Actually, name's Grax!" shouted the man from across the glen. "Grax Hajar. And I'm no blazing Reggie. I'm captain of the king's Harvesting crew."

The king had sent his Harvesting crew to hunt them down? It made sense, in an unconventional way. An experienced Harvesting crew would navigate the island much better than the harbor Regulators. And they wouldn't be short on firepower. Every Harvester was trained with a Roller, illegal for use in the Greater Chain but not on Pekal.

Ard glanced at Quarrah and then at Raek.

"I'm going out there," Ard said. "To talk to him for a minute."

"Flames, no!" Quarrah retorted. "You'll get yourself shot dead in a heartbeat!"

"We gotta move," Jip Kranfel cut in. "Can't you see what's going on here? The rat's stalling us. Probably has men circling around as we speak."

"I think we should get some answers from him," Ard insisted. "It might help us stay ahead of them."

From across the glen, Grax shouted again. "Just want to talk about your purpose here. This island's not for the faint of heart."

"I see him," Lan whispered. "He's next to that rock cluster. Standing between those two birch trees."

Ard peered through a gap in the carriage rubble, eyes strafing through the trees until he spotted the figure.

Grax was a short man, wearing a loose sleeveless shirt that fell open on his hairy chest. He was short and stocky, his once-dark hair now flecked with white. His face was squarish, brown skin weathered and scarred. Not a handsome man by any stretch of the imagination, but clearly a man who had spent the better part of his life on Pekal.

"It seems King Pethredote's taken a special liking to you," Grax continued. "Made my crew anchor within ten miles of Pekal so we could be the first to greet you."

That explained how they had arrived so quickly. A mere ten miles was within questionable range during a Moon Passing, even for the Redeye Scouts. Pethredote had gambled with the lives of his Harvesters because he knew Ard intended to arrive on the island first.

And there were only three people who had known that information before today.

"What the blazes?" Raek muttered. "Pethredote knew we were coming? Sparks, Ard. Someone must have sold us out!"

Something about the way he said it made Ard cringe. Seeds of doubt that Ard had been ignoring for weeks suddenly seemed to sprout. Raekon Dorrel? He was the only one who'd known the extent of their plans this time. He'd been piloting the carriage, allowing him to land conveniently close to the harbor. Ard wanted to push the thoughts aside once more, but this time the idea had lodged in his mind like the crashed carriage in the soft mountainside. There was no other explanation.

But it couldn't be! Raek was his brother in every sense but blood. This wasn't a possibility. It just couldn't be!

"We should go from this place," Ulusal's voice sounded behind Ard, her Trothian accent heavy. She was right. Grax wasn't likely to spill much more information than he already had. Maybe that was all he knew. But it was enough for Ard.

"Not sure if you heard," Grax carried on, "but there are dragons in these hills. You might want to—"

Lan Kranfel took the shot, cutting Grax's sentence short as the Fielder ball tore into his bare chest. Ard saw him slump against the nearest tree before slipping to the grass, a gory wound just below his collarbone. From the woods, Ard heard a woman scream.

Ard spun to face his crew member, Lan's Fielder still smoking from the Blast Grit. "What was that?"

"Too much talking," the rough man muttered, reloading the weapon with startling speed.

A flurry of lead balls from the king's Harvesters pinged off the downed carriage, causing Ard's crew to drop to the damp grasses and cover their heads. Then the Kranfel brothers were up, each cracking a Fielder before drawing their Rollers and unloading into the trees across the glen.

It was time to move out. Past time, really. Ard hated to admit that his desire for answers had led to the firefight. The Kranfel brothers were practiced at laying down cover fire, alternating shots and reloads without leaving a moment exposed.

Raek scrambled to the Drift crate. Ulusal had already hefted the poles on the front of the large wooden box. Raek grunted against the weight, and Ard realized that in their haste to escape, the Drift Grit hadn't been ignited. Too late now. The load was heavy, but it wasn't like lugging a lump of Slagstone. Raek and Ulusal would have to bear the natural weight of the crate's load until they reached the safety of the trees.

Ard reached for Quarrah, but she was already on the move. Moroy was nearly to the trees, and Lence Raismus was moving surprisingly fast for his age. Ard had taken half a dozen steps when he glanced back and saw Nemery.

The girl was still seated on the grass, her back to the wooden hull of the carriage, petrified. Ard certainly wasn't going to leave her to those vagabonds.

Darting back, he dropped to his knees and took Nemery's arm. The sharp tug seemed to jolt her senses, and soon they were running side by side, quickly gaining on Raek and Ulusal.

Ard and Nemery were passing the Drift crate when Raek came to a jarring halt. Ulusal lurched forward, nearly dropping the carrying poles at the front. Nemery sprinted on as Ard turned back to find Raek standing stiffly, gazing toward the enemies in the distant trees.

Ulusal suddenly howled in pain. Ard saw the spray of blood, the dark blue flesh of her calf ripped wide from a Harvester's ball. The

Trothian woman dropped her end of the Drift crate, one of the poles cracking as it hit the ground.

"Raek!" Ard cursed. What was he doing? *Trying* to get shot? Ard leapt to Ulusal's side, hefting the remaining pole and gripping under the crate itself.

Ulusal, grunting on one knee, drew a Roller from her belt and fired twice across the glen. Ard groaned under the weight of the crate. It was much heavier than he had supposed, which spoke volumes about the strength of the two who had been carrying it.

The three of them were almost to the trees when a lead ball ripped through the top of the Drift crate. Splintered wood showered on Ard, and he staggered under the burden. Ulusal, hands bloody and shaking, caught the pole, and together, they limped the remaining distance into the trees.

"Lay down fire for the Kranfel brothers!" Ard shouted. "Somebody ignite the Drift crate, and get Ulusal some cloth to bind this wound! We've still got a lot of running ahead of us."

Quarrah crossed instantly to Ulusal, who was making aimless shots across the glen with her Roller. In moments, Ard's crew was raising a chorus of gunfire, and he saw Lan and Jip Kranfel sprinting toward them.

Ard stepped up to the Drift crate, his hands trembling as he picked up the ignitor. He didn't have time to investigate how much damage the crate had sustained, but he hoped it was intact enough to hold the detonation cloud.

Drift crates were designed to contain a cloud of Drift Grit much the same way a glass lantern contained a detonation of Light Grit. Although there was no way to reduce the weight of the crate itself, by filling the wooden box with a Drift cloud, the contents of the crate would become weightless.

Ard peered into the hopper, confirming that Ulusal had filled it. He closed the seal and inserted the long ignitor into a keyhole on the side. Rapping sharply on the end of the ignitor, he heard the

Slagstone make impact with a metal plate inside. There was a tiny spark and a rush of detonation as the crate filled with a cloud of weightlessness.

"Ard," Raek whispered, coming up alongside the large crate. "Did you see?"

Ard gritted his teeth, trying desperately to hold back the rush of anger and betrayal that surged toward his old friend. "What the blazes happened to you out there? Ulusal took a ball because you couldn't keep your feet moving."

Raek suddenly reached out a hand, seizing Ard's shoulder with an uncomfortable firmness. "You didn't see her?"

Ard tried to weasel out of the man's grasp, but Raek held him firmly against the side of the Drift crate, determined to maintain Ard's full attention.

"What are you talking about?" Ard hissed. "See who?"

"She's here, Ard." Raek finally released his iron grip. "She's in the king's Harvesting crew."

The Kranfel brothers burst into the trees, shouting to get the group moving. Raek never turned his eyes from Ard.

"It was Tanalin."

~

*It is hard for me to accept that I will never
see my loved ones again.*

CHAPTER

27

Quarrah stared at her reflection in the pool of water, the afternoon sun beating on her neck. Did the springtime sun feel warmer here? She certainly felt closer to it, and that was after a few mere hours of hiking. They hadn't made a dent in Pekal's vast altitude, but Quarrah was standing on higher ground than she'd ever known.

It was beautiful country, there was no denying that. But the beauty had a wild edge to it that prevented Quarrah from feeling like she could ever truly enjoy it.

Ulusal was not doing well. She had washed her wounded leg in the pool and rewrapped it with a fresh bandage. But even from a distance, Quarrah could tell that the damage was significant. Maybe the bone had been hit. If that was the case, it was likely that a piece of the ball was still inside her leg. Ulusal's detonation of Health Grit hadn't done much, prompting Quarrah to offer hers. The Trothian woman refused, explaining that she would rather hobble than be responsible for Quarrah's life if something were to happen to her later.

Lence Raismus had chosen this small waterfall as the baiting site. The old man was tinkering with flasks and jars containing various colorful liquids. It was a miracle that the glass hadn't broken during the carriage crash. The Feeder's pack must have been very well padded.

Raek and the Kranfel brothers had been gone a few hours, hunting for any kind of large game for Lence to prepare.

Moroy Peng was in and out of sight, exploring the surrounding area and doubling back along their route to make sure the king's Harvesters weren't following them. It seemed like a good idea, although Ard deemed it unnecessary. The Harvesters had lost their captain. Ard said that was enough to shake any crew.

On the other side of the pool, Quarrah had watched Nemery Baggish unpack her Calling instruments. The young girl was now foraging into the trees for sticks and vegetation.

And then there was Ard, standing alone near the base of the waterfall, where the spray from the rocks was just enough to dampen his shirt.

Quarrah had never seen Ard like this. The surprise arrival of the king's Harvesters had thrown a terrible wrinkle into an already complicated job. She had tried to talk to him about it, but Ard had truncated the conversation with a brusque reply.

"Only three of us knew the plan, Quarrah." His face was intense. "Only three of us knew that our Trans-Island Carriage was headed for Pekal."

She knew what that meant, and it made her feel sick. Ard had given in to the logic, though it must have been as painful for him as a knife in the gut.

Raekon Dorrel was the king's informant.

Quarrah couldn't imagine Raek going against Ardor Benn for any price. The two had been friends and partners for too long. Raek wouldn't suddenly change sides unless there was a catalyst that Quarrah wasn't seeing.

She had seen Raek say something to Ard during the gunfight. The conversation had shaken Ard, and he had obviously been avoiding Quarrah over the last few hours. He'd barely even look at her!

Sparks, could it be that Ard was now suspecting *her*? Had Raek said something to cause Ard to doubt her loyalty?

Only three of us knew the plan, Quarrah.

Oh, how had she ever wound up with these ruse artists? They were a complicated duo. They found a way to convolute even the simplest job. If something needed taking, sneak in and take it. In Quarrah's opinion, talking about it was just a waste of time.

So why did it bother her so much that Ard *wasn't* talking to her now?

Quarrah turned, as Raek and the Kranfel brothers emerged from the trees, Raek's short sword clearing the underbrush. Lan and Jip carried a stout branch between them, propped over their shoulders. Hanging from the branch was a huge dead hog, its cloven hooves trussed tightly and its head dangling limply.

"It's about blazing time." Lence gestured to a clearing of loose rock beside the pool. "Put it there."

The Kranfel brothers lowered the hog, and Raek used his sword to cut the bindings around the hooves. The dead animal slumped onto the rocks.

Ard appeared beside the hog, intensely interested after the long wait, shell fragments in a bag over one shoulder.

Lence Raismus pulled off his shirt and dropped it next to his pack. His frame was extremely thin, with a sparse curl of white chest hair over his pasty skin. He pushed past Raek until he was standing at the hog's exposed belly. Drawing a long knife, Lence plunged it into the animal's tender gut. Quarrah watched as he sliced a line from the hind legs to the throat. Innards spilled onto the pebbly ground, and Lence reached in to carve them loose.

Quarrah cringed at the sight of the gory mess. Lan Kranfel must have seen her and he chuckled. "Welcome to the real world, city girl. Pork chops don't just show up on your table."

"Why didn't you just gut that thing where you shot it?" she

asked. "Would've made it a lot easier to carry back." Not to mention it would have kept their campsite a lot cleaner.

Jip grunted. "Say! That's a good idea, Lan. Why didn't we think of it? Oh, wait. We did."

"Blazing Feeder wouldn't let us," Lan shouted at Lence.

"Eh?" The old man looked up at the brothers. "Someone say something about me?"

"Miss Long Legs was wondering why you didn't let us gut the hog in the field," Jip shouted.

"Presentation. It matters," Lence said. "I needed the gore on these stones." The Feeder rocked back on his heels, glancing at Ard. "This would be the time to plant the indigestibles. I'm assuming you have some?"

In response, Ard dropped the bag from his shoulder, the shell pieces clattering against the ground.

Lence Raismus peered inside, his blue eyes wide. "Ashes and soot," he muttered. "What have we here?" One of his bloody hands withdrew a sizable fragment of fertilized shell. He held it up, sunlight shimmering on its amber hues.

"Dragon shell," Ard confirmed.

"So you're making Visitant Grit," replied Lence. There was no other explanation for planting dragon shell into the bait. "I didn't take you for a holy man."

"Of course," Ard answered. "That's why I limit myself to such holy company." He gestured at the others around him.

The old Feeder upended the bag, spreading the shell fragments across the blood-soaked stones. In contrast to the deep red, the amber shards seemed to glow.

Lence stuffed all the fragments into the empty cavern of the hog's gut before retrieving a long needle and some sinewy thread from his pack.

Quarrah felt she knew a fair bit about sewing. Her dark thieving outfits, with their customized boots and gloves, had been created from scratch by her own hand. But watching an old half-deaf man stitch up a dead pig was a sewing application Quarrah had never considered.

"I'm preparing this as a Proud Kill," Lence explained as he sewed. "Dragons are a lot like people. They like to show off. And they don't get along."

Quarrah balked at the analogy at first. But then, how many people had she really gotten along with in her life?

"Dragons usually forage, but they'll eat anything or anybody that's easy for the taking," continued Lence. "Well, not *anybody*. Back in the days of the Patriarchy, the bulls wouldn't fight one another. There were only three of them to keep the species running. But the sows were always available for a skirmish—against the bulls and one another. Dragons fight. They seem pretty interested in killing one another. Again, like people."

"Doesn't the dragon find it odd that the hog is full of fertilized shell?"

"The dragon will barely taste it; their jaws are so big," said Raek. "For you, it would be like popping a blueberry into your mouth." Raek and Ard had probably seen dozens of Feedings during their time as Harvesters, but everything was new to Quarrah.

"Dragons don't tend to do much chewing," Lence added. "They'd just as soon swallow things whole."

"Then what's the point in having such impressive teeth?"

"Teeth aren't for chewing," said Raek. "They're for ripping things down to swallowable sizes. Haven't you seen Ard eat a pastry?"

Quarrah's eyes flicked up to see how Ard would react to the joke. He met it with a distracted half smile. It seemed as though he had been standing among the group, but absent from the conversation at hand.

Lence finished stitching the hog's flayed underbelly. He tied off the thread and stuck the large needle through the fabric of his filthy trousers.

"The Caller and I are going to lure a dragon to this site," Lence explained, picking up the long knife again. "We're going to make it look like another dragon made the kill and had to brag about it."

Lence suddenly began slashing into the exposed side of the hog. Quarrah drew back as the blade carved through the flesh, mutilating the dead animal until it was barely recognizable. Black flies swarmed the bloody mess as Lence stepped back.

"And that's why we needed the guts here," he finally explained. "To make it look like this hog was torn to shreds by a hunting dragon at this very site."

A hunting dragon? That brought Quarrah's nerves up again. "I thought you said they foraged."

"Most of the time." Lence crossed to the pool and rinsed the hog's blood from his arms and chest. "But sometimes the beasts get a primal itch to hunt. Once they make a kill, they leave it for later feasting, and go off bellowing about how strong and skilled they are."

"Think of it like this," said Raek. "Let's say you baked a right lovely apple pie."

"I don't bake," Quarrah answered abruptly.

Raek rolled his eyes. "It's hypothetical, Quarrah. Use a little imagination." He waved a hand. "So you make a pie, and when it's finished, you're so proud of it that you set it on your porch for all to see. You head off down the road, telling everybody about it, and when you get back to the porch it's gone. Your hollering called somebody in to eat the pie."

"Was it Ard?" Quarrah asked. He was most likely to eat a pie that didn't belong to him. She glanced up to see if he was following the joke, but Ard still seemed distant.

"Most likely," said Raek. "Anyway, Lence simulates the kill. Nemery simulates the bragging Call. And then we wait to see if there are any opportunistic dragons nearby, hungry for some bacon."

Lence uncorked a large flask and poured a viscous green substance into a glass measuring vial. He checked the measurement, and then dumped the liquid over the mutilated hog carcass.

"Everything has to be mixed on-site for maximum potency," said the Feeder. "If a dragon doesn't take this bait by nightfall, I'll have to mix something fresh."

"What is that stuff?" Was Quarrah really the only one that didn't know all this?

"Corriloy Perefon," the old Feeder declared. "Dragon laxative." He removed the cork on another flask. "It takes a typical dragon about twelve days to drop her slag."

Twelve days was too long to track a dragon in these mountains. Depending on how much territory she covered, it might take the rest of the crew an extra week to catch up to the Tracer and the Slagstone mound. And it could take even longer to hike out once they'd made the Harvest. That could put them on Pekal for close to a full cycle, with even the slightest delay exposing them to a Moon Passing and leaving everyone sick.

Lence began pouring another liquid, oily and yellow, into the same glass vial. "The laxative will speed digestion. Takes about three days. Might take up to five if the dragon's a big gal, but I always administer the minimum dosage to avoid any risk of splatting out."

"Splatting out?" Quarrah's question was instantly met with snickers from the rest of the crew, and she suddenly had a good idea of what the terminology meant.

"Yeah," said Lan Kranfel. "The same thing happens to Jip when he eats those garlic shrimp from Gaira's shack in South Beripent." This earned the older Kranfel a punch from his scar-faced brother.

"If the slag is passed prematurely," Raek explained, "the dragon won't stick around to fire it. Reeks like nothing else."

"I don't mind the smell..." Lence poured the vial of yellow liquid over the hog carcass.

"What's the yellow stuff?" Quarrah was anxious to change the topic.

"Binding agent," explained Lence. "Helps solidify the slag in the dragon's digestive tract so it'll hold together when it passes with the laxative."

The casual way they discussed this made Quarrah uncomfortable. She wasn't some royal lady, but Quarrah had a standard of conversational decency, and this fell far below it. "This is disgusting."

"That's the problem with society in the Greater Chain," said Jip Kranfel. "Nobody really understands where the Grit comes from. I mean, they're taught. But there's nothing like seeing it. You'll take nothing for granted after this, missy."

Quarrah didn't appreciate the "missy," but Jip made a fair point. It was beyond educational to see a material turned from an ordinary scrap, to the Grit that fueled the economy of the Greater Chain.

Lence filled a bucket at the pool and deposited it next to the dead hog. "There's one more crucial ingredient." He picked up a canteen, holding it at arm's length as he opened the cap. "Reek Sauce."

"What kind of a name is Reek Sauce?" Quarrah noticed the other crew members moving away from the baiting area, as though suddenly losing interest. "Should I be nervous?"

Lence Raismus poured half the contents of the canteen into the bucket of water and stirred it with a long piece of driftwood.

"It's a man-made dragon stimulant." Lence overturned the bucket on the dead hog, residual liquid running down and soaking the bloody stones. A terrible odor assaulted Quarrah's senses, and she brought her hand up to her nose.

Lence made his way back to the pool and drew another bucket of water, mixing in the remaining pungent liquid from his canteen. "One of the few useful things that came out of probing Grotenisk in captivity," he said. "It's a mix of xanatic, prosium, extract of lithpate—"

"Basically, a lot of potent stuff," Raek cut in, hand over his face. "Its proper name is Daudre Solution—named after the chemist who perfected it. But Harvesters affectionately call it Reek Sauce."

"For good reason." Quarrah thought she might gag.

"It stimulates the bite instinct as dragons draw close to it," Raek explained. "Gives them an almost overwhelming desire to snap down on whatever is doused."

"More than doubled the take rate of bait since its discovery." Lence upended the second bucket on the other side of the bait. "Scary as sparks to walk around with a canteen of it on your back. Got to keep the lid marked with Pichar oil to cover the scent."

"Should we be standing this close?" Quarrah instinctively drew back a step as Lence crossed to the pool to rinse his hands and bucket. He returned, loading his pack with the various containers and flasks.

"Nemery's got a Caller hut set up downwind." Raek gestured across the shallow pool. "We should take cover."

Quarrah didn't see anything unusual where Raek had pointed, just a tangle of trees and a crop of stones. The Kranfel brothers were nowhere in sight, and Ard was helping Ulusal ford the shallow neck, where the pool flowed into a clear stream.

Quarrah wondered if Ard would have left her standing out there, wondering where all the others had gone. His sudden disconnect was frustrating. If a new concern had arisen, Ard needed to be forthright enough to talk to her about it.

Quarrah glanced back at Lence Raismus. "You coming?"

"Flames, yes," answered the old man, slinging his pack over one shoulder. "All the Ashings in the world couldn't convince me to stick around here when the dragon shows up."

Quarrah and Lence followed Raek across the stream, catching up to Ard and Ulusal as they reached the Caller hut.

Quarrah could see it clearly now, a type of camouflaged lean-up that Nemery had constructed about fifty yards from the messy bait. Quarrah followed Raek around a jagged boulder to find the hut's opening next to the repaired Drift crate.

There was so much foliage piled atop the support branches that it gave the illusion of dusk even though it was still hours away. Moroy had returned from his exploring, and the wiry Tracer was seated in one corner of the hut next to the Kranfel brothers. Ard and Ulusal were settling in when Quarrah and the others entered.

"Come on." Nemery ushered them at the doorway. "I realize a Caller hut doesn't typically house the entire crew, but I figured there were so few of us. And it's smarter to stay together with the king's Harvesters out there. This really is the safest place. Downwind from the bait at a distance greater than thirty yards. It's positioned across running water, which should help mask our scent." She was explaining it as though reciting rules from an instructional book. "Oh, and I've stacked Pichar boughs across the top and corners. That should also help mask our smell. Not as strong as the oil extract, but I don't have enough of that to go around—"

"Nemery," Ard cut her off. "The stand looks great."

"You want me to make the Call?" the girl asked.

"In a moment," said Ard. "Now that everyone is together, it's time to make some changes."

Changes? What was Ard talking about?

"From here out, I will no longer be captain of this crew," Ard began. "I relinquish the position to my partner, the Short Fuse."

Raek sat forward, his forehead wrinkled with confusion. "What the blazes, Ard? What are you talking about?"

"I'm also moving Moroy Peng to fill Raek's position as a Harvester," continued Ard. "And I, myself, will be taking Moroy's spot as Forward Tracer."

"You two-faced, conniving rat!" Moroy shouted, leaping to his feet, but standing bent over in the low hut. "I don't care what you say. I was hired to be a Tracer on this crew, and you can't make me lug equipment."

"Actually," Ard went on, "as captain, it is my prerogative to make changes among the crew."

"But you aren't captain anymore," Moroy griped. "Just demoted yourself." He looked to Raek. "Change things back, Short Fuse!

You know it's not right to have me pulling Drift crates. I need to be running these slopes. What does this idiot ruse artist know about Tracing? If you're really captain now, then change things back."

Quarrah thought she understood what Ard was doing. This was a test for Raek. If he rejected the changes, returning captainship to Ard, or worse, relinquishing it to another crew member, then Ard would know that his friend had turned against him.

"I don't know, Ard," Raek muttered. "I don't think this is the right move. You as a Tracer? I've seen you winded from running up a flight of stairs..."

"Blazes, Raek!" Ard shouted. "I know what I'm doing. Do you trust me or not?"

Quarrah saw Ard grimace as the forceful words came out. So much for his test. After a blatant statement like that, there was really only one way Raek could respond.

"Flames," the big man finally muttered. "The matter is settled. Positions stand the way Ardor Benn reassigned them."

Moroy swore angrily and stormed out of the hut, leaving an awkward silence in his wake.

"Nemery," Ard finally said. "Make the Call."

The young girl paused. "What about Moroy?"

"His fault for wandering off," Lan Kranfel remarked.

"Make the Call," Ard repeated coldly.

Nemery looked uneasy about the idea, but she picked her way across the low-roofed hut and dropped to her knees at the front. Quarrah peered over the girl's thin frame, getting a clear glimpse of the instrument she was about to use.

It was hornlike in shape, though Quarrah couldn't see the wide bell of the horn since it extended through the leafy wall of the hut to project the sound outside.

The mouthpiece looked just like those of the brass instruments Quarrah had seen during her orchestra rehearsals as Azania Fyse. But this was unlike any instrument Quarrah had seen.

Valves and pull chords were set into a rectangular box on the neck of the horn. Something else protruded from the top, like the thick double reed of a giant oboe—Quarrah had learned that from her training with Cinza. Curious to see how all the components worked together, Quarrah watched carefully as Nemery primed the instrument.

The girl took hold of one of the pull chords and began tugging it, slowly and rhythmically at first, but increasing speed as she went. Within the rectangular box, Quarrah heard something spinning, faster and faster, until it achieved a steady whirr.

Drawing a deep breath, Nemery placed her lips against the brass mouthpiece and blew with practiced precision. At the same time, she reached up with her left hand, depressed a valve, and oscillated the reeds ever so slightly.

A magnificent, bone-chilling sound surged through the large instrument, and Quarrah felt goose bumps prickle across her skin. It was a howl, a groan, and a shriek all tied into one. It had the low reverberation of a prolonged peal of thunder, with all the grinding aggression of a shrill scream.

Nemery made a subtle movement and depressed a second valve, altering the overall pitch as the Call cut through the trees and rolled across the mountainside.

It didn't last long, maybe five seconds at most. And the silence that followed was almost as awe inspiring. It was as though every bird stopped chirping, and every insect stopped buzzing. The creatures of this island knew that sound. And they knew what was coming.

The chill passed, and Quarrah finally took a breath. That was just the *imitation*! What would it sound like when erupting from the throat of an actual dragon? Quarrah leaned forward, peering through the gaps in the hut's front wall. The hog's bloody carcass remained undisturbed and undiscovered.

"Do you blow it again?" Quarrah whispered.

Nemery glanced up at Quarrah. "Timing is everything. Pacing between the calls keeps the sound organic and believable."

Quarrah looked down at the girl's dark hands. Nemery was shaking. Her breathing was steady and full, but her hands were trembling ever so slightly. Quarrah wondered how many times the girl had Called for dragons, and whether experience would numb her to the sensational rush of adrenaline.

The others in the crew seemed far less impressed with the girl's ability, but Pekal was familiar to them. Quarrah didn't feel like she could ever grow used to this environment. The towering peaks and steep slopes filled her with a sense of wonder and fear—a feeling that the hillside itself could reach out and hold her forever.

They sat in silence for a long stretch. Quarrah thought that all of Pekal must have heard Nemery's Call. Sparks, had they just announced their location to the people that were searching for them?

"What if the king's Harvesters heard that?" Quarrah finally whispered.

"We're ahead of them," Ard replied flatly.

"And they're not going to attack us now," added Raek. "That was the Call of a boasting dragon. Whether those Harvesters think the sound is real or not, they won't be stupid enough to go charging toward it."

In the silence that followed, Ulusal's breathing sounded ragged, her face glistening with a sheen of sweat. It was warm inside the thatched hut, but not warm enough to be sweating like that. Ulusal needed better medical attention than the simple cloth binding, which had already soaked through again.

Nemery leaned forward and began pulling the cord on the instrument, prepping for another Call as Quarrah crawled over to Ulusal.

"How's your leg?" Quarrah whispered in the cramped space.

"It feels like flowers and rainbows." Ulusal grunted. "What do you think?"

Quarrah steeled herself against the chuckles from the Kranfel brothers. Unsavory types without a shred of decency. Just look at Lan Kranfel. He didn't seem the slightest bit troubled that he had killed the Harvesters' captain.

"We should take a look at the wound," Quarrah insisted. Just because she was trapped in a hut with a bunch of lowlifes didn't mean she had to behave like them. "We have medical supplies. Ointments and salves. We can dress it…"

"Muckmus medicine," Ulusal cut her off, followed by a statement in the Trothian tongue. It didn't sound appreciative.

Nemery pealed out another Call, deep, clear, and unsettling. Quarrah paused as the sound rolled out of the instrument. There was no sense in trying to speak over the thunderous resonance.

Quarrah waited until the reverberations echoed away down the steep canyon, then she resumed her discussion with Ulusal as though she hadn't been interrupted. "We should at least make sure that the ball passed clean. And we need to get a fresh bandage around that."

Quarrah glanced up at Ard, half surprised to see that he was actually looking at her. "Where are the medical supplies?" she whispered to him.

Ard gestured toward the Drift crate outside the hut. "The white pack."

Quarrah took a deep steadying breath. She had expected Ard to fetch the supplies for her while she began to undress Ulusal's dirty bandage. Well, if Ard was going to lower his standards to fit the current company, then Quarrah would have to do it all herself.

She ducked out of the brush hut. The Drift crate was already open, but it took Quarrah a moment to locate the white medical pack amidst all the other supplies. She found it shoved near the back and had to crawl into the large crate to reach it. A moment later she withdrew, clutching the white pack against her chest.

Quarrah turned back to the hut and froze. There, beyond the shelter, perched atop the waterfall, was a dragon.

Quarrah couldn't see its entire body, but the portion currently visible was both terrifying and magnificent. The dragon's scales were a deep grayish green, with a texture like tree bark but a sheen like glass. The beast's head was larger than the Drift crate, with horns curling up from its high brow. Nostrils flared in an audible snort, and Quarrah saw shimmering heat waves rise from the snout. The dragon's mouth was closed, but the two primary upper tusks protruded past the beast's jaw.

There was an elegance to the way the sow held herself, and her poise seemed to portray an agility, contrary to her gargantuan size. Forelegs gripped the stone at the top of the waterfall, causing the stream's flow to part around her talons. Her breast was massive, like a piece of the mountain itself, and Quarrah could just see the tips of her wings folded against her back.

The dragon snorted again, her long neck extending, head drooping low until it almost touched the gently rolling water of the pool. Her golden eyes, shimmering like large clouds of Light Grit, studied the mutilated hog lying on the bloody stones.

Quarrah didn't know what to do. Instinct told her to duck into the shelter, but her thief's training told her that any sudden movement could draw the dragon's eye. So Quarrah stood, clutching the medical bag and breathing slowly and steadily.

The dragon had arrived much sooner than Quarrah had anticipated. Sparks, Nemery had only Called twice! Ard would consider this good fortune, assuming the dragon didn't spot Quarrah and eat her instead of the bait.

The dragon inched her giant body forward, bits of rock crumbling from the top of the waterfall. Her forelegs now extended down the cliff face, propping her at a rather precarious angle. The wings unfolded, stretching upward to counterbalance the way she was leaning.

Quarrah couldn't blink. Those wings were like ship sails. A network of veins were scrawled across their leathery surface, and the shining sun made the wings appear almost translucent. In a way, they seemed too delicate to belong to such a heavy creature.

The dragon's body now blocked the natural flow of the waterfall. After a second, water began spilling around her, cascading down foliated rocks, forging a new path to the pool below.

The sow's face hovered just above the dead hog. She sniffed the air once more. And then that powerful jaw split wide. Her head came down, mouth snagging the hog carcass. It dangled from her razor teeth, causing the dragon to snap her head back, flinging the hog into the air. She caught the falling carcass in her open maw, those incomparable jaws slamming together, throat contracting as she swallowed the bait.

The dragon's wings came down in a rush of wind that caused the surface of the pool to ripple. The action boosted the dragon's body back to stability on the short clifftop. The sow opened her mouth once again, a bit of shimmering heat wave filtering upward as she bellowed a boasting cry of her own.

If Nemery's artificial Call had given Quarrah chills, then this nearly dropped her in a dead faint. The sound washed over Quarrah, almost like a tangible substance. She felt a gentle warmth radiate from the creature's breath. The monster's cry hit every point of the spectrum—high and low, shrill and soothing. All the components of Nemery's instrument were present, but there was no substitute for the real thing. In comparison, the imitation now seemed hollow and weak.

The cry subsided and the dragon turned with a mighty crashing of underbrush. With such an unbridled departure, Quarrah was surprised she hadn't heard it coming. Could an animal that size move quietly through the brush? The idea terrified her.

Quarrah saw the tip of the dragon's tail as it flicked around, and then the sow vanished into the forest above the cliff. Quarrah remained rigid, the white medical pack clutched against her pounding heart.

Suddenly, Ard was facing her outside the hut. A large pack rested across his shoulders, and there was a brightly colored spear in one hand. "She took the bait." Ard's voice was soft, their faces close together in the late-afternoon light. "All of it."

"That was a dragon," Quarrah muttered. The simple remark brought a smile to his face, and for a moment, Ard seemed to let go of whatever new trouble had been bothering him.

"I have to follow her. I'll see you at the Slagstone," Ard whispered. "Don't trust anyone, Quarrah." He suddenly leaned forward and kissed her softly on the lips. She remained standing in that same place long after Ard had departed. In that place where she had seen a dragon.

~

Of all the music my ears have taken in, nothing can rival the harmonic dissonance of a dragon's cry.

CHAPTER
28

A rd moved swiftly up a treeless incline, his legs burning from exertion as the midday sun beat down upon him. What was he thinking, making himself Forward Tracer? Ard wasn't cut out for this kind of physical activity. He was an idea man. He should have been sitting in the upper room of the Bakery on Humont Street, devouring scones.

Still, changing the crew assignments had been the only move.

Tracers set a path for the rest of the crew, following the baited dragon, sometimes waiting days before the other Harvesters reached the fired Slagstone. That gave the Tracers too much power—perhaps even more power than the captain.

Ard needed to know exactly where the crew was going. If Moroy Peng was working with Raek—and it was a real possibility, since Raek had hired him—it would be too easy to lead the crew into a trap.

Ard's only regret about the reassignment was leaving Quarrah behind. At least she knew of his suspicions toward Raek. Quarrah could keep an eye on him, while Ard marked the trail.

He paused halfway up the hill, leaning on his marking spear and gasping for breath. It was risky to stop in the open, but Ard thought it highly unlikely that the dragon would double back along this path. He had seen her vanish into the trees at the top of the slope. Once he reached that point, he'd have to locate her again, maintaining a safe distance while keeping her within eyesight for as long as possible.

Ard couldn't decide if the solitude was good for his mind. He spent the time pounding out the facts again and again. And each time, the facts pointed to Raek as the king's informant.

Ard shouldn't have let himself be so blind to it. For weeks, he had refused to consider the thought that Raek could lie to him like this. But lying was what ruse artists did best. Was it really a stretch to think that his best friend could have deceived him? Hadn't Ard once done something similar to the woman he loved?

Tanalin Phor. She was here.

It could have been a trick, of course, like so many other things his partner might be lying about. But there was something too gen- uine about the way Raek had said her name. It was logical, too. Ard had heard that Tanalin was working with the king's Harvest- ing crew.

But more than anything, Ard seemed to *sense* that Tanalin was near. It wasn't something he could have deduced on his own, but once Raek had made the comment, her presence began to resonate in him.

Ard couldn't let Tanalin see him. It wasn't supposed to happen like this. Finding Tanalin again had always been his long-term plan. This ruse, with Isle Halavend's million-Ashing payout, would be enough for Ard to leave this life, but he knew everything would be ruined if he had to face Tanalin prematurely.

It was terrifying. More frightening than the dragon he was chasing. The woman he had never stopped loving was on this island. She was coming for him, though she had no idea who he really was.

Ard reached the top of the bare slope and stopped at the tree line. Time for another mark. He twisted the spearhead free from the shaft and dropped it to the grass. Reaching into a leather pouch hanging at his side, Ard withdrew an orange cartridge wrapped in thin paper with twisted ends.

Tracer's Dye. It was the proven method of leaving a path for the rest of the crew to follow. Usually the Forward Tracer paused only to make a few necessary marks, while the Secondary Tracer followed, reinforcing the trail with more dye. But Sojin Wint was dead, leaving it all up to Ard.

He untwisted one end of the paper cartridge and emptied the powdered dye into the hollow shaft of his marking spear. Ard rapped the butt of the spear against the ground a few times before uncorking his water skin.

He took a long swig of water, warmed by the beating sun. But the second mouthful, Ard spit into the hollow shaft of his spear.

Ard spit two more mouthfuls and waited a moment for the dye to mix. Freshwater wasn't a scarcity on Pekal, so the waste didn't bother Ard. The habitat was lush, with all those streams and springs.

The water reacted with the dye to create a frothy foam. Ard heard it fizzing as it increased in volume, nearly filling the hollow spear.

At the butt of the spear was a metal cap with a groove in one side. Ard untwisted the other end of the paper cartridge and emptied a tiny pinch of Blast Grit into the groove.

Rising to his feet, Ard took aim, pointing the open end of the hollow spear toward a large tree. He gave the metal cap a sharp twist, which simultaneously deposited the Blast Grit into the shaft and sparked a Slagstone ignitor to create a small explosion.

The detonation blasted the foamy dye across the limbs and trunk of the tree, making a bright orange mark in a spot easily visible from the bottom of the slope. The spear was still smoking when Ard twisted the pointy head back into place and trudged into the trees.

The marking spear was a versatile tool. In a bind, it served as a weapon. The long pole was a helpful trekking stick when ascending steep slopes. And the hollow shaft doubled as a blow sprayer to mark the trail with the foaming dye.

The dye was designed to linger on rocks and vegetation for up to three weeks. Harbor Regulation assigned the color, assuring that no two Harvesting crews would use the same color within the same cycle. Doing so lessened the likelihood that paths would cross and people would get lost in the mountains.

Ard didn't know if orange was an approved color for this cycle. It was simply the only dye Raek was able to secure for the trip. It showed up well enough, even if Ard found spraying a mark every few hundred yards rather tedious.

It was risky for Ard to play at being a Tracer, since he didn't really know what he was doing. A typical crew covered significant distances across difficult terrain. If the marks he was leaving weren't easily seen, the following crew would have to fan out and search for the trail. From what he'd heard, that was a major reason people got lost and abandoned on Pekal. If a bad storm rolled in while the crew was spread out like that, it would be easy for anyone to get disoriented, even if they had experience on the mountain.

Ard determined which direction the dragon had gone, noting matted grasses and flattened underbrush. The huge creatures did surprisingly well at snaking their way through trees without demolishing the forests. Dragons were more flexible than most people assumed, and they had no desire to ruin their singular habitat.

The creatures didn't move extraordinarily fast unless they wanted to. Ard's sow had meandered across the mountainside at a steady pace. But she navigated ravines and cliffs with much greater ease than a human Tracer.

Gratefully, the dragon had bedded down last night, giving Ard a chance to string his hammock downwind and get some much-needed rest. The morning had been grueling, and Ard's legs were already sore from yesterday's hike. But as lunchtime drew near, the sow's pace seemed to slow.

Ard paused, his ears honing on a sound from the trees behind him. He would have dismissed it as wildlife if the same snapping twigs had not followed him all morning. Had Raek sent someone from the crew to keep an eye on him?

If it was a sneaky follower, it was time to flush them out. Ard clutched his spear loosely and took off at a sprint toward a cluster of crumbled Slagstone rocks.

Old chunks of Slagstone dotted this entire island, broken to bits by the natural Dross layer. The explosive properties of the once-organic material greatly diminished with time, so Harvesters rarely bothered with it, spending their time instead on chasing a baited dragon to claim fresh Slagstone.

Ard paused behind the heaped rocks, tense legs burning. He dropped his pack, drew a dagger from his belt, and rested against one of the cool shaded stones. For a long spell, he heard nothing but the distant rumblings of the foraging dragon. Then there was a crunch of old leaves just down the hill from Ard's hiding place. His follower was drawing nearer, attempting to walk with careful, quiet steps.

Ard would spring on them once they came into view. If it was one of his crew members, he'd question them. If it was someone from Tanalin's crew, he'd tie them up and leave them. Ard's heart suddenly skittered. And if it was Tanalin herself?

A twig snapped, and Ard saw a figure step cautiously into view. He sprang from his hiding place, tackling the figure before realizing that he recognized her.

"Nemery?" Ard lowered the dagger and rose quickly to his feet. "What the blazes are you doing here?"

The girl was trembling, attempting to recover her breath while lying in the underbrush, making no effort to stand. Ard reached down to help her up. Nemery's pack looked as big as she did.

"What are you doing?" Ard asked again, dusting off his pants.

"Following you," Nemery said.

"Yes, I can see that," replied Ard. "Technically, everyone is supposed to be following me. That's a Tracer's job. Where are the others?"

"I went ahead of them."

"Well, you can't stay with me." He gestured back in the direction he had come. "Get back to the group. I've got a dragon with a belly full of valuables that better not get too far ahead of me."

"I can help," Nemery begged. "I know a lot about dragons. Did you know that their ability to breathe fire is reserved almost singularly for hardening Slagstone? Granted, the bulls had an additional purpose for breathing fire to fertilize gelatinous eggs. A lot of folk think that the dragons use their fire as their primary form of attack and defense, but that's a myth that started when Grotenisk razed Old Beripent. Practically speaking, recklessly breathing fire in a forest would be foolish. This island is home for the dragons. They can't afford to burn it all to ash."

Ard stared at the girl in amazement. She was like a talking book! The information was all accurate, but that wasn't the way to make conversation. "So, what *is* a dragon's primary defense?" Ard decided to goad her a bit.

"Aside from the obvious teeth and talons, a mature dragon can swing her tail at a bone-crushing velocity," said Nemery. "They can also breathe heat vapor. It's essentially a cloud of intense heat that is every bit as dangerous as regular fire but doesn't catch the surrounding vegetation."

Ard sniffed the air. There was a distinctive smell to the girl. "Are you wearing Pichar extract?"

"Of course." Nemery fumbled with her pockets, producing a small vial with a cork stopper. "At this proximity to the sow, we are easily within range of her powerful olfactory. A dragon can smell its surroundings up to a hundred yards, depending on the wind..."

"Nemery." Ard gripped the girl's thin shoulder to stop her rambling.

"What?"

"This is your first time on Pekal, isn't it?" Nemery dropped her chin, her unblinking wide eyes studying Ard's boots. "It's okay," Ard continued. "You can tell me. What am I going to do, send you home? You're here now, and you did an impressive job Calling that sow yesterday."

Nemery let a moment of silence hang before answering. Her voice was far less chipper than it had been while explaining dragon defenses. "I lied. I've been apprenticing with a Caller outside Panes. When the Short Fuse was assembling the crew, my master vouched for me. A few others did as well. I knew you were only taking people with experience, but how was I supposed to gain experience if nobody would hire a person with no experience?"

"How old are you?" Ard asked.

"Fourteen."

"Sparks, Nemery!" She was even younger than Ard had suspected. "When I was fourteen, I was far more focused on meeting girls than dragons." He swung his pack onto his shoulders. "Somebody send you out here to find me?"

"No." Nemery slipped the vial of Pichar oil back into her pocket.

"So, you just...missed me? Wanted to catch up?"

"I don't like them," Nemery said.

"You don't like who?" replied Ard.

"Those brothers, Ulusal, Moroy, the Feeder," she listed. "Raek."

Ard studied her, trying to decide if her anxiety was genuine. "To be honest, I'm not sure how much I like the crew lately, either." Ard meant the comment for Raek, but he didn't want to say it outright in case Nemery was working with him.

"But what about Quarrah?" Ard asked.

"No, I don't like her, either."

"Really?" Ard scratched his head. What was there not to like about Quarrah Khai? As thieves and criminals went, she was among the most upstanding.

"They're criminals," Nemery went on.

This got a good chuckle from Ard. "So are you, Nemery. And I'm their leader! What does that make me?"

"Different," said Nemery. "You're different from the others."

"What do you mean?"

"Your name," Nemery said. "It's religious. You're a Wayfarist, right?"

This startled Ard enough that he couldn't find a proper answer. He *had* been Wayfarist once. But that was in his youth. It seemed like ages ago.

"I am, too," Nemery went on. "The others might have been at some time in their lives. But they're obviously pretty Settled now. They don't care about the Homeland, I can tell. Not like you."

The conversation made Ard suddenly uncomfortable, as though a prickly leaf had dropped into his shirt. He should have stopped the girl right then. Set her straight about his religious beliefs. But there was something innocent in those eyes, and Ard didn't have the heart to quash it.

"That's the thing," Nemery went on. "I knew you'd watch out for me. It's what the Homeland commands all good Wayfarists to do for one another. I mean, I know what we're doing is illegal. That goes against the teachings of the Islehood, so technically our actions right now are very Settled. But I need the money and the experience. And we're making Visitant Grit. That's a holy purpose. The Homeland has to understand why we're here, right?"

Oh, Nemery had no idea. A Holy Isle had hired him! And, half a million Ashings aside, deep down, Ard felt more and more like he was doing the right thing. He'd looked into King Pethredote's eyes and felt a zeal drive him onward. An Urging, perhaps? If the Homeland really did exist, Ard thought it must be rooting for him.

"You can stay with me." Ard saw the effect of his words on the young girl's face. "But there's no complaining allowed." He started down the hillside.

"Oh, I won't complain," Nemery said, jogging to keep up. "Did you know that a mature dragon can consume up to two thousand panweights during the course of a regular digestive cycle? Of course, the extruded Slagstone doesn't weigh half that much..."

"I have another rule," Ard said. "No talking."

"Okay," replied Nemery. "I can do that. I mean, I *won't* do that. Talking." She seemed to realize what she was saying and fell silent.

Poor girl. How did a good Wayfarist like her end up in a crew of criminals chasing dragons on Pekal? Nemery was a talented Caller. Her time on a legitimate Harvesting crew surely would have come if she'd exercised a little more patience. She was on a rough road now, assuming she even survived this trip.

It made Ard remember how he'd gotten where he was. This was his first time on Pekal in seven years. Last time he was here, he'd been a different person. Last time he'd stood on these slopes, he'd made a decision—a selfish one, no matter how he justified it. This was where it had all begun for him.

It took Nemery's innocence and a return to these forests for Ard to truly see how far he had fallen. If it came down to meeting Tanalin on this mountain, would she even recognize who he'd become? Yet, Nemery had seen some good in him. The spirit of Wayfarism. Maybe Tanalin would see it, too.

It was midafternoon when Quarrah finally demanded that the crew take a rest. The past day had been rough without Ard. Quarrah was sore from the hiking, but even more tired of her current company.

Nemery had been missing since dawn. Quarrah had no idea what happened to the poor girl. There were no signs of foul play, and no one seemed to have any indication of where she might have gone.

Nemery must have run away. It was all Quarrah could figure. Didn't the girl know that separating herself from the group was an inevitable way to get killed?

Quarrah had searched for Nemery that morning, venturing farther from their campsite than she felt comfortable. Raek had scoured the woods a bit, too, but the others seemed to dismiss her absence with insensitive nonchalance.

Raek had given the order to move on, a death sentence for Nemery Baggish. Quarrah was furious with the big man, but it wasn't like they could wait around with hopes that Nemery might show up.

They had followed Ard's orange markers all day. He had obviously tried to leave them in conspicuous places, but even still, the crew spent a lot of time scouring the area for the next stain.

The Kranfel brothers were crude and crass. Quarrah didn't care to hear a single thing that came out of their mouths, especially since most of their idle comments were directed at her.

Moroy was a fountain of negativity. Owing to the reassignment, the ex-Tracer was now taking turns carrying the Drift crate. Quarrah helped, too, the poles rubbing blisters on her hands, and the cumbersome crate slowing them down. And that was with a detonation of Drift Grit to make the contents weightless.

Lence Raismus hiked with surprising agility, a trekking stick with a whittled handle in each hand. But Ulusal was the primary reason Quarrah had demanded that they take a break.

The Trothian was really struggling to keep up. Raek had carried the Drift crate during her shift, since it was all she could do to hobble on her injured leg. She was silent and strong, but her body was soaked in a feverish sweat brought on by more than the hike.

Quarrah crossed to where Ulusal had collapsed in the grass. She handed the Trothian her water skin, urging Ulusal to drink what was left. The woman silently obliged, propping herself onto one elbow and tipping back the skin.

"Let's take a look." Quarrah gestured to the stained bandage around her calf. The wound was still seeping heavily. And not all the fluids were red.

Yesterday, Lence had stitched the wound closed after Ard's departure. But by nightfall it was clear that something more needed to be done. Raek had built a small fire, heated a blade, and attempted to cauterize Ulusal's torn flesh. This had gotten her through the night, though to be honest, Quarrah didn't think the Trothian slept much for the pain.

"Have you ever been shot?" Ulusal muttered, lying back in the grass without even protesting as Quarrah began peeling away the bandage.

"Thankfully, no," answered Quarrah. "And I hope to keep it that way." The bandage was stuck in a mixture of blood and yellowish seepage. Quarrah had to tug, tearing bits of burned flesh and causing Ulusal to groan.

"You wasting bandage," Ulusal gasped. "Air heals best."

"I don't think so." Quarrah was no trained healer, but she knew that keeping the wound under pressure was supposed to slow the loss of blood.

"Let's get moving," Raek ordered, returning from a brief moment of solitude in the trees. "Jip and Moroy are on the Drift crate."

"Hold on, Raek," Quarrah called. "I just got her bandage off. I've got to get this covered up again."

"It's good," said Ulusal.

"It's not good," corrected Quarrah. "You can't walk like this."

"I know," answered Ulusal. "You all go on."

It took Quarrah a moment to realize what Ulusal was implying. "And leave you here? Sparks, no!"

Jip Kranfel lifted the front poles of the Drift crate. "You heard the woman. She wants to be left behind. She's not carrying her share of the load anyway."

"We're not going to leave you," Quarrah insisted. "We can stay here until the bleeding stops."

"That'll put us days behind the Tracer," said Moroy.

"The Slagstone's not going anywhere," Quarrah retorted. Wasn't this woman's life more important than getting to the stone a day sooner?

"The king's Harvesters are still looking for us," said Lan. "Staying in one place is like asking to be found."

"Or they find the Slagstone before we do," Lence hypothesized. "We go home empty-handed. I have a feeling Ardor Benn wouldn't be too happy about that."

So maybe sitting still wasn't the best idea. But surely they could find another solution that didn't involve abandoning Ulusal to the wilds of the mountain!

Raek crossed to the spot where Ulusal was lying. He was the captain of this crew. Ultimately, his decision could trump anyone else's word. The big man dropped a small pack into the grass beside the injured Trothian.

"There's some food and water in here," Raek said. "And extra lead balls and Blast Grit cartridges. You have a Roller?"

Quarrah's mouth fell agape at what she was witnessing. Ulusal nodded, pulling back her coat to reveal the holstered gun.

"Get yourself to the Harbor," Raek said. "You can claim the Fourth Decree."

"Fourth Decree?" Quarrah cut in. "What's the Fourth Decree?"

"It states that no person on Pekal can be declined passage off the island," answered Raek. "It was designed as a merciful law in case someone was marooned here."

"That's great." Quarrah turned back to Ulusal. "If you can just get yourself to the harbor, they can't deny you passage to Espar."

Ulusal scoffed, staring at Raek with her vibrating eyes. "You cannot fool me. Fourth Decree only good for legal Harvesters. They will know I am poacher."

"Legal Harvester?" Quarrah turned to Raek. "What's she saying?"

His face was flat. "In order to honor the Fourth Decree, her name would have to be on the manifest of a legal incoming ship. But since we came in on a carriage..."

So Ulusal would be turning herself over to the Regulators. Wouldn't that be better than dying alone on Pekal? Wouldn't Ulusal rather be arrested than wait in the darkness for a dragon to devour her?

"At least try to get yourself to North Pointe," said Raek. "That's where we'll be departing from once we Harvest the Slagstone. We'll keep an eye out for you."

Ulusal nodded as Jip and Moroy passed with the Drift crate between them. "Glad to hear that there *is* an exit plan," muttered Moroy. "Hope it's as half-baked as our arrival."

"Nothing so fancy," Raek replied, moving up the hill away from Ulusal. "We'll be taking a more traditional mode of transportation away from Pekal..."

And just like that, the others were moving on. Raek didn't seem the least bit compassionate. But then, why would he want Ulusal to survive? As their numbers dwindled, the payout got cheaper. Or, if Raek *was* selling secrets to Pethredote, as Ard now suspected, then leaving the injured Trothian meant one less problem he'd have to clean up later.

Quarrah remained crouched beside Ulusal, struggling with the moral implications of abandoning her. Ard wouldn't do this. If he were here, still in command, Ard would have found a way to keep Ulusal with the rest of the crew.

The Trothian woman had her eyes closed, sweaty face tensed as dappled sunlight played across it. Quarrah quietly stood up and took a step away from Ulusal.

First Sojin. Then Nemery. Now Ulusal? Their numbers were dropping too rapidly. Not to mention how this didn't bode well for the women on the crew.

Quarrah reached into her belt and withdrew her rationed bit of Health Grit. Wordlessly, she set the clay pot beside Ulusal. Maybe the Trothian's leg was too far gone, but the Grit could provide at least a few minutes of relief from the pain. She had to believe that Ulusal had a chance at getting off the island before the Moon Passing.

Failure to do so would lead to an inescapable punishment. It was a constant threat lurking in the mind of every individual who dared step foot on these forested slopes. A burning fuse. And the same time was given to each person. Thirty days. And then... Moonsickness.

Quarrah moved stiffly up the hillside, not daring to look back at the injured crew member lying in the grass. It could have been any one of them. That Fielder ball could have torn through Quarrah's calf just as easily as Ulusal's.

What was she doing here, hiking with a gang of criminal men and a traitorous friend? Quarrah didn't belong on this island. Pekal was equally terrifying as it was beautiful. Quarrah belonged in a city of smoke and Grit. With walls to scale and locks to pick.

Quarrah had followed Ard into this wild land, but where was he now? He had been suddenly cold toward her, from the crash site until the moment he departed to track the dragon.

But Quarrah remembered his kiss, genuine and concerned. He had kissed her as Dale Hizror, but this was different. This was Ardor Benn, and the look in his eyes had been real. Quarrah knew he cared for her, but there always seemed to be something in the way. Most recently, a dragon.

This would be over soon. If Quarrah could survive the next few days, she'd be back to the Greater Chain. Back to a familiar world where companions weren't left alone to die in the grass.

～

I have found a steady pace, though sometimes it seems I will never reach the summit.

CHAPTER

29

A rd knelt at the edge of a small pool, his little orb of detonated Light Grit reflecting like a brilliant star in the glassy surface of the water. He needed the extra light, in addition to the small campfire flickering behind him.

Ard was experimenting like a Mixer, trying to be as calculated and mathematical as he could, which seemed to go against his very nature in a highly frustrating manner. He glanced at the ball of ice floating in the pool. At least he had improved from last night's attempts. But there was still a long way to go before deciding if his plan would even work.

Ard spread an empty dye paper cartridge on a flat stone in front of him. He took a pinch of Cold Grit from a pouch and placed it in the center of the paper. To that, he added two equal-sized pinches of Compounding Grit. Digging into another pouch, Ard withdrew a Slagstone fragment. They were supposed to be replacements for the hammer of his gun, but one would serve well in this experiment.

Ard carefully placed the Slagstone chip atop the mound of Grit. Pinching the ends of the paper, he rolled the cartridge, securely containing the contents. He selected a rock from the edge of the pool. It was smooth and oblong, roughly the size of his fist.

Delicately placing the cartridge against the stone, Ard used a length of string to tie it in place. He stood up, extending his arm as high as he could over the pool and dropping the contraption.

The stone hit the water with a splash and sank out of sight. The Grit was soaked, not worth salvaging. Ard cursed softly and turned from the pool.

"Sank like a stone," said Nemery, who had been watching curiously from the campfire.

"Maybe because it was one," answered Ard. What he needed was Raek's expertise. His Mixer friend could probably solve this problem in mere minutes. Ard had come so close to telling Raek this part of the plan, but he was grateful now that the gunshots had interrupted him.

"What was it supposed to do?" Nemery popped a handful of fresh berries into her mouth.

"I thought the impact of the rock would spark the Slagstone and ignite the Grit. It was supposed to..." Ard waved her off. "Never mind. It doesn't matter." It *did* matter. Immensely. But Ard didn't need to trouble Nemery with it.

"Maybe you need to increase the impact," suggested the girl. "Drop it from higher up. Or throw the rock down."

Ard blew off the suggestions. They wouldn't have much relevance in the actual application of his plan. When it came to executing this idea, the rock would be dropping from a fixed height.

"You could boost me onto your shoulders and I could drop it," Nemery went on. "Or we could…"

"Nemery," Ard said. "I'm done with that for tonight."

It had been a relatively easy day, and Ard thought the slower pace might help the rest of the crew catch up a bit. The dragon had taken a midmorning nap, foraged a bit around noon, and then moved into a gentle canyon during the afternoon. She was sleeping for the night now, curled against a cliff face with a roof of trees overhanging her position.

Ard and Nemery were camped far enough away that they could converse easily, but close enough that any movement from the sow would quickly be noticed.

Nemery had vast knowledge of Pekal and the dragons, but her obvious lack of experience betrayed her. The previous night, she hadn't even known how to string up her hammock. Ard had taught her the knots, showed her how to test them, and talked about which trees she wanted to string between.

Tonight hadn't been much better. Nemery had forgotten the knots, but was clearly too anxious to prove her independence to admit it. The hammock had slipped when she tested it, and Ard helped her restring.

Ard liked the young girl. Nemery didn't belong on this mission, surrounded by criminals. Ard thought she finally realized that, now that it was impossible to turn back.

"You know, that was my first time in a Trans-Island Carriage." Nemery prodded at the fire with a short stick. Behind them, Ard's Light Grit detonation burned out with a puff.

"They're usually a bit more stable," Ard said.

"Is that how we're getting home?" she asked. "On the carriage?"

"Sparks, no," answered Ard. "That thing's never flying again." Nemery didn't respond. Ard could tell that the girl wanted to ask how they were going to get back to Espar, but she didn't want to appear weak by focusing on home.

"We have a way off Pekal." Ard satisfied her need to know without making her ask for it. "We're each going to ride a dragon."

He watched her face stretch, her eyes nearly popping out at the ludicrous idea. Nemery's reaction was too priceless, and Ard couldn't contain a snicker.

She reached across the fire and swatted his arm. "That's not funny, Ardor."

"You would have thought it was funny if you saw your face," he replied. "Actually, we've arranged for a ship to pick us up somewhere near North Pointe."

"There's no harbor by North Pointe," said Nemery. "It's just cliffs." Like the rest of the shoreline.

"There'll be some jumping involved," Ard mentioned. "And some swimming."

"We'll have to swim ten miles!"

"That would be the legal way of doing things." The Regulation had set up a no-sail zone of ten miles around Pekal to discourage smugglers from climbing the rocky shoreline or escaping with contraband.

"What if we get caught?" Nemery asked.

Ard thought it was a little late to be asking that question. The answer seemed fairly obvious. Look at Sojin Wint. "The people picking us up are extremely good at what they do."

"Breaking the no-sail perimeter?" Nemery clarified.

"Well, that's not *all* they do," said Ard. "They're pirates. They plunder other ships, too."

Nemery rolled her eyes. "I'm going to pretend like you're teasing me again." She looked up at the dark sky. "The stars look brighter here."

"It's because we're closer to them," Ard replied. "Some people think that's why Moonsickness strikes here but nowhere else."

Nemery scoffed. "But we know that's not true." She was staring at him like he'd suggested something absurd. "It's because there's no Holy Torch on Pekal. This island isn't protected."

"Of course," Ard recovered. "Obviously that's just a Settled theory."

"Did you hear the rumors about that farming village in southern Espar?" Nemery followed up.

Ard hadn't heard anything. But it wasn't like he had a lot of time for gossiping about distant townships. "What's it about?"

"They're saying the whole town got Moonsick," Nemery said. "But that would be impossible. The southern tip of Espar is as far from Pekal as you can get. And the Islehood is vigilant in burning the Holy Torch in Beripent. That would shield even the southern-most reaches."

Ard dismissed the gossip. It wasn't the first time he had heard rumors about Moonsickness touching down in the Greater Chain. But the stories were always proven false. "Probably nothing more than a Settled scare tactic."

They stared into the flickering flames for a silent moment. A bit of sudden movement caught Ard's eye, and he looked up in time to see a Karvan lizard scamper through the underbrush. It moved fast—nothing like that useless lump of a reptile in Pethredote's throne room.

Nemery had noticed the creature, too. Not the first one they'd seen on Pekal, but the closest.

"Did you know that some Islehood philosophers think the Karvan lizard might be a distant relation to the dragons?" Nemery said.

"I did not know," answered Ard.

She nodded earnestly. "Different evolutionary paths, but there's a possibility that they stem from the same ancestral lizard. I find that hard to believe, though. In my opinion, there is no creature alive that can compare to a dragon. Just their size alone. Can you believe it?"

"I can't."

"I'm not sure what to think. Most of the credible theories I take from the early writers like Toom, Kalep, and Eilmer. But there are some interesting modern studies on dragons. Did you know that Isle Davis's latest book hypothesizes that the dragons themselves impart some sort of regenerative properties to the flora and fauna of Pekal?"

"I did not know."

"Crazy, right?" Nemery chuckled. "The study is based on the question of whether or not the ecology of Pekal could sustain as many large carnivores as it has during peak dragon population periods. I mean, it's not as big of an issue now because of the dwindling numbers. But he raises some interesting points. What do you think?"

Ard cleared his throat and looked straight at the girl, firelight flickering on her youthful face. "What are you doing out here, Nemery?"

She looked up at him. "Same thing the rest of you are doing. Trying to earn some Ashings."

"There are better ways for a person your age to do that," replied Ard. "You clearly have musical ability. Have you looked into auditioning for an orchestra?"

"You sound like my mother," said Nemery. Ard waited to see if she'd go on. The words built up inside her until eventually, she did. "Two years ago, I began taking lessons to play the horn. Low brass."

It made sense. The girl had impressive lung capacity, and the mouthpiece on her Caller instrument was just like that on a trombone.

"My tutor said I was extremely talented. She told my parents she could get me into the Youth Musical Institute on Talumon, but they had to pay two years of tuition up front." Nemery paused. "It was all the money they had."

"So why aren't you there?" Ard asked.

"Never went." She used her stick to turn a burning log in the fire. "Whole thing was a lie. My tutor took the money and the Youth Musical Institute never knew I was coming."

Sparks! Nemery's tutor was a ruse artist. Did Ard's targets end up as devastated as this young girl? That was why he only rused crooked folks and stuffy nobles. They deserved it, right?

"My chance at a legitimate musical career was shot," Nemery explained. "So my pa introduced me to a Caller—the one outside Panes who I've been apprenticing with. The first time I heard that sound, I felt..." She trailed away. "I just knew what I was supposed to do with my life."

Nemery's eyes were wet as she looked up at the dark sky.

"My mum and pa split after that. Mum was too angry at him for coaching me down a path where my skills would only be useful on a faraway island, Calling to the most dangerous creatures alive. Not to mention the coming extinction. Not a lot of people talk about that, but my master told me that without the Bull Dragon Patriarchy, there won't be a long future in Calling dragons."

"That's why you couldn't wait," Ard surmised. "You had to Call a real dragon before they went extinct."

Nemery nodded. "It's not really about the Ashings. Though Homeland knows my pa needs some help."

The fire popped. "Well, Nemery Baggish," said Ard. "I guess that's something we have in common."

"Your pa needs money, too?"

Ard chuckled. "No. Not anymore. What I mean is that I'm not really here for the Ashings, either. Not like the others."

Ard had been thinking about Halavend's payout less and less. It was the old Isle's hidden motives that drove him on. His *new doctrine*. Ard had seen Halavend's desperate eyes, glowing with a righteous hope for Ard to complete his task, no matter the cost.

"I know," Nemery said. "You're here for her. For Quarrah."

"Whoa!" Ard rebutted. That wasn't exactly his line of thought. "What makes you think that?"

"You kissed her," Nemery pointed out. "Right outside the hut."

"Oh." Ard felt slightly abashed. "Did everyone see that?"

"I don't know," Nemery said. "But it's obvious that she cares for you. You're all she could talk about after you followed the dragon. Is she Wayfarist?"

Ard scratched his head. "Sort of, I think. We haven't talked about it much."

"You should," Nemery encouraged. "You could be together."

"It's complicated," said Ard. And the complication's name was Tanalin Phor.

Tanalin had held Ard captive for some ten years now. Three years enjoying her actual company, and seven years in his mind, preparing for the day they could be together again. It had taken Quarrah Khai for Ard to realize that his dreams of Tanalin were misplaced. The perfect pedestal that Ard had created for Tanalin was a standard to which no other woman could hope to measure.

But Ard couldn't give it up. What if his view of Tanalin was even half right? What if his image of her really did hold up when he finally saw her again?

"Do you want to talk about it?" Nemery asked.

Ard had only ever discussed the topic with Raek. But now, any advice his big friend might have shared seemed tainted. And what light could young Nemery hope to shed on a subject so complex?

"I'll tell you when you're older." Ard grinned, knowing full well that the statement would annoy his young companion.

Nemery scoffed and tossed her stoking stick into the fire. "I'm going to sleep." She rose from the rock she'd been sitting on and turned toward her hammock. "Maybe tomorrow I'll be old enough to hear about your big-boy problems."

Ard chuckled. When she put it that way, it sounded ridiculous. And maybe it was. Either way, he had an ominous feeling that things with Tanalin were going to resolve soon. It frightened him, but at the same time excited him.

Tanalin was here. Not just hunting for him, but her memory was in these woods. Ard remembered late nights, side by side in their hammock, talking about everything. He remembered her laugh. The way she made him feel like every moment spent together was worthwhile.

Sparks, he still missed her. After all these years.

Quarrah rolled the broad leaf between her palms. It stung at first, but then a cooling sensation washed over her blistered hands. She rested her head back, hammock swinging gently as she stared through the dense treetops into a starlit sky.

A little over two days on the dragon's trail and Quarrah knew for sure. Thieving was her thing. Not Harvesting. If she had to pick up that stupid Drift crate one more time, she thought her arms might rip right out of her shoulders.

Quarrah tossed the leaf over the edge of her hammock. It was a plant that Lence Raismus had introduced to her yesterday. The icy relief would last only a few minutes, but it might be enough for her to drift off to sleep.

It had been another exhausting day, chasing those blazing orange markers through the mountains. There was still no sign of Ard. From what Quarrah gathered, it was common not to see the Tracers until they reached the mound of fired Slagstone.

Since that first day, when the dragon had arrived to eat the bait, Quarrah hadn't glimpsed another sow. She'd seen deer, goats, and hogs aplenty. She'd even seen a number of those Karvan lizards. But the rulers of Pekal, the mighty dragons, seemed scarce.

Quarrah didn't know what she had expected. Dragon population was way down, and the creatures were furtive. Lence said they *had* likely come across a dragon in the last day or two, but the beast had heard or smelled the crew and moved to avoid them. That wasn't the popular stereotype portrayed in the Greater Chain. Quarrah had basically grown up thinking that a dragon's main food supply was human beings.

They had seen *signs* of dragons, however. A few shed scales, rough and uncut. White scrapes across cliff faces. Dead, charred trees that must have been collateral in the Slagstone firing process. Earlier today, they had even come across an unfertilized egg.

Quarrah had seen the gelatinous egg on display in the Mooring once. The soft orb was suspended in a clear liquid, housed inside a giant glass box. But after seeing the egg in the wild, Quarrah wondered if the Mooring's display was even real.

Moroy happened upon the gelatinous egg by accident as they fanned out to search for Ard's next marker. It was lying amidst the tall grass in a small basin. There was no birdlike nest to receive the soft egg. In fact, Quarrah thought it looked abandoned.

Lence Raismus explained that female dragons laid their eggs without nesting, because the hatching took place in a separate location. The sows selected a place in full shade with natural protection from wind and sun. Predators weren't a problem, since consuming the egg was poisonous to other animals.

The soft egg Quarrah had seen today was a male. Lence explained that the bull eggs were a golden color, while the eggs which would produce a sow were milky white. Of course, the same was true of the hardened fertilized shell.

Quarrah had been uneasy observing the gelatinous egg in the basin. She knew a mother's instinct was strong, and she'd always been taught to stay away from the offspring of wild animals.

Dragons were different, according to Lence. After laying a soft egg, the sow made it a point to depart from the place. This allowed one of the three bulls in the Patriarchy to come along unopposed. The bull would lift the delicate egg and remove it to another location. Once in place, the bull would breath his fertilizing fire to harden the shell.

The mother dragon had the ability to sense the timing and location of the fertilization. She would fly to the fertilized egg, carry it to her nest, and nurture the egg until the hatchling appeared.

It was a fascinating process to be sure, but one that was now obsolete. The soft golden egg Quarrah had observed in the grass would stay there, eventually withering and drying out. There were no bulls in the Patriarchy to carry on the circle of life. The dragons were a dying breed.

"You did good today." Raek's voice sounded quietly beside her. Quarrah lifted her head out of the hammock to find the big man leaning against the tree by her feet. His bald head was covered with a knit cap. There was a slight chill whipping down the canyon tonight.

"I know it's not easy," Raek said. "We covered a lot of ground the past two days."

Quarrah's excellent sense of direction told her that their path had wound mostly northward, cutting through ravines and traversing canyons. The dragon had led them deeper into the mountains, but depending on where she dropped her Slagstone, it might be a straight shot down to the North Pointe shoreline.

"At least we're moving in the right direction," Quarrah said. "You think the pirates will show?" Raek had finally told the crew about their arrangement to escape the island. "I've heard they're not the most trustworthy types."

"I paid them only a third in advance," said Raek. "Two-thirds on returning us safely to the Greater Chain."

"How long are they willing to wait for us?" Quarrah was

thinking of Ulusal. The Trothian woman had been on her own for a day and a half now. She could escape with them from North Pointe. But Quarrah knew Ulusal was likely already dead.

"I told them to be in position on the fourth day after the Passing," said Raek.

"That's tomorrow."

Raek nodded. "They agreed to patrol the area for five days. We just have to send up a Light Grit flare when we're ready for them to sail into illegal waters and extract us."

"What about the Slagstone?" Quarrah knew that North Pointe was a high cliff. Getting the fired mound to the pirate ship was going to be nearly impossible.

"Ard's got a plan."

"He didn't tell you?" Of course not. Ard hadn't even told Quarrah, let alone the man he now suspected to be the king's informant.

"No," Raek said. "But I think I understand why Ard kept his lips closed about it." He lowered his voice. "We have a traitor, Quarrah."

She swallowed hard. Directly addressing the issue was a strategy Quarrah hadn't anticipated. If she played this conversation correctly, she might get some illumination about which side Raek was really on.

Quarrah sat up to show that she was interested in pursuing this conversation. "What do you mean?"

"The king's Harvesters knew we were coming," Raek continued. "Their captain said Pethredote knew our plans! I thought only the three of us knew where that carriage was going this morning. Did Ard tell Isle Halavend?"

"I don't know," Quarrah answered honestly. She dangled her legs over the edge of her hammock. "Ard seemed really shaken after the attack at the crash site. He barely spoke to me at all that day." If she could victimize herself alongside Raek, perhaps he would open up to her.

"That probably has something to do with the fact that Tanalin is hunting us." Raek sighed. "Ard has every reason to be shaken up."

"Wait," Quarrah cut in. "Tanalin? Who's Tanalin?" She'd heard the name before. More than once, in fact. But only ever discussed between Ard and Raek in hushed tones. Almost like a secret.

Raek's eyebrows furrowed beneath his knit cap. "Ard's never told you about Tanalin Phor?"

"Not unless I forgot," Quarrah said pointedly.

"You wouldn't forget." Raek drew in a deep breath and slowly let it out. She could tell that he had started down a conversational road that he now wanted to abandon.

"Who's Tanalin?" Quarrah asked again.

"She's..." Raek began. "Well, she's the reason that Ard is who he is today."

"What's that supposed to mean?" retorted Quarrah, trying not to feel jealous. She didn't even know who she was feeling jealous of. Or why. "She's a ruse artist?"

"Oh, flames, no! Tanalin's the opposite." Raek reached up and plucked a twig off the branch overhead. "Has Ard ever told you about his first ruse? How he started into this insane business?"

Quarrah had asked him, but Ard always seemed to avoid questions about his past. For a man so eloquent in speech, Ard sure had a hard time communicating the most important things to Quarrah.

"What happened?" she asked.

Raek debated for a moment, and then waved his hand dismissively. "Really isn't my place to tell you."

"Seriously, Raek? You can't start a story like that and leave it dangling."

"I don't think Ard would be happy if I told you."

Quarrah took a deep breath. It was late. They were tired. Raek seemed susceptible. "Ard talked to me about the traitor. And he wouldn't be happy if I told you, either."

Raek clenched his jaw. "What did he say?"

"It actually started cycles ago," she began. "Someone tipped off the Reggies that Ard would be at Farasse's concert."

"Well, I knew that," Raek said. "But there are a number of ways that information could have leaked. Doesn't mean there was a traitor."

"And then there was the first night we tried to steal the regalia. The night that Ard got arrested," she continued. "The king told Ard he had an informant. They set a trap for me."

Raek paused. "That's not the story I heard. Ard told me his disguise slipped and he had to make a desperate attempt to get you out." He wiped a hand over his face, shoulders slumping with a heavy sigh. "He thinks it's me," Raek whispered. "After all these years... Did he tell you not to trust me? Did he accuse me?"

Oh, flames. This wasn't a conversation Quarrah wanted to be having. "I think Ard is under an incredible amount of pressure."

"I know Ard under pressure," said Raek. "This isn't how he acts. Pressure makes him bolder. Stronger."

"He isn't sure who to trust right now."

"He should always trust me." A bitterness broke through Raek's voice. "I'm not... I would never do anything to betray him. He's my little brother."

Quarrah sat awkwardly, a long moment of silence passing as she swung gently in her hammock, feet just off the ground. She believed Raek. Not because of what he said, but because of how he said it. There was a hurt in his voice that Quarrah didn't think anyone could feign.

No, Raekon Dorrel was not the traitor. A single conversation on the topic had revealed that to Quarrah. Ard's strategy to separate himself from the crew was a mistake. He needed to talk to Raek, not avoid him.

"We met Tanalin Phor at a pub in Beripent's Western Quarter," Raek suddenly began. "She was a gorgeous woman sitting by herself. The kind Ard always had to meet. There was something about

her that captivated him. I could see it from the moment their conversation began. Tanalin was different from Ard's usual type. She
was grounded, smart, extremely driven, and a rule follower. A solid
Wayfarist. Tanalin didn't pay him much attention that first night.
Why would she? In the morning she was setting sail for Pekal as a
newly enlisted Harvester for Lord Creg—a royal heap of lard based
in Talumon.

"Ard followed her. And I followed him. That's what people tend
to do: follow Ard. Except for Tanalin. I think he liked the chase.
There were no available Harvesting positions in Creg's crew that
cycle, but Ard and I signed on as ship hands to get them to and
from Pekal."

Raek took a deep breath, his head tipping back to rest against
the bark of the tree he was leaning on. "Eventually we got in with
the crew. Ard and Tanalin became very close over the three years
of Harvesting. She was better at it than him. Probably had to do
with Ard's inherent laziness when faced with physical labor. I was
useful muscle, but most of my focus was on mixing Grit.

"One afternoon, late in the Seventh Cycle, our crew was following the Tracer markers. The dragon was a big one. We were already
four days in, skirting right along the shoreline. I had stepped away
from the crew to take care of some personal business, when I came
across a husk."

"A dragon husk?" Quarrah clarified.

Raek nodded. "Basically a complete set of scales, shed right there
next to a big rock. I pulled Ard and Tanalin back to show them my
find. Tanalin's instinct was to shout to the crew captain. It was procedure for a find like this. But Ard held her back. He realized that
the thing in front of us meant money."

"But the scales were uncut," said Quarrah. "They're practically
useless that way."

"Actually, there's a market for uncut scales if you know the right
channels," said Raek. "We didn't, at the time. But Ard had a crazier

plan. You see, my cousin worked at a Coinery on Dronodan. Ard thought maybe we could cut the Ashings ourselves."

"And your cousin went along with it?"

"Sparks, no!" cried Raek. "He was just our way inside. Poor Andus had no idea..." Raek slowly pulled off his knit cap. "Tanalin didn't like the plan, but we marked the spot so we'd be able to find the husk again. By nightfall, what started out as an idea to steal a few scales had escalated to taking the entire husk."

Quarrah scoffed. "Of course." They were talking about Ardor Benn. "The more Ashings the better."

"It wasn't really about the Ashings," Raek said. "I mean, it *was*. But not just for the sake of getting rich. I'm guessing Ard never told you anything about his parents?"

Quarrah thought back to that carriage ride so long ago. She'd been quick to tell him about her father's death and mother's abandonment, but now that she gave it some thought, it seemed like Ard had never told her anything real. Certainly nothing about his life before rusing.

"All the years I'd known him, Ard's father worked the silver mines a few miles south of Beripent. About two years into our stint on Pekal, Ard got word that his pa had been in an accident. Rail cart smashed up his leg something awful. Healers said the leg had to come off at the knee unless he had significant amounts of Health Grit to reknit the bone. The mine owner, a real gem of a guy named Baron Siv, had a policy in place for injuries like that. He loaned the Grit, and Ard's father took it. Better than losing a leg for a working-class citizen. He made a full recovery and was back in the mine five cycles later. That was when Baron Siv's collectors came knocking. There was no way Ard's parents could get out from under a debt that large, even with his mother taking an extra shift at the garden plots."

"What about Ard's income?" Quarrah asked. As she understood it, Harvesters usually made good money.

"We weren't making as much as we should have been. Wasn't until later we learned that Lord Creg allowed his Captain and Tracers to skim off the top of our earnings," Raek said. "Anyway, Ard saw the husk as a way to get his parents out from under the baron's thumb and set them up right. That was a cause even Tanalin Phor could get behind. She knew and respected Ard's folks. Good Wayfarists."

Add that to the list of things making Quarrah feel hurt. It was becoming more and more obvious that this Tanalin had known the *real* Ard. Quarrah knew only a face.

"After our crew had Harvested the Slagstone, we made our way back toward the harbor," Raek went on. "One of the nights we ended up camping just south of the husk. This was when things were about to get risky, and Tanalin was a nervous wreck. In order for our plan to work, we needed to steal a Drift crate, and that's a crime punishable by death. Ard was nervous, too, but not about making the theft. He was in love with Tanalin, and he couldn't bear the thought that something could happen to her if things went wrong."

Pah! Tanalin sounded like a wimp. It was hard for Quarrah to imagine Ard in love with anyone, let alone someone who trembled at the thought of breaking a law.

"Ard developed a backup plan," Raek said. "He brought me in on it, but he didn't tell Tanalin. It was dangerous and complicated—classic Ardor Benn. Early in the evening, Ard slipped away and spent a few hours making preparations. He moved the husk, dragging it south and dropping it right at the edge of the shoreline cliff, fairly close to our camp. But we were going to need a Drift crate to get the thing all the way to the Harbor."

Raek waved his knit cap absently at a nighttime insect fluttering past. "In a regular crew, shifts are taken to watch the Drift crates at night. I rigged up a fuse to detonate a small bit of Light Grit in the trees to draw their attention. Once their backs were turned, the three of us grabbed the crate and ran."

"That doesn't sound overly tricky for the ruse artist I know," said Quarrah. Stealing a Drift crate under cover of darkness was something she would do.

"Yeah. We were pretty new at this kind of stuff. And apparently we weren't as sneaky as we'd hoped."

"They caught you?"

"They saw us making off down the slope and shouted to wake up the rest of the crew," said Raek. "Obviously, we'd hoped to make a clean getaway, but now that they were on to us, Ard initiated the backup plan." Raek stuffed the cap back on his head. "Ard steered us down to the shoreline. Tanalin was panicking. Ard explained that he'd moved the husk to a closer spot, and maybe we'd still have time to get it loaded before the others caught us.

"We reached the husk. Tanalin helped me load it into the Drift crate, but it was clear there was no chance of getting away. That was the whole point of Ard's backup plan. He never would have let Tanalin get involved without a way to prove her innocence if we were caught."

"I'm not seeing the plan." So far, stealing a Drift crate and a husk of dragon scales was *very* incriminating.

"I shot him," Raek said. "I shot Ard twice in the chest. At least, that's what it looked like. I was firing blanks and Ard had capsules of pig's blood hidden beneath his shirt."

"Sounds familiar," Quarrah muttered.

"It's a good trick," replied Raek. "Tanalin screamed, and the gunshots sent the crew directly to us. I detonated a cloud of Prolonged Barrier Grit around the Drift crate and put the smoking Roller in Tanalin's hand. She was frozen. Numb. One of the Tracers came out of the trees just as Ard's bloody body tumbled off the edge of the shoreline cliff."

"How did he survive the fall?" Quarrah asked.

"While Tanalin and I loaded the husk, Ard roped himself into a harness that he'd prepared," explained Raek. "Tanalin couldn't see it in the dark."

Raek had said the backup plan was dangerous and complicated. With the fake blood, the blank shots, the harness and ropes...

"No one could see Ard's body from the clifftop," continued Raek. "The Tracer claimed he witnessed Tanalin pull the trigger. She couldn't speak, but I smoothed over the rest with a preplanned story about how Ard had tricked us into taking a Drift crate because he'd found an injured person at the shoreline. When we arrived, it turned out to be a dragon husk. He loaded it into the crate and tried to convince us to help him take it to the harbor. I refused and threw a Barrier cloud around the Drift crate to stop him. He tried to attack me, and Tanalin shot him twice."

"Your crew bought that story?" Quarrah asked.

"All the evidence was laid out for them," Raek replied. "Ard was known for being a bit of a wild card. The hatch on the Drift crate was open, so the captain could see Ard's dragon husk. Just couldn't get to it because of the Prolonged Barrier cloud."

"And the smoking Roller exonerated Tanalin," Quarrah surmised.

"She never even tried to contradict my story," Raek said. "We were counting on her grief to solidify the whole thing. The captain was actually pleased with the discovery of the husk. Bringing home some uncut scales would get him a nice bonus. He ordered camp to be moved to the shoreline so he could keep a close eye on that Drift crate until the detonation cloud burned out."

"So you never got the dragon husk?" Quarrah asked.

Raek raised one eyebrow. "Do you really think Ardor Benn failed his first ruse? He was counting on our captain to move camp to the shoreline. In fact, Ard helped us do it."

"What? How?"

"Ard pulled himself up from the cliff, tugged his hat down low, and met me back at the campsite," Raek went on. "It was dark. The action was over. People were tired. They weren't looking for a dead man. Ard and I grabbed a new Drift crate and slipped away in the commotion. Of course, I couldn't stay with him. I had to get back to the shoreline and make sure that all eyes were on that first Drift crate, because the husk inside was actually nothing more than a papery skin."

"It wasn't real?"

"Earlier that evening, Ard had spent hours cutting all the rough scales out of the husk and piling them up at the first site. More than eight hundred usable scales. That's the only reason the husk was lightweight enough for him to move down to the shoreline. The captain was pretty chapped to find out the truth, once the Prolonged Barrier cloud burned out. And Tanalin was downright sick. Ard had died for a worthless skin . . ."

"Didn't the captain notice that a second Drift crate had gone missing?" Quarrah asked.

Raek nodded. "Chalked it up to poachers that must have raided the camp while everyone was out looking for the first stolen crate. Stuff like that happens in a big crew. Captain accepted the loss and our crew sailed back to Talumon to disband for the rest of the cycle."

"So how did Ard get off Pekal?"

"He emptied the tools from that second Drift crate and loaded it with his bounty of uncut scales," Raek explained. "Then he dragged that blazing Drift crate all the way down to the harbor, arriving the moment before the final Reggies set sail to avoid the Moon Passing. He claimed the Fourth Decree, and said he and the Drift crate had been separated from the rest of the crew during a storm. They checked his name against our earlier manifest, took him on board without question. That night, I commandeered a fishing boat and sailed out to meet the Reggie ship on its way to Beripent. Ard flagged me down, insisting that he get the Drift crate back to Talumon to appease an angry employer. Since a stop at Talumon would add hours to their trip home, the Reggies approved me to take him. So we loaded the Drift crate and sailed away.

"Eventually, we took advantage of my cousin and got all those scales coined into seven-mark Ashings," Raek said. "Freed Ard's parents from their debts and got them set for life in a little country home on leeward Espar. But Ard had to start a new life. He couldn't risk letting his parents know that he was alive in case Tanalin spoke to them."

"Why didn't he go to her?" Quarrah asked. "Once everything had settled, why didn't Ard tell her the truth?"

Raek shrugged. "The thrill of the ruse, I guess. We'd been so successful with the scales that Ard wanted to do another scheme. And another. Kept thinking that he'd eventually have enough money to go back to Tanalin and sweep her off her feet. He even mentioned that this ruse might be the one. With a payout like this ruse offered, he could finally be with her again. So it's not hard to see why Ard was a little rattled to discover that Tanalin Phor is hunting him."

Quarrah swallowed hard. Raek's words stung in her chest. It was a silly sense of jealousy, for a bygone relationship. But maybe the relationship wasn't as bygone as Quarrah wanted to believe. It seemed like Ard was still in love with this woman. That's why he had never mentioned her to Quarrah.

She felt a pit of anger boiling up in her stomach. Had her affections toward Ard been misplaced all this time? Had she deluded herself to believe that he felt something for her?

Quarrah wanted Raek to walk away now. It would be easier to be alone with her thoughts than to try to keep a conversation going. Perhaps it would have been better to hear that story from Ard. But then, Quarrah doubted he'd ever tell her.

So why had Raek suddenly been so willing to divulge Ard's story?

Perhaps it was some measure of emotional revenge. Raek was upset that Ard had gone to Quarrah about the traitor, when he should have talked to him. And Quarrah felt the same way about this Tanalin Phor.

Quarrah tucked her legs into her hammock and leaned back, giving a not-so-subtle hint to Raek that their conversation was over. But the big man didn't leave for a very long time. He stood beside the tree at Quarrah's feet, staring into the dark forest.

Both were hurt by each other's words. Not because they'd heard them, but because they hadn't heard them from Ardor Benn.

～

Undertaking this task has caused me to ponder the choices that led me here. I steel myself against regrets. There is no place for them now.

CHAPTER

30

The dragon was flying.

Ard flinched as Nemery grabbed his arm, her fingers biting nervously into his bicep. "Look at that. Look at that!" Nemery whispered frantically, as though Ard hadn't noticed the massive beast rise above the trees. "Why is she flying?" she persisted. "Dragons are only supposed to fly if threatened by a larger dragon, or roosting at the summit for the Moon Passing. Or if the mother's sense tells her that her egg has been fertilized, but that can't possibly be the case."

"That may be what your books taught you," Ard answered quietly, "but out here in the real world, the dragons don't always follow the rules."

"Then why is she flying?" Nemery asked again.

"Let's find out." Ard ran into the muddy glade where they had been observing the dragon.

It was hard to gauge what time it was, though Ard guessed it was edging toward late afternoon. A rainstorm had rolled in early that morning and persisted heavily until after midday. Now the island was a slippery, muddy mess, the sky still thick with dark clouds, and an occasional drizzle reminding them that the storm had not fully passed.

Ard didn't dare pause to spray an orange Marker. He'd have to double back and do it later. If the dragon was in flight, she would be capable of covering a tremendous amount of ground. It was a move like this that led most Tracers to lose their dragons.

Nemery followed right behind, as Ard had found she liked to do. The girl was strong and determined, two characteristics that made her an excellent companion. The more time he spent with her, the more he realized the truth.

Ard *was* something of a Wayfarist.

It took Nemery assuming it to jar the roots of his belief. Ard didn't know if he really believed in the Homeland, but there were certain principles of Wayfarism that still lived on in his heart. The driving desire to progress. Never Settle. Make yourself into someone stronger and smarter than you were the day before. Weren't those his primary motivators whenever he ran a ruse?

Who was Ardor Benn? He was something of a contradiction. A Wayfarist ruse artist. It was why he always found himself caring so deeply, and investing so fully in whatever job he took on. It was why this current job, no matter how crazy it seemed, was worth doing. Because at the root of this ruse was a Holy Isle.

Halavend had more power over Ard than he cared to admit. Because at the end of the day, how different were he and Isle Halavend? Halavend, too, was something of a contradiction, and that united them.

Halavend must have known, deep down, that threads of belief were still woven inside Ardor Benn. From Ard's willingness to trust Halavend, to his familiarity with the Mooring, to the very fact that he had not changed his religious name.

Nemery Baggish was a different level of devout. The girl followed Ard based solely on belief. Because Wayfarists had a moral obligation to watch out for one another. Nemery felt safe with Ardor, and that alone rekindled a bit more of his faith.

Ard burst through the trees and came to a grinding halt, Nemery gasping alongside him. They stood at the edge of a cliff, the face dropping some eighty feet in front of them. The bottom of the cliff met a bare rocky slope that climbed away from them at a gentle angle.

"That's why she flew," Ard said. The dragon had landed on the opposite slope, roughly the same altitude as Ard and Nemery. But between them was a significant drop-off. The big sow folded her muscular wings and paused.

"She knew the terrain," Ard explained. "Flying was the quickest way to get across."

"But why would she risk exposing herself just to cross the cliff?" Nemery glanced sideways. "She could have worked her way around over there."

"She was surveying the area," Ard said. The dragon started back down the scree slope she had just flown over, her tail swiping sharply to the side and sending small fragments of rock skittering downward.

"She's about to do it, isn't she?" Nemery asked. "Deposit the slag."

"I think so," muttered Ard. To be honest, he hadn't ever witnessed the event. Typically, the Harvesting crew didn't arrive on the scene until long after the Slagstone had been deposited.

Nemery was grinning. "It's the perfect location," she gushed. "The lack of vegetation on the rocky hillside will reduce the amount of preparation she'll have to do for the firing. They're cautious about breathing fire, and they have surprising control over the flames. But they always have to clear around the slag to prevent fire from spreading across the mountain."

"Come on," Ard said, impressed by Nemery's constant fount of knowledge. "We need to find a way down this cliff and mark it for the rest of the crew."

"Wait. We're not going to watch?"

"You do know what Slagstone is, right?" he answered. "Let's give the dragon some privacy."

Nemery seemed a little disappointed, but she followed Ard, casting frequent glances to the opposing hillside where the dragon was digging and stamping to prepare the area. Ard was anxious to obtain the fired Slagstone, but he had absolutely no desire to witness it coming out.

They found a rough ramp-like cleft carved into the cliff face. Ard took some quick arm measurements and determined that the path would be wide enough to accommodate the crew's large Drift crate.

Tree roots had found purchase there, creating a forested wall along some stretches. The slag-depositing dragon was hidden from view as they descended the steep notch, much to Nemery's disappointment.

Ard could hear the dragon, however, and that was quite enough. It was beyond strange to think that the dragon's current act could possibly save the world. Sparks, she was just doing what came naturally.

The fact that the greatest power came from the dung of a beast was the perfect illustration of society in the Greater Chain. Rich folk talked of Grit as though it were some blessing from the Homeland. They used it to light their homes, construct their buildings, silence their crying babies. The Regulation used it to enforce the law, to wage war. But what was this substance that ruled them all? What was it really?

The most vile, undesirable excretion.

By the time Ard and Nemery reached the bottom of the cliff, the fresh slag had been deposited. But the dragon was not finished. A crucial step remained, and without it, this whole venture would be an utter waste.

Ard held Nemery's shoulder so she wouldn't be tempted to step around the boulder they were hiding behind. The girl had been right about the ideal setting of this rocky hillside. There were dozens of Slagstone boulders that had survived their own Dross, rolling to the bottom of the cliff as the rains washed through.

Tucked behind the black boulder, Ard immediately realized that they were still downwind of the dragon. The stench was choking, but it brought back a flood of memories from his time as a legal Harvester. From his time with Tanalin. Strange to think that she was here now, looking for him.

The thought occurred to him that the same orange marks that guided his crew could also guide Tanalin straight to him. No use dwelling on that. Ard's crew just needed to be faster. It was going to be a race to get this Slagstone packed up and carried out before the king's Harvesters tracked them down.

Ard glanced at Nemery who was frantically applying the scent-masking Pichar extract to her neck and arms. It really wasn't necessary, with the wind in their favor. Besides, hadn't Nemery just splashed some on before the dragon took flight?

The girl held out the small vial in a silent offering. Oh, why not? A little extra precaution wouldn't hurt, even if the stuff curled his nose hairs. Ard stuck out his finger, and Nemery dabbed a drop of oil onto it. He swiped the extract across his forehead and peered around the edge of the boulder, Nemery following his lead.

The dragon was still there, hunched halfway up the slope. Her tail was curled up like a scorpion, and her forelegs scratched the loose rock, sending it tumbling down toward Ard and Nemery. In front of the dragon was the slag pile—black, steaming, revolting. The awful mound had been deposited in a slight dugout, excavated in the loose rock by the dragon's powerful legs.

"It's huge," Nemery whispered. "Although the firing process does tend to shrink the Slagstone as it dries under the extreme—" Ard reached around and covered the girl's mouth. The last thing they needed was for Nemery's nervous, albeit knowledgeable, rambling to spook the sow.

The two of them watched in silence as the dragon drew a deep breath, torso expanding. She began to glow from within, a web of red cracks that shone between her rough scales. Then the breath came tumbling out as bright yellow fire.

The flames were precise, just as Nemery had said. The fire streamed from the dragon's long neck, enveloping the slag until it glowed like a white-hot coal. Ard stared, unblinking at the absolute power of the beast. He was pretty sure Nemery tried to say something, but his hand still muted her as the rush and crackle of raw fire echoed off the cliff behind them.

Then the dragon was done. The stream of flames ended abruptly. Her wings unfurled and she leapt into the air. She soared directly over Ard and Nemery's hiding place, disappearing into the trees at the top of the cliff.

Ard released Nemery and she stepped out from behind the boulder, mouth agape. The fired Slagstone was still burning on the hillside. In the gloom of the storm it seemed bright and enchanting.

"That's it," Nemery whispered, fighting to keep her voice down with excitement. "She did it!"

"*We* did it," Ard replied.

Nemery turned to look up at him, her face breaking into a massive grin. She let out a laugh and threw her arms around him. The victorious feeling was contagious, but Ard knew they still had a long way to go before they got off this island. Especially with Tanalin's crew searching for them.

"That's enough." Ard peeled her off. "We need to retrace our steps and set the final Markers for our crew."

"Can't I stay with the Slagstone?"

Ard shook his head. "The king's Harvesters could already be here, watching. We'll be exposed on that slope. We need to scout the perimeter and make sure we're alone." He glanced at the smoldering stone. "That Slagstone needs to cool off anyway."

"They say the Dross layer forms during cooling," Nemery said. "Did you know that Dross explosions are *still* the leading cause of death among Harvesting crews?"

Ard hefted his orange-stained spear, sighing. "I had no idea."

"Bet your pretty eyes have never seen something so ugly as a pile of Slagstone," Jip Kranfel called to Quarrah as she arrived at the large mound.

"Sure she has," Lan said to his little brother. "She seen you."

Both men were tending to the piece of fired Slagstone, with Raek standing on the opposite side. The mound came nearly to their shoulders, resting in the divot excavated by the dragon.

Quarrah had always supposed that Harvesting the Slagstone mound would be as simple as loading the large stone into the Drift crate. But Raek had explained that there was much more to it.

During the firing process, each mound of Slagstone developed a highly flammable, explosive outer crust called Dross. It was far too volatile to be of any practical use to humans. After processing, Blast Grit was just as explosive and not nearly as finicky.

The Dross layer detonated under even the slightest bit of pressure. A falling rock, a hailstorm. Raek said that Dross was even known to ignite on a hot day if the mound was in direct sunlight. The resulting blast would blow the Slagstone into small chunks whose detonative properties would quickly depreciate.

Nature's purpose for the highly explosive Dross layer actually made a lot of sense to Quarrah. Dragons had lived on this island for all of human record. If each dragon passed a mound of Slagstone on an average twelve-day period, then Pekal should be nothing but a giant heap of boulders. Dross was nature's way of maintaining Pekal's lush environment.

Raek and the Kranfel brothers had already begun to remove the Dross layer. Their cork chisels probed for weak spots, allowing them to pry up small pieces and set them a safe distance away.

Farther down the slope, Quarrah saw Ard pulling supplies from the Drift crate. Their reunion had been painfully awkward, Quarrah choosing to walk away so she didn't say something she'd regret.

Ard still loved Tanalin.

According to Raek, it had always been Ard's plan to find her again. Once he had enough Ashings, they were supposed to live out the rest of their lives like happy little lovers.

It made Quarrah sick. Like an idiot, she had imagined a future with Ard. And, over the last eight cycles, Quarrah had convinced herself that Ard saw the same.

Well, at least Quarrah would get two hundred thousand Ashings. And she was already devising a way to steal a good portion of Ard's payout, too. Maybe that would teach him not to play with Quarrah Khai.

"Let's get that crate into position!" Raek shouted down the rocky hill.

The Drift crate was empty now, the supplies unloaded at the base of the cliff. Raek had decided that they would abandon all supplies that couldn't be carried in packs for the quick hike out. That would include the Kranfels' Fielders, some of Lence Raismus's Feeder supplies, and Nemery's Caller instruments. The crew's agreement to do so came with the promise of ample compensation for their lost items.

Ard and Moroy picked up the wooden crate, making their way up the scree. Quarrah was grateful she didn't have to lug that box any farther today. Raek had begun rationing the Drift Grit to make sure they had enough for the hike out. This meant a lot of Prolonging Grit was added to the crate's hopper. It extended the effect of the Drift cloud, but as time wore on, the box got progressively heavier. Today, they had even hiked a few stretches with no Grit at all.

Ard and Moroy set the Drift crate beside the Slagstone where Raek instructed. Nemery Baggish was at Ard's side like a talking shadow. Quarrah still couldn't believe the girl was alive. She had risked so much, leaving the entire crew just to be with Ard.

Quarrah found their sudden friendship annoying. It was an embodiment of Ard's charm and personality. He put people at ease. It was his nature. Like how Quarrah stole things, or how a dragon breathed fire.

Moroy wandered away from the Drift crate. Ard said something to Nemery who moved off to check on Lence Raismus.

From the trees at the top of the slope, a strange sound echoed downward. It was like the cry of a loud bird: a grating chirp with a gravelly undertone. Everyone looked up from their tasks for a moment. The noise sent a shiver down Quarrah's spine. This island was wild. It seemed Pekal itself spoke a language Quarrah didn't understand.

"I was sorry to hear about Ulusal," Ard said, hiking up to where Quarrah stood. "The others told me you did everything you could to help her."

"Didn't seem right to leave her like that," Quarrah answered. Had she cooled off enough to have a conversation with Ard?

"I'm glad you're all right." Ard's voice matched the soft evening light. Quarrah felt his hand gently grasping for hers. She made a subtle movement, pulling away as she turned to look out over the rocky slope.

"You never saw Tanalin's crew?" Quarrah decided to tackle the subject. It would eat her up if she had to wait any longer.

"Tanalin," Ard muttered. "What did Raek tell you?"

"I don't care what you did in the past, Ard." Quarrah turned back to him. "I don't care who you were with. But I do care about *now*. Raek's explanation helped me understand something. That wall. The wall you keep around yourself that I've been trying to climb. But I don't want to climb it anymore. Not if I'm going to find Tanalin inside."

Ard lifted a hand to his forehead, jaw tightening with discomfort. "It's not like that, Quarrah. Tanalin and me. She's the reason I did a lot of the things I did. But she has nothing to do with *this*." He reached out and took her hands.

"But you love her," said Quarrah. "A woman who you haven't seen in years. As long as she has you, I can't."

"I owe it to Tanalin," Ard replied. "I abandoned her that night. She thinks I'm dead. I have to—"

"You don't *have* to do anything!" Quarrah cut him off. "So she thinks you're dead. Let her think it. The only thing that could hurt her worse is finding out you're alive."

That same guttural chirp echoed down the rocky slope from the trees above. At the Slagstone mound, the Kranfel brothers commented on it, and Raek glanced upward to see if he could spot the source.

But Ard and Quarrah remained on the hillside with their eyes locked. "What are you going to do if you see Tanalin before we leave the island?" Quarrah probed. "You really think she's going to be happy you're here? Think she'll be proud of the name you've made for yourself and all the dirty Ashings you've earned?"

Ard dropped the eye contact, unable to withstand the torrent Quarrah was sending his way. He hadn't denied any of it. He hadn't even bothered to rebut. Tanalin's obvious power over him made Quarrah feel exposed, like her emotions were something comical to be paraded around, while Tanalin was kept close to Ard's heart.

A few loose rocks tumbled down the slope as Nemery came running up behind them. "Ardor!"

"Not now, Nemery." All the energy and charisma was gone from Ard's voice. Perhaps it would be good for the young girl to see him boiled down to this unusually humbled state.

"I'm sorry," said Nemery, "but that sound. Did you hear it?"

"Of course," Ard answered. "Why?"

"I couldn't place it at first. It's a Call my master said I'd never need to learn," explained Nemery. "It's a hatchling dragon in distress."

Ard stepped back, casting his eyes up to the trees. "What?"

"How is that possible?" Quarrah asked.

"It's not," said Ard. "That sound isn't coming from a hatchling. It's coming from a Caller."

"The king's Harvesters?" Nemery asked, but Ard was already scrambling up the slope, scanning the tree line. Quarrah glanced in that direction, but she didn't even know what to look for. A Caller with an instrument like Nemery's?

The rest of the crew picked up on the sudden tension. Raek and the Kranfel brothers redoubled their efforts, chipping away the Dross with calculated, steady movements.

Lence, Moroy, and Nemery were fanning out along the hillside, their eyes trained upward, when the Call came screeching out again. But this time it didn't stop. The Caller knew his trick had been uncovered. There was a true desperation behind the grating chirp. The race was on to see how long he could Call before his exact location was uncovered.

"There!" Nemery pointed into the trees some fifty yards away. Moroy was closest, and he set off at a sprint. Quarrah watched those long legs churn over the damp, loose rocks with the agility of a practiced Tracer.

At first, Quarrah couldn't see what he was running toward. Then she saw a structure to the vegetation that didn't seem quite natural. It was a hut. Similar to the one Nemery had constructed, only much smaller.

The hatchling distress Call continued with a wild freneticism until Moroy was mere feet from the hut. A gunshot cracked, echoing down the rocks, and vegetation ripped as the Caller fired from within the small hut.

The ball must have gone amiss, because Moroy didn't even hesitate. From the side of the hut, a man emerged, dressed in fringed attire of brown and green. The Caller made to run, leveling his gun behind him in a blind shot.

Moroy fired first, his Roller smoking as the Caller fell with a scream of pain.

"Moroy!" Ard shouted. But the Tracer closed the distance, angled his Roller downward and finished the man at point-blank range.

Quarrah felt her stomach twist in an anxious knot. To see a man's life ended so abruptly. So violently. She felt nauseous, rooted in place on the slippery rocks.

"Sparks, Moroy!" Ard screamed. "We needed him alive!" Changing direction, Ard raced toward the Slagstone mound, stones cascading under each step. "How much longer?" he called to Raek and the Kranfel brothers.

"It's a delicate process," muttered Jip.

"Where are the rest of them?" Quarrah's eyes scanned the clifftop for Harvesters.

"We have to assume they'll be here any moment." Ard drew a short knife and stepped up to the Slagstone mound. "Their Caller must have been sending a signal to the other Harvesters."

Lan Kranfel looked up just long enough to swat Ard back. "Not with the knife, Bloodeye. You'll blow the whole thing to chunks, and us with it."

"We have to speed this up." Ard stowed the knife but managed to peel off a flake of Dross with his bare fingers.

"You want to speed things up?" called Lan. "Then make like a legitimate Harvesting crew and form a line to pass the Dross bits."

Ard moved past Quarrah and carefully deposited his piece of Dross on the distant discard pile. Quarrah stepped into line with Nemery, but they didn't have a chance to pass a single piece of Dross.

Something came careening over the clifftop like an ominous cloud.

It was a dragon.

Quarrah felt her legs instantly threaten to give out. The beast was massive. She didn't know if it was the same creature they had baited, but it looked so much bigger displayed against the dusky clouded sky.

It dove with a thundering shriek, landing in a spray of rocks. Its neck darted forward like a powerful snake. Those tremendous jaws opened.

Lence Raismus was snatched from the rocks midsprint. He screamed, his body tossed skyward before the jaws crunched together, a shower of blood soaking anew the rain slicked rocks.

Quarrah couldn't breathe, the horror slamming into her like a tangible wall. The Caller from the hut hadn't been signaling the other Harvesters. He had been signaling a dragon!

The hatchling's cry of distress had been answered, the angry sow looking to destroy anything that might be threatening a young of her species.

Was this Tanalin's plan? This diabolical method for disposing of the criminals without even dirtying her hands? This was the justice of Pekal. A monster unleashed to judge and execute.

Moroy's Roller cracked twice, and Quarrah saw the lead balls ping off the dragon's impenetrable scales. The lean Tracer altered his route, making huge downward leaps through the loose rock.

The dragon sprang for him just as he reached the bottom, diving headlong into a gap between two boulders. The dragon's broad forehead smashed into the nearest stone, shattering it.

In the cloud of dust, Quarrah couldn't see if Moroy had survived. The dragon seemed uninterested, instead turning her attention to the group of six people huddled near the Slagstone mound.

Nemery suddenly broke from the group, sprinting up the slope toward the trees. "Nemery! Get back here!" Ard shouted, running another flake of Dross to the discard pile. Nemery didn't stop. She didn't respond. The girl just kept running as the dragon lumbered toward them in no apparent rush.

"Blazing girl," Ard muttered.

"I'll go after her," Quarrah said. With experience at handling Dross, Ard would be of more use to the Harvesters. But Ard drew a Roller from his holster and sprinted after the girl muttering, "She's my responsibility."

Since when had Ardor Benn felt responsible for anyone other than himself?

Quarrah set off after him anyway. The dragon was coming for the group at the Slagstone pile. Staying together would only give her an easy meal.

Ard fired three shots from his Roller into the dragon's face. The balls seemed to sting a little, but proved to be merely a nuisance. Like a biting fly.

The dragon lunged for the trio at the Slagstone mound, teeth stained red from Lence's blood, her jaws spreading wider than Quarrah thought possible. Wide enough to hook all three big men at once.

Quarrah flinched as the jaws came together, Raek and the Kranfels not even attempting to flee. But the dragon whipped her head back, growling some sound that Quarrah thought indicated pain. A hazy Barrier cloud arched over the men at the Slagstone mound like a protective dome. Raek must have detonated a pot as the dragon lunged for them.

Angered, the sow recoiled before attempting another bite with her incredible jaws. This time, Quarrah saw the teeth strike the invisible perimeter and stop fast. A dragon could chew through rock and bone, but a cloud of Barrier Grit was its match for strength.

The dragon withdrew, grunting once more. This time she swatted at the three Harvesters with a mighty foreleg. But even the huge sideways impact on the detonation cloud couldn't cause it to budge. Despite the seemingly tangible perimeter, the Barrier Grit dome would stay exactly where it had been ignited.

Suddenly, from the top of the hill, the hatchling Call pealed out again. Quarrah whirled in surprise as the grating shriek sounded. Ard had paused in the rocks just above her, but Quarrah didn't see Nemery anywhere.

Sparks! The girl was in the hut!

Quarrah and Ard both began a desperate sprint to the small disguised stand. Now closer to the temporary structure, Quarrah could see the wide bell of the horn protruding out the front of the hut.

The dragon, keying into the sound once again, spun a wide circle on the hillside, her tail spreading rocks in a massive spiral. The sow seemed confused, hearing the sound of the hatchling's distress, but unable to locate the offspring.

In a rage, the dragon leapt up the hill, bypassing Ard and Quarrah, and smashed into the nearest trees. The dragon's guess was to the left of Nemery's hut, but the space was cleared with startling speed. Entire trees came up by the roots, branches and timbers flying.

The sow carried on her frenzied search, as Nemery continued to Call with barely a breath between blasts. Quarrah and Ard were both ignored by the angry beast at the moment, and advancing on Nemery's location would only draw attention to her hidden instrument.

"We have to get her out of there," Ard said. "I want you to take Nemery and run down the valley as far as you can."

Before Quarrah could respond, the sow turned sharply, her tail swinging around like a hammer's blow and striking into the disguised hut. Nemery's hatchling Call was instantly silenced. As the tail swept away, Quarrah saw only rubble where the camouflaged structure had been.

Ard cursed, lunging through the slippery rocks. But something new drew Quarrah's attention skyward. A rush of wind, and a darkening above the trees.

By the Homeland. It was *another* dragon!

The new arrival was a close match in size to the first. The airborne beast immediately acknowledged the dragon demolishing the tree line, and she dove with a shriek.

The physical impact of the two giant creatures sent Quarrah tumbling backward in a gust of hot wind. A scaly tail slammed the earth beside her, sending a shock wave through the stones.

Quarrah gasped, crawling upward behind Ard, the feuding beasts each mistaking the other for the reason the hatchling had cried for help. What Nemery had just done would either save their lives or get them all eaten twice as fast.

Ard reached the ruined hut, desperately flinging branches and boughs aside in search of the young girl. Quarrah helped him push aside the trunk of a fallen tree, noticing bits of bent metal that had surely belonged to the instrument.

"Ardor!" The girl's voice was faint, and Ard frantically pulled back a few thatched boughs to find Nemery lying on her back. "It hurts." Quarrah saw blood all over her hands.

"You're going to be all right." Ard dropped to his knees in the wet soil. He pushed away another branch, and Quarrah saw the wound. A stick had been pushed into Nemery's leg, just above the knee. It was roughly the size of Quarrah's index finger, and protruded like a broken spear, passing clean through.

"You're going to have to leave me behind." Nemery was shaking terribly, her chin quivering as though she were freezing cold. "Like they did to Ulusal."

"Don't talk like that," Ard said. "I'm getting you out of here if I have to carry you on my back." He began tearing the fabric away from the injury. "I'm here for you, Nemery. *Two souls aligned in this journey. One to help the other. The other to help the one.*'"

Quarrah leaned forward, sure she had misheard him. Was Ard quoting Wayfarist scripture now?

The girl smiled, but her eyes rolled back, her body finally still from the shaking. Ard glanced over his shoulder at Quarrah. "She's going to make it home," he said. "I've got to get her out of here, but that doesn't make me much use in loading the Slagstone."

"I can do that," Quarrah said. Outside the trees, the grating sounds of the sparring dragons raged on. Raek's Barrier cloud would close in a few minutes. Quarrah wanted to be in position as soon as it did.

"That was a brave thing she did." Quarrah gestured to Nemery. Then she turned and sprinted back onto the exposed hillside.

By the time she reached the Drift crate, it was raining again. Her dirty hair was matted and the rocks were treacherous underfoot. Quarrah found the latch on the crate and pulled open the door.

"I've got a pot of Drift Grit we can use to load this," Raek said as the Barrier cloud burned out. The three men had successfully removed the Dross, but it was now piled at their feet like a deadly mine. Could the force of a raindrop cause the Dross to explode?

"Here." Raek carefully stepped around the Slagstone and tossed a pot against the rocks. There was a quick spark, and Quarrah felt the sensation of weightlessness ripple past her.

The Kranfel brothers seized the huge black Slagstone and tipped it up, trying to guide it as it drifted through the detonation cloud. The open side of the Drift crate was inside the cloud, but the back of the wooden box was grounded firmly outside the perimeter.

Raek hopped over to the brothers as Quarrah held on to the edge of the crate. Bits of Dross were now afloat in the cloud, making it dangerous to maneuver without bumping them. Quarrah hoped she and the others were long gone by the time gravity returned and the highly explosive flakes fell earthward.

Lining up the hovering Slagstone, the Kranfel brothers tried to load it into the Drift crate. It bumped once, twice, jarring the crate backward and nearly knocking it out of the cloud.

"It's too big," Jip Kranfel said. "Gotta split it."

Raek cursed, but Quarrah could see that Jip was right. The Slagstone mound was slightly too long to fit into the crate.

Lan floated out of the detonation cloud and jogged a few steps to where the tools had been dropped. He reentered the cloud a second later, with a hammer and slag pick in each hand.

"Brace the crate from the outside," Lan instructed.

Quarrah followed Raek to the back of the crate, getting her feet under her as gravity returned outside the cloud. Side by side, Quarrah and Raek braced their shoulders against the wooden structure.

The Kranfel brothers felt the ends of the Slagstone mound, running their hands along natural cracks and crevasses in the stone to find a weak spot. In a moment, they found what they were looking for.

Wedging the heads of their slag picks into a fissure, Lan pulled one way, and Jip the other. They wrangled the picks back and forth, sparks showering with every movement. Using the hammer, they pounded the picks deeper, the tooth material of the points holding up well against the Slagstone. At last, Quarrah heard a resounding *crack*.

The Kranfel brothers made some crude expression of victory, letting the splintered piece drift away. It wasn't a very big fragment, maybe a foot wide and twice as tall. But it was just enough to allow Lan and Jip to slip the rest of the large lump into the Drift crate. The broken chunk followed, clattering into the top of the box. Quarrah and Raek stopped bracing the backside, and the whole crate slipped out of the cloud.

Quarrah sealed and latched the door while Raek loaded the hopper, using the ignition key to detonate a new cloud of Drift Grit inside the airtight crate.

Quarrah glanced up to the tree line. There was no sign of Ard or Nemery. The dragons were still locked in combat, and their skirmish had led them downhill from the loaded Drift crate.

"Let's go!" Raek hoisted the front poles. Quarrah grabbed the back end, finding it no heavier than when it was empty. She heard the Slagstone mound rattling around inside the damp wooden box, throwing sparks with each little collision.

They hadn't gone ten steps when Quarrah heard Jip Kranfel shout for help. "Brother!"

She turned to see the younger sibling still adrift in the detonation cloud, his arms and legs flailing uselessly with nothing to propel him. Lan had just touched down outside the Drift perimeter. But Quarrah saw the problem and realized there was nothing he could do.

Two large flakes of Dross were drifting slowly toward one another, just out of Jip's reach. He pointed to them, his eyes wide. And then the crusty pieces of explosive met.

Quarrah felt a rush of air pummel her back, the exploding Dross reverberating like cannon fire. Lan was thrown uphill, but his younger brother was tossed with tremendous force down the rocky slope.

Jip slid down the scree, into the direct path of the fighting dragons. One of the sows broke away, her foreleg coming down to pin Jip before he could rise. She threw him as the second dragon moved in. Jip's body hurtled through the air, smashing into the cliff face with bone-shattering force.

Lan belted a scream of rage, sprinting down the hill toward his younger brother. He slipped on the wet rocks, tumbling as the enraged dragons snapped at him. The first sow missed, her jaws picking up loose stones.

Lan righted himself, clutching the slag pick with both hands, and thrust upward as the second dragon struck. The pick's head, fashioned from a dragon's tooth, pierced the scales of the beast's neck and drove into the flesh with a spray of black blood. The handle of the pick snapped from the force, and the dragon's head slammed down on Lan Kranfel. He crumpled, and the first dragon knocked aside the second, scooping his broken body into her jaws and swallowing him whole.

It all happened so fast. Quarrah stood stunned until Raek pulled the Drift crate forward again. Her feet seemed numb. Lence, Jip, Lan, Moroy. Was everyone going to die here? How would any of them escape this valley of terror?

Behind her, the dragons were fighting again, the injured one clearly unable to match her previous fury. Their battle was inseparable from a hot wind racing across the slope. Quarrah was sweating. They had almost reached the bottom. From there it would be an easy sprint on level ground along the base of the cliff until they reached the trees.

A gunshot sounded across the scree. It was followed immediately by a thundering boom. The ground seemed to lift beneath Quarrah's feet as stones pelted into her back. She was thrown away from the Drift crate, skittering down the last bit of the slope to rest against a smooth boulder.

Her vision was spinning, stars circling in her peripheral vision. What kind of explosion was that? Her ears felt like they were bleeding. And who was shooting? Quarrah looked up and saw Ard sprinting toward her, a look of panic on his face.

Something hit the ground beside Quarrah, and the familiar haziness of a Barrier cloud sprang up around her. Ard faltered for a moment. He said something that she couldn't hear. Their eyes locked.

Then he broke away, picking up the rear of the toppled Drift crate. Ard and Raek ran, the crate rattling with its weightless payload. He was leaving her there!

Quarrah heard voices through the ringing in her ears. Urgent shouting. The king's Harvesters were coming.

In that moment, Quarrah knew there would be no rescue. She wasn't worth the risk. Tanalin was here.

Of course Ard was running.

～

I can only imagine the kind of devastation those jaws could wreak. Homeland see that I stay downwind long enough to complete my task.

CHAPTER

31

It was dawn, but Ardor Benn had not even lain down. The first six hours of the night had been spent running. His hands were blistered and raw from the poles of the Drift crate he and Raek had been carrying, and Ard's head was pounding.

Nemery was alive, but her condition was worsening. Ard regretted having used his Health Grit at the crash site when the girl could obviously benefit from the detonation. And Raek's allotment had been left behind in his pack.

Ard had removed the stick from Nemery's leg and used his shirt and belt to make a tight bandage to staunch the bleeding. There was no way the girl could walk, so Ard lashed her to the top of the Drift crate and they carried her through the forest. She was small, but her added weight to their load was painfully noticeable.

They had to stop every ten minutes or so and reload the Drift crate hopper. Raek had tried using Prolonging Grit, but its effect gradually decreased the potency of the Drift. As a result, the weight of the Slagstone increased, coupled with the natural weight of Nemery and the crate, becoming simply too heavy to maneuver at any significant speed.

As a result, they were nearly out of Drift Grit when they finally arrived at North Pointe in the dark hours just before dawn. Surprisingly, Moroy Peng was waiting for them. Apparently, the man had survived the dragon's attack and fled during the chaos of the second dragon's arrival. He barely had a scratch, and his trained running legs had carried him to the rendezvous point much faster than Ard and Raek.

But Quarrah was gone. Taken by the king's Harvesters.

They had opened fire, a Fielder ball striking a pile of discarded Dross. The explosion had been huge, blasting a crater in the hillside and showering bits of stone like hail.

Quarrah had been thrown by the explosion, and before Ard could reach her, a crossbow bolt loaded with Barrier Grit struck the stones, trapping Quarrah at the base of the cliff. Ard told himself that the Harvesters needed Quarrah alive for questioning. Otherwise they would have used a Roller.

Ard felt a swell of anxiety. Tanalin questioning Quarrah. There was no favorable ending to that scenario.

"Ardor!" Nemery suddenly called. Ard raced to her side, dropping to his knees in the soft gathering of vegetation he had pulled together for her bed. He had placed her very near the shoreline cliff to allow the ocean breeze to wash over her.

The girl's face was sweaty and her dark skin looked pale. Sparks, she needed Health Grit and a legitimate healer. Still, it was good that she was awake. Nemery hadn't stirred since he laid her down nearly three hours ago.

"How are you feeling?"

"Thirsty," she mumbled. Ard retrieved his water skin and uncorked it. Nemery took it from his hands, tipping it back and nearly draining the vessel.

"Are they coming?" she whispered.

"The king's Harvesters?" Ard took the skin back and replaced the cork.

Nemery shook her head. "The pirates."

Ard looked over the vast horizon of water. From here, it seemed like it went on forever. Like Pekal was the only island in the archipelago.

"They're on their way to get us now." Ard hadn't spotted the escape vessel yet, but Raek had lit the flare. If the pirates had been waiting at the ten-mile line, then they were probably already making their way to North Pointe.

Nemery closed her eyes. "I don't think I'll be leaving with you."

Ard touched her hand. "Why would you say that?"

She shrugged. "Just an Urging from the Homeland, I guess."

"The Homeland would never Urge you to stay on Pekal," replied Ard. "It's too dangerous. Even for someone with your talents." This made Nemery smile, so Ard continued to bolster her with praise. "I'm serious. You saved us back there. If you hadn't thought to Call in that second dragon, the first one would have killed us all." He squinted at her in mock suspicion. "I thought your master told you not to bother learning that Call. The hatchling in distress."

"He did," Nemery admitted. "But that doesn't mean I listened to him."

"Get some rest," Ard said. "I'll wake you when the ship arrives." Nemery didn't protest, lying her head back against Ard's bundled coat.

Ard turned his attention to the tip of North Pointe, where Raek crouched, tinkering with the flare. Ard sighed heavily and then strode out to meet him, watching his step on the dangerous ascent.

North Pointe was a craggy peninsula of rock, jutting out from the northeast corner of Pekal like a pointing finger. It was at most thirty feet wide but extended some fifty yards. The rocks were naturally chiseled like a rugged staircase, reaching upward as it stretched away from the island.

North Pointe was an excellent place to display a signal, its tip standing more than a hundred feet above the InterIsland Waters. As Ard drew closer, Raek stood, striking his ignitor and sending a fresh streamer of light blaring off the tip of the narrow peninsula.

They'd been burning the flare since they'd arrived, getting a few hours of glow before the sun came peeking up. The flare was usually fueled by a mix of Light Grit and Prolonging Grit. Now that the sunrise was competing for brightness, it looked like Raek had replaced the Prolonging Grit with Compounding. The signal now burned so brightly that Ard couldn't stand to look directly at it. But without the Prolonging effect, Raek would have to reload every ten minutes or so. They'd burn up their remaining Light Grit in a hurry.

"Think they'll see it?" Ard asked, coming up behind Raek.

The big man didn't turn from where he stood looking out over the ocean. "They already have." He held out a spyglass.

Ard stepped up to the highest rock, taking the magnifier from his friend's hand. Raek pointed and Ard peered through the lens, slowly strafing the horizon. He saw the ship, its prow turned directly toward Pekal.

All this time traversing the mountain, assuring Nemery that their escape would come, but Ard didn't truly believe it until right now. Raek had arranged things with the pirates, and Ard wondered for the hundredth time what his partner's final goal was. The best ruses took time and patience. But at some point, Raek would have to try and turn the tables.

"How long until they get here?" Ard handed the spyglass back to Raek.

"I'd say we have about two hours." Raek glanced back along

the peninsula to the trees where Nemery slept. "She's not going to make the jump, Ard. You know that, right?"

Ard looked down the steep cliff to where the waves smashed against the rocks with a steady cadence. They wouldn't jump from here. Ard had scouted a spot closer to where Nemery was resting. There, the cliff was almost perfectly vertical with no rocks at the bottom to conflict with landing. But the jump would still be over sixty feet. And once they hit the water, there would be a fair swim to reach the ship.

Raek was right. There was no way Nemery would survive the jump.

"We'll figure something out," said Ard.

"In the next two hours?" Raek replied. "And what about the Slagstone? You claim to have some brilliant idea to get it off the island, but you won't tell me a word about it! Is that going to be ready in time? Or do we just leave the digested shell and forget all about this ruse?"

"I'm working on it!" Ard shouted, clenching his fists. The tension was tangible. Raek was pressuring him. Trying to get him to break down. "There are a few complicated calculations that—"

"Then tell me!" Raek bellowed. "Homeland knows that your mathematical skills will be the death of us all. That's *my* expertise, Ard."

Ard glanced back toward the Drift crate. Raek was absolutely right. Ard's experiments had never even been successful on a miniature scale. What hope did he have of executing them properly at full size?

"I had a real fancy drink at one of the orchestra receptions," said Ard. He had to tell Raek if he wanted his plan to succeed. That was all there was to it.

Raek looked puzzled at first, and then muttered, "Well, that's more like the Ard I used to know."

"The bartender used Compounded Cold Grit to make a sphere

of ice," Ard continued. "As the reception went on, the drinks got more elaborate. The last one I ordered had a grape frozen in the center of it."

"Why are you telling me this, Ard?" Raek's tone was slightly annoyed as he rubbed a hand over his bald head.

"The grape floated," Ard said. "A grape usually sinks. But when it was surrounded by a sphere of ice, the grape floated to the top of the glass." He paused to see if Raek would figure it out. Met with a blank stare, Ard went on.

"If we mix enough Compounded Cold Grit and strap it to the Slagstone mound, we could throw the whole thing off the cliff," he explained. "The Grit will detonate on impact and should freeze a sphere of water around the Slagstone. It'll float."

Raek stared at him unblinking for several moments. Now that Ard had finally divulged the plan, he actually felt quite desperate to hear Raek's opinion.

"I don't know if that'll work," Raek finally said.

"It has to," Ard pointed out. "We don't really have another option."

"There are a lot of variables." Raek shook his head. "Size, weight, density of the Slagstone. External air temperature. Water temperature. Mixing ratios between Grit types."

"I've done a few calculations already," said Ard. "I ran some tests while I was chasing the dragon…"

"Freshwater," Raek interrupted. "You ran your tests in freshwater, Ard. We have to drop the Slagstone into the ocean. The rate at which salt water freezes is significantly different than freshwater. Your calculations are useless."

"Then I'm glad I decided to tell you." Ard knew his work was subpar, but he didn't know he'd been so far off. "You can figure this out."

"I could have," said Raek, "a week ago. You're asking me to do this in two hours, with the few materials we happen to have left? What if we don't have enough Grit?"

"I've got nearly a full panweight of Cold Grit in my pack. And twice that in Compounding Grit," said Ard. "I came prepared for this."

"We'll see about that." Raek turned back to the open sea, shutting one eye and peering through the spyglass at the approaching ship. "Even if I figure this out and we get the Slagstone off Pekal..." He took a deep breath as if debating whether or not he should say what he was thinking. "What about Quarrah?"

"I've sent Moroy to look for Quarrah," Ard answered without a pause. The Tracer should have been back with a report by now.

"But I see that you didn't go yourself."

Raek's words were like a gunshot to the heart. Ard *wanted* to go after Quarrah. He hated the fact that he'd bribed Moroy to investigate for him. Ard told himself that it was because he couldn't leave Nemery. Because he couldn't leave the Slagstone under Raek's suspicious care. But those were hardly reasons to keep him from chasing Quarrah.

It was Tanalin.

They were so close to escaping Pekal. Mere hours away. If he went looking for Quarrah, he'd risk meeting Tanalin. And Ard didn't know what he would do if he came face-to-face with that ghost.

Raek shook his head. "The Ardor Benn I know would do anything for the people he *trusts.*"

Ard's eyes locked on to his companion's face. The game was up, then. Raek had sniffed out his suspicions.

"I'm sure I don't know what you mean." If this were a common ruse, Ard would identify this moment as the Final Distrust. A last opportunity for both parties to turn away and pretend like nothing was afoul between them.

"You think I'm the king's informant," Raek said. Ard felt his stomach drop. "Why else wouldn't you tell me your plan for moving the Slagstone off the island? And the way you changed the crew's command structure to distance yourself from me... I didn't let myself believe it. I couldn't allow myself to think that you'd accuse me. *Me!* Turned against you. Like I could be bought. A traitor!"

"Well, are you?" Ard shouted, unable to hold the question back any longer.

Raek stared down at him, scarred face shadowed. Ard had seen the man shot, sliced, and battered, but here on the peninsula of this Homeland-forsaken island, the pain in Raek's dark eyes was beyond anything Ard had witnessed.

"I'm not going to answer that, old friend." Raek took a steadying breath. "That's a question you shouldn't have to ask."

It was Ard's job to read people. He didn't have proof, but the look in his friend's eyes was enough.

"I'm sorry, Raek." Ard was surprised at the emotion in his own voice. "I don't know what I was thinking. All the evidence led me to believe it was you. I didn't want it to be true—"

"It's not," Raek snapped, his expression steely once more.

"I know." Ard rubbed a hand across his forehead. It was as though a costume had been dropped, exposing an old friend he hoped was still beneath. But it was a costume that Ard alone had put on Raek. How could he ever have suspected Raekon Dorrel?

"It's this blazing ruse. Halavend's hidden motives," Ard muttered. "It's all been playing tricks with my mind. Sometimes I feel as if the Homeland itself is running a ruse on me." He looked up at his big friend. "I trust you, Raek." Flames, it felt good to say those words and mean them. "But if not you, then who?"

Raek shook his head in confusion. "There were only three of us that ever knew all the plans."

"Not Quarrah," Ard whispered.

"There's no way. We would have seen through her by now," Raek said. "Maybe it's Isle Halavend. Or what about the Agrodite priestess working with him?"

Ard shut his eyes, listening to the waves roll against the cliffs so far below. For a moment, he didn't care who the king's informant was. He knew it wasn't Raek, and that was all that mattered.

Ard's reverie was interrupted by the sounds of someone approaching across the peninsula's rocks. He opened his eyes and spun to see Moroy, his angular face dirty and weary.

"One of my snares just caught a deer," he reported. "If we get a fire going, we could have something decent to eat."

Ard raised his hands in frustration. "Did you do what I asked?"

"Yeah, yeah," he said. "I found Quarrah. The Harvesters have her. She was alive when I saw her. Looks like the woman Tracer has taken over as captain. She was questioning Quarrah. Don't know if she got any useful information against us."

Tanalin.

Tanalin Phor was now captain of the king's Harvesting crew.

Ard felt Raek's eyes boring into him. This inevitable moment, which had been slowly brewing for seven years, had just reached a full boil. The only way to reach Quarrah was to face Tanalin.

He was going to have to choose. Tanalin Phor or Quarrah Khai.

One was a long-lost relationship. A dream that Ard held on to with all his might. The idea that he could, one day, under the perfect circumstances, make Tanalin understand why he'd done the things he'd done. They could be together, with more Ashings than they knew how to spend.

The other was something much more real. Not a dream but a growing, developing organism. What Ard and Quarrah shared was flawed, and at times difficult. He had come to know Quarrah well over the last eight cycles, and whether or not he wanted to admit it, he had come to love her.

What did the Homeland want him to do? Ard tried to focus on the Urgings—those feelings of the heart that he had learned about from his mother. But even without the Urgings, Ard knew which was the right choice.

Wayfarism taught that its followers should ever be progressing, advancing. Settling was a sin. Quarrah represented one doctrine in his mind, and Tanalin the other. And when he thought of it that way, the choice was obvious.

Homeland help me, Ard thought. "Where are they?"

Moroy pointed southward along the shoreline. "They've got a camp about a half hour's jog along the coast. They're keeping Quarrah in shackles."

Ard stepped past Moroy, making his way down the craggy peninsula. "Where are you going?" Raek asked.

"You know what I have to do, Raek. You've been telling me for cycles, but I've been too stubborn to trust you." For the first time in years, Ard felt a distinct and undeniable Urging from the Homeland. It was a powerful twist of his insides that couldn't be ignored. "I'm going to get Quarrah."

"They've got a lot of men," Moroy said. "A lot of weapons. You'll never fight your way to her."

"I'm not going to fight."

"What are you going to do?" Moroy asked. "Ask them nicely to release her?"

"Something like that," replied Ard. "I have an advantage with this particular Harvesting captain. She won't kill me."

"How can you be so sure?" Moroy asked.

Ard glanced at Raek. "Because everyone thinks she already did."

~

I am not above doubt. But I believe that facing it will show me the truth.

CHAPTER

32

Ardor Benn sat in the captain's map tent, awaiting the moment he had dreamed of for years. But now those dreams had turned to nightmares, and the prospect of the coming conversation caused him to tremble.

He was seated on a low wooden stool, his back to the tent's entrance flap. Ard leaned forward on his knees, head downcast, trying to keep his emotions under control. Two big Harvesters stood on either side of him, Rollers drawn as though they might shoot him point-blank if he so much as breathed funny.

It was dim inside the tent, with only the first rays of sunshine stretching through the trees and dappling across the walls. The trees dripped steadily from the night's rain, giving the illusion that the storm had not yet passed.

Ard was prepared—as prepared as he could be. As much as he wanted to pretend that things would go smoothly, he couldn't ignore the facts. He was a wanted man, and Tanalin was the captain of a crew sent to find him. The situation would be problematic, even if the two of them didn't have a history. But Ard was counting on that history to prevent Tanalin from killing him on the spot. Of course, there was also a chance that it would backfire...

Behind him, Ard heard the sodden canvas tent flap pull open. A plume of smoke from a dying campfire wafted in. *Oh, flames.* He wasn't ready for this!

"My crew said you wanted to see me?"

Her voice! That was Tanalin's voice! It made Ard's heart race and his breath come short.

"Yes," he whispered. "I've wanted to see you for many years, Tanalin Phor." He stood, slowly turning to look at her.

Tanalin gasped, a sound akin to a drowning woman sucking in her final breath. She took a step backward, and her legs gave out. The man next to her—a new face that had entered the tent with Tanalin—caught her, muscular arms wrapping around her for stability.

"Tanalin and I would like a moment alone," Ard said to the three men in the tent. He needed to be alone with her. They needed to speak freely—not just of his plans to rescue Quarrah, but of their past.

"You're insane!" spat the man supporting Tanalin. Who was he, anyway? What right did he have to hold her like that?

"The poacher is right, Omith," Tanalin finally spoke. She was standing on her own now, but her hand lingered on his arm. "You must leave us."

"What?" Omith whispered. "Tana…"

Tana. Just like Ard used to call her. She had always been *Tanalin*. To everyone else.

"Go," said Tanalin. "I don't want to have to make it an order."

Awkwardly, Omith moved backward, ducking through the tent flap with the two big Harvesters right behind. The subtle sound of water droplets splattering on the tent's canvas roof was like gunfire in Ard's ears. His own breathing was a hurricane.

"Who are you?" she whispered. Ard saw that he wasn't the only one shaking.

"It's me." Didn't she recognize him? Had she not thought of his face as often as he had pictured hers? Still, there was no substitute for seeing the real thing. The years had been good to her. And Tanalin's shocked expression only enhanced her natural beauty.

Her stark black hair had been cut shorter than Ard had ever

seen it. Her face looked browner, tanned by years of Harvesting expeditions. But her eyes were the same. Pale blue and sparkling, like the midday summer sun reflected in a calm mountain pool.

"But how are you here?" Tanalin's speech was slurred. "Illusion Grit? What kind of trick is this?"

"No trick," he said. "It's really me. It's Ardor."

Tanalin was shaking her head. "No. No. You died. Raek shot you. The cliff…"

Ard took a deep breath. Part of him wanted to lie. He even had a story prepared about how he had miraculously survived the fall. But that wouldn't settle anything between them, and any measure of acceptance he received from Tanalin would only be based on deceit.

No. It was time to come clean.

"I didn't die that night," he started. "I didn't even get shot."

"But the Roller…I saw—"

"It wasn't real," he interrupted. "I had to stage the whole thing to protect you. I had to make sure no one in the crew would suspect your involvement in stealing the husk."

"No," she whispered. "You're lying."

"I'm afraid not," he said. "Raek helped me pull it off. There were blanks in the Roller. I claimed the Fourth Decree and got off the island with the last ship to depart that cycle."

Ard saw the truth working in her. He saw Tanalin's face go flat with the numbness of disbelief. But she couldn't deny the man standing before her very eyes.

"Where have you been?" she asked. Ard saw the tears starting, running silently down her beautiful face.

"I wanted to find you sooner," he said. "I didn't want us to meet under these circumstances—"

"Sparks, Ard!" Tanalin stepped forward and punched him squarely in the chest.

Okay, so she was angry. Ard understood that. He held up his arms in case she wanted to punch again.

"You wanted me to think you were dead!" she shouted. "How were we supposed to meet again? What circumstances were you hoping for?"

"I've been working hard," Ard tried to explain, lowering his hands. "I've been saving Ashings. All these years! It's always been my plan to come back for you!"

Tanalin punched him again, this time in the jaw. He grunted, dropping to one knee from the blow. Tanalin always had been a spitfire. Ard supposed he should have expected this.

"Do you have any idea what you put me through?" Tanalin continued. "I was blamed for your death! And Raekon... Oh, if I could get my hands on him..."

She clenched her fists, and Ard brought his hands up in defense once more. But Tanalin seemed to resist striking him again.

"I can explain." Ard rose slowly. "My parents, Tanalin. You remember? They were in a terrible debt."

"I cared about them, too," she said. "I was willing to help you. Why, Ard? Why?"

"I protected you, Tana," he answered. Now that he called her that, it felt odd on his tongue. Like saying a word in Trothian, even though he didn't know its meaning.

"I couldn't allow my bad decisions to get you in trouble," Ard continued. "I had to make you believe I was dead. It was the only way to prove your innocence. I didn't have a choice."

"Didn't have a choice?" she fumed. "You lost everything for an empty husk. Did you know that? There wasn't a usable scale on it."

Ard dropped his eyes to the damp dirt floor. For a moment, he considered telling her the truth about that first ruse. But Ard could tell that tales of his success as a ruse artist would only drive Tanalin into a deeper rage.

"I understand how upset you must be..." Ard tried.

"You don't understand anything!" Tanalin yelled. "If you did, you wouldn't be here now." She drew a step closer to him, and Ard could see that her whole body was trembling. "I had to watch you die," Tanalin whispered. "I loved you, Ard." Those words stirred up memories powerful enough that Ardor Benn nearly broke. "I loved the *memory* of you."

"I'm still the same man," he replied, though Ard couldn't even convince himself that those words were true.

"No," said Tanalin. "Looking at you, I can *almost* see a glimpse of him. The man who cared for me...But something else moves you now."

Ard swallowed hard, fighting tears. It was over now. Ard knew it. Tanalin knew it. This was the closure he'd been seeking, but that didn't make the truth easy to accept.

"Who are you now?" Tanalin asked. "A poacher? A murderer?"

Ard shook his head. "It's not like that."

"Your people killed my captain!" she shouted. "Grax Hajar! You probably didn't even know his name. He was my friend. And a blazing good man! An honest one, at least."

"I told my crew not to shoot," Ard said. "He was a goon. Nothing more than hired muscle—"

"*You* brought them here," Tanalin cut him off. "You can't pretend like you weren't involved. Like your hands aren't dirty. You were always so blazing good at that!"

Ard clenched his teeth, a bit of anger stirring inside him, too. Now that he'd finally set his emotions aside, it was time to get serious. "Well, you'll be pleased to know that your dragon ate him."

That struck a chord in Tanalin. Ard could see it in her face. She had surely ordered her Caller to summon that dragon to act as executioner. From that clifftop, Tanalin and her Harvesters could have easily used Fielders to pick off every person in Ard's crew. But the dragon was nature's way of dealing with trespassers on Pekal. It would seem that Tanalin didn't like to get her hands dirty, either.

"Why are you here, Ard?" Tanalin finally asked, looking anywhere but at his face.

"I've come for Quarrah Khai."

"My prisoner?" Tanalin clarified. "You expect me to release her just because you dropped in to say hello?"

"There's a good reason for all of this, Tanalin."

"Well, I'm still waiting to hear it."

They stared at one another for a long moment as Ard tried to decide how much to tell her.

"My crew has to get that Slagstone off this island," Ard began. "You're the only person who can make sure that happens."

"Oh!" She raised her eyebrows. "Oh, really? You show up from beyond the grave, don't even apologize for the pain you've caused me, and now you expect me to do something that could cost me my career? Or worse!" She shook her head. "I have to take you in. I have to turn you over to the harbor Reggies."

"You know what'll happen to me?" Ard asked. "The moment Pethredote hears I'm alive, he'll give the order to execute me."

"That's supposed to appeal to my mercy? You already died, Ard."

"So you know exactly how it felt," he cut in. "Send me to my death, and you'll have to experience it all over again."

"Oh, I have a feeling it'll be a lot easier this time," Tanalin blurted.

Ard grunted in frustration. This wasn't going well. He never had been able to talk circles around Tanalin the way he could everyone else. Ard had a weak spot for her, but he needed to hedge it up or this was going to end very poorly.

"What I'm doing is important," Ard said. "My employer isn't the usual type. I swear to you that he hired me for the good of the Greater Chain."

"That sounds awfully altruistic for you," replied Tanalin. "Who is this employer?"

"Someone you wouldn't suspect, but someone you would instinctively trust," Ard answered, thinking of Halavend's desperate conversation from their first meeting. "I can't explain it all. I don't understand it myself, but I know that what I'm doing is the right thing. I have to get that Slagstone off Pekal. Lean to the Homeland. Feel its Urgings, Tanalin. You'll know I'm telling the truth."

"So you're a Wayfarist zealot now?" Tanalin retorted. "The Ardor I knew wasn't nearly so religious. I find it hard to believe that you've rediscovered your faith while living like a criminal."

When she said it so bluntly, Ard realized how ironic it was.

"Let's suppose I let you go," she said quietly. "My crew saw you enter this tent. I'd be charged with treason."

"It's quite the mess we're in," Ard agreed. "If I leave the tent unscathed, you'll be tried and executed. If I leave the tent in chains, I'll be tried and executed."

"You have to know which option I'll choose."

"What if there was a third option?" he proposed. "One where we both get away." The moment had come for Ardor Benn to explain his plan. This was the man he was now. A man of clever words and daring plans. Ard felt his anxieties ease as he set out to do what he did best.

"I'm listening," Tanalin whispered.

Ard reached into his vest and withdrew a slender piece of metal with a slight bend at the top. It wasn't one of Quarrah's genuine lock-picking tools, but it was the closest thing he could find in his pack—part of a cheap ignitor with the spring and the Slagstone removed. Ard trusted that Quarrah would have no trouble getting herself free, even with such a makeshift tool.

"I need you to give this to Quarrah Khai." He handed the item to Tanalin.

"What is it?"

"She'll know what to do with it," Ard assured. "In a moment of lax security, she'll be gone." Tanalin tucked the metal tool into her pocket. "My crew is camping at North Pointe. A ship is coming for us, but it won't arrive for another hour or so. If you direct your crew inland, away from the peninsula, it will buy us time to get off the island. Once we're gone, I have a favor to ask."

"You're hardly in a position to ask for more favors."

"There is a girl in my company, Nemery Baggish," said Ard, ignoring her statement. "She's young, Tanalin. Only fourteen. She signed on to be our Caller, but she's no criminal."

"Why are you telling me this?"

"She was injured in the dragon attack," Ard explained. "She won't survive a jump to the ship."

"You want me to take her off the island."

"She's talented, Tanalin," said Ard. "Homeland knows she needs a better role model than my motley crew. And she's not going to find that in a Reggie Stockade."

"I can't just let her go free," she said. "The girl is underage, undocumented, and she threw in her lot with poachers."

"She's not a criminal," Ard said again. He didn't know what to do if Tanalin refused to help. Ard was hardly willing to leave Nemery behind.

"I thought your crew was just hired help. Why do you care so much about this one?" Tanalin asked. "I've always been told that there was no honor among criminals."

Why did he care about Nemery Baggish? Was it because she was so young? Was it because she had awakened a Wayfarist sentiment within his heart? Or did it have something to do with the fact that another ruse artist had taken her parents' money and left Nemery's family broken?

"She's just a good Wayfarist kid who made a bad choice in coming here," Ard said. "You'll see what I mean when you meet her."

Tanalin sighed, and Ard knew that he had reached her. The Tanalin he remembered had always been compassionate.

"I'll fetch the girl at North Pointe," she said. "But I make no promises about what I'll do once she's in my custody."

"You'll do the right thing," said Ard. "Meeting you will be a crossroads for Nemery. In a big way, you'll determine which road she goes down. You can save her life, Tanalin. And I don't just mean from the Moonsickness."

Ard's words were crafted to instill a sense of responsibility in Tanalin. They proved that Ard respected the woman she was, despite the fact that his lifestyle was so different.

"You still haven't explained how we get out of this tent," said Tanalin.

Ard nodded. Now they were getting to the good part. "Let me see your Roller."

She hesitated for a moment, but Ard assuaged her fears by holding out his hands and making a harmless expression. Tanalin couldn't possibly think that he would hurt her. Finally drawing the Roller from its leather holster, she passed him the gun.

Ard popped open the rotating side and pulled all six cartridges and balls from the chambers. He handed five of them back to Tanalin, but kept the gun and the final piece of ammunition. Carefully, Ard worked the metal ball from the tip of the cartridge, loosening the adhesive that held the thin paper to the lead projectile. Once finished, he dropped the ball into his pocket and reloaded the blank cartridge into the Roller's first chamber.

Spinning the gun around, Ard offered the handle to Tanalin. "At the risk of repeating a good trick..." Ard pulled open the collar of his shirt so Tanalin could see what he had strapped to his chest. It was a soft pouch, tied securely around his chest with a long piece of string.

"What is that?" Tanalin asked, taking the Roller.

"Blood," Ard answered. Fresh from Moroy's snared deer at North Pointe. "You're going to have to shoot me, Tanalin."

She almost dropped the Roller. Ard knew what this meant for her. Tanalin hadn't pulled the trigger last time, but she'd held the smoking gun. Raek said the crew had recoiled from her. A woman who would shoot the man she loved, just to stop him from carrying out a theft. That smoking Roller had branded Tanalin a figure of brutal justice. And now he was asking her to do it again.

"You pull the trigger," Ard said. "Your crew comes bursting through the tent flap and they find me dead on the ground. Leave me where I lie, pack up the tent, and lead your team inland. Quarrah will use the tool to escape. I'll rendezvous with her and take her to North Pointe. Give us a couple of hours to get away, and then circle northward to retrieve Nemery."

Tanalin was staring at him, breathing heavily. Ard, usually so good at reading people, had no idea what she was thinking.

"You summed it up so well," she whispered. "Your little *ruse*."

"Tanalin," he said. "I—"

She pulled back the Slagstone gun hammer and fired. Through the puff of smoke, they stared into each other's eyes for one brief moment. Then Ard slapped his chest and felt the pouch of blood explode.

Ard dropped to the ground in what he hoped was a convincing display, but the look on Tanalin's face was not acting. It was reliving. Watching Ard fall, bloodied and dying, with a smoking Roller in her hand.

Omith came flying through the wet tent flap. Ard sputtered once, closed his eyes, and relaxed his body. The deer blood ran down his sides, his shirt soaked. He heard Tanalin drop the gun.

"Sparks, Tana!" Omith's voice was intense. "What did you do?"

Ard heard Tanalin draw several deep, steadying breaths before she spoke. Everything now hinged on what the woman chose to say.

"He lied," Tanalin whispered. "He lied to me." Well, that part was true. "He told me his crew was camped at North Pointe." Ard felt his hopes falling. "But I'm sure they went inland. They're trying to skirt around us and make for the harbor."

Ard resisted a big sigh of relief. Dead men didn't sigh.

"Leave his body there," Tanalin continued. "We'll pack up and move inland at once."

"I'll tell the crew," Omith replied. Ard heard the swish of the wet tent flap, and he could still hear Tanalin breathing. The two of them were alone in the tent again, but Ard didn't even dare crack his eyelids open.

"Flames, Ard," she whispered. "I'm getting too good at this. You better hope we never meet again. One of these times, there'll be a real ball in the gun."

Quarrah twisted, legs tucked back, testing the true measure of her flexibility. Her fingers slipped into the top of her boot, feeling the tip of the metal tool as she worked it from the lining pocket.

The gunshot was finally the distraction she'd been waiting for. It had resounded from the center of camp, causing the king's Harvesters to jerk like puppets on a string.

For a hopeful moment, Quarrah thought the disruption might be some sort of rescue attempt from her crew. But the hubbub died as quickly as the shot had sounded, leaving Quarrah to realize that any escape would have to be of her own making.

As the fear of attack waned, curiosity among the Harvesters piqued, and Quarrah's guard finally wandered far enough for her to make her move.

She slipped the tool free of her boot lining, spinning it between her fingers and inserting the tip into the lock. The jagpin wasn't the best choice for releasing one's own hands from shackles, but it was the only thing the Harvesters hadn't taken from her.

Her treatment had been fair, for a prisoner. Quarrah had been given water and a strip of dried meat as camp was set. They'd pressed her for information, but their methods had remained humane.

Quarrah had spoken with Tanalin.

She didn't even remember what she'd said to the stern woman. Simply standing before Tanalin sent a thrill of jealousy through Quarrah's stomach. And it was then, looking into the eyes of

Tanalin Phor, that Quarrah knew Ard would abandon her. Any attempt at rescue could bring Ard and Tanalin together. Quarrah knew she wasn't worth that risk.

With a satisfying click, the lock popped open and Quarrah felt the metal shackles loosen around her aching wrists. She slipped free, leaping to her feet and sprinting into the dimness of the trees where the morning light had not yet penetrated. There was no immediate call of alarm at her escape, and Quarrah fell into a steady run.

Well, that was easy.

She needed to reach North Pointe. Quarrah's impeccable sense of direction, along with snippets of conversation she'd picked up from the king's Harvesters, told her which direction to go.

Quarrah was slicked with sweat, her breath coming in weary gasps, when Moroy Peng stepped out of the trees with a Roller leveled in her direction.

"Sparks, Moroy!" She skidded to a halt in the damp soil. "Put that thing down! It's me."

He sniffed nervously and lowered the gun. "How do I know you're not leading the king's Harvies right to us?" He glanced behind her. "Where's Ardor?"

Quarrah brushed the painful question aside. "We need to get to North Pointe."

"You're there." Moroy gestured vaguely over his shoulder, his gaze still trained on the trees behind her. "The blazing fool get himself killed?"

"Ard?" Quarrah clarified. "I thought he was with you."

"Was," Moroy replied. "He went looking for you. Said he was going straight to that woman captain to negotiate your release."

Quarrah felt her breath catch. Ard had faced Tanalin for her? He . . . The gunshot! Sparks, had Tanalin killed him?

"For the record, I thought it was a bad idea." Moroy finally holstered his Roller and turned. Quarrah fidgeted, her feet torn between following Moroy to North Pointe, and sprinting back to the Harvester camp to search for Ard.

"The Short Fuse is nearly finished rigging up some harebrained idea," Moroy continued. "It's time to get off this Homeland-forsaken island."

Quarrah stood rigid for one more moment before jogging to catch up with the lean man. "What about Ulusal? Did she make it?"

Moroy let out a cold laugh. "You're the only one who thought she would. She's been dinner for the wolves by now."

So many dead. Was Ard one of them? He had come for her! How could she leave Pekal not knowing if he was alive?

Quarrah followed Moroy out of the trees, the bright morning sun glinting sharply off the water far below. The rocky peninsula of North Pointe extended like a pointing finger, but Moroy led her past it. The familiar Drift crate came into view, but it was empty. The massive lump of Slagstone now rested at the edge of the cliff.

All around, the earth had been cleared to bare dirt. Quarrah stepped carefully over a series of numbers that had been scratched into the rich soil. Arithmetic of some sort. Raek must have been hard at work here, scribing madly on his poor man's chalkboard.

"Quarrah!"

She turned as Raek appeared from behind the empty crate. The big man was holding a detonation pot marked with the colors of Drift Grit.

"Well, call me a Paladin Visitant," Raek said. "Tanalin actually let you go!"

"She didn't let me go," Quarrah said. "I escaped."

"Of course it had to look that way." He glanced around. "Where's Ard?"

Quarrah sighed. "I never saw him."

"Well, the guy has a knack for showing up at the last minute." Raek distracted himself with some final adjustments on the Slag-stone, but in her mind, Quarrah heard the gunshot once more.

Moroy Peng stepped up to the edge of the cliff, shedding his boots, belt, and shirt. "I'm not waiting around for the ruse artist. I expect full payment within a cycle. Assuming you survive the jump."

"Jump?" Quarrah asked.

In response, Moroy leapt from the cliff, plunging some sixty feet into the InterIsland Waters below.

"Flames! He jumped!" she cried.

"That *is* the quickest way down," Raek remarked.

Quarrah saw the pirate ship waiting below, anchored illegally close to Pekal's shoreline cliffs. Moroy surfaced and began the two-hundred-yard swim to the vessel.

"This thing is all set." Raek gently patted the lump of Slagstone. Detonation pots were carefully strapped around the black rock. "All we need to do is detonate some Drift Grit and float it off the edge of the cliff. Impact with the water should be enough to spark the pots and envelop the whole mound in a ball of ice."

But Quarrah wasn't paying attention. Ardor Benn's voice suddenly cut through the morning stillness.

"Spark it all, Raek!"

Quarrah turned to see Ard scrambling over some rocks at the base of the peninsula. "I can't find her anywhere! Tanalin promised that she'd give her the ..." Ard froze when he saw her. Quarrah watched an expression of frustration melt into a broad smile. But his shirt! It was stained red in a gruesome pattern. "Oh, there you are, Quarrah Khai."

Quarrah opened her mouth to reply, but what could she say? He was always the one with the words.

"You were faster than I expected," Ard said to her.

"You were expecting me?"

"Of course," he said. "I negotiated your release. Did you think Tanalin Phor slipped you that lock-picking tool out of the goodness of her heart?"

"Lock-picking tool...?" Was he talking about the hidden jagpin in her boot?

"I knew those shackles wouldn't give you any trouble if I got the right instrument into your hands," Ard carried on. "I found the tool in your pack and coerced Tanalin into making the delivery."

As far as Ard was aware, _he_ had rescued Quarrah. She wondered what Tanalin must have thought when she came to drop off the tool and found Quarrah's shackles empty.

She smiled, deciding not to tell Ard the truth of her escape just yet. He had come for her. He had finally faced his bygone lover for Quarrah's sake. He'd chosen her over Tanalin in an apparent display of his affection. Quarrah thought it best to let him revel in the moment.

"Did you send Tanalin my warmest regards?" Raek asked.

Ard nodded. "She said we should all get together for lunch sometime."

"And then she shot you in the chest?"

"That was a formality." Ard plucked at his stained shirt. "It hurt a lot worse when she punched me in the face."

Quarrah had only been apart from them for a single night, but something had obviously changed between the two partners. An old level of trust seemed to be reemerging, like sunlight breaking through clouds after a heavy storm.

"We should get moving," Ard said. "It won't be long before Tanalin leads her crew this way."

"She knows where we are?" Raek asked.

"I had to tell her," answered Ard. "But she agreed to turn a blind eye while we escape. Then she promised to circle around and retrieve Nemery."

Quarrah started. In her worry over Ard's return, she'd forgotten about the girl. "Where is she?"

Ard pointed back toward the trees. "Asleep," he said. "And she needs to stay that way until we're gone."

It seemed harsh to leave Nemery behind, but Quarrah knew it was the right choice. She'd seen the girl's wounded leg. Nemery would never make the swim to the waiting ship. Still, turning her over to Tanalin was a gamble. But Quarrah supposed it was better that Nemery be a prisoner than a corpse.

"Time to test Ard's frozen grape theory." Raek's statement made no sense to Quarrah, but she watched as the big man placed the pot of Drift Grit he'd been holding. Ard seemed to know what to do, moving around to brace himself against the Slagstone as Raek detonated the Grit.

With a slight discoloration of the air, a weightless cloud sprang up, enveloping the huge black stone. Raek took his place beside Ard, the two men planting their feet outside the blast perimeter for leverage.

"Hey, Ard," Raek said with a cheeky grin. "If this doesn't float, we're *sunk.*"

Ard rolled his eyes. "Thanks for *buoying* my confidence."

They counted down from three and shoved against the Slagstone, sending it spinning through the hazy Grit cloud and over the cliff's edge.

Quarrah stepped forward anxiously as it plummeted. Far below, it struck the water. In the mist from the crashing waves, Quarrah couldn't tell if the Grit detonated like Raek said it should.

The Slagstone sunk out of sight, the three of them holding their breath as they peered down. And then a massive chunk of ice rose from the depths and bobbed upon the surface.

Raek let out a huge sigh, and Ard laughed victoriously. When Quarrah realized what they'd done, she shook her head at the brilliant idea.

"Won't it melt?" she asked. The detonation cloud would stay where it originated, but the Slagstone had already floated yards away.

"Eventually, yes," Raek said, pulling off his shirt in preparation for the big dive. "But ice is ice, whether it's in the freezing atmosphere or not. Which reminds me…" He held up a finger of caution. "Make sure you don't jump into the Cold cloud below or it'll freeze you solid in the blink of an eye."

Quarrah glanced down at the Compounded Cold cloud on the ocean's surface. Continuous shards of ice formed as water passed into the detonation radius, the current pushing and pulling the frozen fractals in multiple directions. Quarrah suddenly realized the urgency of their dive, since every moment they waited filled their landing space with deadly icebergs.

She was standing there as though frozen, fear filling up her insides, when Ard's warm hand slipped into hers.

"We'll jump together." The morning light shone on his crimson-stained bare chest. Quarrah nodded wordlessly, slipping out of her boots. Her clothes were tight-fitting enough not to bog her down, and she had no other excess to shed.

Hand in hand, Ard and Quarrah sprinted a handful of steps, and then the ground fell out from beneath them. It was a paralyzing plunge, and Quarrah was sure they would hit one of the icebergs below.

Water wrapped around her like a forceful hug. She felt Ard's hand separate from hers as she strained upward, breaking the surface with a gasp.

Quarrah was by no means an expert swimmer, but she found the rhythm of it, kicking hard in the direction of the waiting ship. She felt as though she had left all of her strength in the water when they hauled her up, cold hands clinging desperately to the rope ladder.

"Welcome aboard the *Shiverswift*," a new voice greeted Quarrah as she pulled herself, sopping, onto the deck. "Frightful good fortune to pull a fine young lass from the water."

Quarrah looked at the speaker. The man's hair was gray and comely, pulled back in the popular fashion. He wore a striking blue shoulder cape and a pressed shirt with impressive sleeves. His chin was shaved smooth, leaving only a neatly trimmed mustache.

The early light played on his blue feathered hat, the left side of the huge brim turned up. If Quarrah hadn't known better, she'd have thought the man was dressed for an orchestra concert in Beripent.

"I thought," she gasped, "you were pirates."

"What makes you think we aren't?" the man asked, proffering a dry handkerchief.

Quarrah glanced across the deck. Ard and Raek had apparently beaten her to the ship and were already conversing with a few well-dressed sailors at the stern. A ship hand walked by with a glass of red wine. An actual glass!

"I thought you'd be more…" Quarrah dried her face. "Rough."

"Homeland, no!" the man exclaimed. "A bit of scented grape-seed oil softens the calluses nicely." He produced a long-stemmed pipe and began to light the tobacco. "We consider ourselves high-class pirates, madame. We're in it for the finer things. Leave the ravaging and murdering to the tasteless folk."

Quarrah shouldn't have been surprised. After all she'd been through with Ardor Benn and Raekon Dorrel, she should have expected them to contract with classy pirates.

The ship lurched, and Quarrah barely kept her feet planted. Raek ran past, shouting something as a handful of sailors readied the cargo nets. A few minutes later, they had managed to ensnare the floating, ice-encrusted Slagstone. Sails whipped in the wind, and the *Shiverswift* towed its valuable cargo away from Pekal's high shoreline.

Ard came alongside the finely dressed pirate. "Our ice is melting fast. The cargo won't stay afloat much longer."

"We'll pull her aboard once we reach legal waters," the gray-haired man said.

"Thanks, Captain," Ard replied. "We'll get payments squared away within a cycle."

"Aye. I'll expect the deposit into my treasury account at the Symphonette guesthouse." The captain offered them each a butter mint, took a long puff on his pipe, and strode away.

"Good winds," Raek said, coming up behind Ard. "We should be to Strind by suppertime."

"Tell us about the factory," Ard said.

"Well, I've picked out the perfect place," Raek began. "Cozy, quaint. And wait until you see the views."

Quarrah lifted an eyebrow. "We *are* talking about a Grit processing factory, right?"

Raek chuckled. "Actually, the place is a perfect dump. It'll fit our needs nicely."

"We'll move in after dark?" Quarrah clarified. "Process the Grit while no one is there?"

"There's always *someone* there," Ard said. "And it's going to be nearly impossible to sneak that lump of Slagstone in after hours. Besides, Raek's not sneaky. Just look at him."

"Then what's the plan?" Quarrah wondered why they hadn't talked about this? All this time she had imagined that they'd sneak in.

"I left a stash when I visited a few cycles back," Raek said. "It's got uniforms, documents, everything we need to bring that Slagstone through the front door right under the workers' noses."

"Another ruse?" Quarrah sighed. Why couldn't they ever do things her way?

"Yes and no," said Ard. "We'll move the Slagstone into the factory during the hustle and bustle of regular hours. Then we'll need someone to slip in undetected in the middle of the night, steal some keys, open some doors, and get us access to the machinery." He rubbed his chin. "If only I knew someone with that specific skill set..."

Quarrah grinned. Maybe they would do something her way after all.

———

I envy all those who can so easily sail away
from this place.

CHAPTER

33

Quarrah slipped into the dark corner of the Grit factory, melding with the midnight shadows and waiting for the scheduled security guard to walk past. She altered her breathing. Low and shallow, but steady. It was the common temptation to hold one's breath while hiding, but that tactic inevitably led to audible gasping.

It wasn't like the handful of guards would be listening to the shadows anyway. It was just an ordinary night at Mordell and Sons Grit Processing Factory.

Quarrah, Ard, and Raek had barely arrived before the factory closed, the pirates dropping them at a quiet harbor on Strind before departing with Moroy Peng.

Raek's stash of uniforms and forged paperwork had served them well, allowing the three of them to move the Slagstone into a holding room without any trouble. Now it was Quarrah's turn to get them all inside again, with full access to the Slagstone, the machinery, and the processing pits.

Quarrah heard the footsteps she'd been expecting. A single pair of boots, slow, heavy gait. A bit of a shuffle, which would imply either fatigue or intoxication. Perhaps a bit of both.

The guard walked past, a heavyset man with a bored expression. Quarrah waited until the sound of his steps faded around a corner before ducking out of her shadowed nook and moving down the hallway.

It felt good to be a thief again! Like rinsing in a clear stream after a day on the dusty road.

Mordell and Sons was the perfect place. Private security was lax, locks were outdated, and half of the standard safety protocols were ignored.

Quarrah had already lifted a ring of keys from a "secure" room. These would allow Ard and Raek to open doors without her. And it would make it much easier to relock doors behind them, so as not to leave any evidence of their intrusion.

This was really the end of the ruse! Quarrah hadn't given much thought to it on Pekal, with all her focus on basic survival. By morning they'd be back in Beripent, delivering the Visitant Grit to Isle Halavend and collecting their million Ashings.

Where would Quarrah go next? Things weren't perfect with Ard, but she hoped they might begin to build something real together. They'd be as rich as nobility, and Ard would have no excuses but to focus a bit of that brilliant mind on cultivating a relationship with her.

Quarrah moved around another corner. The factory was a large hexagonal structure, the six exterior corridors pocked with rooms to house equipment and supplies. The center of the hexagon was an open-air courtyard where the processing pits and stationary machinery were located.

Listening for any sounds of security guards, Quarrah paused at an outer personnel door. Most of the factory entrances were large cargo gates, designed to bring in cumbersome Slagstone mounds. But this small door would be more subtle.

Quarrah inserted the key that corresponded with that particular style of lock and pushed open the metal door, wincing as it groaned on its hinges.

Ard and Raek stepped quickly inside. The stolen factory uniforms they'd been wearing earlier were replaced by more traditional clothes—billowing sleeves and a vest for Ard, cutoff shirtsleeves for Raek.

"This way." Quarrah took off down the hallway at a jog. Her boots from the stash weren't nearly as comfortable as her usual soft leather. And the soles seemed to scuff noisily.

In a moment, they were standing in the room where the Slagstone was stored. Ard rested one hand gently on the cool, dark stone as if he'd hated being apart from it.

"There are four security guards patrolling the hallways," Quarrah said. "How do we stop them from coming into the courtyard once we start processing?"

"We'll need to keep the loud machinery in a cloud of Silence Grit at all times," Ard said.

"I've also got these." Raek held out a handful of curious devices. Each looked like a detonation pot with a metal prong extending off one side.

"Door mines full of Memory Grit," he explained. "Once we get into the courtyard, I'll attach these to each of the doors. If a guard tries to walk in on us, the mine will detonate. He'll be instantly enveloped by a cloud of Memory Grit, so he won't remember anything he sees in the courtyard."

"What's to stop him from stepping through the cloud?" Quarrah asked. Memory Grit only erased the person's ability to recall things that happened while they were contained within it.

"That's what these are for." Raek gestured to a bundle of thin tubes at his belt.

"You rascal!" Ard cried. "Where did you get those?"

"Had some left over from the Dewdow ruse," he said. "I stashed them here with the other stuff."

"That's why I keep this guy around," Ard said.

"What are they?" Quarrah asked.

"Trothian Air Darts," Raek explained. "They blow needles

laced with tranquilizer. I'll rig them to the door frame with an ignitor and the smallest pinch of Void Grit. The detonation will shoot the needle across the threshold when the door opens. As long as it hits the guard while he's in the Memory cloud, he won't remember any of it. When he wakes up, he'll think he must have dozed off. It is the night shift, after all."

"Remind me to give you a raise," Ard said.

"I would," Raek replied, "but I'm not your employee."

"Quarrah and I will set up the equipment while you place the door mines," Ard went on. "When you finish, start mixing the solution for the pits. We'll begin Chipping, but we need to move through this as quickly as possible. We're looking for seventeen fragments of fertilized shell in this mound." He patted the Slagstone, the broken end resting in the cart beside it.

"You got it." Raek swung open the wide loading door. Quarrah glimpsed the dark courtyard beyond as Raek moved out of sight.

"Here's a list of materials we're going to need." Ard handed her a slip of paper. "Supply rooms are usually located with easy access to the pits. Check the doors around the perimeter of the courtyard."

Quarrah squinted at the list. She'd have to step closer to the Light cloud if she hoped to read it. There wasn't much she missed about being Azania Fyse, but Quarrah regretted not keeping her spectacles in moments like these.

"I'll move the Slagstone into position and prime the machinery." Ard seemed to sense her nervousness and tried to break it with a winning smile. "Don't worry, Quarrah. This'll be fun."

"Have you done this before?" she asked. Ard knew so much about it, Quarrah assumed he had experience working in a Grit factory.

"That depends on what you mean," answered Ard.

"I thought it was a straightforward question."

"If you're asking if I've ever broken into a factory and processed my own Grit in the middle of the night, then the answer is no," he said. "If you're asking if I've ever processed Grit in a factory at all, then the answer is . . . no."

"So, basically, the answer is no," said Quarrah.

"Hey. Try not to be so negative." He winked at her. "Raek read a book about Grit processing once. He told me what it said. I'm sure we'll be fine."

Quarrah rolled her eyes, unable to decide if Ard was telling the truth or trying to lighten the mood. He pulled the handle of the Slagstone cart, Quarrah giving a good shove from the back as it rolled onto the packed dirt of the courtyard.

Alone now, Quarrah stepped over to the floating cloud of Light Grit, mumbling aloud as she read the list that Ard had scribed for her.

"Weighted Light Grit lanterns, glass eye lenses, steel gauntlets, nose plugs, breathing reed . . . What the blazes?" Quarrah shook her head. She couldn't have predicted a single bizarre item on this list.

Knowing Ard, half the items could have been a joke. But Quarrah knew he wasn't in the mood to waste time tonight. She'd get the supplies as quickly as possible and hope that he and Raek really knew what they were doing.

The night was nearly spent, but Ard felt confident that they'd be done by sunrise. Raek's Memory Grit door mines had captured only one would-be intruder. But Raek had dragged the unconscious guard back into the hallway before resetting the mine and Trothian Air Dart.

The Mill's steady pounding was as rhythmic as Ard's heartbeat, sending tremors through the dirt as the plate of sharp dragon teeth pulverized the shell fragments.

Fortunately, the factory's machinery hadn't given them any trouble. Quarrah and Raek had used the Chipping Vise and Blast Chisels to rough out the pieces of shell, breaking away excess

Slagstone. They had uncovered bone, wood, and chips of rock. Normally, a factory would carefully extract every indigestible embedded within the Slagstone. But tonight, Ard was only interested in dragon shell.

To Ard's frustration, they had only been able to uncover fifteen pieces of the golden shell. Likely, two of the smaller fragments hadn't survived the dragon's digestive acids and had dissolved and incorporated into the organic slag. Whatever was the case, Ard had decided to move on so they could be sure to finish by sunrise.

Ard had spent most of the night underwater, submerged in the salty anti-ignition solution of the Scouring Pit, glass lenses over his eyes and a long breathing tube in his mouth.

His hands still ached from the Scouring gloves—leather mitts with flat bits of dragon bone overlapping like small scales. Ard had used his rasp-like gloves to rub off the remaining Slagstone that couldn't be removed with the imprecise Blast Chisels. Submerged in the anti-ignition liquid, there was little risk of the scoured powder igniting like Blast Grit.

After his prolonged time underwater, Ard relished the cool bite of the spring air on his bare chest as he turned the Mill's crank, Quarrah beside him.

Now that Tanalin was finally out of his mind, Quarrah's presence meant more than ever. He wanted to stop right there and tell her how he felt. But judging by the position of the stars overhead, Ard suspected the sun would rise in about two hours. There was still one more step in this process, and they were running out of time.

Inside the cloud of Silence Grit, the Mill was a deafening piece of machinery. At the top was a circular plate, slightly convex and loaded with dozens of razor-sharp points—the tips of dragon teeth set so closely together that it looked almost like a bed of nails facing downward.

Quarrah poured Blast Grit into a narrow trough, Ard's crank

forcing the Grit into a funneled hopper, where it ignited on a spark-ing chip of Slagstone. The resulting explosion pushed the teeth plate down with significant force.

Raek had primed the machine by detonating a pot of Barrier Grit on the underside of a wooden tray, creating an upside-down dome. Sliding away the tray, they were left with a Barrier Grit bowl, hanging suspended in the place it was ignited. The convex teeth plate was designed to fit the concave opening of the Barrier bowl. Milling was easy. Ard simply needed to drop a piece of Scoured shell into the bowl and fire up the machine.

At least they weren't Milling Blast Grit. Due to its explosive nature, that operation required the entire Mill to be submerged in one of the anti-ignition liquid pits.

But Visitant Grit was not explosive in the same manner. As long as they kept sparks away from it, there was no risk of a premature detonation.

Funny, Ard thought. *We're taking the very thing we spent cycles trying to get, and smashing it to powder.*

In a few more hours, all of this would be behind them. Ard had sent word of his progress to Isle Halavend as soon as they reached Strind. The old man would be relieved to know that they'd suc-ceeded on Pekal.

As a cool drip of anti-ignition liquid ran down Ard's bare back, he found himself thinking of the Mooring and its unique watery passageways. He had a sudden nostalgic desire to visit that sacred building again. Not just to deliver the Visitant Grit to Halavend, but to ponder a few things for himself.

He had questions for Isle Halavend. Questions of a spiritual nature. The Homeland had been speaking to Ard more and more. Not real audible words, but Urgings within. Those Urgings had led him to trust Raek. To confront Tanalin. To finish this job. But then what?

The idea of a future with Tanalin Phor had finally melted away.

Like an ice sphere from one of those fancy receptions, left too long in the sun. Now Ard saw new possibilities opening before him.

Possibly even a future with Quarrah Khai.

At last, Ard let go of the Mill crank, his aching arms falling limply to his sides. Quarrah stepped through the smoke from the Blast detonations, using a small horsehair broom to sweep the final bit of Grit out of the inverted Barrier dome, and into a wooden bowl.

They crossed quickly to the Tumbler where Raek was waiting.

"Is this enough?" Quarrah held out the bowl of powdered shell.

"Halavend didn't really specify how much we needed to bring him," Ard pointed out. "What size of blast cloud do you think he'll get with this amount?"

Raek puzzled over it for a minute, turning his sweaty head this way and that. "Maybe a forty-foot radius, depending on its natural potency. Hard to say. I'm not exactly familiar with the detonation rate of Visitant Grit. Some documents say it's comparable to specialized bone Grit like Health, Memory, and Illusion. But I'd tell old Halavend to use it all in one shot. If he's going to detonate a Visitant cloud, he should probably err on the side of having too much."

"Hey, that's usually *my* philosophy." Ard leaned forward to peer into the bowl. Under the faint glow of Raek's Light Grit lantern, he examined the golden powder for the first time. It looked like perfectly functional Grit, though it shimmered with a brilliance that Ard had never seen in any other type.

"We still have to run it through the Tumbler?" Quarrah asked.

"Won't take long," answered Raek, pointing to the machine. It looked like a large barrel with a cloth lining. "It's designed to wick away any residual moisture from the anti-ignition solution. Leaves the Grit ready for immediate use."

Ard had purchased bad batches of Grit before, from cheap factories that skipped the Tumbling. As a result, the Grit was tainted from the anti-ignition liquid, so it wouldn't ignite under spark or flame. Nothing like fireproof Grit.

Quarrah moved over to the Tumbler, her steady hands carefully emptying the wooden bowl into an open hatch at the top of the barrel. Shutting the lid, Raek took hold of a cord and gave a sharp pull.

The cord unwound, spinning the cloth lined barrel with a whir. As it began to slow, Raek gave another pull. And another. The whole Tumbling procedure took less than five minutes, Quarrah and Ard watching anxiously.

As the barrel rolled to a stop, Raek reached inside with the same little brush Quarrah had been using. He swept the dry, golden powder into a Grit keg. There must have been nearly a quarter panweight of it, filling it almost to the top.

Ard accepted the Grit keg from Raek, staring down at the glittery gold dust.

Visitant Grit. The stuff of legend. The stuff of children's dreams and the Islehood's musings. The stuff that had the power to topple kings and lead uprisings.

For the first time in his life, Ardor Benn held true power in his hands.

~

It is humbling to think that all Grit originates here. We have worked so hard to tame its properties. But it all begins in the viscera of a wild thing.

CHAPTER

34

The desk in Cove 23 was littered with loose parchments and meaningless books. Isle Halavend stared blankly at the stone wall, a strange calm enveloping his old mind.

Like the tepid air before a winter rainstorm. The latter, which chilled to the bone and brought the mighty running for cover, was yet ahead.

Tomorrow, they would save the islands, or all hope of ever delivering mankind from the Moonsickness would be lost. Ardor Benn, against all odds, had completed his ruse. Halavend had received word that the shell was being processed.

The Visitant Grit was ready.

For over a year, he had worked to see this moment. He no longer felt afraid or anxious. Halavend had pondered all he could, researched harder than he ever had. Now the Homeland would have to see the rest through.

There was but one thing left for him to do. And no amount of reading and study could truly prepare him for what was ahead. He needed to choose someone to detonate the Visitant Grit.

Ardor Benn was worth considering, if only for a moment. The ruse artist was as Settled as they came, but Ardor was passionate—his very name implied it. Perhaps his passion would have been enough to drive them to the finish if Halavend had done what Lyndel suggested and told him everything. But now time was up.

No, Ardor Benn was not really an option.

Oh, that he could have chosen Isless Malla! She was clearly the best candidate for detonating the Visitant Grit. But she had played her role too soon, leaving Halavend alone in the final stretch.

The pressure was tremendous. Ardor Benn was currently in possession of the only Visitant Grit in existence. There would be no second chances. All life on the islands, though they didn't know it, depended on an old Isle to make the correct choice.

Who was Halavend, to play at being Prime Isle in such a way? He was a heretic. An Isle who had disproved the doctrine of the Holy Torch and cast his lot with criminals. But Halavend still felt he was experiencing the Urgings of the Homeland. Urges to press on.

Were those feelings truly from that sacred land? Or had he instilled them in himself through a desperation to prevent Moonsickness from descending upon the Greater Chain? Halavend knew he was not the worthy candidate to detonate the Visitant Grit. But was he at least worthy enough for the Homeland to Urge him?

Halavend rubbed his wrinkled hands together. Despite the weeks of spring, it was cool in his cove, but he hadn't burned Heat Grit in the hearth for days now. He found that the chill edge kept him alert and focused.

Ha! Most Isles his age would have retired from the Mooring years ago. They would have a cozy cottage from the Islehood's pension, Heat Grit burning year-round, as they dozed in a padded chair.

Halavend's life had not grown calmer with age. He danced a careful step now, suspicious of everyone but Lyndel. The king and Prime Isle had conspired, consorted, and ultimately led to the inevitable destruction of all life. If the two most powerful men in the Greater Chain were guilty of such crimes, then no one was beyond their reach.

Halavend's hand moved to the sheathed dagger on the desk beside his manuscripts. The Trothian Assassin Blade terrified him, and Halavend still felt that using it would not be necessary.

So many risks could have been avoided if Prime Isle Chauster had listened to Halavend when he first approached him about the coming Moonsickness. But Chauster had been covering for the king, silently standing behind Pethredote's decision to poison the Bull Dragon Patriarchy.

Halavend didn't believe that the king or the Prime Isle fully understood the ramifications of that action. Surely, they realized that the dragon extinction would undermine the economy of the Greater Chain. But that must have been a fair price for Pethredote to ensure that no one else could detonate Visitant Grit.

But why? With the Islehood controlling the dragon shell, Visitant Grit could be used only by worthy people fighting for worthy causes.

It seemed like a situation that was already under control. What motive could have driven the king to eliminate every fragment of fertilized shell?

No matter. These were answers that Halavend would never receive, and he had come to terms with that. The Homeland Urged him with his own cause now, and Pethredote be Settled for whatever motives had led him to poison the Bull Dragon Patriarchy.

Halavend turned his tired gaze back to the parchments on the desk before him. They were not important documents. By now, all of those had been smuggled out through the aqueduct with Lyndel. She was storing them safely. And once all this was over, they could make their findings public.

In the meantime, Halavend had to finish his paper on Teriget's summoning. It was this shred of legitimate work that seemed to keep Chauster's suspicions at bay. Halavend was an old man, and this project should have been enough to consume a full work schedule. As long as he wrote the paper, he felt that no one would consider him capable of accomplishing anything else.

But this evening, Halavend could not even muster enough interest to pick up a quill. He had made up his mind about the Visitant

Grit, and he wanted the decision to percolate through every fiber of his old body.

He had chosen Lyndel.

It was as unorthodox a decision as he could make, selecting a Trothian Agrodite priestess to summon a Paladin Visitant. But at the end of all his stewing and searching, Lyndel was really the obvious choice. The only choice.

Halavend hadn't known Lyndel long. As to her younger years, he could not speak. Some would consider that problematic, as Oriar had been scrutinized about his Settled teenage years. To Halavend, it didn't matter. Lyndel's character today was inscrutable. And the Homeland whispered that, despite her Trothian lineage, she was worthy of the Paladin Visitant. The last and definitive Paladin Visitant, who would set all things right again.

Lyndel would refuse at first. Halavend knew she was much too humble to accept the responsibility straightaway. But he would help her see the reasoning behind his decision. Ultimately, Lyndel would take the Visitant Grit because it was the right thing to do. And she would save them all.

Halavend was expecting her soon. Their penultimate secret meeting before everything came together, for better or worse.

Halavend's head perked up, snapping him out of his reverie. Was that a soft knock? Sliding back his chair, he peered beneath his desk. He hadn't even pulled back the rug to expose the trapdoor.

Behind him, the door to the cove swung inward. Halavend startled at the unexpected movement, barely managing to slide a loose leaf of parchment to conceal the Trothian Assassin Blade on his desk. A figure stepped silently into Cove 23, deep violet robes swirling about his ankles.

Prime Isle Chauster.

Halavend stood up sharply, his knees cracking at the jolt. But the old Isle's fragile body was numb with alarm, a rush of blood to his face, and a tingling in his fingertips. He resisted the urge to grasp for the dagger. Chauster's presence did not yet mean accusation, but brandishing a weapon against him would not plead Halavend's innocence.

"Good evening, Isle Halavend." Chauster's voice filled the cove with its deep reverberations. His prominent eyebrows curled together in a worrisome furrow. "I hope you are well."

"Quite well," Halavend answered, relieved that his voice did not betray him. "Only startled, that's all. I wasn't expecting any visitors."

"In my experience," said Chauster, "unexpected visitors are often the best kind. They can offer a needed reprieve from the toiling of your daily schedule. Help you see something you might not have otherwise noticed."

"Is that why you're here?" asked Halavend. "To relieve me of my studies?" He gestured innocently back at his desk.

"Actually, I'm here on behalf of another," said Chauster. "My companion awaits you on the dock outside the cove. Indeed a rare and surprising visitor to the Mooring."

Homeland save us! Halavend gripped the back of his chair for stability. *They've captured Lyndel!*

"I need—" Halavend stammered. "I need a moment to collect my things." If he could manage to roll a parchment around the dagger, he might be able to slip it into his deep robe pockets without Chauster noticing.

The Prime Isle stepped forward, his thin hand gripping Halavend's arm just above the elbow. "That won't be necessary," he said. "We shouldn't keep our visitor waiting."

Halavend's breath caught in his throat as he stumbled across the cove. He cast a final backward glance at the hidden weapon and stepped through the door.

The visitor waiting on the dock was not Lyndel.

It was King Pethredote.

"Your Highness!" Halavend stood stunned for a moment before dropping his head in a respectful bow. The king! The king himself had come to the Mooring to see Halavend.

Pethredote stood on the dock, his shoulders squared and his feet firmly planted on the planks. He was shorter than Halavend had supposed, after seeing him give so many public addresses over the years. The man before him looked plain without the bulk of the Royal Regalia.

"So you're the Holy Isle I've heard so much about." Pethredote's hands were clasped behind his back. A sword hung at his side, the hilt mostly concealed by his long, unbuttoned coat.

"Oh?" Halavend said. "I wouldn't presume to think that my name should ever have entered your royal ear."

"Don't be so modest," replied King Pethredote. "It is not Settled to claim responsibility for notable deeds."

"And what might those deeds be?" Halavend's jaw was tight, his head beginning to ache from the stress of maintaining a composed face.

"I'm referring to your research, of course," said the king.

"Ah, yes," answered Halavend. "You have a particular interest in Teriget's Paladin Visitant of 1157? I would be honored to have you—"

"Let's talk about the *other* research," Pethredote cut him off.

"I'm afraid I don't understand," Halavend said. "Other research?"

It was Prime Isle Chauster who answered, his voice harsh and threatening. "Where is the Royal Regalia, Halavend?"

He felt his security slipping away. Had he come so far only to be hounded out the night before the Grit was to be used? Halavend glanced down the dim waterway of the Mooring. How did Chauster dare speak so boldly? The Mooring was quiet tonight, but surely some Isle would see the confrontation.

"We're quite alone," said King Pethredote, following Halavend's gaze. "Chauster took the opportunity to close the Mooring for my visit tonight. My personal guard awaits my return outside."

Halavend attempted to pull his arm away from Chauster's grip, but the Prime Isle held him fast. Was this how the others had felt? Reejin, the shell forger, the Harvesting crew that administered the Turroc and Stigsam? Domic Chauster? Had they been confronted by the king and the Prime Isle, given a chance to plead their innocence?

"We know you have been working with a Trothian priestess," said the king. "We know you hired a ruse artist named Ardor Benn to steal my regalia and process the shell into Visitant Grit."

The king's eye twitched. This was personal to him. *What a fool!* Halavend thought. It wasn't personal at all! This was about saving the future of the islands. Had the Prime Isle believed Halavend's new doctrine about Moonsickness, it would never have come to this.

"I don't know what you're talking about." Halavend clenched his fists at his sides.

"You can't escape this," Chauster said. "I have suspected foul play from you for cycles now. Our source has finally confirmed that you are the founder of Ardor Benn's entire ruse. And she hasn't been wrong yet."

"*She . . .*" Halavend muttered.

Quarrah Khai? Could that thief have been trading secrets behind Ardor's back all this time?

"Yes," said Chauster. "The Trothian woman."

Halavend felt a sickness wash over him. *Lyndel!* His stomach cramped, and he thought he might vomit. He tried to reconcile the thought that his only friend had betrayed everything they had worked toward. It was beyond unexpected. Not once had Lyndel shown reluctance in his plotting and planning. She had expressed many questions, yes. But those were the questions of an eager mind. Questions that had guided all his research.

"No," Halavend whispered.

"The woman's name is Mearet," said the king. "A Trothian baker."

"What?" Halavend felt the skin on his entire body prickle like gooseflesh. "What?" he stammered a second time, his eyes trained on the king.

"She has a bakery on Humont Street," the king continued. "She came to us shortly after Ardor Benn purchased the establishment and set up his space in the upper room. Mearet was concerned that she'd heard disparaging remarks about my kingship. She is a loyal subject, grateful for the opportunity my rule has given her people. So Mearet installed a listening device through one of the chimneys. It kept her useful by eavesdropping on Ardor's meetings."

Halavend exhaled sharply. Lyndel was clean after all! Homeland be praised, since Halavend wasn't likely to escape this night unscathed. Lyndel would have to finish his work. She knew what needed to be done, though she might never know that Halavend had decided she should be the one to detonate the Visitant Grit.

"Our source led us through every stage of the ruse," said the king. "The tip to the Regulators that Ardor would be at the concert. Dale Hizror's first attempt to steal my regalia at the reception. An unauthorized Harvesting crew running an expedition on Pekal. But the baker began to grow self-important toward the end, demanding increasing monetary compensation for her information. Threatening to expose my involvement if we didn't pander to her every demand. Confirming your involvement was the final bargaining chip she stubbornly held on to. But my people were able to beat that out of her. See, we knew about everything."

Halavend's lip quivered into something resembling a grin. "And yet, despite such useful information, Ardor Benn still managed to succeed."

King Pethredote's hands suddenly unclasped, drawing his sword in a fluid motion. Halavend staggered backward and the tip of the thin blade hovered just inches from his neck.

"Ardor Benn is dead," the king declared.

Halavend's brow furrowed. That wasn't possible. He'd received a message from the ruse artist just hours ago.

"My Harvesting crew shot him dead on Pekal just last night," Pethredote continued. "But it would seem that Ardor's associates are still at large. A citizen fishing vessel reported seeing a ship in the InterIsland Waters using cargo nets to bring a mound of Slagstone on board. They will no doubt sail to Strind. In the next few days, they will attempt to access a factory so they can grind the shell to Visitant Grit."

In the next few days. Ha! Pethredote *was* a fool! "Perhaps they have already succeeded," ventured Halavend. "Perhaps you are too late."

The king's jaw tightened in anger. "We will catch Ardor Benn's partner when he returns to the bakery, but you could help speed that process. Withholding information does not make you valuable. The Visitant Grit is useless in the hands of your criminal associates. What makes you think you could ever choose a hero worthy of summoning a Holy Paladin?"

"What makes any of us worthy?" Halavend asked. "The heroes chosen by the Prime Isles of old have been failures, more often than not."

"How dare you speak against this holy station!" Chauster shouted. "Those heroes, which you are so quick to call failures, have each served a very specific purpose."

Halavend's head began to spin. What was he saying? The Prime Isles of old had intentionally chosen unworthy heroes?

"What is it, then?" Halavend's scholarly mind began digging for answers despite his current danger. "What makes a worthy hero?"

"None are worthy," said Chauster. "The king and I know things about Visitant Grit that your feeble mind could never comprehend."

"Tell us where the Slagstone is," said the king.

"What will you do if I don't speak?" Halavend dared. "You said it yourself. We are quite alone in here. How will you explain the murdered body of an old Isle when the two of you were the only ones in the Mooring tonight?"

"Quite easily," said Prime Isle Chauster. "We found the poor man dead when we came in. It's understandable for a feeble old Isle to slip on the wet planks of the dock."

With one swift movement, Chauster kicked the side of Halavend's knee. The old Isle felt something pop, followed by an excruciating pain. He toppled, Chauster's hands striking him in the chest.

Cold water enveloped Halavend in a drowning embrace. His mouth was full before he could even take a breath. The terror paralyzed his mind, but his arms thrashed through the water until his fingers felt the edge of the dock. His feet touched the bottom of the waterway, and at last he was able to pull his head above the surface.

He sputtered and coughed, opening his eyes just in time to see Chauster crouched at the edge of the dock. The Prime Isle reached down, gripping a fistful of soaking silver hair atop Halavend's head.

Before Halavend could react, Chauster was forcing him under the water, yet again without time for a proper breath. Halavend should have been able to hold himself up. But his knee! It throbbed, collapsing uselessly beneath him. He released his grip on the dock to claw at his oppressor, but Chauster had every advantage.

A sharp tug on the top of his head, and Halavend was brought above the surface once again, choking, frantic.

"Our records indicate its been over a hundred years since an Isle has drowned in the Mooring," said the Prime Isle. "Tell us where to find the Slagstone, and we won't have to start the count anew."

Halavend drew a shaky breath, water streaming off his chin. He would face his death with honor. It was something he had resigned to the moment he embarked on this dangerous quest. He would not beg and grovel. He would not give them the information they were seeking. Halavend was an old man. If death had arrived, he would stand up to it bravely. As Isless Malla had done.

Prime Isle Chauster pushed him down again, the force snapping his head back sharply. His eyes were open wide in the clear water, staring panic stricken at his murderer. Halavend waited for Chauster to pull him up again, but each second passed like a knife in his chest.

His lungs felt as if they would burst. Helpless, submerged, his old body wracked with pain. This was what it felt like to die. This was death. In the place where he had spent most of his life. Under the hand of the man he had served for decades.

Suddenly, Chauster was pulling his head out of the water again. Halavend sucked in deep breaths, gagging, and vomiting into the water around him. His sight seemed to clarify a bit more with each gasp. He hadn't noticed it was going black under the water. Pinpricks of light danced across his vision, and his heartbeat seemed to pound in his temples like a striking hammer.

"This will be your final opportunity, Isle Halavend," said Chauster. At the end of the dock, Halavend noticed that King Pethredote had stepped onto the raft, the tether released, anchoring the vessel with the long pole in his hands.

"You will tell us where to find—" Chauster's threat was suddenly cut short as the door behind him swung open. A figure leapt from Cove 23, blue-skinned, with arms wrapped in the religious red cloth of her people. Halavend tried to shout her name, warn her to get as far away as she could.

But Lyndel did not seem frightened. The king cried out from his raft, and the Prime Isle turned abruptly to face the unexpected arrival. Chauster's hand released Halavend's head, and the old man caught the edge of the dock for support.

There was a flash of steel in Lyndel's hand, and Halavend recognized the Trothian Assassin Blade she had given him. The priestess shouted a cry in her native tongue, brought the dagger around, and thrust it into Chauster's stomach.

The two halves of the blade grated against each other as they cut into his flesh. The Slagstone threw unseeable sparks into the groove, instantly igniting the Void Grit that Lyndel had loaded.

Prime Isle Chauster exploded.

The blast might have only been a foot or so, but the Void Grit worked with tremendous force, creating a clear space that originated inside Chauster's torso.

Blood and gore spattered like spilled paint. Lyndel's hand was pushed backward, the blade thrown from her grasp. The weapon clattered against the doorway to the cove as the mangled corpse of the Prime Isle fell from the dock.

He hit the water beside Isle Halavend, staining the Mooring a deep crimson. Chauster's shredded body floated—a buoy of death in sacred waters. Halavend looked up at Lyndel, crouching on the dock in front of the cove door. She was unrecognizable—a canvas entirely painted in carnage.

Lyndel retrieved the fallen dagger. Its explosive Grit properties were spent, but it was still a fine blade. She turned her bloodstained face across the Mooring to find King Pethredote on his raft, a short distance up the waterway. He looked frightened, stunned, making a hasty retreat to the guards waiting outside. Halavend understood the king's panic. Lyndel had come seemingly from nowhere and butchered the second most powerful man in the Greater Chain.

And she was not finished.

Lyndel sprinted three long-legged steps across the dock, building momentum as she pulled her arm back, the dagger gripped loosely in her fingers. She hurled the weapon hilt over blade at the fleeing king.

In the dimness of the Mooring's Light Grit torches, Halavend could not see if the blade struck. The king dropped to a crouch, the long rafting pole still held in one hand.

Halavend's numb fingers groped along the edge of the dock until he found the short ladder. The water was so red, opaque. Bracing with his arms, he planted the foot of his uninjured leg on one of the submerged rungs and tried to hoist himself. He teetered, too weak to rise, fighting against his crippled balance so he wouldn't fall back into the pool of blood.

A hand reached down, seizing the sodden shoulder of his robe and pulling him partway out of the water. It was Lyndel, turned back to help him. She was a visage of death, the whites of her jittery eyes contrastingly bright against the crimson blood on her navy face.

"You shouldn't have come," muttered Halavend. "They know about everything. Ardor must not go to Humont... The Trothian baker—she was the spy. They're looking for the Visitant Grit."

"I will find Ardor," Lyndel promised. "But we have to get you out of here." She managed to hoist him until he was sitting sideways on the stained planks, his broken leg trailing back into the water.

"Lyndel," he whispered. "There is something more. The Prime Isle said no one is worthy to detonate the Visitant Grit. Only he and the king know the truth about its success. But I have decided that you should be—"

Halavend's sentence was cut short as the deafening crack of a gunshot echoed down the Mooring's spacious tunnel. Lyndel went rigid beside him, falling back to brace herself against the stone wall of the cove. He locked eyes with her.

"Halavend," she whispered, dropping to her knees. "No."

Then he felt it. The intense burning pain in his chest. Halavend looked down to see his own blood seeping from a hole below his rib cage.

In the distance, King Pethredote was standing on his raft once more. Halavend's vision was darkening, and he could not see the Singler in the king's hand. But Pethredote's posture identified him as the shooter, his arm still extended toward the dock, and a puff of smoke above his head.

Lyndel reached for Halavend, her wide eyes frantic. But the old man's strength was gone. He slipped silently from the edge of the dock, his own shade of red mingling with that already swirling in the water.

It was cold. Isle Halavend was far from the Homeland, adrift without a vessel to bear him. Pain gave way to a benumbed reverie, and the old man finally closed his eyes.

The sacred waters of the Mooring wrapped around him.

~

I must believe that my soul will find the Homeland. My faith must carry me into death.

PART V

Hear, O islands, and hearken yonder seas. The Homeland will forever Urge to keep that Holy Torch alight. Beside this, there is no greater duty.

—Wayfarist Voyage, *Vol. 3*

Death is painted with the Moon's red fire. But none are burned by the highest torch.

—*Ancient Agrodite song*

CHAPTER

35

Beripent was in a state of disarray like Ard had never seen before. Rioting. Looting. Sparks, there were dead bodies in the streets! And this wasn't even the sketchy part of town.

The harbor had been a mess of confusion, crawling with Regulators. In the disorder, Raek had managed to moor the *Double Take* without paying so much as a docking fee. Now they navigated the streets, Quarrah at his side, with Raek trailing a few steps behind.

These were hardly the conditions Ard expected, coming back from Strind with a keg full of Visitant Grit. Part of him feared that it was no coincidence. That the sudden, unexplained riotousness was the result of his return. Isle Halavend had warned him numerous times that chaos and anarchy would ensue, should the true motives behind the ruse be discovered.

Well, wouldn't that be painfully ironic, Ard thought, *if the rest of the citizens knew why I was doing what I was doing before I did.*

Perhaps Tanalin had something to do with this. The king's Harvesting crew would be back from Pekal by now, and Ard hoped that Nemery Baggish was getting the treatment she needed. Ard didn't know what kind of report Tanalin would make to King Pethredote. The only way to preserve her innocence would be in claiming to have shot the poacher, Ardor Benn. Which, in a way, she had.

Ard kept one hand on his satchel, feeling the bulky Grit keg.

His other hand was tucked under the flap of his coat, resting on the handle of his holstered Roller.

It seemed risky to take a public carriage, so Ard and his companions went by foot, maneuvering their way quietly toward the Bakery on Humont Street. Once they arrived, Raek would fix the Visitant Grit into a secure detonation pot.

It was almost time to make the delivery to Isle Halavend.

Ard gathered bits of information as they made their way. Conflicting stories, but the Trothians appeared to have made some sort of hostile attack on the Mooring. Some said the king was dead. Others said it was the Prime Isle.

Now there were bodies in the streets. Most of them Trothians.

"We need to get out of sight," Quarrah muttered as something smashed through a high window. She'd probably prefer slinking through back alleyways.

"We're almost to the bakery," Ard replied.

He didn't want to jump to any conclusions, patchy as the stories on the street were. But why would the Trothians attack? King Pethredote had been a wonderful king for them, extending more fairness and opportunity than any ruler in recent history.

The rumors seemed to agree that the assault had taken place at the Mooring. Maybe this was an attack on Wayfarism, since the Prime Isle wouldn't allow conversion for Trothians due to their intrinsic ties with Agrodite ritual. Ard worried about Isle Halavend. But the old man was wise enough to stay out of trouble—at least the kind that didn't involve him.

"How do we know the bakery will be safe?" Quarrah asked.

"We don't have much choice," Raek said. "All my materials for mixing Grit are in the upper room."

"Besides," Ard added, "what kind of secret meeting would it be without Mearet's cinnamon scones? We have standards, Quarrah."

They rounded the corner to Humont Street, and the bakery

storefront came into view. It was quiet here, and Ard wasn't sure if he should be grateful or fearful.

"Quarrah." Ard handed her the satchel. "Raek and I will make sure the bakery is secure. If something goes wrong, it'll be up to you to get the Visitant Grit to Isle Halavend."

Quarrah was the perfect fail-safe. Ard had no doubt she could navigate the streets of Beripent and enter the Mooring without detection.

Raek moved toward the shopfront, Ard jogging to catch up. He quietly slipped his Roller free of its holster, keeping it concealed beneath the flap of his coat as he opened the bakery door. The bell chimed, but otherwise, all was still inside. The counter displayed a picked-over selection of baked goods, and Ard could tell they were at least a day old.

The ovens hadn't been lit this morning. Ard could always smell the baking as soon as he entered the shop. He stopped before the counter, Raek moving around to approach the false oven leading to the upper room. Ard saw movement, his ears training on a shuffling step coming from the hallway that led to the back of the shop.

Ard whipped out his Roller, but he holstered the weapon the moment he saw who it was.

"Flames, Mearet!" Ard stepped toward her. "What happened to you?"

The short Trothian baker looked terrible. One of her eyes was completely swollen shut, her lip was split, and there was a cut across her cheek. Her arms hung limply by her side, as though any strength to lift them had been beaten out of her.

"The streets are a dangerous place for a Trothian today," muttered the baker.

Ard leaned across the counter, shaking his head upon closer inspection of the wounds. "We need to get you to a healer," he said. "You need stitches…"

The bell chimed on the door behind him. Ard whirled around, his hand darting to his Roller once again.

A hooded figure streaked forward, knocking Ard back before his gun cleared the leather holster. Raek turned away from the false oven, drawing a dagger, but the lithe figure hurled something at the secret entrance.

A clay Grit pot. It smashed against the oven entrance to Ard's hideout, throwing an instant blast of hazy Barrier Grit. The detonation cloud filled the fake hearth, blocking any possibility of getting up to the hidden room.

With a bound, the cowled intruder leapt onto the bakery counter in front of Mearet. The baker cried out, and a Singler appeared in the stout woman's hand. But the hooded figure was swifter. A gloved hand reached out, a dagger glinting in the morning light. Then the blade plunged into Mearet's neck. The person kneeling on the counter quickly released the dagger, Mearet falling forward onto the day-old pastries in a red mess.

Ard rose to his knees, Roller drawn, Slagstone hammer cocked back. He was only feet away from the sudden murderer, an easy shot.

"Hold your weapons!" the figure shouted, gloved hands coming up to throw back the hood. "It is I, Halavend's companion, Lyndel." She turned to face Ard, startled recognition the only thing stopping him from pulling the trigger.

Ard's gaze fell back on the murdered baker. "What the blazing sparks, Lyndel?"

"You wondered about the spy in your group?" Lyndel pointed to Mearet. "There is your answer."

"What?" Ard shouted. Mearet? He'd never seen that coming.

"Ha!" Raek exclaimed, tucking away his knife. "Told you it wasn't me!"

"Well, it's nice to finally have proof," Ard said. "I was beginning to suspect you again after my breakfast went missing on the *Double*

Take." He glanced sorrowfully at the dead woman. "You sure it was her?"

Lyndel nodded. "Information Halavend received directly from the king."

Halavend talking to King Pethredote? That didn't sound like good news. "We need to—" Ard's sentence was cut off as the upper wall to the hideout exploded in a hailstorm of Roller balls.

Raek pulled Ard to the floor, rolling to the base of the wall as the upper portion splintered and chipped, spewing dust and broken boards. Lyndel dropped behind Mearet's dead body on the pastry counter.

Ard glanced over at the priestess, grateful that her detonation of Barrier Grit kept whoever was shooting from coming down to the bakery shopfront. There was a sudden lull in the gunfire. Ard tried to say something, but Raek clamped a hand over his mouth, ear tilted upward, listening.

"Gotta move," Raek whispered. "They're mixing Blast Grit to blow through the upper wall."

"You can tell all that by listening?" Ard interjected, pushing his friend's hand away.

"It's my mixing gear," answered Raek. "I know that sound like a mother knows her baby's cry."

Lyndel sprinted for the bakery exit, throwing the hood over her head again as Ard and Raek followed close behind. The upper wall was a perforated mess of splintered wood, and Ard could see men in uniforms through the gaps.

Lyndel kicked open the door with a pleasant chime of the bell. Ard and Raek had barely cleared the shop when an explosion sounded from within the bakery. It was Blast Grit, just as Raek had predicted, and the force shattered every window in that building and the neighboring ones.

Quarrah met them, her face creased with worry, as they sprinted after the lean Trothian woman. Lyndel led them to an open-top carriage waiting just yards down the street. Leaping onto the driving bench, Lyndel seized the reins as Ard and his two companions clamored aboard.

Quarrah passed the satchel with the Grit keg back to Ard. He slipped the strap over his shoulder, calling out to Lyndel. "We have the Grit. We need to get to Halavend—"

"Isle Halavend is dead," Lyndel said abruptly.

Ard froze, a hundred questions shooting through his mind like gunfire. "What?" He barely noticed the group of Reggies pouring out of the burning bakery. "Dead?"

Lyndel snapped the reins and they tore down the street, the two yoked horses pulling them at a faster rate than a typical hired carriage. Raek fired two shots from his Roller, causing the pursuing Regulators to dive for cover. There was little threat of pursuit, since the Reggies didn't have a horse or carriage, and soon Lyndel had left Humont Street behind.

"Did she say Halavend is dead?" Quarrah called over the bumping carriage.

"That's what she said." Ard was still trying to process it.

"So..." Raek replied. "Does this mean we're not getting paid?"

Ard felt a spear of despair in his gut. This wasn't the first job to end in his employer's death. But this was Isle Halavend! Forget the Ashings, what had happened to the poor old man?

Raek and Quarrah hadn't seen Isle Halavend's face as he pled for him to take the job. That genuine desperation had spurred Ard through it all, with a motive more powerful than money. It was more than a simple feeling.

The Homeland had been Urging him all along, driving Ard to this moment.

He had wanted to discuss it with Halavend. He burned for this unknown cause with a fervor. A deep-seated passion.

An ardor.

Lyndel slowed the horses, eventually stopping the carriage outside a tall apartment building. As soon as everyone had climbed down, she slapped the horses' flanks, sending the empty ride bumping down the street.

"This way." Lyndel cautiously approached the door to the building.

"What happened, Lyndel?" Ard asked. "The city's falling apart! What is going on?"

Lyndel led them inside, and up a light of narrow stairs. "The king made an announcement at dawn. He has rescinded the Trothian Inclusionary Act," she said. "And he has placed an expulsion order upon my people. He intends to have us all dead or driven back to the Trothian islets by the end of the cycle."

"What?" Quarrah cried. "That's outrageous! He's always been an advocate for Trothians in the Greater Chain. Why would he do that?"

"I will explain everything inside," she said. They had reached a landing on the fifth floor. The priestess listened through the door before inserting a key and ushering everyone inside.

The apartment was a single room, dusty and quiet. Heavy drapes hung across the only window, and Ard noticed a straw mattress tucked into one corner with a thick blanket. The room would have been quite unremarkable if it weren't for the array of parchments, books, and documents spread in an orderly fashion across the wooden floorboards.

Lyndel locked the door, fitting a cover over the keyhole.

"Writing a book?" Raek asked sarcastically, turning his big feet sideways so as not to step on any parchment. Indeed, there were so many papers on the floor, it was difficult to find a place to stand.

"I didn't think Trothians could read," Quarrah said.

"Our eyesight prevents us from seeing text on a page," answered Lyndel, removing her hood and cloak. Her clothing beneath was plain; a tan tunic and sash, with red fabric wrapping her arms from the elbows to the wrists. "Technically, we are capable of learning to read, but the methods to achieve visible text are highly impractical."

Raek pointed at the display on the floor. "Then what's all this?"

Lyndel maneuvered to the center of the small room and dropped silently to her knees. "This is evidence—proof that what we are doing will save mankind."

Raek tilted his head skeptically. "By the sound of it, you've been spending too much time with that old Isle."

"Isle Halavend. Yes," said Lyndel.

"What happened to him?" Ard asked.

"There is much to discuss. Seat yourselves." She gestured at the floor.

Ard placed his back against the wall and slowly lowered himself to the floorboards as Raek strode to the far corner and plopped down on the small mattress. These must have been Halavend's books. Ard couldn't imagine how Lyndel had managed to get them out of the Mooring.

"Isle Halavend was murdered last night," Lyndel began. "By the hand of King Pethredote."

"What?" Ard cried. "In the Mooring?"

"Prime Isle Chauster brought King Pethredote to the Mooring to question Halavend about the ruse," Lyndel explained. "The king shot Halavend and escaped, but I arrived at the cove with enough time to kill Chauster."

"Blazing flames!" Ard ran his hands through his hair. "You killed the Prime Isle of Wayfarism?"

"Well, that explains the expulsion order against the Trothians," Raek said.

"Yes." Lyndel seemed frighteningly calm after such an admission. "He knows I am out here with information about his dark secrets. An island-wide assault against my people is the only way he can be sure that I am either killed or driven away."

"The Lander citizens won't go along with it," Quarrah said, finally seating herself beside Ard. "The king can't expect people to turn on their neighbors just because he rolls out a new order."

"Look outside! It is happening already," cried Lyndel. "Some of your people have always harbored ill feelings toward my kind—rooted in unfounded fear and centuries of cultural separation. Pethredote has played on that fear and incited the Landers against us. To cover the murder of Halavend, he announced that a Trothian Agrodite priestess broke into the Mooring, shot an old Isle, and stabbed Chauster to death. The king's expulsion order against my people isn't just a new law. He's made it a Wayfarist cause."

Ard could almost see the islands falling apart. The chaos in the streets would spread with the king's new decree. Thousands of Trothians would be uprooted from the lives they had been laboring to build here.

All because of the ruse. Because Ard had taken on something too big. How many would die because Halavend fell in with criminals and an Agrodite priestess?

"You think a Paladin Visitant can set this right?" Ard asked.

"Possibly, one could," answered Lyndel. "But we must rely on the Visitant Grit for something greater."

"People are dying out there!" Quarrah gestured out the window. "*Your* people."

"It is better that some should perish than for us to give up our cause," said Lyndel. "Did Halavend warn you of the coming Moonsickness?"

Ard shook his head. "The old Isle didn't say anything more than he had to. Despite my best efforts."

"Halavend kept many secrets that I urged him to share with you," said Lyndel. "Now he is gone. And I am in charge."

"You're going to tell us what this was all about?" Ard asked.

"There is a Trothian saying," replied Lyndel. "The water is as warm as the one who swims in it."

"Pretty warm if you're swimming with Ard after he's had a lot to drink," joked Raek.

"Hey, now," Ard began. "That's just—"

"What does the saying mean?" Quarrah cut in.

"It means, if I tell you something and you don't believe me, it will seem false to you. It will seem nonsense." Lyndel paused. "It means there are certain things you should tell only to those who will believe."

"But how do you know if someone will believe unless you tell them?" asked Raek.

"Therein lies faith," said the priestess. "What do you know of the Wayfarist Holy Torch?"

"The Islehood lights it," Ard answered. "There's one in every Mooring in the Greater Chain. Keeping the Torch burning through the night of a Passing shields the islands from Moonsickness."

"The Holy Torch is not what you think it is," said Lyndel. "Based on our joint studies, Isle Halavend was able to disprove the doctrine of the Holy Torch."

"How?" Quarrah asked.

"Many cycles back," Lyndel said, "on the night of a Moon Passing, Isle Halavend was assigned to tend the Holy Torch. But that night, he did not light it."

"Sparks!" Ard shouted. Halavend had gambled with everyone's life! If he'd been wrong about the Wayfarist tradition, everyone on Espar would have contracted Moonsickness. Ard grinned. The old man had mettle, there was no disputing that.

"How would he do that?" Quarrah asked. "The Mooring is full of people offering prayers to the Homeland on the night of a Moon Passing."

Quarrah had a point. Surely, everyone would have noticed that the big torch was dark.

"Illusion Grit," Lyndel explained. "Halavend had detonated some in the Torch the cycle before to record the image. When it was his turn to tend, he simply detonated a second cloud, making the Torch appear to be lit without any actual fire. An addition of Heat Grit was enough to convince even those who stood near."

Ard slapped his knee, a broad grin on his face. "The old Isle was a blazing ruse artist!" he cried. "He had hundreds of people praying to an illusion!"

"No one got sick," Quarrah muttered. "The doctrine of the Holy Torch is false..."

"Not entirely," said Lyndel.

"What do you mean?" asked Ard.

"The Torch *is* real," Lyndel explained. "It protects mankind from the Moonsickness. Only, the Torch is not what Wayfarists think. We discovered the truth. Halavend called it our new doctrine. This was what Prime Isle Chauster refused to hear."

"What is it?" Ard asked. "What is the Holy Torch?"

Lyndel's voice was soft. "Dragons."

What Lyndel was suggesting was beyond blasphemous. It was unfathomable! Ard couldn't wrap his head around it. How would the dragons protect mankind from Moonsickness?

"The dragons provide much more than Ashings and Grit," Lyndel continued. "They act as a buffer between us and the Crimson Moon. The Moon radiates a kind of energy—*fire*, in the Agrodite doctrine. The dragons high on the mountains of Pekal absorb this energy, preventing it from reaching the rest of the islands and sickening the humans."

"But if the dragons are absorbing the Moon fire," said Quarrah, "then why does a person get sick if they stay on Pekal?"

"The absorption of the dragons is limited," explained Lyndel. "What energy the beasts cannot take in spills down the slopes of Pekal."

"And the village in southern Espar?" asked Ard. "Rumors say the Moonsickness struck there."

"Not rumors," said Lyndel. "With the number of dragons

dwindling, they cannot capture the full rays of the Moon. The dragons' protective ring is weakening, and the fallout is spreading as the Moon rays touch down in other places. The rays have always fallen upon the distant seas. It is why your Wayfarist Voyages have never succeeded. Those who sail from these islands eventually find themselves beyond the reach of the dragons' absorption. That reach is diminishing, Moonsickness falling upon the outlying villages of the Greater Chain. And we should expect to see more outbreaks in the coming cycles."

"That's why the dragons never leave Pekal," Quarrah said. "They're protecting us."

"Dragons need the Moon's energy," Lyndel went on. "They are dependent upon it, and we are dependent upon them. If either goes without, the Moonsickness sets in."

"Wait," said Ard. "You're saying that dragons can get Moonsick?"

"There have been many humans that have fallen sick to the Moon's rays while stranded on Pekal," said Lyndel. "But there has been only one dragon taken out of the mountains."

"Grotenisk."

Lyndel nodded. "In much the same way that you or I contract Moonsickness by taking in the Moon's rays, a dragon is sickened by being deprived of them. Grotenisk exhibited all of the signs. Muteness, blindness, irrational violence. Isle Halavend read me the histories. It all seemed quite apparent, though none of your scholars made the connection."

"That's because our scholars don't believe it," Raek said. Ard wasn't sure what to think about it, either. "I've read a lot of interesting theories about Moonsickness. But to say that the dragons are a shield against it—"

"Our doctrines confirm it, when studied together," continued Lyndel. "Halavend and I united Agrodite poems and Wayfarist scripture. Each helped to clarify the other, revealing the true nature of the dragons on Pekal. Halavend wrote it all down." Lyndel gestured to the writings on the floor of her apartment. "It is all here for your examination."

"Religious texts," said Raek. "You're asking us to go on faith. I'm a man of proof."

"How can you prove something like that?" Quarrah asked. "You can't exactly ask the dragons if they're absorbing deadly Moon fire."

"We needed a witness." Lyndel picked up a cloth-wrapped item. Peeling it back, she revealed a piece of red glass. The edge was wrapped with rawhide, a loop of frayed leather on each side.

"Moon glass." Lyndel slipped her hands into the loops and lifted the glass, looking at Ard directly through it.

"Whoa," Ard whispered, staring back at Lyndel through the glass. The image he was seeing was so different, he could barely make sense of it.

Lyndel's face was glowing. Her skin was still blue, but it radiated. It was almost as if Ard were not looking at her face itself, but rather some kind of energy that her face was emitting. Ard had never seen anything like it.

"Is this what you see?" he muttered.

Lyndel panned across the room, letting Raek and Quarrah glimpse through the glass.

"Halavend supposed that this glass allowed the Lander eye to see as the Trothian sees," Lyndel said. "But in fact, it is more than that. This is one of three shards of Moon Glass kept by the Agrodite priestesses. It was originally formed by our Trothian ancestors centuries ago, before recorded history. In my religion, the Crimson Moon is the focus of our worship. It is our *Homeland*. This glass is meant only for the most devoted Agrodites to watch the Moon."

"What does it show you?" Ard asked.

"The glass shows the Moon uncovered," said Lyndel. "It shows the fire of the Moon, normally hidden, even to the Trothian eye." Ard must have looked confused, because Lyndel went on. "When I told Halavend of the glass's power, he didn't understand, either. But he saw for himself. The glass makes the rays visible. As the Crimson Moon crests the horizon, the fire leaps to the mountains, passing the islands of the Greater Chain, drawn to Pekal like a boat pulled by a strong current. Through the glass, you can see that the Moon's energy is focused only on Pekal."

"But not necessarily the dragons," said Raek. "Pekal is the only mountainous island. It's a Settled belief, but a lot of folks think the Moonsickness has to do simply with the altitude and Pekal's proximity to the Moon."

"It has nothing to do with the mountain!" Lyndel cried, raw frustration edging her voice as she set down the Moon Glass. "Halavend could have explained so much better." She reached forward and picked up a small, leather-bound book. Holding it for a moment, Lyndel seemed to regain her composure.

"There was another who began this search with us," continued Lyndel. "Halavend's young pupil. Her name was Isless Malla. She was the witness we needed to prove our theory. Malla took the Moon Glass and went to Pekal for the Passing."

Ard raised his eyebrows. Sparks, what was Lyndel saying? "You gave a Wayfarist Isless an Agrodite relic and sent her into the mountains during a Moon Passing?"

"She chose that path," Lyndel said. "Isle Halavend was too feeble for the trek. I would have gone myself, but I cannot write. And writing would be necessary, since the Moonsickness would take her voice before she could escape the island. She had to see the truth. The Moon Glass had always shown us that the rays fell upon Pekal. But Isless Malla proved that the dragons were taking the energy into themselves." Lyndel gently tossed the book to Ard. "Her journal."

Ard felt the smooth leather of the covers, a thin cloth bookmark hanging limply from the pages. A reverent respect flooded through him. The author had given her life to write these words. This was Halavend's proof. His motive for the entire ruse.

The journal fell open to a bookmarked page somewhere near the end. Ard glanced at the practiced handwriting and began to read aloud.

"'The Moon is glaring down on me, even as I write this. But Homeland knows, I have seen enough. So high upon Pekal's snowcapped summit, the Red Moon dominates the sky and lights the peaks like day.

"'The dragons are here. All of them. They came to the summit at dusk, powerful wings bearing them up to the highest point. There is no quarrel between them tonight. They come as wolves to a watering hole, an unspoken peace treaty governing their actions under the giant Moon.

"'Here, far above the trees, they stretch their massive bodies. The warmth of their bodies has cleared the ice and snow, and the tip of the mountain is a bald crown of stone. Their majestic figures are displayed upon the rocks like cats basking in a warming ray of sunshine. But these rays are something altogether different.'"

Ard turned the page and continued.

"'I have seen the Moon's energy, exposed through the red glass of this Agrodite lens. The rays from the Moon swirl toward the dragons, flowing into a brilliant arc of crimson light. I cannot see it with the naked eye, but the glass exposes the currents, streaming from the Moon and funneling into the dragons like water flushing through a drain.

"'Their bodies are ignited. This I can see, even without the Moon Glass. As the energy pours into their basking forms, a blaze burns hot beneath their scales. They are transfigured, full of light and power. But they cannot capture it all.

"'Some of the Moon's energy is cascading toward me. I see it rolling down the snowy mountainside like deadly waves. I am awash in it, sitting in a sea of bloodred ripples that move behind the Agrodite Glass like a current. I can see the *energy claiming Pekal, roiling all the way down to the InterIsland Waters. It is but a trickle at the shoreline, the dragons soaking in the brunt of it.*

"'Through the Glass, I can see more rays afar. There is a pink glow on the distant horizon, the Red Moon's toxic power touching down somewhere far abroad, much beyond the farthest reaches of the Greater Chain.*

"'From these heights, I can see that the islands are a ring of purity. Everything beyond the Greater Chain seems to be at the mercy of the Moon. But the rays are drawn away from our islands, honing into the bodies of the glowing beasts above me.*

"'Why are we so fortunate to have these regal protectors to shield us from the Moonsickness? Homeland preserve them. Without the dragons, these rays will surely spread. The sickening fire will seep into every man, woman, and child below. Just as it seeps into me now.*

"'I can feel it. I am absorbing the rays like the dragons above me. But I am not suited for this power. It bleeds through my flesh, and, while I feel no different, I know that it is taking me. I cannot stand against it. I have strayed out of the dragons' shield, Homeland help me. And tonight, I am a victim of Moonsickness. This is what I came here for. But now that it has claimed me, I am more frightened than ever.'"*

Ard shut the journal. He didn't need to read anymore. His chest felt tight. His hands were shaking. Sparks, he was struck with genuine fear. Looking at his companions, he saw that Isless Malla's words had achieved similar impact. Quarrah stared unblinking, and Raek sat on the straw mattress with his face downcast. The weight of the dead Isless's words settled around them like fog after a spring rain.

The dragons were the only thing standing between the Red Moon and the sickening of all human life on the islands.

And the dragons were going extinct.

"It is spreading as the dragons die," said Lyndel. "That is what happened to the poor Landers in the southernmost part of Espar."

The village of Brend. Rumors were that the people had torn each other to shreds.

"It's like a doughnut," said Raek. He had his big hand raised, his index finger and thumb joined together to make a ring in the air. "The hole of the doughnut—Pekal—has always been poisonous. Too many Moon rays falling on the dragons there. And beyond the ring, the rays touch down in the oceans again, too far away to be absorbed. But the doughnut ring—the Greater Chain—is protected."

Ard nodded. It seemed to be a sound metaphor, based on Lyndel's explanation. And to take it one step further... "And now the doughnut is shrinking," said Ard. "As the dragon population decreases, the poisonous doughnut hole expands, and the outside edges press in. The ring of protection will get thinner and thinner."

Beside him, Quarrah sighed sharply, and Ard caught her rolling her eyes. "The world is ending, and you two find a way to compare it to a doughnut."

"I always told Ard too many pastries would kill him," Raek replied solemnly.

Ard reached into his satchel and withdrew the keg of Visitant Grit. Slowly, he placed it on the floor. "What can this do?" he asked Lyndel.

Ard and his team had run the most elaborate ruse of their lives to obtain this Grit, but now that the dire situation had been fully explained, Ard didn't see any hope.

"I don't understand how a Paladin Visitant could fix this," said Ard. "They're unrivaled warriors, but we're not in need of a fight. We need to preserve the dragons."

"Halavend believed in a Wayfarist scripture," Lyndel said. "It speaks of how the Paladin Visitants have the power to save mankind from its own annihilation."

"I've heard the verse," Ard said. "But how does it apply?"

"With faith," said Lyndel. "We have to believe that in

summoning a Paladin Visitant, he will see mankind balancing on the brink of destruction. How he will save us, we do not know. But we must believe."

And there it was. The motive for everything.

Faith.

Ard lifted a hand to his forehead. Sparks. Did *he* believe that a Paladin Visitant could save them?

"Who's going to summon him?" Ard asked. The Islehood claimed that only the most worthy would succeed. "Who's going to use the Grit?"

"That was a point of great concern for Isle Halavend," said Lyndel. "He struggled with the dilemma from the start. And unfortunately, his life was taken before he could come to a decision. That leaves it in our hands to decide."

It fell silent as all four occupants looked at one another. If Isle Halavend had been unable to come to a conclusion regarding a worthy candidate, how would this ragtag crew have any chance? An Agrodite, a thief, a Mixer, and a ruse artist.

It should have ended today. Ard should have given the Visitant Grit to Isle Halavend, collected his Ashings, and moved on. But now, at the end of his assignment, he felt the Homeland Urging him once again. Urging him to finish what the old Isle had started.

"Can we back up a minute?" Raek cut into the silence. "When I signed up for this job, I distinctly remember that I was supposed to walk away with a clear name and half a million Ashings. Payable on delivery of the Visitant Grit." He scratched his bald head. "Just wondering if that's, you know … still on the table?"

"I can pay you nothing," admitted Lyndel. "And as to your criminal record, I have no say."

"All right." Raek slowly stood up from the mattress. "I was afraid this was going to happen. There was always this little tickle in the back of my brain that seemed to say, 'Ard is crazy, and you should have stayed home this morning.'"

Raek picked his way carefully across the room, making for the exit. Ard quickly positioned himself to block Raek's path. "Come on, Raek."

Was he really going to walk out on them now? Raek could endure danger and setbacks. Even false accusations of his loyalty. But not getting paid was where he drew the line?

Raek pushed past him and stepped through the doorway.

"Where are you going?" Ard asked.

"Where am I going?" Raek paused on the landing. "Well, all my supplies got blown up in the bakery, so I'm going to need a high-grade Detonation keg, size six. A pin-trigger Slagstone ignitor. Dampener funnel, tamping rod, cotton wadding, and a tall mug of ale."

"What are you going to blow up, Raek?" Ard had never known his old partner to go on a careless explosion spree.

"Nothing," answered Raek. "But somebody's got to fix up that Visitant Grit so it's ready for detonation."

Ard's face broke into a slow grin, but Raek just rolled his eyes. Perhaps things weren't perfectly smoothed between them, but at least Raekon Dorrel wasn't going to abandon him.

"You'll only have one shot at detonating the Visitant Grit," Raek said. "I don't want to be the reason it's a dud."

"Me?" Ard glanced back at the two women in the room. Raek expected *him* to detonate the Visitant Grit? "What about Lyndel? She's a priestess."

"I also assassinated the Prime Isle last night," Lyndel said. "I do not think I am the right choice."

"Whoa, I don't know about this." Ard held up his hands. He was flattered, truly. But that didn't make him worthy of a Paladin Visitant! Ard turned to Quarrah. "What do you think?"

"You're a terrible choice," she said.

"Thanks, Quarrah..." Ard turned back to Raek. "See? I'm hardly worthy; you should know that better than anyone."

"Oh, I never said you were worthy," Raek replied. "But if there is anyone in the Greater Chain who can trick a Paladin Visitant into appearing for him, it's Ardor Benn."

Ard looked down at the Grit keg on the floor. Run a ruse on a Paladin Visitant? He had to admit, it sounded like the tiniest bit of fun. There were no Ashings to be had, but a new reward had presented itself. If Ard's actions could somehow restore the dragons and save the world from imminent Moonsickness, wasn't that payout enough?

Ard turned to Lyndel. "I'm going to need a chalkboard."

~

This is what I came here for. But now that it has claimed me, I am more frightened than ever.

CHAPTER

36

The accommodations weren't nearly as nice as the Bakery on Humont Street. Quarrah shifted uncomfortably upon the dirt floor, suddenly missing the soft couch. She missed the pastries, too, though she wouldn't be so quick to admit it, seeing as how the Trothian baker had caused them such trouble. But there was no disputing the fact that she made a perfect chocolate croissant.

Their meeting place was now an abandoned butchery on the outskirts of Beripent's Eastern Quarter. It had taken them nearly a week to establish this new hideout. Longer than anticipated, but worth it to make sure the location was secure. Aside from the shop-front, the building had no windows. The rear of the store had been excavated to create a subterranean room for curing and keeping meats cool. And it was large enough for Raek to set up his new equipment for mixing Grit.

They couldn't stay at Lyndel's upper-story apartment. Too close to the Mooring. But this part of town was already home to questionable characters. No one was likely to speak to the new activity surrounding the old butcher shop.

Then there was the smell. Stale blood and spoiled meat. It was enough to keep all but the boldest squatters away. They'd only had to chase out one vagabond while moving in.

Ard didn't seem to mind the new hideout at all. He had a chalkboard, pitched on the dirt floor, leaning against the bricked subterranean wall. A blast of Prolonged Light Grit burned low in the corner.

Their discussions so far had led to one undeniable truth. King Pethredote knew what made Visitant Grit work. According to Lyndel, Halavend had heard from the Prime Isle's own lips that worthiness was nonessential. That meant there must be some other, quantifiable aspect that made for a successful detonation. Pethredote knew it, and was thus desperate to destroy any scrap of fertilized dragon shell.

Quarrah didn't believe, however, that King Pethredote understood the dragons' connection to Moonsickness. Chauster might have secretly believed what little he'd heard of Halavend's research, but the Prime Isle wasn't going to be the one to tell Pethredote that their actions had led to a side effect that would bring Moonsickness upon the entire Greater Chain.

After so many cycles, and against all odds, Ardor Benn had enough Visitant Grit for one good detonation. Quarrah knew he wasn't going to rush into it now. He wouldn't use that Grit until he had discovered everything that could be learned about it. And that meant talking to the only person alive who knew what went into a successful detonation.

That meant talking to King Pethredote.

Lyndel crouched against the far wall, her braided hair falling over her blue shoulders, exposed by the sleeveless tunic she wore. Quarrah studied her as Ard paced the smelly room, deep in thought.

The Agrodite priestess stayed with them for discussions, but she had been happy to pass the torch of command to Ard once she had shared all her valuable information. Other concerns now demanded Lyndel's attention. Following Pethredote's expulsion order, the Trothians were in turmoil. Quarrah knew that Lyndel was spending most of her time helping her people hide in Beripent or get safely back to the Trothian islets.

Lyndel would do what she must. Ardor Benn would take care of the rest.

Quarrah drew in a deep breath for a sigh, and crinkled her nose at the stench of their hideout. There she was, sitting in the blood-soaked dirt, finally feeling like she belonged. But belonging had changed her. Quarrah Khai had been so independent once. Now she seemed to spend all her time waiting for Ard to come up with a brilliant plan.

Quarrah was a follower.

As Azania, she had followed Cinza's coaching. On Pekal, she had taken direction from Raek. In many ways, Ardor Benn had commandeered her entire life. The way she thought about her job, the way she interacted with others, the way she felt for him...

What would things be like when this ruse was done? Could she return to her previous lifestyle, or would she flounder, waiting for a ruse artist to tell her what to do next?

Ard suddenly tossed his piece of chalk into the air, clapped his hands, and caught the chalk as it came down.

"We write a letter!" His face was bright with enthusiasm. "Get some parchment and a scribing charcoal. This is going to work."

Raek, who had been sitting on a rickety chair by his mixing station, produced the materials Ard had requested.

"A letter?" Quarrah asked. "We kindly ask for information?"

"Exactly," Ard said. "During times of war, it's common practice for the leader of the enemy forces to meet with the king in order to discuss demands. Parley."

"You want to parley with King Pethredote." Raek rolled his eyes. "What makes you think he'll even be interested in meeting with you?"

"Because he thinks I'm dead," said Ard. "I'm sure Tanalin has made her report by now. There's an old Trothian saying... 'The curious cat bites off its own tail.'"

"There is no such saying," Lyndel cut in.

"Well, there should be," said Ard. "It means that Pethredote will be so anxious to know how I survived Pekal, that he'll agree to a meeting."

"Even if he does," Raek said, "we're not exactly in a tactical position for a parley. It works best with a formidable army breathing down your opponent's neck."

"We have something better." Ard gestured to the keg of Visitant Grit on the dirt floor. A centerpiece for both the room and the conversation.

"Pethredote knows we've been trying to make Visitant Grit," continued Ard. "We might as well use that to our advantage." He shook his finger at Raek. "Write this down... 'To His Majesty, King Pethredote.'" Ard paused before speaking aside to Raek. "You should spell Pethredote wrong."

Raek glanced up from his parchment. "What do you mean?

"I don't know," he answered playfully. "Spell it with an L. Pethredolt."

"Why would we do that?" Raek took the words out of Quarrah's mouth.

Ard shrugged. "It'll aggravate him."

"It'll make us look uneducated," Raek countered. "That's a stupid idea. I'm spelling it the way it's supposed to be spelled." He put his charcoal to the parchment and finished the intro.

"'As I'm sure you are aware,'" Ard continued dictating, "'I, Ardor Benn, am currently in possession of a single detonation of Visitant Grit.'"

"You sure we want to show our hand like that?" Quarrah cut in. "Is it a good idea to tell him we only have enough for one detonation?"

Ard smiled. "Actually, that little nugget of truth is essential to my plan."

"What exactly is your plan?" Raek tucked the long scribing charcoal behind his ear. "I mean, besides the letter—which you can finish writing yourself. I'm sure your prose is only going to get more flowery."

"The letter gets us face-to-face with the king," said Ard. "Once there, we can question him about his knowledge of Visitant Grit and discover what we need to know to make our detonation successful."

"Successful to what end?" Raek asked. "We get a Paladin Visitant to show up. So what? How is that supposed to protect us from the Moonsickness? We stake everything we've got on a Wayfarist scripture."

"I am not Wayfarist," Lyndel said. "Yet I believe." She took a step forward. "If I do not believe, then hope is dead. There would be no reason to go on with any of this."

"Lyndel's right," Ard agreed. "We have to assume that the Paladin Visitant can do something to shield the islands against the coming Moonsickness. I believe it could work. But I'm also a fan of cold, hard facts. That's why I'm proposing this final run against Pethredote. We get him to spill his secrets, and we reconvene to make a plan based on our new findings."

"How do we coerce the king into revealing what he knows?" asked Quarrah.

"We take the Visitant Grit to him," Ard said.

"Absolutely not!" Lyndel began. "You are—"

"Relax!" Ard waved the angry Trothian back. "Not the real Grit. We take a fake pot to our meeting and detonate it on the floor."

"It wouldn't do anything," Quarrah said.

"That's right," answered Ard. "When no Paladin Visitant appears, it'll look like our detonation failed. The king will be far more likely to tell us what we did wrong, once he knows we've used the Visitant Grit and don't have a second shot."

"I don't see an escape plan," said Raek. "Once Pethredote thinks we've used up our Grit, our insurance is gone. We'll be in his palace, surrounded by his Regulators. There's no amount of intimidation we could apply that would get him to talk. He'll probably have us killed on the spot."

"Unless we actually summoned a Paladin Visitant," Quarrah muttered. If history was any indication, those fiery visitors could decimate an entire room with their mere presence.

Ard suddenly clapped his hands. He crossed the room, grabbed Quarrah by the neck, and kissed her forehead. "Quarrah Khai, you are a genius!"

"What?" she gasped, flustered from the public show of affection and completely puzzled at his words.

"We summon a Paladin Visitant!" Ard dropped to one knee and scrawled on the chalkboard.

"Actually…" Quarrah whispered. "I didn't seriously think we could."

"Don't apologize," Ard said. "It's brilliant. Summoning a Paladin Visitant provides the intimidation we need to get Pethredote talking. And like I said earlier, he'll be more likely to talk if he thinks our single detonation is spent."

"But won't it be?" Lyndel asked. "You propose to actually detonate the Grit in the king's presence."

"No, no!" Ard was still scrawling ideas across the board. "That would be a waste. Even if a Paladin did appear, we'd be too late to employ anything useful that we learned from Pethredote."

"What are you suggesting, Ard?" Quarrah asked.

He dropped the chalk and stood up abruptly. Now that Quarrah could see his scribblings, they hardly made sense. Half the words were illegible. Several seemed of little application to the problem at hand. Quarrah saw the words *heat, radius, palace, Grit*. And, seriously, had Ard written *Pethredolt*? The man could be so immature sometimes.

Ard walked across the room until he stood face-to-face with Raek. "Could you light yourself on fire?"

Raek scratched his bald head. "I suppose anyone could. I typically avoid it."

"You know what I mean, Raek." Ard was on a roll. "Could *you* be the Paladin Visitant?"

Quarrah's eyebrows lifted as she realized what Ard was proposing. Her throwaway remark had sparked this plan? She didn't understand how Ard's brain worked. Probably never would. The ruse artist's mind was like the Char on a busy day—with more ideas coming and going than Quarrah could keep track of.

"That'd be a complex trick," Raek responded. "But I know a vendor in the Western Quarter that sells a sunflare cloak. The fabric repels flame. They use them in the industrial forges. Doesn't stop heat, though. Unpleasant work."

"Nothing a bit of Cold Grit won't fix," Ard said. "As Quarrah and I were clever enough to figure out the night we climbed into Grotenisk's burning skull."

"It's not like the Cold Grit made it *pleasant*," Quarrah pointed out.

"But we didn't die," said Ard. "I think that's the takeaway message here."

"Sure," continued Raek. "I could trap a blast of Compounded Cold Grit under the sunflare cloak to keep my body sufficiently cool. The outside of the cloak could easily be fitted with strings soaked in Thrast oil. It burns long and steady."

"See?" Ard reached up and rubbed the big man's shaved head. "You're well on your way to becoming a Paladin Visitant. My boy's growing up so fast."

"Lighting myself on fire isn't the complicated part," said Raek.

Ard sighed, stepping back. "You had to go and spoil our moment."

"Paladin Visitants are supposedly too glorious to behold with the eye," said Raek. "Any creature who looks at them is supposed to burst into flame."

"You're saying you're not glorious enough?" Ard replied.

"He's saying that the whole illusion will be shattered the moment Pethredote sees him and doesn't burn up," said Quarrah. Ard was getting particularly punchy as the plan developed. That was what confidence did to him.

"Pethredote won't dare look." Ard didn't miss a beat. "I will announce that I'm detonating Visitant Grit. Pethredote will certainly shield his eyes. And when he senses a fiery figure standing behind me, he won't risk taking a peek."

"That works in a perfect scenario," answered Raek. "If we had Pethredote alone. But what about the Reggies in the room? We can't count on all of them to have the self-discipline of the king. If one of them looks, the trick will dissolve."

This seemed to stump Ard for a moment. He put a hand to his forehead and turned away, pacing a few steps in front of the chalkboard.

"We need to convince the Reggies, too," Ard finally muttered. "We need the fear of a Paladin Visitant to strike them so deeply that they vacate the room."

"Why don't we catch a few of them on fire?" Lyndel suggested.

All heads turned to the Agrodite priestess. She was crouched against the wall again, her blue fingers knit together and her hands resting just below her chin, shimmering eyes staring at them.

Quarrah didn't know why the comment surprised her. Lyndel had already shown a ruthless side in her dealing with Mearet and Chauster. But for some reason, Quarrah assumed a priestess would seek a more peaceful alternative. But then, Agroditism wasn't Wayfarism. What did Quarrah even know about Lyndel's religion?

"Would you care to elaborate?" Ard asked.

Lyndel remained in her pensive stance. "If several of the Regulators were to spontaneously burst into flame, it would prove to the others that the fiery figure in the room is a genuine Paladin Visitant."

"And if the Regulators are on fire, they're probably going to leave the room in a hurry," said Ard.

"Catching on fire seems to have that effect on people," Raek added.

Quarrah watched the conversation unfold with a mix of disgust and awe. Were they really discussing this option? Now that they knew what was really at stake with the coming Moonsickness, Ard's commitment to this job knew no bounds.

"So, how do we do it?" Ard asked. "How do we spontaneously ignite everyone in the room?"

"Except for you and Pethredote," Quarrah said.

"I thought that went without saying." Ard turned to Raek. "You can do it, right? Mix up some kind of Grit, slip it into the Reggie pockets, have it go *boom* precisely when we need it to?"

"That's not the way Grit works." Raek sighed, putting a hand to his forehead. Quarrah got the impression that this was a recurring conversation between these two. Ard demanded something spectacular, and Raek had to find a feasible way of making it work.

"Fuses!" Ard suggested. "Really slow-burning fuses?"

"And how would we get fuse pots into the pockets of every Reggie in the room?"

"Depends on how many there are," Ard pointed out. "Depends on the size of the room."

"That's a good point," Quarrah said. "Where are you hoping this parley will take place?"

"It'll be at the palace," Ard replied. "We'll never convince Pethredote to meet on neutral ground."

"So, the throne room," said Quarrah. "Homeland knows we've spent enough time there."

"The throne room doesn't present us with any real advantages," said Ard. "In fact, we run the risk that the fire in Grotenisk's skull would detract from Raek's appearance as the Paladin."

"How do we get Pethredote to pick a different room?" Quarrah asked.

Ard snapped his fingers, an early sign that a sharp idea had just entered his mind. "The reception hall! I'll put it in the letter." Ard pretended to quote a passage that he had not yet written. "'We will meet in the palace reception hall, a location familiar to both of us, but one that does not bear the unpleasant memories we share in the throne room.'"

Sparks, Ard was good with words. But Quarrah wasn't sure why he seemed excited about that venue. The reception hall was significantly larger than the throne room, with multiple doors and a sprawling balcony that could all serve as access points for the Reggies.

"The reception hall is illuminated by a Grit delivery system recessed into the walls," Ard said. "A servant in the room below operates a bellows to disperse Light Grit into the pipes. A wall ignitor switch detonates the Grit and leaves orbs of light hanging on the chandeliers."

"And you think we could pump another type of Grit through the system," Raek said. "Fill the room with something that will set the Reggies on fire."

Ard nodded. "What about Blast Grit?"

Raek laughed. "If we pumped Blast Grit into the reception hall, a single spark would blow the palace halfway to the Homeland. You might survive in a Barrier cloud, but I don't think that's the effect you're going for."

"I'm just throwing out ideas," Ard said. "What about Heat Grit? We raise the temperature high enough that those Reggie wool coats ignite."

"That kind of temperature, and we'd all be dead," replied Raek. "Wool is fairly flame resistant. Our skin would scald before the uniforms caught fire." He paused. "There is a substance. A chemical called Kalignine—a potent liquid created from Dross. It spontaneously combusts at around 115 degrees. But it flares almost like a spark. Doesn't burn long enough to catch anything on fire."

"Unless..." Ard probed.

"I didn't have an *unless* planned for that statement," Raek said. "Give me a second." He shut his eyes and yawned. "Particles of Blast Grit diluted fifty parts to one in a solution of corn oil, beeswax, and Kalignine. We apply it to the Reggie uniforms, and they should catch fire if the ambient temperature in the room reaches 115 degrees."

Now it was Quarrah's turn to be astounded by Raek. She'd seen him spout formulas and equations in the past, but this was incredible. She understood exactly why Ard had kept Raek close over all their years of rusing. One was a dreamer. The other a doer. Together, they were practically unstoppable.

"Perfect!" Ard cried. "How do we apply the solution to the Reggie coats?"

"Not while they're wearing them, obviously," Quarrah said.

"The palace Reggies wear red coats," said Raek, in what Quarrah thought sounded suspiciously like the beginning of a bad joke. "But they aren't allowed to wear them into the city. That means somewhere in the palace, there's bound to be a giant closet full of uniforms, just waiting to be tainted."

Ard glanced at Quarrah as though he expected her to know where such a closet existed. She simply shrugged. During her time as Azania Fyse, she had been exposed to many hallways and chambers, adding them first to her mental map before solidifying them with a sketch on a paper. But she didn't know every closet.

"Maybe we do not need to know where these coats are kept," said Lyndel unexpectedly. "We just need them to be taken somewhere we can get them."

"Ideas?" Ard probed.

"Outside," suggested Lyndel. "Why does anyone take their clothing outside?"

"To wash," said Quarrah. "How do we get them to wash all the Reggie coats at the same time?"

"There is a Trothian saying," Lyndel said. "The bird who brings the viper to the nest spoils the meal for everyone."

There was momentary silence in the dugout butchery before Ard said, "Yeah, I don't really capture the meaning of that."

"At the end of a day, we put something into the coat of one *Reggie*." Lyndel said it like she'd never tried out that slang before. "When he returns the uniform to the closet, it spoils the others overnight."

"Something smelly." Ard seemed pleased with the idea.

"Oh, I've got just the thing." Raek rubbed his hands together like an excited little boy. "Remember that Choke Beetle I got in Noriman last year?"

"During the Luthpit job?" Ard asked. "You stank for a week."

"The point is…I still have a vial of the oil I extracted from its glands," he replied. "I'll dispense some into a wax ball. A little Guman's vinegar will slowly dissolve the wax during the night until the Choke Beetle extract spills out."

"The smell is strong enough?" Quarrah asked.

"It'll be enough to pollute a fair-sized room," Raek said. "An enclosed closet with wool uniforms is ideal."

"So how do we place this delightful little bundle of wax?" Ard asked.

"I could do it," Quarrah volunteered. "It shouldn't be any trouble to tuck something into a Reggie's coat and slip away without drawing too much attention."

Ard nodded. "Pull your hair back. You'll want to look as little like Azania Fyse as possible. Some of the palace Reggies might recognize your face."

"I don't really plan to be seen," said Quarrah.

"Obviously, not *all* of the Reggie coats will be affected," said Ard. "Those on duty while the Choke Beetle works its magic will escape the stench. But if we time it right, and strike during the smallest shift, we maximize our chance of reaching the most uniforms. The following morning, they'll bring the uniforms out to air. And if we're lucky, they'll employ some extra hands to wash them down by the river delta."

"I'll make sure my hands are there," said Raek, "with a large basin of flammable Kalignine solution."

"Heavy wool... It'll take the uniforms a full day in the sun to dry," said Ard. "That'll mean most of the Reggies on duty won't have the standard red uniform available. They'll most likely wear street uniforms in the interim. Blue coats. There's going to be some confusion. We'll use that to smuggle a few kegs of Heat Grit into the bellows room below the reception hall."

"You plan to take it in?" Quarrah asked. The sketch of Ard's face had gotten around—especially among the palace Reggies.

"I'll reach out to Cinza," he said. "She's usually game to do a single job without asking a lot of questions. Probably do it for as little as fifty Ashings. That would keep us out of harm's way while still managing to maneuver the Heat Grit into position."

"I'll need to premix it with Compounding Grit if we have any hope of spiking the temperature high enough," explained Raek.

"How much do we need?" Ard asked.

"Well, too little Heat Grit and the blast won't encompass the reception hall. Too little Compounding Grit and the Kalignine solution on the uniforms won't ignite. Too much, and our flesh will turn crispy." Raek sniffed. "Really depends on the size of the room."

"It's a vaulted ceiling," said Quarrah. "Thirty-five feet at its highest point in the center. Maybe sloping down to about fifteen feet on the edges."

Raek stepped past Ard, dropping to one knee and wiping his sleeve across the jumble of words Ard had written on the chalkboard. Fetching the fallen piece of chalk, Raek began sketching the dimensions of the room as Quarrah listed them.

She was proud of herself for providing valuable information that no one else on the team had. Prouder still when she saw the impressed look on Ard's face as he observed the mathematician and the thief estimating the volume of the palace reception hall.

Quarrah was fairly confident in her measurements. Judging length, width, and height was a valuable skill in her line of work.

"Three hundred and thirty-seven granules of Heat Grit," Raek said as he continued to write out his equation. "Plus five hundred and twenty granules of Compounding Grit... That ought to do the trick. I'll run the calculations again before I mix the batch." He circled a few numbers on the chalkboard. "Whoever is running the bellows needs to make sure they pump all of the Grit into the system before we ignite anything upstairs."

"Quarrah," Ard said. "Do you think you could get yourself inside unnoticed and operate the bellows system?"

With Ard and Raek running the ruse in the reception hall, that left only Quarrah and Lyndel available for *backstage* work, as it were. And there was no way a Trothian was getting into the palace.

"Of course," Quarrah answered.

Based on her map of the palace, she already had two or three potential access points in mind. Creeping into the palace once again?

It seemed like a delightful challenge. In many ways, this ruse represented the culmination of her career. When this was all over, wouldn't the manors and estates of the rich folk seem like child's play?

"I think we have our work cut out for us." Ard looked quite pleased with the complex plan they had devised. "The clock starts ticking once the uniforms are tainted. "From there we'll only have a day or two to get the uniforms washed, dried, and back in circulation. Let's make sure everything is going to work before we get that Choke Beetle concoction in place. We set our appointment with Pethredote, say, two weeks from today."

"I think you have overlooked one thing," said Lyndel.

"What's that?"

"Your escape from the reception hall," she answered. "It is naïve to think that Pethredote will let you leave once you have detonated the false Visitant Grit."

"I'll have a Paladin Visitant," Ard replied.

"Who will eventually burn out," said Lyndel. "And your deception will be exposed if Raekon leaves the reception hall. If he were a real Paladin, he would be unable to exit the Visitant cloud."

"Lyndel's right," Quarrah agreed. "You two can't go in there unless you have a better exit plan."

"You should kill the king," stated Lyndel.

"What?" Ard replied. "I think you just said I should kill the king."

"He is an evil man," Lyndel went on. "A man of so many lies."

"I know he's a liar, but Pethredote has brought a lot of peace and growth to the Greater Chain," Ard said. "Killing him would divide the islands. It would be complete chaos."

Lyndel pointed upward, toward the streets of Beripent. "This city is already in chaos. Do yesterday's peace and growth matter if innocent people are dying today?" She stood slowly. "Your plan will put you face-to-face with Pethredote. Once he has given you the information we need about the Paladin Visitant, you must kill him."

Ard stood awkwardly, the dim Light Grit casting half his face in shadow. Quarrah saw the debate in his eyes as he considered Lyndel's suggestion. Assassinate King Pethredote? Ardor Benn was not a murderer. She knew he had killed in defense, killed in escape. His actions had caused collateral damage and taken lives. But murdering the king seemed different. Premeditated.

"I don't see how that would help us escape," Ard pointed out. "Killing Pethredote will only bring the Reggies running in our direction."

"Not if the Regulators are otherwise engaged," said Lyndel. Quarrah took a step closer so as not to miss a word of her accented voice. "Two weeks is enough time to gather some of my followers."

"Sparks," Quarrah whispered. "You're going to lead the Trothians in an attack on the palace?"

"Only a skirmish," Lyndel said. "Enough to provide Ardor and the Short Fuse some cover so they can escape." She stepped closer to Ard, her face intense as she raised her wrapped arms. "I believe that Isle Halavend would agree. Your Homeland wants Pethredote dead." Then Lyndel turned sharply and strode out of the dugout meat cellar.

In silence, Quarrah stared at Ard and Raek, grateful that she would not be the one to make that terrible decision. Ard would probably spend the next two weeks stewing over Lyndel's proposal, as if the burden of preparing this final stage of the ruse were not enough.

"Well, then." Ard snapped the three of them out of the reverie that Lyndel's words had inspired. "Let's make ourselves a Paladin Visitant, shall we?"

~

No amount of planning could prepare me for this.
When will I begin to decay?

CHAPTER

37

This better work, Ard thought, a group of uniformed Regulators escorting him and Raek through the palace hallway. *Sparks! I hope any of this works.*

Despite the washing and drying of the red uniforms, Ard could still smell the residual funk of the Choke Beetle excretions on his escort Reggies. The lingering stench was actually a benefit, masking the milder odor of the Kalignine solution that Raek had applied after washing.

Raek and his hired hands had only managed to taint about sixty of the eighty uniforms being washed. Another twenty had been worn during the night shift, avoiding the beetle extract altogether.

Raek had pointed out the odds. Six out of ten Regulators in the reception hall would be likely to combust today. Ard was counting on the ones who didn't to run screaming when their friends caught fire, knowing that the Paladin Visitant could end their lives with a single word.

It had taken King Pethredote until last night to agree to Ard's letter of parley, igniting the signal over the northeast corner of the palace. Three side-by-side detonations of Light Grit, the middle one larger than the others, just as Ard had specified.

They ascended the steps, just a short corridor until they arrived at the reception hall. Ard glanced at Raek, who had to hike up the hem of his heavy sunflare cloak to manage the stairs. Towering over even the tallest Reggie escort, Raekon Dorrel looked intimidating.

His cloak was thick and padded with liners of Cold Grit, enhancing the man's natural size.

Raek had made the improvements to the sunflare cloak look like decoration. Using more sunflare material, he had sewn long strips from the shoulders down. Each strip had been soaked in Thrast oil, which Raek assured would burn for at least ten minutes—the expected duration of the Visitant cloud.

The cloak had been examined at the palace entrance, of course. Both Ard and Raek had practically been undressed, as the rules of parley demanded that they come unarmed. The sunflare cloak was approved. Ard's boots were not. He had hidden a knife in a disguised boot lining, which was intended for the Reggies to discover. It was a distraction tactic, allowing him to move the pot of fake Visitant Grit from his pants to his jacket, which the Regulators had already inspected. Seriously, their incompetence was laughable at times.

The keg of genuine Visitant Grit, buried in the dugout cellar of the abandoned butcher shop, was much larger than the counterfeit pot Ard carried. But Pethredote would have no way of knowing how much Grit they had obtained.

Ard took a deep breath as they entered the reception hall. The room looked even larger without the social tables, gossiping rich folk, and colorful gowns and capes. The centerpiece tree was still there, surrounded by benches, its planter box full of late spring flowers.

Ard scanned the room, taking a quick count of the Reggies standing guard. There were fifteen visible—twenty, if the men that had escorted them were allowed to stay for the meeting. They all wore red uniforms, but even if this whole thing worked, Raek's estimation at the odds would indicate that eight of the coats would be unaffected by the Heat Grit. Too many.

The glass doors leading to the balcony were as dark as the night outside, and Ard didn't like the idea that more Regulators were likely positioned there, out of the Heat Grit's blast radius.

Ard glanced up at the five large chandeliers. The Grit dishes were each lit with an orb of detonated Light Grit. Soon, Ard was counting on a different detonation flooding the chandeliers.

By this point, Quarrah would be in position in the room below, pumping all of the smuggled Compounded Heat Grit into the chamber. All they needed was a spark, and a massive detonation cloud would be forced through the wall pipes, filling the entire room.

A service door swung open on the far side of the reception hall. Ard had once watched kitchen staff use that entrance to supply food and drink to impatient guests. But this time, it was King Pethredote.

The king looked old and worn, Millguin clinging to his shoulder. The lazy Karvan lizard stared unblinking as two Reggie guards secured the service door behind the king.

Pethredote wore a crimson shoulder cape, with a shirt whose sleeves billowed as he strode slowly toward Raek and Ard. Without the crown and a coat of dragon shell, Pethredote looked like an ordinary nobleman. In a way, that made Lyndel's suggestion to kill him even harder. But then Ard remembered Isle Halavend, a ball of lead in his frail old chest.

Perhaps Ard *could* find the nerve to end the crooked king.

"I heard you were dead." Pethredote stopped with a good distance between them. "I received the report from my own Harvesting crew. The poacher—the *ruse artist*—Ardor Benn was shot and killed."

"Who, me?" Ard cried. "Well, you'll have to do better than that."

"How did you do it?"

"A simple ruse," Ard replied. He had promised Tanalin that pulling the trigger on that blank Roller would save them both from trial and execution. He intended to uphold that promise.

"I sent one of my men to speak with your Harvesting captain, posing to be Ardor Benn," explained Ard. "Your captain shot him dead in cold blood. Suppose I should be glad I sent someone else to do my dirty work. You should be an expert on that topic. As I understand it, there was a trail of bodies to clean up after you had the Bull Dragon Patriarchy poisoned."

A murmur passed around the room, despite the training and discipline that palace Regulators were supposed to possess. King Pethredote took a step forward, his hand on the hilt of his sword. "How dare you speak…" he began, before catching himself.

Good. The king was rattled. Ard would play on that paranoia, coaxing Pethredote into sending away all but his most trusted Reggie guards, just as Dale Hizror had done on the night they entered the throne room to find Quarrah.

The king straightened, took a deep breath, and nervously reached up to stroke the leathery beard of the lizard on his shoulder. He cast furtive glances across the room, subtly trying to gauge the reaction that Ard's words had evoked from his Regulator guards. Ard took the moment of weakness to advance farther.

"Domic Chauster, and his son, Glipp. Reejin, the shell forger. The members of your former Harvesting crew. Isle Halavend…"

"Silence!" Pethredote shrieked. The outburst sent Millguin leaping from the king's shoulder, claws clicking against the stone floor as she scurried away from her angry master. In the same moment, Pethredote's sword flashed from its scabbard, glinting in the steady glow of the Light Grit chandeliers. The thin blade leveled a foot from Ard's face, the king's heavy breaths causing the weapon to waver just slightly.

"Killing me will not help you find the Visitant Grit." Ard's voice was calm with the confidence that Pethredote's sword was an empty threat. "Besides, I thought we were here to converse, not brandish weapons."

"I once told Dale Hizror," whispered the king. "I shouldn't have to repeat myself to you. Certain things are never to be discussed."

"And yet those are the very things I have come here to discuss." Ard gestured around the room.

King Pethredote lowered his sword and turned to the nearest Regulator. "Clear the balcony and the service room. I want everyone but Benthrop's regiment to exit at once. You can await my commands in the hallway. But seal the doors."

Sparks! Pethredote was easy to manipulate. He was a powerful man, but he existed in a state of constant fear. Secrets had a way of doing that to people, Ard would know. And applying slight pressure on Pethredote's insecurities turned him into little more than a puppet on a string.

Ard and Raek stood still, watching the king's new orders carried out with a degree of concern and unspoken disagreement. As the heavy doors to the hallway swung shut, Pethredote had reduced his protective forces to a mere twelve men.

"Now"—the king's voice was low—"let us speak of this Visitant Grit you supposedly have."

"Or perhaps you'd like to see it." Ard plunged his hand swiftly into his jacket. By the time he had withdrawn the clay detonation pot, a dozen Rollers were leveled on him.

Ard stood with his right hand outstretched, palm downward, fingers loosely holding the clay sphere. "You were looking for this?"

The tip of the king's sword scraped the floor as he took a step back in astonishment. Pethredote's hand came up to the Reggies in the room, giving the order not to shoot. Ard had positioned himself in such a way that any attack would cause him to drop the clay pot against the stone floor.

"This wasn't easy to get," Ard said. "I only wish Isle Halavend could have seen the finished Visitant Grit."

"That old man was a fool," Pethredote remarked. "The Prime Isle had warned me, and I regret that it took us so long to silence him."

"Halavend had everything figured out," Ard said. "He knew you had the Bull Dragon Patriarchy killed. And he knew that their extinction would cause Moonsickness to spread across the Greater Chain."

"Halavend was a heretic," Pethredote replied. "He planned to use his holy position to gain a following. His so-called *discoveries* were falsehoods, meant to incite the people against my leadership!"

Ard felt the moment coming. Pethredote was already on edge. He would divulge all under the threat of a Paladin Visitant.

"Isle Halavend was right on all counts," pressed Ard. "But there was one thing he couldn't figure out." Ard stepped closer to the king. "Why was it so important to destroy the shell? That's why you poisoned the Patriarchy. That's why you silenced everyone who might have known about it. It was because of the shell. The Visitant Grit. You were determined that there would never be another Paladin Visitant."

"And I'm right!" shouted Pethredote. "You think some meddling Isle knows more about the Paladin Visitants than I do? I summoned one in my youth. I know their true power!"

"Then you'll be distressed to know that Halavend pronounced me worthy of summoning one."

"You can't!" Pethredote yelled. "No one can know..."

Ard threw the pot of fake Visitant Grit against the floor. The clay shattered on impact, sparking a small fragment of Slagstone. There was no Grit within the pot, but in a moment, the air would be hazy with the blast of Heat Grit, and no one would know the difference.

Ard sensed Raek leaping toward the ignitor switch on the wall behind them. The switch would set everything into motion, the spark igniting the Compounded Heat Grit for the chandeliers, as well as lighting Raek's sunflare cloak.

Ard dropped to a crouch, hands coming over his head to shield himself. The move had two purposes. First, this was the expected stance when detonating Visitant Grit, since seeing, touching, or hearing the Paladin Visitant resulted in bursting into flame.

Secondly, if nothing went right, ducking low seemed like a good idea when the Reggies started shooting.

The reception hall suddenly grew very hot. An intense spike in temperature unlike anything Ard had felt before. It wasn't like standing too close to a bonfire, where one's front seemed scalded, while the rear remained cool. This was an all-encompassing heat that wrapped completely around him like a stifling blanket.

There was a scream across the room, and Ard's head snapped up from his defensive crouch. One of the Regulators was on fire! Blazing sparks, the man was actually burning! And he wasn't the only one. Another Reggie combusted before Ard's eyes, his red coat going up in spontaneous flames.

A short distance away, Pethredote had dropped into a similar defensive crouch, arms shielding his head and his sword lying useless on the floor beside him. But, like Ard, the aging king couldn't help but peek at the reactions of his guards.

Ten Regulators were ablaze. Screaming, flailing, running. The two that weren't had dropped to the floor, crawling with their faces averted from Raek's presence.

The hallway doors flung open, more than a dozen waiting Regulators intent on storming the room. But the awful sight and sounds greeted them, along with the shouted warnings of the two Reggies that had escaped combustion.

"Paladin! Paladin! Shield yourselves!"

There was a sudden belch of smoke and flame, accompanied by a rending shriek as one of the burning Regulators exploded. Ard ducked at the terrifying sight, a spattering of blood and gore painting the reception hall.

Oh, flames, Ard thought. *The Grit sashes.*

All Regulators wore them, stocked with a number of loaded pots and crossbow Grit bolts. The flames from the combusting uniform must have made contact, a violent explosion of Blast Grit ending his life. And that wasn't the only thing to detonate.

Multiple Grit detonations sounded, discolored clouds overlapping and hanging in the spot where the Reggie had exploded.

An orb of Light Grit perfectly illuminated the scene, half trapped within a Barrier cloud as bits of burning cloth and charred flesh hung suspended in a detonation of Drift Grit.

"To the king!" shouted a bold Reggie from the hallway. The rallying call was followed by multiple gunshots, causing Ard to plaster himself against the stone floor.

He glanced over his shoulder. Raek had his back against the wall, standing tall next to the ignitor switch that had thrown the room into chaos. The sunflare cloak appeared to be doing the trick masterfully, protecting Raek's skin from the burning strips of cloth that raged across his body.

Raek had donned an additional hood and mask of the same fabric. As fire danced across his entire form, Ard himself was nearly convinced that the man behind him was a Paladin Visitant. Raek certainly looked true to the description in the history books.

Ard's admiration of Raek was short-lived, as a handful of Regulators from the hallway attempted to storm the room, Rollers and crossbows leading them. Upon entering the tremendous heat, two of the uniforms combusted, disbanding the rescue attempt in a mess of smoke and screams.

Another burning Regulator exploded, this time in the hallway as he fled the reception hall. That was a terribly gruesome side effect Ard had not anticipated. Had the circumstances been any different—had the stakes of this ruse been different—Ardor Benn would have been horrified by their deaths. But this was no longer a simple ruse. Ard was fighting a war for humanity. And as such, he needed to steel himself against the bloodshed.

Ard knelt, scanning the room. Pethredote was attempting some sort of crawl, his eyes shut, and his hands clamped over his ears. The reception hall had nearly cleared. The combusting Regulators had either exploded, fallen to their burns, or managed to flee into the hallway.

Ard saw six more Reggies mounting another attempt in the

hallway, their determined faces already sweating from the mere proximity to the sweltering room. Their loyalty was an admirable quality, even if it was placed in a man unworthy of it. What would it take to convince them to back down?

"Seal the room!" Ard barked the command, altering his voice to carry the authoritative tone of a Regulator chief. "The king is dead! Seal the room and retreat!"

His voice mixed with the chaos, and no one questioned the order. The final burning Regulator passed into the hallway, the men in the threshold disbanding. The doors to the reception hall groaned on their hinges, a resonating *boom* echoing through the spacious room as the area was closed and secured.

Ard stood slowly, not daring to face Raek in case Pethredote was watching him. Overhead, the chandelier Light clouds suddenly extinguished. It was no matter, though. There were three or four Light Grit detonations glowing at random throughout the reception hall—the results of the exploding Reggie Grit sashes. And the sudden dimming of the large room only enhanced the flickering, fiery blaze of Raek's elaborate costume.

Ard strode forward and kicked Pethredote in the ribs. The old man didn't move, his hands clasped securely over his ears, a muttering hum passing his lips in an attempt to block any sound that the Paladin Visitant might make.

Ard stooped, grasped the king's right arm, and tugged it away from Pethredote's head. He cried out in fear, trying to turn away.

"My Paladin stands back," Ard said. "Since speaking would kill us both, he will not open his mouth."

Pethredote's eyes snapped open, wide and blue, full of panic. "You fool! You cannot control him like some pet! He is here to bring change."

"He's here because I summoned him," Ard said. "And I didn't need your Prime Isle to say I was worthy."

Pethredote shook his head wildly. "You aren't worthy! Your

detonation failed once. Your victory today is a rewriting of history. Not for your good, but for the good of the future as someone else sees it. But my reign will forever remain intact. Time will not rewrite the good I've done!"

"What the blazes are you talking about, old man?" Ard muttered.

He reached down and hoisted Pethredote into a sitting position. Both men turned their faces slightly aside as the fiery glow of Raek's Paladin Visitant flickered ominously in the dim chamber.

"I want answers." Ard crouched before the pitiful king. "What do you mean, my detonation failed once? My Paladin Visitant is here, and I will command him to snuff out your life if you do not answer my questions."

Ard had to get him talking. Pethredote would only expect the Visitant Grit to burn for ten minutes or so. Raek had said that the Thrast oil on his sunflare cloak wouldn't be good for much longer than that anyway. Precious time had been spent establishing the veracity of Raek's image and clearing the Regulators from the room.

"I will say nothing to you, Settled warmonger." Pethredote closed his eyes tightly in defiance.

Ard stood, keeping his face tilted away from Raek's burning figure. He didn't have time for this kind of righteous indignation. He snapped his fingers. "Mighty Paladin," Ard said. "Touch this man with your holy fist."

He didn't dare glance at Raek, but Ard imagined that the big man was smiling behind the fireproof mask. Holy fist? Ard would never hear the end of that.

Ard felt Raek drawing closer, the brightness of his blaze coming upon Pethredote. The heat of the room was exhausting, and Ard sucked in a few breaths.

They needed the king to cave. If Pethredote had decided to meet death, he was going to be sorely disappointed to find that Raek's touch would merely scald him.

From the corner of his eye, Ard risked a glance. The massive burning form of Raek loomed above the spot where Pethredote sat. The burning figure reached out, his movements incredibly slow, allowing King Pethredote every opportunity to yield.

Raek's gloved hand was mere inches from Pethredote's face when the king finally cried out, "What do you want?"

Raek paused, and Ard got the impression he was awaiting a command. "Holy Paladin. Withdraw." Raek stepped back, and Ard took his place hovering over the king.

Pethredote still refused to open his eyes. Sweat streamed down his face as he trembled.

"Why did you say I failed?" Ard pressed. "I am obviously worthy—"

"It has nothing to do with worthiness," said the king. "Everyone fails. The Prime Isle told me the truth! The Paladin Visitants. They are not who you think they are."

"Immortal warriors." Ard recited the common Wayfarist doctrine. "Sent by the Homeland."

"The Homeland is a lie!" Pethredote's face twisted at the confession. "It is a lie that every Prime Isle has maintained under sacred obligation."

Ard felt his hopes begin to fall right there. Isle Halavend had believed that the Paladin Visitant would somehow save mankind from the coming Moonsickness. If the Homeland was a lie, if the Paladins were not who everyone thought they were, then what hope remained?

"The Homeland doesn't exist?" Ard had long suspected it. But if that were true, then what power had been Urging him through the past few cycles?

"The Homeland exists," muttered Pethredote. "But it is not a place."

What kind of nonsense was this old fool jabbering? "Explain!" Ard shook the king roughly.

Pethredote cracked his eyes open to peer at Ard's face with

frantic intensity. "The Homeland is the future," he whispered. "Our perfect future."

"That's a blazing lie!" And a downright confusing one.

"Think about it," Pethredote answered. "What does Wayfarism teach of the Homeland? It is a place of peace and prosperity. The Homeland Urges every faithful man and woman to grow, to change, to progress and move forward. What are we moving to? A better future. A Homeland that we ourselves can create through righteous living."

"You're out of your mind." But Ard felt the truth of the king's words sinking in. In a way, what Pethredote explained made more sense than the Wayfarist doctrine. It would certainly explain why the Wayfarist Voyages never found land. They were adrift in the distant sea, out of range of the dragons' protection. Sickened by the Moon rays while searching for a land that didn't exist.

"If the Homeland is the future," Ard mused, "then what about the Paladin Visitants? Where do they come from? Who are they?"

"The Paladin Visitants are the Prime Isles of the future," said Pethredote, "who have traveled backward through time."

"Through time?" Ard muttered. He half expected Raek to burst out laughing, an error that would have completely destroyed their trick. But laughing was what Ard felt like doing. Time traveling? That was a thing of fiction and idle speculation.

It was one thing to describe the Homeland as an idyllic future. That was an abstract concept Ard could eventually wrap his mind around. But now the king was saying that the Holy Paladins, actual, physical beings, were visitors from that future?

"'Behold, the Homeland sendeth those fiery figures. Those Paladin Visitants, who alone can save mankind from its own annihilation.'" The king quoted the familiar Wayfarist verse. He looked squarely at Ard. "'In the day of their coming, mankind is transported as one. As a flock of birds upon the wind, drawing ever closer to that Homeland blessed.'"

That was the verse that Isle Halavend had been counting on.

Now the king was quoting it as if these new revelations didn't disprove its veracity? "The Paladins will take us to the Homeland?" Ard mused. "Into a perfect version of the future?"

"They help us create it," corrected the king. "Man is weak. We bring about our own destruction."

Ha! Pethredote was one to talk, since his own greedy ambitions were leading to an imminent epidemic of Moonsickness.

"It is the sacred duty of the Prime Isle to assess the world in which we live," said Pethredote. "He must identify significant points with potential to change the course of the future. When such a moment arises, he authorizes a hero to detonate Visitant Grit."

"And the worthy heroes succeed," Ard said. "But what makes them worthy?"

This was the very question that held everything stationary. Halavend had fruitlessly sought the answer until the moment his life was taken.

"No one succeeds," replied the king. "The first attempt is always deemed a failure."

"What does that mean?" Ard shook his head. *First attempt*. Pethredote kept saying that. As though any failed hero had been given a chance to try again. "But you," Ard said to the king. "You succeeded in using a Paladin Visitant to take the throne from King Barrid."

"In this timeline, yes," replied Pethredote. "But in another timeline, my detonation of Visitant Grit failed."

"I don't understand." Sparks, this was a lot more complicated than he anticipated. Ard hoped Raek was paying close attention. They'd have a lot to talk about when they got back to the butcher shop. "How did you fail?"

"We can't possibly know what happened in that other timeline," the king rambled. "I was given Visitant Grit and set against King Barrid. I detonated the Grit, but failed to make a Paladin appear. Perhaps I was executed. Perhaps I was jailed. Time passed and history acknowledged me a failure. Then, at some point in the future, maybe a hundred years from now, the Prime Isle considered the islands to be in distress—physical distress, or spiritual decay. Whatever it may be, the Prime Isle determined that life on the islands needed to be reset. Wiped clean and given a fresh start.

"This future Prime Isle would have taken a pot of Visitant Grit to the very place where I had used mine, some hundred years before. He would ignite the Grit, and the two detonation clouds would link across the span of years."

"Like Illusion Grit," Ard said.

"But instead of merely recording an image and displaying it, Visitant Grit physically delivers the person in the second detonation cloud backward through time."

"Why the fire?" Ard asked. "Why the death?" If the Paladin Visitants were simply some Prime Isle from the future, why did they appear so radiant?

"People from the past cannot behold someone from their future. They will burn up, as time cannot allow the interaction. The very Grit cloud from the first detonation burns upon the skin of the Paladin, giving him an appearance of flame."

"What happens next?" Ard asked. "This future Prime Isle, he linked his detonation with yours and traveled back through time. To what end?"

"To change things," answered the king. "From the moment of his arrival, a new timeline begins. In this timeline, I am a successful king, uniting the people in peace and prosperity. Bringing everyone closer to that perfect Homeland."

Pethredote sure had an inflated view of himself. Sure, he'd done a lot of good, but he was leaving out the part where he'd murdered a bunch of people and selfishly brought about the extinction of the dragons.

"And what of that future Prime Isle who was your Paladin Visitant?" Ard asked. "He returns to his time when the Grit burns out?"

"No." Pethredote's blue eyes were fierce. "He has nowhere to return. There can be only *one* timeline. By going back, the Prime Isle knows that he is erasing all that has happened since. He is giving the world a new beginning at the cost of his own existence."

"But time always moves forward," Ard said. "That Prime Isle will exist again someday. What's to stop him from making the same choice and going back in time once more?"

"A time loop," whispered Pethredote. "If he were continually allowed to make the same choice, time would only progress a finite number of years before repeating itself."

"That's what I'm saying," spat Ard. "None of this makes sense!"

"Time will never repeat itself the same way," said Pethredote. "The Urgings of the Homeland prevent it."

"What are the Urgings?" So the feelings *were* something transcendental.

"An Urge to change. Repeating one's actions is Settled." It was a familiar Wayfarist phrase. "The Homeland Urges us to make significant changes, so as time unfolds, the future from which the Paladin Visitant came will never exist. In one timeline I was a failure. In this timeline I am a hero. I have followed the Urgings and shaped the future differently with the power I've been given. Chances are, that the future Prime Isle who visited me will never come into that Holy position. He may never exist. Or he may be nothing more than a vile criminal in our future."

"So by going back in time, he destroyed his own life and surroundings?" Ard asked. "How many have done this?"

"Every Paladin Visitant through recorded history. Most Prime Isles do not need to make the journey through time," said Pethredote. "They assign Visitant Grit to a number of heroes, all of which will fail initially. But the Prime Isles are responsible for creating these checkpoints through history. Each failed detonation is a potential moment to which time could be reset. They give us another chance at shaping the future differently."

"Did Chauster go back in time?" Ard asked.

"No, Homeland be praised," said the king. "Had he gone back, none of us would be here today. It is a terrible price to pay. Everything is erased, and the future is forced to unravel differently the second time. Why do you think this knowledge is limited to our spiritual leader?"

"And yet you learned the secret," Ard pointed out. "How?"

"Chauster told me," said the king. "Shortly after he became Prime Isle, he revealed the knowledge to me."

"Why would he do that?"

"Chauster knew that in the future, someone could return to a time before ours and appear as a Paladin Visitant. Doing so would reset the timeline. The future would shape itself differently, and we may never have a chance to do the good that we've done."

"That sounds pretty altruistic to me," Ard said.

"Chauster and I considered the future. We couldn't trust the next generation. As the crusader monarch, I have no heir. The kingship would be decided upon by a group of nobles who would bicker for the right to take my place. Chauster would depart on a Wayfarist Voyage, and the new ruler of the Greater Chain would appoint whomever he pleased to fill the vacancy of Prime Isle. The Homeland would reveal the truth to this new Prime Isle. Someone we don't even know. How could we trust a future lineage of strangers not to erase our accomplishments? Chauster had to tell me the truth so we could take action."

"By eliminating the dragon shell," said Ard.

"Aside from the Prime Isles, I was the first man to be trusted with this holy information," said Pethredote. "It was my responsibility to do something about it."

Ard made a skeptical expression. "Twelve hundred years, and not a single Prime Isle has been loose-lipped about this holy secret?" He shook his head. "Don't flatter yourself into thinking that you're the first to know, Pethredote."

"But I am! A secret so large could not be contained. If someone had learned about the Paladin Visitants before me, the knowledge would have become common."

Ard nodded. "There's the problem with erasing history. Chances are, others *have* learned the truth about the Paladin Visitants. And just as you said, a leak of such information would have gone public. Someone would detonate the Visitant Grit and travel back in time. They'd reset the timeline and erase any knowledge that the truth had ever been revealed." Ard finally let go of the king, shoving him backward to the tile floor. "You're not an exception, Pethredote. More likely *you* are the information leak, doing the very thing that caused the timelines to get reset in the past."

"But the damage is already done," Pethredote said. "Your final detonation begins history anew from this day on. But you haven't erased my reign. My legacy will live on. Don't you understand? Chauster and I had to destroy the dragon shell to preserve ourselves. Every man, woman, and child. We had to preserve *this* timeline—the only one that really matters."

Ard stared at the old king, the secrecy behind those blue eyes draining out, leaving a pitiful husk of a man crumpled in the dim room. Pethredote actually believed that he had done the right thing—that eliminating every piece of dragon shell was a noble act.

Ard didn't know what to think. Preserving their current timeline seemed important, but if the Prime Isles of the future were coming back to change the past, didn't it mean that the future was in even worse shape?

What about the man who had appeared as Pethredote's Paladin Visitant some forty years ago? Why had he traveled through time to make Pethredote into a hero? Had the islands been on the brink of destruction? If so, that visitor from the future had done no good. The islands were facing destruction *now*, with the imminent Moon-sickness. By resetting the timeline and giving Pethredote power, that Paladin Visitant hadn't spared the people from mass destruction. He had accelerated it.

Ard understood now. He understood how the Visitant Grit must be used, but he hated the idea of it. The only way to save mankind from Moonsickness was to reset the timeline. Ard would ignite this final blast of Visitant Grit in the very spot where someone in history had failed their detonation, transporting himself back in time to turn that failure into a success.

Ard himself would become the Paladin Visitant. Any who looked upon him would burn out of existence. Ard would have the power to destroy anyone with a single utterance.

The timeline would reset. The Homeland would Urge people to behave differently so that history would write itself in a new way. If Ard went back far enough, Pethredote may never be born. The man certainly wouldn't take the throne. The Bull Dragon Patriarchy would be spared of Pethredote's poison, and mankind would live on, never knowing that the winged beasts upon Pekal absorbed the sickening rays of the Red Moon.

But Ard, too, might not exist. Or if he did, he'd likely be a very different person. *This* Ard would never exist. And worse than that—neither would his friends. Resetting the timeline would doom them all to an altered existence. Would they be happy in their new skins? Raek might be his enemy, Elbrig his brother. Quarrah Khai may never cross his path...

Ard shook his head. Deep thoughts were not supposed to trouble him. If he'd wanted to be weighed down by burdensome philosophies, he would have joined the Islehood.

Through the glass doors leading to the balcony, Ard heard the blaring of a trumpet. He quickly scooped up the king's fallen sword as Pethredote began to rise. Ard felt better with a weapon in his hands. Especially if Raek's costume failed prematurely.

"The palace defense alarm," the king whispered. "What army have you persuaded to help you win the night?"

"Not my army," said Ard. "This one belongs to somebody else you sparked off."

The alarm meant Lyndel's Trothian force was striking the palace, creating the distraction that Ard and Raek would need to escape. Just in time, too. Raek's fire seemed to be dwindling. The trick would probably last only a few more moments. But Ard had learned what he needed from King Pethredote, even if he couldn't yet make sense of it.

"What will you do now, Ardor Benn?" The king was on his knees. "Take my place? Rise to the throne? The people will not accept you as they once did me. Not even with the backing of your Paladin Visitant. You are Settled. A criminal. These people need a hero to follow."

Ard brought the sword around and placed the slender blade against the king's neck. *Your Homeland wants Pethredote dead.* Lyndel's words rattled in Ard's head.

The Homeland was a perfected version of the future, slowly being crafted as the timelines reset with each Paladin Visitant, until perfect harmony could be achieved. There was no room for a man like Pethredote in such a paradisiacal future. Lyndel was right. The Homeland *did* want him dead.

Ard's grip tensed on the hilt, his arm flexing in preparation to thrust the blade through the king's sweaty neck. But he faltered. Frozen despite the heat.

Ard was no assassin. And becoming one today would do nothing to help Ard reach the Homeland. Didn't Ard already share many of Pethredote's flaws? Manipulative, deceitful, cunning.

Strange. Until seeing those qualities in Pethredote, Ard would have considered them positive in himself. And under that pretext, Ardor Benn knew that there was no place for him in the Homeland, either.

Ard cast the king's sword down, the metal clattering harshly against the stone floor. The tremendous heat in the room suddenly reprieved. The Compounded Heat Grit must have burned out. That meant about ten minutes had passed since the trick had begun. It was time to make their escape.

"Let's go," Ard said to Raek, keeping his gaze averted from the smoldering man as he strode for the doors. Hopefully, Lyndel's attack had proven a sufficient distraction to draw the Regulators away.

Raek had performed exceptionally well as a Paladin Visitant. It was the easy part, Ard wanted to point out. Raek had stood virtually motionless to avoid getting burned through the sunflare cloak. As usual, Ard had done all the talking and most of the quick thinking. Raek hadn't even been allowed to say a word. His big friend was surely enjoying the role. Standing as still as a stump while managing to portray the most powerful being in the world. Raek would say that the only thing that could make it better was doughnuts.

Ard pulled open the doors. They would have to flee the moment Raek shed that burning cloak. If Pethredote saw the costume come off, he would know he'd been tricked.

Leaving Pethredote alive was the right choice, wasn't it? Lyndel would be disappointed in him. But soon enough, Ard would detonate the actual Visitant Grit and the king would be erased from existence anyway. They all would. No one would know what they had accomplished here today because today would never occur in this way.

From behind him, Raek grunted—the first sound he had made since entering the palace. From the corner of his eye, Ard risked a glance to see what his big friend might need.

The king's sword protruded from Raek's chest.

Ard felt his body go numb, the sweat from the last ten minutes seeming to ice over his flesh. Raek, still in full costume, his strips of cloth burning low over his black cloak, fell to his knees.

Pethredote stood behind him, still gripping the hilt of the sword whose blade had passed clean through Raek's back and emerged several inches from his chest.

"Millguin." The king's voice was barely audible. "She saw him."

"Raek!" Ard staggered a step away from the open door. It had to be a trick. Some sort of illusion. He and Raek had survived too many narrow escapes together. Cheated death too many times. The dying man before him couldn't be Raekon Dorrel.

Pethredote withdrew the sword with a sharp pull, the action tugging the smoldering body backward and causing him to sprawl upon the floor of the reception hall. Ard saw the blood. Deep rivulets of crimson flowing along the grooves of grout between the floor tiles. Blood. Raek's blood. So much of it.

Ard knew it was real then, and the shock of it paralyzed him. The king's voice was tinny and distant as it reached his ears, echoing past the disbelief and numbness of what had just transpired.

"Millguin saw the man and did not burn," the king explained. Ard was barely aware of the Karvan lizard, sprawled lazily upon the hot stone floor, several feet behind Pethredote. The creature was staring disinterested, the room reflected in those big black eyes.

"A trick," Pethredote mumbled. "Somehow it was all a clever trick." The thin blade in his hand dripped, its glossy red appearance lit by the flickering flames on the body of the dying man.

Pethredote stepped toward Raek, but Ard barreled into him, leaping over the still form of his friend and knocking the king backward. They tumbled, the sword clattering away, Ard losing control as he brought his fist down against Pethredote's face. He punched again and again, releasing the fury that was building inside of him.

His partner. His conscience. His best friend.

It couldn't be. Raek wasn't dead. Not yet. Ard could save him.

He rolled away from the king, his knuckles tingling and bloody, cut to the bone from the beating. Maybe the king was dead. Pethredote certainly wasn't moving.

Ard scrambled to his friend's side. Under that heavy, smoldering cloak, it was impossible to tell if he was breathing. Ard stripped back Raek's mask, not even caring if it singed his fingers.

"Raek," he whispered. The man's face was drained of color. There was blood in his mouth, but Ard could tell now that he was indeed breathing. Shallow, labored.

"All right," Ard muttered. "You're going to be all right. Let's get you out of here." He pulled Raek's arm around his neck, the sunflare cloak singeing his skin. Ard heaved, eliciting a moan from his dying friend. "Well, it's not my fault you're so big," Ard muttered. "Homeland, Raek! You've got to be two hundred and fifty panweights. I told you…"

"Ard…"

He froze at the sound of his friend's voice, Ard still squatting and Raek halfway into a seated position.

"Ard…" he said again. His voice was so weak. So unlike the Raek he knew. "Get the blazes out of here."

"What do you think I'm trying to do?"

"Leave me."

"Ha!" Ard replied. "Now, what kind of friend would I be if I left you behind?"

"Ard!" His voice was a little more forceful this time. "It's the only chance…Go!"

"Not happening," replied Ard, making another attempt to heave his big friend to his feet. "The least you could do is try to get your feet under you." He didn't know how to handle this. Ard's emotions were hanging at the edge of a cliff. He talked to Raek the only way he knew how—like everything was okay.

Raek's other hand suddenly reached out, pointing across the large room. "That…" he muttered. "Get that…"

Ard looked in the direction he pointed. "What?"

"Grit belt…" Raek rasped.

Of course! A Regulator would carry Health Grit on his sash. It obviously wouldn't be enough to heal Raek, but maybe it could keep him alive until Ard could get more help.

He scrambled across the room in the direction Raek had pointed. He didn't see a Grit belt anywhere. From behind, Ard suddenly heard the distinctive shattering of a clay Grit pot. He whirled in time to see the detonation surround Raek.

Barrier Grit.

Ard leapt toward him, slamming his fist against the impenetrable shell of the detonation cloud. Peering through the haze, he saw that the shards of the pot were scattered under Raek's own hand. He must have smuggled the pot inside his large cloak. Raek had detonated it himself!

"Blazes, Raek! What did you do?" He pounded hopelessly against the Barrier's perimeter.

"I'm a goner, Ard," Raek wheezed. "Now get your stubborn self out..."

A gunshot echoed through the reception hall, and Ard felt a terrible sting in his left shoulder, a flecking of his blood peppering across the dome of the Barrier cloud. The sudden jolt of pain caused Ard to stumble.

The shooter stood in the open doorway. A Reggie in a red uniform, probably doubling back to check on the status of the room, eager to find the king's body. He fired a second shot from his Roller, but this one went wide, pinging off the hard barrier of Raek's cloud.

Ard gripped his shoulder, blood seeping between his fingers. He could tell from the flow that the ball had passed. Must have missed the bone. Numb from the pain, it was really impossible to tell.

The Regulator took a step farther into the room, crying out as he saw the king. Pethredote was breathing shallow breaths, sputtering on his own blood that seemed to flow from every opening on his face.

Ard glanced once more at Raek's fallen form. His friend's eyes were closed. Had he stopped breathing? He'd be dead before Ard could get to him. If he wasn't already.

Ard knew that was why Raek had detonated the Barrier Grit. It was his way of giving Ard a chance to escape. The big man knew that Ard wouldn't leave the palace without him. Not if there was any hope in saving his life. Well, there wasn't hope now. And if Ard didn't get moving, they'd both end up dead.

Ard muttered his friend's name, tears welling in his eyes. Then he was on the move, scrambling across the large room. He passed the tree and surrounding ornamental flowers, all of which had wilted from prolonged exposure to extreme heat. A third shot cracked through the reception hall, missing Ard and shattering the glass in one of the balcony doors.

Three more balls, assuming the Roller was fully loaded when the Reggie barged in. There was no chance of rushing him and fleeing into the hallway. The balcony was Ard's best option.

As Dale Hizror, Ard remembered taking Azania onto that very balcony one cool night. She had looked radiant in the soft glow of the chandelier. He had told Raek about how he'd felt toward Quarrah. Sparks, he'd told Raek everything. Always.

Ard knew the second-story balcony overlooked the manicured grass and dotted bushes. A large detonation of Drift Grit would have bridged the gap to the ground, allowing him to leap down and land with little more force than a regular jump. But Ard had no Drift Grit.

He truly had nothing. No weapons. No Grit. No Raek.

Ard burst through the glass door as the fourth gunshot rang behind him. He staggered, cut now from the shattered glass as well. Hoisting himself upon the stone railing, he looked down. The night was too dark to judge the distance accurately, and perhaps that was a good thing.

As the fifth shot sounded behind him, Ard jumped. He struck the ground, attempting to roll through the landing like Quarrah had once showed him.

There was a searing pain in his leg. He hadn't heard the bone snap, but he knew it must have. Grimacing against the wash of agony, Ard pulled himself forward, crawling through the grass, his left arm numb and his injured leg trailing behind.

Glancing back, Ard saw the Regulator reach the edge of the balcony, peering down, waiting for his eyes to adjust to the darkness outside. The man had one shot left. Ard was an easy target, helplessly displayed upon the lawn. Even if the Reggie missed, he would alert others. There was no chance Ard could clear the outer wall and make the cover of the Char before more Regulators converged on him.

There was a gunshot, and Ard tensed. A strangled cry came from the balcony, and Ard saw the Regulator topple limply over the railing. Confused, his mind a foggy jumble, Ard redoubled his efforts, crawling forward and fighting to maintain consciousness.

Suddenly, Lyndel was there beside him, a long-barreled Fielder on a strap over her shoulder. She dropped to her knees on the lawn, bending to pull Ard's arm around her neck. Lyndel said something, but her words seemed far away. She hoisted him upright, and Ard felt the earth spinning beneath his feet.

The pain. The shock.

Raek.

~

*They will grieve for me. I will die without
speaking a word.*

CHAPTER

38

Ardor Benn was adrift, his surroundings a jumble of incorporeal blackness and disjointed visions of places he had been. One moment wandering the heavy underbrush of Pekal, the next standing in the king's throne room. At times in the hidden room above the bakery, and sometimes floating through a vacant Char.

He might have thought himself dead. A ghost. A tortured soul made to oversee the places where the final cycles of his Settled life had played out.

Adrift. Adrift and alone.

But Ard knew he was not dead. There was still pain. He felt it most in his right leg, just below the knee, at times sharp enough to spike the length of his entire body. His left shoulder ached, too, causing a numbness that bled into his arm and chest.

Those moments of searing, burning pain anchored him to one tangible place. It was a dark, cool room, ripe with the smell of spoiled meat. The dugout at the back of the abandoned butcher shop.

During rare snippets of physical awareness, Ard often felt a gentle hand. It was familiar, though the voice that accompanied it was too far away to distinguish. And any attempt to make a verbal reply sent waves of pain crashing through his insides.

Awake, Ard's thoughts were indecipherable, his mind a clouded mess like a dozen detonations igniting within his skull. But in his dreamlike drifting—in his haunts—Ard's mind was startlingly clear. The facts were displayed before him. Secrets that he knew. Knowledge that had once seemed as intangible as he now felt, was verifiable truth.

Alone in this state, floating from landmark to familiar landmark, Ard could process everything. He knew what needed to be done. Sparks, he even knew how to do it. But using the Visitant Grit to go back in time would change everything. This entire existence would be erased. Rewritten.

The Homeland would Urge people differently in the new timeline, preventing history from repeating itself. Preventing any possibility of catching all of existence in a never-ending time loop.

The dramatic summoning of a Paladin Visitant gave mankind a chance to start anew and flourish. A chance to recover from the brink of utter destruction. And wasn't such destruction the very thing that mankind now faced? An unstoppable epidemic of Moonsickness. The fabled Paladins of fire could, as Wayfarist doctrine stated, eventually deliver them to the Homeland. Though not even the Homeland was what Ard had been led to believe.

The Homeland was a future that could be created, through careful, calculated uses of Visitant Grit. It could be shaped by the Prime Isles who knew the secret of time traveling. But could the Visitant Grit actually forge a future perfect enough to satisfy *every* soul?

It was a point that Ardor could not reconcile. He believed what Pethredote had told him about the Homeland, but knowing it made him loathe the place. Whose version of the future would be represented? And what about all the rejected timelines? Considering that his was about to become one, those lost lives seemed very real, and their erasure akin to mass genocide.

The future wasn't supposed to be crafted. It wasn't clay or wood. It was something organic. Time was supposed to roll forward like a ship on the waves. And the events that buffeted the sojourners of life were best if unexpected and surprising. The thought that Ard's actions could be erased at any moment made his life seem like it amounted to little more than a pile of unfired slag. Ard didn't want someone shaping the future. Not a Wayfarist Prime Isle. Not a Paladin Visitant.

Ard himself didn't feel comfortable making that call. And he was a ruse artist. He'd dedicated most of his adult life to manipulating people, controlling situations, and getting what he wanted.

Cheating time, giving history a chance to do things over. That should have been right down Ard's alley. Making this decision would be the ultimate manipulation. He would alter the destiny of every living soul.

But it took no finesse or craftiness. All it took was a well-placed detonation, and the power of the Visitant Grit would do the rest. That wasn't Ard. That wasn't his style. There had to be another option—to cheat time but preserve the timeline.

What if he could find a way around the rules? What if he could run a ruse on time itself?

"Well, that's presumptuous," spoke a familiar voice.

Ard swiveled around, finding himself standing on the stage of the Royal Concert Hall. The large theater was vacant, the seats wispy and not fully formed in Ard's hallucinatory state. The curtains hung like columns of black smoke, and Raekon Dorrel stood in the center of the empty stage.

The big man was wearing tall boots and dark pants. A wide Grit belt was fastened around his middle, and Raek had on a sleeveless tan shirt. He looked every bit himself, the mirrored stage lights reflecting on his shiny bald head, his expression preparing Ard to hear some wry comment. But his chest...

Oh, flames! Raek's chest was soaked in blood. The red stain flowered across his shirt, dripping down to his belt in lines of gore. At the center of the mess was King Pethredote's blade. The thin length of steel protruded from Raek's ribs, a visual reminder of the scene that had burned itself into Ard's memory.

"What are you doing here, Raek?" Ard didn't want to point out that his friend was dead. Drawing attention to that fact might send Raek away, and Ard would lose his partner to the darkest recesses of his mind.

"Every time I leave you alone," Raek said, striding forward, "you manage to get yourself in trouble." He reached down and pulled up a chair that suddenly materialized on the stage. "I'm here to make sure you don't mess this up." The sword in his chest didn't seem to bother him, the hilt passing through the back of the chair as he sat.

"I'm sorry," Ard muttered.

"Hey." Raek shrugged. "How were we supposed to know that Pethredote would bring his blazing pet?"

It was that unforeseeable variable. The biggest risk in any job. And Raek had never blamed him when one of those variables threw a spark into the mix at the wrong time.

"Even if we'd known the lizard would be there," Raek went on, "we couldn't have controlled it. We couldn't have stopped it from looking at the sunflare cloak. It wasn't your fault, Ard."

"It got you killed," Ard whispered. A confounded pet! A useless, overfed animal!

"You can't let this slow you down," Raek replied. "Not until the job is finished. You finally understand the Visitant Grit. How can you use it?"

Ard scratched his head, glancing over the empty seats in the audience. "It's all going to change, Raek."

"Everything changes," he replied.

"But change is supposed to happen naturally," answered Ard. "Not like this."

"It's happened before," said Raek. "You and I are little more than the product of the latest Paladin Visitant."

"I hadn't thought of it like that," whispered Ard.

"The timeline reset just forty years ago," Raek continued. "You weren't even a twinkle in your mother's eye at the time. Did you ever stop to think what our lives would have been in that other timeline? That first timeline when Pethredote's detonation failed?"

"I would have been the same person I am today," Ard tried to justify. "It wasn't that long ago. How much could I have changed?"

"A great deal," answered Raek. "You're making history, Ardor Benn. History can't play out the same way twice, and something tells me that you were not so significant in that other timeline."

"But we would have been friends, right?" said Ard. "Maybe we would have been merchants, or miners... Sparks, maybe even Holy Isles. But we would have been partners in that other timeline. Don't you think so, Raek?"

He shook his head casually, a bit of blood spilling out his mouth. "Not if we're making history together," he said. "This sort of partnership is powerful trouble." He grinned. "The Homeland would have Urged us apart. I don't think the timeline would allow us together in any other conceivable history, past or future."

"Then I can't detonate the Visitant Grit," said Ard. "I can't erase what we've done!"

"That sounds an awful lot like a certain king I know." Raek rose, the chair vanishing beneath him. "I don't see what choice you have." He strode past Ard, walking along the very edge of the stage. "If you don't detonate the Visitant Grit, Moonsickness will claim everyone. This is a chance for a new beginning."

Ard turned to face his dead partner. As he did, their surroundings suddenly shifted. The vaulted ceiling of the concert hall was replaced with bright blue sky, seagulls squawking overhead. The vacant audience chairs were swapped for lapping waves, and Ard found himself aboard the *Double Take*.

Raek was wearing his sailor's hat, the wide brim casting his crooked nose in shadow. The Grit belt was gone, replaced with a broad knife that slapped against his thigh as he reached up and adjusted the ship's single sail.

Raek was shirtless now, a sheen of sweat on his dark skin. But the sword was still there, rising from his bare chest like the mast of a ship. Ard grimaced at the bloody wound, averting his gaze across the expanse of water.

They were somewhere between Espar and Pekal, catching a light southeastern across the InterIsland Waters. A fishing boat bobbed at a short distance, but otherwise the sea was open and calm.

"Eggshell." Raek positioned himself, pulling on the rudder handle.

"What do you mean?" Ard subconsciously took hold of a rope to steady the sail.

"Why eggshell?" he asked. "Grit is derived from a number of indigestibles: bone, rock, metals. Why would the shell of a dragon egg summon a Paladin Visitant?"

"Is there an explanation for any of it?" Ard asked.

Raek gave him a disapproving glare. The kind he often dealt when Ard skirted an answer by asking a question of his own.

"Dragon eggshell," Ard mused. "It's scarce and valuable. Durable enough to pass through the digestive tract—"

"What does it *mean*?" Raek cut him off.

"Birth?" Ard ventured. "Life?"

Raek nodded his approval, using his weight to hold the rudder steady as the ship swiveled toward Pekal. "A new beginning," Raek said. "Isn't that what this is all about?"

"I don't want a new beginning," Ard said. "I agree that something has to be done. Time must be rewritten. But I want the same beginning. I want *this* life."

"A dragon is born when that shell *breaks*," Raek went on. "A tiny monster climbs out of that shattered cage and begins a life of endless possibilities. Up until a certain point, that shell was everything to the creature inside. It provided warmth, comfort, protection. But the dragon within eventually outgrew the shell. If the shell didn't break, the animal would suffocate and die within its limited confines."

"Waxing philosophical, I see."

Raek shrugged good-naturedly. "All I'm saying is that sometimes, in order to start something new, something old must be shattered."

"You're not just talking about the timeline," Ard said. It was one of the perks of having a delusional conversation within his mind. Ard knew the intent and direction of both parties.

"Quarrah's a good fit for you, Ard."

"*You're* my partner, Raek. Nobody's going to replace you."

"Oh, I know that," Raek replied. "I'm the best Mixer you'll ever meet, Ard. There's no replacing me."

"What does it matter, anyway?" Ard asked. "I have no future with Quarrah. If I reset the timeline, none of us have a future together. I can save the world, and nothing we've done will ever be remembered."

"You telling me I died for nothing?" Raek wrinkled his brow.

Ard shut his eyes and drew in a deep breath of salty sea air. When he opened them again, the *Double Take* was gone.

Ard was standing in the hidden room at the Bakery on Humont Street. The chalkboard hanging on the wall was covered in writing—Ard's handwriting, though the jumble of words were scrawled so closely together that he had a hard time making them out.

"So my death was pointless," Raek said, causing Ard to whirl around. The big man was seated on the padded couch. He was wearing the stolen Reggie uniform that he'd gotten so much mileage out of. The Regulator helmet was beside him on the couch, and a plate of Mearet's fresh pastries rested in Raek's lap.

But the sword was still there, piercing through the thick wool. Blood seeped through the uniform, and Raek's hands were smeared with red as he scooped a chocolate croissant from the plate.

"Time restarts, lives begin anew, and no one ever knows that the blazing king stabbed me in the back?" Raek shook his head, taking a bite of the pastry.

"Who's being selfish now?" Ard asked, but the injustice of it was filling him up. Raek had struck a nerve by calling attention to his sacrifice. Didn't Halavend's death mean something, too? And young Isless Malla? Ard had never met her, but her written testament of the sickening Moon beams had moved him to care about this ruse more than anything he had previously undertaken.

"See, it's something of a conundrum," Raek said. "We can't ignore the fact that Pethredote has actually done a lot of good for the Greater Chain. Sure, he's unraveling now, with that expulsion order toward the Trothians. But a new ruler could still salvage the progress Pethredote has made. If you reset the timeline, the politics of the islands will regress. And Homeland knows how long it'll take for those same advancements to be made in a new timeline."

Ard thought of his father's words of praise for the crusader monarch. He thought of his own education as a lad, made possible only because of the king's policies. He thought of countless enterprising Trothians carving out a place for themselves in the Greater Chain.

Oh, sparks. Was Ard actually siding with the king? Ard truly could understand Pethredote's motive for destroying the dragons in order to preserve his legacy. But that didn't make it right.

"Pethredote will get what he deserves," Ard said.

"Not if you reset the timeline," answered Raek. "Sure, in the new timeline Pethredote might become a peaceable fisherman. But that doesn't change *this* Pethredote. He gets away free—unpunished for all his crooked deeds."

Raek was right. Giving Pethredote a new beginning sickened Ard beyond any previous thought. And he wasn't going to let that happen.

"What are you doing?" Raek asked, as Ard set off across the room.

"I'm going to figure out another way." He stopped in front of the chalkboard, his eyes flicking over the scrawled words.

"Another way for what?" Raek polished off a blackberry tart.

Ard saw two words he'd written on the board. *Dragons* and *Moonsickness,* with a line connecting them. "We don't have to reset the timeline," he muttered. "We just have to save the dragons. If we can bring them back, they'll continue to shield us from the Crimson Moon."

"You can't just wish them back," Raek said. "There are only sows left, and that's an inevitable path to extinction. Do I need to explain the birds and the bees?"

Ard spotted *Paladin Visitant* written in the center of the chalkboard, with several words connected to it in a spiderweb. *Worthy. Homeland. Fire. Timeline.*

Ard felt a piece of chalk materialize between his fingers. Reaching up, he crossed out *worthy.*

"There's your problem," Raek said from the couch. "All this time we were acting under Halavend's directions. Wayfarist doctrine."

"I know," answered Ard. "But we know the truth about the Paladin's nature now."

Ard stared at the remaining words. *Fire. Timeline.*

"The only way to save the dragons is by fertilizing another male egg," Ard said. "A bull dragon fertilizes with fire. The Paladin Visitants have the ability to move through time."

An idea began to take shape. It was difficult to put into words, and Ard had no idea if it would work.

"We've been thinking about this all wrong, Raek," he said. "According to Pethredote, the Paladin Visitants come from the Homeland. From the future. They use their power to affect the past." He wrote the word *Future* with an arrow connecting it to *Past*. "But what if we could do the very opposite?" He reversed the direction of the arrow. "Instead of using the future to change the past, we can use the past to change the future."

He glanced at Raek, who sat scratching his head in confusion, a bit of cream filling in the corner of his mouth. Raek's confusion represented Ard's uncertainties. But that's why Raek had always been there—to force Ard to explain the ruse from every angle and make an ironclad plan.

"You're thinking about transporting a bull dragon from the past to the present day," Raek said. "Not going to work. Visitant Grit doesn't work like that. Once you've entered the past, everything begins to change. By the time the Visitant cloud burns out, there is no present day to go home to. The timeline has reset."

"There has to be a way..." Ard whispered. "Once I detonate the Grit, I become the Paladin Visitant. I go back in time, the most powerful being ever to exist. Shouldn't I be able to decide if I want to change things or not?"

Raek shook his head. "You make that decision the moment you ignite the Grit. Even if you don't speak a word. Even if you don't touch a soul. People in the past will still see you and burn at the sight. And whatever failed past hero you visit would now be a worthy success. That's where the change begins."

"But what if no one saw me?" Ard said. "What if, at the end of the day, the failed hero I visit is still deemed a failure? What if I could visit the past without making a mark upon it?"

"I don't see how that's possible," Raek replied. "And even if it was, nothing would be accomplished."

"But if I could do it," Ard said, "then this timeline, *our* timeline, would be maintained, right? I'd have somewhere to come home to when the Visitant Grit burned out."

"Theoretically," Raek said, "I suppose that's accurate."

"Raek, I've got it!" Ard cried. "I know what to do!" He spun to find his big friend, but Raekon Dorrel was gone. The hidden room of the bakery dissolved, and Ard felt the heat and pain of his physical condition washing over him.

A foul smell filled his nose, and the cool air seemed to smart against the fever of his flesh. The hand that had so frequently tended him was there at once, resting gently upon his chest. It was Quarrah Khai's hand. Ard wondered how he didn't recognize it before.

With a sudden expenditure of strength, Ard reached up and seized the fingers that lay against his heart.

"Ard!" Quarrah's voice still seemed distant, but he understood his name. His eyes fluttered open and through a surge of dizziness and nausea, he saw her beautiful face. "I'm here," Quarrah whispered. "I'm right here. You're going to be all right, Ard."

"Egg," he sputtered. "Bring me an egg." The request would sound like madness to her, but Ard hoped Quarrah would understand his urgent sincerity. "Bull dragon," he said. "I need the egg of a bull dragon."

And then his pain spiked. Ard cried out, his hand slipping from Quarrah's as darkness closed upon his vision.

And he was adrift again.

~

I feel it in the back of my mind. Like a black spot of mold, ready to spread.

CHAPTER

39

Quarrah stood motionless above the docks as her hired carriage rambled away down the rainy street. She stared down at the ships, big fancy ones whose construction had gone so far as to include useless wooden ornamentation on the prow. Quarrah wouldn't have been surprised to find out that the sails were embroidered.

She squinted across the lineup, disinterested in all but one ship. It was there, just as her sources had said it would be. Quarrah set off down the path that led to the secluded harbor.

It hadn't been easy to learn the ship's schedule. Quarrah had, of necessity, reached out to some rather unsavory former acquaintances who could get access to such information. Calling on old sources was like looking into a mirror after a long time away. It startled Quarrah to see how much she had changed when held up to old associates who hadn't. But they had gotten her results. And they were the only people Quarrah had to call on at the moment.

It had been two weeks, and Quarrah remembered the night of Raek's death with terrible clarity. After pumping all of the Compounded Heat Grit into the reception hall, Quarrah had made a silent escape from the palace.

Those hours had been horrible, waiting alone in the abandoned butcher shop. As the night crawled on, Quarrah knew something had gone wrong. It wasn't just that the others were late in returning. She could feel it.

But it had still been a terrible shock when Lyndel burst into the butcher shop, traipsing a bloodied Ardor Benn along. They formed a makeshift bed in the dugout meat storage room and Lyndel immediately saw to his wounds.

On that first night, Ard had revived just enough to tell them that King Pethredote had killed Raek. He had been distraught beyond any emotional extreme Quarrah had witnessed, so she was relieved when Ard finally drifted off to sleep.

But that sleep was fitful, and Ard couldn't seem to come out of it. Quarrah had stayed at his side from that first night, changing bandages, and mopping an increasing sweat from his face.

Fortunately, Quarrah had a fair amount of Health Grit at her disposal. Ironic that the king had once gifted that Grit to heal a supposed gunshot wound for Dale Hizror. They had stored the valuable Health Grit in a lock box in the upper room of the bakery. After the Reggies blew the wall apart, Raek had found the box intact in the rubble and brought it to the butchery.

Quarrah didn't know all the rules pertaining to Health Grit. She knew prolonged use caused some people to acquire a dependence on it. An expensive addiction, to be sure. Still, Quarrah didn't hold back. She had even risked mixing a bit of Compounding Grit with the Health detonation, intensifying the healing process in a way that some considered dangerous.

The Moon Passing had come and gone, marking the start of the Third Cycle. Over the last two weeks, Ard had only awakened long enough to choke down scraps of bread and wet his throat with a trickle of water. Ard seemed unusually somber. So deep in thought that he barely seemed aware of his surroundings. He hadn't shared any information he might have gathered from King Pethredote, and Quarrah didn't press him. He hadn't expounded on his demand that someone bring him a dragon egg. And who was supposed to do that, anyway?

The team was shattered. Raek and Halavend were dead. Cinza

and Elbrig were impossible to find. Quarrah had reached out to the forger, Tarnath Aimes, but he wanted nothing more to do with them. Sparks, she had even tried to find Moroy Peng.

With Halavend's death, their funds were utterly depleted. And although Quarrah, Ard, and Raek had been willing to continue working for the salvation of mankind, others didn't seem interested in joining their crusade without a hefty bag of Ashings.

Lyndel was the only person Quarrah could lean on, but the priestess hadn't been around since delivering Ard on the night of his injuries. Enraged by the king's sudden announcement against the Trothians, Lyndel's followers had responded to the assault on the palace with frightful enthusiasm. Her people were in hiding now, and Lyndel was working to procure better weapons and supplies so they'd be prepared for another attack.

Another attack? Quarrah knew Lyndel was furious over the death of Isle Halavend, but how far was she going to take this?

Sparks! They had done this! Did Quarrah have a hand in this anarchy that was spreading like mold on a rotten apple? What had begun as a well-paying ruse was turning out to be something far more than any of them had signed on for.

Quarrah believed Halavend's research. And with that belief came a responsibility to act. But what more could she do? Ard seemed to be brewing a plan, but Quarrah hardly had the experience and know-how to extract an unfertilized dragon egg from Pekal. She was alone with an impossible task. Which was what had brought her to this harbor for the only help she could think of.

Tanalin Phor.

Quarrah had decided not to tell Ard of her plans. He was still weak, and there was no way he would agree to involve Tanalin. But the Harvester captain had the resources and the experience to get what Ard needed.

Quarrah strode onto the long dock. The rainy day made for a quiet harbor. The workers kept their heads down, so Quarrah didn't draw any unwanted attention. Quarrah assumed Tanalin would be on board the *Crown's Ashing*, which was scheduled to leave for a Harvesting trip to Pekal within the hour.

Quarrah hoped what she planned to say would be enough to convince Tanalin. Words were Ard's thing. And while Tanalin had made it quite clear that she wasn't interested in hearing another word from him, Quarrah hoped she might be received with a more open mind.

The *Crown's Ashing* was the king's primary Harvesting ship. It was built for speed with plenty of storage, and well armored in the unlikely event of a pirate strike in the InterIsland Waters.

Quarrah brushed her fingertips across the Singler under her jacket as she moved up the ramp to the ship. If it came to blows, the weapon would be seriously insufficient. Quarrah was risking a lot coming here, where a single word from Tanalin could lead to her immediate arrest. Or worse. But Quarrah desperately needed help. She needed direction.

Once, Quarrah had been entirely independent. She prided herself on having accomplished so many solo thefts. Planning, plotting, scouting, thieving... Quarrah had done it all. Now that she was alone again, she felt paralyzed. Desperate for someone to turn to.

Quarrah reached the top of the ramp, only to be stopped by a callused hand. A stout sailor, nearly as broad as he was tall, barred access to the ship's deck.

"Don't know your face," he said, rain pattering off his hood. Quarrah was quite grateful for that. Some of Tanalin's crew might recognize her from her time as their prisoner. "Let's see those papers."

"I'm here to see Captain Tanalin Phor," Quarrah answered, skirting the fact that she didn't have the necessary papers for admittance.

"Captain's busy," said the man. "Due to set sail in half an hour."

"It's an urgent matter," Quarrah pressed. "I need help."

"We all need help," he answered.

"The captain knows me," she insisted. "If you'd just give her my name. Or ask her to peer out of her cabin to see my face."

"It is a face worth seeing," the man said. "Now get yourself back down that ramp, or I'll have the pleasure of handling you myself."

Quarrah scowled. If she couldn't talk her way past this salty sailor, what hope did she have in convincing Tanalin to help her? Ard would have talked his way on board in half as many sentences, but words never got her anywhere.

Impulsively, Quarrah reached into her jacket, drew the Singler, and fired it directly into the air. So much for that shot. Oh, well. Not like one ball would have made a difference if things went that way.

The squat sailor stumbled backward in shock, composing himself as he drew a Singler of his own. All motion on the *Crown's Ashing* had ceased, half a dozen guns trained on her. On the docks behind, Quarrah saw the harbor Regulators rushing in her direction. She would certainly be at Tanalin's mercy now, assuming that the Harvesting captain showed herself before the Reggies hauled her away.

"Quarrah Khai." Tanalin moved into view around the ship's mast, wide-brimmed hat sheltering her face from the rain. "You must have some death wish, coming here and taking shots like that."

Tanalin strode forward, her gate unimpressed, with a long-barreled Singler over one shoulder. She was a small woman, but looking tough as any sailor, with that tanned skin and jet-black hair. "What are you doing on the deck of my ship?"

"I tried to hold her back," said the callused sailor. "She drew a gun on me..."

"I need your help, Tanalin," Quarrah blurted.

"Someone put you up to this." Tanalin wouldn't say Ard's name. As far as the crew knew, their captain had shot Ardor Benn dead in that tent on Pekal.

"He doesn't know I'm here," Quarrah said. "He's hurt. I had no one else I could turn to for help."

"Raekon finally grew tired of the manipulation?" Tanalin asked. "Big fool's been a blind follower for so many years—"

"Raek's dead." Quarrah spat the words out and saw them take

immediate effect on Tanalin. The other woman froze, her mouth opening slightly, but not a word coming out.

A pair of harbor Regulators reached the bottom of the ramp, Rollers drawn and aimed at Quarrah's back as they issued commands for her to move slowly off the ship.

Tanalin was still for one more moment. Then she stepped up to the ship's rail and called down to the Reggies. "It's all right. Just a misfire. No trouble here."

Quarrah glanced over her shoulder, the Regulators holstering their Rollers and moving away from the ramp.

"Thank you." Quarrah tucked the spent Singler back into her jacket.

"Don't thank me yet," Tanalin replied, turning from the rail. "Come with me."

She led Quarrah across the deck of the *Crown's Ashing* and gestured for her to enter the captain's cabin set into the ship's raised stern.

Once inside, Tanalin shut the door, significantly reducing the amount of daylight that spilled into the room. Tanalin stepped past Quarrah and seated herself on a short bench against the wall.

"How did he die?" Tanalin resumed their conversation as though it had never been interrupted.

"Pethredote killed him," answered Quarrah, brushing her plastered wet hair from her forehead. "Raek and Ard were attempting to get information out of the king and something went wrong."

Tanalin swallowed. "Of course they were," she muttered. "What information?"

Quarrah shrugged. "Don't know. Ard was injured in the escape. He hasn't been well enough to say much."

"Ard? Not saying much? Well, that's highly unusual." Tanalin leaned back against the wall and studied Quarrah. "How'd you get away?" she asked. "On Pekal. Ard arranged for me to deliver you a lock-picking tool. You were gone by the time I came by."

"I can take care of myself," said Quarrah. "Have been for a long time."

"Why are you here?" asked Tanalin.

Quarrah didn't know if she should feel encouraged by the fact that Tanalin had brought the matter up. "I'm looking for an unfertilized dragon egg."

Tanalin squinted her eyes. "There's one in the Mooring. Anyone's welcome to take a look at it."

Quarrah had already considered the Mooring's gelatinous egg. She was sure she could steal it. Trouble was, the egg displayed in the glass case was milky white—indicating that the hatchling would be female if the egg were ever fertilized. Ard had been specific in his request.

"It has to be a bull egg," Quarrah explained. "That's what he said."

"Oh?" Tanalin raised her eyebrows. "Now that Raek is gone, Ard has you running his errands?"

This flustered Quarrah, and she hoped it didn't show. In many ways, she was blindly following Ard's request. But she had seen a look of sincerity in his eyes when he first awakened to make his desperate plea. And Ard had repeated his request in the days following. In fact, it was nearly all he had said, spending every ounce of energy to verify that she was trying to do something about it. Surely, he was planning something important.

"Why does Ard think he needs a gelatinous egg?" Tanalin continued.

"I don't know," Quarrah admitted. It had to have something to do with the information he learned from King Pethredote. "He must have discovered a way to hatch a bull dragon." It was the most she could hope for.

Tanalin rolled her eyes. "Only Ard would think himself above the laws of nature. Without the Bull Dragon Patriarchy, there's no way to fertilize another egg."

"Ard must have found a way," Quarrah insisted. She didn't know his game, but Quarrah trusted Ard, which was something Tanalin would never understand.

Quarrah had always known the type of person Ardor Benn was, and she had approached him as she would a venomous snake. Poor Tanalin had never suspected Ard's trickery until it was too late.

"Even if Ard could do this," said Tanalin, "why bother to bring back the dragons? There are sufficient stores of Grit, so it's not like he'll ever know a life without it. With the extinction of the dragons, the value of Grit would increase. In his line of work, Ard stands to gain from it."

"He's doing it for—"

"Don't tell me he's doing it for posterity," Tanalin cut in. "Ard is inherently selfish. I understand that better now than ever before. He doesn't care about the future. That man is only concerned with what he can gain today."

Quarrah took a deep breath. It was time to hit Tanalin Phor with a good dose of the truth. Hopefully the woman would believe her and respond sensibly.

"Have you heard about that case of Moonsickness on southern Espar?" Quarrah asked.

Tanalin seemed taken aback. "News has a way of warping as it travels. Can't trust everything you hear."

"Moonsickness is spreading to the Greater Chain, and that village is just the beginning." Quarrah took an urgent step forward. "We've learned things, Tanalin. Things about the dragons. They protect us from the Moonsickness." When Tanalin didn't say anything, Quarrah pressed on.

"The dragons absorb energy rays from the Moon Passing. For centuries, they have shielded us from certain death. A death that is now beginning to spread as the number of dragons on Pekal dwindles. Ardor has a plan. I don't know what it is, but it may be our final shred of hope to save the islands."

Quarrah finished her monologue, surprised at the fluidity of her speech. Her chest was heaving from the passion behind her words, and Quarrah felt rather proud of the way she had presented things. Perhaps a tiny bit of Ard's eloquence had rubbed off on her after all.

Tanalin stood up slowly, lacing her fingers together. "That's a blazing big story," she said, voice soft. "And I have to say, it reeks of Ardor Benn."

"What do you mean?" Quarrah felt her confidence begin to slip away.

"The story is so complex it's almost impossible to grasp. The stakes are high and full of emotion. The call to arms is dramatic and enticing." Tanalin shook her head. "Sparks, Quarrah. How can you believe anything that man says?"

Quarrah suddenly realized that coming here was a mistake. Tanalin was blinded by an overwhelming betrayal. She wasn't going to help them, because she refused to see facts. As far as Ard was concerned, Tanalin Phor could see only deceit and manipulation. He wasn't the man she'd once known.

But Ard wasn't the man Quarrah had once known, either. The Ardor Benn that had auditioned her skills against a supposed Lemnow painting wouldn't do anything unless the right sum of Ashings was backing it up. But the Ardor Benn lying injured in the abandoned butcher shop hadn't shirked away when he discovered that Halavend was dead, and their funds dried up. He was a man attuned to the Urgings of the Homeland, willing to finish this job for the payout of saving numberless innocent souls.

"It's all true," Quarrah said, though she could now see that Tanalin wasn't going to believe any of it. "You can take me to Pekal so I can fetch an unfertilized egg. Or you can stand by and watch Moonsickness spread until it infects every man, woman, and child."

Tanalin stared at her. "It's going to take a lot more than altruistic rhetoric to convince me."

Quarrah took a deep breath, preparing to shift tactics. If the logic and reason of truth didn't move Tanalin to help, perhaps something more brusque would do it. "My people have ten panweights of Blast Grit rigged into an explosive keg with instructions to detonate on the *Crown's Ashing* unless I sail out of here with you."

The lie was something Quarrah had concocted on the carriage ride to the docks. She had no idea what effect it would have on Tanalin, but it was a tactic worth investigating.

"It's unwise to threaten me," Tanalin said. "Especially when your threats are empty lies."

"That's a risk you're willing to take, then?" Quarrah asked. "Willing to blow up your crew and half this harbor just to show that you're not afraid of my words?"

"Absolutely," Tanalin said. "I've done some research on you since our last encounter. It's important for both of us to know what we are and what we aren't. You're a thief, Quarrah. Not a killer. If I'm to believe that you would stand by and watch my crew of thirty people blown to chunks, along with Homeland knows how many casualties on the docks, then that would make me a fool. Which I am not."

Quarrah felt her face turning red. Ard would have sold that threat differently. Whatever he would have said would have caused Tanalin to feel doubt, at the very least. "You have to understand—"

"I see what you're trying to do," Tanalin said. "And I will not be manipulated. As captain of the king's Harvesting crew, I have responsibilities to the crown and the Greater Chain. Not to thieves and ruse artists. You will leave this ship at once, unless you'd like me to shout for those Regulators to return."

Both tactics had failed, making Quarrah's appeal to Tanalin an utter waste of time. The two women ducked out of the small cabin and into the dreary daylight, crossing the wet deck in silence.

"You can tell him that I saw the girl safely home," Tanalin said. Quarrah paused on the ramp and looked back at her. "Nemery Baggish. She's with her mother now."

Quarrah nodded. Ard would be glad to hear the report. He had really worried for young Nemery.

"She thought he was a Wayfarist," Tanalin continued. "You should have heard the things that girl said about him. You'd think she was describing a Holy Isle." Tanalin chuckled bitterly. "Does anyone know the real Ardor Benn?"

It was a question that had crossed Quarrah's mind countless times. She'd seen him as a bantering ruse artist to Raek, as a suave composer to Cantibel Tren, as a gruff Harvesting captain to his criminal crew, and as a good Wayfarist to Nemery Baggish.

But who was Ard to Quarrah Khai?

"I could have left the girl on Pekal," Tanalin continued. "Or turned her over to the Regulators."

"Nemery isn't a criminal," Quarrah answered. "Ard didn't doubt for a minute that you'd do the right thing. You're a hard act to follow, Tanalin Phor." She turned and started down the ramp toward the docks.

"Quarrah," Tanalin called, causing her to stop once more. When Quarrah looked back, Tanalin seemed hesitant to say what was on her mind. At last, she spoke. "You're not much for words." Quarrah wrinkled her brow. Tanalin had called after her just to make an insult? "But I hear you're good at other things." Tanalin cast a sidelong glance down the dock. "His way isn't the only way to get what you need."

With that, Tanalin spun around and strode across the deck. Quarrah had reached the bottom of the ramp by the time Tanalin's words really sank in.

Appealing to Tanalin, asking for help, attempting to trick her into providing passage to Pekal. Those were all Ard's tactics. If Quarrah was in charge, which she now was, there would be a different skill set used in obtaining a gelatinous egg.

Steal it.

The *Crown's Ashing* was a busy atmosphere in preparation to set sail. Quarrah could easily get herself on board and stay concealed during the journey. The king's Harvesting ship was fast, likely to make it to Pekal in just under ten hours. The expedition would take at least five days for the dragon to pass the indigestibles and the Harvesters to haul out the fired Slagstone.

Quarrah had been planning to go with Tanalin anyway, and had left plenty of food and water within Ard's reach. He would survive her absence.

Quarrah turned back and stared at the big ship. The real difficulty would be working alone to acquire an egg on Pekal. Ard would never approve of this radical, underprepared plan, but Ard wasn't running the ruse anymore. Quarrah Khai was in charge now.

Quarrah moved quietly along the docks to get a good glimpse of the ship's stern. There had to be an opening she could slip into somewhere...

~

If only there was someone I could turn to for help. But I am more alone than ever. And my condition is fixed.

CHAPTER

40

Quarrah dropped the Drift crate as the Grit burned out, the weight of the gelatinous egg inside causing her to stagger a few steps. She collapsed beneath a tree, sweaty back pressing against the bark as she tipped her water skin to drink. And she thought the Drift crate was cumbersome to carry in pairs! Lugging this thing on her own was going to break her back.

Pekal was even more frightening than Quarrah remembered it. Last time, her comrades had been shot and torn to bits by dragons. But there had been a measure of security in numbers. This time, Quarrah was enduring the ominous grandeur of the mountain island in complete solitude.

Quarrah had spent the first night aboard the *Crown's Ashing* in Pekal's harbor, too afraid to disembark, even long after Tanalin and her crew had gone into the mountains. The next morning, she had finally crept ashore, easily navigating the lax Reggies on patrol.

Quarrah had run as far as she could, staying along the eastern shoreline until she reached North Pointe. The Drift crate they had used to transport the Slagstone was exactly where Ard had left it. After being abandoned for only a cycle, Quarrah was surprised to see thin vines already creeping up the sides of the box.

Quarrah's nights on the island had been rather sleepless, and she found herself hyperaware of every sound. Every cracking twig or rustling leaf. Every gust of wind or coo of a nighttime bird. All these sounds had been dragons to her. Dragons coming to eat her as they had done to Lence Raismus and the Kranfel brothers.

During the daylight hours, Quarrah had made treks from North Pointe, scouring the slopes for a gelatinous dragon egg. She mapped the island in her head, making a few rough notes on a piece of parchment. Quarrah learned to stop viewing the island as an overgrown mountain. In her mind, she transformed Pekal into a city.

Instead of canyons and ravines, she saw alleyways and roads. Instead of unique, gnarled trees, she saw noteworthy buildings. Instead of boulders, she saw parked carriages.

Quarrah had narrowed her search by remembering what Lence Raismus had told her about egg sites. The sow dragons selected a place in full shade with natural protection from wind and sun. But it wasn't until the third evening that Quarrah had found the egg.

It was resting in a low grassy ravine, an overhang of rocks

providing the textbook shade and shelter. The gelatinous orb was a rich gold color, distinctly marking it as that of a bull.

Quarrah had retrieved the egg the following morning, dragging the Drift crate to the site. She had been afraid to approach the egg, even though Lence Raismus had explained that the sows left them unattended to allow a bull to carry it away for fertilization.

But that morning, as Quarrah ignited a cloud of Drift Grit and loaded the egg into the crate, she couldn't shake the feeling that something was watching her.

Quarrah was worried now, making the descent. It was midafternoon on her fourth day in the mountains. If Quarrah didn't make it back to the harbor by nightfall, there was a real possibility that she'd miss Tanalin's departure.

Quarrah knew there was little possibility of sneaking back onto the *Crown's Ashing*. Her cargo would be much too cumbersome. Quarrah would need to change her tactic for the sail home.

She was going to have to claim the Fourth Decree.

Quarrah knew it wouldn't work, since her name was not on any arriving ship's manifest. She would have to appeal to the mercy of Tanalin Phor.

Tanalin had to suspect that Quarrah had crept aboard the *Crown's Ashing*. She'd actually given Quarrah the idea! Surely, the Harvesting captain wouldn't abandon Quarrah to the wilds of Pekal. The next Moon Passing was less than two weeks away, and that would definitely finish her off. Well, the Moon Passing might finish everyone off anyway, if Ard didn't have something brilliant up his sleeve.

Quarrah rubbed that numbing leaf between her blistering palms and felt the momentary cool relief. She took another sip from her water skin and convinced herself that it was time to get moving. According to her mental map, she was only a few miles from the harbor. Assuming nothing unexpected happened, she'd reach the ship by dark.

Quarrah had just ignited a fresh bit of Drift Grit in the crate's hopper when something came crashing through the underbrush behind her. It wasn't the first deer or hog that had startled her, but Quarrah spun with a sharp intake of breath.

There was a person standing in the brush, head tipped slightly to one side, face downcast. It was a woman, dressed in filthy rags, dark blue skin identifying her as a Trothian.

As sunlight dappled through the branches overhead, the woman reached up and tucked stringy strands of black hair behind her ear. Quarrah saw her face clearly.

It was Ulusal.

"Sparks," Quarrah muttered. "Ulusal!" She was alive! Quarrah had never thought it possible. A wave of relief washed over her—relief from the guilt of abandonment that she hadn't realized she still felt. Quarrah stepped toward her old crew mate as Ulusal's head snapped up.

Those eyes. They were lifeless, crimson. Like pools of blood.

Oh, flames! In the exuberance of seeing Ulusal, Quarrah had forgotten the primary rule of Pekal. The Moon Passing had changed this woman.

Ulusal opened her mouth, a bloodstained slit with missing teeth, but no sound escaped her torn lips. The woman sprinted forward, blundering haplessly through the underbrush, clipping her shoulder against a stout tree.

Quarrah gasped, scrambling backward. What the blazes was happening? She'd never seen a Moonsick person up close. Let alone someone she had known!

"Ulusal!" Quarrah shouted. "It's me. It's Quarrah Khai!" There was absolutely no recognition in those terrible eyes. The Trothian looked almost corpse-like, her body stiff, and movements jarring. Her skin was deeply cracked and flaking, deprived of a saltwater soak for weeks now. But she moved with surprising speed and a frantic sort of desperation.

It had been a full cycle. Ulusal's Moonsickness would be well into the third stage, her cognitive abilities drowned out by a driving need for violence that overruled any sense of self-control.

"Get away!" Quarrah shrieked as the frightening version of Ulusal closed the distance between them. What was she supposed to do, stand and fight?

Run! Quarrah could lead the demented Ulusal into the forest. Then she could circle back, grab the Drift crate and make a final dash to the harbor.

As Quarrah turned, Ulusal seemed to change tactics. Instead of giving chase, the sick woman fell upon the Drift crate. She threw her body against the side, fingers clawing at the airtight boards, leaving bloody streaks across the crate.

Ulusal must have sensed the gelatinous egg inside—something organic with potential for life—and it seemed to enhance her frenzy.

Ulusal's fingers were bent at odd angles, as though the bones had already been broken in a previous rage. The flesh of her hands was torn and oozing, but no semblance of pain crossed her deranged face.

"Hey!" Quarrah didn't dare advance a single step toward Ulusal, but she couldn't let the Trothian's fury reach the gelatinous egg.

Quarrah stooped and picked up a fist-sized rock. She hurled it at Ulusal, the stone striking the sick woman's shoulder. The rock thudded to the ground, but Ulusal didn't even turn.

One of the crate's boards was peeling back, Ulusal redoubling her efforts at the success. Quarrah swung the pack from her shoulders and reached inside, fumbling for the Singler she had swiped from the *Crown's Ashing*.

Quarrah quickly loaded the Blast cartridge into the empty chamber. With trembling fingers, she dropped in the lead ball, using the gun's tamping rod to pack the shot. Snapping the chamber closed, Quarrah pulled back the Slagstone hammer, slipped her index finger over the cold smooth trigger, and took aim.

"Ulusal!" Quarrah screamed. But the woman ripping at the crate was not the Trothian who had been a part of Ard's Harvesting crew. The sickness had taken her. What Quarrah saw here was a monster, masquerading in the dried skin of an old companion.

"I'm sorry!" Quarrah squeezed the trigger.

In a puff of Blast smoke, the Singler cracked, spitting fire. The ball didn't have to travel far, and Quarrah saw a spray of blood as the piece of hot lead tore into Ulusal's neck. The Trothian woman buckled, tumbling away from the Drift crate and landing heavily in the dirt.

Quarrah lowered the gun slowly. Her hand was shaking now, though it had been still when the shot was fired. While the idea of what Quarrah had just done made her sick, she knew that ending Ulusal's life had been a favor to the suffering woman.

Quarrah leaned through the clearing smoke, drawing a few uncertain steps toward the downed body. The Drift crate would need some repairs before it would hold a detonation airtight, but Quarrah couldn't work on the box so near the dead woman.

She reached down to pick up her pack, when Ulusal suddenly sprang from the dirt. Quarrah screamed, the large Trothian falling upon her with silent mouth open wide.

What was this devilry? Hadn't Quarrah's shot killed the poor woman?

They rolled to the side, and Quarrah managed to slip free. Ulusal's body was covered in blood. Quarrah couldn't count the wounds, though all of them looked roughly scabbed.

As Ulusal crouched in the tall grass, Quarrah saw the hole in the side of the woman's neck where her lead ball had entered. A yellowish foam was frothing at the damaged flesh, staunching the blood flow and clotting the wound. Quarrah had heard that Moonsick victims had bodies that were more resilient to damage. But what was this? The sickness was *healing* Ulusal?

Quarrah fumbled for the thin-bladed short sword on her pack.

It was a standard item, used by Harvesters to hack through Pekal's dense vegetation. The tip of the weapon had barely cleared Quarrah's scabbard, when Ulusal sprang forward.

Quarrah leapt back, swinging the sword in a way she hoped would intimidate her opponent. Ulusal seemed oblivious to the careening blade. It was more than the fact that she was blind. It seemed as though Ulusal didn't care about the danger.

"Back!" Quarrah yelled, though *she* was the one making a steady retreat. "Get back! I will kill you!"

The threats, the weapons—nothing seemed to dissuade Ulusal from coming forward, her broken, bloody hands reaching out, clawing at the air in manic gestures.

Ulusal suddenly pounced like a cat. Quarrah shut her eyes and swung the thin sword. Not for the head, that was just too brutal, but she had to stop this horrendous monster! Quarrah felt the blade sink in, initially soft, then jarring against something hard. A warm spray spattered up her arm and across her face. Despite all these obvious signs, Quarrah thought she must have missed because there was no scream of pain, no grunt of shock. It was absolutely silent.

Quarrah's eyes snapped open and what she saw sickened her. The sword was buried in Ulusal's left shoulder. Her collarbone was shattered, and her arm dangled, barely attached. Everywhere Quarrah looked was red.

But Ulusal's face was a mask at odds with the rest of her body. The woman showed no pain or discomfort, only that same frenzied expression, damaged mouth still agape.

Quarrah's hand slipped from the hilt of the short sword. The blade remained embedded in Ulusal's shoulder, blood and yellow foam fountaining around the hard steel. Quarrah fell to the earth, scooting on her backside to get away, as Ulusal resumed her advance.

What more could Quarrah do? She'd shot her. She'd hacked her.

And still, Ulusal was unfazed. Quarrah needed heavier weaponry. A few Grit pots were stashed in her pack. If she could get to it, there might be something useful in taking down this monster.

Hurling a useless handful of dirt at Ulusal's face, Quarrah began crawling. Ulusal paused, her dirty nose sniffing the air, head cocking to one side as she listened. Then she lunged in a silent fury, missing Quarrah by mere inches as she leapt up and ran the final distance to the pack.

Quarrah dumped out the contents, trying desperately to remember where she had stored those Grit pots. A handful tumbled into the dirt, and Quarrah snatched a few, turning them over to see what markings they bore.

Drift Grit. So much Drift Grit! It was to be expected with the task she had been undertaking. But Quarrah needed Barrier Grit. If she had brought any, there wasn't time to dig through the pack looking for it. Ah! She'd never be so unprepared if Raek were still alive to outfit her!

Ulusal had risen again, her wounded arm looking even more likely to fall off now that the sword had dislodged.

With a pot of Drift Grit in hand, Quarrah ran back along the trail, trying to think of a way to eliminate the deranged enemy. Quarrah could Drift Jump into a tree, but judging by the look in Ulusal's blind red eyes, the afflicted Trothian would tear down the trunk before giving up.

Perhaps Quarrah could use the Drift Grit like a trap. Capture Ulusal in a weightless cloud and escape with the crate before the Trothian managed to get free. But Ulusal was moving too quickly. If the Trothian entered the Drift cloud at a run, she'd float right through and exit out the other side.

Quarrah turned sharply and ducked into a cluster of large broken rocks. Maybe if she held very still, careful to make no sound at all, the blind Ulusal would wander past, grow frustrated, and move on to exercise her violence elsewhere. Hopefully they were far enough from the Drift crate that Ulusal wouldn't find her way back to the egg.

Quarrah took a series of deep breaths, trying to regulate her oxygen flow so she could breathe naturally without gasping in fear. She was still sputtering nervously when Ulusal stepped into view. Against her better judgment, Quarrah drew in a deep breath and held it. She would need to exhale eventually, and when she did, the chase would be on again. But if Quarrah could hold out long enough, perhaps she could think of something.

Ulusal stood in the trail, head tilted in that unnatural way. The only sound she made was an occasional sniff. Quarrah had heard that Moonsick victims had an acute sense of smell, and their hearing was unrivaled.

Move on, Quarrah screamed inside her own head. *Just keep walking!*

A sharp sniff. Ulusal's head tilted another direction. Her damaged face was staring straight at Quarrah now. Ulusal's eyes were wide, but her sockets were filled with sightless crimson orbs. Like miniature versions of the Red Moon that caused this malady.

Quarrah's lungs were going to burst. Ulusal took a shuffling, curious step toward the rocks where Quarrah crouched, the Trothian's mangled hands stroking the air.

A horrific, brutal idea occurred to Quarrah. But she'd have to act quickly.

Quarrah gasped for air, the sound causing Ulusal's head to snap up. At the same moment, Quarrah shattered the pot of Drift Grit at her feet, casting a small cloud around her and the rocks.

Bracing herself against one of the rocks that was lodged in the ground, Quarrah reached out and picked up a large boulder, her arms barely reaching halfway around its jagged surface. In the weightless environment, Quarrah managed the stone quite easily, keeping her legs anchored against the rooted rock behind her.

Ulusal broke into a maniacal sprint, damaged arm trailing behind and twitching as the other clawed savagely in Quarrah's direction. Quarrah paused for only a second, leveraging herself against the grounded stones behind her, and hurling the boulder.

The rough boulder exited the Drift cloud, immediately subject to gravity's natural pull. But it had height, and a little velocity. And Ulusal was utterly reckless, unflinching as the large stone came down on her.

It smashed into the Trothian with a horrifying sound. The weight of the rock threw her backward, crushing Ulusal against the dirt before rolling a few more feet.

Quarrah pushed off the grounded stones and drifted out of the cloud. She didn't want to look at the mess on the trail, but she had to be sure that Ulusal wouldn't rise again.

There was no chance of it. The only bit of the Trothian that was even remotely recognizable was her legs, which the tumbling boulder had somehow missed. On Ulusal's left calf was a bandage, so filthy and shredded that Quarrah couldn't believe it was still there. It covered Ulusal's first injury. The gunshot wound that had caused Quarrah and the rest of the crew to leave her behind.

Quarrah felt suddenly light-headed and sick to her stomach. She turned away from the carnage and staggered down the trail to the damaged Drift crate. She needed to fix the cracked board so the crate would properly house a Drift Grit detonation and lighten her load. She needed to check on the gelatinous egg and make sure it wasn't damaged in the attack.

But Quarrah couldn't bring herself to do any of those things. Instead, she slumped to the dirt and stared into the trees. Unblinking. Unmoving.

It must have been an hour before Quarrah felt like she could move again. At last, she pulled herself up, still shaking. She rifled through her pack and found a measure of Drift Grit. Tearing off the end of the paper cartridge, she poured the contents into the funnel-shaped hopper chamber in the side of the Drift Grit. Closing the seal, she found the long key ignitor and stuck it into the keyhole.

She paused. Ulusal had done significant damage to the corner of the crate. A hole that size was likely to cause a loss of containment of the Drift cloud. Quarrah stepped back, trying to devise a way to patch it. She was so underprepared for this kind of setback. No real tools or materials. Quarrah thought of using the shirt off her back, but she wasn't sure if the material would be thick enough to hold the detonation.

Quarrah suddenly remembered that run-down old tenement on Dal Street where she had spent her sixteenth birthday. That winter had been cold, and the sill had fallen out of the room's only window. When Quarrah had complained to the landlady, the cranky spinster had given her a bucket of water and a wheelbarrow full of dirt. The patchwork had been crude but effective.

Quarrah drew her knife and began digging through the soil. This was the windward side of Pekal, so the earth was already moist. She had a heap of loose dirt in a matter of minutes. Unstopping her water skin, Quarrah poured what she had left onto the pile and began working it until the dirt had become a thick, muddy paste.

Using handfuls of the mixture, she packed it into the damaged corner of the Drift crate. It wasn't pretty, but it filled the gap nicely. Quarrah inserted the ignition key and detonated the Grit, her eyes on the patch.

Homeland be praised, her mud seal was successful in containing the cloud! She grabbed the front carrying poles and continued down the mountainside, the back poles dragging ruts in the ground as the crate bumped and bounced over the uneven terrain.

It was significantly easier once Quarrah reached the well-trod shoreline trail. The mud had dried on her hands, but she felt blisters raw and painful underneath. Quarrah was pulling as fast as she could, but it was already dusk.

She needed to be at the harbor *now*. No, she needed to be at the harbor an hour ago. There was a chance that Tanalin's crew might still be days out, but if they had been quick to Harvest their Slag-stone, then they could be departing to sail through the night.

What was she going to do when she reached the harbor, anyway? Sneaking away from the *Crown's Ashing* had been simple. Getting back on board with a stolen Drift crate full of dragon egg would be something else.

Quarrah reached the harbor long before she had any kind of a plan. It was fully dark, but she'd been following the glow of the tall lighthouse that overlooked the harbor. From her place on this raised bluff, Quarrah could see past the gate and checkpoint and down to the ships waiting below.

A large detonation of Light Grit had been set above the docks, and Quarrah could see dozens of figures milling around the *Crown's Ashing*.

Tanalin's crew was back. They were loading the ship for departure. Quarrah could see all the equipment from their expedition arranged on the docks.

Quarrah saw three other ships below, quiet and out of the light. Smuggling her crate onto one of those would be far more doable. One of the ships would belong to the harbor Regulation. It wouldn't depart until just before sunset on the night of the Passing. Quarrah didn't have the supplies to survive that long in the wilds of Pekal.

There was no way to know the schedules of the two other ships. One of them had been in the harbor when she arrived, so it would stand to reason that it should be departing soon. But there was no telling where those other ships would sail. The last thing she needed was to end up on Talumon or Strind with the dragon egg.

Quarrah needed to get aboard the *Crown's Ashing*. And she needed to do it before they finished loading.

Pekal's harbors were developed with security in mind. From her position, the only reasonable way to reach the docks with a Drift crate was by descending a wide man-made ramp that switch-backed twice. At the bottom of the ramp, Quarrah would need to pass through the checkpoint gate—the only break in the wall that skirted the entire harbor.

Picking up the blazing Drift crate once more, Quarrah started down the dark ramp. Tanalin's crew had either arrived before nightfall, or been on the docks long enough that any Light Grit used to illuminate the ramp had burned out.

Still, Quarrah knew she would be seen. And the Regulators would stop her. It left her with only one recourse, and she didn't have much confidence in her ability to pull it off.

Surprisingly, Quarrah reached the bottom of the ramp without attracting any attention. She was aware of the Drift crate's rear poles *thump-thump*ing across the wooden planks of the walkway as she moved toward the gate. At least it was still open! Although a bright cloud of Light Grit hung directly above it. Even from here, Quarrah could see three Reggies in the checkpoint booth beside the gate.

Quarrah ducked her head low and pressed forward, holding her breath against the inevitable confrontation. She actually passed through the open gate, which was farther than she expected to make it.

Quarrah was twenty feet onto the damp docks when she heard the Regulator shout from behind her.

"Hoy! Stop right there!"

Instead of halting, Quarrah picked up her pace. Every foot closer to the *Crown's Ashing* increased her chances of pulling this off.

She heard running footsteps from the Regulators behind, but Quarrah didn't stop until she heard the click of a Roller hammer beside her ear. Slowly, Quarrah lowered the Drift crate to the dock and turned to face the Reggie, hands raised.

"I claim the Fourth Decree," Quarrah muttered. "I came here with a Harvesting ship earlier this cycle, but I was separated from my crew. The law states that you are required to allow me and my belongings to board that ship and receive safe passage back to the Greater Chain."

"Oh, you think you know the law?" asked the Reggie with the gun. His partner stood just beside him, a deep dimple in his chin full of whiskers.

"I claim the Fourth Decree," Quarrah said again. This needed to work.

"I heard you the first time," the Reggie replied. "If your paperwork checks out, we'll get you on the king's ship out of here." When Quarrah didn't respond, the Reggie shrugged impatiently. "Let's see those papers!"

"Don't have them," admitted Quarrah. She'd feel a lot better if he'd lower that blazing Roller. "Lost them." She tried to remember how she had lied so convincingly as Azania Fyse. Those skills felt rusty now, and Quarrah hoped it wouldn't give her away.

"Well, why don't we start with your name?"

"I don't..." She couldn't make something up. They'd check whatever name she gave them against earlier manifests. "I don't know."

"Don't know your name?" The Regulator let out an incredulous laugh. "You're not doing yourself too many favors, miss."

"Sparks, Hedris," the dimple-chinned Reggie said to his companion. "Lighten up. Look at her. Homeland knows what this lady's been through out there."

Quarrah suddenly realized that she must have looked something awful, caked in dried mud and speckled with Ulusal's blood. She hadn't had time to clean herself up. The only thing that mattered was getting off Pekal with the dragon egg.

"Can anyone verify your identity?" chin Reggie asked.

Finally, something was going right! This might work after all. "Tanalin Phor," said Quarrah. "Tanalin Phor can vouch for me."

The two Regulators looked at one another. Then the one with the chin said, "I'll fetch her." He took off in the direction of the *Crown's Ashing.*

Well, all hope was now resting on Tanalin. It was an idea so risky that Quarrah would never have resorted to it if she'd seen any other way. Tanalin would have to lie on her behalf. She'd have to tell the Regulators that Quarrah was not an undocumented poacher. But a part of her believed it would work. Tanalin had all but invited her to stow away. Quarrah was hoping that the Harvesting captain wouldn't get hung up on semantics now.

Sooner than Quarrah expected, she saw the Reggie returning along the docks. At his side was the athletic figure of Tanalin Phor.

Quarrah drew in a deep breath when Tanalin saw her, bright light perfectly illuminating her face. Quarrah didn't know what to make of the captain's expression. It wasn't surprise so much as appraisal.

"Woman says you'll vouch for her, Captain," said the Regulator who was waiting at Quarrah's side. "Trying to claim the Fourth Decree, but she can't seem to remember her own name!"

Tanalin stood just out of arm's reach, eyeing Quarrah from head to foot, studying her filthy appearance. Quarrah stared straight ahead, her gaze fixed over the dark harbor, unwilling to look Tanalin in the eye. Her heart was pounding, and every second seemed to draw out like dripping honey.

"Can't you see she took a blow to the head?" said Tanalin. "Poor woman's been on Pekal since the first week of the cycle. You were a Harvester in Captain Munyan's crew, weren't you?"

Quarrah broke her distant gaze to look directly at Tanalin. "Yes," she muttered. "Yes, I was…"

Tanalin strode past Quarrah to inspect the damaged Drift crate. Only now was Quarrah realizing that it didn't look much better than she did, smeared with dried blood.

"And you carried this down by yourself?" Tanalin tapped softly on the side of the crate.

"I did."

"Equipment from your crew, I presume?" said Tanalin.

"Small piece of Slagstone," Quarrah answered. "Tools."

It was a ludicrous story. Quarrah was a terrible liar. Tanalin surely knew what was in the Drift crate. Quarrah had told the captain her reason for coming to Pekal. Still, Tanalin looked impressed—no, astonished—that someone with as little experience as Quarrah could successfully extract a gelatinous egg.

Tanalin circled around the Drift crate and spoke to the two Regulators. "We're good here. You can make a note that I've personally inspected the woman's cargo. Looks like everything checks out."

"We still need her name for our records," said the gun Reggie.

"Why don't you bring me the last cycle's worth of manifests and we can look it over together?" Tanalin said.

"We'll get them over to you right away," said the chin.

"In the meantime," Tanalin said, "would you two be so kind as to load this woman's Drift crate onto the *Crown's Ashing*?"

At last, the Regulator holstered his Roller. With his companion taking the back poles, the two men hoisted the crate and moved down the docks.

Slowly, Quarrah turned to look at Tanalin. The captain was staring up at the dark hillside of Pekal, a distant expression on her face.

"Tanalin," Quarrah whispered. "Thank you."

"Well, I can't leave you here," she replied, her attention turning away from the mountain grandeur. "This island is wicked."

"You'll be able to clear my name on the manifest?" Quarrah asked.

"I'll make something work," she answered. "This is a different shift of Regulators from the ones who were here during Captain Munyan's expedition. I can convince them that there was a discrepancy."

"Thank you," Quarrah said again. She realized what Tanalin was risking. "When do we sail?"

"At first light," answered Tanalin.

Now it was Quarrah's turn to cast a glance at the dark mountain. "I hope I never come back." She turned to Tanalin. "How do you do it?"

"It's all I know anymore." Tanalin's expression darkened as she gestured toward the InterIsland Waters and the Greater Chain. "I've got nothing out there." Her voice was a whisper.

"There was a time when I didn't have anything, either," Quarrah said.

"That's why you became a thief?"

"Sometimes you have to chase the things you want."

"And sometimes you have to *stop* chasing them," said Tanalin.

Quarrah nodded. "It took Ardor a long time to figure that out."

"You think he has?"

Quarrah realized that the captain wasn't just talking about Ard's feelings for Tanalin. She was talking about his lifestyle. The insatiable drive of the ruse artist.

"Did Ardor ever tell you about his death?" Tanalin asked. "Did he tell you why he did it?"

"The husk of dragon scales." No, Quarrah hadn't heard it from Ard. But Raek had told her enough.

Tanalin nodded. "Once he decided to take it, he couldn't stop chasing it. He gave up everything he had to steal that husk." She stepped forward and gripped Quarrah's shoulder. "Ardor doesn't know when to stop. He gave me up for a husk of dragon scales. What's he chasing now?"

Quarrah didn't respond, staring back at Tanalin in the steady illumination of the harbor Light Grit. The captain's words upset her. Tanalin didn't know Ardor Benn like she did.

"He'll stop," Quarrah finally managed. "Ard has to see this through. Just a little farther. Then it'll all be over."

"Will it?" Tanalin asked. "How far will he try to push you, Quarrah? Sparks! Just look at what you've done for him. You're covered in blood, for Homeland's sake!"

Quarrah didn't answer, but Tanalin dropped her hand and stepped away. She had a point. Ardor Benn had pushed Quarrah into doing things she never would have done on her own. But that wasn't all bad, was it? The Islehood taught that the Homeland wanted people to progress. Ard had forced Quarrah way out of her comfort zone, but she was a better person for it. She was proud of her accomplishments over the last year.

"Keep your head down," Tanalin instructed, striding toward the *Crown's Ashing*. "Someone in the crew might recognize you as our escaped prisoner." Quarrah moved to keep up with the captain. "And take a minute to wash yourself off. You look terrible."

Quarrah cast a final glance over her shoulder at the towering blackness of Pekal. This place took too much out of people. She hoped to the Homeland that she'd never find her way back here.

~

My scribing must be brief. There is little time left. I am running. If I do not reach the harbor in time, this writing will fall into the hands of a deranged monster.

CHAPTER

41

Quarrah leapt down from the wagon's driving bench, pausing beside the blood-spattered Drift crate lashed to the back. All was quiet around the butchery hideout, and Quarrah couldn't help but feel extremely nervous. She had been gone less than a week, but a lot could happen to an injured, wanted man in that amount of time.

Quarrah was back in her city, having survived a second venture to Pekal. She had scrubbed herself clean on the *Crown's Ashing*, and with her feet on Beripent roads, Quarrah's terrifying ordeal with Ulusal seemed like a fading nightmare.

It would be dark in about an hour. Standing outside the butcher shop, Quarrah was anxious to see Ard. But she was too uneasy about leaving the Drift crate and its precious contents unattended in the quiet street.

She crossed to the dilapidated shopfront door and knocked. Who was she kidding? Ard wasn't going to answer the door, regardless of his health. The only people who pounded on doors in this part of town were Reggies.

"Quarrah Khai." The voice came from behind, causing Quarrah to whirl around. Lyndel stood beside the wagon. There was a thin sword strapped to her hip now, and the wooden butt of a Roller rose from a holster on her thigh.

"Lyndel," Quarrah sighed with relief. "Where were you?"

She gestured across the street to a derelict building. "I watch the shop to make sure no one finds him."

"Is it safe for you to be here?" Politically, it was obvious that nothing had changed during Quarrah's days away. King Pethredote's expulsion order was clearly still in effect, though Quarrah was relieved to see that the unchecked violence in the streets had ceased. It had been terrible for a few days following the king's announcement. Now that the general fear and frenzy had subsided, it seemed like the king's order was being carried out in a much more civilized manner. More deportations and fewer hapless murders. Just that afternoon, Quarrah had seen an entire ship of Trothians leaving the harbor.

"It is not safe for me anywhere," said the priestess, scratching at her arm. Quarrah noticed that the woman's blue skin looked chapped and dry. The need for a saltwater soak would eventually drive all the Trothians to the sea. The Regulators would be waiting for them, ready to pack them up and ship them back to their islets.

"I'm so sorry, Lyndel," Quarrah said. "What are you going to do?"

"I have distrusted your king for many cycles now," said Lyndel. "My people are made furious by his betrayal. All my time with Isle Halavend, I was anxious to get back to the islets. But after what Pethredote has done, there are many of us who will not go quietly."

"You're going to stay and fight?" Fight who? The Regulation? Lyndel was hinting at war. But it was a war she couldn't hope to win, outnumbered as her people were in Beripent.

"Isle Halavend did not want his discoveries to lead to violence," said Lyndel. "But my people stand ready to move at my command. They will fight for this cause. They will fight for Ardor's *Kram Udal.*"

"*Kram Udal?*" Quarrah had never heard those words before.

"The Paladin Visitant," Lyndel whispered.

Ardor's Paladin Visitant? The way Lyndel was talking made it sound like Ard had learned what he needed to make the detonation work. Perhaps the conversation with King Pethredote had been worthwhile, and Raek's death was not a total waste.

Lyndel placed a hand on the dirty Drift crate strapped to the wagon. "You found what Ardor asked for?"

Quarrah nodded. "It was no easy task." Sparks, it was probably the most difficult thing she'd done in her entire life. Certainly the most frightening. "What is he planning, Lyndel?"

"Ardor is a man of many ideas," said the priestess. "There is a Trothian saying. Feed the strongest ox first, or none will be well enough to pull the feed wagon."

Quarrah wrinkled her forehead, trying to decipher the phrase. "Is Ard the ox or the feed wagon?"

Lyndel smiled a half smile. "Ardor Benn is mankind's greatest chance at survival right now. My people will support him. They will fight and die because I have told them that Ardor pulls the feed wagon."

So he's the ox. Quarrah scratched her head. She still didn't understand exactly how the Trothian saying applied to this situation. But it was enough to know that Lyndel had pledged her people to their cause. Whatever Ard was planning, he wouldn't have to undertake it alone.

Lyndel gestured toward the butcher shop. "Go see him." Quarrah cast a hesitant glance at the Drift crate, still unwilling to leave it unattended. "I will guard it," Lyndel said, noting her obvious concern.

Quarrah thanked Lyndel and turned, pushing through the squeaky door of the butchery shopfront. Crossing the room, she pulled open the cellar entrance, descending hastily into the earthy dugout, the faint glow of a small Light Grit detonation illuminating the way.

"Lyndel," Ard's voice sounded. "I was thinking we could..."

He trailed off when he saw Quarrah. Ard was standing—that was a good sign. But as he muttered her name, he staggered slightly, collapsing onto his heap of a straw bed.

"Praise the Homeland you're back." Ard smiled that roguish smile, melting Quarrah's insides. It had been almost three weeks since she'd seen him on his feet, heading to the palace with Raek, the pair of them filled with confidence.

So much had happened since then. Now that she was facing him again, Quarrah didn't know how to explain everything she'd done. *I found the dragon egg, brutally killed Ulusal, and hitched a ride with your old girlfriend.*

"How are you feeling?" she asked instead.

"Well, I burned through all the Health Grit." Ard gritted his teeth. "I'm not out of the woods yet, but I'm doing much better. Lyndel's been checking in on me."

"I got it, Ard," Quarrah whispered, unable to hold back the news any longer. "I got the dragon egg from Pekal."

Ard's gaze, already steady, seemed to intensify a hundredfold. "You're sure it's a bull?"

She nodded. "Lence Raismus told me what to look for in the different genders of the gelatinous eggs, and I found—"

Ard cut her off, springing from his mattress and crossing the room in a blur. Their lips met, forceful yet somehow delicate. Quarrah felt her body trembling as he tucked back a strand of her hair. His hand lingered on her neck, so warm and familiar.

Their lips parted, but their faces remained close, foreheads pressed gently together. Quarrah's eyes were closed, but she thought she could *hear* Ardor smiling.

He pulled away suddenly. Quarrah's eyes snapped open, the intoxicating moment falling away as Ard winced in pain, gripping at his wounded leg. She caught him by the arm, and in a few steps they were both seated upon the straw mattress.

"Nothing like a broken leg to spoil the moment." Ard reached out and took her hand. "You're something else, Quarrah Khai."

For once, she didn't even blush. Quarrah had craved a moment like this. It felt so real. So…right. Quarrah pushed Tanalin's warnings even further from her mind. Tanalin didn't know this man like Quarrah did.

They sat side by side in the dimness of the dugout butchery, the malodorous surroundings a strange juxtaposition to the feelings in her chest. For a moment, she was content not to know the answers about Ard's plans. She was perfectly satisfied not to think of dragon eggs, Moonsickness, and Paladin Visitants.

"I don't want anything to change," Quarrah whispered. Ard looked at her sharply. Almost accusatory. "Between us, I mean," she added. Why couldn't this moment, this *feeling*, last forever?

"Change," he mumbled. "Everything changes. If we're not changing, we're Settled."

"That's awfully Wayfarist, coming from you, Ardor Benn."

"I understand so much now," he replied. "About the Homeland."

"What do you mean?" Quarrah hadn't expected this level of spiritualism from Ard. But then, the man had undergone so much with his injuries and Raek's death. Grief had a way of defining one's beliefs. It either drew people closer to the Homeland, or turned them Settled.

"The summer Raek's parents died..." Ard closed his eyes, as if deep in thought. "I was fifteen—fresh out of school. Raek had been tutoring me for a couple of years, so the two of us were already into a lot of shenanigans." He chuckled quietly. "After the accident, Raek came to stay with my parents and me. He was old enough to be on his own, but I thought he needed us. Still, Raek spent a lot of time off on his own. My folks said that was right. Said he needed time to grieve. Some nights he didn't come home at all."

Ard opened his eyes, but he wouldn't look at Quarrah. She noticed silent tears welling.

"One night I woke up with a real twist in my gut," Ard continued. "Couldn't shake it. Finally decided it was the Homeland Urging me to get outside. It was the night of a Moon Passing, so I didn't need any light. I took off down the street. I felt led by the Urgings, and soon I was running, though I didn't know where I was going. Ended up clear out on the eastern coastline of Beripent. That's where I found Raek."

Ard sniffed, and Quarrah wondered if he would go on.

"He was standing at the shoreline cliff," Ard whispered. "Blazing toes hanging right off the edge. I saw him in the red light of the Moon and I screamed his name so loud my throat felt like it ripped. He turned and looked at me. Wasn't crying or anything. But I was. He stepped away from the edge and we sat there at the shoreline, watching the big Moon crawl across the night sky. Talking about our dreams, about girls, about anything except the reason he was there. When the sun came up, we headed down to this tavern in the Eastern Quarter and ate all the pastries, bacon, and eggs we could manage. Sparks, that guy could eat..."

Ard's voice cracked with a sob, the tears falling faster than

Quarrah could brush them away. He didn't say anything, pressing his face into Quarrah's shoulder as she cradled his head.

After a moment, he seemed to compose himself. Ard looked at her, those brown eyes glistening in the dwindling glow of the Prolonged Light Grit detonation.

"The Homeland Urged Raek and me together," Ard said. "It needed us together so we would do the things we've done. The Homeland has always driven me forward. Maybe not in the exact way the Islehood preaches, but does it matter that they have it wrong? I was never truly *Settled*. Even in my darkest moments, something Urged me to go on. The Homeland has brought me to this very moment. I know what I have to do now, but there's no way to be sure it will work."

"What are you talking about, Ard?" she asked. "What did you learn from King Pethredote?" It was high time to get some answers about what happened on that dreaded night of Raek's death.

"We have a plan, Quarrah." She noticed how he didn't answer her question. "Isle Halavend had Lyndel smuggle a lot of valuable text out of the Mooring before he died."

Quarrah nodded. She remembered seeing the pages scattered across the floor of Lyndel's apartment.

"Lyndel and I have worked everything out," Ard continued. "I understand why the old Isle spoke so highly of her. She's brilliant. Lyndel is committed to this cause, Quarrah. She believes in the research, and she'll do anything to protect and preserve her people."

"I spoke with her outside," Quarrah replied. "She said the Trothians are willing to follow you." *That's what people do—follow Ardor Benn*. Quarrah remembered Raek's words.

"The Trothians don't truly understand what's at stake," Ard said. "No one does. But Lyndel has persuaded them that our cause is of the utmost importance. They will stand and fight when the time comes."

"When the time comes for what?" Quarrah asked. "Tell me what you're doing, Ard. Why did you need a dragon egg? Why is Lyndel rallying the Trothians?"

He took both her hands in his. "I'm going to detonate the Visitant Grit," Ard continued. It didn't answer her questions, and it brought up a whole slew of new ones.

"But despite all my efforts to correct my mistakes," said Ard, "I worry that the Homeland will find me unworthy."

Was this the reason Ard had been waxing spiritual lately? He wanted to make himself worthy of a Paladin Visitant. But was it enough to reform? The Islehood taught that a worthy Wayfarist was one who had never wavered in belief of the Homeland.

"I feel that I am almost ready, Quarrah. But there is one more mistake I need to rectify," said Ard. "I abandoned a good Wayfarist on Pekal."

"Nemery Baggish?" That was Ard's biggest guilt? He hadn't really abandoned the girl. In fact, he'd risked a lot to arrange her passage with Tanalin. And according to the Harvesting captain, Nemery was now safely home with her mother. Of course, Quarrah couldn't very well tell that to Ard without letting him know that she'd spoken with Tanalin Phor.

"I've got to find her." Ard struggled to rise, falling back with another wince of pain. "I have to know if Nemery still considers me a worthy Wayfarist after what I did."

"You're in no shape to go anywhere." Quarrah put a heavy hand on his shoulder. "Besides, you're the most wanted man in the Greater Chain." She paused. "I'm sure the girl has forgiven you."

"It's more than that," Ard whispered. "I need to give her a message. I have to tell her—'*The prepared shall stand untouched, like a spire of stone amidst a blaze.*'"

"A scripture?" Of all the things!

"It's a verse about preparing for a Paladin Visitant," Ard explained. "I need Nemery to know that we succeeded in getting the Grit."

"Why does it matter?" Weren't there more important things to do right now?

"My worthiness may depend on it." He looked pained. "Nemery was only willing to justify my Settled acts because she knew I was trying to create Visitant Grit. If she thinks I failed…"

Quarrah sighed. "If this is really so important to you, I can go."

Ard's expression softened, and Quarrah knew that her offer had been just what he needed to hear. Sparks, she'd do nearly anything for that man. After Quarrah's ordeal on Pekal, checking on Nemery Baggish seemed a minuscule favor. Besides, wasn't this why she had stayed with Ard through such a long ruse? Tending to each other, doing each other favors, providing a shoulder to cry on. This was belonging.

"It's not just important to me," Ard said. "Nemery's feelings may determine whether or not I'm worthy of the Paladin Visitant who can save us all."

"What's the verse, again?" she asked, quoting it back after Ard repeated it.

She kissed the side of Ard's head and stood up. It would probably only take her a few hours to locate the girl. Quarrah had an idea where Nemery lived from talking with Tanalin on the voyage back from Pekal.

Ard leaned back and closed his eyes, sighing as though a great weight had been lifted from his shoulders. "I'll tell you everything the moment you get back. Pethredote, the egg, our plan…" He took a deep breath. "Everything."

She didn't press the matter. Of course, Quarrah wanted answers now, but Ard looked so weary. It would do him good to rest. He could launch into the full explanation when his emotions weren't so near the surface.

"I'll tell Lyndel to stay with the wagon." Quarrah crossed to the stairwell, pausing halfway up. "Thank you, Ard."

His eyes opened. "For what?"

She thought of Tanalin Phor, with no sense of belonging outside the Harvesting job she hated. In comparison, Quarrah felt like she was right where she was meant to be. She might have said she was *settled* in this new life, if the word didn't have such a sinful connotation.

"For helping me find my place."

He smiled, and Quarrah moved swiftly out of the dugout.

~

*I feel death's kiss upon my face. I am
betrothed to the grave.*

CHAPTER

42

A rd glanced over his shoulder to check the straps holding the Drift crate in the back of the wagon. Everything was still secure, despite the bumpy ride they had taken through the back streets of Beripent.

"Turn here." Lyndel leaned across the driving bench and pointed down a dark pathway leading into the Char. The path was not designed for a horse and wagon, but Ard was sure they would fit.

So much was riding on tonight. Everything, really. Ard felt a stab of anxiety at the thought of what was ahead. He felt up to the task, at least physically. His damaged leg and shoulder were actually much better than he'd led Quarrah to believe. He might still favor them, but they certainly wouldn't slow him down.

Ard was ashamed of what he'd done to Quarrah Khai, sending her away on a useless errand to quote scripture to young Nemery. But that little deceit had been necessary to remove her from harm's way. It wasn't all a lie. Ard hoped Quarrah would know. Seeing her beautiful face had nearly overwhelmed him after days in that rotting butchery dugout. The kiss was real. The passion he had felt surprised even him.

And Quarrah's comforts had been a needed salve for his grief. Homeland knew he'd been doing plenty of genuine grieving. Without Raek, Ard felt an indescribable void in his soul. It was an emptiness that screamed for revenge. A pit in his stomach that could only be filled by seeing justice served to King Pethredote.

"Slow a bit," Lyndel instructed.

Ard pulled back on the horse's reins, branches and brushes scraping the sides of the crate. It was stealth over speed here. A load this large would attract attention from the nighttime Regulators patrolling the Char. He glanced once more at the Drift crate behind him. The last thing they needed was for a nosy Reggie to go peeking inside.

Ard wasn't surprised that Quarrah had succeeded in getting the egg. After all this time together, he had little doubt about her skills and her mettle to see a job through.

Ard truly loved Quarrah Khai. It was a different kind of love than he had wasted on Tanalin all these years. It was real, current, which made it far more potent.

I don't want anything to change. Neither did Ard.

And that was precisely why he had to send Quarrah away.

Ard was about to venture back in time. If anything went wrong, his actions would obliterate the future, which, for them, was today.

Quarrah's presence tonight would only have distracted him. Ard didn't need any more reason to doubt what he was about to do. Keeping Quarrah out of sight might make his near-impossible task a little bit easier.

"There." Lyndel pointed again. Ard saw nothing through the dark trees, but he knew better than to question Lyndel's eyesight.

"Your people are ready?" Ard asked, directing the wagon down another narrow pathway.

"They are anxious for our arrival," she replied.

The Trothians.

Lyndel had arranged for her followers to meet them at this specific time. Well suited for gathering in the dark, Ard hoped that the Trothian crowd had not yet been noticed by the Regulators patrolling the Char.

When they were close enough to distinguish individual figures in the crowd ahead, Lyndel put a hand on Ard's shoulder and he eased back on the reins, bringing the wagon to a complete halt. His Trothian companion leapt off the driving bench and landed gracefully beside the horse's flank. Slipping quietly forward, she took the animal by the bridle and led it the remaining distance, Ard and the wagon in tow.

They cleared the trees and entered Oriar's Square. The open space was packed with bodies. There must have been over two hundred Trothians, their dark blue skin rough and peeling from being deprived of the Agrodite soak.

The crowd tensed, seeming to flinch collectively at the sudden arrival of the wagon. But any fear of a Reggie assault abated when they saw Lyndel leading the horse. The expression of the gathering changed then, an anxious enthusiasm spreading across the crowd. Lyndel was right. Her people had been prepared for tonight. Although Ard was sure that none of them truly knew what they were supposed to be excited about. A man with a wagon. A promise of a large detonation.

Now that they were closer, Ard could see that there were many Landers in the crowd, too. Most of them were young men and women, incensed by their king's sudden mistreatment toward their

Trothian neighbors. Ard didn't know how Lyndel had reached them, but it was obvious that these Landers also stood ready to fight.

The group continued to part as Lyndel led the horse and wagon to the base of the Old Palace Steps, a chain cordoning off the historic ruins. The crowd was beginning to silence itself, as if expecting someone to address them. Lyndel shouted something in Trothian, and suddenly the area was lit with several Light Grit detonations. A pair of glowing orbs now framed the steps, hanging just outside the chain.

The atmosphere was electrifying. Ard could sense the coming conflict in the air. Like the smell of hot oil before the dough dropped into it.

Ard leapt down from the carriage, his fingers tingling with anticipation, his head swooning with the thrill. He realized that everyone gathered had some expectation placed on him, seeded by Lyndel's Agrodite preachings.

Ard didn't know much about the Trothian religion, but he thought that these good people actually embodied the best of Wayfarist teaching. They were here because they were not willing to settle peacefully back into their islets. They had come to the Greater Chain out of a desire for progress and change. Now they would stay and fight for that cause.

Ard and Lyndel knew that the cause was so much bigger. But this crowd of brave souls couldn't possibly know that Ardor Benn held the fate of time itself in a Grit keg stowed beneath the wagon's driving bench.

Ard strapped on a Grit belt stocked with four specific pots, each prepared the best way that Ard knew how. It was an added stress to think that Ard's calculations, which he had arrived at largely with Lyndel's input, might be incorrect. Grit was a finicky substance, and Ard would never forgive himself if tonight's efforts failed because of the substandard loading of a Grit pot.

Just another reminder of how much he had depended on Raekon Dorrel.

Ard lifted the keg of Visitant Grit onto the driver's bench, checking the Slagstone pin-trigger ignitor on the lid. A sharp tug would throw a spark, and the detonation would rush through the gaps at the top of the keg, forming the cloud. Raek had loaded it before his death, estimating a single blast with a radius of some forty feet.

Ard would only have one shot at this. But one was all he'd need. If his plan didn't work, the timeline would reset, erasing the current day and eliminating any chance of trying again.

A Trothian man stepped out of the crowd, a long-barreled Fielder over one shoulder, and a belt of cartridges around his waist. In the glow of the Light Grit detonations, Ard realized that he recognized the man.

"Darbu!" Ard cried. "*Omligath.*" The greeting was the extent of Ard's knowledge of the Trothian language. Darbu nodded, a grin on his face as his oscillating eyes studied Ard.

"You know Darbu?" Lyndel asked.

"We've done business." Ard remembered the look on the Trothian's face as he sat atop those crates of Rollers in the Avedon apartment while Ard and the king shared a drink.

"Darbu has been collecting weapons for me," said Lyndel. "Guns, swords, Grit."

"Huh," Ard remarked. "Small world."

"I have always believed that my people should be prepared," continued Lyndel. "Especially those of us living in the Greater Chain. I remember a time before the Inclusionary Act. I always believed it could end as quickly as it came to be."

"I guess your paranoia is paying off," Ard said. The Trothian rebellion was certainly well armed, with extra ammunition being divvied among the insurgents.

Ard handed the keg of Visitant Grit to Lyndel and climbed into the back of the wagon to release the straps that secured the Drift crate.

Lyndel spoke for a moment to Darbu and another robust Trothian who stood nearby. The two men stepped forward and seized the carrying poles of the Drift crate, easily lifting it with the weightless detonation still burning inside. Lyndel directed them to wait beside the cordon chains at the bottom of the Old Palace Steps.

Ard directed the wagon away and the crowd shuffled backward, clearing a wide arena for Lyndel, Ard, and the two Trothians holding the Drift crate.

Lyndel began to speak in Trothian. Ard wasn't catching a word of it, but her speech was obviously having a powerful effect on the Trothians present. Murmured translations spread to the Lander sympathizers in the crowd, but Ard was too far away to hear.

He scanned the dark trees at the edge of Oriar's Square. By now, the Regulators would surely have been alerted to the gathering. To strike against a crowd so large, the Reggies would need significant reinforcements. Once they arrived, the fight would begin. But Ard only needed about ten minutes.

Lyndel finished her speech, pointing back at the Old Palace Steps. The Trothian rebels broke into a cry of determination.

"What did you tell them?" Ard asked.

"I spoke to them of the *Kram Udal*," said Lyndel.

"You told them there would be a Paladin Visitant?" Ard cried.

"There will be," Lyndel replied. "But my people know they will not see him. I told them to stay clear of the blast cloud and protect the detonation from the Regulators at all costs."

"Thank them for me," Ard whispered. He unhitched the chain that cordoned off the Old Palace Steps and dropped it to the packed dirt at his feet. Lyndel instructed Darbu and his companion to move the Drift crate into position at the bottom of the stairs.

Ard pulled open the hatch, and the gelatinous egg slid out of the box with a squelching sound, striking the hard ground and sliding until it came to rest against the bottom stair of the ruined Old Palace Steps. Accompanying the soft golden egg was a pungent smell. A smell that transported Ard back to the mountains of Pekal. An odor he had only smelled at frightening proximity to a dragon or something left behind by one.

There was an array of gasps from those in the crowd close enough to see what had just arrived. The Light clouds glimmered against the gelatinous egg, the full spectrum of colors dancing in rainbow-like patterns through the amber translucent orb. It wobbled against the stone stair, firm enough to hold its shape, but soft enough to jiggle like lard.

Lyndel said something to Darbu and the other Trothian, who promptly carried the empty Drift crate away. Then the priestess turned to face Ard, her steel-gray eyes quivering as she studied him.

"May you return to us again, Ardor Benn."

She handed him the keg of Visitant Grit and dashed through the clearing to be greeted by the anxious crowd.

Ard was alone beside the unfertilized bull egg, the ring of spectators anxiously looking on but obediently maintaining a wide berth. He strode up the Old Palace Steps, stopping just five stairs above the gelatinous egg.

The ruins rose some thirty steps more before ending at a crumbled platform. The history books claimed that Oriar himself had stood there, detonating a hopeful blast of Visitant Grit to defend the city against a rampant Grotenisk.

Now standing just yards from the site of that historic failure, the only thing separating Ard from Oriar was two hundred and fifty-two years. And those were years that could be instantly bridged by a second detonation of Visitant Grit in this very place.

Ard cast a quick glance over the steps. Anything within the radius of the Visitant cloud would be transported back in time with him.

He had to make sure there would be no accidental stowaways—just himself and the unfertilized dragon egg.

The soft amber egg had finally settled. It needed the fire of a bull dragon to harden that shell. To activate the potential life inside that gooey orb. And Ard was about to deliver that egg to the one moment in time where he was sure that dragon fire had pervaded.

Grotenisk would fertilize this egg. And when the Visitant cloud burned out, Ard would return to the present day with a rebirth for the dragon race. That was the payout. But the ruse was still to be run. A ruse on history. A ruse on time itself.

Ard believed it would work. Isless Vesta's lyrics that Dale Hizror had used for the cantata confirmed it. Ard could almost hear Quarrah's off-tune voice rehearsing in the bakery's upper room.

The midnight blast enveloped Oriar. But he was left alone. No Paladin Visitant was his rearguard. No flaming form to bring the dragon low. Just a cloud of darkest night where the bright warrior should have been.

Shadow Grit.

Ard unclipped the first Grit pot from his belt and dashed it against the stone steps at his feet. The cloud instantly formed around him, the detonation encompassing himself and the gelatinous egg. This was the trick. And like the best of all ruses, it was a simple solution to circumvent the most complex issue.

Ard and the egg were now completely concealed in a cloud of impenetrable blackness. He could see out with perfect clarity, but gauging by the gasp of the onlooking crowd, Ard had seemed to suddenly disappear in the darkness.

The timeline would only reset if things in the past were altered— if lives were lost, or if Oriar was hailed a hero. But under the cloak of Shadow Grit, no one on that fell night long ago would ever see Ard—the Paladin Visitant who actually came. Oriar would continue to be the failure that history had made him. If all went right, nothing from the past would change, so the timeline would remain intact. But Grotenisk's centuries-old fertilizing fire would save the future from the ravages of Moonsickness.

A gunshot sounded through the Char, and Ard looked up to see the back of the Trothian crowd erupt into chaos.

The Regulators.

As cowardly as it felt to flee now that a conflict was breaking out, Ard knew it was time to detonate the Visitant Grit. He had a date with history. And if everything went as planned, he was about to come face-to-face with a very angry dragon.

Ard crouched on the stair, placing the keg beside him. He reached his finger through the pin-trigger and pulled sharply upward. He heard the Slagstone ignitor grinding inside. He didn't see the sparks, but he felt the rush of detonation as the cloud surrounded him.

In the blink of an eye, Ard was ablaze. He still crouched on the Old Palace Steps, but they were no longer ruins.

He had traveled through time, and in so doing, had become the most powerful being ever to exist. Ardor Benn was a Paladin Visitant. He could wreak death and destruction with a single word.

Quarrah sprinted through the trees, leaves and twigs lashing at her, slowing her down. She had left the beaten pathways of the Char to cut a more direct route to Oriar's Square.

Blazing Ard! What was he thinking? Had he been planning to do this behind her back all along? Had she played right into his rusing little hands by agreeing to check on Nemery Baggish?

And what kind of plan was this, anyway, taking the egg to the Char? Putting it on display in front of hundreds of people! It was *her* egg, spark it all! Getting cut out, after everything Quarrah had risked to steal it...

She was lucky to have figured out what was going on at all. After unsuccessfully checking the neighborhood where she thought Nemery lived, Quarrah had been cutting across the Char to search the Southern Quarter.

On a back trail, some hundred yards out from the Square, Quarrah had seen the bright detonation of Light Grit. With the caution of a practiced thief, Quarrah had drawn her spyglass. She'd seen the large crowd of armed Trothians, but Quarrah focused on the figures at the center of the crowded Square. She might not have known it was Ard from such a distance, but the wagon and Drift crate were an instant giveaway.

There was a gunshot, and Quarrah dropped to a crouch in the bushes beside the footpath. She really wasn't equipped for a fight. Her belt was stocked with only a few useful items—Light Grit, Drift Grit, and a single small pot of Barrier Grit.

Quarrah rose from the bushes, teeth grinding in frustration. She sprinted down the narrow dirt path toward the crowded Square. Sounds of conflict were increasing by the footstep. Another gunshot. Shouts and screams. What the blazes was Ard doing down there?

In the darkness, Quarrah didn't see the trail that merged with hers. She nearly stumbled into a pair of Regulators running the same direction she was. Quarrah reeled back as the two shouted in surprise. One of them fired a Roller, and Quarrah heard the ball tear into the brush behind her.

Frantic, Quarrah dropped to her knees, hand plunging into her belt for the Barrier Grit. She hurled the pot, but it didn't strike the trail with enough force. The clay might have cracked, but the pot didn't shatter in a way to spark the Slagstone.

"Sparks," Quarrah muttered, the irony of her expletive woefully apparent. She scrambled on hands and knees into the brush before realizing that the Reggies had moved on, careless to pursue her while the real conflict raged at the Square.

Too afraid to rejoin the footpath, Quarrah scooped up the failed pot and moved at a cautious pace until at last she emerged into the open Square.

The place was a war zone!

Regulators pressed in from various points, but the Trothians repelled them. Quarrah saw muzzle flashes as guns rang out, swords and daggers gleaming in the bright clouds of Light Grit. There were already bodies on the ground!

Some of the Regulators took shots into the crowd, assured to strike someone in the tight throng. But the Trothians had detonated bunkers of Barrier Grit around the perimeter, popping around the impenetrable domes to fire off their own rounds.

Regulators scrambled for cover, shouting commands to one another. This skirmish was only going to escalate. So close to the palace, the Reggies would have a steady stream of reinforcements coming fast.

The horrific scene seemed to seize Quarrah by the throat and steal her breath. She knew she should leave. Turn away from the Square and escape the Char as quickly as her lithe legs would carry her.

But Ard was here. And she had to know what that blazing fool was doing with her dragon egg!

Quarrah sprinted from the cover of the trees toward the crowd of angry Trothians, hurling the cracked pot of Barrier Grit behind her. It detonated this time, at least creating some sort of cover. She ran with her head bowed, hands up, hoping desperately that the mob would recognize her as a sympathizer. Miraculously, she reached the line of Trothians, dark blue hands pulling her roughly into the crowd.

The woman next to her screamed, and Quarrah felt a spray of blood speckle the back of her neck as the stranger fell soundlessly to the stones. Quarrah fell, too, from the shock of the scene. On hands and knees beside the corpse, she tried not to wretch. Quarrah crawled deeper into the crowd, someone stepping on her knuckles before hands pulled her upright again, taking shelter behind a Barrier bunker.

At last, Quarrah broke into the inner ring of the Square. There was nothing here but the Old Palace Steps, the Trothian mob tactically positioned around it in a defensive perimeter.

Quarrah glanced at the historic ruins, but they were dark. So dark that the steps seemed untouched by the glow from the nearby Light clouds. Quarrah squinted. There was a hazy quality to the air. Some sort of detonation, though it was impossible to tell what type of Grit from here. Well, Quarrah would just have to step into that detonation cloud and find out.

She was halfway to the Old Palace Steps when someone called her name from the crowd.

"Quarrah Khai!"

She ground to a stop, whirling to find the speaker.

It was Lyndel. She had a long dagger in one hand and a Roller in the other. Her long braids spilled over her bare blue shoulders, and the light spilled across her face.

"Where's Ardor?" Quarrah shouted as Lyndel reached her.

"You must come away from the steps," said Lyndel.

"Where is he?"

Lyndel pointed to the Old Palace Steps. "He has detonated the Visitant Grit."

Quarrah swiveled to study the empty cloud around the ruined stairs. That was the Visitant cloud? Ard had already detonated it without even telling her? There was no Paladin Visitant standing in fiery glory. There was nothing but blackness on the steps.

"He failed?" Quarrah cried.

"It is far more complicated than that," said Lyndel. "You must stay clear of the detonation."

"You knew he was coming here tonight?" Quarrah felt the betrayal intensifying. Ard had trusted Lyndel over her? It was obvious. The Trothians and their sympathizers were a respectable force. Ard must have been planning this for days.

"He cares for you," Lyndel said.

Quarrah drew a deep breath. There was no time for this conversation right now. If Ard truly cared for her, as he'd led her to believe, then he wouldn't have sent her away. He would have told her what he was doing.

"He said you would be a distraction to him," uttered Lyndel.

"Distraction?" Quarrah laughed bitterly. "Like I might get hurt?"

Azania and the bulk of the ruse aside, Quarrah had stowed away, to and from Pekal, on the king's own Harvesting ship. She had stolen the gelatinous egg and pulled it with bleeding hands down the mountain. She had killed Ulusal. She'd done it all on her own. And Ard didn't want her to be a *distraction*?

Quarrah felt as though a fire had been lit beneath her cheeks. Both hands clenched into tight fists.

"Please," Lyndel urged. "Ardor Benn is doing what he must to save us all."

"Right," Quarrah said sarcastically. Even old Lyndel seemed to have fallen under his manipulative spell. "We're talking about Ard. Don't act like he's some hero!"

"Not a hero." Lyndel glanced toward the cloud of Visitant Grit around the steps. "He is a Paladin Visitant."

Ard stood slowly. His skin appeared to be on fire, but he felt no pain. The flames upon his flesh were merely a response to the time travel. The air here, hazy with Grit from Oriar's detonation, was touching his skin. On contact with a flesh-and-blood figure from the future, the airborne Grit from the past was consumed in fire.

The gelatinous egg resting against the bottom step also blazed like a bonfire, burning up the Grit that was out of sync with its own time.

He had done it! Ard had actually succeeded in using the Visitant

Grit to launch himself backward through time, though he only had about ten minutes before the cloud burned out. Pethredote's secret had been wholly accurate, and Ard now felt a sudden surge of confidence that the rest of this ruse might actually work.

Like the surroundings he had left, it was night. Very dark—a historical fact that Ard was relying on, so his cloud of Shadow Grit would go unnoticed. There was so much to take in. So much that seemed familiar, and yet wildly different.

This was the site of Oriar's Square at the heart of the Char. But the Char was a preserved piece of land set aside to celebrate the regrowth following Grotenisk's destruction. Destruction that was happening this very night.

From Ard's view on the lower steps, countless buildings were collapsing, flames leaping higher than a tree could grow. Human figures streaked through the fiery chaos, screaming and dying, looking small and insignificant against a backdrop of so much red and yellow.

The stairs upon which Ard now stood had not yet been attacked. The platform above did not crumble away into nothing, but instead comprised a beautiful landing before a set of regal doors leading into the massive palace.

Standing on that landing was a man in a decorated breastplate, a broadsword in his gloved hand.

Captain Oriar.

It had to be, standing at the palace entrance exactly as history had described him. His face was downcast, eyes closed in preparation for the appearance of a Paladin Visitant. He was muttering something, though Ard could not hear the words over the sounds of wreckage in the city. Ard's sudden presence in the past meant that Oriar had already detonated his infamously failed pot of Visitant Grit.

Ard's detonation would have transported him back to the very

moment that Oriar's Grit ignited, linking the two events geographically through time. Ard saw bits of shattered ceramic on the steps
below the hopeful Oriar.

Presumably, Oriar's detonation had occurred just a few yards
above Ard. The centers of both blasts had not been in the exact
same place, so Oriar's cloud and Ard's cloud were probably not
lined up perfectly. But this was good. Ard and the egg were close
enough that the overlapping portion of the Visitant cloud transported them through time. Any closer and Oriar might have
appeared inside the Shadow Grit detonation, burning up at Ard's
presence.

The hero on the landing risked an outward glance, paling to find
that no Paladin Vistant had appeared. Oriar gazed down the palace steps, eyes full of hope, staring directly through the space where
Ard was shrouded in blackness.

There was a rush of wind and Oriar's attention was drawn out
over the burning city. Ard spun on the step, knowing full well what
had commanded Oriar's gaze.

It was Grotenisk.

The dragon landed in a flurry of wings that fed the flames
behind him like a giant bellows. His tail snaked down the burning
street behind him, and leathery wings folded inward as stout hind
legs supported his body. Grotenisk dropped forward onto powerful
forelegs, his massive talons crushing stone and churning soil.

The dragon's eyes were like pools of blood—crimson spheres as
large as wagon wheels. There was a madness behind those eyes,
a desperate and violent frenzy. Grotenisk snorted, smoke curling
from his black-pit nostrils. He opened his mouth as if to bellow, but
only a noiseless gust escaped his throat, the air shimmering with
heat waves.

By the Homeland, Ard thought. *Halavend was right about everything.*
Grotenisk was clearly suffering from the same symptoms that

plagued a Moonsick human. The bull dragon razing the city was not born a violent monster. His captive life away from Pekal had deprived him of the Red Moon's rays. The same rays that poisoned humans clearly sustained these mighty beasts.

How did the historians miss this? Perhaps the facts were lost in the chaos of the night. Or perhaps no one wanted to see Moonsickness in a dragon. Admitting to Grotenisk's true condition would, in the same hand, imply that his violent behavior was helplessly involuntary. Then the finger of blame could only be pointed to King Kerith and the people who'd made Grotenisk this way.

The dragon suddenly turned, his long head snapping sideways toward a brave battalion of soldiers that had been creeping forward. Grotenisk leveled his face toward them, dropping his hooked jaw right against the road.

The soldiers immediately engaged, hurling spears and shooting bolts from heavy crossbows. The dragon waited a moment, letting the sharp projectiles wash over him. The bolts pierced his nose between those impenetrable scales. One spear found its mark, lodging in a soft spot beneath the creature's blind eye.

The attacks triggered no response from Grotenisk. Like a Moonsick human, Ard knew he could feel no pain. The sound of ringing metal echoed as the soldiers drew their swords.

Grotenisk lashed out.

He devoured the first two soldiers in a single bite, dismembered parts falling in a rain of blood to the street. The next man he smashed with his mighty chin, shattering bones with the weight of his massive head. The final two soldiers were making a hasty retreat when Grotenisk released a plume of fire with as little effort as a child blowing out a candle.

The fire peeled out, precise, targeted. It struck the fleeing soldiers with such a blast that they were both thrown forward. The dragon held a stream of flames upon their downed bodies as they writhed and screamed. When at last they were still, the incinerating subsided and Grotenisk's head swiveled back around, the spear hanging limply from his bloody eye.

"Beast!" cried a voice from behind Ard. He glanced back at Oriar, who stood with broadsword extended in challenge. "Your destruction tonight is over! Behold, my Paladin Visitant comes to save us all!"

The man on the landing dropped his head, eyes squinting shut again. But Ard remained unseen in the cloud of Shadow Grit.

Captain Oriar. The Folly of Beripent. His bravado against the dragon was misplaced. The Grit had already been detonated. No verbal summoning would call forth a Paladin Visitant.

As long as Ard remained hidden within the cloud of blackness, Oriar would fail. He would flee, and Grotenisk would lay waste to the Old Palace. His fires would rage on. There were still so many people destined to die from Grotenisk's destruction.

The dragon himself would kill a thousand people tonight. Ard couldn't put out the fires with his presence, but he could stop the monster.

A thousand deaths.

Ardor Benn could prevent those. He could make Oriar a success. All he had to do was shout the dragon's name. Ard's voice, out of sync with this time, would be picked up by the dragon's enhanced hearing, and Grotenisk would wither in flames. Captain Oriar would be a worthy hero. But with that, the timeline would reset, extinguishing everyone and everything in Ard's world. He couldn't let that happen.

A thousand deaths now for millions of lives later.

Ard told himself that these people were already dead. The five soldiers Grotenisk had just obliterated had already died two hundred and fifty-two years ago. Things couldn't be changed. They *shouldn't* be changed. This was *supposed* to happen.

But his justifications felt empty upon hearing the chorus of screams ringing through the city. These people were dying *now*, for the first time. Ard had the power to help them. To stop any further desolation. But that was not why he had come. He must let them die again, in the exact same manner as they had in the history books. It was the only way to preserve the future timeline. To preserve the good that existed in the world that Ard had left.

I'm sorry, Ard thought as Grotenisk advanced.

Oriar stumbled backward as the dragon reared up, drawing a huge breath of air that caused his broad chest to expand to a terrifying size. This was it. This was the blast that would fertilize the egg hiding at the base of the stairs. The only problem was, the same rush of fire would no doubt incinerate Ard.

His hand flashed to his belt, unclipping the two remaining Grit pots. Ard dropped into a crouch on the stairs, slamming the ceramic pots against the stone between his feet. Two detonation clouds formed simultaneously, both of them just large enough to surround Ard's crouched figure, leaving the gelatinous egg unprotected on the steps in front of him.

The first was Barrier Grit. The cage that formed around him was tight, making Ard feel claustrophobic as he couldn't stand up within its confines. The Barrier Grit would protect him against Grotenisk's flames, but not the heat of the fire. He had essentially created an inescapable oven in which any exposure to Grotenisk's fury would bake him.

That was why the second pot contained Compounded Cold Grit. The temperature within the cloud plummeted instantly as the Grit ignited. Ard gasped, a sharp intake of breath at the nip of iciness against his skin. It was strange to see his flesh aflame with the power of a Paladin Visitant, and yet feel so cold.

The Grit clouds were layered around him, a complex interweave of the best defenses Ard could hope for. The largest was the Visitant Grit that both he and Oriar had detonated, though done at different times. Within that cloud was the blast of Shadow Grit, still concealing him and the unfertilized egg from the eyes of anyone living in the past. And within the Shadow Grit, Ard himself was hunched under a protective cloud of Barrier Grit and surrounded by a blast of Compounded Cold.

The bull dragon dropped once more onto his forelegs, and with the impact of touching down, released a tremendous gush of flames from deep within his scaly body. The fire rushed forward like a living thing, swirling and leaping its way up the palace steps.

Ard flinched, his eyes shutting though he knew the fire could not pass through the outer edge of the Barrier cloud. The temperature began to increase until sweat formed on Ard's forehead despite the active Cold Grit.

After a second, he dared to open his eyes. Encased within his cloud of safety, Ard was at the heart of a fiery storm. Reds and yellows, with streaks of blues, greens, and whites, surrounded him on all sides. It was a tapestry of color, heat, and destruction, woven before his very eyes while he crouched unnoticed at its heart.

It was bright. So bright he could barely keep his eyes open. Ard peered downward, desperate to see how the gelatinous egg was faring in this oppressive fire. If it were anything else, he would have expected it to burn to cinders, reduced to ash. But Grotenisk's fire was precisely what this egg needed to spring alive and flourish.

He resisted the urge to cry out, though he doubted his voice could be heard in the torrent of flame. Then suddenly, the fury was past. The brightness of the fire gave way to the darkness of night, leaving Ard blinking madly as his eyes adjusted. Half-blinded, he saw Grotenisk leap forward, wings unfurling just enough to bear him up the palace steps.

The beast landed behind Ard, the serpentine tail draping across the stairs, hardly more than arm's reach from where Ard was crouched. There was a cracking of timber and stone as the dragon began to force his massive figure into the Old Palace.

Oriar was gone, retreated inside the building. He would survive the night, though his future was grim due to the negative response he'd receive for failing with the Grit.

Little did history know that Oriar was no failure. A Paladin Visitant had indeed come to his detonation. He had not saved them from Grotenisk the Destroyer. But in a way, Grotenisk's destruction of the past would save all mankind in the future.

Something changed suddenly. It was still dark around Ard, but the fires in the streets winked out abruptly. The buildings were gone, replaced with dark trees. And the frightening dragon vanished along with the palace he was destroying.

There were still shouts around him, a skirmish of bodies in the darkness. Ard couldn't see clearly from where he crouched on the steps, and he couldn't stand due to the frigid Barrier still shrouding him.

"Ardor!"

His name! Someone had shouted his name. The cry could only mean one thing. He had returned to the present. And the present still knew him!

The speaker was Quarrah Khai, racing to the steps as a full-scale battle waged behind her. Sparks, what was Quarrah doing here?

She paused beside an object that Ard first mistook for a sculpted stone. It was round, oblong, and perfectly smooth. In the flickering torchlight, he saw the amber color, a glossy sheen to its surface.

It was the egg. No longer gelatinous, but fertilized into an exterior shell, a nearly indestructible cradle of life.

He wanted to reach out and touch it, but his detonation clouds still held him prisoner—an egg of his own.

"I don't understand..." Quarrah muttered.

"We have to move the egg," Ard said, impatient for the Grit to burn out around him. "We have to get it out of the Char. Away from these people."

"Lyndel is fetching the wagon." Quarrah seemed distanced from him. As if it wasn't just the Barrier cloud separating them.

"Quarrah, I shouldn't have sent you away." Ard's jaw shivered at the pocket of cold that enveloped him. "I should have told you what I was doing tonight."

"It's who you are." Quarrah looked small next to the massive fertilized egg, as though four of her could have fit comfortably within that mighty shell.

"It's not who I want to be," Ard said. "I need you."

"You need me to do what?" Quarrah replied flatly.

"It's not like that..." Ard tried. Sparks, they didn't have time for this conversation now. Couldn't Quarrah see how he felt for her? His feelings weren't part of any clever game or ruse.

Lyndel suddenly appeared, leading the horse and wagon with the Drift crate. "Ardor!" she called. "My people cannot hold much longer."

"We have to get the egg away from the Char," Ard replied. "We have to get it as far away from the city as we can."

"We have to get it to Pekal," Quarrah whispered.

Ard shook his head. "That's not up to us."

"What do you mean?" Quarrah cried. "Who else is going to do it?"

"We just have to get it out into the fields." Ard needed to tell her everything. Quarrah deserved to know. But there would be time enough for that conversation on the wagon ride out of Beripent.

"Quarrah," Lyndel called. "Give me help." The priestess had positioned the Drift crate beside the fertilized egg, hatch open to receive it. A pot shattered on the ground, and Ard saw a detonation cloud envelop the solid egg.

Quarrah grunted in frustration and turned away from Ard to help Lyndel with the precious load. Ard watched helplessly from his confines, his breath coming out in frosty plumes as he shivered against the Compounded Cold Grit.

Something slapped against the Barrier cloud behind him,

causing Ard to whirl on his knees. A familiar face was peering in at him, hands pressed against the Barrier's solid perimeter, as though attempting to push it aside.

"Sparks, Elbrig!" Ard cried. "What are you doing here? How did you find me?"

"It was easy," the man replied. "I followed the sounds of utter chaos."

Elbrig was dressed in the manner that Ard was most familiar with—the appearance he had used when tutoring Ard to become Dale Hizror. Had Elbrig come to help the Trothians fight?

"We did it, Elbrig," Ard whispered. "Do you see that?" He gestured toward the fertilized dragon egg that Quarrah and Lyndel were sliding into the Drift crate.

"I've come to tell you something," Elbrig replied.

"That's a dragon egg," Ard persisted. "A fertilized bull. Do you realize what this means?"

"Listen to me, Ardy!" Elbrig's voice was stern. "There's something you need to know. Something very important."

What could possibly be more important than securing the egg to the back of the wagon? Ard was becoming accustomed to mind-boggling revelations. After what he'd learned about Moonsickness, the Homeland, and the Paladin Visitants, what could Elbrig Taut possibly say to Ardor Benn that would even give him pause?

"Raekon is alive."

Ard's Barrier cloud burned out, but he didn't move. The Compounded Cold Grit expired, but he still felt frozen. Elbrig's words rattled in Ard's head.

"What?" he finally mustered.

"Raekon Dorrel is alive," Elbrig repeated. "The king must have found a way to preserve his life after you left the reception hall. He's being kept in the palace dungeon."

"What?" Ard muttered again. Surely this was some deception. "You're certain it was him?"

"Pah!" Elbrig scoffed. "I'd know that big oaf anywhere. He's one of a kind."

Ard was shaking, his face suddenly wet with tears. Could this be true? What reason would Elbrig have to lie to him?

"What can we do?" Ard could barely form the words.

"He's under heavy guard," Elbrig replied. "It'll be nearly impossible to extract him. He's still very weak."

Ard let out a choked sob, overwhelmed by the sudden elation that swept him up as a rising tide. It was like coming up for air after a dive that had nearly drowned him. For a second, Ard forgot about timelines, dragon eggs, and the fate of all mankind. He let himself hover in a moment of relief and euphoria. Then he came down, his mind racing, spinning, his focus kicking in and the fervor within him burning fiercely.

Plans. He needed a plan to rescue his friend before it was too late. If Pethredote had saved Raek from the brink of death, it was probably because he wanted to question him about the Visitant Grit. Raek's usefulness would run out if the king got word of Ard's detonation tonight.

Ard glanced over at Quarrah and Lyndel. The two women had successfully loaded the cargo, and they were just checking the straps to make sure the Drift crate would ride safely on the wagon.

It suddenly became perfectly clear what Ard needed to do. Like all his best ideas, it took the threads of multiple problems and wove them into one simple solution.

King Pethredote.

Justice.

The egg.

Raekon Dorrel.

The plan was sheer recklessness—risky and ultimately selfish. But wasn't this kind of plan Ardor Benn's specialty? He shut his eyes, thinking through every angle, chasing down every possible variable. Yes, it was a gamble, but sparks, if it worked—and it *would* work...

Ard looked at Elbrig Taut. "I need you to do something for me."

The disguise manager raised an eyebrow. "You've got that brazen look in your eye, Ardy. You won't be any good to Raekon if you're dead. And there's no way you can get into the palace alone."

"I won't be alone." Ardor Benn glanced skyward, into the dark night. "She's coming."

~

I write this blindly. In terms of both eyesight and faith. Would that I could see what impact my actions will have.

CHAPTER

43

Quarrah had heard Ard explain some pretty outlandish things...but this was beyond compare. Traveling through time?

Ard had told her everything that he'd learned from King Pethredote as they drove the wagon out of the Char. He paused only once to ignite more Drift Grit in the crate to reduce the weight of the payload.

Quarrah couldn't wrap her mind around it. On its own, the concept of time travel was complex, convoluted. And Ard had managed to take it one step further by cheating time itself. He had obviously succeeded. Had the timeline been reset, as Pethredote cautioned, none of this would be happening. History would have unraveled differently, and Quarrah might never have crossed paths with Ardor Benn.

Would that have been a better life for her? Perhaps in that life, she would have had parents to care for her. Perhaps in that life, she would have found joy in more wholesome things, and her thrill for thieving would never have flourished.

"And the egg?" Quarrah asked, as Ard drew the wagon to a halt in the dark street. "Why do we need to get it out of the city?"

"We don't."

"But you said—"

"Plans change," he cut her off. "This is as far as we're taking the egg."

They were in the middle of a Beripent neighborhood in the Western Quarter. Regulators would definitely be patrolling this area. They couldn't leave it here!

"We have to get it back to Pekal," Quarrah insisted. "So it can hatch."

Ard shook his head. "The sows have a sense. A maternal sense," he began. "When one of her eggs is fertilized, she knows it. She traverses Pekal to find the spot where the bull fertilized it. And when she does, she takes the egg to a nest and nurtures it until the hatchling emerges."

Quarrah stared at Ard in the dark street, the horse stamping its hooves on the cobblestones behind her. "You think she's coming here?" she whispered. "The mother. You think she'll leave Pekal to get her egg from Beripent?"

She glanced back at the Drift crate lashed to the wagon. She now understood Ard's original urgency to get the egg out of the city. Sparks, if the sow dragon was really coming, her arrival would turn this city upside down. But why had Ard changed his plan?

"It's forty-five miles from Pekal to Beripent," Ard explained.

"Pekal itself is twice that far across. If a sow can sense her egg over that distance, then she should be able to span the InterIsland Waters."

"Forty-five miles," Quarrah muttered. "How fast does a dragon fly?"

"Fast. It's impossible to know how long it will take her instinctual sense to kick in," said Ard. "But I imagine she'll be here within the hour."

"Then why are we leaving it here?" Quarrah cried. "We need to let the mother take it back to Pekal. This thing *has* to hatch, Ard. Otherwise, everything we did will have been in vain."

"I know," said Ard. "But I have one more card up my sleeve."

"This..." Quarrah leapt from the driving bench to land face-to-face with him on the street. "*This* is the problem." She jabbed him in the chest with two fingers. "You've done this since the moment I met you, Ardor Benn. All I can figure is that it gives you some twisted sense of pleasure to feel like the only person who knows what's going on."

"Quarrah, look. I'm..."

She held up her hands to cut him off. "Don't apologize, Ard. It doesn't become you." Life was a ruse to him. Quarrah was tired of playing Ard's games. "All that talk about correcting your mistakes, following the Homeland's Urgings so you'd be worthy of a Paladin Visitant...It was a load of slag! You sent me to check on Nemery because you didn't want me near you."

"Let me explain..." he tried again.

"Some things shouldn't need explaining," Quarrah retorted. "I've listened to your explanations for cycles. I did everything you asked. Played my part. And you cut me out when it really mattered. Went behind my back. Traveled through time and made everything okay again." She took a deep breath. "But not this. You can't make this okay."

She stepped back from him, Ard's countenance seeming to

diminish a bit. Quarrah had bottled this up, but it felt good to finally let loose. She only regretted waiting this long, and that her feelings were cast on a night when the city itself seemed to be spiraling into war. Perhaps it was this very atmosphere that Quarrah needed to express herself. A night like tonight, when the air was tainted with recklessness. Why not throw her heart into the mix?

"What do I have to do, Quarrah?" Ard said. "I've been at your side all this time. I've listened to you. I've protected you. Sparks, I faced Tanalin for you!"

Quarrah felt her blood boil. Oh, Ard was *so* proud of that. Like all of his other decisions were excusable because he'd "*faced Tanalin Phor.*"

"I escaped!" Quarrah spat. "You didn't *save* me from Tanalin. I picked my own lock. I got myself to North Pointe."

"But…" She reveled in the look of confusion on his face. "I arranged for Tanalin to give you the tool—"

"No," Quarrah cut him off. "You don't do everything, Ard. Sometimes people succeed without your help. I know that's hard for you to comprehend."

She watched the realization sink in. If Quarrah had escaped on her own, then Ard's visit to Tanalin hadn't truly been necessary after all. She watched Ard wrangle with the thought that he could have kept the fantasy going.

"I'm giving the egg to the Regulators." Ard distracted himself by checking the latch on the Drift crate. "I picked a well-patrolled neighborhood because I know they'll find it soon."

"What?" Quarrah's head reeled. After all her efforts to procure the egg, Ard was just going to give it up?

Ard turned to face her, his brown eyes glistening in the darkness. "Quarrah," he whispered. "Raek is still alive. Elbrig saw him in the palace dungeon."

She didn't know what to say. Was this another trick, like the time she'd seen Ard shoot Elbrig with a blank Roller? Like the time Tanalin shot Ard?

"Is this a thing with you ruse artists?" Quarrah finally asked. "You like to make people think you're dead?"

"I didn't know! Sparks!" Ard ran a hand through his hair. "He was still alive when I left the reception hall. Barely. Pethredote must have got to him with Health Grit just in time. We have to get Raek out of there."

"We will," Quarrah said. Raek was her friend, too. The news of his survival was both shocking and thrilling, if she could let herself believe that it was actually true. "We'll make a plan. I can get into the palace within the next few days and—"

"No!" Ard cried. "I have the plan. *She's* the plan." He pointed skyward. "This is the final step of the ruse, Quarrah. It's the answer to everything. Don't you see? If I give the egg over to the Regulators, they'll take it to the palace. The sow will bring justice to King Pethredote, and in the chaos, I'll be able to get Raek out of there."

Quarrah couldn't help but let out a bitter laugh as she pieced it all together. "Ard," she whispered. "You're insane."

"Does that mean you like the plan?" His stony expression softened a little.

"Sparks, no!" cried Quarrah. "It means I can't let you do it. The hope of all life rests inside that egg. What if Pethredote cracks it open?" This was madness, even for Ardor Benn. There were other, more sensible ways to rescue Raek.

"Oh, come on!" Ard moaned. "The shell is nearly indestructible. You know that. The only chance he'd have of cracking it would be to move the egg to a Grit processing factory. And there isn't one within sixty miles of the palace."

"Then what if he decides to sail it out to sea and drop it overboard?" Quarrah went on.

"That would take resources and time," rebutted Ard. "The dragon will be here by then."

"What if she doesn't come?" Quarrah cried. "What if the mother's sense doesn't engage? What if she decides it's too far from Pekal? We don't know enough about this, Ard. We need to hide the egg and arrange safe transport for it back to Pekal."

Ard grunted. His hand flashed to his side and Quarrah saw a Roller in his grasp. She wasn't afraid that Ard would hurt her. She had never been afraid of that. Quarrah actually believed that somewhere in his manipulative heart, Ardor Benn truly did care for her. The question was how much?

"What are you going to do, Ard?" She whispered the words. They stood so close, his gun pointed at the street, his eyes pockets of shadow. "Stop. Please," Quarrah breathed. "We will find another way to save Raek. I'll help you. But you have to stop this, Ard."

Tanalin's words echoed in Quarrah's head. *Ard doesn't know when to stop. He gave me up for a husk of dragon scales. What's he chasing now?*

"It's almost over, Quarrah," he muttered. "I have to do this. I know it'll work. It's the answer to everything we've been fighting for. The sow will get her egg. Pethredote will get justice. And I will get Raek back."

"Is that what we've been fighting for?" Quarrah asked. "You said Isle Halavend didn't want violence. He wouldn't want this."

"I'm doing this for him. For Halavend. For that Isless that died on Pekal." Ard was breathing heavy. "I chose not to reset the time-line because doing so would erase the meaning of their deaths. In another timeline, Pethredote would get away, and I can't let that happen. I had to save what we have here, Quarrah. What we have *now.*"

"What do we have?" she asked. "The Trothians have been driven out of the Greater Chain. Lyndel is leading those who remain to war. The leader of Wayfarism is dead, and the king has lost control of the peaceful reign he worked so hard to establish. We did that. We did all of that!"

"Pethredote is a liar!" Ard lifted the Roller, pointing it skyward.

"So are you." Quarrah regretted the words as soon as they passed her lips.

Ard stood stunned as Quarrah's heartbeat hammered in her ears. She saw the hurt in his eyes, but it didn't last long. Ard's expression slowly morphed. From stunned disbelief at Quarrah's words to resolute hardness.

He fired the gun into the air. Four consecutive shots that caused Quarrah's ears to ring from the proximity to the firearm. Smoke from the Blast cartridges drifted between them. That screen of smoke suddenly made Ard seem farther away than ever before.

Quarrah knew she had lost him then. Lost him to the zeal that bespoke his very name. She had never met a man more driven than Ardor Benn. He was fueled by a power. An ardor. Nothing could come between him and his goals.

Quarrah suddenly felt strangely safe. A man so possessed would not fail. His risks in using the egg would play out just as he planned. Pethredote would be brought down, and Raek would be saved.

But Ard had to do it alone. His ambitions allowed for no measure of distraction. He'd lost Tanalin once, over a husk of dragon scales. And with those four shots in this darkened street, he'd just lost Quarrah Khai.

"The Reggies will be here any moment." Ard lowered his Roller, fitting it into his holster. "We should slip away."

"I think we already have." Quarrah turned and ran, darting through a narrow alley between two brick buildings. There were tears on her face, though she hadn't felt them coming. Each step that bore her farther from Ard, grounded her into a new reality.

She was alone again, though not like before. Once, she had thrived on solitude, balking at the notion of their working alongside another. Ardor Benn had changed that. He had changed so much in her. And now, as Quarrah sprinted back into her old life, it felt much like a coat she had outgrown.

Quarrah didn't stop running until she reached the shoreline. Drawing to a halt among a few leaned-up shanties beyond a wealthy Beripent neighborhood, she cast her eyes over the great black expanse of the InterIsland Waters.

Pekal was out there, somewhere in the midnight dark. Quarrah cried out in frustration, falling to her knees at the top of the cliff-like shoreline. She felt a wild sense of freedom, having finally parted ways with Ardor Benn. But there was a sorrow, too. And a fear that their paths would never cross again.

Quarrah crumpled forward on the clifftop, giving in to the night. She was still there when the sow dragon appeared like a ribbon of fire on the horizon.

~

I cannot speak, but it matters not. Anything I would say has been recorded here. My determination has seen me to the shoreline, but I cannot rest until I reach the harbor.

CHAPTER

44

Ardor Benn crouched outside the low wall of the palace grounds, awaiting the dragon. News of her arrival traveled faster than she did, which was remarkable, considering.

She had come from the southwest, a straight shot from Pekal. The harbor watchmen spotted her from afar, the dragon's massive airborne form like some luminescent cloud on first glance.

The sight of a dragon flying at night was something to behold. Ard had only seen it once on Pekal. The exertion of propelling such a massive body through the air created a furnace within the beasts. Cracks between scales glowed with a reddish fire, stoked by the mighty wings. In the dead of night, after such a long flight, Ard imagined that this particular sow must have looked like a soaring ember.

Once her identity was confirmed, the watchmen sent a rider inland. On the shoreline, the approaching threat was met with a wartime signal, sending Regulators scrambling to tactical positions which, before tonight, had never been more than a rehearsed station.

Pethredote's reign of peace meant the coastal defenses were rusty at best. The Reggies were trained to fire the cannons, but it was more a principle of tradition than actual military training.

Nevertheless, the shoreline Regulation seemed to be putting up some kind of fight against the sow. Even from here, Ard had heard a few resounding cannon shots. His money was on the dragon, though, circling in irritation to decimate the threats that prodded harmlessly at her. The shoreline defenses would be sorely inadequate in a skyward strike from a fire-breathing dragon.

Never in recorded history had a dragon flown from Pekal. There was Grotenisk, yes. But he had been hatched in captivity on Espar, the mother sow killed in the skirmish to steal Grotenisk's egg.

But tonight, a dragon egg had been fertilized *here*. And the fast-approaching mother would stop at nothing to reunite with her lost egg.

Ard thought that her desperation must have been greater than ever before. The sows had to know that their race was heading for extinction, despite the number of eggs they laid. But tonight, after years of barren sorrow, one mother's sense had awakened.

Busy night. Every Reggie in Beripent must have been in uniform. Between the Trothian rebellion in the Char, and the incoming sow dragon, the Regulators would be pulled in a dozen directions.

Ard knew the feeling. One half of his broken heart demanded that he follow the egg, making sure the Regulators reached the palace in time for all his plans to come together. In time to save Raekon Dorrel. But the other half wanted to chase Quarrah Khai down that black alley, not stopping until he caught her.

But alas, he was here now, having followed the Reggies back to the palace, once they recognized the precious cargo inside the wagon's Drift crate. Ard hated himself for making that choice, but he wasn't surprised by his decision. This was the final stage of a ruse that had taken everything he had. But it wasn't going to take his best friend.

Ard was obsessed. He knew it. For a time, he'd thought a future with Quarrah might have been possible. He honestly loved her, but in the end, the ruse had left him alone again, reminding Ard of one huge difference between himself and Quarrah Khai.

She was a thief. Quarrah stole whatever she needed in the quiet moments. The moments when no one was watching or listening. The very opposite was true for Ard. He was his best, and his worst, whenever the spotlight was upon him.

Simply put, Quarrah was Quarrah when she wasn't thieving. But Ardor Benn was always a ruse artist.

Ard bit back the flood of emotions. He needed to steel himself now. He could find Quarrah in the aftermath, once Raek was freed and the dragon had brought down Pethredote and carried her egg safely to Pekal.

A group of Lander civilians was gathering at the front gate of the palace grounds, clamoring for the king. These would be concerned Wayfarists, possibly even some nobility, demanding answers about the Trothian uprising in the Char and the rumors of a coming dragon.

Regulators in uniforms of red and blue stood against the growing throng with guns and crossbows, sashes laden with Grit. Some were on horseback, riding to keep back the crowd, which was already bordering a righteous frenzy. Good. Elbrig and Cinza would have no trouble manipulating the crowd's emotions.

Ard had met up with Elbrig just moments ago, the man having prepared a Grit belt with all the supplies Ard would need to carry out his risky plan. The disguise managers were happy to help. Working a crowd like this was enough fun that they hadn't even asked for payment.

Ard glanced toward the distant Char, where the Trothian fight had escalated. Somehow, in the struggle, a blaze had broken out among the trees. Ard could see bright flames and smoke raging through the monument that was supposed to represent regrowth.

The Trothians and their sympathizers were stronger than Ard had anticipated. Lyndel had estimated her numbers, but tonight's battle had brought more fighters out of the woodwork.

Quarrah had been right. Lyndel was trying to start a war. A real war. The first Ard had known in his lifetime. It was frightening, to be sure. He hadn't wanted this. Isle Halavend certainly hadn't wanted this.

Maybe he should have reset the timeline. Maybe Ard should have allowed himself to be seen during his Paladin transfiguration. If he had done so, none of this would be happening. But who was he to decide that these events should not transpire? War was a terrible thing, but it had a way of bringing about change. And wasn't that what this was all about? Shaping each day in an effort to bring to pass that perfect, Homeland future?

The dragon arrived.

She came so suddenly that Ard fell back, clutching the smooth handle of his Roller, though such a tiny weapon was insignificant against a monster her size.

With a rush of leathery wings, the dragon landed atop the palace roof, wrapping her forelegs around one of the tall corner turrets. The sow's torso was glowing from her long flight from Pekal. Ard had never seen an internal blaze so bright, as though liquid fire wanted to burst through every seam between her deep green scales.

The dragon's fiery bulk settled across the rooftop, causing timbers to crack and stone to chip. Her immense tail draped over the side of the elaborate building, the tip twitching just yards from the ground.

Her silent arrival threw the Regulators into a frantic scramble. Dozens of shots rang out, long-range Fielders spitting lead balls at the perched beast.

In response, the dragon craned her long neck upward and bellowed. From his hiding place, Ard felt the rumble of her cry. The sound was like shattering glass and stones dragged across a chalkboard. Several of the Reggie horses bolted.

The dragon's side twitched as a crossbow bolt of Void Grit struck its mark. The beast turned, her eyes seeking the minuscule aggravators below.

Those massive jaws opened and fire rolled out as easily as a man could spit. The column of flame and smoke peeled down the front of the palace, scattering or consuming the closest Reggies. When the fiery breath subsided, the earth was charred black, and vegetation was aflame.

With a groan, the sow swung her head around, blunt forehead smashing into the pointed roof of the turret. The impact sent shingles and beams flying, sufficiently weakening the turret so the dragon could crush the rounded walls with her muscled forelegs.

Debris rained down on the burning palace grounds as the dragon brought her long tail up like a whip. It came down again, fast as a striking snake. The action cracked mortar and stone as she plunged her forelegs through the roof.

Sparks! She was burrowing into the palace from the very top! Well, it wasn't like Ard expected her to enter through the front doors. But still, this level of devastation hadn't touched Beripent since Grotenisk.

It was chilling to think that Ard had witnessed both events in the same night. Though separated by more than two centuries, the Visitant Grit had spanned the years. There was something cyclical about seeing the new palace burn. It was proof that the city's dated victory over Grotenisk was merely provisional. That another Grotenisk could humble them at any moment.

Yet the nature of the two beasts could not have been more different. The legendary Grotenisk had been afflicted with Moonsickness, growing manic and deranged. He had killed and burned with no apparent purpose. Ard had seen his bloodred blind eyes and mute throat. Estranged from the rays of the Crimson Moon, Grotenisk had truly become a monster of man's own creation.

In contrast, the sow's destruction was a means to a very significant end. She didn't hesitate to crush or kill anything that presented itself as an obstacle to her objective. She was a mother beast, and by nature's instincts, she would save her unborn son, regardless of death or collateral damage.

Ard ducked as a far-flung scrap of debris sailed over the outer wall of the grounds. The Regulators were distressed, scattering for cover. Time to get inside and find Raek.

Ard vaulted the short stone wall, landing between two clusters of shrubs that had escaped the dragon's first wave of fire. In the zoo of panicked Regulators, Ard's presence was barely noticed, let alone questioned as he sprinted forward.

The horseback Regulator didn't even see Ard until he was being pulled from the saddle. He cried out, striking the ground as Ard leapt onto the mount, digging his heels and riding hard for the palace steps.

The sow was delving deep into the palace now, her catastrophic intrusion compromising the integrity of every wall. Ard didn't know where the Regulators had taken the fertilized egg, but if the dragon didn't find it soon, the palace was going to crumble entirely.

Sparks! This was happening too fast. Ard hadn't anticipated the dragon tearing through stone walls with such ease.

Ard spurred his horse up the palace steps and through the open door. Inside, one corridor had completely collapsed, and Ard could hear wailing from beyond the rubble. Another hallway shone with a blinding brightness. Something was on fire, and Ard guessed the flames had found a storage of Light Grit, the resulting blast flooding the passageway with startling brilliance.

Elbrig had given him directions to the dungeon, but the main passageway was blocked with rubble. He'd have to take the long way around. Good thing he'd stolen this horse.

With hooves hammering against the stone floor, Ard set off through the palace at a gallop. He passed several Reggies, but they paid him no more than a frightened glance as they sprinted for the exit.

A moment later, Ard had found the door that led to the palace dungeon. He leapt down from the saddle and drew his Roller, firing a ball directly into the keyhole.

Ard steadied the horse as the shot echoed down the hallway. At least there wasn't a Reggie guard to contend with. Anyone with sense would have abandoned their post the moment the dragon slammed into the building.

Hastily, Ard holstered his gun and lashed the horse's reins to a wall sconce. The door handle was jammed from the shot, but after a hard kick, it pulled open.

Moving into the dark stairwell, he drew a pot of Light Grit from his belt and pitched it forward, the cloud glowing on the bottom step. He raced down, turning the corner into the dank stench of the dungeon.

The cell doors were solid wood, with a thin viewing slat that slid open at eye level. The first two cells stood open and empty. It was too dark to see into the third. Taking another Light Grit pot from his belt, Ard smashed it against the door beside the viewing slat. The Light cloud shone through the gap, casting a flat ray like a sunrise over the horizon.

And there was Raek, lying on his side, facing the wall. A moldy blanket covered his broad shoulders, but his bare feet were exposed. That unmistakable bald head glinted in the light, but he didn't so much as turn to see who was peering through the viewing slat.

Ard's breath caught in his throat and an irresistible grin spread across his face. He hadn't come to terms with Raek's supposed death—not even close. But this was a sight Ardor Benn had never expected to see again.

"There's a dragon literally tearing apart this building, and you're down here catching a nap?" Ard spoke through the slat.

Raek's still form rustled, his head raised. "Ard?" He turned, squinting at the door.

"I mean, I can come back later if this isn't a good time." Ard stepped back and examined the lock on the cell door. Quarrah would have had it silently sprung in moments, but Ard would have to resort to a more brute tactic. Not that anyone would notice, with the palace burning down.

"Sparks, Ard. Is that really you?" Raek's voice sounded diluted, like he couldn't muster the strength to speak with his usual tone.

"Stay back!" Ard shouted, sliding a pot of Blast Grit from his belt and pitching it at the lock. The Slagstone sparked, and the Grit exploded in a deafening bang. The mangled lock fell to the floor, smoldering, as the cell door swung inward.

Raek was standing, clutching that ratty blanket across his shoulders. His face looked broken and bruised, lips swollen and eyes blacked. His forehead glistened with sweat despite the coolness of the dungeon. But at the sight of Ardor Benn, Raek's face broke into a crooked smile.

"You don't look half bad for a dead man," said Ard.

Raek stepped forward. He was just past the threshold of his cell when his legs gave out. Ard caught him, throwing one of the big man's arms around his shoulder.

"But you don't smell too pretty," Ard said.

"It's a new perfume I'm trying," replied Raek. "They call it Rat Piss and Mildew. It's not for everyone."

"Well, I think you're making it work." Ard helped his injured friend across the dungeon. "What happened, Raek? I thought you were dead."

"So did I," he answered. "Last thing I remember was watching you escape out the balcony. Then I woke up to find a healer wrist-deep inside my chest."

"Was she pretty?"

"Well, it was a guy. And no."

"Health Grit?"

Raek nodded. "Compounded. I had a cloud burning inside me for over a week."

"Sparks, Raek! That could have serious side effects!"

"It wasn't like I asked them to do it," he mumbled.

They had reached the bottom of the stairs and the Light cloud shone brightly. Raek leaned away from Ard for a moment, pulling aside his blanket to expose his bare chest.

Ard flinched at the sight of the wound. What the blazes had they done to him? Something was embedded in Raek's muscular chest, just below his heart. It looked like a length of pipe, or a funnel. Scar tissue had formed around it, fusing the metal piece into his torso and leaving a hole that sank straight into his chest.

"Does it hurt?" Ard asked.

Raek grunted. "Can't yet tell what really hurts. Right now I'd say everything does."

"Well, at least they saved your life." Ard helped Raek into the stairwell.

"Only saved it so they could torture me for information…about the Visitant Grit."

"Did you crack?" Ard asked, stopping to readjust halfway up the stairs. "It's okay if you did…"

Raek nodded. "The king demanded that I tell him everything. So I started at the very beginning. But I only got a year in. Pethredote didn't seem to care about the time we caught that skunk and slipped it into old man Wilmfet's carriage…"

"Yet another time you didn't smell pretty."

Raek smiled, but it looked painful on his damaged face. As good as it felt to speak with his friend, there was an undercurrent of anger flowing through Ard's heart. King Pethredote would pay for this before the night was over. The dragon would find him and exact justice. Ard would make sure of that.

Far overhead, something rumbled like a peal of thunder that lasted too long. Raek glanced upward. "Is there really a dragon?"

"Just one," Ard replied. "I called her over to help me break you out."

"Oh, that's nice." Raek attempted a chuckle as Ard heaved him through the door at the top of the stairs. "Wait, are you serious?"

"There's a blazing load to explain, Raek, but it's going to have to wait. Just get on the horse."

"Ha! There's a horse."

With considerable effort, Ard helped his friend into the saddle, Raek's blanket finally slipping free and falling to the floor. Once he was situated, Ard handed him one of his Rollers.

"You remember how to use one of these?"

"Parry, thrust," he said. "Got it."

Ard unhitched the reins and passed them over. His friend's hands, usually so careful and steady, were trembling. Up a nearby staircase to the second floor, Ard heard distant shouting. He could just make out the words. "To the king! Rally to the king!" Pethredote was somewhere up there, still struggling to escape.

"What about you?" Raek asked.

"That's a strong horse, but she's not meant for two riders," he pointed out. "I'll see you on the outside, Short Fuse." Before Raek could say anything, Ard slapped the horse's flank, sending it galloping down the dim corridor.

All right. That part of his plan had gone as well as could be expected. And seeing Raek alive had given Ard a fresh rush of determination. He was tingling now, buzzing with a drive to finish this.

Ard sprinted up the nearby stairwell to the second floor. He wasn't eager to ascend more stairs in a building that seemed to be actively collapsing. Ard could hear the dragon somewhere above him, uncomfortably close now. Smashing, breaking, bellowing that bone-chilling cry.

The cries were more apparent here, and they led Ard forward.

"To the king! Homeland save the king!"

It was dark and hot on the second floor, the warmth of the dragon's fire reaching him from above. Ard moved forward following voices down the corridor to a heap of broken timbers and shattered stone. The rubble choked the hallway, a dozen Regulators shouting commands and heaving aside any manageable pieces. All their effort seemed concentrated on one spot near the front of the pile, the uniformed workers shoulder to shoulder.

"He's alive!" The shout seemed to redouble their efforts.

Ard drew cautiously nearer as the Reggies extracted the king. Pethredote was covered in dust, a matted bloody wound on his forehead.

Good, Ard thought, *at least the old fool is conscious.* His plan wouldn't be nearly as dramatic if Pethredote couldn't speak.

Ard wiped sweat from his face, sprinting forward and positioning himself to receive the injured king as the Regulators helped Pethredote down the rubble. In the frantic darkness, no one questioned the ruse artist's presence. They would take him for a loyal civilian. But sparks! The Reggies were literally handing King Pethredote over.

The king, face downcast, slipped an arm around Ard's neck, leaning heavily as they stepped away from the debris. With his free hand, Ard unclipped a pot of Barrier Grit from his belt as he sized up the situation.

There were three red-coat Regulators standing much too close.

A sharp twist sent the king tumbling to the floor behind Ard. A kick to the chest knocked the first Reggie backward. Ard's Roller flashed from its holster. The second man went down with a shot to the knee. The third Regulator was drawing his gun when Ard's lead ball tore through his hand.

Ard leapt backward, dragging the downed king by the lapels of his coat as he hurled the pot of Barrier Grit at the heap of rubble. The detonation filled the corridor, trapping some of the Reggies within, and the rest behind.

There was a tremendous thump, and the ceiling overhead groaned, dust falling like heavy snow, as a sudden heat washed over the hallway. *Oh, flames!* The dragon was right above them! What separated them from the frenzied mother dragon? A few floorboards and some timber joists? Those would never hold if she dropped her full weight upon them.

"Come on, you big load of slag." Ard hoisted the injured king, dragging him down the hallway. Overhead, boards cracked and sparks rained. The ceiling was on fire now, fingers of flame scraping away at the integrity of the floorboards.

Ard stumbled at the upper landing of the stairs, falling to his knees beside the heavy king. "Do you know why she's here?" Ard asked. The king's eyes barely flickered open. He wasn't faring well. The blazing king was supposed to die on Ard's schedule! This just simply wouldn't do.

Ard lifted the pot of Health Grit from the belt that Elbrig had given him outside the palace grounds. The disguise manager would be furious to know that Ard had wasted the detonation on the crooked king, but Pethredote needed to be lucid.

With a shattering of clay, the Grit ignited, catching king and ruse artist in a Health cloud. Ard felt instantly stronger, the ache of his leg injury vanishing. Pethredote took a deep breath, his blue eyes snapping open with renewed clarity.

"Have you finally come to kill me, Ardor Benn?" Pethredote's voice was tired and raspy.

"Do you know why she's here?" Ard asked again.

"You think the dragon has come to fetch that fraudulent egg," answered the king.

"The egg is not counterfeit," replied Ard.

"You and I both know that is *impossible*!" sputtered Pethredote. "No matter how real it may seem."

"Did you touch it?"

"Of course I have examined it!" Pethredote rose onto one elbow.

"Good," Ard answered. "I was counting on that." He grinned. "Now your scent is all over that egg. You see, *I'm* not going to kill you, Pethredote. That's what the sow is for."

"Bah!" The king's voice was growing stronger with every

moment in the Health cloud. "You delivered that egg. *Your* scent is as condemning as my own."

"You think I wouldn't have thought of that?" Ard replied. He drew a metal flask from his belt. "Pichar oil—a fragrant extract from the needles of the Pichar boughs. Tracers use it to mask their scent on Pekal. Makes them blazing near invisible to the dragons."

The king's eyes fell upon the shiny flask.

The ceiling exploded. One of the dragon's hind legs crashed through the weakened floorboards in a hail of ash and sparks. In the disorienting cloud of smoke and falling debris, long talons raked the floor beside Ard and the king. The leg began to flail, the desperate back-and-forth thrashing of a trapped animal.

There was a terrible crunching sound and Ard saw the exterior wall begin to slough away. Stones moved in a disorienting cascade as the crumbling palace came down. More of the dragon appeared, her blazing body smashing through the finest edifice man had built. Her tail swung like a mighty pendulum, tearing through stone as though it were parchment.

With a sudden surge of energy, the king lunged for the flask in Ard's hand. The two men tumbled down the staircase, leaving the upper stories of the palace to utter ruin. Ard felt a sharp pain in his ribs as they rolled, both men trying to use the other to take the brunt of the fall.

They skidded to a halt in the grand entrance foyer. Ard rolled away from the king, reaching for his gun. The holster was empty, his hand clawing for a weapon that must have tumbled loose in the struggle.

In the exploded brightness of the Light Grit–flooded hallway, Ard saw the old king rise to his knees. The metal flask gleamed in Pethredote's hand as he uncorked the opening.

Ard watched as the king doused his head with the contents of the flask, wincing as the fragrant liquid ran across his bleeding scalp. Ard wrinkled his nose at the smell, but the king seemed unfazed by its potency.

Pethredote rose slowly to his feet, gasping, grimacing, dripping. "Lost at your own game, Ardor Benn." His speech was once again slurred with pain, eyes flicking upward to the cacophonous devastation of the sow dragon. "Looks like she's coming for *you* after all."

Pethredote staggered through the open doorway and onto the exterior steps. Ard crawled forward as the palace seemed to cry out. He saw one of the foyer walls shift suddenly. There was a lot of weight crashing down on the upper stories. Being at the bottom of it all suddenly seemed like a horrible idea.

Ard rose to his feet, limping toward the palace exit one painstaking step at a time. The distance was less than a dozen yards, but it seemed a mile to Ard. He watched that open entryway, its tall doors hanging wide on heavy hinges. That threshold was a portal to survival. Ard prayed to the Homeland that it didn't collapse.

A gush of flames filled the foyer as he passed through the entryway. The grand stairs leading to the burning grounds were cluttered with chunks of stone and wood. Ard felt the cool night air touch his face, filling him with an extra repository of strength.

The crowd that Elbrig and Cinza had gathered was now thrice the size, pressing through the crumpled gate to invade the grounds as their king paused halfway down the steps, swooning from the pain of his injuries.

"They know what you've done!" Ard shouted down to Pethredote. "Your people want answers."

"The dragon has come for the king!" someone shouted. "She has come for vengeance! For the Bull Dragon Patriarchy!"

The crowd of impassioned Wayfarists was indeed agitated. Sparks! Was that a noblewoman hurling a stone in the king's direction? It was probably Cinza Ortemion in costume. Regardless, the disguise managers had done an excellent job tonight.

The king held out his hands, either too weak or too fearful to descend the steps to the citizens. "No!" he shouted, with an effort that nearly buckled his legs. "The dragon has come for this man!"

He pointed to Ard, who was crouching behind him on the upper stairs. "He is a criminal and an anarchist!"

"Let the dragon decide!" cried a man with a long mustache at the front of the crowd. He wore a miniature sculpted anchor on a chain around his neck—the symbol of a Wayfarist zealot. Although Ard didn't recognize him, he knew it would be Elbrig.

With a blast of hot wind, the dragon landed in a full display of her size and terror. She dropped to the broad stone steps, situating herself directly between Ard and the king. Her body was not glowing as fiercely as it had upon arrival. It was now a deep green, illuminated by the blaze of her desolation all around.

The dragon's long tail draped across the wreckage, and her elegant neck craned upward as she let out a rumbling bellow. She sat on powerful bent haunches, one foreleg touching the steps and the other drawn close to her breast, the talons pointed inward as she gripped something.

The egg.

The mother sow held it close to her heart, as though using the furnace heat of her massive body to warm the stony shell.

"The dragon has come to judge!" the disguised Elbrig shouted as the crowd quieted in the sow's presence. "She knows the scent of the man who poisoned the bulls. She has come for justice!"

It was all part of the script that he and Elbrig had discussed, although Ard wasn't sure how he was feeling about it now, as the beast's gaze fell upon him.

"Good girl," Ard muttered, trying to hold very still. "You know what you need to do," he urged in a whisper, voice shaking as he looked into those giant emerald eyes.

Did she know? Could the dragon somehow sense what he had done for that egg? That he had traveled through time to give her this gift of birth?

That was crazy thinking. She was an animal. How could she possibly know such a thing? Ard suddenly thought he might be way off the mark. Perhaps it wasn't acknowledgment in those eyes. Perhaps it was simply a bestial hunger that chased after the rage of her destruction.

She's going to eat me, Ard thought, his blood chilling. *My plans were too blazing arrogant this time.* He knew that, in truth, his scent was all over that egg. And while the scent-masking Pichar oil was certainly a good idea, Ard didn't have any.

The dragon dropped her head, jaws parting slightly, and a thin wisp of smoke curling off her tongue. Ard could feel the hot vapor upon his face, smell her fetid breath.

King Pethredote's voice drifted up the stairs as he gained confidence. He shouted to the citizens in an attempt to confirm Elbrig's theory. "Behold! The dragon knows..."

The sow's neck snaked out, curling away from Ard, those incomparable jaws snapping around King Pethredote midsentence. He screamed as she lifted him into the air, shaking him with a violent crunching of bones and a shower of blood. In a single gulp, the king was gone, downed like a cream-filled pastry from the Bakery on Humont Street.

Ard fell backward, gasping in shocked relief as the citizens scattered with screams of horror.

The dragon's wings snapped outward, her hind legs thrusting as her torso flared like coals under the breath of a bellows. Ard watched her rise, higher and higher into the dark sky, cradling that egg as she winged her way in the direction of Pekal's glorious peaks.

Ard lay still for several moments, the fear of his encounter having sapped all strength from his aching limbs. Then another piece of the burning palace gave way, rubble raining dangerously close.

With slow, deliberate movements, Ard picked himself up and descended the steps, not even pausing at the red spatter of Pethredote's remains. A group of bold Wayfarists stopped him at the bottom of the stairs, their frightened expressions somewhat awestruck.

"Is she coming back?" a man asked, glancing skyward.

"Are more dragons coming?" cried a woman.

Ard held out a weary hand. "The dragon got what she came for. We are safe now."

"They're saying the king poisoned the Bull Dragon Patriarchy," said a woman in the group. "That he killed an innocent Isle in the Mooring."

Excellent. People were talking. The facts had been sown, and the dragon's finale had germinated those seeds.

"It's all true," Ard confirmed. "The crusader monarch was not the man he claimed to be."

"Who are you?" whispered the first man.

A year ago, Ard would have claimed this moment. He would have proudly professed his name and taken responsibility for delivering the king to justice. He probably would have even gone so far as to say he'd commanded the dragon to fly away.

But Ardor Benn was a different man now. And his answer to the question was honest.

"I'm a servant of the Homeland."

Ard stepped past, the people letting him go in silent awe. The chaos of fleeing citizens churned around him as Ard made his way through fire and ash to the broken outer gate.

"You had me scared for a moment," Raek's voice sounded at his side. He was soaked in sweat and shaking, still clinging to the saddle of the stolen Reggie horse. But his face carried an old familiar expression of mischief.

"I had everything under my thumb, Raek."

"Sounds like the people know the truth," Raek said, guiding his horse to stay by Ard's side as they moved away from the burning palace grounds.

"Not all of it," answered Ard. "Not yet. We just told them the parts that would get them fired up."

"We?"

"The crazies," Ard replied. "They were working the crowd."

"Ah, that explains all that blazing nonsense about the dragon bringing justice to the king," said Raek.

"*Poetic* justice," Ard replied. "I thought the dragon added a nice touch. Plus, a vengeful sow lends a bit of veracity to our wild accusations against the king."

"This will change the political dynamic of the Greater Chain," Raek said. "The crusader monarch was supposed to end his term peacefully. Now the nobles will be scrabbling over who gets to rule the islands."

Ard hadn't really intended any of this. He'd been swept into dangerous waters, compelled to swim on as the ruse got bigger and bigger.

"How did you know, Ard?" Raek asked. "How did you know the dragon would eat Pethredote instead of you?"

For a moment, staring into those big green eyes, Ard hadn't been so sure. "Reek Sauce," he answered. "Elbrig picked up a flask for me. I convinced the king to pour it all over his head, essentially marking himself as irresistible dragon bait."

Raek burst into a laugh that instantly caused him to grimace in pain. "Talk about a foul supper!"

Ard shook his head in mock pity. "Poor dragon."

"It was a blazing genius plan, though," Raek admitted.

"Hey. I was just doing what I always do."

"Feeding corrupt monarchs to dragons?"

Ard chuckled. "Manipulating the other guy." Strangely, it was what the Homeland had always Urged him to do.

The Homeland.

Ard wanted to make it to that perfect future. But he wasn't going to leave the Homeland to be crafted at the discretion of one almighty individual with the power to rewrite time. Ard would reach his own Homeland by the natural unveiling of day upon day. By the choices he made.

Ard glanced up at Raek. His friend would have his skin for

thinking such elevated Wayfarist sentiments. Ardor Benn, a religious man? Stranger things had happened. Ard himself had become a Paladin Visitant. He couldn't wait to fill Raek in on that particular accomplishment.

"So, what's next?" Raek asked. "The Greater Chain happens to need a new ruler and a new Prime Isle. And there just so happens to be two of us."

"Ha!" Ard laughed. "Let's wait at least until they build us a new palace."

"Good point."

What *were* they going to do next? Ard had become accustomed to holding the world on his shoulders as it turned upside down. Could he really let that burden go? Along with the political and religious upheaval, Lyndel's people would need protection and justice. Pekal would need safeguarding to ensure that the bull dragon hatched. Moonsickness would likely touch more outlying villages before the dragon population recovered enough to fully absorb the rays.

Perhaps Ard could position himself...

No.

"We can't go on like this, Raek," whispered Ard.

You have to stop this, Ard. Quarrah's words rattled in Ard's head.

"You want to go clean?" the big man asked.

Ard wanted Quarrah Khai. He remembered her face in that dark alley as she pleaded with him to be done.

Well, he was done now.

~

My part in this is over. What becomes of the truths I gathered is no longer up to me. I chose this fate. And now I go to die, a victim of my own impassioned ardor.

GRIT
CLASSIFICATION TABLE

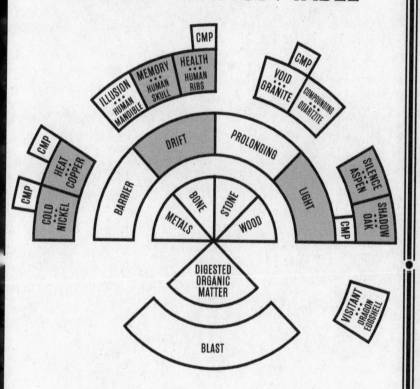

CMP — ILLUSION ··· HUMAN MANDIBLE
MEMORY ··· HUMAN SKULL
HEALTH ··· HUMAN RIBS

CMP — VOID ··· GRANITE
COMPOUNDING ··· QUARTZITE

CMP — HEAT ··· COPPER
CMP — COLD ··· NICKEL

SILENCE ··· ASPEN
SHADOW ··· OAK
CMP

DRIFT
PROLONGING

BARRIER
LIGHT

METALS
BONE
STONE
WOOD

DIGESTED ORGANIC MATTER

BLAST

VISITANT ··· DRAGON EGGSHELL

 CAN BE FULLY CONTAINED

 CAN BE COMPOUNDED

GLOSSARY

Common Grit: Barrier, Blast, Drift, Light, and Prolonging Grit are classified as *Common Grit*. These are derived from common types of source material, including digested organic matter, most metals, most bone, most wood, and most stone. All organic material can be digested and becomes Slagstone, although bone and wood typically pass through the dragon intact and are then processed to become various other types of Grit. In contrast to Common Grit, types of Specialty Grit are each derived from a single, specific indigestible source material. For example, all types of wood but oak and aspen are classified as *Common* and produce Light Grit. Oak, however, produces Shadow Grit and aspen produces Silence Grit, both are types of Specialty Grit.

Contained detonations: Any cloud that is met with physical resistance sufficient to inhibit the cloud's natural spherical shape.

> **Partially contained:** Any detonation where part but not all of the cloud's natural spherical shape is contained. This is the most common detonation (as it includes the familiar dome), due to the fact that most detonations occur as Slagstone sparks against a solid surface, frequently placing the cloud's center against the ground or a wall. Partially contained detonations cannot be moved or altered.

> **Fully contained:** Any detonation where every part of the cloud's natural spherical shape has been completely contained. Once

enclosed in this manner, clouds resulting from the following types of Grit can be moved: Drift, Light, Shadow, Silence, Cold, Heat, Memory, and Health. Any attempt to fully contain other Grit types will effectively render their detonation null.

Loss of containment: A partially contained cloud cannot lose containment, since a portion of the detonation was fully formed, reaching stability by achieving its natural spherical shape. That said, should a wall (upon which a partially contained cloud is formed) collapse, the cloud dome will remain suspended in the exact place where it was originally detonated. In the event of a fully contained cloud losing containment, however, the detonation will suddenly assume its desired spherical shape, rendering the cloud immovable.

Granule: Smallest standard unit of weight measurement. 450 granules = 1 panweight.

Ignition rate: The time it takes for Grit to make a fully formed cloud after detonation.

Natural cloud duration: All detonations (with an exception of Blast Grit) result in a cloud that lasts between eight and ten minutes, depending on the quality of the Grit.

Quality: Quality is lowered when contaminates are introduced to the Grit during or after processing. Contaminates may include trace particles of other Grit types, or other natural contaminates such as dust, dirt, or sand. Low quality Grit, results in a cloud whose duration can be shortened by up to two minutes. It is important to note that the quality of the Grit does not alter the potency of the cloud's effect, only the duration of the cloud.

Overlapping detonations: These clouds occur when multiple detonations (of the same or differing Grit types) are separated by enough time that each cloud is fully formed before the next ignites. In the likely event that the center of the two detonations are not in the same place, the resulting clouds will partially overlap, with no apparent change to their effect in the overlapping area.

Radius: The distance between the detonation center, where ignition occurs, and the surface of a detonation cloud. In the event of a contained detonation cloud, the radius is still considered to be the distance to the point where the cloud's surface would have formed, given the chance to achieve its natural spherical shape.

Simultaneous detonations: Any two or more detonations of the same Grit type that occur within the space of the ignition rate will effectively merge into one cloud, its dimensions reflecting the sum of all detonating Grit. This is not to be confused with overlapping detonations.

Slagstone: Digested organic matter that has passed through a dragon's digestive tract and subsequently been fired into a stonelike material. The term *Slagstone* frequently is applied to the entire mass of fired excrement, although, technically, the indigestible materials within are entirely different. While Slagstone is frequently reduced to Blast Grit, the stone itself has notable properties. Any measurable impact against Slagstone results in a spark. Thus, small Slagstone fragments are used for gun hammers, ignitor tools, and the catalyst within detonation pots and Grit kegs.

Source Material: The original material from which each type of Grit is derived.

Specialty Grit: Cold, Heat, Illusion, Memory, Health, Void, Compounding, Silence, Shadow, and Visitant Grit are classified as *Specialty Grit*. These are derived from a single, specific indigestible source material. The source materials for Specialty Grit, while technically falling under one of the five common classes, are in fact exceptions. As an example, all types of metal but nickel and copper are classified as *Common* and produce Barrier Grit. However, nickel produces Cold Grit and copper produces Heat Grit, both types of Specialty Grit.

Types of Common Grit

Barrier Grit

Cloud effect: Perimeter hardens into an impenetrable shell.
Source material: Common metals
Ignition rate: 0.4 seconds
Notes: The distinctive hard shell of a Barrier cloud forms as soon as the detonation has reached its full size. The shell-like perimeter develops

upon contact with air, and once formed, cannot be altered. If detonated against a wall (forming a dome), it will remain in place, even
if the wall is removed, leaving the dome like an open bowl. Because
of this feature, digging under the edge of the solid perimeter is one
of the only known ways to bypass a dome of Barrier Grit. The Barrier shell is considered impenetrable, even fireproof. However, clouds
from other Grit types can pass through a Barrier wall (with the
exception of Blast Grit). When mixed with Prolonging Grit, the Barrier shell grows weaker after the natural ten minutes of full potency.
Eventually, things within or without can forcefully press through the
softening perimeter. Detonations cannot be fully contained.

Blast Grit

Cloud effect: No lingering cloud. Detonation results in a short-lived forceful
explosion of fire and sparks.

Source material: Common digested organic matter (Slagstone)

Ignition rate: 0.2 seconds

Notes: Blast Grit's notable absence of a lasting detonation "cloud" has led
some to question even its basic classification as *Grit*. Its unique nature
likely has to do with it being the only Grit type obtained from *digested*
organic material, while all other Grit types are derived from *indigestible* materials that have passed through a dragon's tract and subsequently been fired. Thus, every mound of fired dragon dung yields
Blast Grit in large quantities. Its abundance makes this Grit significantly less expensive than any other, which led to its most common
use in ammunitions.

Drift Grit

Cloud effect: Weightlessness.

Source material: Common bones

Ignition rate: 0.4 seconds

Notes: Objects within a Drift cloud act as if they are at rest with regards
to the outside world. They can neither act nor be acted upon by any
force or object outside the Drift cloud. While objects within a cloud
of Drift Grit are considered weightless, the cloud itself is subject to
the planet's gravity. Without such a caveat, the objects within the

cloud would theoretically be flung outward at the speed of the planet's rotation. Although the cloud itself is tied to the gravitational pull, its actual weight and mass is insignificant, allowing a contained cloud to be carried with no noticeable payload. Objects within a fully contained cloud move with the cloud.

Light Grit

Cloud effect: Light.
Source material: Common wood
Ignition rate: 0.6 seconds
Notes: The brightness of detonated Light Grit is comparable to firelight. A fist-sized Light cloud yields approximately the same illumination as a fist-sized flame. While both fire and Light Grit draw light from wood, there are several notable differences. Light Grit detonations are odorless, smokeless, and devoid of any discernible warmth. The glow resulting from a cloud of Light Grit is steady, lacking the characteristic flicker of common flame.

Prolonging Grit

Cloud effect: Prolonged effect of another Grit type when detonated simultaneously.
Source material: Common stone
Ignition rate: 0.2 seconds
Notes: The nature and use of Prolonging Grit is reliant upon simultaneous detonation with another type of Grit. Ignited on its own, Prolonging Grit burns out in a useless burst, providing no effect and leaving no lingering cloud. Prolonging Grit allows a detonation to stretch beyond its natural duration. The length of this sustaining effect is determined by the amount of Prolonging Grit added to the other Grit type at the time of ignition. The addition of Prolonging Grit causes the effect of the other Grit to decay slowly after the natural detonation duration, rather than dispersing immediately as usual. Any additional minutes produced by the presence of Prolonging Grit will gradually wane until the cloud burns out. Prolonging Grit is extremely useful and widely used. It is ineffective only on Blast Grit, as there is no detonation cloud to sustain.

Types of Specialty Grit

Cold Grit

Cloud effect: Cold air.
Source material: Nickel
Ignition rate: 0.6 seconds
Notes: The baseline temperature for a cloud of Cold Grit is around 35 degrees (Shwazer), just above the freezing point of water. The cloud's potency is self-sustaining and largely unaffected by external air temperature.

Compounding Grit

Cloud effect: Compounded effect of another Grit type when detonated simultaneously.
Source material: Quartzite
Ignition rate: 0.2 seconds
Notes: The nature and use of Compounding Grit is reliant upon simultaneous detonation with another type of Grit. When ignited on its own, Compounding Grit burns out in a useless burst, providing no effect and leaving no lingering cloud. Compounding Grit intensifies the effect of another Grit type. This intensifying effect is determined by the amount of Compounding Grit added to the other Grit type at the time of ignition. Not all Grit types can be effectively Compounded. It is ineffective on Blast, Drift, Barrier, Shadow, Visitant, Silence, and Memory Grit. It can be used with Prolonging Grit to supplement any other Grit type, but does not affect the distinctive waning that results from the use of Prolonging Grit.

Health Grit

Cloud effect: Capable of healing wounds and purging imperfections in all living lifeforms.
Source material: Human ribs
Ignition rate: 0.8 seconds
Notes: The primary function of Health Grit is to heal, or retain the health, of any living being inside its cloud. It has the remarkable ability to speed the healing of physical injuries, including aches and pains, bruising, broken bones, and damaged flesh, though it is ineffective in regrowing body parts. A cloud of Health Grit can also

purge imperfections from the body, such as allergic reactions, poisons, and toxins. It does not, however, cure common illnesses. This has led some healers to believe that flus and colds are actually living organisms within a human host, and are thus strengthened by a detonation of Health Grit. There are some risks inherent to overuse of Health Grit, specifically when the healing effect is Prolonged or Compounded. Such risks include debilitating addictions and weakening of the body. Application of Health clouds should be limited and localized to injured areas to prevent overexposure.

Heat Grit

Cloud effect: Warm air.

Source material: Copper

Ignition rate: 0.8 seconds

Notes: The baseline temperature for a cloud of Heat Grit is around 95 degrees (Shwazer), about half the boiling point of water. The cloud's potency is self-sustaining and largely unaffected by external air temperature. While many have adopted the use of Heat clouds to warm their residences, it is quite an impractical and expensive practice. Without a significant amount of Compounding Grit, a regular Heat cloud emanates very little warmth, and one must reach inside the detonation to benefit from it. The detonation is smokeless, odorless, and emits no light.

Illusion Grit

Cloud effect: Capable of recording, and then replaying an image specific to one location.

Source material: Human mandible

Ignition rate: 0.3 seconds

Notes: A first detonation makes a record tied to a specific geographic location. A second detonation in that same location displays the recorded events without sound. This effectively resets the area, meaning that a third detonation in the same spot would make a new record. Overlapping, but offsetting, the second detonation will allow for the overlapped section of the first detonation to be viewed, but will not record the outlying portions of the second cloud. In essence, any contact between two clouds of Illusion Grit will render the link satisfied and reset the area. Detonations cannot be fully contained.

Memory Grit

Cloud effect: Erases memories.
Source material: Human skull
Ignition rate: 0.5 seconds
Notes: Memory Grit's sole purpose is to remove memories of those within
  its cloud, but it is important to note that the erasure does not occur
  until the detonation burns out. While operating within a cloud of
  Memory Grit, a person retains full knowledge of events leading up to
  the detonation, as well as what is transpiring within the cloud. The
  stretch of memories from ignition to burn out are then erased the
  moment the detonation closes.

Shadow Grit

Cloud effect: Darkness.
Source material: Oak
Ignition rate: 0.6 seconds
Notes: Clouds of Shadow Grit have been measured at absolute darkness,
  comparable to being in an underground cave with no light source.
  While it is impossible for anyone outside the detonation to see in,
  those within the Shadow cloud are able to see out. This effect is much
  like a person sitting inside a dark room looking through an open
  door. It is easy for that individual to see what is happening on the
  illuminated street, but difficult for those on the street to see into the
  room.

Silence Grit

Cloud effect: Silence.
Source material: Aspen
Ignition rate: 0.4 seconds
Notes: A detonation of Silence Grit will contain any sound originating
  from within the cloud. A person within the cloud cannot hear anything outside. Similarly, a person outside the cloud cannot hear anything within.

Visitant Grit

Cloud effect: Capable of summoning a Paladin Visitant.

Source material: Dragon eggshell

Ignition rate: 0.6 seconds

Notes: A successful detonation will summon a fabled Paladin Visitant, capable of destroying all life with a single utterance. Any who hear, see, or touch a Paladin Visitant will instantly wither in flames. It is notable that most Visitant Grit detonations throughout history have failed to yield a Paladin Visitant. Only the most worthy Wayfarists can succeed in summoning the omnipotent beings. As such, it is the responsibility of the Prime Isle or Prime Isless to carefully select a worthy hero to detonate the Visitant Grit in times of need. Detonations cannot be fully contained.

Void Grit

Cloud effect: Outward-pushing energy.

Source material: Granite

Ignition rate: 0.5 seconds

Notes: The effect of this cloud emanates from the center point: the specific place where the detonation originated. From that center, an equally distributed force constantly pushes outward, ejecting items within the cloud, or repelling items that attempt to enter. While the effect of a Void cloud can be Compounded, its natural force is usually sufficient to expel an average sized person, head on. Detonations cannot be fully contained.

The story continues in...

Kingdom of Grit: Book Two

ACKNOWLEDGMENTS

I had intended for this book to be a pet project—something I could pick away at over the course of several years, something to keep me busy between the deadlines for my middle-grade books. But the moment I started writing it, the story took hold of me and wouldn't let me go. I ended up writing the entire first draft over the space of about six months.

From a young age, I had dreamed of writing an epic fantasy like this. But a book of this size and complexity required me to call on friends and family for valuable feedback. Special thanks to my early readers: Spencer Munyan; Rob, Chris, and Coby Davis; Celeste and Brad Baillio; Tom and Kaleb Elmer; Laura and Martin Wilson; Anna and Maren Lund; and Andy Cunningham. Thanks to my brother, Clayton Whitesides, for answering many random geographical questions, and to Mike Johnson for some technical consultations.

A big thanks goes to my agent, Ammi-Joan Paquette, who got behind this story with so much enthusiasm. Thank you for going the extra mile with your representation, venturing into the realm of adult epic fantasy!

To my editor at Orbit, Lindsey Hall, I can't say thank you enough! Your excitement for these characters and this world was so motivating. It was a pleasure to work with you on this project.

The whole team at Orbit has been fantastic. Thanks to Bradley Englert for your editorial services, and for taking things over without a hiccup. And thanks to Emily Byron (Orbit UK) for her insights and involvement every step along the way.

Thanks to Serena Malyon for creating a map that wonderfully represented my world. It's a beautiful piece of art. And to Tommy Arnold for the amazing cover.

A huge thanks to my mom and dad, who always encouraged my writing and reading habits. And the biggest thanks of all to my wife, Connie. She knows these characters inside and out, and she's always willing to listen to my ramblings.

I hope you've all enjoyed running this ruse with Ardor Benn. I can't wait for his story to continue. Thanks for reading!

extras

about the author

Tyler Whitesides is the author of bestselling children's series Janitors and the Wishmakers. *The Thousand Deaths of Ardor Benn* is his adult debut. When he's not writing, Tyler enjoys playing percussion, hiking, fly-fishing, cooking, and the theater. He lives in the mountains of northern Utah with his wife and son.

Find out more about Tyler Whitesides and other Orbit authors by registering for the free monthly newsletter at www.orbitbooks.net

if you enjoyed

THE THOUSAND DEATHS
OF ARDOR BENN

look out for

THE DRAGON LORDS:
FOOL'S GOLD

by

Jon Hollins

Guardians of the Galaxy *meets* **The Hobbit** *in this rollicking fantasy adventure.*

It's not easy to live in a world ruled by dragons. The taxes are high and their control is complete. But for one group of bold adventurers, it's time to band together and steal back some of that wealth.

No one ever said they were smart.

1
Will

It was a confrontation as old as time. A tale begun back when the Pantheon of old first breathed life into the clay mold of man and set him down upon the earth. It was the tale of the untamable pitted against the master. Of the wild tearing at the walls of the civilized. It was man versus the beast.

Will placed each foot carefully, held his balance low. He circled slowly. Cold mud pulled at his feet. Sweat trickled down the crease between his eyebrows. Inch by inch he closed the distance.

The pig Bessie grunted at him.

"Five shek says she tips him on his arse," said Albor, one of Will's two farmhands. A strip of hairy gut was visible where he rested it upon the sty's rickety old fence. It was, Will had noted, significantly hairier in fact than his chin, which he scratched at constantly. Albor's wife had just departed the nearby village for a monthlong trip to help look after her sister's new baby, and Albor was three days into growing the beard she hated.

"I say it's face first, he lands," said Dunstan, Will's other farmhand. The two men were a study in contrasts. Where Albor's stomach swayed heavily over his gut, Dunstan's broad leather belt was wrapped twice around his waist and still flapped loose beyond the buckle. His narrow face was barely visible behind a thick cloud of facial hair, which his wife loved to excess. She had a tendency to braid sections of it and line it with bows.

"You're on," said Albor, spitting in his muddy palm and holding it out to Dunstan.

Will gave a damn about neither beards nor wives. All he cared about was his father's thrice-cursed prize sow, Bessie. She had been his dancing partner in this sty for almost half an hour now. He was so coated in mud that if he lay upon the sty's floor, he would have been virtually invisible. He briefly considered this as a possible angle of attack, but the pig was as likely to shit on him and call it a good day's work as anything else. There was an uncanny intelligence in her eyes. Still, she was old and he was young. Brute force would win the day.

He closed the distance down by another inch.

Bessie narrowed her eyes.

Another inch.

Bessie squealed and charged. Will lunged, met the charge head-on. His hands slammed down hard against her sides.

Bessie flew through his mud-slick palms and crashed all of her considerable weight into his legs. The world performed a sprawling flip around Will's head, then hit him in the face.

He came up spluttering mud, and was just in time to hear Dunstan say, "That's five shek you owe me then."

Bessie was standing nonchalantly behind him, with an air of almost studied calm.

Will found his resolve hardening. Bessie had to die. With a roar, he launched himself at the pig. She bucked wildly. And yet still one of his hands snagged a bony trotter. He heaved upon it with all his might.

Bessie, however, had lived upon the farm longer than Will. She had survived lean winters, breeched piglets, and several virulent diseases, and was determined to survive him. She did not allow her limb to collapse under Will's weight, advanced years or no. Instead she simply pulled him skidding through the mud. After several laps, he appeared to be done. With her free hoof, she kicked him in the forehead to emphasize the lesson, then walked away.

"I think you almost got her that time," Albor called in what might be generously described as an encouraging tone.

Will did not respond. Personal honor was at stake at this point in the proceedings. Still, there was only so much mud a man could swallow. He clambered to his feet and retreated to consider his options.

Dunstan patted him on the shoulder as he collapsed against the fence. Bessie regarded him balefully.

"She's too strong for me," Will said when he'd gotten his breath back.

"To be fair, you say that about most girls," Albor told him.

"I have to outsmart her."

"That too," Dunstan chipped in.

"Don't usually work, though." Albor chewed a strand of straw sagely.

"This," said Will, his temper fraying, "is not so much helpful advice as much as it is shit swilling in a blocked ditch. That pig has to become crispy rashers and if you have nothing helpful to add you can go back to picking apples in the orchard."

For a short while the only sound was Bessie farting noisily in her corner of the sty.

Above the men, thin clouds swept across a pale blue sky. The distant mountains were a misty purple, almost translucent.

Will softened. None of this was Albor's or Dunstan's fault, even if they did not want to see old Bessie taken to the butcher's block. Deep down—deeper perhaps now than at the start of his ordeal—neither did he. Bessie had been part of this farm as long as he could remember. His father had sat him upon her back and had him ride around the sty, whooping and hollering, while his mother stood clucking her tongue. Dunstan and Albor had been there, cheering him on. Even old Firkin had been there.

But now Will's parents were gone to an early grave, and Firkin had lost his mind. Bessie was old and would not sow anymore. And Will was the unwilling owner of a farm on the brink of ruin.

"Look," he said, voice calmer, "I want Bessie dead no more than you do, but I am out of options. The Consortium increased taxes again, and paying them has left my coffers bare. If I am to have a hope of surviving another year, I need to put her to the knife and sell her pieces for as much as I can get. Next winter she'll be blind and hobbled and it will be a kindness."

Another silence.

"You can't wait a little, Will?" said Albor, straw drooping in the corner of his mouth. "Give her one last good year?"

Will sighed. "If I do, then there won't be anyone to slaughter her. This whole place will be gone to the Consortium and I'll be in a debtors' jail, and you two will be in old Cornwall's tavern without any sheks to pay for his ale."

At that threat, the two farmhands looked at each other. Finally Dunstan shrugged. "I never liked that fucking pig anyway."

Albor echoed his sad smile.

"That's more like it," said Will. "Now let's see if together three grown men can't outwit one decrepit pig."

Slowly, painfully, Will, Albor, and Dunstan hobbled back toward the farmhouse. Albor rubbed at a badly bruised hip. Dunstan was wringing muddy water out of his sodden, matted beard.

"It's all right," said Will, "we'll get her tomorrow."

Later, the farm's other animals locked away for the night, straw fresh on the barn's floor, Will stood in the farmhouse, heating a heavy iron pot full of stew over the hearth. A few strips of chicken roiled fretfully among vegetable chunks.

He never bothered naming the chickens. It was easier that way.

He sighed as he watched the stew slowly simmer. He should be checking the cheese presses, or scooping butter out of the churn and into pots before it spoiled, or possibly even attempting to tally his books so he could work out exactly how much money he owed folk. Instead he stood and stared.

The nights were long out on the farm. It was five miles through the fields and woods down to The Village. The distance had never seemed far when he was a child. But that was when his parents were alive, and when Dunstan and Albor, and even Firkin, would all have stayed to share the supper, with laughter, and jokes, and fiddle music lilting late into the night. That was when performing the chores around the house had never seemed exactly like work, and when stoking the fire so it warmed the whole room had never felt like an extravagance.

The firelight cast the heavy wooden cabinets and thick oak table and chairs in guttering light. Will tried to focus on that, not the shadows of the day. Maybe Bessie did have one more litter in her. Maybe he could give her one more year. A good litter would bring in enough coin. Or near enough, if the taxes didn't go up again. And he could scrimp and save in a few places. Maybe sell a few of the chairs. It wasn't like he needed more than one.

Yes. Yes, of course that would work. And Lawl or some other member of the Pantheon would manifest in the run-down old temple in the village below and shower them all with gold. That was what would happen . . .

His slow-bubbling thoughts were interrupted abruptly by a sharp rap at his door. He snapped his head to look at the thick oak slats. Outside, rain had begun to fall, tapping a complex undulating rhythm against the thatch roof above his head. It was over an hour's walk from The Village. Who would bother dragging themselves out here at this hour?

He had half-dismissed the sound as a loose branch blowing across the yard when it came again. A hard, precise rap that rattled the door latch. If it was a branch, it was a persistent one.

Removing the stew pot from the fire, he crossed the room quickly, unlatched the door, and opened it onto a cold and blustery night.

Four soldiers stood upon his doorstep. Their narrowed eyes stared out from beneath the shadows of their helms, which dripped rainwater down onto their long noses. Swords hung heavily on their large belts, each pommel embossed with an image of two batlike wings—the mark of the Dragon Consortium. Sodden leather jerkins with the same insignia were pulled over their heavy chain-mail shirts.

They were not small men. Their expressions were not kind. Will could not tell for sure, but they bore a striking resemblance to the four soldiers who had carried off most of the coin he'd been relying on to get through the winter.

"Can I help you?" asked Will, as politely as he was able. If there was anything at which he could fail to help them, he wanted to know about it.

"You can get the piss out of my way so me and my men can come out of this Hallows-cursed rain," said the lead soldier. He was taller than the others, with a large blunt nose that appeared to have been used to stop a frying pan, repeatedly, for most of his childhood. Air whistled in and out of it as he spoke.

"Of course." Will stepped aside. While he bore the guards of the Dragon Consortium no love, he bore even less for the idea of receiving a sound thrashing at their hands.

The four soldiers tramped laboriously in, sagging under the weight of their wet armor. "Obliged," said the last of the men, nodding. He had a kinder face than the others. Will saw the lead soldier roll his eyes.

They stood around Will's small fire and surveyed his house with expressions that looked a lot like disdain. Large brown footprints tracked their path from the door. The fourth guard looked at them, then shrugged at Will apologetically.

For a moment they all stood still. Will refused to leave the door, clinging to the solidity of it. Grounding himself in the wood his father had cut and hewn before he was born. As he watched the soldiers by the fire, his stomach tied more knots than an obsessive-compulsive fisherman.

Finally he crossed to them, the table, and his stew. He began to ladle it into a large if poorly made bowl. He wasn't hungry anymore, but it gave him something to do. These soldiers would get to their business with or without his help.

As he ladled, the lead soldier fiddled with a leather pouch at his waist.

"Nice place this," said the fourth, seeming to feel more awkward in the silence than the others.

"Thank you," Will said, as evenly as he was able. "My parents built it."

"Keep saying to the missus we should get a place like this," the guard continued, "but she doesn't like the idea of farm living. Likes to be close to the center of things. By which she really means the alchemist. Gets a lot of things from the alchemist, she does. Very healthy woman. Always adding supplements to my diet." He patted his stomach, metal gauntleted hand clanking against the chain mail. "Doesn't ever seem to do any good." He looked off into the middle distance. "Of course my brother says I'm cuckolded by a drug-addled harpy, but he's always been a bit negative."

The guard seemed to notice that everyone was staring at him.

"Oh," he said. "Sorry. Obviously none of that is related to why we're officially here. Just wanted to, well, you know . . ." He withered under his commanding officer's stare.

The lead soldier looked away from him, down to a piece of browning parchment paper that he had retrieved from his pouch. Then he turned the gaze he had used to dominate his subordinate upon Will.

"You are Willett Altior Fallows, son of Mickel Betterra Fallows, son of Theorn Pentauk Fallows, owner and title holder of this farmstead?" he asked. He was not a natural public speaker, stumbling over most of the words. But he kept his sneer firmly in place as he read.

Will nodded. "That's what my mother always told me," he said. The fourth soldier let out a snort of laughter, then at the looks from the others, murdered his mirth like a child tossed down a well.

The lead soldier's expression, by contrast, did not flicker for an instant. Will thought he might even have seen a small flame as the joke died against his stony wall of indifference. The soldier had the air of a man who had risen through the ranks on the strength of having no imagination whatsoever. The sort of man who followed orders, blindly and doggedly, and without remorse.

"The dragon Mattrax and by extension the Dragon Consortium as a whole," the officer continued in his same stilted way, reading from the parchment, "find your lack of compliance with this year's taxes a great affront to their nobility, their honor, and their deified status. You are therefore—"

"Wait a minute." Will stood, ladle in his hand, knuckles white about its handle, staring at the man. "My lack of *what*?"

For a moment, as the soldier had begun to speak, Will had felt his stomach plunge in some suicidal swan dive, abandoning ship entirely. And then, as the next words came, there had been a sort of pure calm. An empty space in his emotions, as if they had all been swept away by some great and terrible wind that had scoured the landscape clean and sent cows flying like siege weaponry.

But by the time the soldier finished, there was a fury in him he could barely fathom. He had always thought of himself as a peaceable man. In twenty-eight years he had been in exactly three fights, had started only one of them, and had thrown no more than one punch in each. But, as if summoned by some great yet abdominally restrained wizard, an inferno of rage had appeared out of nowhere in his gut.

"My *taxes*?" he managed to splutter. He was fighting against an increasing urge to take his soup ladle and ram it so far down the soldier's throat he could scoop out his balls. "Your great and grand fucking dragon Mattrax took me for almost every penny I had. He has laid waste to the potential for this farm with his greed. And there was not a single complaint from me. Not as I gave you every inherited copper shek, silver drach, and golden bull I had."

He stood, almost frothing with rage, staring down the lean, unimpressed commander.

"Actually," said the fourth soldier, almost forgotten at the periphery of events, "it was probably a clerical error. There's an absolutely vast number of people who fall under Mattrax's purview, and every year there's just a few people whose names don't get ticked. It's an inevitability of bureaucracy, I suppose."

Both Will and the commanding officer turned hate-filled eyes on the soldier.

"So," said Will, voice crackling with fire, "tick my fucking name then."

"Oh." The soldier looked profoundly uncomfortable. "Actually that's not something we can do. Not our department at all. I mean you can appeal, but first you have to pay the tax a second time, and then appeal."

"Pay the tax?" Will said, the room losing focus for him, a strange sense of unreality descending. "I can't pay the fucking tax a second time. Nobody here could afford that. That's insane."

"Yes," said the guard sadly. "It's not a very fair system."

Will felt as if the edges of the room had become untethered from reality, as if the whole scene might fold up around him, wither away to nothingness, leaving him alone in a black void of insanity.

"Willett Altior Fallows," intoned the lead soldier, with a degree of blandness only achievable through years of honing his callousness to the bluntest of edges, "I hereby strip you of your title to this land in recompense for taxes not paid. You shall be taken from here directly to debtors' jail."

"Oh debtors' jail," said the fourth guard, slapping a palm to his forehead. "I totally forgot about debtors' jail. Because," he added, nodding to himself, "it's not as if you can appeal the ruling while you're in the jail. Nobody's going to come down and listen to you down there. But when you get out, you can totally appeal. I think the queue is only four or five years long at that point. Though, honestly, I would have expected it to be shorter given the fairly high mortality rate among inmates in debtors' jail . . . " he trailed off. "Don't suppose that's very helpful, is it?" he said to the room at large.

Will could barely hear him. This could not be happening. Every careful financial plan he had put together. Every future course he had plotted. Each one of them ruined, ground beneath the twin heels of incompetence and greed, became nothing more than kindling for his fury. Rage roared around him, filled his ears with noise, his vision with red.

He tried to say something, opened his mouth. Only an inarticulate gurgle of rage emerged.

"Chain his hands," said the lead soldier.

Something snapped in Will. Suddenly the bowl of stew was in his hand. He flung it hard and fast at the lead soldier's face. It crashed into his nose with a satisfying crunch, shattered. Pottery shards scored lines across the man's face. He'd made that bowl as a boy, he remembered now. A simple pinch pot; a gift for his mother. He'd meant it as a vase but hadn't been old enough to know what a vase had actually looked like. He'd flown into a temper tantrum when he first saw her eating from it. And now it was gone. Along with everything else.

The soldier reeled back, bellowed. Will was barely paying attention. He was already lunging for the larger pot, iron sides still scalding from the heat of the fire.

A guard beat him, steel-encased fist slamming into the pot, sending the contents flying.

Will could hear steel scraping against leather. Swords leaving their hilts.

He brought the ladle round in a tight arc, smashed it into the lunging guard's cheek. The man staggered sideways. Will came up, was face-to-face with the fourth soldier. The soldier's eyes were wide, panicked. Will stabbed straight forward, the spoon of the ladle crashing into the guard's throat. The guard dropped to the floor choking, a look of surprise and hurt on his face.

And then the last guard's sword smashed the ladle from Will's hands and sent it skittering across the floor.

Out of daily kitchenware, Will reconsidered his options. The lead guard was recovering, snarling, red blistering skin bleeding openly. The fourth guard was still gasping, but the other two both had their swords up. They advanced.

As most other options seem to lead to rapid and fatal perforation, Will backed up fast.

"Not sure you're going to make it to jail," said one guard. He was smiling.

The other just stalked forward, weight held low, eyes narrowed beneath dark brows.

Will glanced about. But his mother had always been strict about leaving the farm outside of the house and that habit had died hard. There was no handy scythe, no gutting knife, not even a shovel. His foot slipped in one of the muddy footprints the guards had left on the tile floor. The grinning guard closed the gap another yard.

"Stop fucking about and kill the little shit stain already," snarled the soldier with the blistered face.

The words were the catalyst. Will unfroze as the guards leapt forward. He tore out of the kitchen door, heard the swish of steel through the air, waited for pain, and found it hadn't come by the time his feet carried him through the threshold and into the darkness.

He abandoned the spill of yellow light and tore toward the barn as fast as his feet would carry him. There was a way to fight back there. A way to stop this. There had to be.

"After the little fucker!" The rasping rage of the burned guard chased after him.

"He hit me." The bewildered burble of the fourth guard.

"I'll fucking hit you if you don't bring me his spleen."

The other guards were hard on his heels. Rain slashed at him. Will hit the door of the barn, bounced off, felt the sting of it in his shoulder, his palms. He scrabbled at the door, flung it open. A sword blade embedded itself in the frame as he darted through. A guard grunted in frustration.

Everything was shadows and the smell of damp straw. He could hear the cows, Ethel and Beatrinne, stamping and huffing. The soft lumbering snores of the two sheep, Atta and Petra. It felt like home. Except the guards behind him were some awful violation. Some tearing wound in everything he held dear.

He looked around, desperate, panic making the place unfamiliar. A blade. He needed a blade. The scythe—

"Torch it." The words barely penetrated his consciousness. But then he heard the strike of a flint, the whispered roar of flame igniting. Yellow light blazed in the doorway. He watched the torch as it flipped end over end to land in the straw.

He rushed toward it. Flames raced toward him. He stamped desperately at them.

The second torch hit him heavily in the chest. He staggered backward, slapped desperately at the flame that started to lick at the front of his jacket. In the handful of seconds it took to extinguish, two more torches had arced into the barn. One landed in the hay pile. It flared like kindling. By the time Will was halfway to the pile, the smoke already had him hacking and coughing.

The cows were awake now, starting to realize they should panic. The guards shouted to each other outside the door.

This was his *home*. This couldn't be.

But it clearly was.

He stopped, stood still, fire and smoke swirling about him, the cries of panicking animals filling the air. He was frozen between the future that he had held and the shattered pieces of the present at his feet.

Something splintered. He looked up, fearful of a falling beam. Then the sound of skittering hooves made him realize it was the gate of the pen that he'd been meaning to fix for more than a month now. And then Ethel's shoulder checked him as she scrambled out of the door.

Cursed cow, said some part of his mind. When she comes back tomorrow she'll be full of rage that she hasn't been milked and her udders are heavy.

But there wouldn't be a tomorrow. Not if he didn't get out.

He started to move again, to look for a way out that was not blocked by soldiers and swords.

For the first time ever, he was glad that the farm overwhelmed him. That there were rotten boards up in the hayloft that he hadn't got round to fixing.

He dashed to the ladder, threw open the door to the sheep pen as he went past it. The rungs were rough, slightly spongy with rot. He climbed upward into clouds of smoke that drove him to his knees, hacking, coughing.

He scrambled forward, elbows and knees supporting his weight. He thumped his head against the barn roof, felt his way along the wall, until the wood bowed beneath the pressure. His lungs burned. Bracing himself, he kicked once, twice. The boards gave way on the third heavy kick. He cleared a wider space with the fourth and fifth, shoved through the gap, grabbed the edge with his fingertips.

He hung in the darkness for a moment, smoke pouring out around him, obscuring his vision. How close had he put the vegetable cart to the back wall? The last thing he needed now was to break his neck on its edge. But there was no time to dredge for the memory.

He kicked off blindly, flailed through space.

He landed on the cart's wooden boards with a crash that jarred him from head to heels. His teeth clacked shut so hard he thought he heard his gums groaning. Spots of light danced in the night sky.

A shout crashed into his swampy thoughts. A guard had circled around the barn, seen him jump. He didn't have time to get his bearings, only to run. So he put his head down and did just that.

A fence lurched at him out of nowhere. The rain was coming down hard now, and the wood was slick as he tumbled over into a field. Wheat slapped at him, tall enough to get lost in.

He tumbled forward, barely thinking, just putting one foot in front of the other, simply getting away, and leaving all his hope behind.

In the end, a tree put paid to his flight. Not one to suffer fools or hysterical men lightly, it hit him forcefully with its trunk. Will took the opportunity to sit down heavily and not think about much at all for a while.

Eventually he came back to himself. Not fully. Not enough to totally take in the events of the evening. But enough to know that he was lost, that it was raining, and that home was not an option.

A moment of confused and painful thinking followed. His home was gone. Irretrievably, irreconcilably. The culmination of the bad luck that had begun with Firkin losing his mind, and moved on with the death of his parents. His future was gone. His dreams too. He would not find a way to make the farm profitable. He would not find a good Village girl to bring back. There would be no one to fill the old farmhouse with light, and love, and song. He had failed his father and his mother both in a single night. The chance to achieve their dreams for him had been stolen from him.

As for the future ... That was beyond him. Instead he aimed for something less ambitious. Like where in the Hallows he had ended up. When he solved the problem, he did not arrive at a particularly reassuring answer.

He'd headed into the Breccan Woods—the vast tangle of untamed forest that lay to the north of his farm. It was a hard enough place to navigate in the bright of day, with a known trail beneath his feet. It was a downright foolish place to be at night. The shadows were not safe— every mother told her child so. Goblins, ogres, and worse called this place home. And yet, he had apparently decided that a headlong dash for the hills superseded anything resembling common sense.

He shivered. He needed shelter. He needed rest. He needed time to come to terms with a torched home and a warrant for his death. Because that was what it would be. *Gentle* and *understanding* were not the words one usually used when describing the soldiers employed by the dragon Mattrax. If you resisted their edicts, they would not simply sit you down with a warm cup of mead to gently explain the misunderstanding. They were generally recruited more from the stick-a-sword-in-your-guts-and-kick-you-into-a-ditch mold. On a good day, at least, your friends would find you before the rats did.

This did not feel like a good day.

His body ached, but—given the trouble he'd been through to keep it in one piece that evening—Will decided to stumble forward, and look for a place where he could avoid freezing to death.

The going was slow. Trees hid most of the moonlight, and what came through seemed reluctant to show him where any obstacles might lie. Stones stubbed his toes, tangles of roots and vines tripped his heels. Rain dripped onto him, seeking out the gap between his collar and his neck with unerring accuracy.

He was shivering hard when he came upon the rock face. A ragged wall of granite twenty yards in height, where the land stepped up toward the mountains at the valley's edge. Such diminutive cliffs were a common enough feature of the landscape, often forming natural boundaries between farmsteads. More to Will's purpose, they tended to contain caves.

All he had to do was find one that didn't contain a bear.

Lawl—father of the Pantheon Above, lord of law and life, he prayed silently as he felt his way along the rock, *I don't know what I did to make you piss in my stew tonight, but I hope you can find it in your heart to forgive me.*

No sooner was the prayer uttered than the rock gave way beneath his hand. He stumbled forward, almost cursing, before he realized that the opening was in fact a cave entrance. *Well, that's service for you*, he thought. *Thank you, kindly.*

He stepped under the lip of the cave's entrance, the relief from the rain instant. He sighed, heavily, inhaled—

— and then rather wished he hadn't.

He'd never smelled anything quite like it. If a bear lived in this cave then it had died here. After a rather violent bout of diarrhea. Possibly brought on by the excess consumption of skunks. Who had also died of excess diarrhea. Several weeks prior.

He gagged slightly, and hesitated. But then, who was he to question divine providence? And while the smell of rot might normally attract predators, this was rancid enough that even a crow might decide it had too much self-esteem to stoop to the cave's contents. And it wasn't as if the world was overabundant with options for him at this moment.

Pulling a mostly dry rag from his pocket, he covered his nose and pushed deeper. Despite the rag, the stench grew with each step. When he could take it no longer—his revulsion a physical wall he could not push past—he backed up a step toward the cave entrance and simply lay down. The rock beneath him was cold and hard, but thankfully lacking in murderous intent. He looked back toward the cave entrance, the world outside. He could just make out the forest, a dark blue smudge in a field of black. He looked away, and rolled over, searching for a more comfortable way to lie—

— and collided with something small, furry, and warm.

Will shrieked.

He had always hoped that in a situation like this he would be able to describe the sound as a bellow, but it was definitely a shriek.

Fortunately, from his ego's point of view, whatever he had collided with let out an equally shrill noise. Less fortunately, something else echoed the sound. And then something else. And then ten more voices took up the cry. And ten more. A rippling wave of tremulous, unmanly sound, rushing back through the cavern.

And then, in response, a wave of light came flooding back. Torches flaring brightly in the dark. The light reached Will just as he made it to his feet.

He looked out onto a cavern packed from wall to wall with small, green figures. Feral faces with pointed snouts and pointier ears. Little black eyes screwed tight in anger. Teeth bared.

The shadows of Breccan Woods were not safe, he reminded himself. This one particularly so it seemed, housing as it did an entire fucking horde of goblins.

Lawl above, Will thought, *you're an absolute bastard.*